Sleepyhead

Mark Billingham is a stand-up comedian, appearing regularly at the Comedy Store. He received the 2003 Sherlock Award for Best Detective created by a British writer and won the Theakston's Old Peculier award for best crime novel of the year. He has also written drama for children's television, including *Knight School*, which won the Royal Television Society Award for best children's drama.

Also by this author

LAZYBONES
THE BURNING GIRL
LIFELESS
BURIED
DEATH MESSAGE
IN THE DARK

MARK BILLINGHAM OMNIBUS

Sleepyhead

Scaredy Cat

Mark Billingham

sphere

SPHERE

This omnibus edition first published in Great Britain in 2009 by Sphere

Previously published separately:
Sleepyhead first published in Great Britain in 2001 by
Little, Brown and Company
Paperback edition published by Time Warner Paperbacks in 2002
Reprinted 2002, 2003 (three times), 2004 (twice)
Reprinted by Time Warner Books in 2005, 2006
Reprinted by Sphere in 2006, 2007

Scaredy Cat first published in Great Britain in 2002 by Little, Brown
Paperback edition published by Time Warner Paperbacks in 2003
Reprinted 2003 (six times), 2004 (twice)
Reprinted by Time Warner Books in 2005 (twice), 2006
Reprinted by Sphere in 2006, 2007

A CIP catalogue record for this book
is available from the British Library.

ISBN 978-0-7515-4165-6

Typeset in Plantin by M Rules
Printed and bound in Great Britain by Clays Ltd, St Ives plc

Sphere
An imprint of
Little, Brown Book Group
100 Victoria Embankment
London EC4Y 0DY

An Hachette UK Company
www.hachette.co.uk

www.littlebrown.co.uk

For Claire. For everything. You're chocolate.

ACKNOWLEDGEMENTS

I owe a huge debt of thanks to a great many people, for a variety of reasons:

Dr Phil Coburn, for his expert advice, sick mind and champagne moments; Carol Bristow, for help with matters of police procedure; Professor Sebastian Lucas at St Thomas's Hospital; Nick Jordan, Bernadette Ford and David Holdstock at the Metropolitan Police Press Office; Caroline Allum; Hilary Hale, my brilliant editor, and all at Little, Brown for their boundless enthusiasm; Sarah Lutyens, my agent, for the furniture; Rachel Daniels at London Management; Peter Cocks for pictures; Howard Pratt for sounds; Mike Gunn for jokes; Paul Thorne for in-flight reading.

And my mother, Pat Thompson, for thirty-nine years. Remember what you said about shouting in bookshops . . .

PROLOGUE

Roger Thomas. F.R.C. Path.

Dr Angela Wilson,
HM Coroner,
Southwark.

26 June 2000

Dear Angela,

Following our recent telephone conversation, I write to summarise certain concerns which you might like to include as an addendum to my post-mortem report (PM2698/RT) on Ms Susan Carlish, a twenty-six-year-old stroke victim discovered at home on 15 June.

The PM was performed at St Thomas's Hospital on 17 June. The deceased died as a result of a brainstem infarction due to basilar artery occlusion from what would appear to be spontaneous vertebral artery dissection. Examination being twelve hours post mortem, I was unable to test for Protein C and Protein S deficiency. This aside, and taking into consideration that Ms Carlish was an occasional smoker, there would still appear to be an absence of conventional risk factors for stroke. I also discovered some minor neck trauma with ligamentous damage at C1 and C2 vertebral level though this would not be inconsistent with some previous whiplash or sporting injury. Traces of a benzodiazepine were discovered in the blood. Enquiries have produced a prescription for Valium made out to Ms Carlish's flatmate eighteen months ago.

While I remain in no doubt as to the cause of death, and concede that all police enquiries have drawn a blank, I am consulting a number of colleagues and copying this letter to all pathology departments and Coroners Courts in the Greater London area. I would be interested to confer with anyone who may have dealt with the body of a stroke victim (prob. female 20–30) displaying any or all of the following peculiarities:

Absence of conventional risk factors
Torn ligaments in neck
Benzodiazepines in the bloodstream

If you wish to discuss my findings, with a view perhaps to a second post-mortem examination, I would of course be delighted to chat with you further.

Yours sincerely,

Dr Roger Thomas FRC Path, Consultant Pathologist

P.S. The condition of the body (which honked like a pair of freshly scrubbed wellies!), was as I told you, of no concern to the authorities and delighted the morticians, but it was, to say the least, a little disconcerting!!

PART ONE

THE PROCEDURE

'Wake up, Sleepyhead . . .'

And lights and voices and a mask and sweet fresh oxygen in my nostrils . . .

And before?

Me and the girls are linking arms to belt out 'I Will Survive' and scare the shit out of every white-sock-wearing Camberwell Casanova in the club . . .

And now I'm dancing on my own. At a cashpoint, for God's sake! Unfeasibly pissed. Top night.

And I'm struggling to get the key in the door.

And there's a man in a car with a bottle of champagne. What's he celebrating? One more can't hurt on top of a bucketful of tequila.

And we're in the kitchen. I can smell some sort of soap. And something else. Something desperate.

And the man is behind me. I'm kneeling. If he wasn't holding me up I'd flop on to the floor. Am I that far gone?

And his hands are on my head and on my neck. He's very gentle. Telling me not to worry.

And . . . nothing . . .

ONE

Thorne hated the idea of coppers being hardened. A hardened copper was useless. Like hardened paint. He was just . . . resigned. To a down-and-out with a fractured skull and the word SCUM carved into his chest. To half a dozen Girl Guides decapitated courtesy of a drunken bus driver and a low bridge. And the harder stuff. Resigned to watching the eyes of a woman, who's lost her son, glaze over as she gnaws her bottom lip and reaches absently for the kettle. Thorne was resigned to all this. And he was resigned to Alison Willetts.

'Stroke of luck, really, sir.'

He was resigned to having to think of this small girl-shaped thing, enmeshed in half a mile of medical spaghetti, as a breakthrough. A piece of good fortune. A stroke of luck. And she was barely even there. What was undeniably lucky was that they'd found her in the first place.

'So, who fucked up?' DC David Holland had heard about Thorne's straight-for-the-jugular approach, but he was unprepared for the question so soon after arriving at the girl's bedside.

'Well, to be fair, sir, she didn't fit the profile. I mean, she was alive for a kick-off, and she's so young.'

'The third victim was only twenty-six.'

'Yes, I know, but look at her.'

He was. Twenty-four and she looked as helpless as a child.

'So it was just a missing-persons' job until the local boys tracked down a boyfriend.' Thorne raised an eyebrow.

Holland instinctively reached for his notebook. 'Er . . . Tim Hinnegan. He's the closest thing there is to next-of-kin. I've got an address. He should be here later. Visits every day apparently. They've been together eighteen months – she moved down here two years ago from Newcastle to take up a position as a nursery nurse.' Holland shut his notebook and looked at his boss, who was still staring down at Alison Willetts. He wondered whether Thorne knew that the rest of the team called him the Weeble. It was easy to see why. Thorne was . . . what? five six? five seven? But the low centre of gravity and the very . . . breadth of him suggested that it would take a lot to make him wobble. There was something in his eyes that told Holland that he would almost certainly not fall down.

His old man had known coppers like Thorne but he was the first Holland had worked with. He decided he'd better not put away the notebook just yet. The Weeble looked like he had a lot more questions. And the bugger did have this knack of asking them without actually opening his mouth.

'Yeah, so she walks home after a hen night . . . er, a week ago Tuesday . . . and winds up on the doorstep of A and E at the Royal London.'

Thorne winced. He knew the hospital. The memory of the pain that had followed the hernia operation there six months earlier was still horribly fresh. He glanced up as a nurse in blue uniform put her head round the door, looking first at them and then at the clock. Holland reached for his ID, but she was already shutting the door behind her.

'Looked like an OD when she came in. Then they found out about this weird coma thing, and she gets transferred here. But even when they discovered it was a stroke there was no obvious link to Backhand. No need to look for benzos and certainly no need to call us.'

Thorne stared down at Alison Willetts. Her fringe needed cutting. He watched as her eyeballs rolled up into their sockets. Did she know they were there? Could she hear them? And could she remember?

'So, if you ask me, the only person who's fucked up is, well, the killer really. Sir.'

'Find us a cup of tea, Holland.'

Thorne didn't shift his gaze from Alison Willetts and it was only the squeak and swish of the door that told him Holland had gone.

Detective Inspector Tom Thorne hadn't wanted Operation Backhand, but was grateful for any transfer out of the brand spanking new Serious Crime Group. The restructuring was confusing everybody and at least Backhand was a straightforward, old-fashioned operation. Still, he hadn't coveted it like some he could mention. Of course it was high profile, but he was one of that strange breed reluctant to take on any case he didn't seriously think could be solved. And this was a weird one. No question about that. Three murders that they knew about, each victim suffering death due to the constriction of the basilar artery. Some maniac was targeting women in their homes, pumping them full of drugs and giving them strokes.

Giving them strokes.

Hendricks was one of the more hands-on pathologists, but a week earlier, in his laboratory, Thorne had been less than thrilled at having those clammy hands on his head and neck as Hendricks tried to demonstrate the killing technique. 'What the bloody hell d'you think you're doing, Phil?'

'Shut your face, Tom. You're off your face on tranquillisers. I can do anything I like. I just bend your head this way and apply pressure to this point here to kink the artery. It's a delicate procedure this, takes specialised knowledge . . . I don't know. Army? Martial arts, maybe? Either way he's a clever bastard. No marks to speak of. It's virtually undetectable.'

Virtually.

Christine Owen and Madeleine Vickery both had risk factors: one in middle age, the second a heavy smoker on the pill. Both were discovered dead at home on opposite sides of London. That they had recently washed with carbolic soap was noted by the pathologists concerned, and though Christine Owen's husband and Madeleine Vickery's flatmate had considered this odd, neither could deny (or explain) the presence of a bar of carbolic in the bathroom. Traces of a tranquilliser were found in both victims, and were attributed in Owen's case to a prescription for depression, and in Vickery's, to an occasional drugs habit. No connection between these tragic yet apparently natural deaths was ever made.

But Susan Carlish had no generally accepted risk factors for stroke, and the tranquillisers found in the one-room flat in Waterloo, in a bottle with no label, were something of a mystery. It was down to the torn ligaments in her neck and one bloody clever pathologist that they'd even got a sniff of it. Even Hendricks had to admire that particular bit of path. work. Very sharp.

But not as sharp as the killer.

'He's playing a percentage game, Tom. Loads of people are walking about with high-risk factors for stroke. You for a start.'

'Eh?'

'Still got a gold card at Threshers, have you?'

Thorne had started to protest but thought better of it. He'd been out on the piss with Hendricks often enough.

'He picks three different areas of London knowing there's a hell of a slim chance that the victims will ever be connected. He goes about his business and we're none the wiser.'

Now Thorne stood listening to the persistent wheeze of Alison's ventilator. Locked-in syndrome it was called. They didn't know for sure but she could probably hear, see and feel. Alison was almost certainly aware of everything going on around her. And she was completely and utterly unable to move. Not the tiniest muscle.

Syndrome wasn't the right word. It was a sentence. And what about the bastard who'd passed it? A martial-arts nutcase? Special Services? That was their best guess. Their only guess. None the wiser . . .

Three different areas of London. What a mess that had been. Three commanders sitting round a table playing 'Whose Knob's the Biggest?' and putting Operation Backhand together.

He had no worries as far as the team was concerned. Tughan was efficient at least, and Frank Keable was a good DCI, if at times a little too . . . cautious. Thorne would have to have a word with him about Holland and his notebook. He never put the bloody thing down. Couldn't the division take on a single detective constable with a memory span greater than the average goldfish?

'Sir?'

Goldfish Boy was back with the tea.

'Who put us on to Alison Willetts?'

'That would be the consultant neurologist, er . . . Doctor . . .'

Holland cleared his throat and swallowed. He had a plastic cup of hot tea in each hand and couldn't get out his notebook. Thorne decided to be nice and reached out to take a cup. Holland groped for the notebook.

'Dr Coburn. Anne Coburn. She's teaching over at the Royal Free today. I've made you an appointment for this afternoon.'

'Another doctor we've got to thank.'

'Yeah, and another bit of luck as it goes. Her old man's a consultant pathologist, David Higgins. He does a bit of forensic work. She tells him about Alison Willetts and he goes, "That's interesting because . . ."'

'What? And he says and she says? Bit of a casual post-nookie chinwag, was it?'

'Don't know, sir. You'll have to ask her.'

Standing aside to let a pale ginger-haired nurse through to change Alison's feeding line, Thorne decided there was no time like the present. He thrust his untouched tea back at Holland.

'You stay here and wait for Hinnegan to show up.'

'But, sir, the appointment isn't until four-thirty.'

'So I'll be early.'

He trudged along a maze of cracked red linoleum-floored corridors in search of the quickest way to the exit and an escape from the smell that he and every right-minded person in the world hated so much. The Intensive Therapy Unit was in a newer wing of the National Hospital for Neurology and Neurosurgery, but it still had the smell. Disinfectant, he reckoned. They used something similar in schools but that just took him back to forgotten gym kits and the horror of PE in underpants. This was a different smell.

Dialysis and death.

He took the lift down to the main reception area, whose imposing Victorian architecture made a surprising contrast with the modern, open plan style of the hospital's newer parts. There was a faded grandeur about the stone tablets that lined the walls and the dusty wooden plaques inscribed with the names of the hospital consultants. Pride of place went to the full-length portrait of Diana, Princess of Wales, a former patron of the hospital. The painting was accomplished, unlike the bust of the Princess that stood on a plinth next to it. Thorne wondered if it had been sculpted by a patient.

As he neared the exit, the muttered curses and dripping umbrellas coming towards him through the main doors told him that summer was at an end. A week and a half into August and it was over. He stood beneath the hospital's elaborate red-brick portico and squinted through the downpour towards where his car was parked, tight against the railings that ran around Queen Square. People scurried through the rain, heads down, across the gardens or towards Russell Square tube station. How many were doctors or nursing staff? There were a dozen hospitals or specialist units within a mile of him. He could just see Great Ormond Street Children's Hospital from where he stood.

He turned up his collar and prepared to make a dash for it.

At first he thought it was a parking ticket and he pulled it roughly from beneath the wiper blade. As soon as he removed the single sheet of A4 from the polythene wrapper and unfolded it, he saw it was something else. He carefully inserted it back into its protective wrapping, wiped off the rain and peered at the neatly typed message. After the first four words he was no longer aware of the rainwater running down the back of his neck.

> DEAR DETECTIVE INSPECTOR THORNE. WHAT CAN I SAY? PRACTICE MAKES PERFECT. AND DON'T YOU JUST ENVY HER THAT PERFECT . . . DISTANCE? I INVITE YOU TO CONSIDER THE CONCEPT OF FREEDOM. TRUE FREEDOM. HAVE YOU EVER REALLY CONSIDERED IT? I'M SORRY ABOUT THE OTHERS. TRULY. I SHALL NOT INSULT YOUR INTELLIGENCE WITH PLATITUDES ABOUT ENDS AND MEANS BUT OFFER IN MITIGATION THE THOUGHT THAT A MASSIVE UNDERTAKING OFTEN HAS AN APPROPRIATE MARGIN OF ERROR. IT'S ALL ABOUT PRESSURE, DETECTIVE INSPECTOR THORNE, BUT THEN YOU'D KNOW ALL ABOUT THAT. SERIOUSLY, THOUGH, TOM, MAYBE I'LL CALL YOU SOMETIME.

Pressure . . .

Thorne looked around, his heart thumping. Whoever left the note must be close – the car hadn't been there long. All he could see were grim-set, rain-soaked faces, and Holland dodging the puddles as he loped across the road towards him.

'Sir, the boyfriend's just arrived. You must've passed him on your way out.'

The look on Thorne's face stopped him dead in his tracks.

'Alison is not a fuck-up, Holland.'

'Of course not, sir. All I meant was—'

'Listen. This is what he wants.' He pointed back towards the hospital. 'Do you understand?' His shirt was plastered to his back. Rain and sweat. He could barely understand it himself. He could hardly believe what was struggling to come out of his mouth. Holland stared at Thorne open-mouthed as he spoke the words that would cost him so much. Words which even as they formed on his lips, told him he should never have agreed to become part of this.

'Alison Willetts is not his first mistake. She's the first one he's got right.'

*Tim's not handling this very well. He had that funny choke in his voice when he was talking to Anne. Anne? First-name terms and we've never met. She sounds nice, though. I like our chats in the evening. Obviously a bit one-sided but at least somebody knows there's something going on in here. There's still some*body *going on in here.*

Did I mention the tests by the way? Absolutely fucking excellent. Well, some of them. Basically there's some sort of kit, literally a kit, in a special case, which tests if you're a complete veggie or not. To see if you're in Persistent Vegetative State. PVS. Which I keep mixing up with VPL but PVS is a bit more serious. They just test all your senses. Banging bits of wood together to see if you can hear, to see if you react. Not quite sure what I did, really, but they seemed pleased. I could have done without the pinpricks and that stuff they waft under your nose that's like the stuff you inhale if you've got a really bad cold. But the taste test makes up for it. They give you whisky. Drops of whisky on your tongue. This is my kind of hospital.

Anne did the tests. She looks dead attractive for somebody quite old. I can't see her very well but that's the image I get of her. I'm not even seeing shapes, really. More like the shadows of shapes. And some of those shadow-shapes are definitely policemen. Tim sounded really nervous when he was talking to one of them. He was pretty young, I reckon.

The man outside the house with the bottle of champagne did . . . what? Turned me into a pretty dull conversationalist but what else? Hurt me somewhere but nothing feels like a wound.

Everything feels like a scar.

Did he touch me? Will he be the last one ever to touch me?

Come on, Tim. I'm alive. It's still me. More or less. You're cracking up and I'm the one singing 'Girlfriend In A Coma' to myself . . .

It was nice that Carol and Paul came in. Christ, I hope all this business didn't bugger up the wedding.

TWO

'Are we looking at a doctor?'

As soon as he had asked the question, Thorne knew what Holland would be thinking. It was undeniable that Anne Coburn was the sort of doctor most men would look at. About whom most men would contrive painful jokes about cold hands and bedside manners. She was tall and slim. Elegant, he thought, like that actress who was in *The Avengers* and plays the old slapper in that sitcom. Thorne put her in her early forties, maybe a year or two older than he was. Although the blue eyes suggested that her hair might once have been blonde, he liked it the way it was now – short and silver. Perched on the edge of a small, cluttered desk, drinking a cup of coffee, she seemed almost relaxed. By comparison with the day before at any rate.

She'd sent him away from the Royal Free with a flea in his ear. Thorne could still hear the laughter of thirty-odd medical students as he'd trudged away up the corridor. It was evidently a treat to take a short break from brain scans to watch the teacher give a high-ranking police officer a thorough bollocking. Anne Coburn did not like to be interrupted. She'd apologised for the incident over the phone when Thorne rang to rearrange their appointment back at

Queen Square where she worked. Where she treated Alison Willetts.

She took another swig of coffee and repeated Thorne's question. Her speech was crisp, efficient and easy on the ear. It was a voice that could certainly wow impressionable medical students or frighten middle-aged policemen. 'Are we looking at a doctor? Well, certainly someone with a degree of medical expertise. To block off the basilar artery and cause a stroke would take medical know-how. To cause the kind of stroke that would induce locked-in syndrome is way beyond that . . . Even if someone knew what they were doing, the odds are against it. You might try it a dozen times and not succeed. We're talking about fractions of an inch.'

Those fractions had cost three women their lives. Thorne flashed on a mental image of Alison Willetts. Make that four women. Perhaps they should count their blessings and thank God for this lunatic's expertise. Or, more likely, worry that now he thought he'd perfected his technique he'd be eager to try again. Dr Coburn hadn't finished. 'Plus of course, there's the journey to consider.'

Thorne nodded. He'd already started to consider it. Holland looked confused.

'From what I can gather, you're presuming that Alison had her stroke at home in south-east London,' said Coburn. 'He would have had to keep her alive until he could get her to the Royal London, which is at least . . .'

'Five miles away.'

'Right. He'd have passed any number of hospitals on the way. Why did he drive all the way to the Royal London?'

Thorne had no idea, but he'd done some checking. 'Camberwell to Whitechapel, he'd have passed three major hospitals, even on the most direct route. How would he have kept her alive?'

'Bag and mask's the most obvious way. He might have had to pull over every ten minutes or so for half a dozen good squeezes on the bag but it's fairly straightforward.'

'So, a doctor, then?'

'I think so, yes. A failed medical student possibly – chiropractor, perhaps . . . a well-read physiotherapist at a hell of a stretch. I've no idea where you'd even begin.'

Holland stopped scribbling in his notebook. 'A hypodermic needle in a haystack?'

Coburn's expression told Thorne that she'd found it about as funny as he had.

'You'd better start looking for it then, Holland,' Thorne told him. 'I'll see you tomorrow. Get a cab back.'

Every step that he and Dr Coburn took towards Alison's room filled Thorne with something approaching dread. It was a terrible thought but he would have found it easier had Alison been one of Hendricks's 'patients'. He couldn't help but wonder if it might not have been easier for Alison too. They walked through to the Chandler Wing then took the lift to the second floor and Medical ITU.

'You don't like hospitals, do you, Detective Inspector?'

An odd question. Thorne couldn't believe that anybody liked hospitals. 'I've spent too much time in them.'

'Professionally or . . .?' She didn't finish the question because she couldn't. What were the right words? 'On an amateur basis?'

Thorne looked straight at her. 'I had a small operation last year.' But that wasn't it. 'And my mother was in hospital a long time before she died.'

Coburn nodded. 'Stroke.'

'Three of them. Eighteen months ago. You really *do* know how brains work, don't you?'

She smiled. He smiled back. They stepped out of the lift.

'By the way, it was a hernia.'

The signs on the walls fascinated Thorne: Movement and Balance; Senility; Dementia. There was even a Headache Clinic. The place was busy but the people they passed as they moved through the building were not the usual walking wounded. He saw no blood, no bandages or plaster casts. The corridors and waiting areas seemed full of people moving slowly and deliberately. They looked lost or bewildered. Thorne wondered what he looked like to them.

Much the same, almost certainly.

They walked on in silence past a canteen filled with the casual chatter that Thorne would have associated with a large factory or office building. He wondered if they ever got that smell out of the food.

'What about doctors? Are we on your shit list?'

For a ridiculous second he wondered if she was coming on to him. Then he remembered the faces of those bloody medical students. This was not a woman about whom he could presume anything. 'Well, not at the moment anyway. Too many of them responsible for putting us on to this. You for a start.'

'I think my husband can take credit for that.' Her tone was brisk, without an ounce of false modesty.

She caught Thorne's fleeting glance towards where a wedding ring should have been. 'Soon to be ex-husband, I should say. It was a chance remark, really. One of the more civilised moments in a rather bloody how-shall-we-handle-the-divorce session.'

Thorne looked straight ahead, saying nothing. Christ, he was so English!

'What about the china? Who keeps the cat? Did you hear about the lunatic who's stroking out women all over London? You know the sort of thing . . .'

Phobia. Death. Divorce. Thorne wondered if perhaps they should move on to the crisis in the Middle East.

'Forty-eight hours after she was brought in we gave Alison an MRI scan. There was oedema around the neck ligaments – bright white patches on the scan. You see it in whiplash victims, but with Alison I thought it was unusual. On top of what my husband had told me—'

'What about the Midazolam?'

'His benzodiazepine of choice? It was a very clever choice, as a matter of fact, especially as there was every chance it would be the same drug given to Alison in A and E. How's that for muddying the waters?'

Thorne stopped. They were outside Alison's room. 'Can we check that?'

'I did. And it was. I know the anaesthetist who was on duty at the Royal London that night. The toxicology report showed Midazolam in Alison's bloodstream but it would have done anyway – that's what was used to sedate her in A and E. But we also take blood routinely, on admission, so I checked. Midazolam was present in that first blood sample too. That's when I decided to contact the police.'

Thorne nodded. A doctor. He had to be. 'Where else do they use Midazolam?'

She thought for a moment. 'It's pretty specialised. ITUs, A and E, Anaesthetics, that's about it.'

'Where's he getting it from? Hospitals? Can't you get this sort of stuff over the Internet?'

'Not in these quantities.'

Thorne knew that this would mean contacting every hospital in the country for recorded thefts of Midazolam. He wasn't sure how far back to check. Six months? Two years? He'd err on the side of caution. Besides, he was sure Holland could use the overtime.

Coburn opened the door to Alison's room.

'Can she hear us?' Thorne asked.

She brushed Alison's hair off her face and smiled at him indulgently. 'Well, if she can't, it's not because there's anything wrong with her hearing.'

Thorne felt himself redden. Idiot. Why *did* people whisper at hospital bedsides?

'To be honest, I'm not sure. The early signs are good. She blinks to sudden noises but there are still tests to be done. I talk to her anyway. She already knows which registrar is an alcoholic and which consultant is doing it with three of his students.'

Thorne raised an inquisitive eyebrow. Coburn sat and took Alison's hand.

'Sorry, Detective Inspector, girls' talk!'

Thorne could do little but watch her among the mess of wires and machinery. Wires and machinery with a young woman attached. He listened to the hiss of Alison's ventilated lungs and felt the throb of her computerised pulse, and he thought about the one doctor out there somewhere who was most definitely on his shit list.

He sat on the tube trying to guess how much longer the businessman opposite him had to live. It was a game he greatly enjoyed.

It had been such a wonderful moment the day before

when Thorne had looked straight at him. He hadn't really seen him: it had been no more than half a second and he was just a passer-by with his hood up, but it had been a lovely bonus. The look on the policeman's face had told him that he'd understood the note. Now he could relax and enjoy what had to be done. He'd lie in the bath when he got home and think about it some more. He'd think about Thorne's face. Then he'd grab a few hours' sleep. He was working later on.

The man opposite looked flushed. Another tough day at the office. He had a smoker's face, pale and blotchy. The broken veins on his cheeks were probably a sign of bad circulation and excessive drinking. The small, creamy blobs on the eyelids, the xanthelasma, almost certainly meant that his cholesterol was way too high, and that his arteries were well furred up.

The businessman gritted his teeth as he turned the pages of his newspaper.

He gave him ten years at most.

As his battle-scarred blue Mondeo moved smoothly through the early-morning traffic on the Marylebone Road, Thorne nudged the Massive Attack tape into the stereo and leaned back in his seat. If he'd wanted to relax and switch off he'd have plumped for some Johnny Cash or Gram Parsons or Hank Williams, but there was nothing like the repetitive, hypnotic thud of music he was twenty-five years too old for to concentrate his thoughts. As ever, when the mechanised beat of 'Unfinished Sympathy' started thumping from the speakers he pictured the incredulous look on the face of the teenage assistant in Our Price. Smug little git had looked at him like he was some old saddo trying to pretend he still had his finger on the pulse.

The spotty teenage face became the infinitely more attractive one belonging to Anne Coburn. He wondered what sort of music she liked. Classical, probably, but with a Hendrix album or two stashed away behind the Mozart and Mendelssohn. What would she make of his penchant for trip-hop and speed-garage? He guessed that she'd go for the saddo theory. He stopped at the lights and rolled down the window to let the beat blast out at the snooty-looking woman in the Saab next to him. Thorne stared straight ahead. When the light hit amber, he turned, winked at her and pulled gently away.

And when he got back to HQ? There would be a convincing babble of efficient-sounding voices, a scurrying back and forth with files, and the buzzing and beeping of faxes and modems. Thorne smacked out the rhythm on his steering-wheel. And as a backdrop to this montage of proper procedure there would be the wall; a blackboard detailing names, dates and ACTIONS, and lined up above it there would be the pictures: Christine, Madeleine and Susan. Their unmarked faces sharing a pallid blankness, but each, to Thorne, seeming to capture a dreadful final instant of some unfamiliar emotion. Confusion. Terror. Regret. All *in extremis*. He turned up the music. In factories and offices across London, workers were copping furtive glances at calendar girls – Saucy Sandra, Naughty Nina, Wicked Wendy. The days, weeks and months that lay ahead for Thorne would be counted off by the reproachful faces of Dead Christine, Dead Madeleine and Dead Susan.

'How's it going, Tommy?'

Christine Owen. Thirty-four. Found lying at the bottom of the stairs . . .

'Shake 'em up, will you, Tom, for fuck's sake?'

Madeleine Vickery. Thirty-seven. Dead on her kitchen floor. A pan of spaghetti boiled dry . . .

'Please, Tom . . .'

Susan Carlish. Twenty-six. Her body discovered in an armchair. Watching television . . .

'Tell us what you're going to do, Tom.'

They would make lists, no question, long lists they would cross-reference with different ones. DCs would ask hundreds of different people the same questions and type out their notes and DSs would take statements and make phone calls and type out *their* notes, which would be collated and indexed and, perhaps, several thousand fields full of cows' worth of shoe leather later, they might get lucky . . .

'Sorry, girls, nothing yet.'

They weren't going to catch this bloke with procedure. Thorne could feel it already. This wasn't the convenient copper's hunch of a thriller writer – he knew it. The killer might get himself caught. Yes, there was a chance of that. The profilers and psychological experts reckoned that, deep down, they all wanted to be caught. He'd have to ask Anne Coburn what she thought about that the next time he saw her. If that turned out to be sooner rather than later he wouldn't be complaining.

Thorne pulled into the car park and killed the music. He stared up at the dirty brown building in which Backhand had made its home. The old station on Edgware Road had been earmarked for closure months ago and was now all but deserted, but the vacant offices above had been perfect for an operation like Backhand. Perfect for the lucky buggers who didn't have to work there every day. An open-plan monstrosity – one enormous fishtank for the minnows with a few smaller bowls around the edges for the bigger fish.

For a moment he was deeply afraid to go in. He got out of the car and leaned against the bonnet until the moment passed.

As he trudged towards the door, he made a decision. He wasn't going to let anyone put a picture of Alison on the wall.

Fourteen hours later Thorne got home and rang his dad. They spoke as often as Thorne could manage and saw each other even less. Jim and Maureen Thorne had left North London for St Albans ten years before, but since his mum had died Thorne felt the distance between him and his dad growing greater all the time. Now they were both alone and their telephone conversations were always desperately trivial. His dad was always keen to pass on the latest dirty story or pub joke, and Thorne was always pleased to hear them. He liked to let his old man make him laugh – he liked to hear *him* laugh. Aside from the forced lightheartedness of these phone calls, he suspected that his father wasn't laughing a great deal. His father knew damn well that *he* wasn't.

'I'll leave you with a couple of good ones, Tom.'

'Go on then, Dad.'

'What's got a one-inch knob and hangs down?'

'I don't know.'

'A bat.'

It wasn't one of his best.

'What's got a nine-inch knob and hangs up?'

'No idea.'

His dad put the phone down.

He sat down and, for a few minutes, he said nothing. Then he began to speak softly. 'Perhaps, in retrospect, the note on the windscreen was a little . . . showy. It's not like me, really. I'm not that sort of person. I suppose I just wanted to say sorry for the others. Well, if I'm being truthful, I must admit that a part of me wanted to boast just a little. And I think Thorne's a man I can talk to. He seems like a man who will understand how proud I am about getting it right. Perfection is everything, isn't it? And haven't I been taught that? You can believe it. I have been well taught.

'I mean, it's been a struggle and I'm certainly not saying that I won't make any more mistakes, but what I'm doing gives me the right to fail, wouldn't you say? The one . . . frustration is that I can only imagine how good it feels on the machines. Safe and clean. Free to relax and let the mind wander. No mess. And if I feel proud at liberating a body from the tyranny of the petty and the putrid then I can't be condemned for that, surely. It's the only real freedom left that's worth fighting for, I'd say. Freedom from our clumsy movement through air. Our bruising. Our . . . sensitivity. To be released from the humdrum and the everyday. Fed and cleaned. Monitored and cared for. All our filthy fluids disposed of. And, above all, to *know*. To be aware of these wonders as they are happening. What does a corpse know of its washing? To know and to feel all these things must be wonderful.

'God, what am I thinking? I'm sorry. I don't have to tell *you* any of this.

'Do I, Alison?'

Sue and Kelly from the nursery came to see me yesterday. My vision's a lot better already. I could see that Sue was wearing far too much eyeliner as usual. There's plenty of gossip. Obviously not as much as usual with me in here, but still good stuff. Mary, the manageress, is really pissing everybody off, sitting on her arse and correcting the spelling on the happy charts. Daniel's still being a little sod. He cried for me last week, they said. They told him I'd gone to Spain on my holidays. They told me that when I came out we'd all go and get completely pissed and that they'd rather be in here any day than changing shitty nappies on three pounds sixty an hour . . .

There wasn't much else after that.

And, at last, a bit of real excitement. Some bedpan-washer or something got blocked up. I know it doesn't sound earth-shattering, but there was water everywhere and all the nurses were sloshing round and getting really pissed off.

Excitement is relative, I suppose.

I dreamed about my mum. She was young, like she was when I was at school. She was getting me dressed and I was arguing about what I was going to wear and she was weeping and weeping . . .

And I dreamed about the man who did this to me. I dreamed that he was here in my room, talking to me. I knew his voice straight away. But it was also a voice I recognised from after it happened. My brain has gone to mush. He sat by my bed and squeezed my hand and tried to tell me why he'd done it. But I didn't really understand. He was telling me how

I should be happy. That voice had told me to enjoy myself as he handed me the champagne bottle and I took a swig.

I must have invited him in. I must have. I suppose the police know that. I wonder if they've told Tim?

Now that dreams are the closest thing I have to sensation, they've become so vivid. It would be fantastic if you could press a button and choose what you were going to dream about. Obviously someone would have to press the button for me, but a selection of family and friends with a healthy degree of filth thrown in would be nice.

Mind you, once you've been fucked to this degree, a shag is neither here nor there, really, is it?

THREE

Thorne had been wrong about the summer: after a fortnight's holiday of its own, it had returned with a sticky vengeance, and the siren call of the launderette could no longer be ignored. He was horribly aware of the smell coming off him as he sat sweltering in Frank Keable's office. They were talking about lists.

'We're concentrating on doctors currently on rotation in inner London, sir.'

Frank Keable was only a year or two older than Thorne but looked fifty. This was more due to some genetic glitch than any kind of stress. The lads reckoned he must have started receding at about the same time he hit puberty, judging by the proximity of his hairline to the nape of his neck. Whatever hormones he had left that stimulated hair growth had somehow been mistakenly rerouted to his eyebrows, which hovered above his bright blue eyes like great grey caterpillars. The eyebrows were highly expressive and gave him an air of wisdom that was, to put it kindly, fortunate. Nobody begrudged him this bit of luck – it was the least you could hope for when you looked like an overfed owl with alopecia.

Keable put one of his caterpillars to good use, raising it questioningly. 'It might be best to look a bit further afield,

Tom. We'd be covering our bases, should the worst happen. We're not short of manpower.'

Thorne looked sceptical but Keable sounded confident.

'It's a big case, Tom, you know that. If you need the bodies to widen things out a bit, I can swing it.'

'Let's have them anyway, sir, it's an enormous list. But I'm sure he's local.'

'The note?'

Thorne felt again the heavy drops of rain that had crawled inside his shirt collar and trickled down between his shoulder-blades. He could still sense the polythene between his fingers and thumbs, as he'd read the killer's words while the water ran down into his eyes, like tears coming home.

The killer had known where Alison was being treated. He was obviously following the case closely. Theirs as well as hers.

'Yes, the note. And the locations. I think he'd want to be around to keep an eye on things.'

To monitor his work.

'Is it worth putting a watch on the hospital?'

'With respect, sir, the place is crawling with doctors . . . I can't see the point at the minute.' His eyes drifted to the calendar on the dirty yellow wall – views of the West Country. Keable was originally from Bristol . . . The heat was making it hard to concentrate. Thorne undid another button on his shirt. Polyester. Not clever. 'Is there any chance of moving that fan round a bit?'

'Oh, sorry, Tom.'

Keable flicked a switch on his black desktop fan, which started to swing backwards and forwards, providing Thorne with a welcome blast of cold air every thirty seconds or so. Keable leaned back in his chair and puffed out his cheeks. 'You don't think we're going to crack this, do you, Tom?'

Thorne closed his eyes as the fan swung back in his direction.

'Tom, is this about the Calvert case?'

Thorne looked at the calendar. Two weeks now since they'd found Alison, and they were nowhere. Two weeks of banging their heads against a wall, and getting nothing but headaches.

Concern, or what passed for it, crept into Keable's voice. 'Cases like this, it's completely understandable . . .'

'Don't be silly, Frank.'

Keable leaned forward quickly. In charge. 'I'm not insensitive to . . . moods, Tom. This case has a taste to it. It's not . . . in the run of things. Even I can sense it.'

Thorne laughed. Old colleagues. 'Even you, Frank?'

'I mean it, Tom.'

'Calvert is ancient history.'

'I hope so. I need you focused – and focused is not fixated.'

Keable wasn't sure but he thought that Thorne nodded. He continued as if the exchange had never happened.

'I think we'll make a case if we get him. We should be able to match up the note to the typewriter for a start.'

Keable sighed and nodded. The old-fashioned typewriter was a bit of luck, a lot easier to identify than a laser printer, but still, they needed a suspect first. He'd been in the same position plenty of times. It was hard to sound enthusiastic about evidence which was only of any use when someone was in custody. The procedure had to be followed, but at the end of the day they had to catch him first. Keable knew that procedure was his strong point. He was a good facilitator. It was this self-awareness that had allowed him to leapfrog other officers, Thorne included. It also ensured that those officers didn't resent it. He recognised the talents of others and the lack of them in himself. He was a forger of team spirit. He was well liked. He helped where he could and left the job at the office at the end of the day. He slept well and had a happy marriage – unlike other officers. Thorne included. 'He'll make a mistake, Tom. When we get a hit on a drugs theft we can start narrowing things down a bit.'

Thorne leaned in close to the fan. 'I'd like to get over to Queen Square, if that's okay. It's been a while and I'd like to see how Alison's doing.'

Keable nodded. This hadn't been his most successful attempt at one-on-one morale-building but, then, he hadn't expected a backslapping gagfest from Tom Thorne. He cleared his throat as Thorne stood up, walked to the door and then turned.

'That note was spotless, Frank. It was the shortest forensic report I've ever seen. And he doesn't wash the bodies in a ritualistic way. He's just very, very careful.'

Keable turned the fan back on himself. He was unsure exactly what Thorne expected him to say. 'I'd been wondering whether we should get the boys to chip in for some flowers or something. I mean, I thought about it but . . .'

Thorne nodded.

'Yes, sir, I know. It hardly seems worth it.'

'These are really lovely. It was a very nice thought.' Anne Coburn finished arranging the flowers and closed the blinds in Alison's room. The sun was streaming in through the window, causing the girl's face to flush a little.

'I meant to come in sooner, but . . .'

She nodded, understanding. 'You could have written a note to say congratulations, though.'

Thorne looked down at Alison and immediately understood. It was difficult to notice one less machine amid the confusion of life-preserving hardware. She was breathing. The breaths were shallow, almost tentative, but they were her own. Now a tube ran into a hole in her windpipe, covered with an oxygen mask.

'She came off the ventilator last night and we performed the tracheostomy.'

Thorne was impressed. 'Exciting night.'

'Oh, it's non-stop excitement in here. We had a small flood a while ago. Have you ever seen nurses in wellies?'

He grinned. 'I've seen the odd dodgy video . . .'

It was the first time he'd heard her laugh: it was filthy.

Thorne nodded towards the flowers, which he'd picked up at a garage on the way in. They weren't quite as lovely as Anne Coburn had said. 'I felt like such an idiot last time, you know, whispering. If she can hear I thought she must be able to smell so . . .'

'Oh, she'll smell these.'

Suddenly Thorne was aware again of the stickiness beneath his arms. He turned to look at Alison. 'While we're on the subject . . . sorry, Alison, I must really hum.' He was embarrassed at the silence where a response should have been. He hoped he could get used to talking to this woman with a tube in her neck and another up her nose. She was unable to clear her throat. She was unable to lift the hand that lay pale and heavy on the pink flowery quilt. She was . . . unable. And yet, selfishly, Thorne hoped that she thought well of him, that she liked him. He wanted to talk to her. Even now he sensed that he would *need* to talk to her.

'Just fill in the gaps yourself,' Coburn said. 'It's what I do. We have some cracking chats.'

The door opened and an immaculately suited middle-aged man walked in with what at first glance appeared to be candyfloss on his head.

'Oh . . .' Thorne saw Coburn's features harden in an instant. 'David. I'm busy I'm afraid.'

They stared at each other. She broke the uncomfortable, hostile silence. 'This is Detective Inspector Thorne. David Higgins.'

The soon-to-be-ex-husband. The helpful pathologist.

'Pleased to meet you.' Thorne held out a hand, which the immaculate suit shook without looking at him – or at Alison.

'You did say that this would be a good time,' said the suit, half smiling.

He was obviously trying hard to be pleasant for Thorne's benefit but clearly it did not come naturally. On further inspection the candyfloss was in reality a teased up and hairsprayed dyed vanilla quiff – a ridiculous affectation in a man who was at least fifty-five: he looked as if he'd walked off the set of *Dynasty*.

'Well, it would have been,' said Coburn frostily.

'My fault, Mr Higgins,' said Thorne. 'I didn't have an appointment.'

Higgins moved towards the door, adjusting his tie. 'Well, I'd better make sure I have an appointment in future, then. I'll call you later, Anne, and we can arrange one.' He closed the door soundlessly behind him. There was a muffled exchange outside and the door was opened again by a nurse. It was time for Alison's bedbath.

Anne Coburn turned to him. 'What do you usually do for lunch?'

They sat in the back of a small sandwich bar on Southampton Row. Ham and Brie on a baguette and a mineral water. A cheese and tomato sandwich and a coffee. Two busy professionals.

'What are Alison's chances of regaining any significant . . .?'

'Nil, I'm afraid. I suppose it depends a little on your definition of "significant" but we have to be realistic. There have been documented cases of patients regaining enough movement to operate a sophisticated wheelchair. They're doing a lot of work in the States with computers operated by headsticks, but realistically it's a bleak prognosis.'

'Wasn't there somebody in France who dictated an entire book with an eyelash or something?'

'*The Diving Bell and the Butterfly* – you should read it. But it's pretty much a one-off. Alison's gaze reacts to voices and she seems to have retained the ability to blink, but whether she has any real control over it is hard to say at the moment. I can't see her giving you a statement just yet.'

'That wasn't the reason I asked about . . . It wasn't the *only* reason.' Thorne took an enormous bite of his sandwich.

Anne had done most of the talking but had already finished hers. She looked at him, narrowing her eyes, her voice conspiratorial. 'Well, you've been privy to my disastrous domestic situation. What about yours?' She took a sip of mineral water and watched him chew, her eyebrows arched theatrically. She laughed as, twice, he tried to answer and, twice, had to resume his efforts to swallow the sandwich.

Finally: 'What – you mean is it disastrous?'

'No. Just . . . is there one?'

Thorne could not get a fix on this woman at all. A vicious temper, a filthy laugh, and a direct line of questioning. There seemed little point in going round the houses.

'I've moved effortlessly from "disastrous" to just plain "bleak".'

'Is that the normal progression?'

'I think so. Sometimes there's a short period of "pitiful" but not always.'

'Oh, well, I'll look forward to that.'

Thorne watched as she reached into her bag for a cigarette. She held up the packet. 'Do you mind?'

Thorne said no, and she lit up. He stared as she blew the smoke out of the side of her mouth, away from him. It had been a long time since his last cigarette.

'More doctors smoke than you'd imagine. And a surprising number of oncologists. I'm amazed that more of us aren't smackheads to be honest. Do you not, then?' Thorne shook his head. 'A policeman who doesn't smoke. You must like a drink, then?'

He smiled. 'I thought you worked too many hours to watch television.'

She groaned with pleasure as she took a long drag.

Thorne spoke slowly but was still smiling when he answered the question. 'I like more than one . . .'

'Glad to hear it.'

'But that's pretty much it, as far as the clichés go. I'm not religious, I hate opera, and I can't finish a crossword to save my life.'

'You must be driven, then? Or haunted? Is that the word?'

Thorne tried to hold the smile in place and even managed to produce a chuckle of sorts as he turned away and looked towards the counter. When he'd caught the eye of the woman at the till he held up his coffee cup, signalling for another.

'So, does "desperate" and "bleak" involve children?'

Thorne turned back round. 'No. You?'

Her smile was huge and as contagious as smallpox. 'One. Rachel. Sixteen and big trouble.'

Sixteen? Thorne raised his eyebrows. 'Do women still get upset if you ask how old they are?'

She plonked an elbow on the table and leaned her chin on the palm of her hand, trying her best to look severe. 'This one does.'

'Sorry.' Thorne tried *his* best to look contrite. 'How much do you weigh?'

She laughed loudly. Not filthy, positively salacious. Thorne laughed too, and grinned at the waitress as his second cup of coffee arrived. It had barely touched the table when Coburn's bleeper went off. She looked at it, stubbed out her cigarette and grabbed her bag from the floor. 'I might not be a smackhead, but I do an awful lot of indigestion tablets.'

Thorne lifted his jacket from the back of his chair. 'I'll walk you back.'

On the way towards Queen Square things became oddly formal again. Small-talk about Indian summers gave way to an awkward silence before they were half-way there. When they reached her office, Thorne hovered in the doorway. He felt like he should go, but she held up her hand to stop him as she made a quick call. The bleep had not been urgent.

'So how is the investigation going?'

Thorne stepped into the office and closed the door. He had thought this was coming over lunch. His capacity to bullshit members of the public had once been endless, but he spent so much of his time exercising that particular skill on superior officers that he couldn't be bothered trying it on with those who had no axe to grind.

'It's a . . . bleak prognosis.'

She smiled.

'Every day there's some stupid story in the paper about armed robbers tunnelling into the shop next door to the building society or burglars falling asleep in houses they've broken into, but the simple fact is that most people who break the law give serious thought to not getting done for it. With murderers, you've got a chance if it's domestic, or when there's sex involved.'

She leaned back in her chair and took a sip from a glass of water.

Thorne watched her. 'Sorry, I didn't mean to make a speech.'

'No, I'm interested, really.'

'Any sort of sexual compulsion can make people sloppy. They take chances and eventually they slip up. I just can't see this bloke slipping up. Whatever's been driving him isn't sexual.'

Her eyes were suddenly flat and cold. 'Isn't it?'

'Not physically. He's perverse . . . but he's—'

'What he's doing is grotesque.'

There was a matter-of-factness about the statement that Thorne had no argument with. What shook him was her use of the present tense. There were those who thought or hoped (and, by Christ, he hoped) that perhaps there'd be no need for new pictures on the wall. But he knew better. Whatever mission this man thought he was on, whatever it was he hoped to achieve, he was *actually* stalking women and killing them in their own homes. And he was enjoying himself. Thorne could feel himself start to redden.

'There's no conventional pattern to this. The ages of the victims seem unimportant to him, as long as they're available. He just picks these women out and when he doesn't get what he wants he just leaves them. Shiny and scrubbed and slumped in a chair or lying on a kitchen floor for their loved ones to stumble across. Nobody sees anything. Nobody knows anything.'

'Except Alison.'

The awkward silence descended again, more stifling than the air trapped inside the tiny office. Thorne felt the retort of his outburst bouncing off the walls like a sluggish bullet. There was none of the usual irritation when his mobile phone rang. He grabbed for it gratefully.

DI Nick Tughan ran the Backhand office: an organiser and collator of information, another embracer of procedure. His smooth Dublin brogue could calm or persuade senior officers. Unlike Frank Keable, though, Tughan had the self-awareness of a tree-stump and little time for characters like Tom Thorne: The way the operation had been going up to now meant that it was very much his show and he ran it with an unflappable efficiency. *He* never lost his temper.

'We've got a fairly major Midazolam theft. Two years ago, Leicester Royal Infirmary, five grams missing.'

Thorne reached across the desk for a piece of paper

and a pen. Anne pushed a pad towards him. He began to scribble down the details. Maybe there had been a slip-up, after all.

'Right, let's send Holland up to Leicester, get all the details, and we'll need a list of everyone on rotation from, say, ninety-seven onwards.'

'Ninety-six onwards. Already sorted it. It's been faxed through.'

Tughan was well ahead of him and thoroughly enjoying it. Thorne knew what he would have done next. 'Obvious question then . . . any matches?'

'A couple in the South-East and half a dozen in London. But there's an interesting one. Works at the Royal London.'

Interesting was right. Anne Coburn had spotted it straight away. Working on the assumption that Alison had been attacked in her home, then why the Royal London? Why not the nearest hospital? Thorne took down the name, kept the compulsory, if distasteful, backslapping brief and hung up.

'Sounded like good news.' She didn't apologise for eavesdropping.

Thorne was starting to like her more and more. He stood up and reached for his jacket. 'Let's hope so. Five grams of Midazolam. Is that a lot?'

'That's a hell of a lot. We'd use anywhere up to *five milligrams* to sedate an average-sized adult. That's intravenously, of course.'

She stood up and moved round the desk to see him out. As she walked to the door she glanced at the scrap of paper, which Thorne had not yet picked up, and stopped dead in her tracks.

'Oh, God!' She reached for it just as Thorne did – he should never have let her see it, but a tussle would have been . . . unseemly. What harm could it do? He opened the door. 'Is this man your . . . match, Detective Inspector?' She moved back to her side of the desk and sat down heavily.

'I'm sorry, Doctor, I'm sure you understand. I can't really—'

'I know him,' she said. 'I know him extremely well.'

Thorne hovered in the doorway. This was starting to get awkward. Procedure dictated that he leave straight away and send someone back to get a statement. He waited for her to continue.

'Yes, he certainly worked in Leicester, but there's no way he'd have anything to do with stealing drugs.'

'Doctor—'

'And he's got something of a cast-iron alibi as far as Alison Willetts is concerned.'

Thorne shut the door. He was listening.

'Jeremy Bishop was the anaesthetist on call at the Royal London A and E the night Alison was brought in. He treated her. Do you remember? I told you I knew him. He told me about the Midazolam.'

Thorne blinked slowly. Dead Susan. Dead Christine. Dead Madeleine.

'*Come on, Tommy, you must have* something *to go on?*'

He opened his eyes. She was shaking her head. She'd seen the date on the piece of paper. 'I'm sorry, Detective Inspector, but much as you dislike Detective Constable Holland . . .'

Thorne opened his mouth and closed it again.

'. . . it's a waste of time to send him to Leicester. The

man you're looking for is certainly clever, but there's no guarantee he ever worked at Leicester Royal Infirmary.'

Thorne dropped his bag and sat down again. 'Why am I starting to feel like Dr Watson?'

'August the first is rotation day. Normally it would be a reasonable assumption that in order to steal a large quantity of drugs from a hospital you'd have to work there. Yes, hospital staff are overstretched and occasionally inefficient, but as far as dangerous drugs are concerned there *is* a procedure in place.'

Thorne's favourite word again.

'But on rotation day, things can get a bit lax. I've worked in hospitals where you could walk out pushing a bed and carrying a kidney machine on August the first. I'm sorry, but whoever took these drugs could have come from anywhere.'

Susan. Christine. Madeleine. '*Something, Tommy. A lead. Something . . .*'

Thorne took out his phone to call Tughan back.

It was Helen Doyle's first round of drinks, but already she was worrying about how much she'd spent. A few designer bottles and a couple of rum and Cokes and it was three times what she earned in an hour.

Sod it. It was Nita's birthday and she didn't do this very often.

She loaded the drinks on to a tray and looked across to where her mates were sitting at a corner table. She'd known three of them since school and the other two for almost that long. The pub wasn't busy and the few people in there were probably pissed off with the noise they were making. On cue the gang began to laugh, Jo's high-pitched cackle the loudest of all. Probably another one of Andrea's filthy jokes . . .

Helen walked slowly back to the table, the other girls cheering when she put the tray down and diving on to their drinks as if they were the first of the night.

'Didn't you get any crisps?'

'Forgot, sorry . . .'

'Dizzy bitch.'

'Tell her the joke . . .'

'How much fucking ice has he put in here?'

Helen took a swig and looked at the label on the bottle. It didn't actually say what was in it. She'd got through plenty already. Hooch, Metz, Breezers. She was never really sure what she was drinking, what the booze was, but she liked the colours and she felt fashionable with the slim, cold bottle in her hand. Sophisticated. Nita drained half of her rum and Coke. Jo emptied the remains of a pint of lager and belched loudly.

'What do you drink those for? It's like pop!'

Helen felt herself blush. 'I like the taste.'

'It's not supposed to taste nice, that's the point.'

Nita and Linzi laughed. Helen shrugged and took another swig. Andrea nudged her. 'Like you know what!'

There was a groan. Jo stuck two fingers down her throat. Helen knew what they were talking about, but part of her wished they wouldn't. Sex was pretty much all Andrea ever talked about.

'Tell us how big his cock was again, Jo.'

The strippergram had been Andrea's idea and Nita had seemed to like it. Helen thought he was really fit, all covered in oil, and he made her go very red, but the poem about Nita hadn't been that good. She could tell that he'd been as embarrassed as her when Jo grabbed his crotch, and for a second he'd looked really upset. Then he'd smiled and grabbed his clothes from off the floor while everybody whistled and cheered. Helen had whistled and cheered too, but she wished she'd been a bit more pissed.

'Big enough!'

'More than a mouthful's a waste.'

Helen leaned across to Linzi. 'How's work?'

She was probably closest to Linzi, but they hadn't spoken properly all night.

'Shit. I'm going to chuck it in . . . do some temping or something.'

'Right.'

Helen loved her job. The money was poor, but the people were nice and even though she had to give her mum and dad a bit, it was still cheap living at home. She couldn't see the sense in moving out, not until she met someone. What was the point in renting a grotty flat like Jo or Nita? Andrea still lived at home anyway. God knows where she was having all that sex she was always on about . . .

'Let Me Entertain You' came on the jukebox. It was one of her favourite songs. She nodded her head to the rhythm and sang the words quietly to herself. She remembered a fifth-form disco, and a boy with an earring and sad brown eyes and cider on his breath. When the chorus came, the rest of the girls joined in and Helen shut up.

The bell rang and the barman shouted something incomprehensible. Andrea and Jo were all for another round. Helen grinned but she knew she should be getting back. She would feel bad in the morning and her dad would be waiting up for her. She was starting to feel woozy and knew that she should have gone home and had her tea before she came out. She could have changed too. She felt frumpy and self-conscious in her black work skirt and sensible blouse. She'd grab a bag of chips on the way home. And a piece of fish for her dad.

Andrea stood up and announced that they'd all put in for one more. Helen cheered along with the rest of them, drained the bottle and reached into her purse for a couple of pound coins.

Thorne sat with his eyes shut listening to Johnny Cash. He rolled his head around on his neck, enjoying every crack of cartilage. Now the Man in Black with the dark, dangerous voice was insisting that he was going to break out of his rusty cage. Thorne opened his eyes and looked around at his neat, comfortable flat – not a cage, exactly, but he knew what Johnny was talking about.

The one-bedroom garden flat was undeniably small, but easily maintained and close enough to the busy Kentish Town Road to ensure that he never ran out of milk or tea. Or wine. The couple in the flat upstairs were quiet and never bothered him. He'd lived here less than six months after finally selling the house in Highbury, but he already knew every inch of the place. He'd furnished the entire flat during one wretched Sunday at IKEA, spent the next three weeks putting the stuff together and the succeeding four months wishing he hadn't bothered.

He couldn't say he'd been unhappy since Jan had left. Christ, they'd been divorced for three years and she'd been gone nearly five, but still, everything just felt . . . out of kilter. He'd thought that moving out of the house they'd shared and into this bright new flat would change things.

He'd been optimistic. However close to him the objects around him were, he had no real . . . connection to any of them. It was functional. He could be out of his chair and in his bed in a matter of seconds but the bed was too new and, tragically, as yet unchristened.

He felt like a faceless businessman in a numberless hotel room.

Perhaps it would have been better if Jan had gone because of the job. He'd seen it often enough and it was the stuff of interminable TV cop shows – copper's wife can't stand playing second fiddle to the job, blah blah blah. Jan had never been an ordinary copper's wife and she'd left for her own reasons. The only job involved in the whole messy business was the one she'd been on every Wednesday afternoon with the lecturer from her creative-writing course.

Until he'd caught them at it. In the middle of the day with the curtains drawn.

Candles by the bed, for Christ's sake . . .

Jan said later that she never understood why Thorne hadn't hit him. He never told her. Even as the scrawny bastard had leaped from the bed, his cock flapping, scrabbling for his glasses, Thorne knew that he wasn't going to hurt him. As he let the pain wash over him, he knew that, reeling and raw as he was, he couldn't bear to hear her scream, see the flash of hatred in her eyes, watch her rushing to comfort the little smartarse as he sat slumped against the wardrobe, moaning and trying to stop the blood.

A few weeks later he'd waited outside the college and followed him. Into shops. Chatting with students on the street. Home to a small flat in Islington with multi-coloured bicycles chained up outside and posters in the window.

That had been enough for him. That simple knowing.

You're mine if I ever decide to come and get you.

But after a while even that seemed shameful. He'd let it go. Now it was the stuff of late nights and red wine and singers with dark, dangerous voices.

Yes, he'd brought the job home – especially after Calvert, when things had slipped away from him for a time – but they'd got married far too young. That was all, really. Perhaps if they'd had kids . . .

Thorne scanned the TV pages of the *Standard*. Tuesday night and bugger all on. Even worse, Sky had shown the Spurs–Bradford game at eight o'clock. He'd forgotten all about it. At home against Bradford – should be three points in the bag. Teletext, the football fan's best friend, gave him the bad news.

She was slumped, her back against his legs, buttocks pressing down on her heels and knuckles lying against the polished wooden floorboards. He stood behind her, both hands on the back of her neck, readying himself. He glanced around the room. Everything was in place. The equipment laid out within easy reach.

Her mouth fell open and a wet gurgling noise came out. He tightened his grip, ever so slightly, on her neck. There was really no point in trying to talk and, besides, he'd heard quite enough from her already.

An hour and a half earlier, he'd watched as the group of girls had begun to thin out. A couple had wandered off towards the tube and a couple more to the bus stop. One tottered off down the Holloway Road. Local, he guessed. Perhaps she'd like to join him for a drink.

He'd taken a left turn and driven the car round the

block, emerging on to the main road twenty yards or so ahead of her. He'd waited at the junction until she was a few feet away then got out of the car.

'Excuse me . . . sorry . . . but I seem to be horribly lost.' Slurring the words ever so slightly. Just the right side of pissed. And so well-spoken.

'Where are you trying to get to?'

Wary. Quite right too. But nothing to worry about here. Just a tipsy hooray lost on the wrong side of the Archway roundabout. Taking off his glasses, looking like he's having trouble focusing . . .

'Hampstead . . . sorry . . . had a bit too much . . . Shouldn't be driving, tell you the truth.'

'That's OK, mate. Hammered meself as it goes . . .'

'Been clubbing?'

'No, just in the pub – mate's birthday . . . really brilliant.'

Good. He was glad she was happy. All the more to want to live for. So . . .

'I don't suppose you fancy a nightcap?' Reaching through the car window and producing it with a flourish.

'Blimey, what are you celebrating?'

Christ, what was it with these girls and a bottle of fizz? Like a hypnotist's gold watch.

'Just pinched it from a party.' Then the giggle. 'One for the road?'

About half an hour. Thirty minutes of meaningless semi-literate yammering until she'd started to go. She was full of herself. Nita's boyfriend . . . Linzi's problems at work . . . a couple of dirty jokes. He'd smiled and nodded and laughed, and tried to imagine how he could possibly have been less interested. Then the nodding-dog head and the sitcom slurring, and it was time for the innocuous-looking man to tip his paralytic girlfriend into the back of his car and take her back to his place.

Then he'd made the phone call, and put her in position.

And now Helen wasn't quite so gobby.

Again the gurgling, from somewhere deep down and desperate.

'Ssh, Helen, just relax. It won't take long.'

He positioned his thumbs, one at either side of the bony bump at the base of the skull and felt for the muscle, talking her through it . . . 'Feel these two pieces of muscle, Helen?'

She groaned.

'The sternocleidomastoid. I know, stupidly long word, don't worry. These muscles reach all the way down to your collar-bone. Now what I'm after is underneath . . .' He gasped as he found it. 'There.'

Slowly he wrapped his fingers, one at a time around the carotid artery and began to press.

He closed his eyes and mentally counted off the seconds. Two minutes would do it. He felt something like a shudder run through her body and up through the thin surgical gloves into his fingers. He nodded respectfully, admiring the Herculean effort that even so tiny a movement must have taken.

He began to think about her body and about how he might have touched it. She was his to do with as he pleased. He could have slipped his hands from her head and slid them straight down the front of her and beneath her shirt in a second. He could turn her round and penetrate her mouth, pushing himself across her teeth. But he wouldn't. He'd thought about it with the others too, but this was not about sex.

After considering such things at length he'd decided that his was a normal and healthy impulse. Wouldn't any man feel the same things with a woman at his mercy? So easily available? Of course. But it was not a good idea. He did not want them . . . classifying this as a sex crime.

That would be easy, would throw them too far off the scent. And he knew all about DNA.

A growl came from somewhere deep in Helen's throat. She could feel everything, was aware of everything and still she fought it.

'Not long now . . . Please be quiet.'

He became aware of a drumming noise and, without moving his head, glanced down to where her fingers were beating spastically against the floorboards. Adrenaline staging a hopeless rearguard action against the drug. She might make it, he thought, she wants to live so much.

One minute forty-five seconds. His fingers locked in position, he leaned down, his lips on her ear, whispering: 'Night-night, Sleepyhead . . .'

She stopped breathing.

Now was the critical time. His movements needed to be swift and precise. He eased the pressure on the artery and pushed her head roughly forward until chin was touching chest. He let it rest there for a few seconds before whipping it back the same way so that he was staring down at her face. Her eyes were open, her jaw slack, spittle running down her chin. He dismissed the urge to kiss her and moved her head back into the central position. Back into neutral. Then he took a firm grip and entwined his fingers in her long brown hair before twisting the head back over the left shoulder.

And holding it.

Then the right shoulder. Each twist splitting the inside of the vertebral artery. Now it was up to her.

He laid her down gently and placed her body in the recovery position. He was sweating heavily. He reached for a glass of cold water and sat down on the chair to watch her. To wait for her to breathe.

His mind was empty as he focused, unblinking, on her face and chest. The breaths would be short and shallow, and he watched and willed the smallest movement. Every few seconds he leaned forward and felt for a pulse.

Helen's body was unmoving.

He reached for the bag and mask. It was time to intervene. Ten minutes of frantic squeezing, shouting at her: 'Come on, Helen, help me!' Screaming into her face. 'I need you to be strong.'

She wasn't strong enough.

He slumped back into the chair, out of breath. He looked down at the lifeless body. A button was missing from her shirt. He looked across at the plain black shoes, neatly placed one next to the other by her side. The small pile of jewellery in a stainless-steel dish next to them. Cheap bracelets and big, ugly earrings.

He mourned her and hated her.

He needed to move. Now it was just about disposal. Quick and easy.

He began to strip her.

Thorne picked up the bottle of red wine from the side of his chair and poured another glass. Maybe forty-year-old men were better off on their own in neat, comfortable but small flats. Forty-year-old men with bad habits, more mood swings than Glenn Miller and twenty-odd years off the market had very little say in the matter. A taste for country-and-western hardly helped.

Johnny was singing about memories. Thorne made a mental note to programme the CD player to skip this track next time. Had Frank been right when he'd asked if the Calvert case was still part of the equation?

Take one fresh and tender corpse . . .

Fifteen years was too long to be lugging this baggage around. It wasn't his anyway. He couldn't recall how it had been passed on to him. He'd only been twenty-five. Those far above him had carried the can, as it was their job so to do. He'd never had the chance to take the honourable way out. Would he have done it anyway?

One man, released . . .

He'd had no say in letting Calvert go after the interview. The fourth interview. What happened in that corridor and later, in that house, seemed like things he'd read about like everybody else. Had he really felt that Calvert was the one? Or was that a detail his imagination had pencilled in later, in the light of what he had seen that Monday morning? Once everything started to come out, his part in it all was largely forgotten anyway.

Four girls, deceased . . .

Besides, what was his trauma – God, what a stupid word – compared with the family of those little girls who should still have been walking around? Who should have had their own kids by now.

Memories are made of this.

He pointed the remote and turned off the song. The phone was ringing.

'Tom Thorne.'

'It's Holland, sir. We think we've got another body.'

'You think?'

His stomach lurching. Calvert smiling as he walked out of the interview room. Alison staring into space. Dead Susan, dead Christine, dead Madeleine, crossing their fingers.

'Looks the same, sir. I don't think they'd even have passed this one on to us but she hasn't got a mark on her.'

'What's the address?'

'That's the thing, sir. The body's outside. The woods behind Highgate station.'

Minutes away, this time of night. He downed the rest of the glass in one. 'You'd better send a car, Holland. I've had a drink.'

'Best of all, sir . . .'

'Best?'

'We've got a witness. Somebody saw him dump the body.'

I could sense that Tim really wanted to know who the flowers were from. He didn't say anything, but I know he was looking at them. He didn't ask me. Maybe that's because it was a question he actually wanted an answer to, and not just a pointless conversation with his ex-girlfriend who's now a retarded mong.

Sorry, Tim. But nothing can prepare you for this, can it? I mean, you go through all the usual stuff, holidays together, meeting each other's friends. He never had to deal with meeting the parents, jammy sod. His were a nightmare! But this was never part of the deal, was it? 'How would you cope if I was on a life-support machine and completely unable to move or communicate?' never really comes up in those early intimate little chats, does it?

Oh, and I've got an air mattress now, to stop me getting bed sores apparently. It's probably hugely comfy. Makes a racket, though. Low and electrical. Sometimes I wake up and lie in the dark thinking that somebody's doing a bit of late-night vacuuming in the next room.

Anne's got the hots for that copper, I reckon. He does seem nice, I grant you. Nicer than her ex anyway, who sounds like a tit. The copper's funny, though. I was pissing myself when he apologised for being a bit whiffy. I heard Tim asking one of the nurses about the flowers. There was no card and the nurse went away to ask one of her mates. Now I think Tim suspects I'm having an affair with a policeman. Obviously, he must be a fairly strange policeman with a taste for cheap yellow nighties and extremely compliant girlfriends who never answer back.

What's that old joke about the perfect woman? If I was a nymphomaniac and my dad owned a brewery, he'd be quids in . . .

FOUR

The Sierra pulled up behind the operations van. As soon as Thorne stepped out of the car he could see that things were going to be difficult. Even at two o'clock in the morning it was still muggy but there was rain coming. Valuable evidence would be lost as the scene turned quickly to mud. The various photographers, scene-of-crime-officers and members of the forensic team were going about their business with quiet efficiency. They knew they didn't have very long. Anything useful was usually found in the first hour. The golden hour. Tughan would still have everything covered anyway: he'd have rung for a weather forecast. This was their first sniff of a crime scene, and nobody was taking any chances.

Thorne set off down the steep flight of steps that led to Highgate tube station and gave access to Queens Wood – the patch of woodland bordering the Archway Road. As he walked he could see the glare of the arc lights through the trees. He could see the figures of forensic scientists in white plastic bodysuits, crouched over what he presumed was the body, in search of stray fibres or hairs from the girl's clothing. He could hear instructions being barked out, the hiss of camera flashes recharging and the constant drone of the portable generator. He'd been at many such scenes in the past, far too many, but this was like watching the A-team work. There was a determination about the entire process that he'd seen only once before. There was a distinct absence of whistling in the dark. There was no gallows humour. There wasn't a flask of tea to be seen anywhere.

It was only when he ducked under the handrail and began to pull on the plastic overshoes provided by a passing SOCO that Thorne realised just how difficult a crime scene this would be to examine. He also saw at once how callous the killer had been in his choice of dumping ground. The body lay hard against the high metal railings that bordered the pavement all the way down the hill. On one side lay the main road and on the other, some hundred feet of dense woodland on a steep hill leading down to the underground station at Highgate. The only access to the body was up the hill and through the trees. Though a well-trodden path had already emerged, it was still a slow process negotiating the route to the body. The ground was hard and dry but it would take only ten minutes of rain to turn it into a mud chute. By the time they'd got the scene protected with polythene tents it would hardly have been worth the effort. He hoped they got what they needed quickly. He hoped there was something to get.

Dave Holland came jogging down the slope towards him. He was backlit beautifully by the arc lights. Thorne could quite clearly make out the silhouette of a notebook being brandished. He doesn't look like a policeman, thought Thorne, he looks like a prefect. Even with a hint of stubble, his tidy blond hair and ruddy complexion made him the obvious target for comments of the aren't-policemen-looking-younger-these-days variety. Pensioners adored him. Thorne wasn't sure. Holland's father had been in the force and, in Thorne's experience, that was rarely without problems. He doesn't even move like a copper, he thought. Coppers don't skip down hills like mountain goats. Coppers move like . . . ambulances.

'Cup of tea, sir?'

OK, perhaps he'd been a bit naïve. There was always tea.

'No. Tell me about this witness.'

'Right, don't get too excited.'

Thorne's heart sank. It was obviously not going to be earth shattering.

'We've got a vague physical description, not a lot.'

'How vague?'

'Height, build, a dark car. The witness, George Hammond . . .'

That fucking notebook again. He wanted to ram it up the cocky little gobshite's arse.

'. . . was at the top of the path a hundred yards further up the main road. He thought the bloke was chucking a bag of rubbish over.'

That was what Thorne had already worked out. He must have pulled up and heaved the body over the railings. She might just as well have been a bag of rubbish.

'And that's it? Height and build?'

'There's a bit more on the car. He says he thinks it was a nice one. Expensive.'

Thorne nodded slowly. Witnesses. Another thing he'd had to become resigned to. Even the more perceptive ones gave conflicting accounts of the same event.

'Mr Hammond's eyesight isn't brilliant, sir. He's an old man. He was only out walking his dog. We've got him in the car.'

'Hang about, those railings are six feet high. How big did he say he was?'

'Six two, six three. She's not a big girl, sir.'

Thorne squinted into the lights. 'Right, I'll have a word with the optically challenged Mr Hammond in a minute. Let's get this over with.'

Phil Hendricks was crouched over the body, his pony-tail secured beneath his distinctive yellow showercap. The scientists had finished their scraping and taping, and Hendricks was taking his turn. Thorne watched the all-too-familiar routine as the pathologist took temperature readings and conducted what, until the body was removed, would be a cursory examination. Every minute or so he would heave himself on to his haunches with a grunt, and mumble into his small tape-recorder. As always, each tedious detail of the entire procedure was being immortalised on film by the police cameraman. Thorne always wondered about those characters. Some of them seemed to fancy themselves as film-makers – he'd actually had to bollock one once for shouting, 'That's a wrap.' Some had a disturbing glint in their eye that said, 'You ought to come round to my place and have a look at some of the footage I'll be showing the lads at Christmas.' He couldn't help wondering if they were all waiting to be headhunted by some avaricious TV company eager for more mindless docusoaps. Maybe he was being too harsh. He was too harsh about Holland as well. Perhaps it was just the perfectly pressed chinos and loafers he didn't like. Maybe it was just that Holland was a young DC eager to please.

Hadn't *he* been like that? Fifteen years ago. Heading for a fall.

Hendricks began to pack away his gear and looked up at Thorne. It was a look that had passed between them on many occasions. To the untrained eye this 'handing over of responsibility' might have seemed as casual as two pool-players exchanging a cue. Pathologists were supposed to be colder than any of them but despite the Mancunian's flippant, nasal tones and dark sense of humour, Thorne knew what Hendricks was feeling. He'd watched him crying into his pint often enough. Thorne had never reciprocated.

'He's getting a tad fucking casual, if you ask me.' Hendricks began fiddling with one of his many earrings. Eight the last time Thorne had counted. The thick glasses gave him an air of studiousness but the earrings, not to mention the discreet but famous tattoos and the penchant for extravagant headgear, marked him out as unconventional to say the least. Thorne had known the gregarious goth pathologist for five years. He was ten years his junior and horribly efficient; Thorne liked him enormously.

'I didn't, but thanks for the observation.'

'No wonder you're touchy, mate. Two–one at home to Bradford?'

'Robbed.'

'Course you were.'

Thorne's neck was still horribly stiff. He dropped his head back and gazed up into a clear night sky. He could make out the Plough. He always looked for it: it was the only constellation he knew by sight. 'So, it's him, then, is it?'

'I'll know for sure by the morning. I think so. But what's she doing here? That's a hell of a busy road. He might easily have been seen.'

'He was. By Mr Magoo, unfortunately. Anyway, I don't think he was here very long. He just stopped and chucked her out.'

Hendricks moved aside and Thorne looked down at the woman who in a few hours would be identified as Helen Theresa Doyle. She was just a girl. Eighteen, nineteen. Her blouse was pulled up, revealing a pierced belly-button. She was wearing large hoop earrings. Her skirt was torn, revealing a nasty gash at the top of her leg.

Hendricks clicked his bag shut. 'I think the wound's from where she got caught on the railings as the bastard hoicked her over the top.'

Something caught Thorne's eye and he glanced to his right. Standing twenty or so feet away, staring straight at him, was a small fox. A vixen, he guessed. She stood completely still, watching the strange activity. They were on her territory. Thorne felt a peculiar pang of shame. He'd heard farmers and pro-hunt lobbyists ranting about the savagery of these animals when they killed, but he doubted that a creature killing to feed itself and its young could enjoy it. Bloodlust fed off a particular kind of intelligence. There was a shout from the top of the hill and the fox prepared to bolt but relaxed again. Thorne could not take his eyes from the animal as it stared into the artificially lit reality of a warped kind of human bloodlust. Of a genuine brutality. Half a minute passed before the fox sniffed the ground, its curiosity satisfied, and trotted away.

Thorne glanced at Hendricks. He'd been watching too. Thorne took a deep breath and turned back to the girl.

Conflicting emotions.

He felt revulsion at the sight of the body, anger at the

waste. Sympathy for the relatives, and terror at the thought of having to confront them, their rage and grief.

But he also felt the buzz.

The rush of the crime scene. The first crime scene. The thing that might smash the investigation wide open might be under their noses, waiting, asking to be found.

If it was there, he'd find it.

Her body . . .

There were leaves in her long brown hair. Her eyes were open. Thorne could see that she had a nice figure. He tried to get the thought out of his mind.

'He's always taken a bit of time before, a'n't he?' mused Hendricks. 'Nice and easy. Taken the trouble to lay them down like they'd stroked out watching telly or cooking dinner. He didn't really seem to care this time. Bit of a rush job.'

Thorne looked at him, asking the question.

'An hour or two at the most. She's not even cold yet.'

Thorne bent down and took the girl's hand. Hendricks pulled off his showercap then snapped off his rubber gloves, releasing a small puff of talcum powder. As Thorne leaned forward to close the girl's eyes, the hum of the generator filled his head. Hendricks's voice seemed to be coming from a long way away.

'I can still smell the carbolic.'

Anne Coburn sat in the dark room at the end of a horrible day that by rights should have ended three hours earlier. The papers were forever banging on about the intolerable hours worked by junior doctors but senior ones didn't exactly have it easy. A meeting with the administrator that should have taken an hour, and lasted three, had given her a headache that was only just starting to abate. It had raged through two lectures, a consultation round, an argument with the registrar and a mountain of paperwork. And David was still on the warpath . . .

She sat back in the chair and massaged her temples. Christ, these chairs were uncomfortable. Had they been designed that way deliberately to encourage visitors to deposit their fruit and bugger off?

Maybe if David had still been at home she'd have left the paperwork, but not any more. The house would be quiet. Rachel would be tucked up in bed by now, watching some emaciated drug casualty with too much eyeliner prancing about on MTV.

She thought about her daughter for a while.

They hadn't been getting on very well recently. The GCSEs had put them both under a lot of strain. Rachel was just letting off steam, that was all, having slogged her guts out. Anne had decided to buy her a present when she got her results, to say well done for working so hard. A new computer, maybe. She thought about getting it now instead.

And then she thought about Tom Thorne.

She looked at the flowers he'd brought with him and smiled as she remembered his apology to Alison for . . . what was the word he'd used? Humming. She'd thought he'd smelt good. She thought he smelt honest. He wasn't a hard man to find attractive. She probably had a few years on him, but knew instinctively that he wasn't the type that would be bothered by that. He was chunky. No . . . solid. He looked like he'd been round the block a few times. He was the sort of man to whom she'd found herself drawn since things had begun to fizzle out with

David – many years ago, if she was being honest with herself.

It was odd that there was more grey in Thorne's hair on the left-hand side. She'd always liked brown eyes as well.

Anne was suddenly aware that she was voicing her thoughts. These late-night conversations with Alison were becoming routine. Nurses were used to discovering her wittering away in the middle of the night. She had begun to look forward to talking to Alison. Engaging with Alison's brain was vital as part of her treatment but Anne found it therapeutic too. It was strange and exciting to be able to speak your mind and not be . . . judged. It was confession without the spooky stuff. Perhaps somewhere Alison *was* judging her. She was probably full of opinions – 'Sod the crusty copper! Find yourself a tasty young medical student!'

One day Anne would find out exactly what Alison had been thinking. Right now, the hum of the machinery was making her sleepy. She stood up, reached across and gently squeezed the lubrication drops into Alison's eyes before taping them shut for the night. She took off her jacket, scrunched it up and put it beneath her head as she sat down again. She closed her eyes, whispered goodnight to Alison and was immediately asleep.

By seven thirty the next morning the body had been formally identified. Helen Doyle's parents had rung to report that she hadn't come home at about the same time as George Hammond was watching her tumble over the railings into Queens Wood. Within hours of that first concerned phone call, Thorne was leaning against a wall, watching them walk slowly down the corridor, away from the mortuary. Michael Doyle sobbed. His wife, Eileen, stared grimly into the distance and squeezed her husband's arm. Her high heels click-clacked all the way down the stone steps as they walked outside, to be greeted by the dazzling, crisp and completely ordinary dawn of their first day without a daughter.

Now Thorne stood with his back to a different wall. Dead Helen had taken her place alongside the others. She hadn't spoken up yet but it was only a matter of time. Now, forty or so officers of assorted rank, together with auxiliaries and civilian staff, sat waiting for Thorne to speak to them. As ever, he felt like the badly dressed deputy headmaster of a run-down comprehensive. His audience exchanged bored pleasantries or swapped laddish insults. The few women on the team sat together, deflecting the casual sexism of colleagues for whom 'harass' was still two words. The wisps of smoke from a dozen or more cigarettes curled up towards the strip-lights. Thorne might as well have been back on twenty a day.

'The body of Helen Doyle was discovered this morning in Queens Wood in Highgate at just after one thirty a.m. She was last seen leaving the Marlborough Arms on Holloway Road at eleven fifteen. The post-mortem is being carried out this morning but for now we're working on the assumption that she was killed by the same man responsible for the deaths of Christine Owen, Madeleine Vickery and Susan Carlish . . .'

The dead girls: '*Oh, come on, Tommy. You know it was him.*'

'. . . as well as the attempted murder of Alison Willetts.'

But it *wasn't* attempted murder, was it? The killer was actually attempting to do something else. Thorne didn't know the word for it. They'd probably have to invent one if they ever caught him. He cleared his throat and ploughed on.

'George Hammond, who discovered the body, has given us a vague description of a man seen removing the body from his car and dumping it at the scene. Six feet one or two, medium build. Dark hair possibly. Glasses maybe. The car is a blue or possibly a black saloon, no make or model as yet. The victim was abducted at some point on her journey from the pub to her home on Windsor Road, which is no more than half a mile away, sometime between eleven fifteen and eleven thirty. Nobody's reported seeing anything but somebody did. I'd like them found, please. Let's get a make on that car and a decent description . . .'

Thorne paused. He could see one or two officers exchanging glances. It had taken him less than a minute to impart the essential information, the paltry scraps of fact that were supposed to shift the operation up a gear.

Frank Keable stood up. 'I don't really need to tell you, but the usual press blackout, please.' The media hadn't got hold of the killings, not as the work of one man at any rate. The fact that the murders hadn't been concentrated in one area and had been so well disguised had made it hard for them. It had taken the police long enough to put it together themselves. Still, Thorne was surprised: Backhand had been up and running for weeks now and they usually had sources within most high-level operations. In time there would be a leak and then the usual buck-passing would begin. The tabloids would come up with a lurid nickname for the killer, publicity-hungry politicians would bleat about law and order, and Keable would give him a speech about 'pressure being brought to bear'. But so far so good.

Keable nodded at Thorne. He was free to continue.

'Helen Doyle was eighteen years old . . .' He stopped and watched his colleagues nod with due disgust. He had not paused for effect. He was feeling the knot in his stomach tighten, slippery and undoable.

Helen was not much older than Calvert's eldest.

'Unlike the other victims she was not attacked in her home. It's a fair bet he didn't do it on the street and the method of killing would suggest that he couldn't do it in a car. So where did he take her?' Thorne talked some more. The usual stuff. Obviously they were still waiting on the results from the forensic team. These were the first real tests they'd been able to carry out and he was hopeful. They should all be hopeful. This might be the breakthrough. It was time to pull their fingers out. They were going to get him. Come on, lads . . .

The house-to-house was allocated. There was talk of a television reconstruction. Then chairs were scraped back, sandwiches ordered, and Frank Keable was summoned to the office of the detective superintendent.

'What's the point? He knows I'll have sod all to tell him until this afternoon.'

'Maybe he just wants to share a power breakfast with you. Mind you, you've already had yours.' Thorne pointed at the ketchup stain on Keable's shirt.

'Bollocks.' He spat on a finger and tried to rub out the bright red splodge.

'He got it wrong again last night and he doesn't like it,' Thorne said.

Keable looked up at him, still rubbing, reaching into his pocket for a handkerchief.

'The way he dumped the girl's body so quickly. He just

wanted shot of her, Frank. He thought he'd cracked it after Alison and when he botched it again I think it really pissed him off. He's getting impatient. And he's getting arrogant. He took a big risk snatching this one off the street. These women, these girls, are just bodies to him, dead or alive. He's just carrying out a procedure on them and I think he blames them when he gets it wrong. There's no real violence, but he's angry.'

'If he's in such a hurry to get rid of them, what's the washing all about?'

'I don't know. It's . . . medical.'

'The fucker probably scrubs up.' Keable snorted. Thorne stared over his head. 'Oh, come on, Tom. Listen, isn't this what we want? If he's getting impatient or whatever, he's far more likely to screw up somewhere and give us what we need to get him.'

'Or just start killing faster. It's been twenty-two days since Alison Willetts was attacked. Susan Carlish was six weeks before that . . .'

Keable stroked the top of his head. 'I know, Tom.' It was a declaration of efficiency, a statement of competence, but Thorne saw something else: a quiet instruction to calm down. A warning. So often he glimpsed the same thing concealed behind a gentle enquiry or a concerned stare. He'd see it most, of course, when there was a suspect. Any suspect. It scalded him, but he understood. The Calvert case was part of a shared history. Folklore almost, like Sutcliffe. A guilt they all inherited at some level or other. But he'd been part of it and they hadn't. He'd been . . . in amongst it.

Keable turned and marched away towards the lift. A car would be waiting to take him across town for the meeting. He pressed the button to go down and turned back to Thorne. 'Let me know as soon as Hendricks gets in touch.'

Thorne watched Keable get into the lift and each shrugged their way through the fifteen seconds of dead time waiting for the doors to close. Keable would tell the chief superintendent that while they were obviously waiting on the results of all the tests, there was the distinct possibility of a breakthrough. Somebody must have seen the killer taking the girl. This was definitely the break in the case that they needed.

Thorne wondered if they would bother broaching the subject that had hung in the air since the note was discovered on his car. It might have been saying 'come and get me', and dumping Helen Doyle's body so clumsily may well have been a taunt, but one thing was obvious: the killer was no longer bothering to disguise what he was doing because he knew they were on to him. If knowing the police had put it together was making him careless, then Thorne was happy that he knew. What really bothered him was how.

Why can't they fucking well fix this? They can stick a human ear on a mouse and clone a fucking sheep. They clone sheep, for Christ's sake, which is the most pointless thing ever since how the bloody hell are you supposed to tell when every sheep looks like every other sodding sheep and there's NOTHING REALLY WRONG WITH ME!

Nothing really . . . wrong.

A stroke. It sounds so soothing, so gentle. I don't feel like I've been stroked by anything. I feel like I've been hit with a jack-hammer. My nan had a stroke, but she could talk afterwards. Her voice was slurred and the drugs made her go a bit funny. Up to then she'd just wittered on about . . . you know, old people's stuff. She never went as far as telling complete strangers how old she was at bus stops, but you know the sort of thing. The drugs they put her on turned her into a geriatric performance poet. She'd lie there ranting about how motorbikes were driving through the ward at night and how the nurses all wanted to have sex with her. Honestly, it was hysterical – she was eighty-six! But at least she could make herself understood. This man gave me a stroke. Anne told me what he did. Twisted some artery and gave me a stroke. Why can't they just untwist it, then? There must be specialists or something. I'm lying here screaming and shouting, and the nurses wander past and coo at me like I'm taking a lazy afternoon nap in the sun. They must have finished all the tests by now. They must know that I'm still in here, still talking to myself, ranting and raving. It's doing my head in! See? I've still got a sense of humour, for fuck's sake.

I was right about Anne and the copper. Thorne. I've met women like Anne before. Always go for the two types of men – the ones that spark something off in their brains or the ones that get it going in their knickers. A man who does both? Forget it. I think it's fairly obvious which category her ex falls into. Time to ring in the changes. So the copper's luck's in, if you ask me.

I reckon I *might have to stick to the brainboxes from now on.*

Tim just sat by the bed this morning and held my hand. He doesn't even bother talking to me any more.

FIVE

Thorne sat perched on the edge of Tughan's desk in the open-plan operations room. As Tughan's hands manoeuvred his mouse and flew across his keyboard, Thorne could almost see the Irishman's back stiffen. He knew he was annoying him.

'Isn't there something you should be doing, Tom?'

Phil Hendricks had worked through the night, and even before Keable had settled down to coffee and croissants with the chief superintendent, Thorne had received the information he'd wanted. Helen Doyle had been heavily drugged with Midazolam and had died as a result of a stroke. In spite of the body's location and the apparent break with his routine, there was no doubt that she had been the killer's fifth victim. That was pretty much all they knew, other than that Forensics had gathered some fibres from Helen Doyle's skirt and blouse. Thorne got straight on the phone.

'Any joy on these fibres?'

'Give us a bloody chance.'

'All right, just give me your best bloody guess, then.'

'Carpet fibres, probably from the boot of the car.'

'Can you get a make?'

'Where do you think this is? Quantico?'

'Where?'

'Forget it. Look, we'll get on to it. Something to match it to would help . . .'

The change in the pattern bothered Thorne, but they were left trying to answer the same questions. How had he talked his way into these women's houses and perhaps, in Helen Doyle's case, talked her into getting into his car? Helen Doyle's body, like that of Alison Willetts and Susan Carlish, was unmarked yet full of drink and drugs. The tranquilliser had to have been administered with alcohol. But how? Had the killer been watching Helen all night and spiked her drink before she left the pub? That would have been difficult – she was with a large group of friends and, besides, to have got the timing of it right would have been near impossible. How could he have known exactly when the drug would start to take effect? It was still the best guess, so Thorne had set about rounding up as many people as possible who had been in the Marlborough at the time. This, on top of the general canvassing along Helen's route home, meant that they were going to need every extra body that Frank Keable could deliver. If he could deliver. Thorne was hopeful of finding somebody who'd seen Helen after she'd left the pub. He still couldn't fathom why the killer was being so brazen but it made him more optimistic than he'd felt in a long time.

'Is there something I can help you with?'

Tughan smiled a lot but his eyes were like something on a plate. He was as skinny as a whippet and fiercely intelligent, with a voice that could cut through squad-room banter like a scalpel. It was always Tughan's thin lips Thorne imagined whispering into the mouthpiece whenever some lunatic phoned Scotland Yard with a coded warning. It wasn't that Thorne didn't appreciate what Tughan was capable of or what he brought to the investigation: Thorne could just about find his way into a file, if he had to, but he couldn't type to save his life and always found himself strangely hypnotised by the screensavers. When new evidence came in, Tughan was the man to make sense of it with his collation programmes and filefinders. Thorne knew that if they'd had a Nick Tughan fifteen years earlier instead of a thousand manilla folders . . . if they'd had a Holmes computer system instead of an antiquated card index, then Calvert might not have done what he did.

'*Hey, Tommy, bugger the Calvert case, what about* our *case?*'

'Tom?'

'Right . . . sorry, Nick. Have you got a copy of the Leicester/London matches handy?'

Tughan grunted, scrolled and double clicked. The printer on the far side of the office began to hum. Thorne had actually been hoping that Tughan might have had a hard copy lying about. It would have been quicker to walk across to his own little goldfish bowl and fetch the copy on his desk, but he couldn't begrudge Tughan his little triumphs of efficiency. He begrudged him virtually everything else, and the feeling was entirely mutual.

Thorne stared at the list. Half a dozen doctors who had been on rotation at Leicester Royal Infirmary at the time of the Midazolam theft and now worked in local hospitals. Anne Coburn's information about the significance of the date had somewhat dampened any enthusiasm for this line of enquiry, and the discovery of Helen Doyle's body had rightly demanded everybody's attention, but

Thorne still sensed that it might be important. It was possible to look at the date of the drugs theft as significant in quite the opposite way. Might not the killer (if indeed it *was* the killer) have chosen that date to make it look as if he might have come from anywhere when in fact he *was* working at the hospital? Besides, they were still working through the far bigger list of all doctors currently on rotation locally so they'd have to get round to this lot eventually.

Jeremy Bishop's name was second on the list.

Thorne was aware of what could only be described as a smirk on Holland's face as they rode the lift down to the car park. 'Isn't he Dr Coburn's friend?'

'She knows him, yes. And his alibi certainly checks out theoretically, yes.'

Jeremy Bishop had unquestionably been responsible for treating Alison Willetts in A and E.

'But Alison Willetts was taken to the Royal London for a reason,' Thorne explained, as if talking to a child. 'I want to check exactly when Bishop came on duty in relation to when she was brought in.'

The smirk stayed on Holland's face. He knew all about Thorne's visit to Queen Square. Was he visiting Alison Willetts or the doctor who was treating her? He was well aware that they could have checked out Bishop with a phone call or, at the very least, sent somebody else.

Thorne felt no compulsion to explain himself to Holland any further. As they stepped out at the ground floor and walked towards the car, he tried to convince himself that Bishop's friendship with Anne Coburn, about whom he was thinking more than he should, wasn't the main reason he was keen to eliminate him from the enquiry as quickly as possible.

As he tucked into a late breakfast, he thought about how tired Thorne had looked at eight o'clock that morning arriving at work. He'd watched him from the greasy spoon opposite as the policeman leaned against his car for a moment before plodding towards the door. He hadn't considered Thorne the plodding type at all. That was why he'd been so delighted when he discovered that he was on the case. That, and the other obvious reason. Thorne, he'd decided, was definitely dogged. And stubborn. These were qualities he required. Plus, of course, the capacity for being too clever for his own good. He certainly needed that. All in all, Thorne was perfect. But it had troubled him to see Thorne looking so worn out. He hoped that the fatigue was just physical and that the detective inspector wasn't burning out. No, he was justifiably exhausted after the . . . demands of the night before. They'd found her quickly. He was impressed. So Thorne had had a rough night. That made two of them.

One out of five. Down from twenty-five to twenty per cent. He'd known straight away, of course. He'd made the necessary phone call then gone about his business, but it was obvious within a minute or two that she'd let him down. Stupid drunken sow. His heart, which had been pounding with the oncoming rush of the dash to hospital with another one for the machines, had quickly slowed to its habitual steady thump. *Her* useless, cholesterol-soaked heart couldn't be bothered to thump at all. What an opportunity he'd given her. But she'd let her sad, silly little life ebb away. Oh, he'd almost certainly have been seen getting rid. They'd have a description of sorts by now. So what? They might even have seen the car. So much the better.

He chewed his toast and stared out of the window at the view across London. The mist was starting to lift. It would be another glorious day. Helen had been just as easy as the others to prepare. Easier. He was getting better at it. There had been those couple of disastrous attempts earlier on, but he was more relaxed about it these days.

Christine and Madeleine had been cautious at first. They were naturally reluctant to let him in but they were lonely women and he was an attractive man. They wanted to talk. And more. And he was very persuasive. Susan and Alison had both invited him in almost instantly and happily drunk themselves into oblivion. Literally. He giggled to himself. The champagne had been an inspired idea. He'd thought about a jab but it would have been messy and he didn't want any sort of struggle. The wait was a little longer with the champagne, naturally, but he liked watching them go slowly. He savoured the frisson of their impending malleability. The other one – the one whose name he hadn't had time to find out – had positively guzzled it down. But then he'd had to leave because the timing had not been . . . judicious. Still, he felt sure that she'd said nothing about it. She would have had a hard enough time explaining to her husband or boyfriend or girlfriend why she was so utterly out of it when they got home. She certainly wouldn't have mentioned inviting a strange man into the house.

It had been such a relief to be able to work on Helen in his own home. He so hated dissembling. He'd hated creeping about in those dreary houses. It had made his flesh crawl to leave the bars of soap and bottles of pills in those dirty, greasy bathrooms. Rolled-up tights and shit stripes in the lavatory bowls. He hated putting his hands on them. On their heads. Even through the gloves he could feel the dirt and grease in their hair. He could swear he almost felt things . . . moving. But now he could work in clean, comfortable surroundings. Now *he* knew that *they* knew that *he* knew that . . .

He whistled his own invented melody to accompany this comforting refrain as he tried his best to stay awake. Thorne wasn't the only one feeling the strain. He needed more coffee. For a moment he closed his eyes and thought about Alison. She hadn't let him down. She'd wanted to live. He thought about going to visit her again, but it was perhaps a little risky. Security in ITUs was fairly tight, these days. The flood had been an inspired idea but could only be a one-off. He began to drift away. Yes, he'd need to think of something else if he wanted to go and see Alison again without getting caught.

Without bumping into Anne Coburn.

'Are you in any pain, Alison?' Doctors Anne Coburn and Steve Clark watched the pallid, peaceful face intently. There was no response. Anne tried again. 'Blink once for yes, Alison.' After a moment there was the tiniest movement – the ghost of a twitch around Alison's left eye. Anne looked across at the occupational therapist who scribbled notes on his clipboard. He nodded at her. She carried on. 'Yes, you are in pain? Was that a yes, Alison?' Nothing. 'Alison?' Steve Clark put his pen away. Alison's left eyelid fluttered three times in rapid succession. 'OK, Alison.'

'Maybe she's just tired, Anne. I'm sure you're right. It's just a question of her gaining sufficient control.'

Anne Coburn had a lot of time for Steve Clark. He was

a brilliant therapist and a nice man, but he lied very badly. He wasn't at all convinced. But she was. 'I feel like somebody who's called out the TV repairman and then there's nothing the matter, only the other way round . . . oh shit, you know what I mean, Steve.'

'I just think that maybe you're rushing things a bit.'

'I'm following well-established guidelines, Steve. The ECG shows normal brain activity.'

'Nobody's arguing with that but it doesn't mean she's got the ability to communicate. I agree that there is movement but I've seen nothing to convince me that it isn't involuntary.'

'This isn't just me, Steve. You can talk to the nursing staff. I'm sure she's ready to communicate.'

'She might be ready—'

'And she's able. I've seen it. She indicated to me that she was in pain, that she was tired. She . . . greets me, Steve.'

Clark opened the door. He was eager to be on his way. 'Maybe she's not comfortable with the pressure of . . . performing.'

Later, when she felt calmer, Anne would realise that he'd been trying to be genuinely sympathetic. At that moment she was angry and frustrated, for herself and for Alison. 'She isn't a performer and these are not cheap theatrics . . .'

But that's exactly what it felt like.

As Holland steered the unmarked Rover into a quiet tree-lined street in Battersea, he took a deceptively vicious speed bump just fast enough to take several layers off the underside of the car and to awaken his boss somewhat rudely.

'Jesus, Holland . . .'

'Sorry sir . . .'

'I know it's only a company car, but for Christ's sake!'

The sunshine was dazzling and Thorne felt every one of the twenty-eight hours since he'd last slept. Holland actually held the car door open for him! Thorne felt that it wasn't so much in deference to his rank as a subtle reminder that the fifteen years he had on the younger man were starting to show.

Jeremy Bishop lived in an elegant three-storey house with a small but well-maintained front garden. Probably four bedrooms. Probably tastefully decorated Thorne guessed, and crammed with what the slimier estate agents, if you could quantify slime, would refer to as 'periods'. Probably worth a piffling half a million. All this, and a nice Volvo parked outside. Clearly Bishop was not struggling.

Holland rang the bell. Thorne looked up at the windows. The curtains were still drawn. After a minute or two the door was opened, Holland made the introductions and he and Thorne were ushered into the house by a sleepy-looking Jeremy Bishop.

While Holland stood efficiently with his notebook at the ready, Thorne slumped into a chair, gratefully accepted a cup of coffee and racked his brain as to why Jeremy Bishop looked so familiar. He was, Thorne guessed, in his mid- to late-forties and, despite the stubble and redness round the eyes, looked ten years younger. He was tall, six two or three, and he reminded Thorne of Dr Richard Kimble, the character played by Harrison Ford in *The Fugitive*. There was plenty of grey in the short hair, but along with the wire-rimmed glasses, it served only to make him look 'distinguished'. This irritated Thorne enormously: his own grey hair simply made him look 'old'. Bugger probably didn't even have grey pubes. Bishop would, without question, be a regular performer in student nurse fantasies – 'Oh, Doctor! Here in the sluice room!?' He thought about Anne Coburn. He tried not to think about her stripping in the sluice room. Weren't doctors ugly any more? He remembered the rancid old GP he'd been dragged to see regularly as a boy: a hideous crone with a man's haircut and moustache, who smelt of cheese and always had a Craven A dangling from the corner of her mouth as she mumbled in an incomprehensible eastern-European accent. No such worries with Jeremy Bishop. His modulated tones would have calmed a thrashing epileptic in an instant.

'I presume this is about Alison Willetts,' he said.

Holland looked at Thorne, who sipped his coffee. Let the constable handle it.

'And why would you presume that, sir?'

Thorne stared at Holland through the steam from his coffee-cup. Nice start: sarcasm, superiority and a hint of aggression. Make your subject feel at ease.

Bishop wasn't fazed at all. 'Alison Willetts was attacked and seriously injured. I treated her, and they don't send detective inspectors round when you haven't paid your parking fines.' He smiled at Holland who could do little else but move on to item two in the do-it-yourself guide to interviews.

'We are investigating a very serious crime, which—'

'Has he done it again?'

Thorne almost spilt his coffee as he sat bolt upright in his chair. Holland looked across at him, thoroughly nonplussed. Bishop's amusement at the look on Holland's face was not lost on Thorne. He guessed that Bishop had seen that look many times as a junior doctor found themselves suddenly out of their depth and sought reassurance, or preferably hands-on assistance, from a senior colleague. Thorne decided that the hands-on approach was best. 'Done what again, sir?'

'Look, I'm sorry if I'm not supposed to know about the other victims. As far as I'm concerned it's simply a question of putting my patient's condition in context. I was informed that there had been other attacks. Anne Coburn and I are very old friends, Inspector, as I'm sure you're well aware.'

Thorne was very well aware that, despite Frank Keable's best intentions, the lid was not going to stay on this case for very long. Not that he ever really thought of cases as having lids . . . saucepans had lids . . . cases had . . . what? . . . locks? . . . well, only open and shut ones. Mind you, was there any point in a case that didn't open and shut. God he was tired . . .

'I'm sorry if we got you out of bed, sir.'

Bishop spread his arms across the back of the sofa. 'Oh, well, I obviously look as rough as you, Inspector.' Thorne raised an eyebrow. 'I spend a lot of time with people who don't get much sleep for one reason or another. The eyes give it away instantly. I've been on call all night. What's your excuse?' His laugh was somewhere between a chuckle and a snort.

Thorne laughed back at him through a good impression of a yawn. 'Yep . . . busy night. What about you, sir?'

Bishop stared at him. 'Oh . . . no, not really. Went in to treat an overdose at about three o'clock and got home about five thirty. But even when you're not called in, it's hard to relax when you're bleeper-watching. Thank God for cable TV.'

'Anything good on?'

'I'm a confirmed channel-hopper, I'm afraid. A lot of old sitcoms, the odd black-and-white film and a fair bit of smut.' He looked up and grinned in disbelief at Holland. 'Are you actually writing all that down, Constable?'

Thorne had been asking himself the same question. 'Only the bit about smut. Detective Constable Holland's life lacks excitement.' Thorne was astonished to see Holland actually blush.

Bishop stood up and stretched. 'I'm going to get another coffee. Anybody else?'

Thorne followed him into the kitchen and they chatted over the growing grumble of the kettle.

'So what time did you go in the night you treated Alison Willetts?'

'I was bleeped at about three o'clock, I think. One sugar, wasn't it?' Thorne nodded and waited for Bishop to continue. 'The patient was found outside by a service entrance . . . I'm sure you know all this . . . and brought straight into A and E.'

'Did you call in when you were bleeped?'

'No need. It was a message saying red trauma. You just go. Sometimes you might get an extension number to ring, or sometimes it's just a message to phone in, but with a trauma call you just get in the car.'

'And when Alison Willetts was brought in, you were the first person to treat her?'

'That's correct. I checked her pupils – they were reacting. I bagged and masked her, intubated her, Midazolam to sedate her, ordered a CT of her head and an ECG, and handed it over to the junior anaesthetist.' Bishop took a sip of his coffee. 'Sorry, I must sound like an episode of *Casualty*.'

Thorne smiled. 'More like *ER*. On *Casualty* it's usually a cup of sweet tea and a couple of aspirin.'

Bishop laughed. 'Absolutely right. And the nursing staff aren't quite so attractive.'

'So if you were bleeped at three o'clock you got there, what, about half past?'

'Something like that, I suppose.'

'And Alison, the patient, was brought in about quarter to four?' Bishop sipped and nodded. 'So why were you bleeped in the first place?'

'I really couldn't tell you, I'm afraid. It isn't unusual – sometimes you can spend ages trying to find out why you've been called in. I've been bleeped before when I shouldn't have been. As for that particular night, I've never really thought about it. I mean, if I'd known exactly what had happened – or, rather, what we'd later discover – I might have a better grasp of the sequence of events that night. It was just a routine emergency at the time. Sorry.'

Thorne put down his coffee-cup. 'Not to worry, sir. I'm sure we can find out.'

Bishop smiled as he picked up Thorne's cup, poured the unfinished coffee into the sink and opened the door of the dishwasher. 'Why I might have been bleeped four Tuesdays ago? Good luck, Inspector.'

As the car moved slowly through the traffic on Albert Bridge, Holland chose not to ask his superior officer a number of questions. Why did we bother driving all that way? Do you think Jeremy Bishop is giving Anne Coburn one? Why do you take the piss out of me all the time? Why do you think you're so much better than everybody else?

He looked across at Thorne, who was slumped in the passenger seat with his eyes shut. He was wide awake.

Thorne spoke only once, to tell Holland that they weren't going back to the office just yet. Without opening his eyes he told him to turn right and drive along the river towards Whitechapel. They were going to call in at the Royal London Hospital first, to see just how cast-iron this alibi of Jeremy Bishop's really was.

Just call me the Amazing Performing Eyelid Woman! Only I can't sodding well perform, can I?

I went out with this actor once. He told me about a recurring dream where he was onstage ready to do his luvvie bit and then all the words just tumbled out of his head like water running really fast down the plughole. That's what it felt like when Anne was asking me to blink. Christ, I wanted to blink for her. No . . . I wanted to blink for me. I can do it, I know I can. I've been doing it all the fucking time when there's nobody there and I've been blinking when Anne's asked me to before. She asked me if I was in pain and I blinked once for yes. One blink. A fraction of a movement in one poxy eye and I felt like I'd just won the lottery, shagged Mel Gibson and been given a year's supply of chocolate.

Actually, I felt like I'd just run the London Marathon. A couple of blinks and I'm knackered. But when that therapist was watching I couldn't do it.

I was screaming at my eyelids inside my head. It felt like the signal went out from my brain. But slowly. It was like some dodgy old Lada beetling along the circuits, or whatever they're called. Neuro-highways or whatever. It was on the right road and then it just got stuck at roadworks somewhere. Like it lost interest. I know I can do it but I haven't got any control over it. When I'm not trying I'm blinking away like some nutter, but when I want to I'm as good as dead.

If blinking's all I've got left, I'm going to be the greatest fucking blinker you've ever seen. Stick with me, Anne. There's so much I want to tell you. I'll be blinking for England, I swear.

I could feel the disappointment in her voice. I wanted to cry. But I can't even do that . . .

SIX

'Where to, sir?'

'Muswell Hill, please.'

'No problem, sir. Where is that, please?'

Thorne sighed heavily as the simple journey from his flat in Kentish Town suddenly became an altogether trickier proposition. It was his own fault for calling a minicab. Why was he such a bloody cheapskate?

He was trying not to think about the case – this was a night off. He fooled himself for about as long as it took the cab to reach the end of his road. He would have loved to spend an evening without his curious calendar girls, but it was going to be hard, considering where he was going and who he was going to see. The subject of Jeremy Bishop might be strictly off limits with Anne Coburn. It was becoming clear that they were extremely close. Were they perhaps more than that? Thorne tried not to think about that possibility. Whatever, their relationship made things awkward in every sense, not least procedurally.

Thorne hated the cliché of the instinctive copper as much as he hated the notion of the hardened one. But the instinctive copper was only a cliché because, he knew, it contained a germ of truth. Hunches were nothing but trouble. If they were wrong they caused embarrassment, pain, guilt and more. But the hunches that were right were far worse. Policemen . . . good policemen, weren't born with these instincts. They developed them. After all, accountants were only good with numbers because they worked with them every day. Even an average copper could spot when someone was lying. A few developed a feel, a taste, a sense about people.

They were the unlucky ones.

'Here you go, sir.'

The minicab driver was thrusting a tattered *A–Z* at him. Christ on a bike, thought Thorne, do you want me to drive the bloody car for you?

'I don't need the *A–Z*. I'll give you directions. Straight up the Archway Road.'

'Right you are, sir. Which way is that?'

Thorne looked out of the window. Another warm late-August evening and a T-shirted queue of eager Saturday night concert-goers was waiting to go into the Forum. As the cab drove past he strained his head to see the name of the band but only caught the word '. . . Maniacs'. Charming.

He now lived no more than half a mile from where he'd grown up. This had been his adolescent stamping ground. Kentish Town, Camden, Highgate. And Archway. He'd worked out of the station at Holloway for six months. He knew the road Helen Doyle had lived in. He'd drunk in the Marlborough Arms. He hoped she'd enjoyed herself that night . . .

Jeremy Bishop.

Yes, it had started as a strange familiarity, which he still couldn't fathom, but it had become more than that. In the few days since he'd first laid eyes on the man, his feelings had begun to bed themselves down on more solid foundations.

Thorne had found out quickly why Bishop had smiled when he'd told him he was going to check out why he'd been bleeped the night that Alison had come in. He was amazed to find that the calls put out to bleep doctors were untraceable. There were no official records. The call could have been made from anywhere by all accounts. It was even possible to bleep yourself. None of the likely candidates could recall bleeping Bishop on the night that Alison Willetts came in. He'd spoken to the senior house officer, the registrar and the junior anaesthetist and their recollection of events that night was as fuzzy as Bishop had known it would be. He was certainly there when she was brought into A and E but his alibi, as far as when she was attacked and when she was dumped at the hospital, was not quite as solid as Anne Coburn had first thought.

He couldn't put any of it together yet, nowhere near, but there were other . . . details.

The canvas of the area in which Helen Doyle had disappeared had started to yield results. She had been seen by at least three people after leaving the pub. One was a neighbour who knew her well. All the witnesses described seeing her talking to a man at the end of her road. She was described variously as 'looking happy', 'talking loudly' and 'seeming as if she was pissed'. The descriptions of the man varied a little but tallied in a number of areas. He was tall. He had short, greying hair and wore glasses. He was probably in his mid- to late-thirties. They thought he was Helen Doyle's new boyfriend. Her older man.

All the witnesses agreed on something else. Helen was drinking from a bottle of champagne. Now they knew how the drug was administered. So simple. So insidious. As the victims' capacity to resist had melted away they'd each felt . . . what? Special? Sophisticated? Thorne sensed that the killer thought of himself in exactly those terms.

The driver turned on his radio. An old song by the Eurythmics. Thorne leaned forward quickly and told him to switch it off.

The cab turned right off the A1 towards Highgate Woods.

'It's just off the Broadway, OK?'

'Broadway . . .'

Thorne caught the driver's look in the mirror. Apologetic yet not really giving a toss.

'If black-cab drivers do the Knowledge, what do you lot do?'

'Sorry, mate?'

'Doesn't matter.'

He'd waited a day before talking to Frank Keable. Stepping into the DCI's office he'd been thoroughly prepared to outline his suspicions – the details that pointed towards Bishop. Ten minutes later he'd walked out feeling like he'd just left Hendon.

'I have to be honest, Tom. No, he doesn't have a rock solid alibi but . . .'

'Not for any of the murders, sir. I checked with—'

'But all you've got is a lot of stuff that, well, it doesn't rule him out, and what about the description? Two of the witnesses say he's early- to mid-thirties.'

'The height's right, Frank, and Bishop looks a lot younger than he is.'

It was at that point that Thorne had become aware that it was all starting to sound unconvincing. He decided to stop before he said something that might make him look vaguely desperate. *'And he's a doctor! And I don't really . . . like him very much . . .'*

The same night he'd walked into his flat and heard a woman's voice coming from the living room.

'. . . at the office. God, I hate these things – sorry. Anyway, please give me a call, I'm very excited about it.'

He grinned. How could a woman who probed about in people's brains be so out of her depth with an answering-machine? He found it endearing, then knew that she'd think he was being patronising. He picked up.

'Tom?'

What was she asking? '*Is* that Tom?' Or 'Is it OK if I *call* you Tom?' Either way his answer was the same.

'Yes. Hi . . .'

'This is Anne Coburn – sorry, I was just waffling away. I tried to get you at the office, I hope you don't mind.'

He'd written his home number on the back of the card he'd given her. He threw his coat on to the sofa and dragged the phone over to the chair. 'No, that's fine. I've just this second walked in the door. So, what are you excited about?'

'Sorry?'

'You said you were excited. I heard it on the machine as I was coming in.'

'Oh, right. It's Alison. I think she's really starting to communicate.'

He was bending to retrieve the half-empty bottle of wine by the side of the chair but instantly sat up again. 'What? That's fantastic.'

'Listen, I do mean *starting*, and I have to say there are people who aren't quite as convinced as me that the movements aren't involuntary but I think you should see it.'

'Yes, of course . . .'

'He's killed another girl, hasn't he?'

Thorne leaned back in the chair. He wedged the phone between ear and shoulder and started to pour himself a hefty glass of wine. Had it made the papers? He hadn't seen anything. Even if it had, there was no link to the other killings. So how did she . . .?

Bishop. He'd obviously told her they'd been round. And just how much had *she* told *him* about the other killings? He'd need to ask her about that, tactfully.

'Look, I understand if you don't want to discuss it. Tom?'

'No, I was just thinking about something. Yes. We've found another body.'

It was her turn to pause. 'I know I said that Alison wouldn't be giving you any statements and she won't, I mean not in any conventional sense, but perhaps . . . Listen, I don't want to raise any false hopes.'

'You think she might be able to respond to questions?'

'Not just yet, but I think so, yes. Simple ones. Yes and no. We could work out a system maybe. Sorry, I'm waffling again. Obviously we need to talk about it but I just wanted to let you know . . .'

'I'm glad you did.'

And then she invited him to dinner.

He proffered the plastic bag containing a bottle of his favourite red wine as soon as she opened the door.

'Thanks, but there was no need.'

'Don't get excited, it's only a plastic bag.'

She laughed and stepped forward to kiss him on the

cheek. Her perfume was lovely. She was wearing a rust-coloured sleeveless top, cream linen trousers and training shoes. He was struck, not unpleasantly as it happened, by the fact that she was an inch or two taller than he was. He was used to that. He felt like he was going to enjoy himself. His good mood evaporated in an instant as he glanced over her shoulder and saw a man in the kitchen at the other end of the hall.

Jeremy Bishop was leaning against the worktop, opening a bottle of champagne.

Anne stepped aside to usher Thorne in and caught his look. 'Sorry,' she mouthed, shrugging.

As Thorne removed his leather jacket and made approving noises about the original coving, he was wondering what she meant. Sorry? She couldn't possibly have any idea what he really thought about Bishop, so what was she sorry for? As he walked towards the kitchen he came to the heartening conclusion that she was sorry they weren't going to be alone. Bishop held out a hand, smiling at him. Thorne smiled back. Sorry? Thinking about it, he wasn't sure that *he* was sorry at all.

'Perfect timing, Detective Inspector.' Bishop offered him a glass of champagne. Thorne felt a chill pass through him as he took it. Bishop looked thoroughly at home, moving easily around a kitchen with which he was obviously familiar. He wore pressed chinos and a collarless shirt. Silk by the look of it. He probably called it a blouse. Thorne felt instantly overdressed in his tie, and instinctively reached up to undo the top button of his shirt, which he definitely called a shirt.

Bishop drained his glass. 'Has the hernia been giving you any more trouble?'

'Sorry?'

'It came to me just after you and your constable left. Come on – don't tell me it hasn't been driving you mad as well. Your hernia op last year . . . I was your gas man.' Without waiting for a response – he would have been waiting for some time – he turned to Anne. 'I've given your sauce a stir, Jimmy, and I'm off to the loo.' He handed Anne his glass and moved past Thorne towards the stairs.

They stood in silence until they heard the bathroom door close.

'Is this awkward for you, Tom? Tell me if it is.'

'Why should it be?'

'I didn't invite him.'

Some good news. Thorne smiled graciously. 'It's fine.'

'I had no idea he was coming. He just dropped by and it would have been rude not to ask him to stay. I know you've questioned him, which is bloody ridiculous . . .'

Thorne took a sip of champagne. It wasn't a drink he was fond of.

'So?'

'So what?'

'So is it awkward?'

Awkward was putting it mildly. Thorne couldn't recall the last time he'd had a cosy dinner with a prime suspect.

He remembered the scene in Keable's office. Make that *his* prime suspect.

Still, it might be interesting. He already knew the basic facts. The two children, the wife who'd died. But there was no question that it would be valuable to get another . . . slant on things. Anne was looking intently at him. He hadn't answered her question. So he asked one instead: 'Jimmy?'

'A nickname from med-school days. James Coburn. You know, *The Magnificent Seven*. He was the one with the knives.'

'Right. Was he any good with scalpels?'

She laughed. 'Whatever misguided reasons you had to question Jeremy, I can fully understand that this might be putting you in a compromising position, but there are two very good reasons why you should stay and have dinner.' Thorne had no intention of going anywhere, but was perfectly happy to let her persuade him. 'One, I would very much like it if you did, and two, I make the finest spaghetti carbonara in North London.'

Dinner was fantastic. It was certainly the best meal Thorne had eaten in a while, but that was to damn it with faint praise. That his eating habits had become a trifle sloppy had been brought home to him on receipt of his BT family and friends list. They might just as well have sent an embossed calling card saying, 'You Sad Bastard'. Thorne's ten most frequently dialled numbers had not exactly been what he'd call kith and kin. He could only hope and pray that he didn't win the holiday. Two weeks in Lanzarote with the manager of the Bengal Lancer and a posse of spotty pizza-delivery boys on mopeds was hardly a prospect that appealed.

'I hope my grilling proved useful, Detective Inspector.' The way Bishop emphasised Thorne's rank, he might have been reading the cast list of an am-dram whodunnit. His evident glee at the situation told Thorne that he was more than willing to play his part but Anne was quick to discourage his interest in the case.

'Come on, Jeremy, I'm sure Tom doesn't want to talk about it. He probably can't, even if he wanted to.'

This was fine with Thorne. He had no need to talk about the case. He wanted to let Bishop talk, and once the boundaries had been established he wasn't disappointed. Bishop was full of stories. He seemed permanently amused, not only at his own patter but at the peculiarity of their cosy little threesome. Again, fine with Thorne. The anaesthetist dominated the conversation, occasionally making an effort to engage the policeman in trite chit-chat.

'Where do you live, then, Tom?'

'Kentish Town. Ryland Road.'

'Not my side of London. Nice?'

Thorne nodded. *No, not particularly.*

Bishop was a witty and entertaining raconteur – probably. Thorne did his best to laugh in all the right places, although he felt clumsy and cack-handed as he watched his fellow diners twirl spaghetti with professional deftness and delicacy.

'. . . and the two old dears were sat talking about the beef crisis and how they were going to exercise their rights as consumers and stick it to the French.'

'Politics in A and E?' Anne turned to Thorne. 'It's usually non-stop babble about football or soap operas or "I know it's a nasty cut but he's never hit me before, honest."'

'But get ready for the killer . . .' Bishop drained his wine glass, letting them wait for the punchline. 'I heard them saying how they were going to boycott French fries!'

Thorne smiled. Bishop raised his eyebrows at Anne and they both giggled before saying as one, 'NFN!'

Stifling her laugh, Anne leaned across to Thorne. 'Normal For Norfolk.'

Thorne smiled. 'Right. Stupid or inbred.' Bishop nodded. Thorne shrugged. *I'm just a copper. Thick as shit, me.*

Anne was still giggling. They'd already polished off two bottles of wine and hadn't finished the pasta yet. 'Somewhere there's a doctor with too much time on his hands thinking up these jokes. There's loads of them, not very nice usually.'

'Come on, Jimmy, they're just a bit of fun. I bet Tom's had to deal with a few JP FROGs in his time, haven't you, Tom?'

'Oh, almost certainly. That would be . . .?' Thorne raised his eyebrows.

'Just Plain Fucking Run Out of Gas,' Anne explained. 'When a patient is going to die. I hate that one . . .' She poured herself another glass of wine and leaned back in her chair, retiring momentarily as Bishop warmed to his theme.

'Jimmy gets a bit touchy and squeamish at some of the more ghoulish jokes that get us through the day. Seriously though, some of the shorthand is actually a useful way to communicate quickly with a colleague.'

'And keep the patients in the dark at the same time?'

Bishop pushed up his glasses with the knuckle of his index finger. Thorne noticed that his fingernails were beautifully manicured. 'Absolutely right. Another of Jimmy's pet hates, but by far the best way if you ask me. What's the point of telling them things they aren't going to understand? If you do tell them and they do understand, chances are it's only going to frighten the life out of them.'

Anne began to clear away the plates.

'So better a patient who's in the dark than a JP FROG?'

Bishop raised his glass to Thorne in mock salute. 'But that's not the best one. I get to deal with a lot of JP FROGs, but Jimmy, specialising as she does in lost causes, is very much the patron saint of TF BUNDYs.' He grinned, showing every one of his perfect teeth. 'Totally Fucked But Unfortunately Not Dead Yet.'

Thorne could hear Anne in the kitchen loading the dishwasher. He remembered the smug look on Bishop's face as he'd put the coffee cups in his dishwasher a few days before. He wore the same expression now. Thorne grinned back at him. 'So what about Alison Willetts? Is she a TF BUNDY?'

Thorne saw at once that if he'd thought this would throw Bishop then he was seriously underestimating him. The doctor's reaction was clearly one of undisguised amusement. He raised his eyebrows and shouted through to the kitchen. 'Oh, Christ, Jimmy, I think I'm outnumbered.' He turned back to Thorne and suddenly there was a glimmer of steel behind the flippancy. 'Come on, Tom, is the moral indignation that was positively dripping from that last comment really meant to suggest that you care about your . . . victims, any more than we care about our patients? That we're just unfeeling monsters while the CID is full of sensitive souls like your good self?'

'*Christ, Tommy, what a smug bastard . . .*'

Susan, Maddy, Christine. And Helen . . .

'I'm not suggesting anything. It just seemed a bit harsh, that's all.'

'It's a job, Tom. Not a very nice one at times and, yes, it's quite well paid after you've slogged your guts out training for seven years then spent a few more kissing enough arses to get to a decent level.' That certainly rang a bell. 'We're paid to treat, we're not paid to care. The simple truth is that the NHS can't afford to care, in any sense of the word.'

Anne put an enormous plate of cheesecake in the centre of the table. 'M and S, I'm afraid. Great with pasta. Crap at puddings.' She went back through to the kitchen leaving Bishop to start divvying it up.

'I always tell students that they have a choice. They can think of the patients as John or Elsie or Bob or whatever and lose what little sleep they get . . .'

Thorne held out his plate for a slice of cheesecake. 'Or . . .?'

'Or they can be good doctors and treat bodies. Dead or alive, they're bodies.'

What had Thorne said earlier to Keable?

'Are you going to let him get away with this shit, Tommy?'

'I'm not sure what I'm going to do. Why don't you help me? Is it him? Is he the one?'

The one question they never answer.

Thorne started to eat. 'So, what do most of your students decide?'

Bishop shrugged and took a mouthful. He chuckled. 'There's another one.'

'What?'

'CID. Another acronym.'

Thorne smiled at Anne as she sat back down and helped herself to a slice. Bishop grunted, demanding the attention of the audience. He'd obviously come up with something wonderful. Thorne turned to him and waited. Get ready for the killer . . .

'Coppers In Disarray?'

Bishop was the first to leave. He'd shaken Thorne's hand and . . . had he winked? Anne led him into the hall to get his jacket, leaving Thorne on the sofa with a glass of wine listening to them saying their goodbyes. Their obvious intimacy disturbed him in every way he could think of. The next part of the evening, whatever that was, would have to be handled very carefully. Their voices were lowered, but there was no mistaking Bishop's low hum of contentment as he kissed Anne goodbye. Thorne wondered how witty and garrulous he'd be with a detective constable's fist halfway down his throat. He wondered how smug he'd be in an airless interview room. He wondered what he'd have to do to get him into one.

He heard the front door shut and took a deep breath. Now he wanted to be alone with Anne and not just because of what she could tell him about Bishop.

She came back into the living room to find Thorne staring into space with a huge smile on his face. 'What's so funny?' Thorne shrugged. He didn't want to get off on the wrong foot by telling her that he'd just come up with his own little acronym for Jeremy Bishop. A highly appropriate one as it happened. GAS.

Guilty As Sin.

'Where's Rachel this evening? Have you locked her in her room with a Spice Girls video?'

'She's out celebrating her GCSE results.'

'God, of course, it was today.' The papers had been full of it. The increase in pass levels. The ever-widening gap between girls and boys. The six-year-old with an A* in maths. 'Celebrating? She must have done well?'

Anne shrugged. 'Pretty well, I suppose. She could maybe have tried harder in one or two subjects, but we were pretty pleased.'

Thorne nodded, smiling. *We?* 'Hmm . . . pushy mother.'

She laughed, flopping into the armchair opposite him

and picking up her glass of wine. Thorne leaned forward to refill his own glass.

'Tell me about Jeremy's wife.'

She sighed heavily. 'Are you asking me as a policeman?'

'As a friend,' he lied.

It was a good few seconds before she answered. 'Sarah was a close friend. I'd known them both at medical school. I'm godmother to their kids, which is why I'm sure that your interest in him is a complete waste of time and I don't want to harp on about this, but it's starting to feel a bit . . . insulting actually.'

Thorne did not want to lie to her, but he did anyway. 'It's just routine, Anne.'

She kicked off her shoes and pulled her feet up underneath her. 'Sarah was killed ten years ago . . . you must know all this.'

'I know the basic facts.'

'It was a horrible time. He's never really got over it. I know he seems a bit . . . assured, but they were very happy and he's never been interested in anyone else.'

'Not even you?'

She blushed. 'Well, at least I know that *this* isn't an official question.'

'Completely unofficial and horribly nosy, I know, but I did wonder . . .'

'We were together once, a long time ago when we were both students.'

'And not since? Sorry . . .'

'My husband thought so, if that makes you feel a little less nosy. David always had a thing about Jeremy, but it was really just professional rivalry, which he liked to tart up as something else.'

Like his hair, thought Thorne.

He'd tried to pace himself and Anne had drunk far more than he had, but he was definitely starting to feel a little lightheaded.

'What do his kids do?'

James, twenty-four, and Rebecca, twenty-six, another doctor. These facts and many others filling three pages of a notebook in his desk drawer.

'Rebecca's in orthopaedics. She works in Bristol.'

Thorne nodded, interested. *Tell me something I don't know.*

'James, well, he's done all manner of things over the last few years. He's been a bit unlucky, if I'm being kind.'

'And if you're being unkind?'

'Well, he does sponge off his dad a little. Jeremy's a bit of a soft touch. They're very close. James was in the car when the— they had the accident. He was a bit screwed up about it for a while.' She blew out a long, slow breath. 'I haven't talked about this for ages . . .'

Suddenly Thorne felt terrible. He wanted to hug her, but instead volunteered to make another cup of coffee. They both stood up at the same time.

'Black or . . .?'

'Listen, Tom, I've got to say this.' Thorne thought she was starting to sound a bit pissed. 'I don't know what you think about Jeremy, I don't know why you had to go and question him . . . I dread to think, actually, but whatever it is I wish you'd stop wasting your time. This is one of my oldest friends we're talking about, and I know he likes to play the hard-bitten, cynical doctor but it's just a party piece. I've heard it hundreds of times. He cares very much about his patients. He's very interested in Alison's progress . . .'

Alison. The one person they were supposed to talk about and hadn't.

'I meant to have a word with you about that, actually. You know we're trying to keep some things out of the papers?'

Her face darkened. 'Am I about to get told off?' She wasn't remotely pissed.

'He seems to know a lot about the case and I just wondered if . . .'

She took a step towards him – not afraid of a fight. 'He knows a lot about the medical case, yes. We've spoken about Alison regularly and obviously he knows about the other attacks because that has a direct bearing on things.'

'Sorry, Anne, I didn't mean—'

'He's a colleague whose advice I value and whose discretion you can count on. I'd say take my word for it, but obviously there wouldn't be much point.'

She stared at him, his first reminder since that morning in the lecture theatre of just how scary she could look. Evidently he didn't have quite the same capacity to intimidate her. Something in his face, he had no idea what, suddenly seemed to amuse her and her expression softened.

'Well, what's it been? A few weeks? And we're already on to our second major row. It doesn't bode well, does it?'

Thorne smiled. This was highly encouraging. 'Well, I'd actually categorise the first one as more of a bollocking, if you want to be accurate.'

'Are you going to get that coffee or what?'

As he filled the mugs from the cafetière, she shouted through to him from the living room, 'I'll stick some music on. Classical? No, let me try and guess what you're into . . .'

Thorne added the milk and thought, never in a million years. He shouted back, 'Just put whatever you want on . . . I'm easy.' As he walked back in with the coffee, he almost laughed out loud as she turned round brandishing a well-worn and wonderfully vinyl copy of *Electric Ladyland.*

As the taxi – a black one, he wasn't going to make that mistake again – ferried him back towards Kentish Town, the evening's conversation rattled around in his head like coins in an envelope. He could remember every word of it.

Bishop had been laughing at him.

The cab drove down the Archway Road towards Suicide Bridge and he looked away as they passed Queens Wood. He pictured the fox moving swiftly and silently through the trees towards its earth. A rabbit still twitching in its jaws, trailing blood across leaves and fallen branches as the vixen carries its prey home. A litter of eager cubs tearing their supper to pieces – ripping away pale chunks of Helen Doyle's flesh while their mother stands frozen, watching for danger . . .

Thorne stared hard at shopfronts as they flashed past. Bed shop, bookshop, delicatessen, massage parlour. He shut his eyes. Sad, soggy men and cold, brittle women, together for a few minutes that both would try later to forget. Not a pleasant image but . . . a better one. For now.

He knew that Helen and Alison and the rest of it would be with him again in the morning, lurking inside his hangover, but for now he wanted to think about Anne. Their kiss on the doorstep had felt like the beginning of something and that, together with the reliably pleasant sensation of being moderately off his face, made him feel as good as he had in a long time.

He decided that, late as it was, he'd ring his dad when he got in. It was ridiculous. He was forty. But he wanted to tell him about this woman he'd met – this woman with a teenage daughter, for God's sake. Rachel had arrived back just as he was leaving. He'd said a swift hello before making a quick escape once the inevitable argument started about how late she'd got back.

He wanted to tell his dad that 'maybe', with a large dollop of 'perhaps' and a decent helping of 'forget it, never in a million years', one of them might not be spending quite so much time alone any more.

He added a two-pound tip to the six-pound fare and headed up the front path, grinning like an idiot. It was always a risky business for cabbies, wasn't it, picking up pissed punters? A healthy tip or vomit in the back of the cab? That was the gamble. Well, one had just got lucky.

Thorne was humming 'All Along The Watchtower' as he put the key in the lock, and was only vaguely aware of the dark figure that emerged from the shadows and ran up the path behind him. He turned just as an animalistic grunt escaped from the mouth behind the balaclava and the arm came down. He felt instantly sick as a bulb blew inside his head.

And suddenly it was much later.

The objects in his living room were at the bottom of a swimming-pool. The stereo, the armchair, the half-empty wine bottle shimmered and wobbled in front of him. He tried desperately to focus, to get a little balance, but all his worldly goods remained upside down and stubbornly unfamiliar. He looked up. The ceiling inched towards him. He summoned every ounce of strength to roll himself over, face down on the carpet and vomit. Then he slept.

A voice woke him. Hoarse and abrasive. '*You look rough, Tom. Come on, mate . . .*'

He raised his head and the room was full of people. Madeleine, Susan and Christine sat in a line on the sofa. Their legs were neatly crossed. Secretaries waiting for a job interview. Not one of them would look at him. To one side Helen Doyle stood staring at the floor and chewing nervously at a hangnail. Huddled into the single armchair were three young girls. Their hair was neatly brushed and their white nightdresses were crisply laundered. The smallest girl, about five years old, smiled at him but her elder sister pulled her fiercely to her breast like a mother. A hand reached towards him and dragged him to his knees. His head pounded. His throat was caked in bile. He licked his lips and tasted the crusty vomit around his mouth.

'*Up you come, Tom, there's a good lad. Now, eyes wide open. Nice and bright.*'

He squinted at the figure leaning against the mantelpiece. Francis Calvert raised a hand in greeting. '*Hello, Detective Constable.*' The dirty blond hair, yellowed by cigarette smoke, was thinner now, but the smile was the same. Warm, welcoming and utterly terrifying. He had far too many teeth, all of them decayed. '*It's been ages, Tom. I'd ask how you were doing but I can see . . . Bit of a session, was it?*'

He tried to speak but his tongue was dead and heavy. It lay in his mouth like a rotting fish.

Calvert stepped towards him, flicking his cigarette towards the carpet and producing the gun in one horribly swift movement. Thorne looked frantically round at the girls on the armchair. They were gone.

At least he was to be spared that.

Knowing what would inevitably follow, he turned his attention back to Calvert, his head swinging round on his hunched shoulders with the ponderous weight of a wrecking ball. Calvert grinned at him, those rotten teeth bared as he clattered them theatrically against the barrel of the gun.

He tried to look away but his head was yanked upwards by the hair, forcing him to watch.

'*Ringside seat this time, Tom. All in glorious Technicolor. I hope that's not a new suit . . .*'

He tried to close his eyes but his eyelids were like tarpaulins, heavy with rain.

The explosion was deafening. He watched as the back of Calvert's head attached itself to the wall and began a slow, messy descent like some comical, slimy child's toy. He moved an arm to wipe away the hot tears that stung his cheeks. His hand came away red, the bits of brain between his fingers. As he slumped towards the floor he was vaguely aware of Helen moving across to join the others on the sofa and lead them in a round of polite but sincere applause.

It was like being horribly drunk and massively hungover at the same time. He knew he mustn't drift off again. The faces were still jumping around in his head like pictures in a child's flick book, but the speed was decreasing. The equilibrium had almost returned but the pain was beyond belief.

He was alone, he was himself, and he was crawling across the puke-ridden carpet, inch by agonising inch. He had no idea what time it was. There was no light coming through the window. Late night or early morning.

His fingers grasped at the nylon fibres of the cheap shagpile. He took a deep breath. Gritting his teeth and failing to stifle a cry of agony, he willed his knees to shuffle another few inches across the vast and merciless eight feet of carpet that separated him from the telephone.

PART TWO

THE GAME

Not spoken to Anne for a couple of days. Not really spoken, I mean. Well, let's get this straight. Perhaps I'm making these conversations sound like bouts of non-stop banter, full of juicy gossip and cracking gags. Let's not be stupid. Basically she spills her guts and I just blink occasionally. Don't get me wrong, they're fucking dynamite blinks, but I don't think I'm chat-show material just yet.

She's probably spending every free moment she's got getting it from her tame copper and his trusty truncheon. There are so many jokes I could make about taking down her particulars and policeman's helmets but I am far too classy.

'Tits first, I'm not a slag.' That's me.

My head is full of corny jokes but, come on, what else have I got to do? I've got shitloads of time on my hands and I'm hardly up to my eyeballs, am I?

I can't even kill myself. Joke!

I hope she hasn't lost faith in me. Anne, I mean. I'm not exactly sending the doctors scurrying about with talk of medical miracles. I know that. There's days when I feel so together it's just like I've got pins and needles or something, and as soon as they wear off I can get up and get dressed and go and call Tim.

And there's other days.

I used to do this thing years ago when I'd lie in bed and try really hard to think of a new colour. One that didn't exist. Or a completely new sound that you've never heard before. I think I read about it in some wanky women's magazine thing about inner calm or some such crap. It's really weird. You start to get dizzy after a while and then feel a bit stoned. I feel like that quite a lot now. Or sometimes I'd lie on my back and stare for ages at the ceiling and try to convince myself that it was the floor. If you concentrate really hard you can actually do it and you start holding on to the sides of the bed in case you fall. It's like that in here, only all the time. And I can't hold on to the side of the fucking bed, can I?

I'm falling . . .

SEVEN

Thorne would later classify the minor physical injury as the easiest of the ways in which he became a victim during the Backhand case. Not that he put himself anywhere near the top of the list. His life was not erased with the twist of a skilful finger or put on hold by the deadly and delicate touch of a hand on his neck. He never felt the sob catch in his throat as a sheet was lifted to reveal the expressionless face of a girlfriend or wife or daughter.

He saw them buried, but they were not his blood.

But still he suffered . . . losses. It was, of course his own doing, but he could only watch as, one by one, they fell away. This process, the honing down, the shedding of those around him was a long and painful journey for all concerned, but it began the moment Thorne opened his eyes and saw David Holland at his bedside, reading a copy of *FHM*. The first thing his brain told his mouth to do was swear, but all it could manage was a gulp and some half-hearted lip-smacking. He closed his eyes; he'd try again in a minute.

Holland was engrossed in a pictorial. The model, a quiz-show hostess, was gorgeous, but he reckoned that actually she wasn't that stupid. He couldn't help but be impressed by quotes like 'The main reason I had breast implants was that I wanted bigger tits.' He wondered what

Sophie would look like with bigger tits. He flinched mentally at the tirade of abuse that would surely be heaped upon him were he ever to bring it up.

Hearing a noise he lowered the magazine. The Weeble was awake and trying to say something.

'Do you want a drink of water or . . .?' Holland reached towards the jug on the bedside table, but Thorne was already closing his eyes.

Holland dropped the magazine and rummaged in a plastic bag beneath his chair. He produced a CD Walkman and, unsure exactly where to put it, placed it on the edge of Thorne's bed.

'I picked this up from your place after you were brought in. Thought you might be . . . .you know . . . and I got this from Our Price . . .' He produced a compact disc and struggled manfully with the Cellophane wrapping. 'I know you're into that country-and-western or whatever. I don't know much about it as it goes – more of a Simply Red man myself. Anyway . . .'

Thorne opened his eyes again. Music. It was a nice thought but some sunglasses would have been better. Or a Bloody Mary. His vision was blurred. He squinted at the CD Holland was brandishing and tried to focus on the sleeve. After a second or two he was able to make out the words *Kenny Rogers*. Before he had a chance to laugh he was asleep.

And Hendricks came. Filled him in on the details. Smacked over the head and drugged. Oh, and Spurs were already thinking about sacking their manager.

Then Keable. They'd got nothing from the flat. They'd fill him in when he was back on his feet. Oh, and the lads sent their best.

And finally Anne Coburn.

Thorne was perched on the edge of the bed putting on his shoes when the curtains were pulled aside. She was grinning. 'Fair enough – if I was in the Whittington I'd want to make a quick getaway.'

Thorne smiled for the first time since he'd last seen her. 'Why couldn't it have been the Royal Free, for Christ's sake? I could have done with a day or two with my feet up.'

Anne sat down next to him and gazed around the ward. 'This place isn't that bad, actually. It's just got a bit of a dodgy reputation.'

'I don't think people stick around long enough to find out. As soon as I saw the name on the blankets I started feeling much better.' He took what he hoped would be a final look around. Perhaps they *had* made an effort but there was something a bit desperate about it. The eastern-European eau-de-Nil on the walls had been replaced by a more optimistic orange, and there was even the odd pair of floral curtains, but it was still a hospital. He had spent the previous night failing to sleep through a cacophony of rattling trolleys, humming floor polishers and anonymous screeching. He would have felt only slightly less miserable in a private room with cable television, intravenous red wine and dancing girls.

Anne reached across towards his head. 'Can I?' Thorne lowered his head and she gently traced a finger along the stitches. 'They'd be happier if you stayed another night. I know you don't like hospitals but concussion is unpredictable . . . and when you've been shot full of Midazolam on top of it . . .'

'He wasn't very gentle about that either. I've got a bruise the size of a cricket ball on my arse. He could have tried the champagne – I might have gone for it, state I was in.'

'Perhaps you're not his type.' The filthy laugh . . .

Thorne finished tying his laces and stared straight ahead. 'Oh, he'll find out exactly what type I am.'

Anne looked away briefly at nothing in particular. She was starting to get a pretty good idea herself. 'He gave you a big dose, Tom. It can't have been . . . pleasant.'

'It wasn't.'

'It might sound strange but that's exactly why we use it. Midazolam fries your short-term memory and detaches you from reality. You go into a dream state. We can stitch up a ten-year-old while they stare at a blank wall and look at the lovely pictures.'

'Mine weren't particularly lovely.' He turned to look at her and tried his best to smile. 'How's Jeremy?'

She tried to look stern, but couldn't manage it. 'He's fine. He seemed rather concerned when I told him what had happened, considering that you two didn't really seem to hit it off.'

'He got home all right, then?'

She stared at him. He knew he was pushing it. He was being stupid and *she* was anything but. 'I mean, if he was half as pissed as I was, he might have had trouble.' The chuckle was forced and he knew she could see it. There was only one other way to go. He reached across and took her hand. 'I don't suppose we did hit it off, but the two of you *were* involved at one time.'

'It was twenty-five years ago.'

'Still, I'm hardly likely to invite him down the pub, am I?'

She squeezed his hand and smiled. They said nothing.

Not telling the truth wasn't the same as lying and he *would* be jealous of Bishop if he didn't feel something a whole lot stronger. Better that she thought it was jealousy. Much better.

Thorne blinked slowly and held his breath. The smell . . . and creaking mattresses, and squeaky shoes, and the uncomfortable smile on the faces of people at bedsides. Was it the same smile he'd given his mother all those times he'd sat by her bed and squeezed her hand and looked into her milky blue eyes and tried to figure out where the fuck she'd gone?

'Tom . . .'

The curtains moved again and Dave Holland appeared. Thorne let go of Anne's hand. 'My taxi's here . . .'

Anne stood up and moved towards the curtain. Before she turned, Thorne saw her smile at Holland and put her hand on his arm. What the hell was that about? *Look after the poor old bugger?*

'Give me a ring, Tom.'

She left and Thorne stared hard at Holland. He looked for the smirk but didn't see it. He couldn't see a notebook either. His vision obviously wasn't back to normal yet.

As they walked towards the car Thorne could feel the chill in the air. August had finally thrown in the towel and now there would be bad weather coming. He preferred it that way if he was honest. He was happier in an overcoat. A security blanket that covered a multitude of sins. The warm night when he'd stepped out of that taxi, pissed and singing, seemed a long way away. If it hadn't been for the wine he'd guzzled while he and Anne had flirted and talked about Jimi Hendrix and failed marriages, he knew that the whole, hideous thing would be over by now. He might even have been what's laughably called a hero. If he hadn't been pissed he might have seen it coming. He might have turned round a second earlier and he'd have had him. He might, at the very least, have avoided the blow. But the man in the balaclava with the iron bar and the needle had had a distinct advantage, of course.

He'd known Thorne was pissed, hadn't he?

Holland held the car door open but Thorne didn't resent it. They pulled out on to Highgate Hill.

'Have you got any food in? I had a quick look and I couldn't see much.'

'Are you inviting yourself round for a meal, Holland?'

'Do you want to stop somewhere? There's a Budgens on the way, isn't there?'

'You can get me a sandwich when we get to the office.'

'Sir?'

Holland looked across at Thorne whose head lay against the car window, his eyes half shut. He'd been wrong about the Weeble. He looked distinctly wobbly.

'There's not much happening at the moment, to be honest. The DCI said it would be best if—'

'Office.'

Holland put his foot down.

He'd stood at a bus stop and watched as Thorne and the young DC had climbed into the car and driven away. Thorne had been in hospital less than thirty-six hours. He was impressed.

So, now what?

Things would pick up a bit, wouldn't they? Thorne would be on the warpath for sure. They'd all have taken it personally, he knew that. That was the copper's way.

Once you involve one of their own, watch out! Like a piss-poor bunch of Masonic East-Enders. Thorne wasn't one of their own, though, was he? He'd hate that idea. He was getting to know the man, little by little, but he knew that for sure. He just needed to get him riled up a little, that was all.

The bus came, and he stood back and watched as people with no place to go hopped on and off, all of them pale and in pain. He turned away in disgust and started to walk down towards the underground station at Archway.

They'd probably see what he'd done to Thorne as a warning. Let them. Thorne would know it was something . . . other than that. He'd know a challenge when he saw one. When he felt one. He'd been personally involved since the first time he'd laid those big brown eyes on Alison. The sentimental idiot had felt sorry for her, hadn't he? He couldn't see beyond the machines. He couldn't smell the freedom. And he really cared about the dead ones. Oh, he really minded about those.

All in all it had worked out quite well and the business with Anne was a lovely bonus.

He stopped to look through the window of a bathroom shop. Mock antique mixer taps and other such shit. Baths with seats in and handles for the old and infirm.

Stupid.

He thought about Thorne's tiny flat. There was the home of a lonely man for sure. No, not a home. Neat and tidy, though, he'd give him that – apart from the empty wine bottles. He knew he'd have the edge on him that night on the doorstep. If Thorne had been sober he wouldn't have fancied his chances.

It was starting to get cold. He pulled down his hat and moved towards the entrance to the tube. Now he wanted some progress. He'd shaken things up for sure and they had to have come up with something. And let the profilers or whatever those over-qualified ponces called themselves, talk about a 'cry for help' or a 'desire to be stopped', if that's what paid their mortgages. Not that Thorne would have any time for psychobabble, he was pretty sure of that. And now that he knew what it felt like, now he knew how those women had felt before he'd laid hands on them, he'd be committed.

He'd known kids like Thorne at school. They just needed to be provoked and there'd be no containing them. Mad kids who would throw a desk out of the window or kill squirrels in the playground if you pushed them a bit – if you punched the right buttons. Thorne was no different. And now he'd kicked him in the shins. He'd rabbit-punched him. Now Thorne wouldn't stop.

A tall skinny woman with a pushchair beat him to the ticket machine. He stared at the back of her slender neck as she fumbled for change in her cheap plastic purse and stared at the station names as if they were printed in Chinese. Single mother, probably. The poor cow wrung out and desperate for a little comfort. Forty fags a day and a couple of Valium to numb the pain and get her through the afternoons.

He thought about any woman he saw now. He considered them all. He could see what each of them needed. Every one was . . . feasible.

'Good to have you back, Tom.'

Tughan's thin lips arranged themselves into what might

pass as a smile. Thorne thought he looked like a gargoyle. Holland made himself scarce and Thorne settled into a chair opposite his fellow DI. The comments of other officers were acknowledged with a nod and a light-hearted comment, and some of the smiles were undoubtedly sincere, but there were other faces he was less pleased to see again.

'*How's the head, Tommy? Now you know how it feels, mate . . .*'

His calendar girls.

Yes, he knew what it felt like to have the power over your own body taken away. He'd been out of control so many times that it was almost familiar, but *that* loss went hand in hand with a warm, sleepy feeling that the booze threw in for good measure. The wine came with a little something special to ease the pain of smashed furniture or grazed knuckles. But the drug had taken him to places he never wanted to see again.

'*He took away everything we had, Tommy . . .*'

'*I wanted to struggle . . .*'

'*We all did . . .*'

'*. . . to fight for my life, Tommy.*'

Tughan's mouth was moving but the sound was coming from a long way away.

Christine. Susan. Madeleine. And Helen. Drugged into oblivion and confronted by a monster. He'd confronted nothing but ghosts. The memories of ghosts. He thought about Alison. He needed to see her. He was still around and he wanted her to know that. He was still around only because that had been what the fucker wanted. He'd realised that straight away and hated the fucker for having the power to spare him. He'd chosen to give him his life.

He had made a mistake.

'*He should have killed me.*'

'*Don't say that, Tommy. Who would we have left to talk to?*'

'Tom? Are you feeling all right? You shouldn't have come in.'

Thorne turned his eyes from the wall. He stood up and walked around the desk, catching Holland's eye as he put his hand on Nick Tughan's shoulder. 'Not caught him yet, then, Nick?'

Tughan laughed. Nails on a blackboard. 'I'll leave that to you, Tom. You're the one with the instincts, aren't you?' Thorne stiffened. 'The one with experience.' He spoke the word as if he were naming a child molester. 'We're just getting on with the job, following leads. One or two of them yours, as a matter of fact.'

'Tom . . . .'

Keable was speaking from the doorway of his office. Thorne looked up and he retreated, the invitation to join him unmistakable.

'I'll catch up with you later, Nick. Why don't you e-mail me what you've got?'

Thorne walked across to Keable's office. He could hear Holland and one of the other DCs laughing as he went. Business as usual. But not for him.

Anne wanted to talk to Alison. Her workload meant that it was becoming increasingly difficult to spend a significant amount of time with her every day and they had stuff to catch up on.

He joined her a second or two after she stepped into the lift.

'David.'

'On the way up to see your locked-in case, I suppose. Any developments?'

'Do you care?'

He pressed the button and the doors started to close. There really wasn't a great deal to look at as a tactic to avoid what was sure to be an unpleasant encounter. She wondered instead if it was possible to escape from a lift using a trap-door in the roof as she had seen people do so often in films.

'I was sorry to hear about the attack on your policeman friend.'

They'd certainly done it in *The Towering Inferno*.

'Just after your cosy dinner *à trois* with Jeremy, wasn't it?'

And Hannibal Lecter did it in *Silence of the Lambs*. Just after he'd cut that man's face off. Hmm.

'Anne?'

'Yes, it was, and no, you're not sorry, you're just a twat.'

The lift reached the second floor and Anne stepped out the moment the doors opened. Higgins stood preventing them from closing. 'Hanging around with police officers is obviously doing marvels for your vocabulary, Anne.'

'You're awfully well informed about what I'm up to, David. Using our daughter as a spy is rather pathetic, though.'

'Oh, I thought you two had no secrets?'

Not usually, but maybe it was time that changed. She'd need to talk to Rachel. He was now wearing that hideous smirk she remembered him reserving for tiny triumphs or the expectation of dutiful sex. She smiled at him, feeling nothing but pity.

'Why are you here, David?'

'Just because we're divorcing doesn't mean that I'm not interested in your life. I am.'

She stepped towards him. Did she see him actually flinch? 'There was an *Oprah* or a *Ricki Lake* recently about divorcing couples, did you catch it? This woman said that it was only when she was divorcing Duane or Marlon or whoever, that she realised how much she loved him. It's weird, because all it's making me realise is how much I wanted to divorce you in the first place.'

The smirk had gone and she could see that the quiff was beginning to wilt slightly, but she could still feel the sharp tingle of the slap in a parked car, and picture the look in his eye after he'd spat at her in an Italian restaurant. Now he tried hard to look world-weary, but just looked old.

'You've become bitter, Anne.'

'And your hair is utterly ridiculous. I'm busy, David.'

The lift doors moved to close again, and Higgins was finding it hard to retain his balance. 'Aren't you at all interested in my life, Anne? What I'm doing?'

He was getting rusty – dollying up the ball like that. She couldn't wait to smash it home. 'OK, David. Are you still fucking that radiotherapist?'

She heard the doors closing as she walked away up the corridor. She knew that he'd never be certain if she'd heard his pathetic parting 'Give my love to Jeremy,' but it didn't matter either way.

She couldn't wait to tell Alison.

'Sit down, Tom.'

Thorne moved to take the uncomfortable brown plastic

seat so generously offered. 'Fuck, this sounds a bit serious. Am I going to get a bollocking for being whacked over the head and pumped full of shit?'

'Why are you here, Tom? Do you think we can't manage without you?'

'No, sir.'

'Stop pissing about, Tom.' Keable passed a hand across his face. He was probably trying to appear thoughtful, thought Thorne, or maybe he was just tired. All he had succeeded in doing was roughing up his voluminous eyebrows and making himself look like a bald wolfman. Keable puffed out his cheeks. 'Do you feel rough?'

'What are these leads that Tughan's talking about?'

'There was a note, Tom.'

Thorne was out of his chair in a second. 'At the flat? Show me . . .'

Keable opened a drawer and produced a dog-eared photocopied sheet of A4. He handed it to Thorne. 'The original's still at Lambeth.'

Thorne nodded. The Forensic Science Services Laboratory. 'Waste of time . . .'

'I know.'

Thorne sat down and read. Typed as before. The same smug familiarity in every sentence. The same enjoyment and belief in a unique and wonderfully detached sense of humour. The same sickening self-love . . .

TOM. I'M NOT A VIOLENT MAN. (HE PAUSES FOR HOLLOW LAUGHTER AND TO LET THE DETECTIVE INSPECTOR TOUCH HIS SORE HEAD.) DID YOU NEED STITCHES? I'M SORRY. I HOPE THE HEEBIE-JEEBIES WEREN'T TOO INTENSE. BOOZE AND BENZOS AREN'T THE MOST

HARMONIOUS OF BEDFELLOWS. SADLY I DIDN'T STAY TO WATCH. I SIMPLY WANTED YOU TO FEEL SOMETHING OF WHAT IT'S LIKE TO SURRENDER YOURSELF. I KNOW IT WASN'T A SURRENDER IN THE TRUEST SENSE OF THE WORD BUT WHO'S GOT TIME TO BE PEDANTIC? YOU'VE GOT MURDERERS TO CATCH AFTER ALL. A LITTLE PAIN WAS NECESSARY TO BRING YOU UP TO SPEED. AND THE GIRLS FELT NOTHING. REMEMBER THAT. I MUST APOLOGISE FOR HELEN BUT SHE REALLY DIDN'T WANT TO LIVE. ALISON WAS THE ONLY ONE WITH ENOUGH FIGHT TO MAKE IT. WHAT WAS THAT OLD ADVERTISEMENT? 'IT'S THE FISH JOHN WEST REJECTS . . .' THAT'S RATHER PAT BUT I'M SURE YOU'LL GET MY POINT. I KNOW YOU'RE ANGRY, TOM, BUT DON'T LET IT EAT YOU UP. USE YOUR ANGER FOR GOOD AS I HAVE AND THERE'S NOTHING YOU CAN'T ACHIEVE. THERE, I HAVE THROWN DOWN A GAUNTLET . . . OR AT THE VERY LEAST A SURGICAL GLOVE!!

SPEAK SOON.

P.S. I HAVE A PERFECTLY HEALTHY SEX DRIVE AND I WASN'T LOCKED IN A CELLAR AS A SMALL CHILD, SO DON'T WASTE VALUABLE MONEY OR RESOURCES ON CHARLATANS.

Thorne felt sick. He took a deep breath and slid the piece of paper back across the desk. Frank Keable raised his head and Thorne looked him straight in the eye. 'It's Bishop.'

Keable put the note into a drawer and slammed it shut. 'No, Tom, it isn't.'

Thorne couldn't look at him. His gaze drifted away to the green metal wastepaper bin, the cheap black plastic hatstand and expensive Barbour jacket. It floated across the dirty yellow walls and settled gratefully on the calendar. September. A particularly uninteresting view of Exmoor in the mist. A two-dimensional and probably long-dead stag the most animated thing in the room.

'So how did you and Dr Bishop enjoy dinner?'

Thorne was irritated that they'd put it together so quickly. He rather felt that he'd had his thunder stolen. He nodded, impressed. And curious.

'There was a message from Dr Coburn on your machine. She hoped you enjoyed your evening. We called her.'

'Right.'

'Did you, by the way? Enjoy your evening?'

'Yes.'

'Was the spaghetti good?'

'How the fuck . . . ?'

'You threw up all over your carpet, Tom. Spaghetti, and a fair amount of red wine . . .'

Thorne sensed that he might have only the one chance and he needed to perform better than he had last time. A matey tone was best. Conspiratorial. Us against him.

'He's a slimy piece of shit, Frank. He left before I did and waited.'

'He predicted your every move, then? He toddled off with the note he'd already prepared, tucked in his pocket, did he? And an iron bar and a syringe hidden inside his overcoat?'

Thorne was thinking quickly. Did Bishop have a bag with him? Had he seen a briefcase in Anne's hall? He couldn't remember. He was pretty sure Bishop had come by car anyway.

'He would have left the stuff in his car.' Standing his ground.

'Come on, Tom . . .'

Thorne stood up a little too quickly. He felt dizzy and casually reached out a hand to steady himself. He looked. Keable had seen it. It didn't matter. 'Surely he's worth looking at, Frank.'

'Yes, and Tughan's done it. We're not completely stupid. There's nothing there.'

'Tughan hates the idea because it's mine . . .'

'Nick Tughan's a professional . . .'

'Bollocks.'

Thorne was trying hard to sound controlled but he knew that by now the rest of the team would be eavesdropping without much difficulty.

Keable raised a hand. 'Go steady now, Detective Inspector.'

'Sir.' Thorne met Keable's eye. He pushed himself away from the wall and lowered his voice. 'I know what you think and I'm well aware of a certain reputation that I may have . . .'

'Let's not get into that, Tom.'

Thorne stared hard at him, breathing heavily. 'No, let's.'

Keable wouldn't hold the stare. 'There's no evidence, Tom.'

'Dr Jeremy Bishop has to be considered a major suspect. He worked at the hospital from which the Midazolam was stolen. He now works at the hospital where Alison Willetts was taken after she'd been attacked. I think he took her there after he'd attacked her to try, unsuccessfully, to give himself an alibi. He has no alibi for any of the murders and he fits the general description of the man seen talking to Helen Doyle on the night she was killed.' He'd said his piece.

Keable cleared his throat. He was going to say his. 'Bishop was involved with Dr Coburn, wasn't he?'

'Some years ago I believe . . . yes.'

'Are you?'

They couldn't confuse what he thought about Bishop with his feelings for Anne, could they? It was necessary to let Anne think that Bishop got to him on that level but Keable would see beyond that surely . . .

'Tughan isn't the only professional . . . sir.'

'Let's talk sensibly, Tom. Everybody agrees we're looking for a doctor.'

'But?'

'The Leicester connection is a red herring due to the date of the theft, if, in fact, the drug stolen was that used on the victims in the first place. Your reasoning as far as the Willetts alibi goes seems to me fanciful at best, and what he was or wasn't doing when the first three victims were killed is irrelevant.'

'What?'

'You know the game, Tom. The CPS isn't even going to look at the first three if we make an arrest. It was all pieced together too long after the event. We've got to go for Willetts and Doyle if we want to secure a conviction. We don't even have an accurate time of death for the first three victims.'

'*When he decided it was time, Tommy. That was when.*'

'Bishop was on call every one of those nights. He's only on call one night a week, it's a hell of a fucking coincidence.' He was almost whispering. 'I know it's him, Frank.'

'Listen to yourself, Tom. This isn't police work, this is . . . obsession.'

Thorne was suddenly very hot. Here it was, then. Calvert. His mark of Cain. Keable was going to pick away the scab.

'I'm sorry, but you were the one who talked about reputations. I'm not interested in reputations, but I wouldn't be doing my job if I wasn't aware of . . . recurring patterns.'

'You're talking like I'm a basket case. How many murderers have I put away in the last fifteen years?'

'You were right fifteen years ago. I know that.'

'And I've paid for it ever since. You've got no idea.'

'You've been right lots of times since then, but it doesn't mean you're always right.'

A minute or so earlier he'd felt like a fight. He'd wanted to get into it, but now he was suddenly exhausted, beyond it. 'Most of those times I was lucky. I could just as easily have fucked it up. I didn't always "know". But I knew fifteen years ago. And I know now.'

Keable shook his head, slowly, sadly. 'There's nothing there, Tom.' Then, an afterthought: an attempt to damp down the flames a little. He waved towards the main operations room. 'And you know full well that half the men in that office fit the general description.'

Thorne said nothing. Jesus, Exmoor looked bleak. Even the majestic stag looked deeply pissed off about the whole thing. Thorne saw himself walking into the mist, a tiny, distant figure leaving this shit behind him and disappearing. He felt the curtain of fog closing behind him, clammy on his shoulders as he marched across the damp, mossy ground with the voices of the girls echoing far behind him.

He knew they'd be the only ones who would care about where he'd gone.

'Now, sit down, Tom, and let's talk about the things we can do. The reconstruction's already been shot. It's going out in a couple of days.'

'Let Tughan do it.'

Thorne was walking quickly towards the door. He'd lost Keable. He didn't care. He opened the door then turned back to the DCI. '*If*, you said.' Thorne shook his head. Keable stared at him. '*If* we make an arrest. Not *when*! You really are an inspiration to us all, Frank.'

'DI Thorne—' Keable was on his feet, shouting, but Thorne was already half-way across the operations room. Those with the imagination picked up conversations where they hadn't left off and those that couldn't be bothered stared at their shoes. As Thorne passed him, Tughan looked up, smiling, from his computer screen. 'I don't know what you're getting so worked up about, Tom. He's a doctor not a lecturer.'

Thorne kept moving. He would make the bastard pay for that one day, but now was definitely not the time.

Holland stood in the corner brandishing a sandwich and watching his boss stride towards him without looking left or right.

'Sir?'

'Right, Detective Constable Holland,' said Thorne. 'Now you can take me home.'

Rachel Higgins lay on her bed, listening to her mother moving about in the bathroom. She had the sound turned down on the TV but every so often she glanced at the screen and tried to figure out exactly what was happening plotwise. It was a trashy late-night Channel 5 skinflick so it wasn't difficult. She heard the toilet flush. Mum was on her way to bed.

She reached over for her Walkman and swept her long brown hair behind her ears before putting on the headphones. The Manic Street Preachers would take her mind off the fight with her mother. It was so stupid the whole thing. It had started with the usual argument about the bloody resits. So what if her grades for IT and chemistry were not what they'd been expecting? She wasn't doing any science subjects in the sixth form anyway. They'd knocked that around for a while and got on each other's nerves and then she'd started on about her 'privacy'. Her right to have a life! Jesus Christ . . .

Maybe she and her mum should stop pretending they were mates in that wanky *Ab Fab* middle-class way. If that was what her mother wanted, that suited her just fine. She'd only been talking to her dad, for fuck's sake. It wasn't like she'd been told not to.

On TV a flabby sound engineer was trying to get some session-singer's bra off. Or maybe he was her manager. He was ugly and she had saggy old tits.

She quite liked the copper, actually, and didn't give a toss if her mum wanted to shag his brains out, but now all of a sudden her mum was moving the goalposts. Certain things were 'her business' and she was allowed to have a private life.

It was obvious that the flabby bloke wasn't going to get his dick out. She picked up the remote, flicked off the TV and lay there in the dark trying not to cry.

The volume on her Walkman was turned up as high as it would go. The noise would send her to sleep eventually and the row would be forgotten in the morning.

It didn't really matter anyway. Her mum could have her secrets if she wanted.

Rachel had plenty of her own.

It sounds as if Anne gave that tit of a husband as good as she got by the lift. She's definitely well shot of him. I wish I could tell her to stop pissing about and make a move on that chunky copper. They've done dinner, now she should go for it, no question. Especially now some nutter's smacked him over the head. Get 'em while their resistance is low. Give him one while he's still dizzy!

I've always been good at getting people together. It was me who got Paul to go and chat Carol up. I wonder if they're back from their honeymoon yet. Presumably not or they'd have been in.

We had a really good laugh, actually, me and Anne. Well, she had a good laugh and I just thought about laughing. It's fucking freaky to tell you the honest truth. When I'm half out of it, which is most of the time (did I mention that the drugs in here are fantastic?) I imagine that all the nurses are actually inside me instead of outside in the real world. I try and pretend that they're like these little munchkins running about inside my body and doing all the things that my brain tells them to do. Sweet little mobile body parts. Nursey to open my eyes. Nursey to wipe away the sweat. Nursey to scratch an itchy tit (well, once I've mastered telling them it's itchy). Remember the Numskulls in that old comic? A funny bunch of dwarfs that lived inside this bloke's head. I think 'hungry' and this little thing in a blue uniform with a stiff cap and an upside-down watch comes and sticks something yummy in my feeding tube. I think 'piss' and, Bob's your uncle, the next little slave empties my catheter. Well, fuck it, you've got to get through the day.

That's another thing. I've got no bloody idea what time of day it is. Anne makes a point of telling me but ten minutes after she's gone I'm confused again. There's a lot of dizziness as well ('No change there, then,' the girls at the nursery would say). I wonder how all the kids are doing? Some of them will have moved up into the next room. A new lot for Daniel to start biting. I really miss them.

I wonder if I could still get pregnant?

EIGHT

Hendricks had arrived laden down with cheap lager and by nine fifteen the pair of them were having trouble staying awake. The reconstruction would be shown in ten minutes. Hendricks, who was far too opinionated for his own good, ranted all the way through the news, while Thorne worked his way quietly through another can of beer and wondered why he hadn't called Anne Coburn.

Of course, he knew full well why he hadn't called her. The real question was how much longer he could maintain the pretence of integrity. Of actually having any.

His resolve was crumbling, can by can.

The most formal of contact, the most banal conversation would, he knew, be tainted by what he wasn't telling her. What he was choosing carefully and deliberately not to tell her. Of course, he was right on a procedural level not to involve her, he knew that. Well done him. But he wanted to see her. He wanted to tell her all sorts of things.

So . . . options.

He could continue to see her and simply not talk about the case. Or about Alison. Or about how he felt every hour of the day . . . but he really wouldn't be giving very much of himself in return for what he needed from her, would he? Or he could tell her the truth. If, however, he confided in her that he thought her oldest friend was a multiple murderer then the relationship might well get off to an iffy start. If he told her that her medical-school chum – and former lover, let's not forget that – was a sociopathic killer then she was hardly going to see him as a prime candidate for getting into her pants, was she?

From the sofa Hendricks let out a long, contented belch. There was nothing like alcohol for bringing out the northern bloke in the southern professional. Or the testosterone-fuelled lad in the tired old man.

And now he'd have to deal with this . . .

It was not a programme he usually watched. He couldn't deny that it often provided useful leads and bumped up the arrest rates. At work they called it *Grass Up Your Neighbour* and it was truly astonishing how many people were only too pleased to do just that. It was the reconstructions that bothered him, and the grainy CCTV footage. He couldn't help but find the whole concept vaguely hilarious. It was usually about the time the orange-coloured presenter talked about 'anything that's jogged your memory' that Thorne stopped paying attention. The city, after all, was chock-a-block with members of the public happily toddling about having completely forgotten that they'd been caught in the middle of a vicious armed robbery a fortnight earlier. That sort of thing can easily slip your mind . . .

They always saved the reconstructions for the really nasty ones. He knew it was down to the tight budgets in both policing and television but there was still something so . . . last gasp about it all. There was a mawkishness to the whole process which made him uncomfortable. Every 'Sleep well', each 'Don't have nightmares' seemed desperately forced. One minute they'd be showing you your neighbour being battered, raped, murdered, and the next they were reassuring you that crimes such as this were 'extremely rare'. The false security of wonderfully malleable crime figures.

Sleep well, if you're a statistician.

Despite the taste, sensitivity and sombre tones it was still television. It was still, at bottom, entertainment or, at its very best, journalism, and it niggled him.

He thought about those police photographers getting Helen Doyle into focus.

'Here we go . . .' Hendricks sat up and grabbed the remote. The presenter and the specially selected media-friendly officers outlined the menu of mayhem on offer for the next forty minutes. Backhand was up first. After a photogenic female DI had looked into the camera and assured him that attacks by complete strangers were very, very rare, Thorne was taken inside the Marlborough Arms.

He watched a young actress sitting with a group of girls, laughing. He watched her go to the bar and buy a round of drinks as the voiceover informed the viewer exactly who she was and what she was doing there and hinted darkly at what was about to happen to her. He watched as the young actress picked up her coat and walked towards the door with several other girls.

And he saw Helen Doyle step out on to the Holloway Road, say goodbye to her friends and stroll away to meet the man who would murder her. He saw the colour reappear in her face and the leaves fall from her hair. Beneath her blouse and skirt he knew that the scar from Hendricks's Y-shaped incision had faded and that her young skin was smooth again and smelling of talcum powder. His throat tightened as the blood pumped around the pallid, crumpled legs that carried Helen Doyle down past Whittington Park towards a house where her parents were waiting for her.

Now Helen is laughing and talking to a man and swigging from a bottle of champagne. The man is tall with greying hair. He is in his mid-thirties. Could he be a little older? Now Helen is starting to get a little wobbly. She all but falls into a dark-coloured car, which moves away to an unknown location where its driver will quietly, and with great skill, rob Helen Doyle and all those that love her of everything she is.

Then there was Nick Tughan at his most user-friendly. Thorne couldn't deny that he came across well. The jacket and tie were sober. That lilting voice sounded good, no question. The appeal for information was simple and heartfelt. Make a difference and come forward. For Helen. For Helen's family. The operations-room number was given out, and it was on to a series of armed robberies in the West Midlands. Thorne closed his eyes.

'*What d'you reckon, Tommy?*'

'*We'll have to wait and see what the calls bring in.*'

'*No . . . I mean . . . was I pretty, Tommy? Tell me. Did I look all right?*'

'*Yes, love. You were gorgeous.*'

'Tughan's got a touch of the Wogan about him, if you ask me.'

'I didn't. And you're pissed. Now, much as I hate to sully my expensive Scandinavian sofabed with Gooner scum such as yourself, you're welcome to stay.'

Hendricks was already clambering to his feet and reaching for his leather jacket. A half-empty can of lager was kicked across the room in the process.

'Sorry . . .'

'Clumsy bastard. Try and make it to the tube in one piece, will you?'

Hendricks waved and pulled a face as he walked past the front window. Thorne mopped up the spilt lager with kitchen towel, stuck on a George Jones CD and settled back in his chair. He was glad Hendricks had gone. He wanted to sit on his own and wait for Holland's call.

Anne turned off the television and moved around the room, switching off the lamps. Thorne had told her about the champagne, about how the killer had drugged that poor girl. And Alison. Seeing it acted out in the places where it had happened had been chilling. Somehow she felt a connection with Helen Doyle, and through her she suddenly felt connected to Alison in a different way. She knew that she was being fanciful, dramatic even, but she knew she wanted to give Alison her life back for more than just professional reasons. She wanted the man who had attacked her and who had killed those other girls to have failed. She wanted to be the reason he failed.

She stood in the darkened living room and wondered why Thorne hadn't been on the programme. Perhaps he hadn't fully recovered yet. He'd seemed on the mend when she'd seen him in hospital, but maybe he shouldn't have checked himself out so quickly. He was pig-headed, but perhaps he was soft-headed as well. She thought about calling him, but she knew it would be a long call. She needed to get some sleep.

Brushing her teeth, she thought about David and pictured him being knocked over by the lift doors. The image made it easy for her to check her laughter lines in the mirror as she rubbed in night cream. She turned off the bathroom light and saw Tom Thorne in the shadows, sitting on the edge of the bed in the hospital ward and staring across the room, a million miles away.

She'd call him tomorrow at work and suggest a drink.

As she went into her bedroom she heard the muffled chirp of the mobile from Rachel's room next door. She heard her daughter mumble a hello before pushing her door firmly shut. Anne was annoyed, but didn't want to challenge her about it. Not so soon after that stupid argument. All the same, she had to be up early for school in the morning.

It was a ridiculous time for her friends to be calling.

Holland called just after eleven thirty. Caller ID told Thorne that he was using his mobile. 'A lot of people saw her walking down the main road. One bloke rang up to tell us that she was singing when she walked past him.'

She'd been happy walking home. Was that a good thing?

'What was she singing?'

'Sir?'

'I can't remember, Tommy. Robbie Williams, maybe . . .'

'What about the killer?'

'Well, obviously there were fewer witnesses once she'd turned off the Holloway Road, but we've had a couple come forward. Nothing really new on a description. Three people rang to say that they thought the car might be a Volvo . . . Can you hear me?'

'Has Keable gone home yet?'

'Yeah, he left a couple of hours ago. Sir?'

Thorne grunted. Was it too late to ring?

'One other thing. We think the killer might have called.'

Thorne had thought it was possible, but it still took the breath out of him. 'Who took the call?'

'Janet Noble. We had the usual load of nutters, but she said this bloke sounded pretty convincing. She was a bit upset, to tell you the truth.'

'Go on.'

'A deepish voice, well spoken . . .'

Thorne knew what he sounded like. 'What did he say?'

'He said he was better-looking than the actor, that Helen Doyle was a lot plainer and that it was a far better brand of champagne.'

Of course. He'd care about details like that.

'And he asked where you were.'

'What did Noble tell him?'

'She said you'd been taken ill, sir.'

Thorne knew how well that would have gone down. If he'd believed it.

'Thanks, Holland, I'll catch up with you tomorrow . . .'

'Goodnight, then, sir . . .'

'. . . and thanks for that CD by the way. I never got a chance to . . .'

'That's all right. Is it any good?'

He felt a twinge of guilt. Kenny Rogers' *Greatest Hits* lay in a box at the bottom of his wardrobe along with a collection of battered paperback books and a self-assembly bathroom cabinet that had got the better of him. He was planning to take it to the charity shop at the weekend.

'Is that it on in the background? Sir?'

Dave Holland clipped his phone to his belt, said goodbye to the officers still taking calls and waited for the lift. He'd known this sort of thing might happen, especially with

Thorne, but none of it was making his life any easier. He wasn't sure exactly what was going on, but you would have had to be stupid not to see that lines were being drawn. He knew what Sophie would tell him to do. Keeping your head down hadn't done the likes of Keable or Tughan any harm over the years, had it?

Or his father.

No harm. Just a nice little pension and some stories and not an ounce of anything like satisfaction in thirty-five years. He'd spoken proudly about 'keeping his nose clean' right up until the day he'd keeled over, stone dead at sixty.

Tom Thorne had never kept his head down in his life. Perhaps he was just . . . losing it. He'd been on the beer when Holland had called, no question about it.

As the ambulance had taken him away from his flat four days earlier, delirious, and Holland had done his best to clear up, he realised that Thorne didn't consider himself better than anyone else. Not Keable or Tughan or ex-Detective Sergeant Brian Holland, four years dead. He was just a different sort of copper. A different sort of man. Maybe the sort of man whose approval meant something. If Holland could get that and still play it safe, then maybe that would be the way to go.

He took out his phone again. If Sophie was still up he'd grab them a curry on the way home. He let it ring four times and hung up. Finally the lift arrived and he stepped inside, knowing deep down that, in the coming days and weeks, playing it safe would not really be an option.

'Frank?'

'What is it, Tom?'

'Bishop drives a Volvo.'

'Right . . .'

'A dark blue Volvo sedan. I didn't put it in my initial report but there was one parked outside his house.'

'It's in Nick Tughan's report.'

'Tughan knew?'

'I told you, he's already looked into all that.'

'All that!'

'Can we talk about this in the morning?'

'And the calls tonight don't make a difference?'

'It's one more thing in the plus column, but there are still too many minuses.'

'You've spent too long talking to Tughan . . .'

'Goodnight, Thorne . . .'

'I'm making a formal request to be taken off this case, sir.'

'We'll definitely talk about this in the morning . . .'

'Anne? It's Tom Thorne. Sorry, did I . . .?'

'Hello?'

'I'll call you tomorrow.'

'It's OK – funny, I was angry about Rachel being on the phone a minute ago. Is it a minute ago? I must have gone out like a light.'

'Rachel's on the phone? I'm—'

'On her mobile. Hate the whole idea of it, really, but . . .'

'It's a safety thing.'

'Hmm.'

'I was just wondering about Alison, really . . . and obviously how are you?'

'Alison's . . . hang on, let's get sat up. That's better . . . Alison's making progress, slowly. I don't want to bring the occupational therapist back just yet, but things are moving. And I'm fine . . . thanks.'

'I'd like to see her. To see how she's getting on. You said about her communicating more.'

'She is, but it's just not . . . reliable, I suppose. I'm putting together a system, which will probably be a complete disaster but anyway . . . How's the head?'

'So, what do you think? Can I come in and see you?'

'Her or me? You said—'

'Sorry?'

'Both of us . . . yep. What about Friday?'

'Fine.'

'I'm up to my eyes in it at the minute.'

'I know . . . That's great. I'm sorry for ringing so late. I've had . . . just . . .'

'A couple of drinks?'

'I've had all sorts of things.'

'Sounds interesting.'

'Not really. I'll let you get back to sleep . . .'

Past midnight. Sitting in an uncomfortable chair with an unpronounceable Swedish name and rearranging his life. Or screwing it up completely. Why did he only ever feel like he was achieving anything if he was pissing someone else off? He was the loudmouth in the pub quiz shouting at the questionmaster until he's proved wrong. He was the irate driver effing and blinding until the other driver points to the sign showing who has right of way. He was the stupid copper who couldn't conceive of being wrong. The idiot whose feelings were written all over his face. That face sent messages. It whispered, 'You're making a mistake.' It murmured, 'I'm right.' It screamed, 'I *know*.' It had got backs up for as long as he could remember. It had alienated colleagues and wound up superior officers.

It had told Francis Calvert to kill children.

There was one can of beer left. He put his favourite track from the George Jones album back on and turned it up. Jones's duet with Elvis Costello . . .

'*There's a stranger in the house no one will ever see . . . but everybody says he looks like me.*'

He'd have to play it carefully with Keable. However much he discredited Thorne's theories about Jeremy Bishop, Keable knew that the killer and Thorne had a connection. That first note had been written before Thorne had even met Bishop. There was a link. The killer wanted Thorne close. So, whatever Thorne did, he knew that Keable would be watching. The truth was that Thorne didn't really know *what* he was going to do and, more disturbingly, he had no idea what Bishop was going to do either. How would he react to Thorne leaving the case? Would he be . . . insulted? Would he do something to demand the attention he thought he deserved?

Thorne tried not to think about those things that might make him bitterly regret what he had chosen to do. He told himself that he'd been given very little choice. They wouldn't listen. Worse, they were judging him. Putting it down to Calvert. Fifteen years, and still he was tainted, any instinct called an obsession. Every observation, every thought weighed up and judged and found wanting.

He couldn't bear that judgement any longer. He didn't need the judgement of the living.

He was being judged every day by the dead.

He needed to be outside an operation that was stifling him. He had to get out and make things happen. While he dicked about following leads and smiling the right smiles, Jeremy Bishop was making a fool of him.

It was time to turn things round.

He had to go to bed. The following morning was not going to be pleasant and he'd need to be as sharp as he could be. But he still needed to make one more call. He got up and went to the mantelpiece for his address book. He couldn't remember the numbers of many pornographers offhand.

I'm glad Anne's spending more time with me again. I'd sort of started thinking that she'd moved on a bit, that the novelty had maybe worn off. I wouldn't have blamed her, but I can't believe she's got many like me. She told me her workload had built up and that the administrator was an arsehole, so fair enough. Mind you, if I don't start making some progress I might find myself out on my ear. Somebody's bound to need the bed.

We've pretty much got 'yes' and 'no' sussed, and 'in pain' is one of my specialities but blinking is hardly Esperanto. One for yes and two for no is all very well in theory but it's the control that's letting me down. And the gaps between the blinks are all over the shop. I try to blink twice but it's hard for Anne to know if I'm saying 'no' or saying 'yes, yes'. There's a lot of 'Is that a yes, Alison? No? Is that a no, then?' We're like a pair of comical foreigners on Benny Hill. *This chicken is rubbery! Dad used to piss himself at that. Mum was never much for comedy shows, but he loved it. Maybe the old sod just fancied the women in bikinis. I caught Mum watching one of the videos a couple of weeks after my dad died. She must have got it out of the video shop. I was doing my NVQs, I think, and I came back from college early one day. She was sitting there watching this sad old fat bloke chasing these dolly-birds round and round a garden and crying her eyes out.*

Tim had better buck up his sodding ideas as well. He just sits there holding my hand. I know he can't come much in the daytime because of work but he should make more of an effort in the evenings. I don't know anything. He doesn't tell me. What's happening on Brookside*? Is he still playing football on Sundays? Has he put that shower curtain up yet? If Dad was here he'd kick him up the arse.*

He's stupid, really, because the weight's dropping off me and if everything else is knackered then there's every chance I might actually have stopped ageing! I'll be walking out of here a slim and sexy shadow of my former self. There's one very tasty male nurse. Probably gay, but fit as fuck. If Tim's not careful I might have to start looking elsewhere.

NINE

When he woke up he was still angry. The previous night's amateur dramatics had been hugely disappointing. And where the hell was Thorne? At least it confirmed what he'd suspected for a while – that the rigorous, high-priority investigation had got precisely nowhere. Perhaps they'd have the car by now, or a slightly better description, but it was still painfully slow. There wasn't even a sniff of the number plate. It was stolen, of course, but come on! It was nearly a fortnight since he'd given them Helen's body to play with and they were still begging for the help of the general public.

Useless wankers.

Thorne. Nowhere to be seen when he should have been grabbing his bit of televisual glory. He hadn't believed for a second that Thorne had still been recovering. No, there was something afoot among the jolly coppers for sure. This was unforeseen but easily dealt with. If all that his thuggish theatrics and beautifully arch little note had done was cause the boys in blue to have some sort of queeny tantrum, then he'd just have to find another way to chivvy them along, wouldn't he?

It was about time anyway. Maniacs were supposed to speed up as the frenzy took hold, weren't they? They'd expect nothing less. He'd considered livening things up a little. Perhaps a gay man or an old person next time. No . . . that would be bound to confuse them and he didn't want them confused. All things considered, he was ready for another bash. Keen as mustard to try, try, try again.

He'd tried kicking Thorne in the shins. It was time to aim for the heart.

Thorne looked around the pub. Businessmen in shirt-sleeves using a basket of scampi or a microwaved chilli con carne as an excuse to sink a couple of pints at lunchtime. It was probably as good a place as any. Informants didn't like to meet too close to home and as it was, of all the people upstairs in the Lamb and Flag, Thorne looked the most likely villain. He was comfortable with that. He knew he looked . . . useful. It hadn't done him any harm by and large, though he would've liked to be taller.

A surly Australian barman emptied the ashtray Thorne wasn't using. 'Are you eating, mate? We need the table.'

Thorne opened his wallet. 'I'll have another mineral water.' He made sure his identification was visible. With a tut the barman wiped the table and went to fetch Thorne's drink.

The Perrier was the one thing slightly at odds with the image he knew he was presenting, but the booze was, as yet, strictly confined to Little IKEA. Besides, he could do with getting straight back to work afterwards. He didn't think rolling in bladdered on his first day would go down too well.

The meeting with Frank Keable the day before hadn't been as prickly as he'd expected. Keable had wanted him to stay on the investigation, but for none of the right reasons. He talked about the integrity of the case, whatever that was, and how he could ill afford to lose an officer with Thorne's outstanding record. As far as the notes and the attack on Thorne, which Keable assured him was being viewed as an attempted murder, were concerned, Keable was predictably vague. He was adamant that this facet of the case would be monitored closely, but Thorne could sense a real fear on Keable's part that, were he to leave, Keable himself might become the object of the killer's bizarre attention.

Thorne knew that this was never going to happen.

The simple truth was that, if Thorne left, Keable was terrified of the press getting hold of it and understandably he did not relish explaining to the detective superintendent why one of his senior officers was jumping ship. Thorne had told him to put it down to a clash with Tughan. Or him. Anything he liked.

Keable asked him to reconsider. Thorne had looked into the bored brown eyes of the Exmoor stag and stood his ground.

By lunchtime he'd been transferred back to the Serious Crime Group (West) out of Hendon, effective from nine o'clock the following morning.

He hoped things were a little clearer than when he'd left.

The Met was in a serious state of flux. Not only was it now under the direct auspices of the GLA and Mayor Livingstone, it was also undergoing major operational restructuring. NHS red tape was impressive, but it didn't even come close.

The old area system had gone. Five areas of London (NW, NE, SW, SE and Central), each with its own Major

Incident Team (AMIT), which had in turn replaced the Area Major Incident Pools (AMIPs) and all now superseded by three Serious Crime Groups (East, West, South) encompassing all existing OCUs as well as the old Organised Crime Department, the Fraud Squad and the Firearms Unit.

The result? Hundreds of officers without a clue what was happening. Or indeed, why. The official line was that the new SCGs were supposed to be more proactive. The Met would no longer sit back and wait for crime to happen.

It was a good theory.

But you couldn't anticipate the likes of Jeremy Bishop.

As the DI on Team 3 out of Beck House in Hendon, Thorne had landed on his feet. He'd worked with DCI Russell Brigstocke for six months at Serious Crime and he knew that, barring anything major going down, Brigstocke wouldn't kick up a fuss should Thorne be unavailable from time to time.

Like since nine o'clock that morning.

'Kodak!'

If Thorne looked useful, the man in his early forties nodding and strolling over to join him was positively indispensable. Six feet four and built like a barn, with bleached blond hair, a nose-ring and, today, a bright yellow puffa jacket. But it wasn't all good news. Dennis Bethell's voice could start a fight at a hundred yards. It was a spilt pint waiting to happen.

'Can I get you one, Mr Thorne?'

Thorne always smiled the first time he heard the incongruous, high-pitched squeak. Whoever was responsible for these things had screwed up big-time or else had a great sense of humour. Somewhere there was an extremely irate cartoon mouse who sounded like Frank Bruno.

He pointed to his water. 'No, I'm fine.'

Bethell nodded for about ten seconds.

Thorne emptied his glass as the barman finally brought over a new one and took the money. Bethell, if anything, was even bigger than the last time he'd seen him.

'Steroids give you cancer, you know, Kodak.'

'Bollocks,' squeaked Bethell. 'They make you infertile. Anyway, this all right for you, Mr Thorne? I know it's a bit busy, but coming up West is handy for me. I do a lot of business round here.'

'Course you do, Kodak . . .'

As porno merchants went, Dennis Bethell was among the least unpleasant. For twenty years Thorne had monitored his career with interest. He was purveyor of everything from soft-focus glamour snaps for car magazines to the more brightly lit and clinical stuff for those publications a little harder to reach. In the eighties his top-quality cumshot work had been much in demand, and his occasional foray into blackmail had caused the abrupt termination of at least one prominent political career. Dennis was old school. In an age where hard-core videos were a tenner and any mug punter with a PC could watch dwarfs doing it with donkeys at the drop of a hat, or the click of a mouse, he was still a firm believer in the power, the truth, of the single still photograph. Deep down, Thorne admired the filthy piece of pondlife.

'This boozer used to be the Bucket of Blood you know.'

Thorne did know. Two hundred and fifty years earlier this had been a brawler's pub. Whores and cut-throats doing business and slicing each other up for pennies while

Hogarth sat in the corner jotting it all down and doing sketches. Thorne looked around him. He couldn't help but wonder if he might not have felt a little more at home.

'Business going well, then, is it?'

Bethell was lighting a Silk Cut. 'Oh, not too shabby. I've got a website, you know . . .'

'You're shattering all my illusions.'

'You've got to move with the times, haven't you? Have you seen the stuff that's out there?'

Thorne had. Plenty of it. 'And you think the stuff you do is any different?'

'I don't do anything with kids, Mr Thorne, you know that. I won't be doing with that filth. Besides, my stuff's a bit more exclusive, I reckon. It's harder to get hold of.'

'Yeah. You've got to stand on tiptoe in the newsagent.'

Bethell looked uncomfortable. Stubbed out the fag long before it was finished. Lit another. 'Can we get this over with, Mr Thorne?'

'Of course. I'm sorry to have kept you.'

'Listen, Mr Thorne, I don't really hear a great deal these days. I've been getting this webcam thing off the ground and apart from that it's just the usual stuff with the models. I don't hang around as much as I did . . .'

The barman returned with Thorne's change. From the table behind him Thorne could hear muffled sniggering. He really hoped it wasn't aimed at the big man sitting opposite him.

Bethell mistook Thorne's silence for disappointment.

'There's a bit of drugs business I could put your way. These young girls are dropping Es and putting Charlie up their beaks like there's no tomorrow. They don't want to eat, see . . .'

More sniggering, and this time Bethell heard it too. Thorne turned round. Four media types. Short hair, square glasses and training shoes that probably cost more than his suit. They wouldn't look at him. He turned back round, lowering his voice as a cue for Bethell to do the same.

'I don't need information, Kodak.'

'Right.'

'I wish to avail myself of your high-quality professional services, which you will provide in return for me not sending Vice to go trampling through your darkroom.'

Bethell thought for a moment or three. 'You want me to take some photos?'

'Simple black and white portrait from as close as you can get. The subject will be unaware that he is being photographed.' Bethell was hardly inconspicuous, but Thorne knew that the man had a great deal of experience in maintaining a low profile. In a parallel universe he might have been a highly paid *paparazzo*.

'No sweat, Mr Thorne, I've got this blinding new three hundred mil Nikon zoom.'

Thorne leaned in close. 'Listen, Bethell, this is a piece of piss, all right? A simple head shot. Coming out of his house, getting into his car, it doesn't matter. Should be simple for you. No beds. No animals. No drugged-up teenage girls.'

He thought about Helen Doyle, sitting in the pub, laughing.

'*I never did anything like that, Tommy. Strictly a Bacardi Breezer girl . . .*'

He gave Bethell the address and finished his drink while the photographer enthused a little more about lenses before lumbering off towards the gents'. As he went, Bethell gave the quartet on the table behind them a good hard look.

Thorne felt pretty sure that Bethell would do a decent job for him. It wasn't just because he'd make his life hell if he didn't, he could sense that the man would take pride in the work. Not for the first time Thorne thought about how much better he functioned with professional criminals. It was a game he was good at. Even the really nasty bastards he had squared up against in his eighteen months on the Flying Squad weren't hard to figure out. Some he caught and some he didn't, but he never had to waste his time wondering why they were doing it. Money, usually. Sex, occasionally. Because they couldn't be arsed doing anything else, often. But the rules of the game were simple: stop them doing it and let somebody else work out why afterwards.

Bishop and those like him were not playing by the same rules. Thorne knew that if he was going to catch Jeremy Bishop he'd have precious little help. He knew that he had to take things carefully, a step at a time. Bethell was the first step, but after that he'd be making it up as he went along. Whatever this new game was, Bishop had a distinct advantage. Thorne was certain that the 'why' was important. The 'why' was probably crucial. But this was where he was up against it.

Thorne didn't give a shit about 'why'.

When Bethell arrived back at the table Thorne stood up and started putting on his coat. 'Are we sorted, then?'

Bethell picked up his cigarettes. 'Yeah. No point me asking how soon you want these photos, is there?'

'Not really, no.'

The laughter from behind them told Thorne that he really should get out, straight away. Bethell was already taking a step towards them.

'Something funny?'

The biggest of the four stood up and stared at Bethell through designer glasses. It was not an aggressive move so much as a reflexive one, but it didn't really matter to Bethell. The thick finger he prodded into the man's chest must have felt like a battering ram. 'Something about how highly I speak of you, was it? Go on, tell me.' Square Glasses moved to swat away the finger; Short Hair moved to protect his friend and it went off.

As Bethell swung a fist bristling with signet rings into Square Glasses' face, Thorne stepped forward and back-handed his friend across the mouth. He fell backwards across the table, the expensive training shoes sending bottles and glasses flying in all directions. It was now two on two and all over very quickly. The third man reached for a large metal ashtray but Thorne was on him in a second, bringing his forehead down across the bridge of the man's nose as casually as if he were bending to tie a shoelace.

It was only as the fourth man backed away in such a hurry as to knock a plate of vividly orange chicken tikka massala into a young woman's lap, that the screaming began in earnest. As the Australian barman hovered nervously, a fearsome-looking landlady with vanilla-coloured hair and a broken pool cue marched from behind the bar. 'Right. Call the police.'

The barman pointed an accusing finger at Thorne. 'They're already here.'

Thorne rubbed his forehead and looked around. Three

men lying, kneeling, crawling across a wooden floor glittering with broken glass, blood splashing on to designer combat trousers, the horrified yet excited faces of two dozen onlookers . . .

He guessed that it was not the right time to mention to the landlady that Hogarth would probably have approved.

Ten minutes later Thorne and Bethell were on the pavement outside the Garrick Club. The landlady had taken a bit of mollifying and those with smashed teeth and shattered noses were predictably aggrieved until Thorne dropped the word 'cocaine' into the conversation and everything was hastily forgiven and forgotten.

Bethell placed an unwelcome hand on Thorne's shoulder. 'Thanks for that, Mr Thorne. Laying into those wankers, that was good of you.'

Thorne could feel the headache starting to kick in. 'I didn't do it for you.'

He stuck out an arm to hail a cab.

And it wasn't them I was laying into . . .

They waited for Alison's boyfriend to leave before they wheeled in the blackboard. Bishop thought that Anne was being a trifle over-sensitive. After all, she'd kept him well appraised of Alison's progress, hadn't she? He'd hardly be expecting her to sit up and start singing.

Anne just wanted to wait a little before she got Tim involved. If all went well then she'd want to bring him in. He'd need to work with Alison himself anyway. She just needed to know that the basic framework was right. Once they were up and running it would be second nature to all of them. She felt that not understanding exactly what her responses signified would give him a skewed idea of Alison's condition.

If he wasn't thinking it already, he would be sure he'd lost her.

The wheels squeaked as the orderly moved the blackboard into position at the foot of the bed. Optimistic as she was, Anne could sense the enormity of the task that lay ahead of her. Alison was twenty-four. This was her first day at kindergarten.

'I wonder what my patients would think if I suggested anaesthetising them with a lump hammer?' Bishop sipped his coffee and stared at the blackboard.

Anne said nothing. It was hardly state of the art, but at this stage it was adequate. She took off her coat and put on her glasses. She picked up the remote control hooked over the head of the bed and pressed a button. With a deep, resonant hum, the bed began to move and Alison was raised up until she was virtually sitting.

'Alison, I've got Dr Bishop with me this afternoon. You might remember him. He treated you the night you were brought in.' She turned to look at Bishop. He was studying the lines of letters, drawn in chalk.

Anne moved up to the top of the bed and took Alison's hand. 'Right, let's see if we can speed things up a bit. Can you see the blackboard, Alison?'

Alison's right eyelid crinkled immediately. She half shut the eye then opened it. Then, five seconds later, a blink. Anne squeezed her hand.

'Good. A to Z in two lines and I've listed a few other things along the bottom. Later on we can increase the list as I get better at this but for now just the basics. "Tired", "in pain", "hungry", "thirsty", "nauseous". You'll have to bear with me, I'm afraid, until we get used to the speed of your responses. I know it'll be frustrating at first, but I think it's going to be worth it. OK, Alison?'

The vein on Alison's forehead was standing out. Ten seconds. A blink.

Anne moved round to the other side of the bed and closed the blind. 'Right, let's just make things as comfortable as possible for you. Can you get the lights, Jeremy?'

Bishop moved to the door and turned out the lights. The room was in semi-darkness. From her pocket Anne produced what looked like a large fountain pen as she moved to the blackboard.

'Right, Alison, this is a laser pointer. It should make it easier to define the letters for you and it makes me feel a little bit less like I'm giving a military briefing. Let's just start at the bottom, make sure you're feeling all right.' She moved the laser pointer until the dot of light lay directly below 'in pain'. 'Don't bother with no if you're not. Just yes if any of them apply.'

Slowly she moved the pointer along the bottom row of words, highlighting each one for nearly a minute. As she waited Anne looked intently at Alison. She could hear the drone of the traffic outside. There was no reaction. She glanced across at Bishop. He nodded.

'Right, let's have a crack at this, shall we?' She began to move the pointer. Bishop removed a small pad from his top pocket and sat holding a pencil, waiting. Anne held the pointer under each letter for nearly a minute but after the first five or six she began to speed up a little. P . . . Q . . . R . . . S.

A blink.

Anne wanted to cheer. 'S. OK . . .'

She reached the end of the alphabet without any further reaction.

Bishop cleared his throat. 'It's a shame there aren't more words in alphabetical order, Jimmy.'

Anne turned to face him, the light from the pointer passing across his chest like the laser dot on a sniper's rifle. He was busily scribbling. 'Almost . . .'

'Almost what?' She could feel herself starting to get snappy.

'*Almost* is one. A word where the letters occur in alphabetical order. And *billowy*. *Aegilops* is actually the longest, which, amazingly enough, is an ulcer in part of the eye, though I can't see her bringing that up.' He smiled. 'Back to the beginning, I think.'

Anne felt stupid for not having considered this. Perhaps there was a more efficient way of laying out the letters. She'd have to work on it later. A second pass added H, O and R.

Anne tried to help. 'Short? Alison . . . short?'

Alison blinked. Anne waited. Alison blinked again. Back to the beginning.

On the third pass Alison blinked as the laser pointer reached M. Anne looked across at Bishop, who was scribbling in his notebook. He stood up, smiling, and moved towards the bed. 'I think she's being a bit over-eager. She's blinking in advance of some of the letters in case she misses them.'

Anne looked at him. There was a hint of impatience when she spoke. 'And?'

'If the S is a T and we go one letter on from the M . . .'

Anne thought for a moment, worked it out, and blushed. Bishop smiled mischievously at her. 'She's asking how our friend the detective inspector is. If I were you I'd add a question mark to the board.' He was standing at the head of the bed. He looked down at Alison. 'And you might want to draw a smiley face on there somewhere as well. There's a definite twinkle in that eye.'

Anne picked up a piece of chalk, a little irritated. Perhaps she shouldn't have asked Jeremy to come along. She'd wanted a colleague who was also a friend to back her up and he'd been only too glad to help, but fond as she was of him, he could be awfully smug. She began to write on the blackboard. 'I'm glad all that time doing *The Times* crossword hasn't been wasted, Jeremy . . .'

Bishop wasn't listening. He was leaning down, his face close to Alison's. 'Do you remember me, Alison?'

A blink.

'From when you were admitted?'

Nothing. Then, a blink.

Bishop nodded. His voice was low and eminently soothing. 'That's good. Now what about before, Alison? Can you remember anything from before?'

A blink.

Anne turned back from the board.

Another one.

Bishop walked back towards Anne, shaking his head. He held out the notepad to her with a grin. Around the single word *THORNE* he'd drawn a heart with an arrow through it. Anne snatched it from him with part-mock, part-genuine annoyance and moved to open the curtains.

'Mr Thorne is very well, thank you, Alison. I'm frankly disturbed that my private life is of such immediate concern to you.' She walked to the bed and looked down. Alison's eyes were still locked on the blackboard. 'Not that I should expect a great deal else from a shameless Geordie hussy with a one-track mind!' She put her hand gently on the girl's shoulder. Her smile was huge and just for Alison.

She turned to look at Bishop, who was staring at the blackboard and smiling at something. She felt sorry for being irritated with him. 'Do you want to pop over for something to eat later?'

He answered without turning round. 'Sorry, Jimmy, I have a date.'

She moved to join him, her eyes wide at the prospect of intrigue. 'Sounds mysterious?'

'Not really.'

'Suit yourself. I'll get it out of you later, though, you know I will. What's so funny anyway?'

Bishop was snorting as he stared at the letters on the blackboard. Anne stared at him, still smiling. 'What?'

'Remember that night in your flat twenty-odd years ago?'

'No . . .'

'Raising the dead, me, you and David. And that girl from Leeds, what was her name?'

'Oh, God, that was freaky.'

'No, it wasn't. David was moving the glass.'

Anne pretended to shudder but felt a genuine chill at the memory. She turned to include Alison, pointing at the blackboard. 'He thinks this looks like a Ouija board.'

The smile on Bishop's face died a little, as he muttered to himself, 'Might just as well be.'

Thorne picked up the Backhand contact list from the kitchen table and walked through to the living room to call Dave Holland. *The Bill* was on with the sound turned down. As good a situation comedy as ITV would ever have.

'Hello . . .'

Holland's girlfriend. Christ, what was her name?

'Oh, hi, is that Sophie?'

'Who's this?'

'Oh, sorry, it's Tom Thorne, I work with Dave. Is he around?'

He heard the distortion in sound as she put her hand over the phone. He couldn't make out what she was saying. As Holland came to the phone he could hear the television being turned down.

'Holland, it's DI Thorne . . .' Best not to be too matey. 'I hope I'm not keeping you from your homework.'

'Sorry, sir?'

'*The Bill* – I heard it in the background. It's not real, you know.'

Holland laughed. 'Yeah, but that one they all take the piss out of is an awful lot like DI Tughan.'

The joke told Thorne a great deal. Holland knew the way things stood. As it happened, Thorne also knew which character he was talking about – he was spot on. He had seriously underestimated this young man. 'Listen, obviously you know I'm back at Hendon now, but I'd still be interested in any developments on the case. Who's come in, by the way?'

'Roger Brewer. Scottish bloke – seems nice enough.'

Thorne hadn't heard of him. Probably just as well. 'So, you know, anything comes up . . .'

'I'll let you know straight away, sir.'

'Anything and everything, Holland . . . please.'

Rachel looked at her watch. He was only five minutes late but she didn't want to miss the trailers. She thought about the nutter who'd sat behind her on the bus from Muswell Hill and decided she'd get a cab back. She checked her purse. If she paid for her own ticket she'd need to ask him to lend her the money. Mum would be happier with a taxi anyway, although she'd wonder why Claire's dad hadn't given her a lift. He usually did after she'd been round there for the evening. Maybe she could say his car was in the garage. But she might see him driving around. Or talk to Claire's mother on the phone. She decided it was probably easier to ask the cab to stop somewhere away from the house. Too many lies weren't a good idea. She wasn't very good at it and she didn't like lying to her mum anyway. She'd just have to pray her mum didn't run into Claire in the next few days.

She was starting to get cold. She did up another button on her denim jacket and stared at the corner of the street, willing him to appear.

She wasn't really lying about him, after all. She just wasn't telling. There'd only be a row and it would be a damn sight bigger than the one they'd had the other night.

These fucking resits that she didn't want to take were the problem. It was so unfair that the time when you started to get serious with people was the same time you had so-called important exams.

Were the two of them serious? It felt like it. They hadn't slept together yet, but not because she hadn't wanted to. It was him. He didn't seem in any hurry. He was obviously waiting for the right time. He was being nice and sensitive because he'd obviously already done it and she hadn't, and he didn't want her to feel like he was putting her under any pressure if she didn't want to . . .

Rachel knew that this would be the big thing with her

mother. His experience. The thing that would send her mum ballistic . . .

Her hand flew to her hair as she saw him coming round the corner. He waved and started to jog towards her. He was really fit. In good condition. Claire would be so jealous. But Mum would not be impressed at all.

Not with him being so much older.

A blackboard! For fuck's sake. Anne brought in a brochure one day with these computers that they were developing in America that you can work with your eyelid or something. They can virtually tell what you're thinking, like something in a film. I've got a mobile phone which predicts what letters you're going to type in when you're sending somebody a text message. Bloody useful, actually, when your spelling is as bad as mine. That cost £29.99 as far as I can remember. And I get a poxy blackboard. Everyone goes on about the cuts in the NHS but this is really taking the piss, isn't it?

And there I was thinking that maybe they might be able to fix up some system so I could read or watch the telly. Nothing too fancy, just a few mirrors and stuff so that I wouldn't have to lie here all day staring at the piece of plaster that's about to fall off the manky grey ceiling up there. Well, there's no chance of that, I suppose. All these machines are probably on their last legs as well. The big one on the left is definitely making a few dodgy noises. I hope they give the nurses enough change to feed the meter. I wouldn't want to pop off in the middle of the night because somebody didn't have a fifty-pence piece.

I know this isn't Anne's fault and I know that you only ever think about these things when you're on the receiving end of it and everything. But still . . .

I was pretty chuffed with myself actually, when it came down to all the alphabet business. We just need to sort out a system so I can tell Anne to go back instead of forward. Otherwise it's sodding interminable. I'm sure she'll work it out.

That doctor she had with her was a right clever sod, mind you, working out that I'd blinked too early. I just had to go for it. If I'd waited and then not been able to blink in time and missed the letter I really wanted, the whole thing would have been cocked up. I'd've ended up spelling out the Czechoslovakian for chemist or something.

I suppose I should be grateful to that doctor if he was the one who sorted me out when I first came in. I do remember his face looking down at me. I remember him telling me to wake up, but I just drifted away. Before that I can only remember bits and pieces. Bits and pieces of a voice. Not the words. Not yet. Just the sound. Smooth and gentle like Dr Bishop.

And there I was, worried that my mobile phone was going to give me cancer . . .

TEN

Thorne got off the train at Clapham Junction. He came out of the station, checked his *A–Z* and began to walk up Lavender Hill. The house was only ten minutes' walk away. He was knackered after five. Carrying the briefcase didn't help.

Not that there was anything in it.

He'd spent precisely an hour at Beck House that morning, not listening as Brigstocke brought him up to speed on a caseload of assorted rapes and robberies-with-menace. He'd picked up the address of a security guard who needed questioning and headed straight for Hendon Central station. He'd have to find time to fit in the interview before he went to Queen Square. Well, he'd see a bit of London today anyway.

He didn't know this part of the city very well but you'd've had to be blind not to see that it was affluent. Wine bars on every corner, delicatessens, restaurants and, of course, more estate agents than you could shake a shitty stick at. Out of curiosity he stopped briefly to peer into a window. An oily-looking article with bad skin and a widow's peak smiled at him from behind a computer terminal. Thorne looked away and took in a few of the details on a revolving display in the window. Kentish Town wasn't cheap but he could have bought a big two-bedroom place with a garden there for the price of a toilet cubicle in leafy Battersea.

His breath back, he started plodding on up the hill. He was already panting again when his phone rang. The squeak was unmistakable. 'Bethell here, Mr Thorne.'

'I know. Are they ready?'

'Oh . . . you recognised my voice, eh?' Bethell laughed.

Thorne had to hold the phone away from his ear. Half the dogs in the area were probably rushing towards him already.

'How did it go, Kodak?'

'Could have gone better, as it goes . . .'

Fucking idiot. He should have brought a camera and done it himself.

'Listen, Bethell . . .'

'Don't worry, Mr Thorne, I got the photos. Good ones too. He was standing on his doorstep pissing about with a hanging basket. What's this bloke do anyway? Some sort of businessman, is he?'

'Why could it have gone better?' Bethell said nothing. 'It could have gone better, you said.'

He could hear Bethell take a long drag on a cigarette.

'Yeah, nothing that I couldn't handle, but after he'd gone back inside this other bloke pulls up outside and when he gets out of his car he looks around and, I don't know, maybe the sun was glinting off the lens or something but he saw me anyway.'

'What was he like?'

'I don't know – tall, in his early twenties, I suppose. Bit of a student type, I reckon – you know, a bit grungy.'

The son. Popping round to borrow a few quid, if what Anne had said was true.

'What did he say?'

'You're breaking up, Mr Thorne . . .'

'What did he say?'

'Oh, you know, he asked me what I was doing. I told him I was composing a portfolio of common urban birdlife and I just stared at him until he pissed off. No sweat. Got a picture or two of him as he buggered off, actually.'

Thorne smiled. He'd sent the right man for the job.

'So when can I have them?'

'Well, they're just drying at the minute. Couple of hours?'

That would work out perfectly.

'Right. Bucket of Blood about one-ish.'

'Is that a good idea?'

Bethell was right. Thorne doubted his welcome would be a warm one.

'Outside, then. Try not to talk to anybody.'

'I'll be there, Mr Thorne.'

'Kodak, you're better than Boots.'

He'd rung the Royal London to check and found out that Bishop's night on call was still Tuesday. He wasn't due in until lunchtime. With a bit of luck Thorne would catch him at home. He certainly looked well rested when he came to the door wearing an expensive-looking lemon sweater and a winning smile.

'Oh . . . Detective Inspector. Should I have known you were coming?'

Thorne could see him looking over his shoulder, searching for a colleague or a car.

'No, sir, this is purely an on-spec sort of thing. Bloody cheeky, if I'm honest.'

'How's the head?' Bishop was relaxed, his hands in his pockets. They were going to have a cosy chat on the doorstep. Fine.

'Much better, thanks. Good job I'm hard-headed.'

Bishop leaned back against the front door. Thorne could see through to the kitchen, but there was still no invitation to come in.

'Yes, I rather got that impression that night round at Jimmy's. Thoroughly enjoyed myself by the way and I hope you didn't mind my being somewhat spiky.'

'Don't be silly.'

'I can't help myself sometimes. I do love a little verbal sparring.'

'As long as you keep it verbal, sir.'

Bishop laughed. He didn't have a filling in his mouth.

Thorne shifted the briefcase to the other hand. 'I had a good time too, which is sort of why I thought I could be a bit pushy and ask you an enormous favour.' Bishop looked at him, waiting. 'I've been to see somebody just round the corner from you, on a totally different case coincidentally, and my constable needed to rush off because his girlfriend's had some sort of accident . . .'

'Nothing serious?'

'I don't think so, trapped her hand in a door or something, but anyway I'm a bit stranded. I've got another interview to do and I'm running late, and as you were only round the corner and seeing as we've already had dinner together . . .'

Bishop stepped forward past Thorne, bent down and began to pull the brown leaves from a large pot on the driveway. 'Ask away.'

'Could I ponce a lift to the station?'

Bishop looked up and stared at him for a few seconds. Thorne could sense that he saw through the lie and was looking to see if it was there in his face. He'd be amazed if it wasn't. Thorne broke the stare and turned his attention to the dying flowers. 'They look as if they were probably lovely a few weeks ago.'

'I'm going to plant evergreens next year I think. Dwarf conifers and Ivies. This is such a lot of work for something that dies so quickly.' He crumpled the dead leaves into his hand and stood up. 'I'm actually going into town. Is that any good to you?'

'Yes. Fantastic. Thanks a lot.'

'I've just got to grab my keys and stuff. Come in for a minute.'

Thorne followed Bishop into the house and stood waiting in the hall. Bishop shouted to him from the kitchen, 'There was a photographer hanging about round here yesterday. Bloody nuisance. I wondered if you knew anything about it.'

So the son had obviously come straight inside and told him about Bethell lurking in the undergrowth or wherever he'd been hiding himself.

'Probably the press just sniffing around. They've been getting worked up since the Helen Doyle reconstruction. Did you see that?'

'No.' Had Thorne detected the hint of a pause before he'd answered? 'I didn't know they'd made any connection to the attack on Alison Willetts.'

They hadn't.

'No, but somebody may have leaked a list of people we'd interviewed or something. These things happen, unfortunately. I'll look into it if you like.'

Bishop came striding up the hall pulling on a sports jacket. He grabbed his keys from the hall table. 'I wouldn't like to see myself splashed across the front page of the *Sun*.' He opened the front door and ushered Thorne out. 'Mind you,' he shut the door behind him and put a hand on Thorne's shoulder as they walked towards the car, 'a discreet photo on page three of the *Daily Telegraph* is a different matter. Might impress a few young nurses.'

Bishop climbed into the car and Thorne walked round towards the passenger side. He stopped behind the car and held up the briefcase. 'Can I chuck this in the boot?' He saw Bishop glance into his rear-view mirror and smiled as he heard the clunk of the boot being opened from the inside.

As the Volvo cruised along the Albert Embankment, Bishop slid a CD into the player. The sound system was certainly a step up from the tinny rattlebox in Thorne's Mondeo. Some people probably thought country music sounded better that way. Bishop glanced across at him. 'Not a classical man?'

'Not really. This is fine, though. What is it?'

'Mahler. *Kindertotenlieder*.'

Thorne waited for the translation – which, amazingly, didn't come. The car was immaculately clean. It still smelt new. When they stopped at lights, Bishop drummed on the wooden gear lever, his wedding ring clicking against the walnut.

'You've known Anne a long time, then?'

'God, for ever. We were pushing beds around the streets together when we were undergraduates. Me and Anne, Sarah and David.' He laughed. 'I'm sure that's why hospitals are so short of beds. They all get pushed into rivers by high-spirited students.'

'She told me about your wife. I'm sorry.'

Bishop nodded, checking his wing mirror although there was nobody behind them.

'I can't believe the time has gone so quickly, to be honest. Ten years ago next month, actually.'

'I lost my mother eighteen months ago.'

Bishop nodded. 'But it wasn't your fault, was it?'

Thorne clenched his teeth. 'I'm sorry?'

'The crash was my fault, you see. I was pissed.'

Anne hadn't mentioned that. Thorne stared at him.

'Don't worry, Inspector, I wasn't driving, there's no case to reopen. But Sarah was tired, and she was driving because I'd had one too many. I have to live with that, I'm afraid.'

You must live with a lot of things.

'It must have been hard bringing up two kids, though? They can't have been very old.'

'Rebecca was sixteen and James was fourteen and, no, it was a bloody nightmare actually. Thank God I was already doing quite well by then.' He stepped on the brakes sharply as the car in front decided against jumping a red light. Thorne jolted back in his seat. Bishop looked across at him, a strange expression on his face. 'Her chest was completely crushed.'

They sat in silence until the lights changed.

Why should I feel sorry for you?

'I saw Alison yesterday. Anne was testing out a communications device. I'm sure she'll tell you all about it . . .'

And then small-talk across Waterloo Bridge and into the West End.

Bishop stuck his hazards on as he pulled over on Long Acre to let Thorne jump out. 'How's that?'

'That's perfect. Thanks again.'

'No problem. I'm sure we'll run into one another soon.'

Thorne slammed the door. The electric window slid down.

'Don't forget your briefcase . . .'

He drove slowly through Covent Garden, up to Holborn, then doubled back towards Soho. Cutting through small streets lined with newly opened shops, their chrome-cluttered interiors bathed in the glow of lava lamps. 'Scouting for locations', he believed this was called in the film world. Locations where he might find the next one. There were many to choose from and he'd have a better selection once it was dark, but he was just getting the feel of things.

He tightened his grip on the steering-wheel. He was still unsure what game Thorne was playing. He was making it all so easy for him and still things were far from satisfactory. The one thing he hadn't bargained for was ineptitude. He should have. He knew what was going on most of the time, and the control he felt at those moments was what would keep everything moving towards the correct and proper outcome. But there were seconds of doubt too. Then he felt as if the unexpected might be round the corner and come rushing at him and send everything spinning into confusion. He did not like surprises.

He hadn't liked them for years.

He'd decided to stick to roughly the same pattern but he fancied a bit of a change. Pubs had proved successful and, of course, the discothèque in south London, but he wanted to adjust the demographics. Perhaps he'd move upmarket a little. Somewhere beset with lacquered wood and polished steel, where decibels inhibited conversation to bellowed soundbites. Set about treating some young thing full of pills and alcopops. Half the job would be done for him already.

All he'd need to do would be to cruise along behind the night bus . . .

Yes, she would probably be very young. Younger than Helen, even. And so much luckier. Success would mean relief from many more years of struggle and stretchmarks. He would get this one right, like Alison. If her heart had the strength, even near death, to keep pumping the blood around the body, then she would be cared for.

He looked around at the other drivers drowning in their cars, the pedestrians choking, the shopworkers being slowly suffocated. All of them dying a little, day by day. He couldn't help all of them, but one was going to be given a fighting chance very soon.

Then Thorne might start doing his job properly.

The kiss, when Anne opened the door to her office, felt awkward. The smiles were genuine and unprofessional. They both wanted more. They'd have to wait.

The blackboard stood against the wall. Thorne took a step towards it. 'This would be the communications device that Jeremy was telling me about?'

She looked stunned. 'You've seen him?'

He shrugged. 'He gave me a lift into town this morning.' *Now he had one or two bits and pieces in his briefcase.*

'Oh.' She walked over and self-consciously rubbed out some of the scrawlier chalk marks. Now, under the lines of letters, there were two small arrows, one pointing forwards, the other backwards.

'It's . . . evolving. I'm hopeful.'

He wished he'd made a move on her that night after dinner. For all sorts of reasons. Now things were so difficult. 'I got one of the blokes at work to have a look on the Internet for me,' he said. 'There were all sorts of . . . gizmos.'

She smiled. 'Oh, there are. If Alison ever recovers significant movement there are powerchairs that are incredibly sophisticated. Even as she is now there's the Eyegaze system, which can be operated by the tiniest eye movement. She could manoeuvre a mouse and type into a computer with vocaliser software. She could speak. She could control virtually any element within her immediate environment.'

'All horribly expensive, I suppose?'

'Believe me, I was lucky to get the blackboard. Do you want a coffee?'

Thorne wanted all manner of disgusting things. Right there on her desk. He wanted to be pushed backwards across it scattering notes on to the floor. He wanted to unzip himself and watch as she walked towards him smiling, hitching up her skirt . . .

'I'd really like to go and see Alison.'

'Well, you go on up and I'll grab us a couple of coffees from the canteen. You remember where it is, don't you?'

The room was not so cluttered with hardware as the last time he'd seen it. It still felt as if he'd taken the lift to the basement and stumbled into the generating room, but there was a lot less of it. Alison seemed less attached. There were fresh flowers – from her boyfriend, he supposed. It suddenly struck him that he'd never met Tim Hinnegan.

He had no idea what he looked like, what he did for a living. He'd ask Holland.

Fuck that. He'd ask Alison. When he had time.

He needed a piss and hurriedly availed himself of Alison's *en-suite* facilities. A low metal pan, a sink, a sharps bin. Handles screwed at a variety of heights and angles into the insipid yellow walls. He flushed the toilet and splashed cold water on to his face.

Thorne sat in the chair nearest the bed and looked at her. Her eyes were wide open, the right eye flickering. The smallest movement but seemingly constant. It was incredibly difficult to maintain eye-contact with her. There was a challenge in that unflinching stare – he was imagining it, he knew, but he still felt embarrassed. How long did you ever hold eye-contact with anyone? Even someone with whom you were intimate? A few seconds? Alison would look deep into his eyes for as long as he was comfortable with it. He quickly realised, with something like shame, that this wasn't very long.

He took her hand and held it tight against the blanket. To have lifted it clear of the bedclothes would have felt like . . . taking advantage.

'Hi, Alison. It's Detective Inspector Thorne.' He reddened, remembering that she'd just been staring at him for nearly a minute. He was starting to sweat. He shuffled the chair a little closer to the bed and squeezed her hand. 'You must be sick of people being as stupid as me.'

Alison blinked. The sluggishness of the eyelid's downward movement was probably normal but, to Thorne, it implied a weary amusement in her answer. He thought he felt a split-second tremor in her fingers and looked into her eyes for confirmation. There was none. How many of her friends had sat where he was and felt the same things? How many had shouted for a nurse and gone home feeling stupid?

He was actually starting to feel genuinely relaxed. The low hum of the machines was soothing and soporific. It wasn't unlike being pissed. There was an enjoyable conversation to be had. But he knew that Anne would arrive with the coffee at any time and there was one question he couldn't ask with her in the room.

Letting go of the small, warm hand was difficult but he needed to open the briefcase. From the stiff-backed manilla envelope he produced the ten-by-eight black-and-white photo, and held it down by his side wondering how best to phrase the question.

She'd recognise Bishop, of course she would. He'd been in the room with Anne the day before, hadn't he? He wasn't really looking for anything like an identification. He just hoped he might learn something else. Get a sense of something else. A recognition beyond the one he knew would be there anyway.

He knew that nothing that happened in this room would ever be admissible as evidence. He also knew instinctively that he couldn't ask her straight out if the face she was about to see belonged to the man who'd put her here. Christ alone knew how fragile she was feeling. She was almost certainly confused, disoriented, even now. He'd have to take it slowly.

Much as he wanted this, he couldn't hurt her.

'Alison, I'm going to show you a picture.' He held up the photo. For a moment he said nothing. There was just the relentless hum. 'You've seen this man before, haven't you?'

His eyes didn't shift from hers for an instant.

She blinked.

His phone rang.

Anne didn't want the coffee to go cold and had tried to keep the conversation with the administrator as brief as possible. He'd collared her at the till and even the few fragments of his monologue that had got through to her had bored her rigid instantly. He was a pathologically dull individual who, were he ever to become a hospital visitor, could set back the treatment of coma patients by decades. She'd smiled and nodded. God knows what she'd actually agreed to.

Now, as she walked towards Alison's room, she wondered if Thorne felt as she did – as though this was some sort of bizarre date, sharing a cup of coffee with Alison as a chaperone.

It was kind of him to have looked into Alison's condition on the Internet. She'd have to check it out for herself: she was well briefed, of course, on all the technological advancements that were making the lives of those with permanent disabilities easier – at least, those with a substantial private income. Things were moving quickly, though, and she was likely to be better informed by the Net than she would be by current medical literature.

She had no idea whether or not Thorne was good at what he did. It was obvious that he cared, that he got involved. As far as his job was concerned, caring might not necessarily be a good thing. She knew what Jeremy would say about it.

Holding a cup in each hand she pushed open the door to Alison's room with her backside and nudged it shut with her hip. She turned to see Thorne standing by the window, staring into space. She looked at the empty chair by Alison's bed and knew instantly that something was wrong.

'Tom?'

She could see the tension in his jaw. His face was the colour of a corpse.

'Someone has contacted my office . . . my former office, anonymously.'

He turned his head slowly towards Alison, but Anne could see that he was looking at a space on the back wall, above her head. His eyes dropped to the girl's face and stayed there for a second or two before he turned and walked slowly out of the room.

Anne put the coffee on the table next to Alison's bed and followed him. He was waiting outside the door. The moment the door was closed, he took a small step towards her and spoke calmly, the fury just held in check.

'I have been accused of molesting Alison.'

The screaming, hypnotic pulse of the music had focused Thorne's mind and steered his thoughts into the dark places in his head that were usually best avoided. He was sitting on the floor, his back resting against the sofa, the beer can cool against his cheek.

Keable had tried to set his mind at rest. 'Don't worry, Tom, it's obviously nothing. Just some nutter who claimed to have heard it from somebody in the hospital. Nobody's taking it seriously – it's not like he could have heard it from Alison Willetts, is it?'

Insensitive to the last, but Thorne was relieved that he couldn't argue with the reasoning. He let his head fall back on to the sofa cushion and stared at the ceiling.

He thought about touching Alison.

He thought about hearing Jeremy Bishop beg.

The doorbell rang. He got slowly to his feet. He opened the door and went straight back to his spot on the floor by the sofa. Formalities seemed pointless. Anne walked in and stood by the fireplace. She dropped her bag, took off the thin raincoat and spent five seconds taking in the room. The first thing she noticed was the beer. 'Can I?'

She walked over, smoothing down her long black skirt. Thorne handed her a can of lager from the broken four-pack by his side. 'Not a brand I'm familiar with.'

'I know. Expensive wine and cheap, piss-weak lager. Don't ask me why.'

'So you can enjoy the drinking without the sensation of being drunk.'

'That's definitely not the reason.'

She sat down on the sofa behind and to his right. 'Tom, that phone call. It's just a crank.'

He half crushed his empty can then stopped and put it down gently next to the others. 'I know exactly who it is.'

'Well, it's stupid to let it upset you.'

He turned and looked at her over his shoulder. 'No. Not upset.'

Anne could see in his eyes that the nice side of him, the side that bought Alison flowers, was far from being the whole story. Though it was difficult to contemplate such a thing, she would not want this man as an enemy.

She took a long swig of beer and gestured towards the stereo. 'Who's this?'

'Leftfield. The track's called "Open Up".'

She listened for a minute. Hated it.

'That's John Lydon doing the vocal,' Thorne said, as if it made a difference.

'Right . . .'

'Johnny Rotten . . . the Sex Pistols?'

'Sadly, I was a little too old even for them. What are you, then? Forty?'

'Forty a few months ago. I was seventeen when "God Save The Queen" came out.'

'God. I was already a third-year med student.'

'I know. Pushing beds into rivers.'

She gave him what his dad would certainly have described as an old-fashioned look. 'So what were *you* doing?'

Not going to university, thought Thorne. For so many reasons, he wished he had. 'I was about to join the force, I suppose, and managing my acne.' Wanting to be a policeman more than anything. Trying to make his mum and dad proud. Wanting to do good, and all the other stupid ideas of which he'd been so brutally disabused.

Anne drained her can and Thorne passed her another. They sat in silence for a minute, remembering, or pretending to remember.

'Thanks for coming over by the way. Did you drive?'

'Yes. Bugger to park, though.' Thorne nodded. 'It's good to get out actually. Rachel and I are getting on each other's nerves a bit at the moment.'

'Yeah?'

'She's got a couple of resits to do and she thought the whole exam thing was behind her. So she's being a bit . . . spiky.'

Thorne remembered his first encounter with Anne Coburn in a lecture theatre at the Royal Free. Spiky obviously ran in the family.

Anne took another long slug of beer. Enjoying it. 'Just run-of-the-mill teenage angst, I suppose. She hasn't pierced her belly-button or painted her room black yet, but it's probably just a matter of time.'

'It'll sort itself out.'

'And so will this business with Alison.'

'It's all right, there won't be an investigation or anything. Nobody's taking it seriously.'

'Except you.'

'If that's what he wants.' The *he* spat out like something sour.

'Why don't you talk about it, then?'

'Anne, I don't need a doctor. Or a mother.'

She shuffled forward to the very edge of the sofa and leaned forward, her head down.

'Fine. Do you want to go to bed, then?'

Thorne had always thought that spluttering your drink out when somebody surprised you only ever happened in *Terry and June*, but he succeeded brilliantly in snorting a decent amount of cheap lager into his lap. The sitcom moment made him laugh uncontrollably.

Anne laughed, too, but she was also blushing to her toenails.

'Well, fuck . . . I don't know what you're supposed to say . . .'

'I think you just said it.'

She slid off the sofa on to the floor next to him. 'So?'

'Well, these trousers have got Tesco's own lager all over them now. They'll have to come off . . .'

He leaned across and kissed her. She put down her lager and placed a hand on his neck. He broke the kiss, looked at the floor. 'Now, this carpet has unhappy memories and

I'm still not a hundred per cent sure I've got the smell of vomit out of it . . .'

'You smooth-talking bastard.'

'So, the palatial bedroom suite?'

She nodded and they stood up. There was still a hint of awkwardness between them. Nothing had yet been abandoned, but taking hands would have seemed a little silly all the same. Thorne held open the bedroom door. 'I have to warn you, I've got a Swedish virgin in here.'

Anne raised her eyebrows and looked into the room, seeing only a small fitted wardrobe, a chest of drawers and a neatly made bed. She didn't get it. 'Eh?'

'The bed . . .' Thorne pulled her to him. 'It doesn't matter . . .'

Thorne woke and looked at the clock. It was nearly two thirty in the morning and the phone was ringing. He was instantly wide awake. He slipped out of bed and hurried naked into the living room where the handset was recharging on the base unit just inside the front door. The heating couldn't have been off for very long but the flat was already freezing.

'Sir, sorry it's so late. It's Holland.'

Thorne pressed the phone tight to his ear and wrapped an arm around his shoulder. He could still hear Leftfield. The CD was on repeat and they'd forgotten to turn it off.

'Yes?'

'We might have something here. A woman rang through. She'd seen the reconstruction – waited a couple of days wondering whether to call.'

'Go on.'

'Nine months ago a man knocked on her door claiming

to be looking for a party. She thought he looked all right – you know, friendly enough. She invited him in. He was carrying a bottle of champagne.'

Thorne stopped shivering.

'I haven't got much more than that at the minute, sir. For some reason he left, and she didn't really think anything of it until the programme. She reckons she can give us a pretty good description, though.'

'Does Tughan know about this?'

'Yes, sir. I've already called him.'

Thorne felt a twinge of annoyance, but he knew that Holland couldn't have done anything else. 'What did he say?'

'He thought it sounded hopeful.'

'Anything about me?'

He could hear Holland thinking.

'Don't spare my feelings, Holland, I haven't got any.'

'There was some crack about you and Miss Willetts, sir. I don't really remember – just a joke, really.'

Nobody was taking it seriously.

'When are you going to interview her?'

'Myself and DI Tughan are going to see her tomorrow morning.'

Thorne took down the details, scribbling the woman's name and address on a Post-it note next to the phone. The initial buzz was wearing off a little and he could feel the cold again. He wanted to get back to bed.

'Thanks for that, Holland. One quick thing . . .'

'Don't worry, sir, I'll call you as soon as we've seen her.'

'Great, thanks. But I was going to say, if anybody should ask, your girlfriend trapped her hand in a door this morning . . .'

He realised as soon as he'd hung up on Holland that he was terribly awake. He turned off the music and scurried around the living room with a bin liner, picking up empty beer cans. For a second he was tempted to look inside Anne's bag, which still lay where she'd dropped it. Had she brought a change of clothes with her?

He thought better of it and instead grabbed the spare duvet from the cupboard in the hall and sat on the sofa in the dark.

Thinking.

Things were moving quickly. There had been cases before where he'd felt like an outsider – he would come at things from a different angle – but he was still, if only nominally, part of a team. This time it was different. He'd felt good marching out of Keable's office but within minutes he was wondering if he'd done the right thing. He still wondered.

He knew why he'd walked away. Whatever Keable had told his bosses about politics and personality clashes, it still came down to judgement.

Their passing of it; his lack of it.

His judgement and theirs, and that of those long gone. But even the judgement of the dead could not always be trusted. Any conviction based on such testimony would surely be flawed. Only one man could judge him.

And Tom Thorne was the harshest judge of all.

He thought about the woman asleep in his bed. Anne wasn't the first woman he'd slept with since Jan. There had been some drunken fumbling with an ambitious young sergeant and a short fling with a legal secretary – but this was the first time he'd felt frightened afterwards.

Once upon a time Anne had been involved with Bishop. Thorne still wasn't sure to what extent, but that hardly mattered. The killer who had all but turned his life upside down had once had sex with the woman who was now, at least for the moment, sharing his bed. He suddenly wondered if Bishop might be jealous. It made sense. The anonymous phone call, the accusation, had seemed a little . . . beneath him. Could the attack here in this room have been, at least in part, a warning to stay away from Anne? On top of everything was there actually a sexual rivalry? The idea was comforting. It began to give him back a sense of control. He'd felt it slipping away as the anger had swept over him after the accusation about Alison. Now he was calmer.

Back in the hospital. *Oh, he'll find out exactly what type I am . . .*

A man trained to save life was taking it in the name of something Thorne could never understand. Didn't care about understanding.

If Thorne was going to stop him, it was important to maintain the initiative.

He went to fetch the phone, curled up on the sofa and dialled 141 . . .

A few minutes later, he crept back into the bedroom, slid under the duvet and lay there blinking, unable to sleep.

Around four o'clock Anne woke up and did her best to help him.

'How do you feel?'

A question I'm asked every day. Sometimes more than once. It's not that I don't understand why. It's that I'd-better-say-something kind of thing. Better than sitting there looking at the clock and wondering which nurse gets to wipe my arse, I suppose. It's hospitals. It makes people feel strangely compelled to buy fruit and breathe through their mouth and ask ridiculous questions. But why questions, for fuck's sake? Don't ask me questions. Tell me things, if you like. I'm a good listener. Getting to be very, very good. Tell me anything you like. Bore me rigid. Sit there and waffle on about how your boss doesn't understand you, or your husband's not interested in sex any more or you want to travel or nursing's badly paid, or you like to drink in the afternoons but don't – ask – me – things.

How do you feel?

It's not like you're actually expecting an answer, is it? You'd be bored off your tits if I decided to play along. If I wanted to respond with a pithy 'Not too bad, thank you for asking, and how are you?' that would take, at present levels of blinking proficiency and taking into account the fatigue factor, approximately forty-five minutes. Sorry you asked? Well, don't, then.

How do you feel?

Grateful that you're there, don't get me wrong. All of you. Visitors, nurses popping heads round the door, cleaners. Say hello. Come in and tell me lies. Just don't be predictable. The only reason you're asking, really, is that you can't tell precisely just by looking at me. Not exactly. I mean, you could take a wild stab in the dark. You could make a pretty good guess. You wouldn't need to phone a friend, would you? I'm lying in hospital. Utterly fucked. I'm hardly going to be over the moon. But most of the time you don't have to ask people how they feel. It's obvious. You can see if someone's happy, or tired, or pissed off because it's there in their face, but my face doesn't give a lot away. It must say something, I suppose, but I can only guess, really. If there's an expression that says, 'Closed,' or 'Gone to lunch,' it's probably there or thereabouts.

How do you feel? OK, then . . .

Angry. Stupid. Optimistic. Bored. Tired. Awake. Frustrated. Grateful. Irritated. Violent. Calm. Dreamy. Shit. Confused. Ignorant. Ugly. Sick. Hungry. Useless. Special. Horny. Pessimistic. Ashamed. Loved. Forgotten. Freaky. Mislaid. Relieved. Alone. Frightened. Stoned. Dirty. Dead . . .

Horny? I know, sorry, very strange. But I'm lying here on a sexy mattress that hums and there's that very gorgeous nurse who actually might not be gay after all. So . . .

Did I say confused? Yes.

A lot of the time. Like why did Thorne show me a picture of Dr Bishop? I had a feeling he was leading up to something. Maybe it's like when you go deaf or blind and your other senses get better to compensate. Because most of me's knackered maybe I'm becoming a bit witchy or something. I know he wanted to ask me things but then his phone rang and he talked quietly and went a bit funny.

Nobody's told me anything yet about what happened. Not really. About the crime, I mean. I know what he did to me . . .

But I still don't know why.

ELEVEN

He got on to the tube at Waterloo. Eight stops, direct, on the Bakerloo line. The carriage was absolutely packed, just the way he liked it. Sometimes he needed to let two or three trains go and wait for the right one. There was no point in squeezing on when the carriage was empty of interest. He watched as the train roared into the station, ignoring his fellow travellers as they inched towards the edge of the platform. He scanned each carriage as it moved past him, making his choice.

It might take a few stops before he'd got to where he needed to be but he moved easily through the crowd of commuters. He enjoyed the build-up. He loved negotiating that sweaty knot of pent-up anger and rustling newspapers to get himself into the right position.

It didn't usually take long to find her.

Today she was tall, only an inch or two shorter than he was. She had dark hair in a bob, and glasses through which she tried to take in as much of her copy of *The Beach* as she could under the circumstances. There was always the danger, of course, that she might get off the train before he did. Before he'd had a chance to get close to her. So many of them got off at Oxford Circus or Baker Street. He wasn't too disappointed when that happened. There was always tomorrow. The rush-hour was wonderfully predictable.

He made his first contact as the train stopped at Piccadilly Circus. That wonderful jolt as the train came to a standstill. Thirty seconds later he would get another chance when they pulled away again. He was behind this one. Sometimes he liked to be face to face. To see their expression as he half looked away or shrugged apologetically. And he loved the breasts, of course. But this was his favourite. He liked the feel of their behinds against his groin. He could place a sweaty hand in the small of their backs to steady himself. He could smell their hair. Best of all, he could turn and look at the person behind him if he needed to, starting a small wave of accusatory looks and sighs as his excitement mounted.

She'd washed her hair this morning. He wondered whether she'd had sex last night. If she'd showered she would have washed the smell away, which was a shame, but he loved the smell of her hair all the same. And a hint of something else at the nape of her neck. The train slowed and came to a halt in the tunnel between Oxford Circus and Regent's Park. Another lovely little push.

With the train motionless, he thought for a minute about what he had to do today. An interview this morning. He enjoyed those. He liked to run things. He could read people well, he knew that. But they could never read him.

The train moved off again with a useful jerk. Only four stops to go. Perhaps one more before the big one. She was looking intently at her book, but he knew she was thinking about him. Despising him. That was fine. Let her think it was over. Let her relax, thinking he'd moved or got off without her seeing. She wouldn't want to look over her shoulder to check. He'd wait until they left Marylebone.

The train moved towards his final destination. He was sure that she'd felt every inch of him that time. It was a second, no more, but he'd felt the crack in her buttocks, the cotton of her long black skirt against the polyester of his work trousers. He'd felt her tense up.

Only once had one of them confronted him. She'd moved away and stepped off the train before turning back and screaming at him. Other passengers looked, but he smiled indulgently and held up his hands and let himself get lost in the mêlée of others getting on the train. Only once. They were pretty good odds. Of course, if it ever came to it, he had a pretty good defence up his sleeve.

This was his favourite moment. One last good one and then away. In that second or two before the doors opened he leaned against her and took everything in. The feeling of his erection against her arse, his face against the back of her head. The intimacy was breathtaking. They might have been lovers, curling up together in bed at night, the sheets damp and smelly . . .

Then off and pushing through the crowd towards the door. As he sidled past her he saw her glance up from her book. Close up she was far from gorgeous but he didn't care. The tension in her face and the heat in his groin were all that really mattered. It was only a game, after all. It was part of the hustle-bustle, wasn't it? He smiled and thought the same thing he always did after such a lovely start to the working day: So don't live in London, love.

Doing up the buttons of his jacket to hide the tiny bulge, Nick Tughan stepped off the train at Edgware Road, and turning his mind towards the day ahead, began moving quickly towards the escalator.

Anne had left early saying she needed to get home before Rachel was awake and Thorne had slept until well after nine. He'd phoned Brigstocke to say he'd be in late. Not that he had anything planned – he was waiting on Holland. He was just plain knackered.

He was enjoying his fourth piece of toast and looking forward to the rare, illicit thrill of *Richard and Judy* when the doorbell rang.

He recognised James Bishop straight away from Kodak's photo. Bethell's appraisal had been about right, he thought: grungy was the word. He was tall and skinny, wearing a long dark coat over T-shirt, jeans and grubby training shoes. What looked like very short, bleached-blond hair was hidden beneath a black pork-pie hat, and he carried a dirty green bag slung across one shoulder.

'Are you Thorne?'

The same well-modulated tones as his father, despite the sad attempt at the oikish London accent, and the same chiselled features, albeit camouflaged by several days of light stubbly fuzz. It was like looking at Dr Jeremy Bishop as a student.

'Yes, I am, James.' That put the cocky little sod on the back foot. Thorne couldn't help smirking. 'Could I ask how you got my address?'

'Yeah. You told my dad which road you lived in . . . I've knocked on virtually every door in the street.'

You should have just asked him, James. He knows exactly where I live.

'I see. Woken up many of my neighbours?'

Bishop smiled. 'A couple. A very tasty housewife asked me in for a cup of tea.'

'We're pretty friendly round here. Fancy a bit of toast?'

Thorne turned from the front door and strolled back into his flat. There was a pause before he heard the young man close the outer door, and another before he shut the door to the flat and came sloping into the living room.

'Not bothered about the toast, but I wouldn't mind a coffee . . .'

Thorne went into the kitchen and watched as his visitor hovered in the middle of the living room. 'James is it, then? Or Jim?'

'James.'

Right, thought Thorne, spooning the coffee into a mug. Jim to your trendy mates but James when you're trying to borrow money off Daddy. He carried the coffee through and handed the mug to him. 'So?'

Bishop looked disarmed. Evidently, this wasn't how he'd wanted things to go. He tried to sound as dangerous as he could, which wasn't very. 'I want you to leave my old man alone.'

Thorne sat down on the arm of the sofa. 'I see. What is it you think I'm doing exactly?'

'Why are you hassling him?'

'Hassling?'

'There was a bloke taking photos outside his house the other day, then when you turn up with some bollocks about scrounging a lift you tell him it was probably reporters. He might have fallen for that, but I think it's crap. What were you doing there anyway?'

'I'm a policeman, James, I can go pretty much wherever I want.'

Bishop was starting to enjoy himself a little. That made two of them. He took a step towards the mantelpiece then turned to Thorne, smiling. 'Shouldn't you call me "sir"?'

Thorne returned the smile with interest. 'If this conversation formed part of an investigation then perhaps I might, yes. But it doesn't, we're in my flat and you're drinking my fucking coffee.'

Bishop's hands tightened around his mug. Wondering what to say next. Thorne saved him the trouble. 'I think your father's overreacting somewhat.'

'He doesn't even know I'm here.'

Right. No. Course not.

'He got these phone calls.'

'When?'

'Last night. In the middle of the night. Four or five, one after the other. He phoned me up in a right panic.'

'What sort of phone calls?'

'You tell me.'

The cockiness had started to return. He needed slapping down harder. 'Listen, I questioned your father as part of an investigation that I'm no longer even part of, all right?' As Bishop's mouth fell open, Thorne felt a twinge of something approaching sympathy. 'Now tell me about the phone calls.'

'Like I said, in the middle of the night. He could hear somebody there. Whoever it was had withheld their number and that was it. One after the other. He's upset – no, he's frightened. He's fucking shit-scared.'

I seriously doubt it.

'So what are you going to do about it?' Bishop was starting to sound genuinely angry.

'I'll tell you what I told him about the photographer. I'll look into it. That's the best I can do.'

'Are you seeing Anne Coburn?'

It was Thorne's turn to be genuinely angry. 'Behave yourself, James . . .'

'Seeing as you're off the investigation it could be that, though, couldn't it?'

'What?' Thorne took a deep breath. Trying not to lose it, knowing it was the father, not the son, he needed to save it for.

'If you and Anne were . . . you know . . . it would be a reason to get at my father.'

Thorne stood up and moved towards Bishop. He saw the slightest flinch, but only shook his head and reached for the empty coffee cup.

'As far as I can remember, Dr Coburn, as your godmother, was responsible for your spiritual well-being. Looking at you, she's obviously failed miserably but that is, I believe, where your relationship with her ends. You probably got a silver christening spoon and the odd birthday present, but who she's sleeping with is not part of the deal.'

Bishop nodded, impressed. Then he broke into a grin. 'So you are, then?'

Thorne smiled as he carried the empty mugs through to the kitchen. 'What do you do, James, when you're not worrying about your father?'

Bishop moved aimlessly around the living room. He stopped to study the pile of CDs. 'I always worry about my father. We're very close. Are you and yours not, then?'

Thorne grimaced. 'Well?'

'I move about a lot. Bit of writing. Tried being an actor. Anything that pays the rent, I suppose.'

Thorne was starting to feel that he understood this young man. Not that he understood many of them any more. This one wasn't quite the good-for-nothing he'd thought Anne had described. Beneath the attempts at nonconformity there was almost certainly an inherited conventionality, which he was trying desperately to escape. Which was *why* he was trying to escape. He was misguided for sure, but essentially harmless. James Bishop had no idea of the poisonous gene pool in which he was splashing around. He could piss in the water as much as he liked, but in all the ways that didn't matter, the poor sod was his father's son.

'Did you study?'

'I wasted a couple of years at college, yeah. I'm not the ivory-tower type.'

Thorne came back into the living room and picked up his jacket. 'Tower Records type, though?'

'Oh, yeah . . .' Bishop self-consciously fingered the T-shirt that carried the shop's logo. 'I'm working there at the moment.'

Thorne gestured towards the hallway. It was time to go. Bishop moved quickly towards the front door, in no hurry to hang about.

'Well, maybe I'll see you in there,' said Thorne. 'What's your country section like?'

Bishop laughed. ' 'Fuck should I know?'

Thorne opened the front door. It was starting to rain.

'Stupid question. What – you more into ambient? Trance? Speed-garage? Could you get me a discount on the new Grooverider twelve-inch?'

Bishop looked at him.

Thorne pulled the door shut. 'You've had quite a few surprises this morning, haven't you?'

Margaret Byrne lived on the ground floor of a small

terraced house in Tulse Hill. She was not what Holland and Tughan had been expecting. A plain and prematurely grey-haired woman, she was probably in her late forties and considerably overweight. Tughan could not conceal his surprise as she peered round her front door at them, one foot held in place against the jamb to prevent a large ginger cat escaping. Once the IDs, which she'd asked to see, had been produced, she was happy to invite them in. She insisted on making them tea, leaving Tughan and Holland to negotiate a route round at least three more large cats before arriving at comfortable chairs in her front room.

Holland was thinking it, but it was Tughan that said it. 'This place fucking stinks,' he hissed, before adding drily, 'No wonder he changed his mind and pissed off.'

After the tea, and a good selection of biscuits, had appeared, Holland sat back, as he'd been instructed to do, and let Tughan run things.

'So you live alone then, Margaret?'

She pulled a face. 'I hate Margaret. Can we stick to Maggie?'

Holland smiled, thinking, Go on, don't make it easy for him.

'Sorry. Maggie . . .'

'My husband left a couple of years ago. Don't know why I call him that, he could never be arsed to marry me, but anyway . . .'

'No children?'

She wrapped her grey cardigan tight across her chest. 'Got a daughter. She's twenty-three, lives in Edinburgh, and I haven't got the first idea where her father is.'

She took another biscuit and began stroking the black-and-white cat that had jumped on to her lap. She muttered to it softly and it settled down. Holland thought she was a bit like his mum. He hadn't seen her for ages. Maybe he'd talk to Sophie about asking her down to stay for a bit.

'Right, tell us about the man with the champagne, Maggie.'

'Didn't you write it down when I phoned up?'

Holland smiled. Tughan didn't.

'We just need a few more details, that's all.'

'Well, it was about eight o'clock, I think. I answered the door and this bloke was standing there waving a bottle about. He asked me if this was where Jenny was having a party?'

'Have you got a neighbour called Jenny?'

'I don't think so. He said he was sure he'd got the right address and we had a bit of a laugh about something or other and he started being a bit naughty, you know, saying how it was a shame to waste a bottle of champagne. He was flirting . . . I think he was a bit tipsy.'

'You said when you called that you could give us a very good description.'

'Did I? Oh, bloody hell. Right, well he was tall, definitely over six feet, glasses, and very well dressed. He had a very nice suit on, you know, expensive . . .'

'Colour?'

'Blue, I think. Dark blue.'

Holland was jotting it all down and keeping his mouth shut like a good boy.

'Go on, Maggie.'

'He had short, greyish hair . . .'

'Greyish?'

'Yeah, you know, not silver, just greying, but he wasn't that old, I don't think. Well, not as old as me at any rate.'

'How old?'

'Thirty-six . . . thirty-seven? I've always been rubbish at that. Well, I think most people are, aren't they?' She turned and looked at Holland. 'How old d'you reckon I am?'

Holland could feel the colour coming to his cheeks. Why the hell had she asked *him*? 'Oh . . . I don't know . . . Thirty-nine?'

She smiled, acknowledging the kindness of the lie. 'I'm forty-three, and I know I look older.'

Tughan, anxious to get back on track, cleared his throat. The cat, startled, shot off Margaret Byrne's lap and flew out of the door. This, in turn, made Tughan jump, which Holland would later remember as the only amusing thing about the entire interview.

'What did he sound like? Did he have an accent?'

'Pretty posh, I'd say. A nice voice . . . and, you know, very good-looking. He was handsome.'

'So you invited him in?'

She brushed more cat hair than there was from her skirt. 'Well, I think he was dropping hints. Like I said, he was waving this bottle around.' She looked at Tughan and held eye-contact. 'Yes. I invited him in.'

Tughan smiled thinly. 'Why?'

Holland was starting to feel uncomfortable. This woman could help them. She might well be the only person who *could* help them. Why she had invited the man who might have killed her into her home was information they didn't need now. This woman wasn't mad or desperate or sex-starved, for Christ's sake. Loneliness was not a crime, much as Tughan seemed to be enjoying touching the tender spot of it. She hadn't answered him anyway. He let it go.

'What happened then?'

'Like I said on the phone, this was the funny part. He opened the champagne – I remember being disappointed because there wasn't a pop – and I said I'd go and get some glasses. He said great and he was just going to make a quick phone call.'

Tughan looked at Holland then back at Margaret. 'You didn't mention that when you called.'

'Didn't I? Well, he did.'

Tughan sat forward in his chair. 'He made a call from here? From your phone?'

'No. Just as I was going off to the kitchen I saw him take out one of those horrible little mobile things. I hate them, don't you? Always beeping and playing daft tunes when you're sitting on a train.'

'And you were in the kitchen?'

'And I was in the kitchen, and I'd just got the glasses down and given them a wipe out because they were a bit dirty, and I heard the front door slam. I came back out and he'd buggered off. I opened the front door but I couldn't see him. I heard a car pull away up the road, but I didn't really see it.'

Tughan nodded. Holland had finished writing.

Margaret Byrne looked quickly from one to the other. 'You reckon he was the bloke who killed that girl up in Holloway, then?'

Tughan said nothing. He stood up and threw Holland a look, telling him to do the same. 'If we send a car for you tomorrow could you come down to Edgware Road and work with one of our computer artists?'

She nodded, and picked up a passing cat as she got to her feet.

When they reached the front door Tughan stopped and looked at her. She smiled nervously at him.

'Why did you wait so long before reporting this matter?' Tughan said. 'I mean, you even waited for four days after the reconstruction went out on TV.'

She pulled the cat close to her neck. Holland stepped forward, putting a hand a little too forcefully on Tughan's shoulder.

'We'd better get going. Thanks for all your help.'

The gratitude in her eyes was obvious. She took hold of his sleeve. 'Was it him?'

Tughan was already on his way to the car. Holland watched him deactivate the alarm, climb in and slam the door. He turned back to her. 'I think you were very lucky, Maggie.'

She smiled and gripped his sleeve a little tighter as her eyes began to fill with tears. 'It would be the first time . . .'

I'm in a much better mood now. I don't mean generally, that's still up and down. Tim said I was moody before and he's probably right. But now, in here, I can be a right bitch. I think that's fair enough, though. I think I deserve a medal for the few nice moods I do have.

Anyway . . .

Even in here there's always something that can cheer you up. It's not exactly Carry On Doctor *but there's laughs to be had if you look for them. Sick ones, usually, but you can't be too fussy. There's this nurse, Martina, who's taken it upon herself to make sure I look pretty all the time. Under normal circumstances, of course, I'd tell her that you can't improve on perfection, but granted, she's got a job on her hands. To be honest, I think she's doing it to get a break from the catheter and arse work, which is hardly brimming with job satisfaction, is it? At first I didn't mind when she was trimming my hair and cutting my toenails but she's started getting a bit ambitious. I think she's a failed beauty therapist or something. She painted my nails the other day and the colour was fucking revolting and yesterday afternoon she decided that a bit of lippy might cheer me up. Putting lipstick on somebody else is like trying to have a wank with your left hand. Forget it. I looked like a clown in a coma, or a tit in a trance, as my nan used to say.*

I think she was trying to make me look like one of those hideous women who work on the makeup counters in department stores – you know, the ones who spend all day surrounded by cosmetics and haven't got a fucking clue how to put them on.

Here's a tip. Don't use a trowel. I always want to creep up behind them and shout, 'Mirror! Use a mirror!'

I didn't plan what happened this morning, I swear, but I quite wish I had. Obviously some of the other nurses had noticed that Martina was spending all her time tarting me up instead of doing any of the dirty work and she got lumbered with cleaning out my breathing tube. I can fully understand not wanting to do it, it's bloody foul. So Martina is supposed to pull it out and clean out all the muck or something so it doesn't get blocked. Imagine somebody was waggling a tube around in your mouth. Well, it's pretty much the same when it's straight into your neck. You'd want to cough, wouldn't you? Coughing isn't one of my best things, these days, but I must have been saving it up. There's Martina trying to be all efficient and I just let one go. I couldn't help it. I coughed out of my neck, for Christ's sake!

Like I said, it wasn't on purpose and she didn't help by screaming the place down, but this enormous lump of phlegmy glop just splattered on to her forehead.

I hope she might stay away for a bit now. Or maybe just stick to the rear-end stuff. At least you know what's coming at you! Come on, though, pearl nail polish?

Everything's moving along on the blink front. Another small complication is that sometimes I screw things up by blinking just because my brain thinks it's high time I did. Same reason you do. That doesn't help. I'm spelling away, then I suddenly throw in an X or a J for no good reason. Like suddenly shouting, 'Bollocks,' in the middle of a conversation.

It's like Newcastle on a Saturday night.

TWELVE

Rachel sat at the desk in her room, the chemistry textbook in front of her long since invisible. She knew that this was what being involved with someone was about. Highs and lows. She'd gone out with a boy for nearly six months when she was a fourth-former and still remembered the dull ache of the phone that didn't ring and the stabbing agony of the undelivered note. This was much worse, though.

She had her own locker now in the sixth-form common room, and had to fight the urge to run and open it every five minutes to check her phone. By the end of the day there would always be at least a text message. She saved them all and reread them constantly. A voice message was always better, though. She loved his voice especially.

She walked over and slumped down on the bed, picking up her phone from where it was recharging as she went. She listened to the message again, that strange part of her that she knew was common to everybody, savouring the pain of it.

Like gnawing at a mouth ulcer.

He wasn't sure if he could make it tonight. He *might* be able to but he didn't want to let her down at the last minute. He was sorry. It was a work thing he couldn't get out of. They'd better cancel. He'd call tomorrow.

As always, she was offered the option to delete the message. She saved it, although it was saved, anyway, in her head. She lay there endlessly pulling to pieces every phrase and analysing every nuance. Had he sounded distant? Was this the start of letting her down gently? He'd call tomorrow, he said, not later tonight. She wanted to call him but knew she wouldn't. The idea of being clingy made her sick. But she knew that if it came to it she would be.

She desperately wanted a cigarette but couldn't risk it. She'd had a couple in the garden the night before when her mum had been out screwing the policeman. She sometimes climbed up on the desk and opened a window to blow the smoke out but her mum would be coming to bed any time. Her mum who smoked, but said that *she* couldn't. Very fucking fair.

She'd speak to him tomorrow and everything would be fine and she'd feel like a pathetic sad cow.

She wasn't a stupid little girl any more. That was why he wanted her.

The carpet fibres that Thorne had scraped from the inside of Bishop's boot were in a small plastic bag. He knew he couldn't take them to Forensics himself and he didn't feel he could ask Holland yet. But there was somebody he could ask.

When the plastic bag dropped on to the pool table, Hendricks didn't shift his gaze a millimetre as he lined up the shot, the cue sliding easily back and forth along the cleft of his chin. He casually potted the eight ball and straightened up. 'That's another fiver.' His eyes shifted to the bag and its contents. 'Where did you get 'em?'

Thorne handed over the money and put his cue down on the table. 'Where d'you think I got them?'

'All right, smartarse, *how* did you get 'em?'

'The less I tell you, the less chance there is of you opening your big Manc gob.'

'I haven't said I'll do it yet, and you're not exactly asking very nicely.'

Thorne knew Hendricks would do it, but still felt bad about asking him. He'd put him up plenty of times, they'd done each other favours, lent each other money, but this was work. This was asking a lot. Hendricks was sharp. If he agreed to do it, he'd do so knowing the risks. He wouldn't lose his job, but he might find himself having to take on a bit more lecture work. He was also sharp enough to see that it was a lot of effort for what would probably be precious little reward.

'If you're so sure it's him, then why are you bothering?'

Two teenagers who had been hovering, waiting for a game, stepped forward. One slapped a fifty-pence piece down on the edge of the table. Thorne moved to the bar. Hendricks picked up the plastic bag and followed him. He was chuffed at the thought of the two teenagers watching them go, convinced they were witnessing a deal in some strange new drug.

'Well?'

'Because it's *only* me that's sure.'

'Fair enough, and when they do match up what does that tell you? Fuck all. We're pretty sure the killer drives a Volvo and I don't think the carpet in the back of each one is individually produced. I know they're nice cars, but come on . . .'

'Tickets to Spurs–Arsenal, on me.'

Hendricks took a long slow drink of Guinness. 'I want a box.'

'How am I supposed to do that?'

'How am I supposed to march into the forensics lab with a plastic bag full of carpet fibres I've produced out of the sodding ether?'

'I'll see what I can do. Listen, Phil, you know that lot, they won't ask questions. They're scientists not taxmen. Just tell them you're trying to help and you've got a mate who drives a Volvo. In fact, take in some other fibres from the back of your car or something – you know, like a comparison.'

'I don't recall a single witness seeing a beige Nissan Micra, do you?'

Hendricks had a point. He did perhaps own the single most repellent vehicle on the road in Greater London.

'Thanks, Phil.'

'Remember, a box!'

'Yeah, yeah . . .'

'Did you know that the Volvo is the only commercially produced car you can't kill yourself in? I mean, obviously you can drive one into a wall if you fancy it, but it has a cut-out device, you know, so that you can't tie a hose to the exhaust, and sit inside and asphyxiate yourself.'

Thorne grunted. 'Pity.'

Thorne had left the pub twenty-five pounds poorer but without the plastic bag that had been burning a hole in his pocket. He'd had a good night.

He hadn't drunk a thing.

Ten minutes after he got in, Holland rang. The DC spoke quietly, almost in a whisper. He told Thorne that Sophie was asleep in the next room and he didn't want to wake her.

He didn't want her to know who he was calling.

Thorne listened as Holland told him about Margaret Byrne. She might have been his first victim if the killer hadn't panicked for some reason. He told him what she'd said about the killer's voice. Nice, she thought. Posh. And soothing, probably, thought Thorne. Gentle.

When he heard about the phone call, Thorne pressed the receiver against his ear so hard that it hurt. Bishop bleeping himself? He dismissed the idea. It didn't make any sense. It was possible, he knew that, but what was the point? There was no record anyway, so why go through the motions?

Dave Holland shrugged off Thorne's question about how he'd got on with Tughan. A flippant remark did the job. He had been trying to forget the discomfort, the unease that had permeated every corner of Margaret Byrne's front room whenever the Irishman had opened his mouth. He wasn't sure whether the unease had been his or Margaret's, but it was stifling. It had stayed with him, following him around for the rest of the day like something rank.

Thorne didn't seem particularly interested in Margaret Byrne herself. When he announced that he'd phoned and arranged to see her the following morning, Holland understood why. He tried to dissuade him. What was the point? They'd already spoken to her and she was coming in anyway to knock up an e-fit.

Thorne was well aware that they'd already seen her.

But they hadn't got a picture of Jeremy Bishop in their pocket.

Anne enjoyed the drive home in the dark. There was usually a play on the radio or a short story or something.

Often, in the forty-five minutes or so from Queen Square to Muswell Hill, she'd become so engrossed that she'd have to sit in the car outside the house and wait for it to finish.

She kept the radio off tonight. She had enough to think about.

That morning, in Alison's room, she'd found the photograph of Jeremy. It was lying on the small table in the corner of the room, probably put there by a nurse. It was obvious to her what Thorne had been doing in Alison's room the day before while she was fetching them coffee and she couldn't bring herself to think about what it might mean. She knew somewhere, of course, what it *might* mean. It could hardly mean very much else, but she couldn't bring herself to even try to deal with it.

Not now.

Feelings for two men. For one man those feelings had been shifting, settling into something else over a period of time. For the other they'd changed overnight.

Her relationship with Jeremy had not been the same since Sarah was killed. They'd always shared everything, which she knew had been the cause of so much tension between herself and David, but since the accident Jeremy had become reserved. His aloofness could be amusing, but had begun to wear her down a little. And recently he had become arrogant . . . more arrogant, and occasionally unpleasant. The work seemed a chore to him. He was going through the motions. He would always be a fixture in her life, she knew that, and so would the children, but there was no joy in it any more. She felt . . . dutiful.

Even so, the things Thorne must be thinking were so shocking. They were unimaginable.

She drove along Camden High Street. She was five minutes from his flat.

If she'd found that photograph twelve hours earlier there would have been a confrontation. She would have demanded to know the answers to questions she could no longer ask. And she would not have slept with him. Might not. The sex had changed everything. She knew it was a horribly old-fashioned outlook on things but it was hers. It always had been and it had cost her too many years of unhappiness to remember.

Now she had to . . . compartmentalise. She needed to ignore a side of the man she was sharing a bed with. It seemed to threaten everything. Her feelings for Thorne gave her little option and those she was losing for Jeremy might just make it possible. For the time being at least she had to make a choice. She could not think about a future with Thorne while having to reconcile herself to the damage he seemed determined to do to her past. And a future with him, however short, was what she felt she should go for.

She would put her fingers in her ears and scream. She had no choice.

She thought about Alison, so removed from everything. More than anything she wanted to bring her back. But with the fear and hate and mistrust that seemed to be so much part and parcel of everything, she couldn't help but wonder if Alison might be better off where she was.

She turned the radio on. There was nothing worth listening to, but she was nearly home anyway.

The bath was starting to get cold.

Thorne sat up and looked at his watch, which was lying

next to his mobile phone on the toilet lid. Nearly one o'clock in the morning.

He'd been lying, completely still, with his head under the water. His eyes were open and he stared up at the ceiling swimming above him, waiting for the water to stop moving around him and seeing how long he could hold his breath. It was a game he had played as a kid, lying in a steaming bath in that big old, echoey bathroom, pretending to be dead. He had stopped the night his grandmother came in, saw him, and took a bit of a turn. He'd sat bolt upright the second she screamed, but he would never forget that look on her face.

It was a look he'd seen many times since.

He'd usually have a glass of wine in the bath, but tonight he had thought better of it. It wasn't that he was on the wagon. He'd clambered aboard that particular vehicle a couple of times and it was a very dull ride. He just didn't think he should have a drink.

Not on a Tuesday night.

It felt, in so many ways, like the beginning of something. Since last night he'd thought about Jan a few times, but not in a maudlin or sentimental way. Being with Anne hadn't made him think about what he was missing. On the contrary, he realised finally that he hadn't been missing it. Missing Jan.

And it might be the beginning of the end of the sweat-stained nightmare that was this case. He thought about Holland and Hendricks out on a limb for him and hoped that what might happen the next day would save them the trouble. It could all be that easy. He wouldn't march back into Keable's office like Charlie Big Potatoes, full of himself, but it would be close.

Thorne got out of the bath, towelled himself off and threw on his dressing-gown. Ignoring the plastic

Thresher's bag in the kitchen, he walked across to the stereo and stuck on *Grievous Angel* by Gram Parsons. Now, there was a man who couldn't say no to a drink.

'*You can, though, Tommy.*'

'*Best not tonight, eh?*'

'*Please, not tonight . . .*'

He lay down on the sofa, thoughts buzzing around in his head like a swarm of fat black flies.

He wanted to ring Anne but thought she'd be in bed by now. His dad would still be up. Or was Anne working late? He couldn't remember. Had James run home and told Daddy all about their little chat? Probably. Had Alison overheard the phone call in her room? Holland's girlfriend didn't like him, that was obvious. How the fuck was he going to organise a box at White Hart Lane?

What would the eldest Calvert girl have been now? Twenty-four? Twenty-five?

The wine would fuzzy up his thinking a little for sure, but it might at least slow things down. He stayed on the sofa and the wine stayed in the bottle. Tomorrow, who could say? There might be cause to celebrate.

Tonight Jeremy Bishop was on call.

There was no way he was going to sleep without calling, so he did. Bishop picked up almost immediately. As the smooth tones gave way quickly to impatience then anger, Thorne flicked the switch that terminated the call, and lay there, relieved, holding the phone. The tension eased in an instant and an overwhelming tide of fatigue began to creep over him. He crossed his arms over the phone on his chest and closed his eyes.

He got into the car and sat for a moment, steadying

himself. He'd had a tough day. Things had come up that needed dealing with and had almost upset his plans for the evening. It was going to be OK, though.

The courtesy light faded away and he began to relax, satisfied that he'd left everything ready at home, should he be lucky enough to bring a guest back. He placed the things he would need on the passenger seat. All could be easily hidden in his pocket when the time came. He was sad that he'd had to dispense with the champagne, but she might have seen that stupid reconstruction. There was no need for it now anyway, but there had been something stylish about it. He'd never skimped: it had always been Taittinger. He'd believed in making their last taste a good one – their last taste in any conventional sense.

The conversations while he'd been waiting for the drug to kick in, though tedious in the main, had at least given him a sense of who he was treating. That was important. The thirty minutes with Alison had made him feel even better about the new life he'd given her. In that half an hour or so of drunken drivel, he'd come to understand the old life he'd be saving her from. From now on it was something of a lottery in that respect.

He smiled. It could be you!

He hoped that the police would be able to see past what were purely practical reasons for this change in his working methods. He didn't want time wasted on irrelevancies. Champagne last time, needle this time, it didn't really matter. Thorne would understand. He might not be involved officially any longer, but that was neither here nor there.

He turned the ignition and switched on his headlights. He felt confident and capable. Once he was back at home and performing the procedure he would not consider the possibility of failure. With the others, it had only been when the light had finally died in their eyes that the word had even entered his head.

He took out his glasses and began to clean the lenses, setting his mind to the immediate task of preparing a new patient. There would need to be some force, unfortunately, as there had been with Thorne, but once he'd found the vein it would be over quickly. Then he just had to keep her quiet for a few minutes and there were ways of doing that. Something sharp would do it nicely. Once the drug began its work she would not be able to cry out anyway, so he shouldn't have too many problems.

The car pulled away and he thought for a while about what he might do when it was all over. There were so many ways that it might end but he wondered how he might look back on what he was doing now. What he'd been forced to do. It would be strange, beginning again, but he would be able to remember certain things with fondness. There would always be Alison and however many other successes time allowed him. He could revel in that. And he would certainly remember and enjoy the symmetry of a punishment justly meted out. Such a fitting punishment. He grinned and began to hum the tune. Someone would certainly wish they'd never dragged him along to Gilbert and Sullivan . . .

He pointed the Volvo towards the West End and leaned back in his seat, feeling as good as he had in a long time.

He'd accomplished so much with skill and rage.

Like I said, some days are a lot better than others . . .

This is the first joke I'm going to tell Anne.

There's this really tasty and sexy young potato and she's walking home from the disco one night, after a top night out with her best friends the parsnip and the runner bean, when she's attacked by this mad carrot. The carrot does all sorts of horrible stuff to her and she winds up in hospital. All her skin's been peeled off and she's been all mashed up and she's just lying there and the only thing that's undamaged are her eyes. The eyes of this potato. So the next day this potato's boyfriend, who's a tall, good-looking swede, comes to the hospital and talks to the doctor and, with tears in his eyes, he says, 'What are her chances, Doc?' The doctor looks down at the poor, sad potato lying in the bed and says to him, 'I'm sorry . . . but she's going to be a vegetable for the rest of her life.'

THIRTEEN

Brigstocke had presumed it was a hangover. 'Sleep it off' was not the traditional response to somebody phoning in sick but Thorne couldn't really argue. Brigstocke had worked with him before and it was a reasonable assumption. It wouldn't be too long before his patience gave out, though, and he went higher up. Thorne knew he didn't have much time. He didn't think he'd need much.

One look at the good weather had made up his mind. He decided to take the Thameslink overground from Kentish Town to Tulse Hill. It was direct, and an attractive alternative to sitting in the car for as long as it might otherwise take him to drive to Birmingham, or getting tense and sweaty on the underground. He'd never seen the attraction of the tube. For Thorne it inevitably meant the Northern line – interestingly the line of choice for most people who chose to jump in front of a tube train. He guessed that they were probably choosing to think of others in their own moment of deepest despair. If you're going to fuck up commuters, then why not fuck up those to whom chaos and delay are barely noticeable any more?

Thorne had decided long ago that, should he ever feel the need, he would be a handful-of-pills-bottle-of-red-wine-lie-on-the-bed-and-drift-away-to-Hank-Williams kind of bloke. Anything else was just showing off.

Though it had to be said, a gun in the mouth looked good on some people.

He looked out of the window as the train rumbled across the Blackfriars rail bridge. If it was a different world south of the river, it was one with its own dividing line. South-west was definitely the more gentrified, Clapham and Richmond and, of course, Battersea. There were *nice* areas of South-east London – he was fond of Greenwich and Blackheath – but, on the whole, that part of the city was as close as London got to a war-zone. South-east . . . *Sarf*-east London didn't need coppers, it needed United Nations peacekeepers. At that very minute in Bermondsey and New Cross there were characters propping up bars in dodgy boozers that would have made Slobodan Milosevic shit himself.

He opened his case and looked at the pictures again. They looked like stills captured in any undercover police operation. A career opportunity for Bethell should he ever decide to hang up his dirty mac for good. Bishop was photogenic, Thorne had known he would be, though when the smile he wore in company was absent, the face was considerably harder, severe even.

Thorne went through the pictures one by one. There was the photo of James walking back towards the house after the confrontation with Bethell. He was glancing back over his shoulder, trying to look tough. He hadn't managed it. Thorne wondered if he had a girlfriend. Probably some horsy type called Charlotte, who called herself Charlie, wore black and hung about in Camden Lock on a Sunday afternoon popping pills. He was looking for the best photo – the one in which Bishop was looking virtually straight at the camera. Perhaps he'd heard Bethell moving about or caught a glimpse of bleached hair bobbing about in the bushes. The photo wasn't there and Thorne realised where he'd left it. The phone call he'd taken in Alison's room had thrown him so completely that he'd all but forgotten why he was there in the first place. Maybe a nurse had found it and thrown it away. Unlikely. Anne had almost certainly come across it by now, which meant that he'd have some explaining to do. By then, of course, it would all have been worth it and she'd realise he'd been right. Who was he kidding? Right or wrong, the deceit involved would probably ensure that what had happened between them two nights earlier would turn out to have been a one-night stand.

The old man next to him had been pretending to be reading his newspaper but had been sneaking furtive looks at the photos on Thorne's lap at every opportunity. Maybe he thought Thorne was some kind of spy or sleazy *paparazzo*. Maybe he thought Thorne had killed his Princess. Either way he was becoming annoying. Thorne turned one of the photos round and held it up so that the old man could have a good look. He quickly glanced back down at his newspaper. Thorne leaned over and whispered conspiratorially, 'It's all right, he's a doctor.'

The old man didn't look up from his paper for the rest of the journey.

Margaret Byrne's house was a five-minute walk from the station. He didn't know the area well but it seemed amazingly calm and suburban, considering that Brixton was two minutes away. Thorne had been on the streets there in 1981. He had never felt so hated. He and many fellow officers had comforted themselves with the thought that it was no more than police bashing. An excuse to torch some flash cars and nick a few TVs. Events since then had made him realise he'd been wrong. And Stephen Lawrence had changed everything.

Thorne rang the doorbell and waited. The curtains in the front bay windows were drawn. The bedroom, he guessed. He looked at his watch; he was ten minutes or so late. He rang the doorbell again. He looked around in the hope of seeing a woman hurrying up the road, having popped out to grab a pint of milk, but saw only a woman in the house opposite, eyeing him suspiciously. He eyed her back.

Thorne pressed himself against the window and peered through a small crack in the green curtains but the room was dark. He turned to see the woman across the road still staring at him. He began to feel uneasy.

'*Calm down, Tommy. She's probably just nodded off or something.*'

'*Oh, Jesus, not now.*'

There was a small passage on the right-hand side of the house all but blocked by a couple of black plastic dustbins. Thorne climbed over them and walked slowly down the passageway. The high gate at the end was locked. He dropped his case over the gate and trudged back to grab one of the bins, having decided that the Neighbourhood Watch co-ordinator over the road would probably have called the police by now anyway.

He tried to lower himself down as far as possible on the other side of the fence but the drop to the patio on the other side still made his teeth rattle. The small garden was neat and tidy. There were blouses and slacks hanging on a washing-line.

The back door had been forced open.

He knew he should unlock the gate and get back to the front of the house.

He knew he should phone for back-up.

He knew the phone was staying in his pocket.

The rush was instant, and breathtaking. There was fear too, pumping round his body, tightening his fists and loosening his bowels. This was the fight-flight reflex at its most basic.

Fight or flight. It was never going to be any contest.

Thorne felt his skin slipping off and falling to the ground like an old overcoat. He felt his nerve-endings vibrate, raw and bloody, his senses painfully heightened. The wind in the trees was a cacophony. A face in a faraway window, an oncoming juggernaut. He could taste the air. Tinfoil on a filling.

There was no theatrical creak as he pushed open the door and tensed every muscle. He stepped into a small kitchen. The surfaces were spotless, a tea-towel folded over a chair, washing-up stacked neatly on the draining-board. Thorne fought the impulse to reach for the breadknife and stood still, trying to control his breathing. To his left was an open door that he could see led on to the living room. He moved soundlessly across the linoleum and scanned the room. It was empty. The brown carpet looked new but was presumably the first stage of improvements – the suite was saggy and threadbare. Thorne hurried across the room, took a deep breath and opened the door at the far end.

He was in a dimly lit hall just inside the front door. There were two more rooms opposite him. The one on the right nearest the front door had to be the bedroom; the other, he guessed, a toilet.

It was worth a try. 'Mrs Byrne?'

Nothing.

From behind the second door he heard a small, muffled thud. The thumping in his chest was anything but.

'*It always comes down to the final door, Tommy.*'

'*Open it . . .*'

'*She'll come walking through the front door in a minute and you'll feel like a right tit . . .*'

Thorne opened the door.

He cried out, staggering backwards in sudden shock as something flew, hissing, out of the room and into his legs. He pushed himself off the wall and watched, his heart smashing against his chest as a cat careered into the living room. He heard the bang as it clattered through the cat-flap in the kitchen door.

Then he could smell it.

Cat shit and something else. Something more familiar and far more disgusting. Tangy and metallic, and so strong he could have licked it out of the air. His tongue on a dying battery.

Resigned to the harder stuff . . .

Resigned to the inevitability of what he was going to see, Thorne stepped forward into the darkened room and reached for the light switch.

There were four more cats. One stared down at him from the top of the wardrobe while a second hopped lazily from a highly polished dressing-table. Two more were on the bed. Curled up across the body of Margaret Byrne.

She lay straight, down the edge of the left-hand side of the bed, her hands by her side, her head back and turned towards him. One eye was half open but not as wide as the scarlet smile across her neck, the incision made gaping by the angle of her head on the pillow.

'*Sweet Christ . . .*'

The blood was pooled beneath her collar-bone and had overflowed across her left side and on to the duvet, from where it still dripped slowly on to the patterned blue carpet. One side of her pink blouse was sopping red. A foot or so from where Thorne was standing, frozen to the spot, there was another bloodstain, already sunk in and brown. Spatter patterns snaked away across the carpet, reaching as far as the wall on the opposite side of the bed. He could see straight away that this was where she'd been attacked, before being laid out on the bed to die, he guessed, a short time later. While her killer watched.

Something glinting on the carpet near the end of the bed caught his eye. An earring, perhaps. He could see a necklace too, and rings, and a wooden jewellery box on its side by the wall.

Margaret Byrne had tried to save the few things she had which were precious. But the man she had tried to save them from had not come to rob her.

Once again the nagging voice of procedure. He was contaminating a crime scene. He needed to get out.

He regretted not asking Holland about her when he'd had the chance. Now he had to stand in a carpeted and perfumed slaughterhouse and piece it together. It wasn't hard to get a feeling for her. Of her. The cats and the neatly arranged bottles and jars on the dressing-table told him enough. He felt behind him for the solidity of the wall, leaned back against it and lowered himself slowly to the floor. The cat that had been sniffing around, a small black-and-white one, ambled over and nuzzled his shins. Thorne reached into his pocket for his phone and held it, dangling between his knees.

He wanted to stay with Margaret for a while before he made the call.

When the cars arrived Thorne was sitting on the doorstep, staring at the woman in the window opposite. The cat, who would not leave him alone, was making itself comfortable on his lap. Holland walked up and hovered. After a few moments Thorne looked up with a twisted smile. He had expected Tughan and was relieved not to see him. He couldn't see anybody he thought might be Brewer either.

'Been promoted, Holland?'

Holland said nothing. Remembering his conversation with Maggie Byrne on the same spot the day before, he was a word, a heartbeat from tears. Thorne watched the SOCOs steaming up the passageway with their equipment. He had felt the same way as Holland fifteen minutes earlier but now a strange calm had begun to settle over him.

'He executed her, Dave. He broke into her house and executed her.'

Holland looked straight back at him and spoke evenly, his face showing nothing.

'He's been busy.'

PART THREE

THE WORD

I'm going to chuck Tim today. Does that sound a bit sudden? Sorry, I know it's out of the blue and maybe I should have built up to it a bit more, but I've been thinking about it for a good while.

Thinking about it.

Like I can do anything else. I'm hardly in a position to discuss boyfriend problems with my best mate, even if I was sure I still had one. Well, I could, but it would be the dullest girly gossip in history. Barley water and blackboards are no substitute for booze and fags and a home-delivery pizza.

And staring isn't laughing, is it?

But I have been thinking a lot about Tim and how unhappy he is. It's a real old line, I know, but it's for his sake rather than mine. Chucking him, I mean. I won't be trotting out shite like 'I love you but I'm not in *love with you,' or 'I think we should just be friends.' To be honest, I'm not exactly sure what I will say. I say 'say'. Obviously I mean 'blink' and 'twitch' while the poor sod tries to keep the smile plastered to his face as he does his best to work out what the fuck I'm on about.*

It's not as if I've got anything to go on, nothing I've ever seen in a film or on telly. Tearful farewells to terminally ill loved ones are ten a penny but this is pretty sodding unique. Never seen this on EastEnders *or* Brookside. *It's probably only a matter of time, of course. They'll drag it out over a couple of months. Milk it a bit. Probably be the big Christmas cliffhanger with the tragic, yet still very sexy young woman in the hospital bed blinking like buggery while her hunky boyfriend kneels by the side of the bed, sobbing his heart out and telling her that he still loves her no matter what.*

Yeah, right . . .

So I don't really know how I'm going to do it, but it's got to be done. I've only ever dumped one person. I was seventeen and he copped off with one of my mates at a party. Had his hand up her bra while I was in the queue for the toilet. Even so, the actual chucking was pretty tricky, and bear in mind, that was when I was vertical with a working gob.

The way I am now, it's shaping up to be a nightmare.

I know that in letting Tim off this very nasty hook, I'm probably coming across like some selfless, saintly figure, but the sad truth is that actually I'm just being a right selfish cow.

Because the fact is that he *won't do it.*

And I can't stand to see the pain in his eyes any more when he looks at me.

He doesn't know what to do, bless him. He talks, slowly. He talks and he uses the pointer like Anne showed him but I know he can't bear it. He's always been a bit of a girl about hospitals and blood and anything like that.

He said that he wished it had happened to him instead of me, and I know he means it. Before it sounds like this is me setting him free, or some cobblers like that, so he can go off and find someone else, I should say that if I ever get out of here and get myself sorted out, he'd better come running straight back, and I won't want to hear about what he's been up to and who with.

The truth is simple. He can't stand to see me hurt, and I feel the same way about him. And he looks utterly crushed all the time he's with me and it's my fault. I'm five feet fuck-all and I can't move a muscle and I'm squashing all the life out of him. So best to knock it on the head for now. Not the best choice of words probably but that's not something I get a lot of say in these days.

He's not going to like it. He'll cry most probably, big soft thing, or shout. Actually that would be good, there's nothing like a bit of a scene to get the nurses going, but I think that when he goes home and thinks about it he'll be relieved. For Christ's sake, our dream ticket, our magic-island scenario, the best we can fucking hope for, involves wheelchairs and computers and one of us winning the lottery to pay for it all, and me about as much use as one of my two-year-olds and I wouldn't wish that on anybody.

Tim cares about me, I know he does. But I couldn't bear to be pitied. Loved is fine. But not pitied.

And 'cares for' is not 'cares about', is it?

So Tim, think yourself lucky, pet, and I apologise in advance if, at the crucial moment in your posh wedding to some drop-dead gorgeous blonde, when the vicar says that bit about 'just cause or impediment', the door to the church crashes open and some spackhead in a wheelchair trundles in. Just ignore me and get on with it. I'll probably be pissed . . .

Fuck me, did you hear what I said before?

'If I ever get out of here.'

If . . .

FOURTEEN

The cat had sat and watched, content, unblinking, as a woman who loved her had been smashed across the back of the head and bled dry like a pig. Now she sat staring down at the face of a man who didn't understand any more than she had. Rising and falling with him as he breathed. Rising and falling and watching his eyes. They were closed but she followed the movements of his eyeballs, darting back and forth behind the eyelids like tiny trapped animals. Looking for a way out. Searching for a weak spot. Heads bulging behind the eyes, threatening to burst through the paper-thin skin . . .

. . . and Maggie Byrne smiled and lay back on the bed. She kicked off her shoes and rubbed her feet together. He could hear the nylon of her tights crackling. He said something – a joke maybe. She threw back her head to laugh and the red line beneath her chin started to gape. She blushed and reached for a scarf and he told her that it didn't matter but she was already starting to cry. She shook her head and sobbed and tried to tie the scarf around her neck. The gash gaped wider until it looked like something on a fishmonger's slab. The not-so-slender neck, hacked into sections like tuna. Pink then a darker pink then red.

And his words would not comfort her. And he tried to

take her in his arms but they slipped from around her neck. And his hands were stroking her collarbone and his fingers were exploring the damp and clammy interior of the wound.

Testing for freshness.

Maggie Byrne tried to scream but it came whistling from her neck.

He opened his eyes . . .

He hadn't been asleep and it wasn't a dream. Just a mental snapshot, twisted. A memory adjusted and warped by the unwelcome addition of an imagination. Something that lived in the ghoulish and morbid corner of his subconscious having its bit of fun.

He opened his eyes . . .

And waited for the images to blur and become distant. Lying on the sofa, hearing his heartbeat slow down. Feeling the beads of sweat on his face evaporate. Letting something creep back into its corner.

Until the next time.

He opened his eyes and stared back at the cat sitting on his chest.

'Fuck off, Elvis!'

The cat jumped off Thorne and slunk away towards the bedroom. Maggie had been a big Elvis fan and had named the cat before it had been sexed. She'd always thought it was funny. Sally Byrne had taken a couple of her mother's cats back to Edinburgh with her, and the rest had gone to the PDSA, but Elvis had been Thorne's from the moment he'd opened the door to Maggie's bedroom and breathed in the blood. The cat seemed drawn to him, Sally had said. To need him, almost.

Almost as much as he needed her.

Just over two weeks now since he'd opened that bedroom door. Just over twenty-four hours since Margaret Byrne's funeral. Thorne didn't know about the arrangements for Leonie Holden. He was what he'd once heard Nick Tughan describe as 'out of the loop' on that one. Her funeral might well already have happened. They'd found her a few hours before he'd found Maggie Byrne, and if Phil Hendricks had got the bits of her he needed, safely labelled in jars, then the body would have been released back to those for whom it still meant something real. Something in their hearts and in their guts. Then they could say goodbye.

There would have been an official presence at her funeral, of course. It was often just some flowers but he could picture Tughan at the back of a church, in black like an assassin. He wondered if Frank Keable would have put in an appearance. Or somebody higher up. If the body count carried on rising they'd end up having to send the commissioner along. A thin smile and a wreath of white lilies spelling out 'Sorry, doing our best'.

Thorne had never made a habit of attending the funerals of his victims . . . the victims of his cases – *on* his cases. He'd go on the occasions when they thought there was a fair chance of the killer turning up. He'd stand at the back then, scanning the mourners, looking for one who didn't belong. There was no chance of the killer attending the funerals of these victims, though. He wanted to forget the dead ones. They were his failures.

It suddenly struck Thorne like a hammer to the chest that he had no idea when Helen Doyle had been buried. Buried, of course, not cremated. Leaving it open for a second post-mortem, should one be needed, or demanded much later by the accused.

Even dead, her body was not her own.

Thorne swung his feet to the floor, sat up and rubbed his eyes. The sweat was making them sting. He was starving. There was a headache starting . . .

It was time to stop hiding.

He'd emerged briefly to pay the respects he felt were due to Margaret Byrne, that he guessed she'd never received when she was alive. He'd hugged the daughter of a woman he'd known only in death. He'd held her close as she wept. He'd laughed as she talked about cats and waved as she climbed into the funeral car.

He'd looked across the all-but-empty church at Dave Holland, who sat stony-faced and stiff, like a sixth-former in an uncomfortable collar. They'd nodded to each other and looked away quickly. It was probably best to keep a little distance with so much accusation still flying around. So much blame to be doled out.

Thorne had given himself a fair bit of explaining to do and hadn't made a particularly good job of it. They knew it was Holland who'd told him about Margaret Byrne and given him her address. They couldn't prove it, but they knew. It didn't change anything. It didn't explain to anybody how the killer had found out. Or how the killer had known that Thorne was close to a positive identification. Or how the killer had been able to pop round to snuff out the threat before calmly going about the business of slaughtering Leonie Holden.

Nothing was easily explained, but what was obvious to everyone was that Thorne had no business being anywhere near Margaret Byrne. He looked unreliable.

He felt responsible.

Margaret Byrne had died because of what she knew

and what she could tell him. That was obvious. She'd died because Thorne knew who the killer was and because she could identify him and because somewhere, in an inept operation that he'd once been a part of, there was a leak big enough to sink a battleship.

Thorne had an idea or two about *who*, but was at a loss to explain *how* or *why*. The press getting hold of stuff, which now they had, was never a mystery. The solution was always there, lurking inside the bank balance of a constable with a gambling problem or some sergeant with too much alimony to pay. But this was something else entirely. This leak had led a killer back to Margaret Byrne's door with an iron bar and a scalpel. This was something infinitely more sinister and something to be guarded much more fiercely.

Ranks were swiftly closed. Eyes turned outwards, fingers pointing. And now, for Thorne, everything was in the balance. Keable had just told him to sit and wait. Thorne had little argument. He was in trouble and decisions needed to be made at a higher level. It sounded good, it sounded like a plan of action, but Thorne knew that really Keable just had no idea what to do with him.

And Thorne was already sick of sitting and waiting.

The nagging headache was starting to scream. He stood and walked towards the bathroom in search of aspirin, but his eye was taken by the small red light winking at him from the table near the front door. Messages on his answering-machine.

'*It's only Dad. Call me when you get a minute . . .*'

'*Tom . . . it's Anne. I'll call back.*'

Then a voice he didn't recognise. A woman's voice. Quiet. Reluctant. A catch in the throat . . .

'*Hello, we've never met. My name's Leonie Holden and I*

was murdered a week or so ago. I would have been twenty-four next week and now I'm alone and I'm cold and frankly I don't give a fuck about who told who what, or your career, or matching carpet fibres and I'd be grateful if you could try and sort all this out, you know . . .'

He opened his eyes.

A cold shower. And hot coffee. And real messages on a real answering-machine.

Time to stop hiding.

Voices, all of them anxious. His father, twice. Anne, twice. Phil Hendricks, needing to talk. Keable, still trying to save his career, or something. Sally Byrne to check on the cat. Dave Holland . . .

And Thorne needed to get out of his flat and talk to all of them, but in the spaces between the messages was a silence that spoke in a voice more insistent than any other. Murmuring the words that had exploded in his head a week or so before and now buzzed around his brain night and day, like aftershocks. He still heard them as they had been spoken to him, announced to him, with undisguised triumph, in Tughan's cold and oddly characterless accent. Words that still numbed him and would force their way, unspoken or otherwise, into any conversation with Anne Coburn or Phil Hendricks or Frank Keable or Dave Holland or anybody else for that matter.

Jeremy Bishop has a cast-iron alibi.

Jeremy Bishop could not possibly have killed Margaret Byrne.

Lunchtime. A sandwich and an energy drink from a nice deli and a stroll around the choking streets of Bloomsbury to stare at the dying.

He could still feel the shockwave up his arm as Margaret Byrne's skull had cracked. He'd felt it shatter like mint cracknel beneath the blow from the bar. That had shut her up. Silly mare had been squealing and running from room to room from the moment he'd kicked open the flimsy back door. It had only been a few seconds but still he wondered, as he followed her into the bedroom and moved towards her from behind, if the neighbours would be able to hear. As he locked his left arm beneath her chin to keep her upright, and his right hand reached into his pocket for the scalpel, he decided it would be all right. Probably just the TV up too loud. Nothing to get excited about.

He might have been seen too. There had been a noticeable bit of curtain-twitching as he'd walked past the house earlier, but it was all a bonus in the long run, despite the confusion it was bound to cause in some quarters. The jewellery on the floor would probably have troubled them a little as well. They could hardly have thought it was a bungled burglary, but perhaps there'd been a struggle? Perhaps the poor thing had thought he was going to rob her. It didn't really matter.

Whatever they were thinking was wrong.

He could still feel the rush as the blade moved across her windpipe. As the blood spurted and sprayed, soundlessly, on to the thick, ugly carpet, he'd jammed a knee into the small of her back and begun hoicking her towards the bed, wishing he'd had the time to do it all properly.

He could still hear the purring of the cats, the only noise that disturbed the silence as he stood watching the life run out of her. Given the time, he'd have liked to make it look like suicide. That way there would have been no confusion. No problems with the timing of events.

She'd needed dealing with quickly, however, and he'd done what was necessary. He now realised that the rushing, and the way his timetable had become compromised, had probably been responsible for the failure with the girl on the bus.

Leonie, the newspaper said her name was. They hadn't had time, of course, to get to know each other properly.

It hadn't helped, that much was certain. He had not been calm enough during the procedure. The excitement of the earlier events had made him clumsy and thrown his timing.

He'd have done it carefully, of course, the suicide. The layman's way. The slash horizontal across the wrist, as opposed to the vertical cut, wrist to elbow along the radial artery, which is far more efficient but hugely suspicious. Mind you, they might not even have spotted that. Everything else was taking them an age.

But then there was Tom Thorne to consider. There was always him. He hadn't known exactly when Thorne was planning to visit Margaret Byrne, but he doubted she had many visitors, so there was a pretty good chance he'd get lucky. When the papers confirmed the name of the officer who'd discovered the body of 'Mrs Byrne – 43' he'd whooped with joy. The one good thing that had come out of all this was Thorne's . . . marginalisation. Looked at that way, he supposed that the timing could not have been any better. Now Thorne was more isolated than ever.

An isolated Tom Thorne, he guessed, was a very dangerous one.

And that was just how he wanted him.

It was a twenty-minute stroll to Waterlow Park. Thorne had toyed with the idea of meeting at Highgate cemetery, but that was his and Jan's place. Or had been. It was a nice spot in which to waste a Sunday morning. She, desperate to feel like the heroine in some arty black-and-white film, and he, happy to kill an hour or two before a boozy lunch in the Old Crown or the Flask. Both content to spend time doing very little, and laugh every single time at the grave of the unknown Mr Spencer that sat opposite that of the far more famous Marx.

Adjoining the cemetery at its north end was Waterlow Park, a small but much loved green space, which those who frequented it never tired of describing as a 'hidden treasure'. The clientele here was odd to say the least: a mixture of the chattering classes, drugged-up layabouts and community-care cases with a smattering of hugely pregnant women sent here from the Whittington hospital to walk about in the hope of bringing on labour.

Thorne was fond of it, not least because of Lauderdale House, the sixteenth-century stately home at its entrance. Now it housed kids' puppet shows, antiques fairs and exhibitions of hideous modern art. It had a decent restaurant and a nice, if overpriced, coffee bar. But four hundred years earlier Nell Gwynne had stayed there as mistress to Charles II. A snotty woman had once told Thorne that Lauderdale House was where Ms Gwynne had 'received her King'. He told her that it was as good a euphemism as he'd ever heard, but the snotty woman had failed to see the funny side. Thorne decided she could have done with receiving a bit of King herself.

Now the place could always raise his spirits. This lovely listed building had basically been a top-of-the-range knocking shop. For this reason alone, the park had become a favourite place for sitting and thinking, with soundtrack courtesy of Gram or Hank on a CD Walkman, an unexpected gift from Jan for his fortieth birthday.

He walked along the huge curving path that ran towards a pair of ropey tennis courts. Every hundred yards or so he came across a figure made of grass, or carved from a dead tree. Organic sculptures. It was probably some Millennium project. What a waste of time and money that had been. He'd spent 31 December 1999 with Phil Hendricks, a chicken vindaloo and an obscene amount of lager. They were both asleep before midnight.

It was as good a place as any for a meeting. Thorne took off his leather jacket and sat on a bench, bolted on to the concrete pathway. He stared across the park at the huge green dome of St Joseph's. The weather was warm, considering that October was just round the corner.

A couple walked towards him hand in hand. They were young, in their early thirties, loose-limbed and straight-backed. He wore baggy-fitting beige trousers and a white sweater. She wore tight white jeans and a cream fleecy top. They walked easily together in step, smiling at something said earlier.

As the pair came nearer to him, brash and bullet-proof, Thorne felt envy burn through his body like caustic soda dissolving the fat in a drain. They were somehow so light and so immaculate, the two of them. An advertiser's dream couple, walking off the coffee and croissants enjoyed in some beautifully converted warehouse. Thorne knew that they had good jobs and cooked exotic meals for perfect friends and had great sex. They enjoyed everything and doubted nothing.

They were undamaged.

He thought of himself and Anne, and wondered if the two of them were not just being utterly stupid.

Why was he finding it so hard to call her?

He'd left a message the day after he'd found Maggie Byrne's body, saying that something had come up, but since then he'd ignored her calls. It wasn't just about the connection with Bishop. It was about keeping something of himself back – that shadowy and indefinable part of himself that he'd need if he was going to get through this in one piece and stop the killing. He was willing to risk everything for that, and he knew that if things with Anne Coburn got any more serious, pieces might start to come away. It was armour and it was also camouflage, and he knew that the smallest crack might render it useless. Given time it would probably renew itself. It would harden eventually, but this was still not a good time to be . . . vulnerable.

Yet still he wanted her close. He wanted her closeness. He watched the young couple strolling away from him towards the pagoda, much favoured by those keen on exchanging bodily fluids in the open air. He decided that he was being an idiot. He'd call Anne as soon as he got back to the flat. What the hell was he thinking of, anyway? He was just a copper, at least in theory.

Cracks in armour? Jesus . . .

He imagined himself briefly as a boxer, unable to fuck before a big fight. It was a ludicrous analogy, but the pictures in his head amused him so much that he was still smiling five minutes later when his date arrived.

There were times when it seemed that a woman deprived of the power of speech was the only person Anne Coburn could really talk to.

Sitting alone in the hospital canteen and pushing a tasteless bit of salad around a paper plate, she contemplated her failings as a professional. The sessions with Alison were going well, but Anne knew that if she wasn't careful there was a danger that they would become fully fledged therapy sessions.

And not for Alison.

Alison was having problems with her boyfriend and things were coming to a head, yet Anne had spent the large part of their last session together bitching about her own problems.

Problems with her daughter. And her ex-husband. And her lover.

Things with Rachel were not getting any better. At least they were talking but they weren't saying anything. There was an element of walking on eggshells on both their parts, the two of them well aware that the smallest comment could blow up into a major row. It was the work she wasn't doing for the resits and the early nights she wasn't getting and the truth she almost certainly wasn't telling.

It was, Anne had begun to suspect – no, to be *certain* – the boy she was seeing.

Anne had brought it up once, casually, but Rachel's reaction, tight-mouthed and defiant, had left her in no doubt that the subject was off limits. It was so stupid. Anne would have no problems with a boyfriend. Why should she? There had been boyfriends before. It was just the timing that was so bloody silly. Important exams were only weeks away and Rachel was in danger of making a mess of everything and Anne couldn't do a thing about it.

Rachel was stubborn, like her father, and now he wasn't speaking to Anne either. Relations between her and David had been distinctly frosty, bordering on downright venomous, for a while, but since she'd told him about Thorne, things had worsened rapidly. He'd seemingly broken off communication altogether, and at a time when a united front, as far as Rachel was concerned, would have been a nice idea.

What was so strange was that he'd seemed to know about the relationship with Thorne even before it happened. She thought back to the confrontation in the lift. He had been making comments about it even then. That was why she'd told him. She wasn't trying to score points – well, maybe just one or two – but his suspicion was already providing him with ample bile to spit in her direction, so why not simply congratulate him on his prescience? But since she'd confirmed her involvement . . . *was it an involvement?* . . . with Thorne, he'd turned really nasty.

Steve Clark walked past and smiled, and she smiled back and wondered if part of this business with Rachel might not have something to do with Thorne as well. Was Rachel jealous? Anne had made an effort to talk to her about Thorne. Since the big flare-up a few weeks earlier she'd tried to be more open. She'd told Rachel about the case and about her connection with it. She'd left out some of the more grisly details and skirted around Jeremy's . . . involvement, as much for her own peace of mind as anything. She'd kept her up-to-date with Alison's progress and, in general, had made a real effort to build bridges. But perhaps she hadn't explained to Rachel how she felt about Thorne.

Anne pushed away the plate of untouched salad and decided that it was because she hadn't actually worked it out herself.

She stood up and moved quickly to the rear of the canteen and out through the swing doors to the fire escape, where she lit a cigarette and took in the view of large steel bins and heaps of polystyrene packaging.

Thorne . . .

He seemed fairly central to all her problematic relationships. Not least the one with Jeremy Bishop.

She'd barely spoken to Jeremy since the night she and Thorne had ended up in bed. This . . . cooling off had been her decision, but she sensed that he was keeping his distance as well. She couldn't deny the possibility that Jeremy was jealous, and that an element of that jealousy might be sexual, but she also suspected that he was becoming involved with somebody himself. He'd made one or two typically oblique comments in the days before they'd stopped seeing each other. He'd seemed distracted and by something other than work. She hoped that it was a woman. She wished Jeremy happy as much as she wished anything.

She missed him.

But she wouldn't pick up the phone. She'd known this man for more than twenty-five years and despite the stupidity of Thorne's suspicions, to do so would have felt vaguely disloyal to the man she'd known for five minutes.

She resented having her loyalty tested. To anybody and by anybody. And why the hell wasn't Thorne calling anyway?

He'd rung to tell her there had been some sort of serious development on the case. Serious, to her, had sounded like another word for 'death', and two days later she'd read all about it. Then the other stuff. No mention of Alison, thank heavens, but plenty of gory grist to the media mill. The press blackout that Thorne had seemed so anxious about early on was well and truly ended. Outraged leader columns and pictures of five dead women.

She'd stopped looking at the newspapers now. She was living with enough sickness already.

Anne didn't want any involvement in this hideous case bar the one she had already through Alison. She didn't want to know anything else.

Until they caught him.

Thorne and Holland had walked down to the pond next to the park's southernmost exit. They leaned against the railings and talked, occasionally needing to raise their voices above the shouts from the children's playground only a few feet away. A father smoked and read a paper, while two children tried unsuccessfully to clamber up a slide and a third stood on a swing, demanding to be looked at.

While Holland stared out across the water, Thorne watched a large brown rat scuttling about in the dust beneath the low hedge that skirted the pond. There were always a few here, on the lookout for badly thrown bits of bread and Thorne was always excited to spot one. It wasn't a beautiful creature, but while Holland's eye was taken by the variety of ducks and geese on display, Thorne's was naturally drawn to the rat. The scavenger, the chancer, the survivor. The villain.

This city could have no more perfect symbol.

'I hadn't got you pegged for a messenger boy, Holland.'

Holland could feel the redness rising up his neck as he turned to look at him. 'That's because I'm not, sir.'

Thorne instantly regretted his tone. It had been an attempt at dark humour but had just sounded sarcastic.

Holland was already past it. 'DCI Keable thought that we might run into each other, that's all. He *had* tried to phone you himself . . .'

Thorne nodded. Lots of people had tried to phone him.

Letting Holland convey this somewhat bizarre offer was a shrewd move. Frank Keable was not the most inspired or inspiring of officers, but he knew what was going on around him. He could read the troops. He always got a sense of the currents within an operation, which went way beyond who had the hump or who might fancy who.

The rat was standing on its hind legs now, sniffing at a litter-bin attached to the railings. Thorne looked across at Holland. 'So, what do you think?'

Holland smiled, part of him flattered at being asked but the greater part well aware that his opinion would probably be worth less than nothing. 'I think it's a good offer, as a matter of fact. Sounds to me like you'll be pretty much a free agent and as long as you don't get into too much trouble . . .'

'Or mention Jeremy Bishop?'

Holland saw no point in sugaring the pill. 'It could be a lot worse.'

Thorne knew that he was right. Keable had hinted at disciplinary action after the discovery of Margaret Byrne's body, but with that and the Leonie Holden killing, castigating a rogue detective inspector with an over-active imagination had become something of a low priority. That's what Keable had said anyway. Either that or he'd had his own reasons for not wanting to make it official just yet and was giving himself time to think of exactly what best to do with Thorne. Either way, at the end of it all there was probably no more than a wrist-slapping in it.

Holland hadn't told him everything.

'They know about the fibres from Bishop's car boot.'

'Fuck.' Thorne kicked at the ground, the dust and grit sending the rat darting momentarily for cover. Somebody in Forensics with a very big mouth. That would explain the call from Hendricks. He needed to talk to him.

'So I'm in a bit of bother, which, if I accept this offer to become some sort of consultant or whatever bollocks title Frank Keable's come up with, might go away. Is that it?'

'He didn't exactly say that, sir.'

Consultant. He wondered what the catches were. Beyond the obvious one.

Leonie Holden was last seen on a night bus bound for Ealing and her body was discovered four hours later on wasteground in Tufnell Park.

Less than a quarter of a mile from Thorne's flat.

The significance of this latest message from the killer to his favourite detective inspector was not lost on anybody.

Consultant? A better word might have been 'bait'.

'What do you think about Jeremy Bishop?'

Holland phrased his answer carefully. 'I don't think he killed Margaret Byrne, sir.'

'He was supposed to have had a cast-iron alibi for Alison Willetts as well, and we found holes in it.'

'I still don't understand any of it, though. I still can't figure out how he could have done what he did to Alison and got her to the hospital in the time. Not to mention why. Why did he go to all that trouble just to give himself an alibi that didn't hold water?'

'I'll work it out, Holland. And I'll work out how he killed Margaret Byrne as well.'

'He didn't, sir.'

'A man fitting his description was seen acting suspiciously outside her flat earlier in the day.'

'Coincidence. Got to be. Besides, that woman opposite is a nutter. She thought *I* was suspicious.' Holland spoke calmly, no element of letting Thorne down gently, just stating the facts. 'I've been to the Royal London and spoken to everybody except the patients in deep comas. She was killed sometime mid- to late-afternoon, and Bishop was at the hospital, working through a routine theatre list. There's dozens of witnesses. Whitechapel to Tulse Hill and back without being missed is impossible.'

Thorne was grateful to Holland for having made the effort. He'd almost certainly done it in his own time, and in the knowledge that if Tughan had found out he'd have been in deep shit.

'No alibi for Leonie Holden.' Thorne was thinking aloud now.

'Sir . . .'

No alibi for Leonie Holden. Because he killed her. The fucker killed her and dumped her on my doorstep.

'So you think I'm barking up the wrong tree as well, then, Holland? Or maybe that should just be barking?'

Holland sighed. The questions just kept getting harder. 'I *had* been sort of coming round to the idea of Bishop as a prime suspect, sir. There's certainly nobody else in the frame, and even though it's all circumstantial I was willing to . . . go with it as an avenue of inquiry. But Maggie Byrne – her and Leonie Holden had to have been killed by the same man.'

They stood in silence. Thorne had nothing to say. Holland had plenty, but thought most was better kept to himself. Behind them, a child tumbled from the roundabout and began to scream.

Holland cleared his throat. 'All the same, as a theory it does have one thing going for it, sir.'

'Yeah?' mumbled Thorne. 'What's that?'

'It's yours.'

Thorne couldn't look at him. He clenched his jaw. He was scared for a second or two that if he looked at Holland his face would show far too much gratitude. It would be shining and desperate and pathetic.

The face that showed too much of everything.

He turned and began to walk towards the gate. His sudden movement caused the rat to bolt again with a small squeal of alarm. The cheeky little bastard had been sitting on its haunches and cleaning its whiskers. They were so unafraid. Thorne had stood there before now and watched one scamper across his shoes.

He glanced over his shoulder. Holland was half a dozen paces behind him.

Whatever journey was ahead, Thorne had no intention of slowing down but sensed that Holland might be the sort of man, the sort of copper, who would close the gap and walk alongside him.

And perhaps, together, they would bring down Jeremy Bishop.

They reckoned that, in London, you were never more than six feet away from a rat. Thorne knew that you weren't a whole lot further from an altogether nastier breed of vermin.

More diseased. More human.

There is definitely no God. Or if there is, he, she or it is a right sick bastard. Like this isn't bad enough!

The way Anne explained it to me is like this.

They have to keep pulling me about every ten bloody minutes so I don't get pressure sores, even on my lovely vibrating bed. So one of the nurses, don't know which one but my money's on Martina as revenge for the neck-coughing incident, accidentally dislodges the nasogastric feed, that's 'tube up nose' to you and me, as she's moving me. Just an inch or two, but that's all it takes. What happens then is that the feed, which is this tasteless white shite that's supposedly full of proteins and other great stuff, instead of going where it's supposed to go, pours into my chest. Loads of it. Now, you and other people who can cough and splutter, just cough and splutter this crap back up and pull a face, and a few days later you might develop a mild chest infection.

Not me, though. Oh, no.

This feed is like nectar to fucking bacteria. They love it. They swarm all over it and, hey presto, I get bastard pneumonia. This sort of thing was bound to happen sooner or later. I'm prone to infection apparently. Well, isn't that just marvellous?

So, here I am back on the ventilator. Big mechanical bellows doing my breathing and I feel like I did when I'd just come in here.

Everything else stops now until I recover. Occupational therapy gets put on hold. The communication was going pretty well, it has to be said. We'd worked out a pretty good system using an alphabet that's based on how many times a certain letter is likely to be used. So it doesn't go A, B, C, D, E. It's not an A–Z so much as an E–X. We've also got shortcuts for going back, for skipping forward, to repeat words, and Anne has become the human equivalent of that thing on my mobile phone that guesses what I'm going to say. She finishes words for me and most of the time she's spot on. She's just about got used to my swearing as well.

Now all that's got to stop until I'm a bit stronger. Until I'm better.

Yeah, well, when you're like this, better is a relative term.

The blackboard's gone from the end of the bed. I am so fucking frustrated.

To be honest, I say the communication was going well and it was *compared to a few weeks ago but it didn't make things any easier with Tim. All the things I'd planned to say went out of the window once we got down to it.*

He just stood there with the pointer in his hand, looking lost.

Even if you can spell the most complicated words in the world as fast as anything, they're just words, aren't they? You can't spell out feelings with an eyelid and a pointer. I couldn't really make him understand.

In the end all I could do was spell out the one word and say it over and over again.

G.O.O.D.B.Y.E.

Goodbye, goodbye, goodbye . . .

FIFTEEN

'I shall be glad to have you around, Tom, but having said that . . .'

Keable was behind his desk making a speech. Tughan leaned against the wall, greasy-haired and gimlet-eyed. Ostensibly Keable was welcoming Thorne back to Operation Backhand, albeit in an unorthodox and somewhat undefined role, but in reality he was laying down ground rules. What those rules were, Thorne would need to clarify later. Now he had one eye on his old friend the Exmoor stag.

He saw new things in this dreary piece of ersatz West Country dross each time he looked at it. Today he glanced up from his chair and was drawn by something in the set of the animal's jaw that seemed overtly aggressive. It was probably just fear, or the readiness to charge the photographer at any moment, but Thorne was mentally adding a thought bubble to the side of the stag's head which read, 'We don't like your sort round here.' It was only a matter of days now until the stunning view that encapsulated October would be unveiled. He was sure that Keable looked forward to this moment every month. What riveting image might Thorne find himself staring at next week? 'Badger At Dusk', perhaps. He wondered if he'd be here long enough to see it.

Keable had finished. 'Well?'

Thorne gave Keable his full attention. The DCI's expression seemed open and amenable. So far this had gone a lot better than might have been expected.

'We should make it clear,' chipped in Tughan, 'that nobody's asking if you're interested in accepting this offer, because it isn't really an offer. You don't have any choice.'

Thorne knew he was hooked and landed, but he still wanted to struggle a little. He ignored Tughan and spoke directly to Keable. 'I appreciate you keeping the disciplinary side of recent events low-key, Frank, but I'm still a bit confused as to exactly what you want me to do in return.' *Because I wasn't really listening. Sorry.* 'Consultant . . . secret weapon . . . supersub, whatever you choose to call it, I'll still be the one DI too many. Brewer's still around, I don't think Nick's planning on going anywhere . . .'

He smiled at Tughan. The Irishman smiled back, his face blank.

'. . . so what am I actually going to be doing day to day, Frank?'

Keable took a few seconds to formulate a response. When it came it was spoken gently but the steel was barely hidden. 'It was you who wanted out in the first place, Thorne, and you got what you wanted. You made a bloody mess of it and here you are again. You're not in any position to be questioning anything.'

Thorne nodded. He needed to be careful. 'Yes, sir.' He glanced across at Tughan. This time the bastard's smile was genuine.

Keable stood and walked round his desk. There was a small mirror on top of the filing cabinet in the corner and he crouched to catch his reflection and adjust his tie. 'I want you as an unofficial part of this operation. I know that you're anything but stupid and you realise that while you're here the killer knows where to find you.'

He'd know where to find me wherever I was. He's watching.

'This seems important to him and what's important to him is important to me. There's not a great deal we're sure of, as far as this case goes, but the killer has some . . . affinity with you, which I intend to take full advantage of. If you're unhappy about that, tough.' Keable stood up. His tie was perfect. 'Are you?'

Thorne shook his head. He was anything but unhappy about it. Not that he intended to sit about and wait for the killer to pop by and say hello. The initiative, which he'd had at one point, had slipped away. He'd *allowed* it to slip away. He wanted it back.

Keable was moving past Tughan, back towards his chair. 'Plus, if you're here, *we* know where to find you as well.'

Thorne almost smiled. 'One question, sir . . .'

'Go ahead.'

'Jeremy Bishop. Off limits?'

Thorne saw the look pass between Keable and Tughan. He could almost have sworn that he *heard* the temperature drop.

'I was getting to that. Dr Bishop is quite aware that you turning up at his house a fortnight ago was a charade of some sort. Be thankful he doesn't know that you were illegally gathering carpet fibres from the boot of his car.'

He still hadn't spoken to Phil Hendricks. He'd call him later.

'They got stuck to my briefcase, which *he* offered to put in the boot.'

'Of course they did,' scoffed Tughan.

'Do they match?'

Keable's mouth actually dropped open.

Tughan pushed himself away from the wall. 'I think people are right, Thorne. I think you've fucking lost it. Yes, they match, but so would fibres taken from any Volvo of that colour and mode made since 1994. Do you not think we checked those things? Have you any idea how many cars that is?'

Thorne hadn't and didn't much care.

Keable picked up the baton. 'Dr Bishop has rung several times to complain about anonymous phone calls. He's making accusations.'

Thorne met his gaze, unblinking. Keable was the first to look away.

'These calls are becoming more and more frequent.'

How many times had he called Bishop since the funeral? He could barely remember. They seemed like things he was doing in his sleep.

'Dr Bishop is predictably angry and upset, as is his son, who has been in to complain, and now his daughter is jumping on the bandwagon. She rang yesterday to ask what was being done.'

The daughter rallying to the cause. That was interesting.

'If I ever get confirmation that you know more about this than you're saying, Tom, I won't be able to save you. I won't want to save you.'

Thorne tried to look suitably chastened. Then a smile. Needing to lighten it. 'You've still not answered the question, Frank. Is he off limits or not?'

Things got no lighter.

'Detective Inspector Thorne, are you in any doubt that the person who killed Margaret Byrne is also responsible for the deaths of Helen Doyle, Leonie Holden and the others?'

Thorne thought for a second or two. 'I'm in no doubt that the person who killed Leonie, Helen and the others was responsible for the death of Margaret Byrne.'

Keable stared at him. His thick, unruly eyebrows knotted in confusion. Then he saw the subtle difference. His face reddened in an instant and his voice dropped to a threatening whisper. 'Don't play fucking silly games with me, Thorne.'

'I'm not playing games . . .'

'I don't want to listen to this rubbish again. Psychopaths do not hire hitmen.'

Jeremy Bishop was no ordinary psychopath, but deep down Thorne knew that Keable was right. The alibi had to be flawed. Else?

He didn't know what else.

'So I'm not even allowed to mention his name?'

'You're being childish. If you want to waste your time you can think what you like, but don't waste mine, or this operation's. Tom . . .' Thorne looked up. Keable was leaning forward and staring deep into his eyes. 'It's been four weeks since Helen Doyle was killed, two months since he attacked Alison Willetts, six months or more since Christine Owen was killed, and Christ knows when he began planning the whole, sick bloody thing.'

When he stole the drugs. Something about Bishop stealing the Midazolam still bothered Thorne. It floated about at the back of his head, but he couldn't grasp it. Like a tune he couldn't place.

Keable got to his point. 'Despite the blather in the papers and the earnest faces at the press conferences, we've got nothing, Tom.'

Tughan looked at the floor. Was that the merest glimpse of guilt? Thorne looked back to Keable.

'I just can't understand your refusal to look at this with an open mind. There are no other suspects. So far, this operation has achieved nothing.'

Tughan wasn't having it. 'Every officer on this operation has been working his balls off, Thorne. We've done everything we should have, everything. We found a very credible witness in Margaret Byrne—'

Thorne cut him off. 'And got her killed.'

The words struck Tughan like hot fat in his face. He marched across the room shouting, the spittle flying on to Thorne's mouth. 'Jeremy Bishop has got nothing to do with it. Nothing. While you've been in Cloud fucking Cuckoo Land we've been doing our jobs. Bishop is not a suspect. The only courtroom he's ever going to see the inside of is the one trying the lawsuit for harassment, which he'll be bringing against you.'

Thorne was out of his chair in a second. He casually took hold of Tughan's wrist and began to squeeze. The blood fled from the Irishman's face. Keable got to his feet and Thorne released his grip. Tughan stepped quickly back towards the wall, breathing heavily.

Thorne wearily raised an arm and made a lazy, swatting motion at something unseen by anybody else in the room. He lifted his jacket from the back of the chair and slowly pulled it on, murmuring, 'No other suspects, Frank . . .' He took a step towards the door.

Keable screamed, 'Then get me some!'

Even Tughan, rubbing his wrist in the corner, looked shocked.

Detective Chief Inspector Frank Keable was trying to look hard; but Thorne met his eyes and saw only desperation.

Holland was working at a computer, unaware that anyone was behind him until he heard the voice.

'It's a nice day, isn't it? I thought I might take a bit of a trip.'

Holland didn't turn round. 'Anywhere in particular?'

'Bristol's nice.'

Holland carried on typing. 'Traffic's a nightmare on the M4 on a Friday.'

'I quite fancied the train anyway. Hour and a half each way. Get the papers, patronise the buffet . . .'

'Sounds good. I'll buy a copy of *Loaded* if you buy the tea.'

'You should probably lie about where you're going . . .'

Holland shut down the computer. 'I'm getting quite good at lying.'

Thorne smiled. Holland was closing the gap.

He glanced inside the newsagent and one headline in particular caught his eye. 'Champagne Charlie', it called him. A day or two after the Margaret Byrne killing the papers had got hold of the whole thing.

The multiple killings.

At first he'd been upset and angry. He was no multiple killer. But he saw that it made sense. Obviously the full story was being held back – the truth of it. He guessed that the police had only agreed to co-operate if the press left out some of the key details to avoid hoax confessions or copycats.

They needn't be worried. When he chose to get in touch again, they'd know it was him.

He was enjoying his daily dose of tabloid speculation and chest-beating. The lack of progress on this 'horrific' case was now a matter of national concern. Making the police look stupid had never been what he wanted, far from it, but the hollow-sounding assurances of assorted commissioners and commanders, in papers and at po-faced press conferences, amused him greatly.

Champagne Charlie. Unimaginative but predictable, and ironic, considering he wouldn't be using the stuff any more. With Leonie, the grab and the jab had done the job nicely. Plus the knife to the throat, of course, to ensure silence while they waited. It was all over very quickly. The champagne had always provided forty minutes or so of small-talk. He'd missed that: it had made what came later that much more interesting. But with the needle, the difference in the speed of everything was fantastic. The adrenaline had fast-tracked the drug through the girl's body so rapidly that she was in the car on the way back to his place within a few minutes of getting off the bus. He hadn't even heard her voice properly.

She'd only said the one word, whispered it really.

Please . . .

And then he'd failed again. The distraction of the Margaret Byrne killing only a few hours earlier, was a convenient excuse but he was beginning to realise that the odds were against him. He had elected to perform a horrendously difficult procedure. He accepted that. The success rate would be small. He'd known that all along. Still, failure was deeply upsetting.

But the results when he got it right made it all worth it.

He had enjoyed killing Margaret Byrne immensely. It had been a jolt of unadulterated shame admitting that to himself, but there was little point in self-delusion.

He had imagined being her. He had imagined feeling the cold blade singing on his skin. Holding his breath for the split second between that sweet song finishing and the blood beginning to flow.

It was a feeling he had once known and loved, and had almost forgotten.

The killing had none of the lingering beauty, none of the grace of his normal work. There was some skill needed, of course, but a pale, stiffening cadaver could not compare to what he had achieved with Alison. That was something truly elevated. Something unique.

All the same, the success rate was incomparable.

His work was ground-breaking, of that he was certain, but he had only succeeded once and now doubts were beginning to creep into his mind and squat there like bloated black spiders. Might not the quick kill be the next best thing? Would not this euthanasia be a service in itself? There was no bright, breathing, painless future like the one he'd given to Alison, but it was . . . an ending.

He tried to dismiss the idea. He could not picture himself stalking the streets with a scalpel in his pocket. That was not who he was.

He carried his newspaper to the counter and fished around for change. A woman stood next to him. A puzzle magazine, a lottery ticket and a fistful of chocolate. She smiled at him and he remembered how important his work still was. Yes, killing her would be simple and she would be far better off, no question. But nothing worth having was ever achieved easily.

Death was something medieval. He could offer people a future.

During the short taxi ride from Temple Meads station to the hospital, Thorne and Holland had worked out their plan for talking to Dr Rebecca Bishop. Simply put, they didn't have one. Holland had rung ahead and established that she was working today, but beyond that they were making it up as they went along.

A year earlier, Bristol Royal Infirmary had been at the centre of a damaging public inquiry into an alarming number of babies and toddlers who had died during heart surgery. The resulting scandal had cast a long, dark shadow across that hospital in particular and the medical profession in general, which some believed was well deserved. Doctors could no longer be trusted to regulate themselves.

Rather like police officers.

Since he'd begun working on this case, nothing that happened in hospitals could surprise Thorne. He was becoming used to the strategies employed to get through the days by those who worked in them. All the same, the Bristol Royal Infirmary inquiry had been disturbing. There had been some shocking revelations. One ward had been known as 'the departure lounge'.

Susan, Christine, Madeleine, Helen. Thorne knew how insistent were the voices of those whose lives had been snatched away. He pitied those who still heard the screams of twenty-nine dead babies.

Rebecca Bishop worked in the department of orthopaedic surgery. Sitting opposite them on moulded green plastic chairs, in a corridor just off a waiting area, her manner left Thorne in no doubt as to the strength of the confidence gene in this particular family. 'I'll give you half an hour. After that, I'm assisting at a riveting lecture on the biomechanics of fracture repair. You're welcome to attend.'

She smiled coldly. Aside from the dark, frizzy hair and slightly elongated chin, Rebecca had the features of her father and brother. She was a handsome woman, as they were handsome men. Handsome but not pretty. There was nothing soft about her. Thorne wondered where the influence of Sarah Bishop was to be found. Had she been soft? Or pretty?

Maybe he'd ask Jeremy one day, when they had time to talk. In an interview room perhaps.

Thorne opened his mouth to reply but Rebecca Bishop had her own agenda. 'You could start by telling me why they've sent the man my father believes is responsible for harassing him to talk to me about it.'

Thorne flicked his eyes to Holland. He got back the facial equivalent of a shrug.

'Nobody is harassing your father, Dr Bishop. Nobody we are aware of anyway. The very fact that I've come down here myself should assure you that we're taking his allegations seriously.'

'I'm pleased to hear it.'

'But you must understand we do have other priorities.'

She got up and walked across to scrutinise a noticeboard. 'Like catching Champagne Charlie? I've been reading all about it.'

Holland was content to play the ebullient sidekick. 'Don't believe everything you read in the papers, Dr Bishop.'

She looked at Holland, and Thorne thought he spotted

the merest hint of a blush. Did she fancy him? So much the better. He tried to catch Holland's eye but couldn't. Rebecca Bishop turned and stared at Thorne, her hands thrust deep into the pockets of a baggy brown cardigan. 'And is my father a suspect, Inspector Thorne?'

Lying was never pleasant, but it was easy. 'No, of course not. He was questioned routinely and eliminated from the inquiry.'

She looked at him hard. He felt nothing. Doctors kept patients in the dark. Ditto policemen and members of the public.

Holland took over. 'Can we talk about this harassment business? Exactly what is happening, as you understand it?'

She sat down. 'I went over all this on the phone.' Holland took out a notebook on cue. Thorne had to admire the timing. She sighed and carried on. 'Right, well, Dad's been getting these phone calls . . . Oh, and there was somebody taking photos outside his house, but it's mainly the phone calls.'

'Your dad told you about this?'

'No, my brother James rang me. Dad's really upset and angry, and James thought I ought to know what was going on. To add another professional voice of complaint, I suppose. James and I don't exactly chat every day, so I guessed it was something important when I got his message.' She began to chew intently at a fingernail. Thorne noticed that they were all bitten to the quick, some raw and bloody.

It was time to dig a little. 'So you and James are not . . . close?'

She looked up and he could see her considering a reply,

and whether to give it. Was this territory she felt safe bringing strangers into? Maybe it was Holland's smile that did the trick.

'We're not a hugely close family. You must know most of this . . .'

They looked at her as if they didn't know anything at all.

'James and I aren't best friends, no. Dad and I don't get on either, if you must know, but that doesn't mean I want to see him upset.'

Holland nodded, full of understanding. 'Of course not.'

She began to speak slowly, but with a detectable relish. 'James and Dad like to think they're close, but really there's a lot of denial flying about. They fell out a bit a few years ago when James went off the rails a little, and now he just sees the old man as a glorified bank manager who's there to dole out cars and deposits on flats, so that good old James can fuck up anything he turns his hand to and not really worry about it.'

Thorne stirred the pot a little. 'I'm sure he does worry about it.'

'Oh, yeah, you've had the pleasure of meeting James, he told me. Christ, how bitter do I sound?' She tried to laugh, but it caught at the back of her throat.

Thorne's voice was quiet, measured. 'And how does your dad feel?'

'Guilty.' An instinctive answer. Word association.

Thorne willed his face to show nothing. Let her carry on dishing the family dirt.

'Guilty that Mum was off her face on tranquillisers and he was too pissed to drive. Guilty that he put her on the fucking tranquillisers in the first place. Guilty that he screwed up both his kids. Guilty that he didn't die instead of her. We're big on guilt, the Bishops. But Jeremy's the top man.'

Tranquillisers. That made a lot of sense. Was the Midazolam doing to his victims in a few short minutes what the tranquillisers had done to his wife over a number of years? Was all this about something as prosaic as revenge? No, not revenge exactly but . . . Thorne didn't know what.

Almost as soon as he'd thought it, he knew that it was too simplistic and, in a strange way, too poetic. The answer to this case wouldn't lie in everyday motives tied up in Christmas cracker psychology.

But he was getting under the skin of Jeremy Bishop.

He gazed across at Bishop's daughter. She looked exhausted. She had been saying something she had not articulated for a while, or so it seemed to Thorne. She was speaking as if he and Holland weren't there. He needed, gently, to remind her that they were.

'And what about you, Rebecca? What are you guilty about?'

She looked at Thorne as if he was mad. Wasn't it obvious? 'That I wasn't in the car.'

While Tom Thorne was questioning Rebecca Bishop, a hundred miles away, her father was having lunch with the woman who, at least in theory, was sleeping with him.

He'd rung the night before. Anne had grabbed at the phone, hoping it might be Thorne, and was more than a little thrown when she'd heard Jeremy's voice. They'd agreed to meet. A pasta place in Clerkenwell, more or less midway between Queen Square and the Royal London.

The hug was perhaps a little forced but the wine soon

relaxed them and the conversation flowed easily enough. They talked about work. Stressful – hard to go home and relax. Tiring – when was it anything else? He was starting to think about a change of direction; she was intrigued. She was disappointed and upset about Alison's setback; he was sympathetic.

They talked about children. Was she expecting too much of Rachel? Was she too pushy? He told her not to give herself a hard time over it. He'd always expected the best from Rebecca and James and almost certainly *had* been too pushy. He was proud of Rebecca, and maybe James would work out soon what he wanted.

She told him he should be proud of both of them.

Then a silence, which was just the right side of awkward, when Bishop broke it. 'Did you not phone because your boyfriend told you not to?'

Anne lit a cigarette, her third since they had finished the meal. 'You didn't call me either.'

'I was worried it might be awkward. I've read the papers and clearly I can't be a suspect any more, but he still seems to have something of a . . . problem with me.'

She flicked non-existent ash into the ashtray. 'I haven't spoken to Tom in over a week.' Bishop raised an eyebrow. More nervous ash-flicking. 'We've never really talked about you, anyway, Jeremy. Best to keep the personal and the professional separate.'

Bishop leaned forward and smiled, interlocking long, slender fingers and resting his chin on them. He stared deep into her eyes. 'I do understand all that, Jimmy, and I know this is hard for you. But what do you really think?'

She held the eye-contact and tried with all her heart

and soul to imagine this man the way Tom Thorne did. She couldn't do it. 'Jeremy, I don't . . .'

'I heard a story yesterday about a GP with a morphine addiction. He'd prescribe it to his older patients, then he'd make house calls and steal it back from them. They'd come into the surgery thinking they'd lost it, you know, going doolally in their old age. He'd smile at them, full of understanding, and prescribe them some more. And so on.'

Anne was not hugely shocked. Many doctors had problems with addiction. There was even a rehab centre exclusively for those who worked in the medical profession. Bishop carried on: 'The guy who told me this had known the man for twenty-odd years and had absolutely no idea.'

She looked at him. Holding her breath. His voice was barely a whisper.

'People have secrets, Anne.'

Anne looked down and fixed her eyes on the cigarette she was stubbing out in the ashtray. Carefully and deliberately she removed any trace of burning ember. What did he expect her to say? Was this just a piece of typically theatrical and provocative weirdness or . . .?

She looked up and signalled for the bill, then turned back to him, smiling. 'Talking of secrets, Jeremy, are you seeing somebody?'

His mood seemed to change in a moment. She saw it, and thought about backing off but decided against it. She wanted to turn the tables a little, to enjoy *his* awkwardness. 'You are, aren't you? Why are you being so coy?' She saw something like an answer in his eyes. 'Do I know her?'

He stared down at the tablecloth. 'It's not really serious and it's probably not going to last very long for all sorts of reasons, but if I talk about it, it will be like I'm cursing it somehow. Condemning it to an early grave.'

She laughed. Why this sudden superstition? 'Come on, since when have—'

'No.' His tone stopped the tail end of her laughter in its tracks. End of conversation.

'It would be like wishing it dead.'

Thorne arrived home fizzing and fidgety. There were people he needed to call. His dad. Hendricks. Anne, of course. But he felt too energised.

It had happened as he'd stepped out of Kentish Town tube station and was wondering which lucky off-licence would have the benefit of his business on the way home. The conversation behind him had gone something like this.

'*Big Issue . . .*'

'Get a fucking job!'

'This is my job, you arsehole!'

And it had gone off.

Thorne had stepped in a second or two after the first punches and kicks began to fly. Wincing as a stray punch caught him on the side of the head, he'd grabbed the get-a-job merchant round the neck and hauled him into a nearby doorway with more force than was strictly necessary. The *Big Issue* seller, having picked up the magazines scattered during the ruck, had moved in close to watch.

Thorne had looked at him, 'Piss off,' then turned his attention back to the one who *had* a home. Drunk, of course, or maybe stoned. A student, Thorne reckoned, with blood from a split lip running on to his white button-down shirt.

Thorne had held him against the door with a stiff arm at

his throat and casually kneed the little tosser between the legs as he removed his badge from the inside pocket of his leather jacket and pushed it into his face. 'Have a guess what *my* job is.'

Now, back at home, opening the first can of cheap lager, he wondered what might have happened if he hadn't been around with a badge in his pocket and some aggression to offload.

If one of them had been carrying a knife.

These were typical murders. Ordinary killings, simple, banal and understandable. People dying because of anger or frustration or a basic lack of space. Dying for a grand cause or a stupid comment. Or a few pence.

Wives and husbands killing with hammers and fists, or men being men with drink and knives, or drug-dealers holding guns as casually as combs.

Thorne understood them, these deaths died in cities. He knew what they were about. Each made its own strange kind of sense.

But not this. Not killing as a side-effect. Bodies as a by-product of some sickfuckingmadness.

He downed the last of the beer, pulled on his jacket, and within forty-five minutes he was standing in a street in Battersea, looking up at the shape that moved behind a light at a second floor window.

He stood for nearly an hour, melting back into the shadows with each twitch of the curtains, real or imagined. Then he stepped back quickly into the anonymous darkness as Jeremy Bishop threw open the curtains and stood looking down at the street.

Bishop stared hard at Thorne, or the place where Thorne *was*, seeing a shape, perhaps, but certainly no more. As Thorne returned the stare, he felt a glacial tremor run through every bone in his body as Bishop's face suddenly changed.

From this distance, Thorne could not be sure.

It might have been a grimace.

It might have been a smile.

I know that I've made jokes before about the NHS and the lack of money and everything. I was taking the piss out of the blackboard when it first appeared, you know, compared with all the flashy stuff they've got in America.

But this?

Anne's been telling me for a while that her and the occupational therapist are going to try to rig up a couple of devices so that I can read and watch TV. Obviously I've been gagging for it, and even more so since I've been back on this bastard ventilator. When a machine is doing your breathing for you, life can get sooo *boring, darling! But I didn't realise they literally meant 'rig up'. Honestly, it's spit and fucking earwax.*

They've screwed some sort of pivoting arm into the ceiling and the TV now hangs down from there so I'm staring up at the screen. Great. If I was in hospital in Fuckwit, Illinois, or wherever, I'd be able to control the volume and, crucially, change the bloody channel *with my eyelid. Here, in good old London Town, on the good old National Health Service, those little details seem to have been overlooked. So I have to wait for a nurse to show up, and blink to indicate that I'd like her to turn over. She does exactly that and buggers off again. Leaving me staring at* Supermarket Sweep *or some moronic cookery programme until she puts her head round the door again twenty minutes later and I'm blinking my head off in an effort to get the football on.*

I don't want to sound ungrateful, but this is heaven compared to my new reading arrangements.

It's based around a music-stand, I think, though there might be a bit of old coat-hanger stuck in there as well. All right, I'm exaggerating, but not much. I get raised up and this metal contraption is placed across my tits with little clamps that fold down to hold in place my book or magazine of choice. Good in theory. First, I'm hardly in a position to make complex requests on the book front. I'm racking my brains to think of books I might fancy reading with really short titles. Same with magazines, though I'm more or less sorted thanks to OK! *and* Hello!. *Not too taxing on the eyelids. The problem is the same as with the telly, though. I'm hardly Brain of Britain, but even I can read a page of pretty much anything in twenty minutes, or however long it is until the nurse comes in again. I don't expect them to come tearing in here every ninety seconds to turn my page for me but there must be something somebody can do.*

I can't pay for anything, and I haven't got family who can pay for anything or try to raise money, but even so . . .

Everything's fucking half-measures.

Half-measures for half a person.

SIXTEEN

Thorne and Anne Coburn had spent most of the day in bed together. He'd been up once, for about half an hour. Just long enough to make a few pieces of toast, put on *American Recordings* by Johnny Cash and fetch the papers. *The Observer* for her (he read the sports section). *The Mirror* and the *Screws* for him (she read the supplements). He wasn't planning to get up again until the pubs opened.

He'd woken, alone, several hours earlier with the image of Jeremy Bishop's face looking down at him, captured in negative when he closed his eyes, as if he'd been staring too long at a lightbulb.

He kept his eyes open and did some catching up. The phone lay on the small cupboard by the side of the bed and he propped a couple of pillows up against the headboard. One extremely comfy office. The call to his dad was surprisingly enjoyable. Jim Thorne hated Sundays, and his irascible commentary on everything from garden centres to 'God-botherers' had made Thorne laugh out loud several times. They'd agreed to have a night out the following week.

Thorne had arranged to meet Phil Hendricks the day after next but this was a less enjoyable prospect. The pathologist had sounded distant and edgy. The call had taken less than a minute. Thorne wondered what Hendricks wanted to see him about. He was pretty sure it had nothing to do with tickets for Spurs–Arsenal.

Then he'd rung Anne.

She'd been having breakfast with Rachel. The two of them were planning to spend the day together and she told Thorne she'd ring back. Within fifteen minutes she was on her way over. Rachel had not seemed too disappointed at the change of plan, and by the time she was climbing back into bed with her mobile phone, her mother was climbing into bed with Tom Thorne.

After making up for lost time they'd dozed for a while but now, surrounded by discarded bits of newspaper, they lay in a bed dotted with toast crumbs and smelling of sex. And began to talk.

It was a conversation of a very different nature from the one they'd had nearly a month earlier, on the night Thorne had gone round for dinner; the night he'd been attacked and drugged in his own home. Then, certainly as far as *he* had been concerned, there had been a lot of lying. There had been the lies implicit in the flirting and the lies behind his questions about Jeremy Bishop.

There was so much he hadn't told her. So many lies by omission.

Now they talked easily, and truthfully. Two people the wrong side of forty with little reason to puff up achievements or suck in stomachs. They spoke about David and Rachel and Jan and the Lecturer. Divorces with children versus divorces without. About her grade-seven piano and the work she'd done on her house and the cups she'd won for tennis before she went to university. About how much he hated poncy tea and brown bread, and how he'd been quite a useful footballer until he'd started putting on weight.

About how often she'd saved a life and how many times he'd fired a gun.

They talked about how utterly unsuited they were, and laughed, and then made love again.

For a few hours on a damp Sunday afternoon at the fag-end of September, the case that had changed both their lives – that would twist and warp their lives, and those of others, even more before it was over – might not have existed.

Then a woman picked up a phone in Edinburgh and changed everything.

He'd enjoyed his Sundays in the past. They had been a vital part of the process. It had been the day when he'd selected several of his early ones. He'd watched Christine on a Sunday – she'd had friends round. And Susan – at home alone in front of an old film. Even after he'd stopped working in other houses, Sunday was still a day to take stock. To plan.

Today, he didn't like what he saw. It was all going to shit. He could feel himself on the edge of a depression that he knew would be crippling if he let it take hold.

The days after Helen had been hard but he'd seen a light at the end of it all. The knowledge that success was possible. That the capacity to achieve success was within him.

And the days after Alison. A happiness he hadn't known before or since.

Today he saw no light ahead. The doubt was taking hold of every part of him and starting to squeeze out the joy and the hope.

It was more than just his own failure, of course. Thorne

was failing as well, or at the very least not being allowed to succeed.

Without Thorne there was really no point.

All his channels of information were clear. The news, the rumour, the word. None of it good. He'd made it all so easy for them and they'd screwed it up. They'd missed every marker he'd left so carefully in their path.

He sat and stared at the pristine white wall. Whatever happened, however it worked itself out, he would always have Alison. She would always be a testament to him and his work. The other part of it, *the other half of it*, might not work out exactly as planned but that was not his fault. That was the result of involving others. There were ways of achieving a similar end on his own.

The punishment was not going to fit the crime, but he would see it meted out nevertheless.

It wasn't over, not yet, but he was starting to feel weary.

Twelve days before, with Margaret Byrne's body cooling where he'd left it and his car effortlessly trailing the night bus carrying Leonie Holden towards him, he'd felt bright and invincible. Today, he wasn't sure he'd even be able to drag himself out of doors.

Even though, later, he would have to.

They were laughing about his taste in music. The track was 'Delia's Gone', which involved Johnny Cash tying his girlfriend to a chair and shooting her a couple of times, essentially because she was 'devilish'. Thorne couldn't see the problem.

Then the phone rang. 'Tom? It's Sally Byrne.'

Thorne laughed. 'Hi, Sally. Elvis is fine. He's destroying the place but he's fine.'

Anne, who hadn't met the cat yet, threw him an odd look from the other side of the bed. He grinned at her over his shoulder, shaking his head. *Don't worry about it.* She picked up a newspaper and snuggled down to read.

'It's not actually about the cat, Tom.'

Thorne began to sit up slowly. He could feel the smallest of sensations, a tingle, a burning, an excitement, building between his shoulder-blades. 'I'm listening, Sally.'

'It's just something a bit odd and I probably should have spoken to the Irish officer. What's his name?'

'Tughan.' *Go on . . .*

'Well, I've been going through Mum's things, you know sorting stuff out for the charity shop or whatever, and I was looking through her jewellery and I found a man's ring.'

Thorne was already out of bed and wandering into the living room, trying to pull on a dressing-gown.

'Tom?'

'Sorry. Which jewellery are we talking about?'

'This is what I'm saying, it's the stuff you lot took away. The scene-of-crime people. They let me have it all back after the funeral, said they didn't need it any more. I don't know where they found this ring, on the floor with the rest of the stuff, I suppose, and they obviously thought it belonged to my mum, but it doesn't.'

'It's definitely a man's?'

'Definitely. It's plain gold. Looks like a wedding ring.'

'Not your dad's?'

'Are you kidding? That bastard would never have worn a wedding ring. Might have spoiled his chances of pulling.'

Thorne was starting to miss what Sally Byrne was saying. A melody was pouring into his brain and filling every corner of it. A classical melody. Mournful and haunting. He couldn't remember what it was called. Something German. But he could remember where he'd heard it. And he could remember a rhythm, a tempo, marked out by the clicking of a wedding ring against a gearstick.

'I mean, I'm sure it's nothing, Tom, but . . .'

When Thorne came back into the bedroom a few minutes later, Anne knew in a heartbeat that something had changed. He was trying to sound casual. He asked if she wanted tea.

She got up and began to dress.

Whatever it was that had actually happened wasn't important. She knew that murder and suspicion were back in the room with them and she needed to leave. They moved around each other awkwardly now, embarrassed, and they froze for half a second as each caught the other's reflection in the long wardrobe mirror.

Thorne saw something like accusation and hated himself for wanting her to leave so that he could ring Dave Holland.

Anne saw the excitement that was running through Thorne like voltage.

She saw a hunger in him.

She saw the face of Jeremy Bishop and the dark sadness that had settled around his eyes as he'd whispered to her.

'*People have secrets, Anne.*'

They sat at a table towards the back of the room, not in total darkness but close to it. It seemed to be the way he wanted it. He'd led her to the table, avoiding the empty seats near the stage. It was probably a good idea considering that they didn't want to get picked on and she was under-age.

Rachel looked around. She wasn't the only one.

Actually she had had no trouble in getting away with it. The club was dimly lit and the woman on the door had barely looked up from her cashbox when the two of them had come in. She'd spent a long time on her makeup. She'd even stood beneath the lights at the bar and bought them both a drink, staring at herself in the mirror that ran along the back wall behind the optics. She looked eighteen easily. Twenty, probably.

This small comedy club below a pub in Crouch End was, he'd told her, one of his favourite places. It was a mixed audience. Nobody cared what you looked like or how old you were. It wasn't exactly the Comedy Store, but you could see some of the same comedians that you were likely to see at the bigger clubs without having to struggle into the West End.

Rachel had liked the sound of it straight away and asked him if he'd take her. He told her about another night at the same club when they did what were called try-out shows or open spots. He came to those as often as he could, if he wasn't working. A dozen or more hopefuls would get up and do a couple of minutes. None of them was any good. It was clearly just therapy for most of them, but it was riveting to watch. Like a car accident. Watching them struggle, watching them 'die', was an amazing experience, he assured her.

The comedian on the tiny stage was a sneering Scotsman with red hair and a loud suit who shouted a lot and swore too much. He talked about sex in graphic detail and Rachel sat blushing in the darkness. She looked out of the corner of her eye at the man next to her so that she could laugh when he did. She didn't want to seem young, or stupid, or unsophisticated.

He was enjoying himself, she could tell. He'd seemed a little tense when he'd picked her up outside the Green Man, but now he looked more relaxed. She watched him far more than she watched what was happening on stage. He stared, engrossed, at the comedian, or at other members of the audience. He was a ferocious watcher, critical and unblinking. She loved that about him. She loved how he lived every moment to its fullest, taking everything in and savouring it. She loved his intensity, his refusal to compromise.

The comedian was telling some joke about his parents and Rachel thought about her mother. Anne had been in a strange mood when she'd come home – from the policeman's place, Rachel guessed. It had definitely been him who'd phoned that morning. Probably at it all day, the pair of them.

She thought quite a lot about Thorne fucking her mother.

She thought quite a lot about fucking.

There had been a bit of an atmosphere when she'd announced that she was going out, but her mother had hardly been in a position to say anything after the way she'd changed their plans earlier.

Around her people started to applaud and she joined in. The compère was coming back on again to introduce another act. He said that there'd be an interval afterwards. She wondered if they'd go out for a meal when the show had finished; there were loads of great restaurants within walking distance. Then they could sit in his car for a while before he drove her home.

The next comedian was a woman. She was gentler and did a really funny song about men being crap in bed to start off.

Rachel took a sip from her half of lager and smiled at him, feeling a little light-headed. He smiled back and squeezed her hand. When he'd let go she slid her arm between his back and the chair.

She was as happy as she could ever remember being.

She rested her hand on his waist . . . the audience laughed . . . he had on a really nice linen shirt which he wore out of his trousers . . . the audience groaned at a corny line . . . he always wore gorgeous clothes . . . the woman on stage started another song . . . Rachel wanted to touch his skin . . . a drunk at the other side of the room started to cheer and clap . . . she moved her hand under his shirt and her fingers crept round to stroke the flesh of his stomach . . .

Then he screamed.

In that split second when everything fell apart, and he was standing up, and her drink was in her lap, and the woman on the stage was pointing at them, it *seemed* to Rachel that he had screamed. Christ, he had. He'd bellowed. As if he'd been scalded . . .

His face was a mask and she reached up to grab his arm, but he called her a stupid little bitch and grabbed for his coat and he was away, moving quickly away, pushing between the tables and knocking over empty chairs.

And the woman on the stage was laughing and saying something to him as he marched out, and he turned and shouted and told her to fuck off, and people in the audience started to boo, and he looked like he wanted to hurt them.

He crashed out through the door, and she could feel the beer soaking through her thin skirt, and the eyes of everyone in the room burning into her. The door slammed shut with a bang, and the woman on the stage leaned in close to her microphone and put a hand over her eyes to stare into the lights and beyond, to where Rachel was sitting and wishing she was dead.

'Bit of a domestic, love?'

A few people in the audience laughed. And Rachel began to cry.

Holland was listening to the sports round-up on Radio 5 Live for the third time in as many hours, when headlights swept across his rear-view mirror and he turned to see Jeremy Bishop pulling up outside his house.

Thorne had called at around six and Sophie was not best pleased. She'd known immediately that it was Thorne. She knew *everything* immediately. She'd have been pissed off at his having to go out anyway but Thorne, as far as she was concerned, represented an unhealthy future for him in the force. A future he should run from at all costs. A future without promotion, without stability, without certainty.

By implication, without her.

He couldn't argue with her. Everything she said made complete sense. But they were words from beyond the grave. His father's words. Sophie was mouthing the sentiments of a man he had loved but had never admired.

It was hard not to admire Tom Thorne.

He couldn't argue with Sophie, so he didn't bother. He left the house in silence and conducted the argument with her in his head as he drove to Battersea and sat waiting. In truth, he was arguing with himself as well.

Thorne was clutching at straws, of course he was. Jeremy Bishop, who, Holland knew, had been at work in the Royal London hospital at the time, had dropped a ring in Maggie Byrne's bedroom as he was murdering her.

Right. Looked at rationally, these were the ravings of a man popularly thought by many of his colleagues to have gone over the edge. But there'd been something in Thorne's voice. Yes, desperation possibly, but more than that. An excitement, a zeal, a *passion* that had Holland reaching for his coat and wondering what he was going to say to Sophie before he'd put down the phone.

He stepped out of the car and crossed the road.

Bishop, who had just locked the Volvo and was about to head towards his front door, saw Holland coming. He sighed theatrically and leaned back against the car, his hands thrust deep into the pockets of his trousers.

Holland was ready with an apologetic shrug and all the appropriate phrases. Just a few more questions. Investigating a fresh lead. Grateful for all your help and co-operation. As he approached he could see that Bishop remembered him. He didn't care. He had his badge in his right hand with the other politely outstretched. 'Detective Constable Holland, sir.'

Bishop pushed himself away from the car and took a step towards him. 'Yes, I know. How's your girlfriend's hand?' The tone impatient, the smile saying he knew it was bollocks.

Holland was thrown, but only for a second. 'Fine.'

'How long is this going to take?'

It wasn't going to take very long at all. As Bishop had started speaking, he had proffered his left hand in return for Holland's. They'd shaken, and with a quick downward glance, Holland had got what he'd come for. What Thorne had sent him for.

No wedding ring.

I've been reading a lot. The same page usually, over and over again, but what the hell? Early on, there was a bit of a scramble to find some interesting reading matter and while they were looking, to sort of test out their new-fangled device, the occupational therapist gave me some official hospital literature to read.

Yawn . . .

Well, that's what I thought until I started reading. Fascinating stuff. This is a quote, and I can remember it very accurately having stared at it for twenty minutes: 'The National Hospital for Neurology and Neurosurgery, incorporating the Institute of Neurology, is a unique resource for teaching, training and research in neurology and the neurosciences. The work of academic staff and their research is closely integrated with the hospital's care of its patients.'

Well, that all seems clear enough to me. The 'care' bit is very much an afterthought, you know, tagged on at the end when somebody remembered that it was supposed to be a hospital. The rest seems to be all about research and training and, frankly, they can just fuck right off.

I'm a patient. Trust me, I'd really rather not be here at all, but if I am then my job description is 'patient', mate. I'm nobody's resource. Nobody's fucking teaching aid.

'Let's have a look at this poor young woman here, utterly buggered thanks to brainstem trauma. Can you try and blink for us, dear?'

No thanks.

All right, I'm being a bit over the top but when I first read that I was really upset. I lay awake all night wondering if anybody here was making any effort at all to help me get better.

I'm still wondering.

Am I more use to them the way I am?

SEVENTEEN

Keable and Tughan had questions ready, and Thorne had plenty of answers. First, there was the small matter of another complaint from Jeremy Bishop.

'He claims there was somebody watching his house on Saturday evening.' Keable looked at Thorne.

Thorne shrugged and turned to Holland innocently. 'Did he say anything about this to you last night?'

Tughan spoke before Holland had a chance to answer. 'You are on such thin ice, Thorne.'

Thorne smiled. He was feeling elated and no amount of sniping from Nick Tughan was going to alter his mood. One day soon they would have it all out. For now, he was best ignored.

Tughan was seated in a chair against the wall beneath the calendar, and Holland stood with his back to the door. The office felt crowded. Thorne placed both hands on Keable's desk and leaned down to him. 'So what are we going to do, Frank?'

Keable slid his chair away from the desk, retreating. He held up a hand. 'First we're going to think about what we've really got here. How on earth can she be sure the ring isn't her mother's?'

'She's sure.'

Tughan snorted. 'She lives in Edinburgh, she never *saw* her mother, for fuck's sake. The ring could be anyone's. Who knows how many men she had round there?'

Holland spoke quietly. 'I don't think Margaret Byrne had any men. Sir.'

Tughan turned round and glared. Holland refused to look away.

'SOC got no prints off the body . . .'

Thorne slammed a hand down on the desk. 'If SOC hadn't fucked up and catalogued a vital piece of evidence as one of the victim's possessions we wouldn't even be here. This would be over by now.'

'No prints on the body, Tom. The killer wore gloves, so how the hell does he lose a ring?'

Thorne took a deep breath. *Answer the question. Nice and calm.* 'I think he put the gloves on once she was unconscious. Surgical gloves. He put them on to handle the scalpel. To make his incision. The ring could have come off anytime before then. There was obviously some sort of struggle.'

Keable looked over at Tughan, who shook his head. 'What does Bishop say?'

Holland stepped forward, placed a hand on the back of Tughan's chair. Spoke over his head. 'He claims to have lost it a few weeks ago.'

Tughan was still shaking his head. Not having any of it. 'How do you "lose" a wedding ring?' He began twisting his own. 'I couldn't get this fucker off even if I wanted to.'

Holland had answers as well as Thorne. 'His comes off quite easily, he told me. He takes it off at work. Takes all his jewellery off. Claims somebody took it out of his locker.'

Keable seized on this. 'Anything else taken?'

'His wallet and a watch. A Tag Heuer.'

'Did he report it?'

'No point. He says stuff goes missing from lockers all the time.'

Thorne's eyes flicked from one face to the other. Holland was doing well. Keable would not go for this without facts. He needed a weight of facts in support, and Holland was supplying them.

'When was this?'

'Nearly three weeks ago. The eleventh.'

Keable nodded. 'The day before Margaret Byrne was killed.'

Thorne said nothing. *The day he'd conned the lift into town. Bishop had been wearing the ring then.* Letting Keable make the decision. It was important he felt that it was his. He was still nodding.

'What do you want, Tom?'

'I want a warrant.'

Tughan stood quickly, his chair shooting back behind him. Keable raised a hand. 'Let's get this ring down here first, and over to the forensic boys. We'll talk about warrants if and when. Nick, get on the phone to Lothian and Borders. I want it driven down here. Understand?'

Tughan was first out of the door. Holland held it open for him. As Thorne went to follow, Keable stopped him. 'There's a press conference scheduled for midday, Tom. I'd like you on the platform, please.'

Keable's tone implied that he would brook no arguments. He wasn't going to get any. The adrenaline was pumping round Thorne's body. He was high as a kite. He'd have happily agreed to appear on *Stars In Their Eyes*.

Thorne . . .

Walking into the operations room. Avoiding eye-contact with nobody. Acknowledging the kind words and approving looks. Putting a hand on Dave Holland's arm and savouring the smile he gets in return. Relishing the scowl on the face of Nick Tughan as the Irishman runs fingers through his thin blond hair and grabs at the phone.

And enjoying the relief in the voices of the girls.

'*It's going to be over soon, isn't it?*'

'*Tommy? Is this it?*'

'*You going to get him, Tommy?*'

'*Get the fucker . . .*'

Christine, Madeleine, Susan. And Helen at the end. Spitting out enough hope for all of them. It was a hope he was no longer afraid of dashing.

'*Yes, I'm going to get him. Very soon.*'

And somewhere in the background, the laughter of Leonie Holden.

He watched it twice. He watched it on each edition of the lunchtime news, BBC and ITV. Both times he was entranced. Both times he laughed out loud, and applauded at the end.

He was in a much better mood anyway. Things were looking up and the despondency of the day before – it had been a dreadful day – had evaporated with one small snippet of news. It was a little overdue, but more than welcome. He still had no great urge to try the procedure again, but it seemed as if things might work out as planned after all.

Commander Sincere, Detective Chief Inspector Eyebrows . . . and Tom Thorne. He'd cheered when Thorne had been introduced, finally, to the nation. So everything was hunky-dory again, was it? Tom was back on the team.

The commander spoke about 'new leads' and 'exciting new avenues of investigation'. And about time too! That said, they were *still* keen to hear from anyone who could supply even a partial number-plate on the blue Volvo, and they were *still* showing that bloody awful e-fit, courtesy of some blind passer-by on the night he'd taken Helen Doyle.

Margaret Byrne would have come up with something far more accurate . . .

Then Commander Sincere introduced the officer who was going to 'make a direct appeal to the man responsible for these terrible killings'. The camera moved along to Thorne. He looked a little nervous. Distracted.

He wondered how Thorne would perform on camera. He must have done this sort of thing before, he was bound to be good at it. The Irishman had been smooth but he guessed that Thorne would bring something else to it. Power, perhaps. Something fuelled by a genuine rage.

Of course he would. Thorne was a man after his own heart.

He wasn't disappointed. There was nothing written down; no need for notes. Thorne looked straight into the camera and spoke calmly, but with precision and strength.

He shuffled his chair forward, his face only inches from the television screen, his mouth open. It was as if Thorne was speaking straight to him.

Which of course he was.

'It's still not too late. You can just stop all of this now. I can't promise anything but if you come forward now, if you come forward *today*, then your case is going to be viewed that much more favourably.

'None of us can even begin to guess why you've chosen to do these things. Perhaps you feel that you *have* no choice. You will get the chance to explain all this if you stop the killing now.

'You know, of course, that we will use any means at our disposal to stop you. Any means at all. I can't guarantee that this will not result in injury of some sort to yourself. Or worse. We do not want to see anybody else hurt and that includes you. You can believe that or not. It's your choice.

'So just stop and think. Right now. Think for a minute. Whatever point you're trying to make, consider it made. Then pick up the phone.

'Let's end this madness. Now. Come forward today and hand yourself over to me . . . to us, and people will be there to help you.'

Then Thorne leaned in towards the camera, his face filling the screen.

'One way or another, this will all be over soon.'

Rachel had forgiven him almost instantly.

He'd called first thing and had sounded so upset about what he'd done. He knew his behaviour had been unforgivable and would completely understand if she wanted to end it.

That was the last thing she wanted to do.

His apology made her feel strangely powerful. It was as if there'd been a sudden shift. He could have just walked away but he hadn't. He'd wanted her forgiveness, and once she'd given it, she sensed that their relationship had moved on to a different footing.

He'd explained that things at work hadn't been going

too well. There were a couple of people he was clashing with and it had all got on top of him. Obviously that didn't excuse what he'd done or anything, but he wanted her to know that he'd been under a lot of stress, that was all. She asked why he hadn't told her. She wanted to share things like that with him. She wanted to share everything with him. She could have helped. He told her that he *wanted* to share everything with her and that one day soon he would.

She felt her mouth go dry. She knew that he was talking about sex.

He'd asked if it had been very bad after he'd stormed out of the comedy club. She told him that the woman comedian had picked on her for a bit but then it had been the interval and she'd sneaked out. They laughed, wondering what the rest of the audience would have been saying about them. He said he'd buy her a new skirt to replace the one that got covered in beer. He told her he'd buy her lots of things.

They'd dallied over saying goodbye, but eventually Rachel said that she really had to go. She told him she'd call him later and that she loved him and they hung up at the same time.

And then she'd carried on getting ready for school.

Anne was in a meeting and would be for the next couple of hours. Thorne was not unhappy about it. He'd asked at Reception and now he walked towards the lifts, breathing a sigh of relief. If he had run into her it would have been fine. He'd have handled it and so would she, but it was probably best to leave it a day or two.

He hoped that it would all be over by then.

The day before, after the call from Sally Byrne, they

hadn't been able to talk about anything. Once an arrest had been made, once *the* arrest had been made, they would be able to talk about it all. It wouldn't be easy for Anne but he would be there to help her through it.

If she still wanted him.

He'd seen it lots of times with those who'd been close to killers. He remembered how hard it had been for Calvert's mother and father, though that had been very different.

It was a kind of death and there would be a proper mourning to be done. Anne would need to grieve for the friend she'd lost. She would be losing him in many ways, and she'd need to grieve for all of them. This was without the guilt she was bound to feel, and the shame at having been his friend in the first place, and the guilt she would feel because of the shame.

In all probability, she would also be the first port of call for his children and would need to comfort them and deal with their feelings. Then she would have the press to deal with. If they couldn't hound a killer, they would hound a killer's friends. None of it was going to be easy.

Anne would be looking for someone to blame.

It was probably best, then, to avoid confrontation for a while. To stay out of the line of fire. It still might all turn to shit anyway. He'd known plenty of cases, a lot more straightforward than this one, where a result had slipped away from them at the last minute. A fuck-up or, God forbid, a legal technicality was waiting around every corner to bury cocksure detective inspectors. Thorne wasn't counting any chickens. However, he was buoyant enough to be here in the first place, stepping into the lift and wondering exactly how he was going to explain everything.

Because it wasn't Anne he had come to see anyway.

Going into Alison's room was a shock. Anne hadn't told him she was back on a ventilator, even though he'd known how susceptible she would always be to infection.

The room was noisier again, more cluttered, but the girl at the centre of it still drew his eye and his heart as she had done from the first time he'd seen her. She'd had her hair cut since the last time he'd been here. That was the day he'd brought Bishop's photo in, just before he'd been told about the 'anonymous' accusations and things had spiralled out of control.

Everything was under control again now.

He moved slowly towards the bed, walking past the blackboard, now folded away and lying against the wall covered in a white sheet. Had Alison heard him come in? He knew how limited her field of vision was and didn't want to make her jump.

He caught himself. *Jump? Silly bastard.* He knew so little about what her life was like. What it had become. He'd promised himself he'd look into it and hadn't. He'd heard about people who'd had amputations and could still feel the limbs that had gone. Was it like that for Alison? Could she still feel or even imagine she was feeling what it was like to jump or run or kick or kiss?

He stopped at the end of the bed where he knew she could see him. Her eyeball skittered back and forth for a few seconds. She blinked.

Hello.

He moved to the side of the bed, reaching for the plastic orange chair and looking around the room, casually, as if he were just another visitor fumbling for a suitable bedside pleasantry. He could see no flowers anywhere.

There was nothing to do but begin talking.

'Hello, Alison. I hope you don't mind me just turning up but there are a few things I wanted to explain. Because nobody else *has*, really, and I think you have a right to know. Dr Coburn will have given you all the medical stuff . . . the medical side of things, but I wanted to try and tell you what happened to *you*. After you left the club that night. Obviously we don't really know how much you remember. Probably nothing.'

He helped himself to a much-needed drink from the water jug on the bedside table. He wondered why there *was* a water jug when Alison couldn't drink.

'Exactly what happened between you leaving the night-club and getting home is guesswork, really, but it doesn't matter. You can tell us about where you met the man with the champagne when you get off this ventilator and get a bit better, but we know that he came into your house, and that the drug in the champagne would have been taking effect, and that there'd have been nothing you could do when he . . . put his hands on you.'

There was a loud crash from the corridor outside. He saw Alison react. A momentary tension in the skin around the eyes. Sounds were obviously so important.

He just needed to get to it now. Stop pissing about. He'd told parents how their children had died. Why should this be so difficult?

'Anyway, Alison, here's the thing. You didn't survive. I mean . . . yes, of course you did, but that was actually what he wanted.'

He patted the edge of the bed, cast an eye towards the machines, the monitors, the tubes, and back to Alison's face.

'*This* . . . is what he wanted, what he was trying to achieve.

'It sounds mad, I know it does, and that's because it is. He wasn't trying to kill you. He might easily have killed you because what he did to you is actually incredibly difficult. He's tried before and since, and not been successful . . . and other women have died. So . . .'

So what? Thorne wondered whether he should ever have started this. What should he tell her now? How *lucky* she'd been?

'That's it. I won't tell you that you were fortunate not to die. That's really something only you can . . . have feelings about. But you were strong enough . . . not to die, so I'm sure you're strong enough to get yourself out of here.

'I have no idea why he did this, Alison. I wish I could tell you I did. I could make something up, but the truth is I haven't got a bloody clue.

'I can tell you one thing, though, and I suppose that's why I've come if I'm honest. He's going to tell me why he did it very soon. I want you to know that. Very soon. He's going to look me in the eye and tell me.'

He took her hand. Squeezed.

'Then I'm going to put the fucker in prison for the rest of his life.'

Really? I see. Well, thanks for popping by and dropping that little snippet into the conversation.

He did this to me deliberately. Wants me like this. Wired up, fucked up.

Right . . .

It's hard to take news any other way than calmly when you're like this. My reactions always tend to look a bit similar. On the outside anyway. I might seem a bit placid. Anybody looking at me would be thinking, Ooh, didn't she take it well?

Inside's another matter.

Raging. Understanding what it means when your blood boils, because I can feel it bubbling. I can feel it moving through my veins like lava. Because I know now. I know for certain.

I'd sort of worked it out anyway.

I've been thinking it had to be something like that.

Something fucking twisted.

I've had a lot of time to think about it and you don't have to be a genius to work out that something strange was going on.

There wasn't a mark on me.

There was nothing sexual. Anne told me.

I thought early on that maybe he was trying to break my neck but there wasn't even a bruise. I reckon it's really quite easy to kill somebody if you want to and I've been wondering why he didn't want to.

Trying to work out what he did want.

So I'm the one he got right? I'm a living and almost breathing testament to this bloke's . . . skill?

While other women died.

Hearing the blood sizzle and hiss through the arteries. Steam coming off my skin.

Thorne sounded pretty confident about getting him. Something in his voice made me think that whoever did this is going to be sorry when Thorne gets hold of him.

Said he was going to make him tell him why he'd done it. I'm not sure that knowing why's going to make me feel better, really. Getting him will, though. Thorne said he didn't know how much I could remember. Neither do I.

But if it's going to help catch this bastard, I'm going to fucking well find out.

EIGHTEEN

12 February 1999. His mother died.

3 September 1994. Jan left him for the first time.

18 June 1985. Calvert . . .

As Thorne drove towards Camden this Tuesday lunchtime, he had no idea that the following day, 2 October 2000, would be another date to add to the list. Perhaps the most significant day of them all. Days that he would choose to forget, but that he would have little choice about remembering.

Days that formed him. Long, long days. Painful days. Days that had taught him something about who he'd been up to that point, and dictated who he was going to be from that point on.

What he was going to be.

This day, the eve of it all, had not begun well and would only get worse. The ring had arrived from Edinburgh the night before and had gone straight to the forensic-science laboratory in Lambeth. Thorne was on the phone to Edgware Road first thing wanting an update on progress. There had been none, and was unlikely to be before the following day. All he'd received for his trouble had been another earful from Keable, who was getting very nervous. Jeremy Bishop had rung, demanding to know what was going on. James Bishop had done likewise. As yet, with Rebecca Bishop remaining silent, it looked as though Thorne and Holland had got away with the trip to Bristol.

Thorne smiled to himself now, as he steered the car through Regent's Park, past the unfeasibly grand houses of diplomats and oil billionaires. He smiled at his cockiness with Keable, his bluff-calling, his fuck-you attitude with Tughan.

He knew that he was on safe ground. All of it, the calls, the carpet fibres, the visits to Bishop's house, would be forgotten as soon as Thorne had got what he was after.

As soon as he'd proved that Jeremy Bishop was a multiple killer.

Then Keable would be too busy accepting the congratulations of the commander (who'd be smiling for the press and getting patted on the back by a thoroughly delighted commissioner) to worry about a few late-night phone calls. A slap on the wrist, perhaps. A word about procedure, probably. A warning about his methods at the very worst.

As long as the vital evidence was collected cleanly, Thorne knew that he would get a conviction. He knew that the evidence was there. In Jeremy Bishop's house in Battersea. He just needed the warrant.

Thorne had passed a very dull morning in what a football manager (the one at Spurs was still clinging on to his job) would call a free role. In practice, this meant answering the phone a lot, handing bits of paper to Nick Tughan, and resisting the temptation to drive down to the forensics lab and oversee the examination of Bishop's wedding ring himself. Being part of this ponderous machine again was hugely frustrating, but he was happy to do whatever was necessary. And it wasn't going to be for long.

In Camden, Thorne parked the car beneath the enormous Sainsbury's next to the canal. There was no charge for customers and buying a few cans of own-brand lager was a fair exchange for free parking in the middle of the day.

He walked up past the old TV-am building where a crowd of youngsters was gawping at the recording of a show for MTV inside a tiny glass-fronted studio in the car park. He stopped and watched for a few minutes. The presenters, a girl and a boy, were young and good-looking, and for a second he thought they might be the young couple he'd seen in Waterlow Park a few days before.

Ignoring the strange looks from the teenagers around him, he watched them for a while, jigging and posturing in dumbshow behind the glass. Then he ambled away, supposing that he probably knew more about the music they were introducing than they did and headed towards Parkway where he was meeting Hendricks.

The café was cheap and miserable, which Thorne far preferred to expensive and cheerful. It was a place where, over a number of years, the two of them had talked about work and football, while indulging their shared passion for fry-ups and stodgy puddings.

When Thorne arrived Hendricks was already there, nursing a cup of tea and looking somewhat less than pleased to see him. Thorne had news that he knew would cheer the miserable bugger up. He signalled to the woman behind the counter for a tea and slid into the booth, picked up a menu and started to read it. Wanting to make it sound casual.

'I think we've got him.' Hendricks looked up but without real interest. Thorne went on, 'I *know* we have, and as soon as we get the forensic tests done I can get a warrant and—'

'Save it, will you?'

Thorne put down the menu. What little appetite he had was vanishing rapidly.

'Well?' Thorne stared at Hendricks. The pathologist looked at his tea, carried on stirring it. 'You've obviously got something to say?'

Hendricks cleared his throat. He'd been rehearsing it. 'Did it not occur to you, even for a second, that when that slimy jobsworth in the forensics lab called up your boss to tell him that a pathologist had just happened to stroll in carrying a plastic bag with carpet fibres in it –'

'Phil, I was going to—'

'– that he might also be calling *my* boss as well? Did that not occur to you?'

'What happened?'

'Deep shit is what happened. Because I was stupid enough to do you a favour. And you didn't even have the courtesy to pick up the fucking phone to see what was going on.'

He'd meant to, more than once, and hadn't. 'I'm sorry, Phil, there was another killing and—'

'I know there was. I did the PM, remember? And considering what the two of us do for a living I hardly think a body is much of a fucking excuse, do you?'

It wasn't, and Thorne knew it. Hendricks had every right to be angry, but to try to explain to him exactly what he'd been thinking . . . feeling . . . after Margaret Byrne's murder wouldn't have been easy.

'So what happened?'

'The wanker of a clinical director, who's been looking

for an excuse anyway, 'cos I don't look like his idea of a pathologist, hauled me up in front of the chief executive and the personnel director.'

'Fuck . . .'

'Yeah, fuck is right. I was given a verbal warning about inappropriate behaviour and they're still talking about the fucking General Medical Council so don't try asking for any more favours, all right?'

Thorne's tea arrived and he took it gratefully, but Hendricks had no intention of letting him off the hook. 'You're completely self-obsessed, do you know that?' Thorne tried to laugh but nothing came out. 'I'm not talking about this case, I mean all the time. You've got no fucking idea what's going on around you, have you?'

Thorne fixed a defiant smile on his face. 'Am I supposed to be answering these questions or is this a lecture?'

'I couldn't give a toss, I'm just telling you. I'm probably the nearest thing to a friend you've got and we talk about fuck all.' Thorne started to speak but Hendricks cut him off. 'Football and work. That's it. Talking shop or talking shit. We play pool and eat pizza and have a joke and talk about sweet fuck all.'

Thorne decided he should fight his corner. 'Hang on a second. What about you? I spoke to you about Jan when we were splitting up, I know I did. You never confide in me about anything.'

'What would be the point?'

'You've never said a word about family, or girlfriends.' Hendricks laughed harshly. Thorne looked at him. 'What?'

'I'm gay, you dickhead. Queer as fuck. OK?'

For reasons he couldn't quite explain, Thorne blushed deeply.

Half a minute passed. He looked up from his tea. 'Why the hell not tell me then? Worried I'd think you fancied me?'

Hendricks laughed again but neither of them was finding anything funny. 'I couldn't tell you. Not . . . you. Everybody else knows.'

'What? Why didn't they say something, then?'

'Not at *work*.' Hendricks's voice was raised. Thorne stared past him, ashamed, to the woman behind the counter who smiled at nothing in particular. 'I mean everybody I care about. My family, my real friends . . . Christ, it's fairly obvious to most people. What do I look like, for fuck's sake? You're so . . . shielded. You couldn't see it because it doesn't affect you. You've got blinkers on and I'm fucking sick of it!'

Anne had slammed down the phone and smoked three cigarettes, one after the other. Now she felt nauseous as well as furious. She marched towards the coffee machine in main reception, going over and over it . . .

She'd called Thorne on his mobile, and although she had no idea where he was or what he was doing, it was obviously putting him in an awful mood.

Now he'd passed it on to her.

They hadn't spoken since Sunday. She'd known then that something important was happening on the case and this feeling had distilled into something else when she'd seen him on the televised press conference.

Something like dread.

She could sense something coming. She could feel the chill, as if a vast shadow were beginning to creep over them. Over all of them – herself, Thorne, Jeremy. She'd reached for the phone needing some reassurance, a tender word. She'd wanted to give those things to *him* too, knowing that he might need them.

And all she'd got was a diatribe. He'd told her, no . . . he'd *ordered* her to stay away from Jeremy Bishop. He assured her it was for her own protection, not that he really believed that she'd be in any physical danger. It was just . . . best. *Best*, he'd said. He explained how he'd tried to keep off the whole subject until now to spare her feelings and to avoid a possible conflict of interests, but now things were coming to a head so he'd decided to get everything out in the open.

Bollocks!

He'd avoided the subject until he'd got into her knickers and now he was laying down the law. She was having none of it and had told him so in no uncertain terms.

The coffee machine was repeatedly rejecting a twenty-pence piece. She carried on putting in the coin, picking it out and putting it in again.

Things had got pretty heated, especially when she'd heard the tell-tale sound of a can being opened. Wherever he was, he was drinking. This, bearing in mind the supposed gravity of what he was telling her – the seriousness of the situation he was trying to make her aware of – annoyed her beyond belief. How fucking dare he?

Then he'd asked her if she could come over tonight.

She smashed the heel of her hand against the front of the coffee machine . . .

It was then that she'd hung up.

Giving up on the coffee, Anne turned and walked back towards the ITU. She had a good mind to go round to Jeremy's tonight. She wouldn't, of course. She'd spend the evening at home with Rachel, if she was in, and drink too much wine and watch something mind-numbing on television, and wonder what Tom Thorne was doing.

And try to keep warm as the shadow grew larger.

The last time he'd stood on this spot, his face had been hidden and his fist wrapped around the end of an iron bar.

Today he had an altogether more subtle message to deliver. He'd rung several times to ensure that the flat was empty, having taken care to withhold his number. He'd smiled each time he'd punched in 141. It was, of course, a trick that Thorne must himself have been familiar with.

Things could not have been going better. The excitement of the procedure, the surge he felt rushing through him, had been replaced by something else, now that he'd admitted to himself that he might never enjoy another success. A different kind of enjoyment, fuelled by a very different purpose.

The enjoyment of the game with Thorne.

The game had been a part of it all from the beginning. A vital part of it. It had gone cheek by jowl with – he smiled – his more hands-on work. It had complemented it, cast a light upon it, put it beautifully into context.

And he had played the game extremely well.

As he moved towards the front door, he wondered if, secretly, Thorne was enjoying it too. He suspected he probably was. There was something in the man's eyes.

He looked around casually and knocked on the door. Just a man of the world paying a visit to a friend. Nobody in? A note would do the trick . . .

He removed a gloved hand from his trouser pocket and reached into his jacket for the envelope. Yes, a different kind of enjoyment. It was not wrapping fingers around a pulsing artery, but he enjoyed its . . . delicacy nevertheless. Popping open a letterbox provided a different kind of thrill from that he garnered when feeling an ordinary life float away under his touch. But, in context, a thrill nevertheless.

The end of the game was in sight.

One way or another, this will all be over soon . . .

He was enjoying it so much, it was almost a shame to let Thorne win.

The car park was starting to empty. Thorne decided it was time to leave. He'd now been sitting in his car for over four hours, during which time he'd drunk six cans of supermarket-strength lager.

He'd never felt more sober.

After his meeting with Phil Hendricks he'd wandered back towards the car in something of a daze. He'd popped into the supermarket to pick up the beer, read the paper, and then sat, listening to the radio, drinking, and mulling over what his friend had said. *Friend?* Had he got any friends?

He knew that Hendricks was right. Everything he'd said was spot on. So he'd thought about it for a while, let one can of beer quickly become four, then turned a bad day into a fucking awful one by deciding to ring Anne.

Where had the caution of the day before gone? He'd decided then that it was probably wise to steer clear of any confrontation until the case had broken. So why, in God's name, had he rung her and told her to stay away from Bishop?

There had been something almost boastful about it.

Some part of him had wanted to flaunt this . . . victory. It was becoming about something more than cracking a case and stopping a killer. It was starting to feel like *defeating* a killer. Like besting a rival. He'd as good as picked up the phone and said, 'Stand back, this isn't going to be pretty.' It was proprietorial.

He wanted her to know how good he was. How right he'd been.

She told him she thought he was pathetic. Fucking pathetic.

He'd hurled his phone into the back of the car, turned up the radio and polished off the last two cans.

Now it was dark outside. The supermarket would be closing soon. The security guard who patrolled the underground car park was starting to give him decidedly dirty looks and mutter into his radio.

Thorne realised that he was starving. Six cans of lager was all that had passed his lips since breakfast. He knew he should leave the car where it was and head for the tube. He was only one stop away from home. Christ, he could walk home in about ten minutes.

Thorne started the engine, pulled out of the car park and pointed the Mondeo south, away from home, and towards the centre of town.

Nobody could say I wasn't comfortable. That's the word hospitals always use, isn't it? When you ring up to ask after someone. They're 'comfortable'. Like they're lying there on feather pillows being massaged or something. Well, I'm certainly comfortable with my state-of-the-art mattress and my remote-control bed and my telly and my magazine holder.

Comfortable.

And all I really want to do is scream until my throat is raw. I want to scream and yell and, maybe it's asking a bit much, but I'd like to punch somebody in the face as hard as I can and smash a few things up as well, if that's all right. Break things. Mirrors. Glass things. Feel blood on my knuckles, anything . . .

Do I sound frustrated? Well, I am. Frustrated.

So. FUCKING. FRUSTRATED!

There's stuff I want to say, to talk about and I've got less chance of doing it now than I had even a week ago. Now that I'm wired up to this superannuated fucking accordion again.

Since I found out why I'm the way I am, since I was told that somebody planned *this, I've been trying to remember. Trying so hard to remember. Something that might help. Anything that might help them get the bastard.*

Now there's some stuff in my head that I know isn't a dream or anything I've imagined. I don't know whether it will help. It'll help me *for sure.*

It's memory and it's fighting to come out.

Memory about what happened after the hen party. It's not so much pictures as words. Actually, not even words. It's sounds. I'm hearing words but it's like they're being spoken to me under water. They're distorted and I can't quite make them out but I can guess the sense of them. I can make out the tone.

Soon I'm going to work out exactly what the words are.

They're the words he said while he was doing it. The man who put me in here.

NINETEEN

A quarter to midnight and Tower Records was heaving. Dozens of late-night shoppers mingled with those who were just there to listen to the music or read the magazines or kill time.

The young man behind the till didn't even look up. 'Yeahcan'elpyou?'

'Yes, I'd like to pay for these, please,' said Thorne, 'and there's a Waylon Jennings import I'd like to order.'

James Bishop reddened furiously. 'What the fuck do you want? I shouldn't even be talking to you.'

Thorne dumped three CDs on to the counter in front of Bishop and fumbled for his wallet. He stared at Bishop until, with a face clouded by resentment, he began picking up the CDs, removing the security tags and running them through the till. He wouldn't look at Thorne, but instead glanced nervously towards his colleagues, thrusting the CDs clumsily into a plastic bag, trying to get it all over as quickly as possible.

Thorne leaned on the counter, waving his credit card. 'What's the matter? Don't want your workmates knowing you've got a friend who buys Kris Kristofferson albums? I did want to get the new Fatboy Slim single but you've sold out.'

Bishop took the credit card, swiped it, and glared at Thorne. 'You're not my friend. You're just a wanker!'

'I don't suppose it's worth asking for the staff discount?'

'Fuck you.'

Thorne shook his head sadly. 'I knew I should have gone to Our Price . . .'

An assistant with a silver spike through his lower lip ambled over. 'Is everything all right, Jim?'

Bishop thrust the plastic bag at Thorne. 'It's fine.' He looked over Thorne's shoulder to the girl waiting behind him. 'Yeahcan'elpyou?'

Thorne didn't move. 'When does your shift finish?'

The girl behind him tutted impatiently. Bishop looked at him with a defiant half-smile. He glanced at the enormous blue G-Shock on his wrist. 'Fifteen minutes. And?'

Thorne pointed towards the door. 'And I'll see you in Dunkin' Donuts. I'd recommend the cinnamon, but it's entirely up to you . . .'

Twenty minutes later, Thorne was just finishing his second coffee and his fourth doughnut when James Bishop strolled in and sat down next to him. He was wearing a red Puffa jacket and the same black woolly hat he'd been wearing in the shop. Thorne took another doughnut and pushed the box towards him. Bishop pushed it back. 'Suit yourself,' Thorne said. Bishop stared at him. 'I've not eaten all day. Do you want coffee?'

Bishop shook his head. Again the strange half-smile. 'So what is it, then? Do you want to know if my dad's flipped out yet, is that it? If you keeping him awake half the night with stupid phone calls is affecting his work? Maybe costing someone their life? Pretty fucking irresponsible, wouldn't you say?'

Thorne stared at him for a few seconds, chewing. 'So has he?'

'Has he what?'

'Flipped out.'

'Jesus . . .' Bishop took out a packet of Marlboro. Thorne's eyes drifted away to the left and Bishop followed them to the no-smoking sign on the wall. He threw the packet on to the table.

'He's pissed off that you're doing it and even more pissed off that you're getting away with it. None of us are going to let it go, you know. Whatever happens, we'll keep making a fuss until you're back in fucking uniform.'

Thorne considered, for a second or two, the uncomplicated life of the woodentop. Domestics. D and D. Traffic. He wouldn't wish it on his worst enemy.

'None of the things that you and your father are accusing me of is against the law, James.'

'Don't hide behind the law, that's pathetic. Especially when you've got no respect for it.'

'I respect the important bits of it.'

'You're not a copper, Thorne, you're a stalker.'

Thorne took a napkin and slowly wiped the sugar from around his mouth. 'I'm just doing my job, James.'

Bishop was agitated. Had been since he'd walked in. Chewing his nails one second, drumming his fingers on the table the next. One part of his body always moving or twitching. Feet kicking, arms stretching. He was jittery. Thorne wondered if he had a drug problem. He didn't find it hard to believe. If he did it was almost certainly funded by his father. Maybe the doctor prescribed something . . .

Another very good reason for wanting to protect him.

'Your sister thinks that you only pretend to be close to your father so that you can keep sponging off him.'

'She's a silly cunt.' Spitting the words out.

Thorne was shocked, but did his best not to show it. 'You do fairly well out of him, though?'

'Look, he gave me a car and he helped with the deposit on my flat, all right?' Thorne shrugged. 'This is nothing to do with money. He's upset and that makes me upset, it's as simple as that. He's my father.'

'So he's not capable of . . . wickedness?' Thorne had no idea why he'd used that particular word. While he was wondering where it had come from, James Bishop was staring at him as if he'd just dropped down to earth from another planet.

'He's my *father*.'

'So you protect him at all costs?'

'Against the likes of you, yeah . . . using the law to act out a vendetta because he happens to have treated some woman who got attacked by the man you're after and because you're shagging somebody he once had a thing with. I'll protect him against that.'

'It's my job to get at the truth, and if that upsets people sometimes, then that's tough.'

Bishop scoffed. 'Christ, you really think you're a hard man, don't you? Part misunderstood copper and part vigilante. I'd call you a dinosaur but they had bigger brains . . .' He stood up and turned to go.

Thorne stopped him. 'So what sort of copper would you be, James? What do you think it should be about?'

Bishop turned and thrust his hands deep into the pockets of his jacket. He sniffed, pursing lips that were the same as his father's. Thorne could see the small boy hiding just beneath the arrogant posturing. 'What about justice?' Bishop sneered. 'I had the stupid idea that was fairly fucking important.'

Thorne pictured a young girl, in a bed with a pale pink quilt, trapped inside a body growing frail and flabby from lack of use. He pictured a face, the features partly shadowed, staring down at him from the second floor of a large house. Now he stared back, hard, at those same perfect features, set in the younger face of the man to whom they'd been passed on. 'Oh, it is, James. Very important . . .'

Thorne followed him to the door. 'Can I drop you anywhere?' Bishop shook his head and stared out of the doorway at the huge stream of people still flowing round Piccadilly Circus in the early hours of a cold October morning. Without a word he stepped into it, and was immediately gone.

Thorne stood for a few seconds, watching the red Puffa jacket disappearing into the distance, before turning and heading in the opposite direction to pick up his car.

Thorne stopped when he saw the shape in the doorway.

He froze when it began to move.

He breathed out, relieved, when the shape revealed itself to be the somewhat wobbly figure of Dave Holland. Thorne's first thought was that he'd been hurt. 'Jesus, Dave . . .' He moved quickly, reaching to gather up the DC by the arms, and then he smelt the booze.

Holland stood up. Not paralytic, but well on the way. 'Sir . . . been sitting waiting for you. You've been ages . . .'

Thorne had given up the whisky a long time ago, at the same time as the fags, but it was still a smell he'd recognise anywhere. Instinctively he reeled from it, just needing a second or two. It was a smell that could overpower him. Pungent and pathetic. The smell of need. The smell of misery. The smell of *alone*.

Francis John Calvert. Whisky, piss and gunpowder. And freshly washed nightdresses.

The smell of death in a council flat on a Monday morning.

Holland stood, leaning against the wall, breathing too loudly. Thorne reached into the pocket of his leather jacket for his keys. 'Come on, Dave, let's get inside and I'll make some coffee. How did you get here anyway?'

'Taxi. Left the car . . .'

There was really no point in asking *where* Holland had left his car. They could sort it out later. The key turned in the lock. Thorne nudged open the front door with his foot, instinctively turning the bunch of keys in his hand, feeling for the second key that would open the door to his flat.

There was a white envelope lying on the doormat in the communal hallway.

Thorne looked at it and thought: There's another note from the killer.

Not 'What's that?' or 'That's odd' or even 'I wonder if . . .?'. He knew what it was immediately and said as much. Holland sobered up straight away.

Thorne knew that neither the envelope nor the note inside it would trouble a forensic scientist greatly. They would be clean – not a print, not a fibre, not a stray hair. But he still took the necessary precautions. Holland held down the envelope with fingers wrapped in kitchen towel while Thorne used two knives to improvise as tongs and remove the piece of paper.

The envelope had not been sealed. Thorne would

probably have steamed it open anyway, but the killer had left nothing to chance. He'd wanted his note read straight away. By Thorne.

He used the knives to flatten the paper out. The note was neatly typed like the others. Thorne knew it was only a matter of time before the typewriter it had been written on was being wrapped up, labelled and loaded into the back of a Forensic Science Services van.

This would be Jeremy Bishop's last note.

TOM,

I HAD CONSIDERED SOMETHING DIFFERENT, AN E-MAIL PERHAPS, BUT I'M GUESSING THAT YOU'RE SOMETHING OF A LUDDITE AS FAR AS ALL THAT'S CONCERNED. SO, INK AND PARCHMENT IT IS.

CONGRATULATIONS ON THE TV PERFORMANCE BY THE WAY, VERY INTENSE. DID YOU MEAN WHAT YOU SAID ABOUT IT ALL BEING OVER SOON, OR WAS THAT JUST HOT AIR FOR THE CAMERAS? THERE'S NOTHING LIKE CONFIDENCE, IS THERE? OR ARE YOU JUST TRYING TO MAKE ME JITTERY IN THE HOPE THAT I'LL MAKE A MISTAKE?

ONE QUESTION . . .

WHAT I WAS WONDERING IS, WHAT WAS IT LIKE FINDING HER? BEING THE FIRST ONE THERE? WAS THAT YOUR FIRST TIME, TOM?

YOU GET USED TO BLOOD, DON'T YOU?

ANYWAY, IF YOU'RE RIGHT, I SUPPOSE I'LL SEE YOU VERY SOON.

REGARDS . . .

Holland slumped on to the settee. Thorne read the note a second time. And a third. The arrogance was breathtaking.

There seemed no great point to it. There was no revelation or announcement. It was all . . . display.

He went into the kitchen, flicked on the kettle and swilled out a couple of coffee-cups. Why did Bishop feel the need to do this? Why was he *baiting* him about Maggie Byrne, when Thorne had so clearly risen to the bait a long time ago?

He spooned in the instant coffee.

There was something skewed about the tone of the note that Thorne couldn't put his finger on. Something almost forced. Maybe the killer was starting to lose the control he had over everything. Maybe his latest failure had tipped him over the edge. Or maybe he was starting to work towards the insanity plea he would obviously try to cop when the time came.

And the time was most certainly coming.

He stirred the drinks. There was nothing artificial about the madness. Nobody sane could do as this man had done, but still Thorne would fight tooth and nail to prevent it cushioning his fall.

He wanted him to fall hard.

There would be pressure, of course, from those who would want to treat his illness, to care for him. There were always those. There were always plenty for whom violent death was a hobby, or a study option or a gravy train. The lunatics who would write to him inside with requests for advice, or signed pictures, or offers of marriage. The campaigners. The writers of books – bestsellers before the bodies had started to decompose. The makers of films. The old women with pastel hair hammering on the side of the van, spitting . . .

And the policemen who remembered the smell of the blood.

Was that your first time?

Thorne carried the coffee into the living room, but stopped in the doorway the second he looked at Holland, who was sitting on the settee and staring at the wall opposite. It was not the faraway look of drunkenness, or tiredness, or boredom.

Thorne felt his heartbeat increase.

He hadn't asked why Holland had come here in the first place.

Holland turned to him. 'We were trying to get hold of you . . .'

Thorne remembered his phone, chucked into the back of his car. 'What's happened, Dave?'

Holland tried to shape an answer and now Thorne recognised the look. He'd seen it fifteen years before, in the bottom of glasses and in shop windows and in mirrors. The look of a young man who's seen far too much death.

Holland spoke, his voice, his eyes, his expression dead. 'Michael and Eileen Doyle . . . Helen Doyle's mum and dad. The next-door neighbour noticed the smell.'

Apparently, the stroke affected only a very small part of my brain. In the brainstem.

The 'inferior pons' this particular bit's called, if you can believe that.

It's just unfortunate that it happens to be the bit that controls things. All the communications pass through it. If your brain's Paddington station, this bit's the signal box. Basically, the signals still get waved or switched on or whatever. When I want to wiggle a toe or sniff or speak, the instruction still goes out. This thing called a relay cell is supposed to make it happen: it fires the signal down the line to the next cell and then the next one. It's like a microscopic version of 'pass it on' all the way to my toe or my nose or wherever. Unfortunately, somewhere in the middle, some of the cells aren't playing the game properly and that's the end of that. In layman's terms, this is me.

Bizarrely, though, as one part of my brain is fucked, it feels like other parts are compensating and changing. The bit that deals with sound. It feels like that bit's been upgraded. I can distinguish between sounds that are very similar. I can place a nurse by the squeak of her shoe and tell how far away things are. The sounds give me a picture in my head, like I'm turning into a bat.

And it's helping me to remember.

Those underwater sounds are getting clearer every day. Words are sharpening up. I can make out a lot of what we said to each other now, me and the man who put me in hospital.

Fragments of a soundtrack.

A lot of it's me, of course, no real surprise there, waffling on about the party and the wedding and stuff. Christ, I sound very pissed. I can hear the champagne going down my throat and I can hear him laughing at my dismal, drunken jokes.

I hear myself playing with the front-door keys. Inviting him inside to finish the drink. Slurred and stupid words. Words that are hardly worth remembering. The last words ever to come out of my mouth.

I'm still groping for the words that came out of his.

TWENTY

As Thorne drove towards the Edgware Road, he found himself fighting to stay awake. The noise of six empty beer cans, rattling around in the footwell, was helping, but it was still a struggle. It had been a long night, and a bleak one. Not even the spectacle of Holland on the phone that morning, squirming and looking pained as he tried sheepishly to explain to Sophie where he'd spent the night, had raised the spirits.

They'd talked long into the night. Holland told Thorne what had happened to Michael and Eileen Doyle. They'd done it with tablets. The police had been called to the house on Windsor Road by a neighbour. She'd presumed they'd gone away to stay with relatives after what had happened to Helen.

A PC found them in an upstairs bedroom. They were holding hands.

In spite of what Holland had already had to drink, Thorne dug out a few cans and they'd sat up talking about everything and nothing. Parents, partners, the job. As the drink met the tiredness head on, Holland had started to drift off, and Thorne began to ramble vaguely about the girls. About Christine and Susan and Madeleine. And Helen. He didn't say anything about their voices. He didn't mention how strange he found it that he never heard the voice of Maggie Byrne.

Thorne wondered if Holland heard it. He never asked him.

The note lay beside him on the passenger seat, safely wrapped up. He saw himself handing it over in exchange for a warrant. He heard himself reading Jeremy Bishop his rights. He pictured himself leading the good doctor away, down the front path, past his terracotta pots full of dead and dying flowers.

Then he arrived at work and it all fell apart.

'They couldn't get a thing. Sorry, Tom.'

Keable did look sorry. But not as sorry as Thorne. They'd been waiting for him, Keable and Tughan, to fuck him up the second he stepped out of the lift.

'A ring's a difficult enough thing to print anyway by all accounts. A small surface area. This one was just a mess. Dozens of partials but nothing worth writing up. We even sent it over to the Yard. SO3 have got better equipment, but —'

'What about dead skin on the inside? Hairs from a finger?' Thorne was trying to sound reasonable.

Tughan shook his head. 'The bloke I spoke to said it was a forensic nightmare. It's been up and down the country, for Christ's sake, handled by God knows how many people.'

Thorne slumped back against the lift doors and felt fury fighting a battle with tiredness for control of him. 'Did you at least check the hallmark? Check it and you'll find out that ring was made the same year Bishop got married.'

Keable nodded but Tughan was in no mood to humour Thorne. 'Listen, even if we do get something, the chain of evidence is non-existent.'

The fury won the battle. 'And whose fault is that? This has been one huge fuck-up from start to finish. I should have had a warrant by now. I should be tearing that bastard's house apart. This case should be over by now – over.'

Tughan moved back towards his desk. 'It was only ever a slim possibility, Tom. We knew that even if you didn't. What were you planning to do anyway? Slip it on to Bishop's finger like a fucking glass slipper?'

Thorne waited until Tughan's self-indulgent chuckle had finished. 'How are you planning to spend the money the newspaper paid you, Nick?'

The colour rose immediately to Tughan's hollow cheeks. Keable stared hard at him, then back to Thorne, deciding finally that accusations would be best left until another day. 'Listen, Tom,' Keable said, 'Nobody's more upset about this than me and I'm going to crack some heads, trust me.'

And now Thorne felt the tiredness come rushing at him. He could barely keep his head erect. He closed his eyes. He had no idea how long they'd been closed when Keable next spoke. 'We've got this latest note. It's a significant development.'

'Another press conference?'

'I think it would be a good idea, yes.'

Thorne called the lift back up. Raising his arm and bringing his finger to the button was a struggle. He had an idea now of the effort it took for Alison to blink. He wanted to go home. He had no intention of hanging around and answering phones. He needed to lie down and switch himself off.

One final question: 'Is Jeremy Bishop this investigation's prime suspect?'

Keable hesitated a fraction too long before replying, but Thorne didn't hear the answer anyway, thanks to the roaring in his ears.

He was driving much too fast along the Marylebone Road. The exertion of steering, of concentrating, was leaving him wringing with sweat, which dripped from him as he leaned forward, crippled with exhaustion. It took every last ounce of energy he had to tap out a rhythm on the wheel, as the music exploded from the speakers.

He turned up the volume as high as it would go. He winced. The cheap speakers distorted the sound, turning the treble into shattering glass and the bass into a collision. The music, if it could still be called that, was shaking the car apart, but he would have made it even louder if he could. He wanted to be bludgeoned by the noise. He wanted to be hypnotised.

He wanted to be anaesthetised . . .

He swerved into the inside lane, reached for his phone and pulled up just past Madame Tussaud's.

He flicked on the hazards, turned down the music and hit the speed dial.

A long queue of tourists was standing in the rain, waiting to get in and gawp at the waxy doppelgangers of pop stars, politicians and sportsmen. And, of course, mass murderers: the Chamber of Horrors was always the most popular attraction.

Anywhere.

The violent death gravy train . . .

She picked up.

'It's me . . . I'm sorry about yesterday.'

'OK . . .' Sounding unsure, hedging her bets.

'Look, Anne, everything's changed, fucked up to be honest, and I just wanted to tell you . . .' *Your ex-boyfriend's off the hook.* '. . . the evidence I thought I had hasn't . . . materialised, so just ignore what I said, all right?'

'What about Jeremy?'

'Can I see you later?'

'Is he still a suspect?'

This time it was Thorne's turn to hesitate too long before replying.

'Can you come over later?'

'Listen, Tom, I won't say I'm not pleased because I am. I'm sorry about yesterday too, though . . .'

In the background Thorne could hear a doctor being paged. He waited until it had finished. 'Anne . . .'

'I'll be over about five-ish. I'm on call tonight so I'll sneak away from here early. All right?'

It was very all right.

He'd legislated for some ineptitude. There had been a little *give* built into his thinking. But this was way beyond anything he'd imagined.

Fucking morons. Stupid fucking idiots.

It was stupid to expect any kind of equilibrium, he knew that, but this kind of unpredictability was so *fucking* annoying.

He'd started to feel the depression take hold again the second he'd put the phone down, wrapping itself around him, like a dark, itchy blanket. Making him scratch. Making him smell.

He walked up and down in straight lines. Up one board and down the other. Moving slowly across the room in vertical lines. Up one, his bare feet cool against the bleached floorboards. Down the other, his toes caressing each knot and whorl of the beautifully smooth wood. Up and down, his fingers stroking the straight, puckered lines that ran across his stomach.

Up and down, his breathing slowing, the white walls soothing . . .

He could roll with the punches. He was adaptable, wasn't he? Champagne or IV. His place or theirs. Hen nights or night buses. Whatever was necessary. This would not be the perfect way to end it but it would certainly do the trick. His plan, of course, the magic-island scenario, the beautiful by-product of his medical work, had involved a little suffering spread out over a very long time. A lot of suffering, *quickly*, might prove just as enjoyable.

He picked up the phone to call her back. She'd be happy he'd called. She'd be thrilled with the invitation. Excited at the hint of what the evening might hold in store. Not as excited as he was, obviously, but then he knew just how good it was really going to be.

Time to get proactive.

Time to find a different way of hurting.

Anne managed to get away from Queen Square even earlier than she'd thought, but by the time she got to the flat, around four, Thorne had already spent the best part of six hours bouncing off the walls.

He'd tried going to bed but it was pointless. Every

muscle screamed out for sleep but his brain wasn't listening. There was a force in him that was now directionless, an energy desperately seeking an outlet. Though his body felt as weary as it had ever felt, his mind was racing. It roared and rumbled and skidded and slipped from its track, then spun around and roared away again.

He could confront Bishop with the ring.

Tell him that they'd found incriminating evidence.

Plant the fucking evidence . . .

He could beat a confession out of him. Christ, it would be good to feel the bones in that face shatter beneath his pounding fists and not stop hitting until Bishop hovered somewhere between life and death and felt what it was like to be Alison Willetts . . .

'*Whatever it takes, Tommy.*'

'*Helen, I'm so sorry about . . .*'

'*It's all right, Tommy. Just get him. You* can *still get him, can't you?*'

Part of him imagined that Anne would come and kiss it all away, fuck it all away, and he would go to sleep and wake up cleansed.

And that was almost how it happened.

She bounded into his living room like a teenager, and the first smile of his day made his face ache. She told him to lie down and went to make them both tea.

He'd told her once that he didn't want a mother. Right now he wasn't arguing.

She brought the drinks through to the living room. 'You sounded a bit manic when you called.'

He grunted. When she pulled away the cushion he was holding across his face, she was relieved to see that he was grinning.

'How do you feel?'

'Like I've taken uppers and downers, hundreds of them.'

She handed him his tea. 'Have you ever?'

Thorne shook his head. 'Booze and fags. Honest working-class drugs.'

'The most dangerous of them all.'

He sipped his tea, staring at the ceiling. 'What I need, I reckon, is about six weeks in one of those nice, cosy rooms you've got on ITU. Just drug me up and lay on some nice, sexy doctor to minister to my needs. Is the room next to Alison available? Do they have Sky? I'll pay, obviously . . .'

Anne laughed and lowered herself into the armchair. 'I'll let you know when we've got one free.'

'How is she? I didn't know she was back on the ventilator.' Anne looked at him questioningly. 'I went in to see her the other day. You were in a meeting, I think.'

'I know. She seemed a little distracted afterwards . . .'

He ignored the implied question. 'Is she any better?'

Anne shook her head, and for the first time felt tired herself. 'She's always going to be prone to infections of this sort. Two steps forward . . .'

A dance with which Thorne was all too familiar.

Anne raised an eyebrow. 'What did you say to Alison?' Remembering the last time. The photograph he'd kept hidden.

Thorne laughed. A splutter of self-disgust. 'I went to let her know I was about to arrest Jeremy Bishop.'

The small-talk had lasted about as long as the tea.

The silence that fell between them was in danger of becoming terminal when Anne spoke quietly, not looking at him: 'Why did you think it was him, Tom?'

Did? Past tense. Not for Thorne.

'It started with the drugs theft obviously. Then the connection to Alison and lack of an alibi for the other killings. The physical description, and the car . . .' He sighed heavily, pushing finger and thumb hard into his eyes and rubbing. 'It's all academic. I've got no evidence and no warrant to go and get any.'

'What did you think you'd find?'

'Typewriter maybe. The drugs probably. Unless he kept them at the hospital, which . . .'

Anne was suddenly on her feet, pacing around the room. 'You keep going on about these drugs but it just doesn't make any sense. Why the hell would he need to steal drugs in those quantities, Tom? Jeremy works with this stuff every day of his life. If he'd wanted to, he could have taken as much as he liked without anyone ever getting suspicious. He could pocket an ampoule, even a couple, every day for six months and nobody would ever notice. So why draw attention to himself by stealing a huge quantity all in one go? It's only when drugs go missing in those amounts that it's even registered. Jeremy would not have needed to do that, Tom.'

And boom! There it was. The tune he'd been unable to place. *That* had been what was bothering him all along, lurking at the back of his brain, slippery and elusive. She was right, of course. Why had none of them ever really sat down and spoken to a fucking doctor? How could they have missed it? How could *he* have missed it?

Easy: he hadn't wanted it to be there.

Hendricks: *You've got blinkers on and I'm fucking sick of it.*

He felt like the breath had been taken from him. Beaten

out of his body. Christ, it was all coming apart in front of him.

'I'm sorry, Tom.'

He closed his eyes. Screwed them shut. He knew it wasn't Anne who should be apologising. There were people *he* needed to say sorry to.

The first time he'd laid eyes on him, he thought he'd looked like the doctor from *The Fugitive*. *That* doctor had been innocent as well.

'I got *thinking* it was him and *wanting* it to be him mixed up, I think . . .'

'Ssssh . . .' She was kneeling beside the settee, stroking his hair.

'It got too personal. There wasn't enough distance.'

'Tom, it doesn't matter now. Nobody was hurt.'

'I was so sure, Anne. So sure Calvert was the killer . . .' He felt her hand stop moving. Shook his head. Tried to laugh it off.

Slip of the tongue.

'*Bishop*, I mean. Bishop.'

'Who's Calvert?'

Whisky, piss and gunpowder. And freshly washed night-dresses. Oh, fuck, no . . .

'Tom, who's Calvert?'

Then the tears came. And he dredged it all up, every heartstopping, malodorous moment of it. For the first time in fifteen years he took himself back completely. Jan never had the time or the stomach for all of it but now he was going to skip nothing. No edited highlights with a warning for those of a sensitive nature.

Thorne fought to bring the sobbing under control.

Then he told her.

TWENTY-ONE

Friday, 15 June 1985. Nearly going-home time.

It's a big one. The biggest since the Ripper. Fifteen thousand interviews in eighteen months and they've got nothing. The press are going mental, but not *that* mental, obviously. It's not like he's killing women or straight blokes, after all. Just the right amount of moral outrage with a smattering of self-righteousness and occasional comments about 'the risks inherent in choosing that kind of lifestyle'.

No lurid nicknames, though if the *Sun* could have got away with 'Poof Killer' they would certainly have used it.

Just 'Johnny Boy'.

The fourth victim had told a friend he was meeting a man called John for a drink. This was an hour or so before his heart was cut out and his genitals were removed. An approximation of what might be Johnny Boy's face stares down from the wall of every nick in the country. He's got dirty-blond hair and a sallow complexion. His eyes are blue and very, very cold.

It's a big one.

Detective Constable Thomas Thorne leans against the wall of the interview room at Paddington station and stares at a man with dirty-blond hair and blue eyes.

Francis John Calvert. Thirty-four. Self-employed builder from North London.

'Any chance of a fag? I'm fucking gasping . . .' Calvert smiles. A winning smile. Perfect teeth.

Thorne says nothing. Just watching him until DI Duffy comes back.

'Surely I'm allowed one poxy fag?' The film-star smile fading just a little.

'Shut up.'

Then the door opens and Duffy comes back in. The interview resumes and Tom Thorne doesn't say another word.

None of it is riveting stuff. Duffy is way past his best. It's purely routine anyway. Calvert is only there because of what he does.

A week before he died, the third victim told a flatmate that he'd met a man in a club. The man had said he was a builder. The flatmate made a joke about tool-kits and builders' bumcrack. Seven days and one body later, the joke wasn't funny any more but the flatmate remembered what his dead friend had said.

Thousands and thousands of builders to be interviewed. Some are seen at their home. Some are questioned at their place of work. Calvert gets a phone call and comes into Paddington for a chat.

Later, of course, it will emerge that he'd been chatted to before.

Duffy and Calvert get on like a house on fire. Duffy gives Calvert his fag.

He wants to get home.

Thorne wants to get home too, he's been married less than a year. He's only got one ear on the answers Calvert reels off.

At home with his wife . . . three little girls are a right handful . . . wishes he could *go out at night gallivanting about . . . not to* those *sort of places obviously. Another flash of that smile. He's helpful, concerned. Wife only too happy to talk to you if you want. He hopes they find this nutter and string him up. It doesn't matter what these pervs get up to in their private lives, what this killer's doing's disgusting . . .*

Duffy hands Calvert the short statement to sign and that's that. Another one crossed off the list. He thanks him.

One of these days they'll strike it lucky.

Duffy stands and heads for the door. 'Show Mr Calvert out, would you, Thorne?' The DI leaves to begin the tedious process of writing it all up. The investigation is awash with paperwork. There are distant rumblings about the arrival of computers that, one day, will simplify all this. But that's all they are. Distant rumblings.

Thorne holds open the door and Calvert steps out into the corridor. He strolls casually past more interview rooms, hands in pockets, whistling. Thorne follows. He can hear a distant radio, probably in the locker room, playing one of his favourite songs – 'There Must Be An Angel' by the Eurythmics. Jan bought the record for him last week. He wonders what she'll have organised for dinner. Maybe he can go and get a takeaway.

Through the first set of swing doors and a left turn along another corridor, which sweeps round towards main reception. Calvert waits, allowing Thorne to catch up. He holds the doors for him. 'Bet you lot are making a fucking mint in overtime.'

Thorne says nothing. He can't wait to see the back of the cocky little fucker. Past another Johnny Boy poster. Somebody's drawn a speech bubble. It says, 'Hello, sailor.' Thorne's humming the Eurythmics song as he walks.

Then the final set of doors. The desk sergeant gives Thorne a nod. Thorne steps ahead of Calvert, pushes open the doors and stops. This is as far as he goes. This isn't a hotel and he isn't a fucking concierge. Calvert steps through the doors, stops and turns. 'Cheers, then . . .'

'Thanks for your help, Mr Calvert. We'll be in touch if we need anything else.'

Thorne holds out his hand without thinking about it. He's looking towards the desk sergeant, who's trying to catch his eye and mouthing something about a party for one of the secretaries who's leaving. Thorne feels the large, callused hand take his and turns to look at Francis John Calvert.

And everything changes.

It isn't the resemblance to the photofit. He'd registered that the instant he'd clapped eyes on Calvert and forgotten it again moments later. It isn't the resemblance but it *is* the face.

Thorne looks at Calvert's face and knows.

He knows.

It lasts no more than a second or two but it's enough. He can see through to what lies behind those deep, blue eyes, and what he sees terrifies him.

He sees boozing, yes, and football on a Saturday and wolf-whistles with the lads and an incandescent rage that is barely kept in check inside the cosy conformity of a loveless, sexless marriage.

He sees something deep and dark and rotting. Something fetid. Something spilling into the earth and bubbling with blood.

He cannot explain it but he knows beyond a shadow of the smallest doubt that Francis John Calvert is Johnny Boy. He knows that the man in front of him, the man shaking his hand, is responsible for stalking and slaughtering half a dozen gay men in the last year and a half.

Thorne is all but frozen to the spot, not sure how he will ever be able to move. He is rigid with fear. He is going to piss in his trousers any second. Then he sees the most terrifying thing of all.

Calvert *knows* that he knows.

Thorne thinks his face is frozen, expressionless. Dead. Obviously he's wrong. He can see the change in Calvert's eyes as they meet his own. Just a slight flicker. The tiniest twitch . . .

And the smile that is beginning to die a little.

Then it's over. The grip is released and Calvert is moving away through the lobby towards the main station doors. He stops for a second and turns, and now the smile is gone completely. The sergeant is wittering at him about this party but Thorne is watching Calvert walk out of the doors. The look he sees on his face is something like fear. Or perhaps hate.

And, somewhere in the distance, a sweet, high voice is still singing about imaginary angels.

He tells nobody. Not Duffy. None of his mates or fellow officers. What's he supposed to tell them? Certainly not Jan. Her mind's on other things, anyway. They're trying for a baby.

At home with her that weekend, he knows he's distant. On Saturday afternoon as they stroll around Chapel Market she asks if there's anything wrong. He says nothing.

On Sunday night she's keen to make love, but every time he shuts his eyes he sees Francis Calvert, one arm round the neck of the young boy he's kissing deeply, pulling at him, holding the soft mouth against his own. As he groans, and comes inside his young wife, he sees Calvert's other hand, strong and callused, reaching for the eight-inch serrated knife in his pocket.

While Jan sleeps soundly next to him, he lies awake all night. By morning he's convinced himself that he's being stupid and within an hour he's sitting in his car in a small street off Kilburn High Road. Watching Francis Calvert's flat.

Monday 18 June 1985.

He just needs to look at him again, that's all. Once he watches him step out of that front door he'll see him for what he really is. A nasty piece of pondlife for sure, but that's about all. A slimy little shit who's probably been done for driving without insurance, almost certainly doesn't have a TV licence and maybe slaps his wife around.

Not a killer.

One more look and Thorne will know he was being stupid. He'll know that what happened in that corridor was an aberration. What Jan likes to call a mindfuck.

He's here in plenty of time. People in the street haven't started leaving for work yet. Calvert's white Astra van is parked outside his flat.

For the next hour he sits and watches them leave. He watches front doors open up and down the street, spitting out men and women with bags and briefcases. They climb into cars or hop on to bikes or stride away towards buses and tubes.

Calvert's door stays resolutely shut.

Thorne sits and stares at the dirty white van. Letters on the side: F. J. CALVERT. BUILDER.

Butcher . . .

Stupid! He's being so stupid. He needs to start his car and get himself to work, and have a laugh with some of the other lads and maybe help to organise this leaving party and forget he ever met Francis John Calvert, and instead he finds himself walking across the street.

He finds himself knocking on a dirty green front door.

He finds himself starting to sweat when he gets no answer.

In the respectfully muted euphoria of the days to come, before the astonishing truth that Calvert had been interviewed on four separate occasions emerges, before the resignations, before the national scandal . . . there will be words of praise for Detective Constable Thomas Thorne. A young officer using his initiative. Doing his job. Putting any thoughts for his own safety out of his mind.

Out of his mind . . .

It is as if he is watching himself, like a nosy bystander. He has no idea why he tries the front door. Why he leans against it. Why he runs back to his car and takes a truncheon from the boot.

Calvert's wife looks surprised to see him. Her eyes are wide as he walks into her kitchen, breath held, heart thumping. She lies on the floor, her head against the dirty white door of the cupboard underneath the sink. The bruise around her neck is beginning to turn black. She still has a wooden spoon in her hand.

She was the first to die. She had to be. The children would tell him that much.

Denise Calvert. 32. Strangled.

Thorne moves through the flat like a deep-sea diver exploring a wreck. The silence is pounding in his ears. His movements feel slow and oddly graceful, and there are ghosts in the water all around him . . .

He finds them in the small bedroom at the back of the flat. They are laid out next to each other on the floor, between the bunk beds and the small, single mattress.

He cannot take his eyes off the six tiny white feet.

Unable to fill his lungs, he drops to his knees and crawls across the floor. He takes in what he is seeing but there is a blunt refusal to process the information correctly. Grabbing at a breath he lets out a scream. He screams at the dead girls. He pleads with them. *Please . . . you'll be late for school.*

He is actually begging them to save him.

With that breath he smells the shampoo in their hair. He smells the freshly washed nightdresses and the urine that has soaked them. He sees the stain on the mattress on the floor where he must have taken each of them. The girls have been laid out side by side, their arms across their chest in some grotesque approximation of peacefulness.

But they did not die peacefully.

Lauren Calvert. 11. Samantha Calvert. 9. Anne-Marie Calvert. 5. Suffocated.

Three little girls, who screamed and fought and kicked and ran to find their mummy and then screamed even louder – their mother already dead, the only state in which she will allow this horror to be visited upon her children – then the man they love and trust closed the bedroom door, and they fluttered around in a panic, like moths trapped inside a light fitting. They crashed into walls, and clutched each other and when he grabbed one and pulled her down to the mattress on the floor, they bit and scratched and cried, and went somewhere far better with their tiny fingers clawing at the flesh of those strong, callused hands.

Thorne has to believe that. He cannot accept that they smiled at their daddy as he laid the pillow across their faces.

He will not accept that.

It might be thirty minutes later when he finds Calvert. He has no idea how long he's spent in that tiny box room trying to understand. Thinking about Jan. The child they are desperate for.

He pushes open the door to the living room and his senses are immediately bludgeoned. He smells whisky, so strong he almost chokes on it, and the pungent aroma of gunpowder, which until this moment he has only ever known on a firing range.

He sees the body on the floor in front of the hearth.

The brain caked to the mirror above the tiled mantelpiece.

Francis John Calvert. 37. Suicide by gunshot.

Thorne walks across the grimy mushroom-coloured carpet like a sleepwalker. Not looking down as his foot sends an empty whisky bottle clattering into the skirting-board. Not taking his eyes off Calvert. The outstretched arm is still holding the gun. The underpants are brown with congealed blood. When had this happened? Last night or first thing this morning?

The hands are unmarked by small fingers.

Thorne stands above the body, his arms hanging heavy by his sides, his breathing deep and desperate. He leans forward, knowing what's going to happen, amazed considering that he's had no breakfast. The spasm, when it comes, moves swiftly from guts to chest and then throat, and he vomits, steaming, wet and bitter, across what's left of Francis Calvert's face.

'It wasn't your fault, Tom. I know it must have been horrible, but you can't think it happened because of you.'

Thorne lay on the settee and stared at his dull magnolia ceiling. Somewhere in the distance the siren of a fire engine or an ambulance was wailing desperately.

Anne squeezed his hand, feeling like a doctor. She thought quickly of Alison. 'You were right when you thought it was an aberration. You finding them was just a coincidence. A horrible coincidence . . .'

Thorne had no more to say. The tiredness that had been clutching at him all day now had a firm grip and he didn't feel like struggling any more. He craved unconsciousness, a blackness that would see everything he'd remembered and described put back where it belonged. The rusty bolts slammed back into place.

He closed his eyes and let it come.

Anne had kept it together while Thorne was telling his story, willing her face to show nothing, but now she let the tears come. Thinking about the little girls. Thinking about her own daughter's tiny white feet.

It was easy to see what drove this man. What had created this obsession with . . . knowing. She hoped in time that he would see his feelings for Jeremy as no more than phantoms. Distorted echoes of a past horror. She hoped they could all move on.

She would be there to help him.

She shivered slightly. The shadow was still moving across them and its chill gathered at her shoulder. She laid her head on Thorne's chest which, within a few moments, began to rise and fall regularly, in sleep.

The pictures are still fuzzy but the words are clearer now. Like watching a film I've seen before, but since the last time I saw it my eyesight's gone funny and it's all a bit jumpy.

We're in the kitchen. Me and him.

I tell him to put his bag down anywhere and I'm still swigging the champagne and asking him if he wants a cup of coffee or a beer or something. He says nice things about the flat. I grab a can of beer that Tim's left in the fridge. He opens it and I'm still talking about the party. About the wankers in the club. Blokes on the sniff. He's sympathetic, saying he knows what men are like, and that I can hardly blame them, can I?

Music comes in for a few seconds as I turn the radio on, and then some static as I try to tune it in to something good, and then I give up.

He says he needs to make a phone call and he does, but I can't hear him saying anything. He's just muttering quietly. I'm still rabbiting on but I can barely make out what I'm saying now. Just gabbling. Something about starting to feel a bit sick but I don't think he's really listening.

I'm apologising for being so out of it. He must think I'm really fucking sad, slumped on the kitchen floor, leaning against a cupboard, hardly able to speak. Not at all, he says, and I can hear him unzipping his bag. Rummaging inside. There's nothing wrong with having a good time, he says. Going for it.

Fucking right I tell him, but that's not how it comes out of my mouth.

I can hear my shoes squeak across the tiles as he drags me to the other side of the kitchen. My earrings and my necklace clinking as he drops them into a dish.

The groaning noise is me.

I sound like I can't actually speak at all. Can't. Like a baby. Or an old person with no teeth in, and half their brain gone. I'm trying to say something but it's just a noise.

He's telling me to be quiet. Telling me not to bother trying.

His hands are on me now and he's describing everything he's doing. Telling me not to worry and to trust him. Talking me through it. He tells me the names of muscles when he touches them.

Stupid names. Medical.

He catches his breath and then he's quiet for a while. A couple of minutes.

And I can't hear myself saying a single thing about it. Not a word of complaint. Just the drip, drip, drip of my dribble as it spills out of my mouth and plops on to the tiles in front of me.

I can make a sort of gargling sound.

There's a couple of grunts but now the sound starts to fade as I begin to slip away from everything.

Then something important. The last thing I can hear. Three words, echoey and strange as if they're from a long way away. Like he's whispering them to me from the end of a long pipe, like my friend saying hello down the vacuum-cleaner tube when we were kids.

I need to tell this, I think.

He says goodnight. Night-night . . .

It's almost silly, what he says. Sweet-sounding and gentle. A word I've heard again since.

A word I heard when I woke up and was like this.

A word that says pretty much everything about what I am.

TWENTY-TWO

When Thorne woke up it was already dark. He looked at his watch. Just after seven o'clock. He'd been out of it for two and a half hours.

He had no way of knowing it, but two hours more and it would all be over.

Anne had gone. He got up off the settee to make himself coffee and saw the note on the mantelpiece.

Tom,
I hope you're feeling better. I know how hard it was for you to tell me.
You mustn't be afraid to be wrong.
I hope you don't mind but I'm going to see Jeremy tonight to tell him that everything's all right. I think he deserves to feel better too.
Call me later.
Anne. X

He made himself the coffee and read the note again. He *was* feeling better and it was more than just the couple of hours' sleep. Talking about what had happened all those years ago had left him feeling cleaner. *Purged* was probably putting it a little strongly but, considering that his case had gone to shit, he had no friends and he was headed for all manner of trouble with his superiors, he might have felt much worse.

Tom Thorne was resigned.

It wasn't so much that he'd been afraid to be wrong. He hadn't even considered it. Now he had to do a lot more than consider it. He had to live with it.

Anne was going to see Bishop to tell him that he was out of the frame. That was fair enough. He'd never really been *in* the frame, if truth were told. Only in Thorne's thick, thick head. It was time to face a few harsh realities.

Anne was doing a good thing. Bishop deserved to know what was going on. He deserved to know how things stood.

He was not the only one.

Thorne picked up the phone and dialled Anne's number. Maybe he could catch her before she left. Rachel answered almost immediately, sounding out of breath, annoyed and distinctly teenage.

'Hi, Rachel, it's Tom Thorne. Can I speak to your mother?'

'No.'

'Right . . .'

'She's not here. You've just missed her.'

'She's on her way to Battersea, is she?'

Her tone changed from impatience to something more strident. 'Yeah. She's gone to tell Jeremy he's not public enemy number one any more. About time as well, if you ask me.'

Thorne said nothing. Anne had told her. It didn't matter now anyway.

'How long ago did she—'

'I don't know. She's going shopping first, I think. She's cooking him dinner.'

'Listen, Rachel—'

She cut him off. 'Look, I've got to go, I'm going to be late. Call her on the mobile or try her later at Jeremy's. Have you got the number?'

Thorne assured her that he had, then realised she was being sarcastic.

He tried Anne's mobile number but couldn't get connected. Maybe she had it switched off. She wouldn't have a signal anyway if she was on the tube. Then he remembered that she was on call and guessed that she'd probably be driving. He had her bleeper number somewhere . . .

He picked up his jacket. He'd do what Rachel had suggested and get her later at Bishop's. This time he wouldn't have to withhold his number.

It wasn't even that important; he just wanted to ask her how late Alison Willetts could receive visitors.

He was wearing one of the crisp white shirts he knew she liked so much. He'd stared at himself in the full-length mirror as he slowly did up the buttons. Watching the scars disappear beneath the spotless white cotton.

Now he looked at his watch as the car cruised sedately north across Blackfriars Bridge. He was going to be a little late. She would be on time as always.

She was very, very keen.

He was meeting her outside the Green Man as usual. It was a bit of a slog to drive all the way across the river just to turn round and drive back south again, but he'd rather do it this way than let her get on the tube or bus. He wanted to be in control of things. If she was late or missed a bus or something it could throw the timing of everything off.

When he'd told her that they would be going back to his place, he knew that she was thinking, *Oh, my God, tonight's the night.* He could almost smell the rush of teenage oestrogen and hear the cogs in her silly little brain whirring as she tried to decide which perfume to dab between her tits and which knickers would turn him on the most.

Well, yes, it would be a night to remember for certain.

Back at his place.

It might be a little crowded . . .

On the drive to Queen Square, Thorne didn't really need to think. He'd worked out what he was going to say to Alison Willetts. Now he just needed to be a little more relaxed in order to say it.

He popped out the Massive Attack tape and slid in Merle Haggard.

Getting relaxed enough to apologise.

'*Tommy?*'

'*Yes, and to you too.*'

After circling the square for nearly ten minutes, swearing loudly, he double-parked and stuck a dog-eared piece of cardboard with 'Police Business' scrawled on it in the front window of the Mondeo.

The evening was turning chilly. He wished he'd grabbed a warmer jacket on his way out. As he walked quickly towards the hospital's main entrance, he felt the first drops of rain and remembered making this same journey in reverse two months earlier. It seemed a lot longer ago, that day in August when he'd first met Alison Willetts. He'd run through the rain towards his car and found the note. He'd begun to understand the nature of the man he was dealing with.

Today, on the same spot, with the rain starting to fall, Thorne was coming to terms with the fact that he still had no idea who that man was.

Nearly eight o'clock. The latest that Thorne had been inside the hospital. It was a very different place after dark. His steps echoed off century-old marble as he strode through the older part of the building towards the Chandler Wing. There were few people around and those he passed, nurses, cleaners, security staff, looked at him closely. They seemed to be studying his face. He'd never been aware of such scrutiny during the day.

Somewhere in the distance he thought he could hear what sounded like somebody weeping softly. He stopped to listen but couldn't hear it any more.

Even the modern part of the hospital seemed spookier. The lights that normally bounced off the bleached wood in the Medical ITU reception area, had been dimmed. The only sounds were the muted tones of a faraway conversation and the low hum of distant equipment of some sort. It might have been cleaning carpets. It might have been keeping somebody alive.

He looked at the row of payphones in Reception. He'd try Anne again as soon as he'd been to see Alison. He'd forgotten to bring his mobile.

As he walked from the lift, he caught the eye of a woman in the glass-fronted office in Reception. She waved at him and he recognised her as Anne's secretary. He couldn't remember her name. He pointed at the doors and she nodded, signalling at him to go on through. He remembered the three-digit code that opened the heavy wooden doors and stepped through them into the Intensive Therapy Unit.

He let the sister on duty at the nursing station know where he was going and set off down the corridor towards Alison's room. As he walked past the other rooms he realised that he knew nothing about the people inside. He'd never spoken to Anne about her other patients. He presumed that none were suffering in quite the same way as Alison was, but that all had seen their lives changed in a few short seconds. The time it takes to trip on the stairs or mistime a tackle or lose control of a car.

The time it takes for a brain to short-circuit.

He listened at the door of the room opposite Alison's. The same telltale hum of machinery from within, like the lazy throb of a dozing beehive coming slowly to life after a long winter. Whoever lay in the bed inside that room was here by accident. That was the difference.

Thorne turned and moved across to Alison's door. He knocked quietly and reached for the handle.

He gasped as the door was yanked open from the inside and David Higgins all but pushed him back into the corridor.

'She's not here.' Higgins was in his face.

'What?' Thorne tried to push past him into the room.

'You're out of luck, Thorne. Sorry.'

Thorne looked at him, not understanding. Higgins began to raise his voice. 'My fucking wife. My fucking wife, who you are fucking. She. Isn't. Here.'

Thorne could smell Dutch courage.

'I'm not here to see Anne. Move out of the way.'

'Of course. Have fun.'

Higgins took a step to his left but Thorne didn't move, just looked at him. 'What does that mean?' Knowing exactly what it meant but wanting to hear him say it.

'Well, in the absence of the lovely Anne, who doesn't actually enjoy it that much anyway, you might as well . . . make hay with someone who really doesn't have a great deal of say in the matter. Like a blow-up doll with a pulse.'

Thorne had always thought that the accusations about his relationship with Alison were a little cheap for the killer. A little beneath him. Now he knew who had been responsible. The motivation was obvious but Thorne asked anyway. 'Why?'

Higgins swallowed, licked his lips. 'Why not?'

As his right arm bent and swung at speed, Thorne unballed his fist. A slap seemed so much more appropriate. Higgins wasn't man enough to punch.

The hard flat hand caught Higgins across the jaw and ear, sending him sprawling across the highly polished linoleum. He lay still, whimpering like a child.

Without looking at him, Thorne stepped across Higgins's outstretched leg and opened the door to Alison Willetts's room.

The second he looked at her, she began to blink. Once, twice, three times. Thorne realised that she'd heard the noise from outside and was disturbed. Maybe he should call for a nurse. What had Higgins been doing in her room anyway? Probably just looking for Anne, but couldn't he have spoken to someone at reception?

Thorne's mind was racing. He needed to calm down if he was going to be able to say what he came to say.

Alison was still blinking. One blink every three or four seconds.

'It's OK, Alison. Look, I'll try and keep this short. It's about what I said the other day, about being close to him, the man who did this to you . . .'

She was still blinking.

Please, for fuck's sake shut up, and listen. Get the board . . .

'What's the matter?' His eyes darted across to the blackboard, still lying against the wall and covered with a sheet. He looked back at Alison. One blink. Yes.

Yes!

He moved across the room, whipped off the sheet and dragged the blackboard to the foot of the bed.

He knew roughly how the system worked. He hurried to switch off the main light and then, using the remote at the end of the bed, he raised Alison up so that she was nearly sitting. Then he picked up the pointer, switched it on and positioned the small red laser dot beneath the first letter: E. He began to move the pointer slowly along the letters.

Nothing.

Starting to speed up, studying her face, watching for the smallest reaction.

Come on . . . come on . . .

Then a blink. He stopped.

'S? Was that an S, Alison?'

Yes, for Christ's sake! Of course it was! Hurry up.

Move. Wait. Watch. Move. Wait. Watch. Move . . .

Another blink. Thorne was sweating. He threw off his jacket. 'L. Yes? OK, that's S, L. Right.'

Back to the beginning again and . . . a blink. No, two blinks.

'Is that a no to the E, Alison?'

No, it isn't fucking no. Two blinks is usually no but when I'm doing this it means 'repeat'. Didn't Anne tell you any of this?

'Or do you mean two Es? Yes? Right. S, L, E, E . . . *sleep*? Do you want to go to sleep, Alison?'

Fuck, fuck, fuck . . .

Two strong blinks. One, two.

No. I. Don't. Have you got any idea how hard this is?

He raised the pointer again. Point. Stop. Look. Point. Stop. Look. Point. Stop . . . a blink. No question about it. A big fat positive Y.

'You're *sleepy*? I'm sorry, Alison, I can come back when . . .'

She was blinking quite rapidly now. Repeatedly.

Do I look fucking sleepy? Well, do I? Come on, Thorne, sort it out . . .

The sweat was running off him. He was making a complete mess of it. One more try and then he'd go and get somebody. Back with the pointer. And Alison blinked. And blinked again.

An H. Another E . . .

And the word became obvious.

And a firework went off in Thorne's stomach.

A memory file, a tiny soundbite was pushed forward in his brain and something pressed the button marked 'play' and lit the fuse. The charge began to churn through his guts and the explosions rang in his ears and the sparks were dancing behind his eyes, green and gold and red and silver, and he was squeezing Alison's hand.

And he was scrabbling in his pockets for change for the phone.

Running from the room.

'Bishop? This is Thorne . . .'

'What?' Weary, but also frightened.

'I know what you said to her. I know what you said to Alison before you stroked her out. What you said to all of them.'

'What are you talking about?'

'"Night-night, Sleepyhead." Same thing you said to me when you put me out for that hernia operation last year.'

His tongue heavy in his mouth, his voice growing weaker as he counts backwards from twenty, wondering if it will hurt when he wakes up, and seeing the smiling face of the anaesthetist looming above him. Murmuring . . .

'Is there a point to any of this, Thorne? I'm expecting somebody.'

'The same thing you said to me, Bishop. "Night-night, Sleepyhead."'

'Look, if it helps you, yes, I say that to patients sometimes when they're going under and I say, "Wake up, Sleepyhead," when they're coming round from the anaesthetic. It's a silly catchphrase. A superstition. For God's sake, I used to say it to my children when I put them to bed at night. Is this helping you, Thorne? Is it?'

'I was about to let it go, do you know that? You were so close to walking away. I thought I was wrong, but I wasn't, was I? Now I'm fucking certain . . .'

'You need help, Thorne. Serious professional help . . .'

'You're the one who needs help, Jeremy. I'm coming for you. I'm coming for you right now.'

Jesus . . . Jesus . . . Jesus . . .

I thought he was never going to get it.

I thought maybe it would be important, you know, because I'd heard it when I woke up as well as when he was doing it to me.

That same word.

I thought it was probably significant and as soon as I heard Thorne outside the door I knew I wanted to try to tell him, but I hadn't expected him to shoot out of here quite like that.

Like shit off a shiny shovel, my old man would have said.

He was obviously still worked up after punching Anne's old man.

Like a blow-up doll with a pulse. What a fucking charmer. I hope Thorne knocked his teeth down his throat.

So it has to be that doctor who brought me round. The anaesthetist who came in here with Anne a couple of times is Champagne Fucking Charlie. The one who's her friend. The one Thorne had the photo of. He obviously suspected him all along.

How can you be a doctor and do . . . this?

Jesus, though, I thought that was going to take for ever. That's the best I've ever done. Anne would have been dead proud, I reckon. I was fucking spot on.

Blinking for England. I said I would, didn't I?

It was so hard, though.

Now I really am *sleepy . . .*

TWENTY-THREE

Dave Holland stared at the film Sophie had rented, not taking in a single word. He pushed bits of cold lasagne round his plate, not really hungry.

Thinking about Tom Thorne.

He hadn't been there that morning when Thorne had stormed out of the office at Edgware Road. He was still trying to bring himself round after the night before when he'd drunk far too much trying to forget about Helen Doyle's parents. They'd made quite a night of it, him and Thorne. Even though he'd been pissed, and asleep some of the time, he could remember a lot of what Thorne had been saying. Lying on the settee late into the night, eyes closed, head spinning, while Thorne talked about blood and voices. Things Dave Holland wouldn't forget in a long time.

Now nobody seemed to know where Thorne was, or even if he'd be back at all.

Those who had been there this morning and seen the state of the DI as he'd walked into the lift, *staggered*, somebody had said, had been only too keen to pass on the details when Holland eventually got into work. 'You'll be interested in this . . .' they said sarcastically. It seemed that a line of inquiry, developed by Detective Inspector Thorne, had now been officially discredited.

It sounded like he'd had the shit kicked out of him.

Holland had gone quietly back to work. Every half an hour or so since, he'd checked his mobile, looking for a message.

Suddenly he noticed that the picture on the TV screen was frozen. Paused. He turned to see Sophie, the remote in her hand, talking to him. Was there really any point in her going to the video shop? Or cooking dinner? Or bothering to talk to him?

He apologised and told her that he was still feeling a bit rough, the worse for wear after his drinking session with the lads last night. Sophie had a go at him, but secretly she didn't really mind. She didn't begrudge him a night out on the beer with the lads. As long as he didn't make a habit of it and had worked out which side his bread was buttered on.

As long as he'd finally decided against throwing in his lot with that loser Thorne.

Anne was annoyed. She had a bag full of shopping – food for the dinner she was going to cook for Jeremy – it was pouring with rain, and she couldn't find a single parking spot on his street. She eventually squeezed into a tight space round the corner and ran back, doing her best to avoid the rapidly growing puddles.

She was amazed to see him sitting in the car outside the house.

She tapped quickly on the glass and laughed as he jumped. The electric window on the Volvo slid down and she leaned in. 'What are you doing sitting out here?'

'Just thinking about things. Waiting for you.' The rain was blowing in through the open window on to his face.

Anne grimaced, confused. 'It's a lot warmer in the house.' He said nothing, staring blankly forward through a windscreen running with rainwater. Anne moved the handles of the plastic shopping-bag round in her hand. It was starting to get heavy. 'Are you coming inside?'

'Can you get in here first? Please, Anne, I need to talk to you about something. Just for a minute.'

Anne wanted to go into the house. She was wet, and very cold. She wanted a cup of tea or, even better, a large glass of wine before she got started on dinner. Still, he seemed upset about something. She hurried round to the passenger side and, dropping the shopping bag on to the floor at her feet, got into the car.

It was nice and warm: the heater had obviously been on for a while. He didn't look at her. She began to think something was seriously wrong.

'Is everything all right? Has something happened?'

He didn't answer and instinctively she began to look around her. Was the answer to whatever was going on here with them in the car? There was something on the back seat, covered with a tartan picnic blanket.

She looked at him. 'What's . . .?'

Instinctively she knew that she wasn't going to get an answer and, with a grunt of effort, she lifted herself off her seat, reached across into the back of the car and pulled off the blanket.

She gasped.

She didn't even feel the needle slip into her arm.

Thorne tried to stay calm. The rain had slowed up the traffic as per usual and it had taken an infuriating twenty-five minutes just to get the half a mile or so from Queen

Square to Waterloo Bridge. Now it had eased off a little and the Mondeo was testing every speed camera it passed as Thorne pushed the car south, through the spray towards Battersea.

The clock on the dashboard said eight forty-five and Merle Haggard was complaining about being let down by the bottle as Thorne drove past St Thomas's Hospital.

He thought about a pathologist whose skill, whose observation, whose *curiosity*, months before, had started it all. He might be working late at this very minute, in one of those lit offices, those bright white squares that Thorne could see as he drove past. Getting tired now, probably, as he stared down into a microscope, then excitement mounting as he spotted some inconsistency, some curious detail that might change the lives of hundreds of people for ever.

He didn't know whether, if he ever met that man, he should thank him or spit in his face. What was certain was that, without him, he would not be on his way right now to confront a killer. He had no idea what might really happen between him and Bishop. Confront him, yes, and what else? Arrest him? Intimidate him? Hurt him?

Thorne would know when he got there.

He hit the brakes too late and too hard approaching the big traffic lights at Vauxhall Bridge. The car skidded a little before stopping, the squeal of tyres attracting the attention of the evening's traffic-light cabaret. Those cleaning windscreens in return for a few coins and a great deal of abuse had now been replaced, bizarrely, by street entertainers. One such, wearing a large, multicoloured jester's hat and juggling three balls, stepped jauntily through the rain towards Thorne's car with a broad grin.

The juggler took one look at Thorne's face and backed

away again quickly, dropping balls as he went. The light, reflected in the puddles of oil and water, turned from red to green, and the Mondeo sped away.

The lights were with him along Nine Elms Lane and Battersea Park Road. He turned left on amber at the Latchmere pub, put his foot down all the way to Lavender Hill, and a few minutes later was turning almost casually into Jeremy Bishop's quiet road.

He turned down the music and began to breathe deeply. There were cars parked along both sides of the street and Thorne drove slowly, looking for a parking spot. The rain was heavier now, and even with the wipers on double speed he had to lean forward, and squint hard through the windscreen to see anything at all.

Suddenly, fifty yards ahead, lights came on and dazzled him as a large dark car pulled out and accelerated. Thorne's first thought was that he'd got a parking space, but a second later he could see that he was in trouble. The car rushed towards him on the wrong side of the road. With one hand shielding his eyes, which closed at the last second in anticipation of the impact, he yanked the wheel sharply to the right to avoid being hit as the car rushed past him with barely inches to spare.

A car with Anne Coburn sitting in the passenger seat.

Thorne slammed on the brakes and watched in his mirror as the Volvo stopped at the end of the road and turned left. They were heading west.

He might have been wrong but he didn't think that either Anne or Bishop had seen him. Both had been staring straight ahead. Where were they going? He hadn't got room to turn the car round quickly. Without thinking, he ground the gearstick into reverse and put his foot down.

For the first few minutes, past the north side of Clapham Common, Thorne was happy to cruise along two or three cars behind the Volvo, watching for its distinctive rear lights, keeping it close. He was sure now that Bishop had no idea he was being followed. Thorne wanted to keep it that way and was content to maintain a relaxed pace. Let them get where they were going. Following procedure for once in his fucking life. Keep it safe, he thought. Keep it sedate.

Sedate. As the word formed in his mind, the car in front turned away giving him a clear view through the Volvo's rear window.

There was something very wrong with the picture.

It took half a second and then he got it. He couldn't see Anne any more.

The car hadn't stopped he was certain of that. She had been there a few minutes earlier, her head against the window. There was only one explanation.

She had to be unconscious.

Things began to speed up in every sense. There was another car between Thorne and the Volvo. He tried to get past it as the traffic swung right on to Clapham Park Road, and as he overtook on the inside, he watched the Volvo accelerate away. It looked as though Bishop knew he was there after all.

Thorne had never been good at this. He'd been in plenty of pursuits but he'd never been the one with his foot on the pedal. Forty-five miles an hour, along busy built-up streets at nine o'clock at night in the driving rain was fucking terrifying.

Why would Bishop hurt Anne? Why now? Thorne knew he should call this in. There was no radio in the car.

His mobile was back at the flat. He thought about pulling over, using a payphone. By the time a unit picked up Bishop's car it might be too late. He had to keep following.

Fifty miles an hour along Acre Lane. The rear fog-lights of the Volvo blinding, the horns of other cars blaring.

Without taking his eyes off the Volvo for a second, Thorne switched tapes and turned up the volume. One type of music for another. Song replaced by sound. Melody by a pumping rhythm that seemed instantly to be emanating from inside his own head. The noise, the beat becoming a low, almost Zen-like hum, pulsing through his skull like the soundtrack to an arcade racing game.

Focusing. The wheel vibrating beneath his fingers. The car in front. The target. Speeding down the hill now towards the lights and the cinema ahead and pedestrians shouting and the wheels squealing as they turn left much too fast on to Brixton Road.

And suddenly, Thorne knows where they're going.

Brixton. SW2. He remembers the address from a page in his notebook. The page headed 'children'. Thorne's never been to this address but why on earth would he have?

Thorne knows now that, even with a warrant, he'd have found nothing at the house in Battersea. Where they're going now is Bishop's place of work. It's where he would have brought Helen and Leonie. A place to which he would have a key. A flat for which he helped pay the deposit. Somewhere almost certainly empty late at night if the occupant is working. Easily established with a phone call . . .

The beat and the speed increasing and rain lashing the windscreen, and Thorne's hands on the wheel guided solely by the movements of the two red lights ahead of him. His eyes fixed on those two red lights, which flash as the Volvo brakes suddenly, like the eyes of some sleek, dark monster, which roars and is away from him quickly as the Volvo jumps the traffic lights and he has no choice but to do the same.

From the corner of his eye he sees the blue and red of the traffic patrol car to his left, and a thousand yards further on the second one pulls out in front of him.

The last thing he needs. A pair of fucking black rats, working in tandem.

As Thorne slowed down, hammering his fists on the steering-wheel, he watched the eyes of the dark monster ahead of him get smaller and smaller.

When the constable, a fat fuck with a pockmarked face and a walrus moustache, finally sauntered up to the Mondeo's passenger door, the first thing he saw was an ID pressed hard against the window. The first thing Thorne saw when he removed it was the smug look the constable gave to his colleague in the patrol car: Look what *we*'ve got.

Thorne took a deep breath. This was going to be interesting.

The walrus made a casual winding motion with his forefinger. *Window down.* Thorne counted to three and wound down the window like a good boy.

'Detective Inspector Thorne. SCG West.' There was no reaction. Thorne certainly hadn't been expecting a tug on the forelock and a polite 'On your way, sir', far from it, but this was going to be a bad one.

Age-old animosities. Uniform and plainclothes. *Anyone* and Traffic.

'Fifty miles an hour plus, through a red light, in the pissing rain. Not clever was it?' The estuary accent trying its very best to drip with sarcasm.

'I'm in pursuit of a suspect,' said Thorne, flatly. The constable turned casually to watch the traffic disappearing into the distance and smiled, the rain dripping off the peak of his cap. Thorne tried to keep his temper. 'I *was* in pursuit of a suspect.'

'You *were* driving like a twat.'

Thorne was out of the car, the red mist ready to come down. 'Is this how you normally deal with members of the public?'

Another sly smile, another glance to his mate in the car. 'You're not public, are you?'

Thorne stood, staring straight ahead, the rain running down the back of his jacket. He thought about the killer's first note again. He thought about Anne lying across leather seats, unable to move. Bishop was probably playing classical music . . . Fuck, they'd probably be there by now.

Jesus fucking Christ . . .

'Have you been drinking, sir?'

'What?' Starting to lose it.

'Simple enough question. You fuckers obviously think you're above the law—'

Thorne grabbed his jacket, spun him round, and pressed him hard against the car, sending his cap tumbling into the gutter. From the corner of his eye, Thorne could see the other one step out of the patrol car. Without even turning to look, he shouted through the rain, 'I'm a DI, now get back in that fucking car.'

The walrus's mate did as he was told. Thorne turned his attention back to the man himself, leaning in close, the rain beating down on the two of them, nose to nose at the side of the road. Passing cars honked their approval, the drivers of Brixton pleased to see a copper getting what was coming to him from an innocent motorist.

Thorne raised his voice just enough to make himself clearly understood over the noise of the rain, spattering off the PC's reflective plastic tabard. 'Listen, you fat, scabby arsehole, I'm getting back into my car now and driving away, and if you so much as raise an eyebrow, you'll be pissing blood for a week. That was a threat. The next bit is an order. Are you following this?'

The walrus nodded. Thorne released his grip but only slightly. 'This is an instruction, understand? Get back into your car right now and get on your radio. I want you to contact someone at Operation Backhand out of Edgware Road. You need to get hold of DC Dave Holland . . .'

In my dream I'm running.

It's nowhere dramatic. Not across a cornfield or through the surf on a storm-lashed beach or anything. And I'm not running towards anybody. There's nobody in the distance with arms thrown wide, aching to kiss me. Not a soldier returned from the war or a film star. Not Tim. It's just me.

Just running.

It's funny because I've always hated running, always done whatever I could to avoid it. Skinny little legs and knock knees. I was always rubbish at any kind of sport and I'm totally unfit. Running for the bus, if I absolutely have to, is about my limit, and that will fuck me up for the rest of the day. But here I am . . .

I'm running, sprinting, and it feels easy.

I don't know what I'm wearing or what the weather's like. None of that seems important. I suppose the wind must be blowing in my hair but, to be honest, I don't really notice. What I do *notice is the wind rushing into my open mouth and inflating my lungs. I notice my lungs pushing the air back out through my mouth.*

I'm running.

I notice my legs moving me along and my arms pumping, and I notice that the muscles in my mouth are working overtime, every last fucking gorgeous one of them. Each muscle working in harmony with the others. Meshing perfectly with its neighbour. Forcing my lips to part, raising the corners of my mouth up, pushing my tongue out slightly against my top teeth. Making me smile.

I'm running away.

TWENTY-FOUR

It was a narrow green door without a window.

Easy to miss between a greengrocer's and a shoe shop in a small street behind the busy Brixton Road. Thorne couldn't see the Volvo anywhere. Maybe there was another way to get in. That would make sense, after all. A back entrance that was easier to carry bodies into unseen.

Yes, and maybe he was wrong about the whole thing. Maybe it had just been coincidence that they'd seemed headed for this address and even now as Thorne was standing in the rain, staring at a narrow green door without a window, Bishop was spiriting Anne away to a place where he would never find her.

Was all this just to hurt *him*?

Thorne put his ear against the door and listened. Not a sound.

He was certain that Bishop had known he was being followed. Thorne had half expected the door to be open. Six inches ajar, tempting him inside. Not a trap, nothing so vulgar.

More like an invitation.

He pressed his hand against the door. It was locked.

Back off now and wait for Holland to arrive with troops. It wouldn't be long, presuming those idiots in the Traffic car had done as they'd been told. Get back into his car and sit tight, that would be best.

He put the side of his head to the door again and this time added the heft of his shoulder. Not a violent movement. Just a sustained pressure, using his weight.

The door gave as easily as if he'd used a key. There was barely any noise.

Ahead of him, by the light from a shopfront opposite, Thorne could see a long straight hallway leading to a staircase that climbed away into darkness. Everything else looked to be on the upper levels, above the greengrocer's.

He stepped smartly inside and tried to shut the door behind him. The lock wouldn't catch against the jamb where he'd forced it, so he just pushed it to. Then he turned inside and listened.

Nothing but the sound of his own breathing and the rain outside and the rumble of the traffic from the main road. He felt for a light switch and found one of those press-in jobs designed to save money. He started up the stairs.

The place was messy. Scattered about on the torn stair-carpet were various bits of junk mail and unopened letters. He could smell fast food of some kind, Chinese maybe.

At the top of the stairs was the kitchen. He found the light switch just as the one on the stairs popped out and the light went off.

It was poky and squalid. The brown vinyl flooring was cracked and greasy, the walls grubby and sweating. Days' worth of used tea-bags squatted in the sink like turds, and a ketchup stain ran down the side of the once white plastic swing-bin. Fast food would certainly be preferable to anything prepared in here.

Thorne backed out of the room. Another half-dozen stairs led up to the second floor. He could see a door ahead of him and two more off to the left. He moved on slowly towards the rooms on the next level, stopping and listening for a few seconds at every step. His doubts outside the front door had given way to a cold, clammy certainty that he was not alone.

It was ending. He could feel it. Somewhere in this building was the wall he would back himself against.

Thorne moved forward and upward, knowing he must be getting closer to where Helen Doyle and Leonie Holden were killed. The walls of the hallway were bare and dusty, the paper peeling and dry as dead leaves. The carpet was stained and gritty. He imagined he felt it moving beneath his feet.

This was not a place anyone should be brought to die.

The first door on the left opened on to a bathroom no bigger than a large cupboard. Thorne put his head round the door for a few seconds. It was enough. No fripperies. Just grimy white fittings and a bad smell.

Then a bedroom. Maybe a little cleaner but stuffed and cluttered and stinking of stale sweat. There were shoes lined up along a mantelpiece. An ironing-board stood in the corner next to a full-length mirror. Piles of magazines spilled out on to the faded cork floor tiles from beneath the unmade bed and cardboard boxes were piled high against the far wall.

Not in here.

As he stepped back on to the landing he heard a noise from somewhere above him. He froze. The lazy creak of a floorboard underfoot.

Underfoot.

Whether or not he'd heard the noise, Thorne would still have skipped the final room. As he stepped towards it and glanced to his right, he could see the way he needed to go. The stairs leading up to what must be the top floor had been stripped and scrubbed. Each tread, along with the handrail, had been meticulously covered in thick, clear polythene.

Sterile.

Thorne looked up. The stairs climbed steeply, at least twenty feet into what had to be an attic or roof conversion. Straight up and into it. Above him, all he could see was a square of light, a hole in the floor of the room above his head. He weighed it up quickly. He knew that he'd be going in blind. He would be able to see nothing of what was in the room above him until the moment his head came up through the floor.

There was nowhere else to go.

'*It always comes down to the final door, Tommy . . .*'

Above his head he heard a floorboard moan quietly. A second later, he heard a small human voice do the same.

Anne . . .

Thorne raised his head and began to climb.

Despite the attack in his flat and the fact that the man had killed at least six women, Thorne didn't think instinctively of Bishop as somebody violent. As he climbed slowly up, one step at a time, towards whatever awaited him in the attic, he never for a second thought it might be something that could hurt him physically. Bishop would have the advantage of surprise and geography, but Thorne guessed that he would not be waiting for him as his head appeared, inch by inch, above the floor of the attic, with a foot drawn back to kick him in the teeth or an iron bar in his hand.

He was nearing the top now. Just a few more feet.

He felt no real sense of physical danger and yet he was as frightened as he'd ever been in his life.

The last couple of steps.

He was not worried about what he was going to feel . . .

He put his foot on the last tread and pushed his body upwards.

. . . he was terrified of what he was going to see.

His head moved up, through the hole and into bright white light. He blinked quickly to adjust then opened his eyes. Thorne's last thought, before his body turned ice cold and he began to shake quietly, was that he'd been right to be afraid.

He hauled himself up on to floor level, like a drowning man clambering aboard a lifeboat full of holes, and stared in disbelief.

White, white walls and smooth, shining floorboards. The light from a row of wall-mounted halogen lamps bounced off the gleaming metal of the sharps bin and the instruments trolley. An elegant chrome mixer tap fed two highly polished white basins. To one side a simple black chair, the only piece of furniture in the room. Everything else, cold and functional. Necessary to the procedure.

Bishop was standing in the very middle of the room. He was busy. He raised his head and smiled at Thorne a little sadly.

Thorne was staring at the girl's eyes, bulging as she fought the movements of his fingers on her neck with every ounce of strength she had and without the slightest success. The drug that was coursing through Rachel Higgins had made her limbs as useless and uncooperative as they would become permanently, if the procedure Bishop was about to perform was successful.

From his left Thorne heard a grunt. He turned. Anne lay motionless against the wall, her eyes wide open, drool spilling from her mouth, the Midazolam doing its work on her too, so that she could do nothing but stare helplessly at the hands working on her daughter.

The voice brought Thorne's head whipping back round. Bishop was caressing the back of the girl's neck. 'Hello, Tom. Come to spoil our party, have you?'

Thorne stood completely still, staring at Bishop. Not wanting to move and spook him. Unable to move even if he'd wanted to. His mouth utterly dry. Voice no better than a whisper.

'Hello, James . . .'

There would be a hundred difficult questions to come, and a complex knot of motivation and psychosis to unravel eventually, but just for a few seconds, in the stark and horrifying tableau in front of him, Thorne saw it all perfectly. Just briefly, for a heartbeat or two, there was clarity, and he knew exactly what and why and who. He saw how he'd been manipulated, how he'd been used. How James Bishop had played him and prodded him and nudged him, exploiting his weak spots and playing to his strengths. How he'd been completely right and horribly wrong. Why Margaret Byrne died and why she might still be alive, were it not for him.

How he'd been led by the fucking nose.

Outclassed.

James Bishop was naked from the waist up. Criss-crossing his stomach were half a dozen straight pink puckered scars, like giant worms beneath his skin. Knife wounds, Thorne thought. Self-inflicted.

Anne : '. . . *he was a bit screwed up about it.*'

Rebecca : '. . . *James went off the rails a little.*'

The scars were the least remarkable thing. The short hair was greying. Spray on dye was the easiest explanation. '*Tried being an actor. Anything that pays the rent.*' He was wearing identical glasses and it was easy to see it, even here in a brightly lit room from a few feet away. At night, outside with only the light from a streetlamp, or no light at all, nobody could be blamed for seeing a man ten years older than he really was.

It was Thorne who had seen Jeremy Bishop.

Thorne looked at Rachel and at Anne. 'What's the point of this, though, James? What's *this* got to do with anything?'

Bishop chuckled. Wasn't it obvious? 'Well, as you've so brilliantly failed in your efforts to arrest and convict the wrong man . . .'

'Your father.'

'My father, yes. I'm having to finish things off a little quicker. With a little less subtlety. It isn't what I wanted but it will have the desired effect.'

'Which is?'

Bishop shook his head. 'You're really not the man I thought you were, are you, Tom?'

'I could say the same for you, James . . .'

'Anne's daughter becoming one of her own patients is pretty tidy, though, isn't it? He may not even be able to live with that.' He was running his thumbs slowly up and down the base of Rachel's skull. 'Mind you, he's lived with himself long enough . . .'

Thorne's eyes didn't move from the long, thin fingers. From the hands encased in the tight surgical gloves. Skilled hands.

James in his flat. Cocky, immature and so easy to read. '*I wasted a couple of years at college, yeah. I'm not the ivory-tower type.*'

The question Thorne had never thought to ask. Four stupid little words.

What did you study?

It was important to keep him talking . . .

'Is that all this has been about, James? Hurting your father? Getting your own back?'

Bishop glared at him. The mask of civility slipping. 'Don't be fucking stupid, Thorne. All this is about?' He looked disgusted at the suggestion. Then his voice softened and changed, becoming almost gentle, concerned, yet with the strength that came from conviction. 'This is about aiming for something like perfection. It's about taking something flawed and weak and rotten and removing the need for it. Eliminating the reliance on it. Letting the brain, which is the only part that's worth anything at all, flourish without the handicap of the body. It's about freedom.'

Thorne threw a quick look to Anne. A look to tell her it would be all right. He put his hands in his pockets, trying to appear relaxed as he turned slowly back to Bishop. Casual, enquiring. 'The frailty of the human body. Something your father taught you?'

'One of many things . . .' The voice had changed again. Casual, disinterested.

'And framing him for it?'

Bishop removed a hand from Rachel's head and ran it slowly across the noughts and crosses scar tissue on his stomach. The other hand stayed where it was, kneading the muscles at the back of her neck. Thorne considered running at him – he could be on him in a second. But a second was all Bishop would need to hurt Rachel. Instead Thorne offered him an answer to the question: 'Killing two birds with one stone.'

'Close enough. Except for the killing bit, obviously. Not very appropriate.'

Thorne disagreed. 'You did plenty of killing, James.' Bishop shrugged.

A weapon would even things up a little. Thorne's eyes flashed to the instrument trolley, to the gleaming tools lined up in a row. Clamps, forceps, a scalpel.

Bishop caught the look. 'Please don't compromise this procedure, Thorne.' He smiled, glancing at the scalpel. 'I think I could reach it before you.'

Thorne nodded slowly. He could feel Anne's eyes on him. Begging.

Bishop stroked the muscle at the base of Rachel's skull. 'The sternocleidomastoid, Tom. Are you familiar with it?'

Thorne was familiar enough. He knew what Bishop was looking for. Feeling for. 'Why the attack on me, though, James? I still don't really understand that.'

'I knew you'd think it was my father. I knew you'd be sure. It was easy. Your relationship with Anne came in very handy. Perhaps your dick clouded your judgement a little. You were so easy to ginger up, Tom, so easy to goad.'

Thorne winced a little at the truth of it: seizing hungrily on every clue Bishop had dropped in front of him; clutching at every straw that had been so deliberately scattered in his path – the drugs, the timing of the killings, the car . . .

'The Volvo?'

'The old man swears by them. When he bought his new one I persuaded him to let me have the cast-off. I gave him a hundred pounds for it, I think, which is obviously less than he'd have got part-ex from a garage but, well . . . he *is* my father.'

That was the key, Thorne realised. Nobody knew Jeremy Bishop better. His son knew his movements, his whereabouts, the words he used. He knew everything his father knew about Alison, about the case. He knew how to steal his wedding ring.

'Sorry it didn't work out with the ring, James. Forensically compromised, I'm afraid.'

'These things happen. *I'm* sorry about the Byrne woman. I'm sorry about all the ones who died, sincerely I am, but I've told you that, haven't I? Of course, she wouldn't have needed to die were you not planning to go charging in there waving your stupid photographs. Have you thought about that, Tom?'

James in his flat. Seeing Margaret Byrne's address on a piece of paper next to the phone . . . .

Thorne had got it so completely wrong. Margaret Byrne hadn't died because she could identify Jeremy Bishop. She had died precisely because she could say for certain that Jeremy Bishop *wasn't* the killer.

They stared at each other, across six yawning feet of gleaming white space, the rain hammering on the roof above their heads.

Thorne jumped, and they both turned their heads when the bleeper went off.

He remembered that Anne was on call. The bleeper was inside her handbag, dumped on the floor next to her.

By the time the bleeping had stopped Thorne had worked something else out. The phone call that Margaret Byrne had seen him make: Bishop had been calling his father, to see if he'd been called in to work. Checking his availability. 'You bleeped your father on the way to the hospital. That night with Alison. You were probably sitting outside, waiting for him to arrive, giving him an alibi that was almost watertight, putting his name on a list.' Bishop smiled modestly. 'Same with the drugs in Leicester—'

Bishop cut him off. 'Yes, a mistake of a sort, obviously. Had you even worked that out?'

Thorne looked across at Anne. *Everything was going to be fine.* 'Anne worked it out.'

Bishop smiled. 'I'm impressed. But it did, as you say, put my father's name on a list. That was the hook. It got you interested . . .'

It had certainly done that.

'But it would never have worked, James. It was all circumstantial. There wasn't any real evidence.'

'That never seemed to bother you, though, did it, Tom?'

Thorne could say nothing, his tongue sticky against the roof of his mouth.

Suddenly Bishop grinned. Thorne could see that his fingers were locked in position, as was the look of something approaching rapture on his face.

'This is my favourite part, Tom. It all begins here.'

The muscles in Bishop's chest flexed as he began to squeeze Rachel's carotid artery. Thorne remembered Hendricks with his hands on his neck, taking him through it. They had about two minutes until she stopped breathing.

Thorne glanced at Anne. The look on her face was desperate. A snarl came from somewhere deep down inside her.

Save my daughter.

Thorne had no idea how. Bishop killed when he

needed to, that much was obvious. The hands that were squeezing away Rachel's life in front of them were as dangerous as any weapon. He could snap her neck in a heartbeat . . .

Thorne felt leaden, useless. Mummified.

Ten seconds gone already. Her tongue lolling out.

'How does this hurt him, James? How does this make him suffer?'

Bishop said nothing. His lips moved soundlessly as he counted away the time in his head.

'This won't bring your mother back, James.' Thorne was shouting now. Anything to get a reaction, to make him stop. James was lost in concentration, readying himself for the difficult part, once the girl had stopped breathing. The manipulation.

Time ticking away. Thorne felt the seconds hurtling past him, Rachel's breath rushing past him as he stood frozen and useless.

'*Please, Tommy . . .*'

'*Helen?*'

'*She's a child . . .*'

'*What can I do? WHAT CAN I DO?*'

Then suddenly, a voice from below them. 'James?'

A reaction from Bishop. A reaction to the *voice of his father*. Fear maybe? Certainly a tension in his body and in his face. Tension in his fingers . . .

'James? I saw you driving away with Anne – what's going on? Is everything all right? Somebody's forced open your front door.'

Half a minute gone . . .

There was no way of knowing what James would do with his father here but Thorne had little option.

Ninety seconds left. Rachel was nearly half-way dead. Thorne shouted, 'Bishop. We're up here!'

Jeremy Bishop appeared in the attic like a ghost rising up through the trap in a stage. The image was completed instantly as the blood deserted his face and the light vanished from the eyes.

Thorne knew what he would look like when he was dead.

'My God – James?' He leaned forward and for a second Thorne thought he was going to pass out. At the last moment Thorne realised he was moving towards his son and reached out an arm to stop him. Bishop glared angrily at him and then, as if woken from a dream, nodded slowly, taking in the full, horrific implications of what he could see around him.

Anne. Rachel. James.

Thorne watched the son glare at the father. Couldn't be much more than a minute now . . .

James's voice was childish, taunting. 'What is it, then? Horror? Outrage? Or just surprise that I know how to do it? A pretty advanced procedure, all in all, considering that I couldn't cut it. Considering what a major disappointment I was . . .'

'Please—'

James screamed, 'Shut up! Fucking shut up, will you?'

Rachel's eyes were rolling up into her head. Sixty seconds, if that . . .

'I always meant to ask you something. When exactly did you start believing the things you do? There must have been a time when you thought the same as the rest of them. About the human body, I mean. All that bollocks about a miracle of design and efficiency. Christ, I'm grateful you taught me what crap *that* was. Your belief in technology was inspiring, did you know that? Truly inspiring. I'm just sorry I couldn't repay the faith you had in me academically. But even when I was fucking it all up, even when I was failing so brilliantly to become the doctor you wanted me to be, I still believed in all the things you did.' He started to cry. 'I still remembered everything you taught me.'

The tears stopped as suddenly as they had started and the voice regained its edge. 'So, when was it? When did you start thinking that the human body was just a worthless piece of shit? Was it when you saw how easily it could be manipulated by drugs? How a body could be slowed up and shaped if you filled it full of tranquillisers? Was she the wife you wanted then? Afterwards? Me and Becks used to call her Snow White – did you know that? Becks said that every time she saw Doc, she went Sleepy and Dopey . . .'

Rachel's breathing was starting to slow. Half a minute . . .

'No, I bet I know when it was. It was when you saw how easily it got damaged, wasn't it? How fragile it was. How easily the skin could be torn by flying glass, or how little it took for a torso to be crushed or twisted. Or perhaps it was both those things. How the body softened up by tranquillisers reacts that much slower in an emergency, in an accident, and becomes a bigger target. Yes, that would make sense. I'd call that a road-to-Damascus sort of moment, wouldn't you? From then on you just saw patients decomposing in front of your eyes. Breaking down, rotting, *dying*, faster than you could stitch them together or prop them up or overhaul them.

'You'd learned a valuable lesson. A powerful lesson.

Once you'd learned that, it was about teaching us. Then pushing and pushing . . .'

Rachel had stopped breathing in. Just the last few messy exhalations.

'I would so like to have seen you in prison. Watched your skin go yellow and your bones turn powdery and your hope evaporate. You're soft and vain, and prison would have killed you very slowly. Then you'd have found out just how frail the body really is. Just how frail, Daddy . . .'

Thorne couldn't hear Rachel breathing any more.

James Bishop closed his eyes and whispered, 'Night-night, Sleepyhead . . .'

Anne Coburn screamed. A roar from somewhere down in her guts, and suddenly the room was full of noise and movement. Jeremy Bishop rushed forward, shouting his son's name as if ordering a dog to drop and play dead. James moved with the instinctive obedience of a frightened child, recoiling, taking his hands off Rachel, letting her tumble helplessly forward on to her face.

Thorne ran to turn the girl over and began searching for a pulse.

Come on . . . .

He got one. She was still breathing. He picked her up, carried her across to Anne and gently laid her in the recovery position next to her mother. Anne's eyes turned up to him, the spark still strong, the relief evident in every tear that rolled down her cheek and dropped on to her daughter's face.

There was a moment of calm.

Just the noise of the rain coming down, like six-inch nails on to the tiles a few feet above them.

Thorne turned to see Jeremy Bishop moving slowly

towards his son, his arms outstretched, his face a death-mask.

James backed into the instrument trolley, which clattered and rolled away from him. He stopped and smiled, his head cocked to one side, and then his arm rose gracefully into the air.

Almost as if he were about to take a bow.

It was a movement so casual that he might have been reaching to scratch a shoulder-blade. Thorne saw the glint of steel at his fist a second before the blood began to spout from the artery in his neck.

'No . . .' Jeremy's voice was a whisper that could have blown down a house.

Thorne leaned against the whitewashed wall and watched as James dropped to his knees and was followed by his father. Jeremy clamped a hand across his son's neck, but the blood gushed between his fingers, running down his arms and pooling across the bleached white floor-boards.

Up one board . . . down another.

Jeremy turned to Thorne, his face already spattered, his hair slick with it. 'Get an ambulance – call somebody.' His voice was thick with desperation. His face implored.

But so did his son's.

James Bishop looked at Tom Thorne and his eyes asked to die. They asked permission to look into his father's face and watch it contort as the blood emptied from the body. He wanted to die watching his father suffer.

Thorne was tempted to let him.

Jeremy's voice was hoarse between the sobs. 'For pity's sake, Thorne . . .'

Then, as Thorne thought about sitting and watching

James Bishop bleed to death, he pictured Maggie Byrne, and Bishop watching as her life poured out on to a cheap duvet.

And he remembered a promise he made to Alison Willetts.

Dying would be easy. He was going to see the fucker tried and put away. He was going to watch James Bishop's hope evaporate.

Jeremy was sobbing uncontrollably, his arms, wrapped tightly around his son's neck, slippery with blood.

With a last look at Anne, Thorne stepped down, out of the white room and on to the stairs, hurrying back towards the street, where he hoped Holland would be waiting.

PART FOUR

THE SILENCE

Don't get me wrong, I'm delighted he's dead.

Thrilled about it. Prison is all well and good but I wouldn't want to lie here thinking about him writing his life story, cock of the fucking walk, probably out before he's fifty. Or else in some hospital somewhere, convincing them all he's mental while he pads around in comfy slippers, making model aeroplanes and remembering the women he killed.

Remembering what he did to me.

Sod that, I'd much rather he was dead. If I could get taken somewhere for the day, you know, loaded up into some special van and taken anywhere I want, I'd like to see his grave. Obviously dancing on it isn't really an option but I'd be happy just to be laid across it. Lifted up and laid down on top of him. And I'd lie there with my face on the ground and think dark thoughts that would seep down into the earth and eat into his box like poison.

I'm glad he's dead. Stiff and still, like me.

No, not like me. He's not scrabbling like a madman at the lid of the coffin, is he? Not tearing his fingers to stumps to try and get out. Not fed. Not wiped. Not breathed for.

On the subject of which – no improvement. No response to the antibiotics and no chance of coming off this ventilator in the near future. Apparently the pneumonia in my lungs has been complicated by a fungal infection. Viruses and fungus. It's like I've become a breeding ground . . .

What I really can't stomach is that it was his choice.

He chose this for me and he chose death for himself.

I'll tell you what's really ironic. I'm actually a dead positive person. I really am. You may not believe that and I know I've been a bit up and down but you can't blame me for that. Try this for a while. Lie on your back and stare at the ceiling until your eyes start to water, and imagine it. Imagine being half dead and half alive, and the two halves not adding up to anything. Cancelling yourself out.

It's not easy to be happy all the time.

I am a positive person. But, lying here, I don't think of myself as a person at all any more. Not even a person alone, without anyone close. I wouldn't feel sorry for myself anyway because of that, but I can't even feel it. I just feel like something in a museum.

I just feel like the thing he created.

And I don't believe in God or anything afterwards. I'm sorry but I just don't, I never have. I believe in the way things are. The way I am. I believe in the capacity for people to do terrible things like he did and I believe that some people can do good.

I'd like to do something good. I want to do something.

Most people don't have a choice about a lot of things. They don't choose to be unhappy or poor, and they don't choose to lose children or get cancer. That's just life, though, that's just the lottery, isn't it? It's the same for all of us. But he chose to kill people and he chose to do this to me, to take away my life and give me the one he decided I should have. And then, when he was good and ready, he chose the manner of his own death . . .

Anne's coming back to work next week, I think. We need to talk.

I can't do very much, but I can choose too. I want to have a say.

I don't want to let him win.

TWENTY-FIVE

Thorne hadn't been able to make good on his promise of a box. Hendricks wasn't pleased, but they were showing the game on Sky anyway, and he agreed to settle for half a dozen cans of cheap lager and a home delivery from the Bengal Lancer.

There had been no great making up, no moment of acceptance or forgiveness. Hendricks called as soon as he heard what happened and they'd talked for a while. It was all that was needed.

Nearly a month now.

When James Bishop died on the operating table, Thorne had blamed himself. Then the post-mortem revealed the drug, and he knew that, even if he'd reacted quicker, the outcome would have been the same. Warfarin. A drug prescribed to treat certain heart and lung disorders and, ironically, used to prevent strokes. An anticoagulant. A drug that prevents the blood clotting.

They couldn't be certain but they guessed he'd been taking it for at least a couple of weeks. Had he been planning it all along? Or had he been taking the drug just in case it ever came down to it? Down to him and his father and a scalpel.

They'd never know for sure.

They'd never know for sure, though Thorne felt pretty certain that Bishop had been the one who'd gone to the press. Leaking the story to free up the channels of information. Once a few decent holes had been torn in the veil of secrecy, he was able to learn so much more about what was happening on the case. The pipeline that fed Bishop information had been a complex one, running back and forth, in many directions and at different speeds from Thorne himself, via Jeremy Bishop, Anne and, of course, Rachel, who James had been seeing for some time.

She never resat her exams.

Anne wasn't sure when Rachel would go back to school or when she herself would go back to work. That's what she'd said a few weeks ago. Thorne had spoken to her frequently in the days following that night in Bishop's attic, but not since. He thought about her a lot, but never without wondering if his stupidity had somehow contributed to what had happened. Had he been responsible for Anne and Rachel being in that attic?

One of many unanswerable questions with which he liked to torture himself.

It wasn't as if he'd done anything that night to make Anne feel inclined to think better of him. There had been no heroics. Just those who died, and those who nearly did.

Perhaps one day she'd call. It needed to come from her.

He knew it would take a while for the bruises he couldn't see to fade, but he *was* starting to feel better. He had got it wrong, and he knew he would do so again. It was a comforting thought. He had been wonderfully, horribly wrong, and in truth, it felt as though a curse had been lifted.

Fucking-up might just have saved him.

And Helen and Susan and Christine and Madeleine and

Leonie? The girls had gone rather quiet. Thorne knew this wasn't because they were 'at peace' or 'avenged' or anything like that. He didn't believe in that sort of crap. He was pretty sure that the silence was only temporary. They would make enough noise when the time came. Them, or others like them.

Right this minute, they just didn't have anything to say.

He watched, confused for a few seconds, as Hendricks jumped from the settee and began to dance around the living room. He glanced at the TV in time to catch the replay. Arsenal had scored. Three more points out of the window and another nail in this season's coffin.

Just one more thing to which Tom Thorne was resigned.

EPILOGUE

Alison and Anne had decided to speed things up.

The process was set down and not open to question. It was ponderous, but that was the way of things when those who took the decisions had to be sure. There was no room for clouded judgement or woolly thinking or, God forbid, overdue haste. The agreement, the rubber stamp of a second consultant, and then, finally, the hearing in front of a judge. These were necessary stages in the process.

Divorce, the custody of children, domestic violence. The High Court Family Division held sway over a great many lives and Alison did not get priority. If anything, her case might be judged less important than some others. So, it was taking time. Alison had first spoken to her over two weeks ago now, and after the tears, the arguments, the doubts, had come a determination on Anne Coburn's part to do what she'd been asked.

To help a friend.

She'd set everything in motion, but it was all too slow for Alison.

Anne walked towards ITU, willing one foot to go down in front of the other and keep moving. Steeling herself.

Jeremy was doing a lot better but it was going to take time. The relationship he'd been having with a junior doctor had ended only a few days before James's death, but even if there had been someone around for him to lean on, to take comfort from, Anne would have wanted to be there as well. As it was, he was alone and desperate, and the twenty-five years she'd known him meant that she would always be nearby, ready to help.

Equally, she could never see Tom Thorne again.

It was as if the two of them had survived the crash of a plane Thorne had been flying. Relieved, but unable to look each other in the eye. Guilt and blame and bad memories were not the stuff of a future.

Her future was Rachel.

Alison had been moved to a side room a couple of weeks earlier. It could not be watched directly from the nurses' station, and they wouldn't disturb her.

Anne opened the door. Alison was awake, and pleased to see her.

She moved across to the window and closed the blind. If anything, the room was even more sparse and functional than the one she'd been in before. Anne remembered the half-dead flowers that Thorne had brought from a garage and wondered for a moment where he was and how he might be feeling. She closed her eyes, wiped away the image of him and turned back to Alison.

They spent a few minutes laughing, and crying, before Anne went to work. Her movements were quick, quiet, professional. She removed the oxymeter peg from the end of Alison's finger and clipped it, at a ninety-degree angle, to its own cable. It was unspoken, but most doctors knew that this would short-circuit the alarm and prevent it sounding when the ventilator was switched off. In twenty minutes or so, she would reattach it, when it was over, and she had turned the ventilator back on again. That had been Alison's idea. Take no risks, make it look natural.

Don't fuck about with your career, pet . . .

Anne moved across to the ventilator and flipped back the plastic cover that protected the switch, as if it were the button that launched nuclear missiles. She looked over at the bed.

Alison had already closed her eyes.

Whatever the quality of the strange, laughable life that Alison had lived these last months, it had been lived to a permanent soundtrack of humming, hissing, beeping, dripping. Twenty-four hours a day. A life defined by noise.

James Bishop had condemned her to that, but Alison had refused to let herself be his victim.

Now, finally, the noise had stopped.

More than anything, Anne Coburn hoped that Alison might hold on to life just long enough to enjoy the silence.

AUTHOR'S NOTE

My research into locked-in syndrome has made one thing abundantly clear: there is no such thing as a typical case. There is certainly no such thing as a typical recovery, if one is made at all.

That said, any liberties that might have been taken with timeframes, procedure and so on have been taken purely in the interests of the story or else are simple, honest mistakes.

No aspersions as to the efficiency, dedication or commitment of medical staff at any hospital mentioned in this book are intended. Any comment on the parlous state of the National Health Service is meant to reflect badly *not* on the workers within it but on politicians and bureaucrats who, while they happily purchase private healthcare, consistently refuse to fund the NHS adequately in the hope that it will die a nice quiet death.

Mark Billingham, 2000

Scaredy Cat

For Katharine and Jack. But not yet.

And in memory of Vi Winyard (1925–2002)

ACKNOWLEDGEMENTS

As always, a great many people have helped, cajoled, suffered . . .

Special thanks are due to DI Neil Hibberd of the Serious Crime Group for his patience and informed creativity and also to Pauline O'Brien (Senior Press officer) and Selina Onorah (Office Manager) at the Metropolitan Police Area West Press Office, for their time and considerable trouble.

For invaluable advice on their own very different subjects, I must thank Jason Schone, Glenda Brunt, Yaron Meron and, as always, the correctly spelled Phil Cowburn.

At Little, Brown special thanks are due and in some cases overdue to: Filomena Wood, Alison Lindsay and Tamsyn Berryman.

There are those whose names, for many reasons, are destined to appear on this, and the corresponding page of all books to come . . .

Hilary Hale and Sarah Lutyens, obviously; Mike Gunn, for his past and his present; Alice Pettet, for notes and a name; David Fulton, for digging me out of a hole; Paul Thorne, for being unconvinced; Howard

Pratt, for knowing most things; Wendy Lee, for missing nothing . . .

And especially Peter Cocks, whose eyes and ears are sharper than most and whose instincts are rarely wrong.

And Claire, for being both Dave and Carmela.

Knock hard, life is deaf.

– Mimi Parent

PROLOGUE

KING EDWARD IV GRAMMAR SCHOOL FOR BOYS

14 August, 1984

Mr and Mrs R. Palmer
43, Valentine Rd
Harrow
Middlesex

Dear Mr and Mrs Palmer

Following an extraordinary meeting of the board of governors, it is with a good deal of regret that I write to confirm the decision to expel your son, Martin, from the school. This expulsion will come into effect immediately.

I must stress that this course of action is highly unusual and is only ever taken as a last resort. It was, however, deemed the only measure appropriate considering the nature of the offence. Your son's activities have been of concern for some time and are all the more disturbing considering his excellent academic record and previously reserved character. The most recent, repulsive incident is only the latest in a catalogue of unacceptable behaviour and flagrant breaches of school regulations.

As you are aware, your son is not the only pupil involved, and indeed, you may take some comfort from the fact that your son was almost certainly not the main perpetrator and has, in my opinion, been to some degree led astray. That said, however, he has shown little remorse for his actions and is unwilling to implicate his erstwhile partner in crime.

In order that the high educational standards of this school are maintained, I feel that similar standards of discipline must be enforced. This being the case, behaviour such as that engaged in by your son cannot be tolerated.

I wish Martin the best of luck in his new school.

Yours sincerely

P.H. Stanley

Philip Stanley, A.F.C., M.A. Headmaster.

Rectory Road, Harrow, Middlesex, MA3 4HL

PART ONE

EIGHT SUMMERS, ONE WINTER

2001

```
Date: 27 November
Target: Fem
Age: 20-30
Pickup: London railway station (Int or
Ext)
Site: TBA
Method: Hands only (weapon permitted to
subdue if necessary)
```

Nicklin watched, unblinking, as the two of them walked hand in hand towards him across the station concourse.

She was perfect.

He was still clutching the book he'd presumably been reading on the train and she was finishing a sandwich. The two of them were chatting and laughing. They kept moving. They looked straight at Nicklin but didn't see him. They weren't looking around for anybody. They were not expecting to be met.

He was sitting and sipping from a can of Coke, gazing casually towards the departure board every few minutes. Just another frustrated traveller monitoring the delays. He turned his head and watched them as they passed him. They were probably heading for taxi, bus or tube. If they were getting a cab then he'd settle back and wait for someone else. Annoying, but not the end of the world. If they were planning to continue their journey by public transport, he would follow.

He was in luck.

Still holding hands, the two of them stepped on to the escalator leading down to the underground. Nicklin put his half-empty can on the floor beside him and stood up, hearing his knee click loudly. He smiled. He wasn't getting any younger.

He reached into his coat pocket for the chocolate bar he'd bought earlier. Moving the knife aside, he took the chocolate out and began to unwrap it as he moved towards the escalator. As he stepped on behind a backpacker, he took a large bite, and after checking that the two of them were still there, twenty feet or so below him, he glanced out through the vast windows towards the bus depot. The crowds were thinning out now; the rush hour nearly over.

It was just starting to get dark. On the streets and in houses.

Inside people's heads.

They took the Northern line south. He settled down a few seats away, and watched. She was in her early thirties, he thought. Tall with dark hair, dark eyes and what Nicklin thought was called an olive complexion. What his mum might have called 'a touch of the tarbrush'. She wasn't pretty but she wasn't a dog either.

Not that it mattered really.

The train passed through the West End and continued south. Clapham, he guessed, or maybe Tooting. Wherever . . .

The two of them were all over each other. He was still looking at his book, glancing up every few seconds to grin at her. She squeezed his hand and on a couple of occasions she actually leant across to nuzzle his neck. People in the seats around them were smiling and shaking their heads.

He could feel the sweat begin to prickle on his forehead and smell that damp, downstairs smell that grew so strong, so acrid, whenever he got close.

They stood up as the train pulled into Balham station.

He watched them jump giggling from the train, and waited a second or two before casually falling into step behind them.

He stayed far enough behind them to be safe, but they were so wrapped up in each other that he could probably have walked at their heels. Oblivious, they drifted along in front of him, towards the station exit. She was wearing a long green coat and ankle boots. He was wearing a blue anorak and a woolly hat.

Nicklin wore a long black coat with deep pockets.

On the street ahead of him, with the gaudy Christmas lights as a backdrop, they were silhouetted against a crimson sky. He knew that this was one of the pictures he would remember. There would be others, of course.

They walked past a small parade of shops and he had to fight the urge to rush into a newsagent for more chocolate. He only had one bar left. He knew that he could be in and out in a few seconds but he daren't risk losing them. He'd get some more when it was all over. He'd be starving by then.

They turned off the main road into a well-lit but quiet side street and his breath grew ragged as he watched her reach into her pocket for keys. He picked up his pace a little. He could hear them talking about toast and tea and bed. He could see their joy at getting home.

He slid his hand into his pocket, looking around to see who might be watching.

Hoping it wasn't a flat. That he'd get some privacy. Praying for a bit of luck.

Her key slid into the lock and his hand moved across her mouth. Her first instinct was to scream but Nicklin pressed the knife into her back and with the pain came a little common sense. She didn't turn to try and look at him.

'Let's go inside.'

Tasting the sweat on his palm, feeling the piss run down her legs, she opens the front door, her hand flapping desperately, reaching down to her side for the one she loves. For the only one she cares about.

For her child.

'Please . . .'

Her voice is muffled by his hand. The word is lost. He pushes her and the boy through the doorway, hurries inside after them and slams the door shut.

The toddler in the blue anorak is still holding tight to his picture book. He looks up at the stranger with the same dark eyes as his mother, his mouth pursing into a tiny, infinitely confused 'O'.

ONE

A little after nine thirty in the morning. The first grey Monday of December. From the third floor of Becke House, Tom Thorne stared out across the monument to concrete and complacency that was Hendon, wishing more than anything that he wasn't thinking clearly.

He was, unfortunately, doing just that. Sorting the material in front of him, taking it all in. Assigning to each item, without knowing it, emotional responses that would colour every waking hour in the months to come.

And many sleeping hours too.

Wide awake and focused, Thorne sat and studied death, the way others at work elsewhere were looking at computer screens or sitting at tills. It was the material he worked with every day and yet, faced with *this*, something to take the edge off would have been nice. Even the steamhammer of a hangover would have been preferable. Something to blunt the corners a little. Something to turn the noise of the horror down.

He'd seen hundreds, maybe thousands, of photos like these. He'd stared at them over the years with the same dispassionate eye that a dentist might cast over X-rays, or an accountant across a tax return. He'd lost count of the pale limbs, twisted or torn or missing altogether in black and white ten-by-eights. Then there were the colour prints. Pale bodies lying on green carpets. A ring of purple bruises around a chalk-white neck. The garish patterned wallpaper against which the blood spatter is barely discernible.

An ever expanding exhibition with a simple message: emotions are powerful things, bodies are not.

These were the pictures filed in his office, with duplicates stored in the files in his head. Snapshots of deaths and portraits of lives lived to extremes. There were occasions when Thorne had gazed at these bodies in monochrome and thought he'd glimpsed rage or hatred or greed or lust, or perhaps the ghosts of such things, floating in the corners of rooms like ectoplasm.

The photographs on the table in front of him this morning were no more sickening than any he had seen before, but keeping his eyes on the image of the dead woman was like staring hard into a flame and feeling his eyeballs start to melt.

He was seeing her through the eyes of her child.

Charlie Garner aged three, now an orphan.

Charlie Garner aged three, being cared for by grandparents who wrestled every minute of every day with what to tell him about his mummy.

Charlie Garner aged three, who spent the best part of two days alone in a house with the body of his mother, clutching at a chocolate wrapper he'd licked clean, starving and dirty and screaming until a neighbour knocked.

'Tom . . .'

Thorne stared out into the greyness for a few more seconds before turning back resignedly to DCI Russell Brigstocke.

As part of the major reorganisation of the Met a year or so earlier, a number of new squads had been established within the three nascent Serious Crime Groups. A unit consisting entirely of officers brought out of retirement had been set up expressly to investigate cold cases. This unit, quickly christened the Crinkly Squad, was just one of a raft of new initiatives as part of a fresh and supposedly proactive approach to fighting crime in the capital. There were other squads specialising in sexual assaults, violence against children and firearms offences.

Then there was Team 3, Serious Crime Group (West).

Officially, this squad was devised to investigate cases whose parameters were outside those which might be investigated elsewhere – cases that didn't fit anybody else's remit. There *were* those, however, who suggested that SCG (West) 3 had been set up simply because no-one quite knew what to do with Detective Inspector Tom Thorne. Thorne himself reckoned that the truth was probably somewhere halfway between the two.

Russell Brigstocke was the senior officer and Thorne had known him for over ten years. He was a big man who cut a distinctive figure with horn-rimmed glasses and hair of which he was inordinately proud. It was thick and blue-black, and the DCI took great delight in teasing it up into a quiff of almost Elvis-like proportions. But if he was a caricaturist's dream, he could also be a suspect's worse nightmare. Thorne had seen Brigstocke with glasses off and fists clenched, hair flopping around his sweat-drenched forehead as he stalked around an interview room, shouting, threatening, carrying out the threat, looking for the truth.

'Carol Garner was a single mum. She was twenty-eight

years old. Her husband died in a road accident three years ago, just after their son was born. She was a teacher. She was found dead in her home in Balham four days ago. There were no signs of forced entry. She'd arrived back at Euston station at six thirty p.m. on the twenty-seventh having been to Birmingham to visit her parents. We think that the killer followed her from the station, probably on the tube. We found a travelcard in her pocket.'

Brigstocke's voice was low and accentless, almost a monotone. Yet the litany of facts simply stated was horribly powerful. Thorne knew most of it, having been briefed by Brigstocke the day before, but still the words were like a series of punches, each harder than the last, combining to leave him aching and breathless. He could see that the others were no less shocked.

And he knew that they had yet to hear the worst.

Brigstocke continued. 'We can only speculate on how the killer gained entry or how long he spent inside Carol Garner's home, but we know what he did when he was there . . .'

Brigstocke looked down the length of the table asking the man at the other end to carry on where he had left off. Thorne stared at the figure in the black fleece, with shaved head and a startling collection of facial piercings. Phil Hendricks was not everybody's idea of a pathologist, but he was the best Thorne had ever worked with. Thorne raised an eyebrow. Was there yet another earring since he'd last seen him? Hendricks was fond of commemorating each new boyfriend with a ring, stud or spike. Thorne sincerely hoped that he would settle down soon, before he was completely unable to lift his head up.

Dr Phil Hendricks was the civilian member of the team. He was there at the beginning, obviously, as the discovery of a body was almost certainly what galvanised the team in the first place. The body that would yield to the knife; the story behind its journey to a cold steel slab whispered in secrets, revealed by its dead flesh and petrified organs. These were the pathologist's areas of expertise.

Though he and Hendricks were good friends, from this point on, in the context of the investigation, Thorne would be happy if he did not see him again.

'Based on when we know she got on a train from Birmingham, we think she was killed somewhere between seven and ten p.m. on the twenty-seventh. She'd been dead for something like forty-eight hours when she was found.'

The flat Mancunian accent conveyed with a simple precision the tawdry and banal reality of genuine horror. Thorne could see the unspeakable thought in the faces of those around the table.

What were those two days like for little Charlie Garner?

'There were no signs of sexual abuse and no indication that she put up any significant struggle. The obvious conclusion is that the killer threatened the child.' Hendricks stopped, took a breath. 'He strangled Carol Garner with his bare hands.'

'Fucker . . .'

Thorne glanced to his left. Detective Sergeant Sarah McEvoy stared down at the file in front of her. Thorne waited, but for the moment it seemed that she'd said everything that was on her mind. Of all of them, she was the officer who Thorne had known for the shortest time. And he still didn't know her at all. Tough, no question, and more than capable. But there was something about her that made Thorne a little wary. There was something hidden.

The voice of DC Dave Holland focused Thorne's thoughts again. 'Do we think he targeted her because of the child?'

Thorne nodded. 'It was her weakness. Yes, I think he probably did . . .'

Brigstocke interrupted. 'But it isn't really significant.'

'Not really significant?' Holland sounded thoroughly confused and looked across at his boss.

Thorne shrugged and threw him a look back. *Wait and see Dave . . .*

It was just over a year since Thorne had first begun working with Dave Holland and he was at last starting to look like a grown-up. His hair was still far too blond and floppy, but the features it framed seemed set a little harder these days. Thorne knew that this was not so much to do with age as experience. Wear and tear. The most wholesome and guileless of faces was bound to cloud a little when confronted with some of the things the job threw up.

The change had begun during their first case together. Three months in which Thorne had lost friends and made enemies, while Dave Holland grew closer to him, watching and absorbing and becoming someone else. Three months that had ended with the slash of a scalpel in a blood-drenched attic in south London.

Holland had learned and *unlearned* a great deal, and Thorne had watched it happen, proud yet saddened. It was an argument that he had with himself on a regular basis. Were they mutually exclusive – the good copper and the good person?

Learning a degree of desensitisation was all very well but there would be a price to pay. He remembered a warning poster he had seen in a dentist's waiting room: the graphic image of a lip bitten clean off by a patient 'testing' the local anaesthetic. You could bite and bite and not feel a thing, but it was only a matter of time until the anaesthetic wore off and then the pain would certainly begin.

The numbness would wear off too, for those colleagues who Thorne watched getting through their days inside their own brand of armour. Whether manufactured in their heads or from a bottle, it would surely wear off one day and then the agony would be unbearable. This was not Tom Thorne's way, and despite the bravado and bullshit that he'd learned, he instinctively knew that it wasn't Holland's either.

The good copper and the good person. Probably *not* mutually exclusive, just fucking difficult to reconcile. Like one of those things in physics that is theoretically possible but that nobody has ever seen.

A silence had settled briefly across what was laughably described as the conference room. It was actually little more than a slightly bigger office, with a jug of coffee and a few more uncomfortable plastic chairs than normal. Thorne considered what he knew about the man who had killed Carol Garner. A man who liked, who needed to be in control. A coward. Perhaps not commanding physically . . . Christ, he was starting to sound like one of those forensic psychiatrists he thought were so overpaid. What he *did* know of course, was that this killer was far from ordinary. Extraordinary, and with a greater *potential*, than Holland or McEvoy yet understood.

Then of course there was the *why*. Always the why. And, as always, Tom Thorne didn't give a flying fuck about it. He would confront it if it presented itself. He would grab it with both hands if he could catch the killer with it. But he didn't *care*. At least, not about whether the man he was after had ever been given a bicycle as a child . . .

McEvoy was shifting on the chair next to him. She had finished looking through her file and he could sense that she had something to say.

'What is it, Sarah?'

'This is horrible, no question . . . and the stuff with the kid, it's very fucking nasty, but I still can't quite see why it's us. As opposed to anybody else. I mean, how do we know she wasn't killed by someone she knew? There were no signs of forced entry, it might have been a boyfriend or an ex-boyfriend . . . so, why us? Sir.'

Thorne looked towards Brigstocke who, with the timing of an expert, lobbed another sheaf of photographs into the middle of the table.

Holland casually reached out to take a photo. 'I was thinking the same thing. I don't understand what makes—' He stopped as he took in the image of the woman on her back, her mouth open, her eyes bulging and bloodied. The woman lying among the rubbish bags in a cold dark street. The woman who was not Carol Garner.

It was a dramatic gesture and meant to be. Brigstocke wanted his team fired up. He wanted them shocked, motivated, passionate.

He certainly had their attention.

It was Thorne who explained exactly what they were up against. 'What makes this different, Holland' – he looked at McEvoy – 'what makes it *us*, is that he did it again.'

Now, it was as if the previous silence had been a cacophony. Thorne could hear nothing but the distant echo of his own voice and the hiss of the adrenaline fizzing through his bloodstream. Brigstocke and Hendricks sat frozen, heads bowed. Holland and McEvoy exchanged a horrified glance.

'It's the reason we know he followed Carol Garner from Euston station. Because as soon as he'd finished killing her, that same day, he went to King's Cross. He went to a different station, found another woman, and did it all over again.'

Karen, it happened again.

Please, let me tell you what happened. I couldn't bear it if you thought badly of me. I know that you can't possibly forgive or condone what I've done . . . what I'm doing, but I know that you'll understand. I've always thought that if I had the chance to explain myself to you, confide in you, that you would be the one person who would truly understand. You always saw me for what I was. You always knew what I thought about you. I could see it in that shy smile.

You knew that you had a power over me, didn't you, but I was never angry with you because of it. Part of me enjoyed the teasing. I wanted to be the one you teased. It felt like I was needed anyway. It just made you more attractive to me, Karen . . .

Jesus, though. Jesus. I did it again. What I was told.

She was alone and frightened of nothing. I could tell by the way she was walking when I followed her out of the station. Not a cocky fearlessness, just a sort of trust. She saw the good in everyone, I could tell that. It was dark and she couldn't see how weak and vile I was. There was no fear in her eyes when I spoke to her.

She knew though, what was going to happen, when she saw the fear in mine.

As soon as she knew, she struggled, but she wasn't strong enough. She was less than half my size, Karen, and I just had to wait for her to fade a little. She was scratching and spitting and I couldn't look at her. And when it was over, I couldn't bear it that her face, which had been so open and warm like yours, now looked like something behind glass, or frozen for a long time inside a block of ice, and I was the one who had made it like that.

And I was hard, Karen. Down there. While I was doing it, and again afterwards, while I was hiding her. I stayed excited until the hissing in my head began to die down and the scratches on my hands started to hurt.

I was hard like I never am, even when I'm thinking about the past.

I don't want to embarrass you by talking like this, but if I can't be honest with you about these things then there's no point to anything. I never really told you what I was thinking when I had the chance, so I'm not going to hide things now.

And I will never lie to you, Karen, I promise you that.

Of course, you're not the only one who knows what I really am but you're the only one who can see what's inside. I'm not making excuses, I know that I deserve nothing, but at the very least I'm being open about everything. Open and honest.

She was nothing to me, this woman from the station. She was nothing to me and I squeezed the life out of her.

I'm so very sorry, and I deserve what is surely coming.

I hate to ask a favour, Karen, but if you see her, the woman I killed, will you tell her that for me?

1982

The kids called it 'the Jungle Story'.

The victim was pinned to the tarmac with one boy holding down each arm and another sitting astride his chest. The fingers were the weapons – tapping, prodding, poking – jabbing out the rhythms of the story on the breastbone. The steps of each new animal marching through the jungle. The story was a very simple one; a straightforward excuse to inflict pain.

The wiry, black-haired boy leaned against the wall, his small dark eyes taking in every detail. Watching as the torment began.

When it was just the monkeys, or whichever of the small creatures the storyteller introduced early on, it was not really much more than a tickle. The victim would writhe around, telling them to stop, to get off; the fear of what was to come worse than anything. Then would come the lions and tigers. Heavier steps, the fingers jabbing harder, tears beginning to prick in the corners of the eyes. Everything, of course, leading up to the seemingly endless herd of elephants tramping through the jungle, the fingers slamming into the chest, the pain excruciating.

The big kid on the floor was screaming now.

The boy pushed himself away from the wall, took his hands from his pockets and moved across the playground to where the crowd of onlookers stood in a circle, jeering and clapping. It was time to intervene.

The one telling the 'story' was called Bardsley. The boy

hated him. He shoved his way through the crowd, which was not difficult as most of the other third formers were scared of him. He was, after all, the 'mad' one, the one who would do anything. The kid who would throw a desk out of the window or wave his tiny cock around in class, or let a teacher's tyres down. He'd had to suffer a great many detentions in his time to earn his reputation, but it was worth it in terms of the respect it won him.

He didn't care about geography or French grammar but he knew about respect.

He reached down, casually took hold of Bardsley's hair and yanked him backwards. There was a gasp from the crowd, which quickly turned to nervous laughter as Bardsley jumped up, furious, ready to transfer his aggression onto whoever was responsible for the terrible stinging on his scalp.

Then he saw who was to blame. The boy, far smaller and slighter than he was, stared calmly back at him, eyes cold and dark as stones frozen in mud, hands once more thrust deep into his pockets.

The crowd dispersed quickly into smaller groups. A kickabout was already starting as Bardsley backed away towards the changing rooms, promising some nasty revenge after school but not really meaning it.

The boy on the floor stood up and began to rearrange his dishevelled uniform. He didn't say anything, but eyed his saviour nervously while doing up his tie and dragging a sleeve across his snotty top lip.

The black-haired boy had seen him around but they had never spoken. He was a year younger, probably only twelve, and the different years didn't really mix. His sandy hair was usually neatly combed with a parting, and he was often to be seen in a corner somewhere, his pale blue eyes peeking out enviously from behind a book, observing the assorted games he had no part in. He was a big kid, at least a foot taller than most of the others in his year and brainy as hell, but he was slow in all the ways that counted. He probably hadn't done anything specific to piss Bardsley off, but that wasn't really the point.

The older boy watched, smiling as a brown plastic comb was produced and dragged through the sandy hair, dislodging pieces of playground grit. He had a comb himself of course, but it was a metal one; far cooler, and used mostly for the lunch-time comb fights of which he was the acknowledged champion. These fights were a more brutal version of 'Slaps' or 'Scissors, paper, rock' and could leave a hand dripping with blood within a few seconds. He was the champion, not because he was quicker than anybody else, but because he could stand the pain for longer.

He could put up with a great deal of pain when he had to.

The sandy-haired boy carefully put away his comb in the inside pocket of his blazer, cleared his throat nervously and produced a rarely seen smile. It quickly disappeared when it was not reciprocated. In its place, a hand, notably free of scratches and scabs, was extended.

'Thank you for . . . doing that. I'm Palmer. Martin . . .'

The wiry black-haired boy, the mad boy, the boy who would do anything, nodded. He ignored the hand and spoke his name with a sly smile, as if revealing a dirty secret.

As if giving a gift that was actually worth far more than it looked.

'Nicklin.'

TWO

'A few less questions, when it's all over, even *one* less than when a case begins, and you're doing all right . . .'

Thorne smiled as he carried his coffee through to the living room, remembering Holland's reaction when he had first passed on this pithy piece of homespun wisdom. It had also, he recalled, been the first time that Thorne had managed to get him inside a pub. An auspicious day.

Questions . . .

In the pub, Holland had smiled. 'What? You mean questions like, "Why didn't I study harder at school?" and, "Isn't there anybody else available?"'

'I think I preferred you when you were an arse-licker, Holland . . .'

Thorne put his mug on the mantelpiece and bent down to light the flame-effect gas fire in the mock-Georgian fireplace. The central heating was up as high as it would go but he was still freezing. *And* his back was playing up. *And* it was pissing down . . .

There were plenty of questions that needed answering right now.

Were the two killings genuinely connected? Apart from

the date and the fact that both women were strangled, there seemed to be no other link, so was the station thing just a coincidence? King's Cross threw up other possibilities. Had he mistaken the second victim for a prostitute? Why kill one at home and one on the street?

And the biggest question of the lot: did he kill twice on the same day because he was out of control, or was killing multiple victims actually the pattern? Blood lust or compulsion? Right now, Holland and McEvoy were earning overtime trying to find out, but whichever it was, the answer was not going to be pleasant.

In the eight months or so that the team had been together, they had only really worked on two major cases that were truly their own. Most of the time they'd been seconded – either individually or together – on to other investigations with other units, and then been reconvened when needed.

The aftermath of the terrorist atrocities of September 11 had seen the teams from Serious Crime involved in an operation unlike any before. Some had expressed surprise that repatriating bodies from New York should be down to them, but it made sense to Thorne. These were British citizens. They had been murdered. It wasn't complicated.

The phone calls had been the hardest: thousands of people eager to trace husbands and wives, sons and daughters who hadn't been in touch and who may or may not have been in the area. So far, of the hundreds whose missing relatives never did get in touch with them, only one had been given an identifiable body to bury . . .

Three months on, and the Met was still stretched – tracking down Anthrax hoaxers, monitoring possible terrorist targets, chasing their tails while street crime grew to fill the hole that was left. If suddenly phone-jacking didn't seem quite so important, there *were* still crimes, like those that Team 3 got handed, that needed to be taken very seriously indeed.

The two cases were both . . . unusual. The first was a series of gruesome killings in south-east London that bore all the hallmarks of gangland slayings. However, the bodies (when they'd been painstakingly re-assembled) were found to belong, not to drug-dealers or loan sharks, but to ordinary, law-abiding citizens. It quickly became clear that the murders were the work of one highly disturbed individual as opposed to an organised gang of them. Whether the killer – a happily married electrical engineer – had been simply trying to disguise his work, or had a psychotic fixation with the disposal methods of gangsters, was as yet unclear. He was still undergoing psychiatric evaluation.

The other case was the more disturbing, despite the lack of bodies. Guests in hotels were being targeted and robbed in their rooms. The minor physical assaults that were part and parcel of the thefts had soon begun to escalate however. Those that willingly handed over cash, Rolexes and other valuables were being tortured anyway. The knife was produced and the PIN number was demanded. The number was given and the knife was used anyway. Small cuts, nicks: wounding for pure pleasure. Thorne knew that this one liked the feel of a blade on skin, enjoyed hearing the intake of breath, and watching the thin red line fill out on the flesh and begin to drip.

The robbery was becoming something else: the robber, *someone* else. Behind his black balaclava, he was starting to enjoy his work a little too much and it was only a matter of time until people started to die.

That was when Thorne had been brought in.

With next to no physical evidence and no real description to work from, the case had quickly become hugely frustrating. Thorne, Holland and McEvoy, in an effort to trap this latent killer, this murderer-to-be, had spent nights in some very nice hotels but without success. Their efforts had evidently been noted and the individual responsible had gone to ground.

Two cases, one arrest. A fifty per cent hit rate, and the numbers would only get worse from here on in. Some had joked that the hotel case, given a few weeks, would get passed on to the Crinkly Squad anyway, but Thorne knew differently. Anybody who enjoyed inflicting pain to the degree this man did, would need to do it again. He would resurface somewhere. The MO might be completely different, but Thorne did not doubt for a second that one day soon he would be providing a pathologist somewhere with some overtime.

Thorne took his coffee across to the sofa and picked up the file on Carol Garner. He sat for a few minutes, not opening it, just staring out into the rain and thinking about the hundreds, the thousands of different people across the capital who owed their employment to the violent death of another. Thinking about the money generated by murder.

Thinking about the industry of killing.

Dave Holland stared over the top of his computer screen at Sarah McEvoy who was avidly studying hers. He thought about his girlfriend, Sophie.

The ongoing argument which they had been having in instalments for the past year, had flared up again. Sophie had a problem with Thorne. She had only met him once and had formed an opinion based entirely on what Holland himself had said about Thorne in the early days of their working relationship. So the man described by Holland over a year ago as 'obsessive' and 'arrogant' had become, in the strange folklore of Sophie's imagination, a pigheaded, self-serving lunatic whose refusal to follow procedure would one day cost him not only *his* career, but those of the people around him. *Those who didn't know any better . . .*

It wasn't that she didn't want Holland to do the job. She just wanted him to do it in a particular way; to be the sort of copper who keeps his head down and gets promoted, and who is universally liked. A copper who does just enough.

A copper like his father.

Once, she'd intimated that if he chose to go a different route then he would be going it alone. He had been furious at the threat and the ultimatum had been quietly forgotten.

At least, they both pretended that it had.

The arguments were never heated. The two of them were sulkers, bottlers-up. It was more a series of snipes and barbed comments, and the intensity had increased as soon as the new case had started. Yesterday evening, after a hectic day that had begun with the team briefing, Sophie had looked up at him across the kitchen table, smiled, and opened her account.

'So how many people did the great Tom Thorne piss off today then?'

He wasn't sure what upset him most about the whole thing. The assumption that as far as *his* career was concerned, she knew best? The lack of support? Or the fact that when it came to her assessment of Thorne, most of the time she was absolutely right?

McEvoy glanced up from her monitor and fixed him with bright green eyes. *Caught you.*

She was tall, 5′ 7″ or 5′ 8″, with shoulder-length, curly brown hair, a broken nose and full lips which smiled easily and, so it seemed to Holland, often. Right now, he reckoned the smile had at least three different meanings.

He didn't understand any of them.

'I heard something very strange today.' Despite the surname, she was pure North London Jewish. Her accent was flattish, hard. Sexy. 'A vicious rumour about the Weeble . . .' The nickname was a reference to Thorne's shape, to how hard people thought it would be to make him fall down.

Holland raised his eyebrows. *Another rumour?* When it came to Thorne, he'd heard most of it, but he enjoyed a good story or bit of gossip as much as anybody else.

'I heard that he likes country-and-western. Is that true?'

Holland nodded, as if confirming a terminal diagnosis. 'Yeah, he loves it.'

'What, all that yee-hah and Dolly Parton and stuff? Does he go line dancing?'

Holland laughed. 'I think it's a bit more obscure than that. He used to listen to a lot of techno and garage stuff as well, but I think that was just a phase.' He blinked slowly, remembering the almost hypnotic noise. Remembering the case it had helped to blot out.

McEvoy looked disappointed. 'Shame. He was starting to sound interesting there for a minute.'

'Oh he's . . . interesting.'

Holland believed *that* about Thorne, if he believed anything. If interesting meant unpredictable and stubborn. If it meant refusing to admit that you might be wrong. If interesting meant determined, and vengeful, and knowing the difference between right and wrong whatever the poxy rules said. And refusing to suffer fools. And possessing the kind of passion that would always make something happen. A passion that Dave Holland, whatever other people might want him to do and be, would have killed to have even the tiniest fucking bit of . . .

He thought about his father. A man who died a sergeant at sixty. Having done just enough.

McEvoy shrugged and her eyes dropped back to her screen. Back to the computerised catalogue of suffering and death from which the two of them were supposed, hopefully, to come up with some answers.

Holland had believed that relatively, London could not be *that* violent a city and that their search would not be overly time-consuming.

He had been wrong on both counts.

Looking for murders committed on the same day *had* sounded fairly straightforward, but Thorne was not a man who did things by half. Both time-frame and search criteria were broadening all the time. McEvoy and Holland had begun by looking for strangulations first and then widened things from there. They couldn't rule out assaults as they might be the work of the same man who had now perhaps graduated to full-blown murder. Even discounting domestics and gang-related attacks, it was a big job. To check thoroughly, to go back far enough to find a pattern – if indeed there was one – was going to take time.

Holland looked up at the clock. Another twenty minutes and they could call it a night. He tried to picture Thorne in a stetson and cowboy boots but the image wouldn't stick.

Thorne was too dangerous to be a figure of fun.

*

Johnny Cash made good music to read post-mortem reports by.

This, after all, was someone who once famously sang about shooting a man just to watch him die. Whether this was big talk or just a very bad case of boredom, he sang as if he knew a great deal about death. Thorne wondered, as he read the words Phil Hendricks had used to describe the manner of Carol Garner's death, how much he really knew. Now, the man with a voice like the long, slow tumble towards hell was singing about flesh and blood needing flesh and blood. Thorne certainly didn't require it, but the proof was there on his lap, right in front of him – the proof that sometimes, flesh and blood needed to *destroy* flesh and blood, too.

The body of the second victim, Ruth Murray, had been examined by another pathologist. Thorne had seen the initial report which confirmed strangulation as the cause of death and revealed that tissue had been removed from beneath the victim's fingernails for DNA-testing. He wasn't going to get too excited just yet. It sounded promising, but he would wait to see what Hendricks had to say once he'd carried out a second PM.

Thorne had once thought strangulation, as ways of dying went, to be a fairly soft option. It could surely not be as terrible as being repeatedly stabbed or bludgeoned. It was certainly not on a par with drowning, or suffocating or swallowing bleach.

He'd thought this, until he'd read his first PM report on a victim of manual strangulation. In many ways, the use of the bare hands to throttle – the flesh on flesh – made it the very worst type of killing. There was no weapon to separate killer from victim. In most cases the victim would lapse into unconsciousness quickly, but the damage inflicted could be massive, often leaving the victim as bloody and bruised as if they had been attacked with a hammer.

Carol Garner had died from asphyxia due to the compression of the carotid arteries, her body displaying virtually every classic trait consistent with violent strangulation.

The eyes were open, the eyeballs distended, the corneas and skin around the eyes showing signs of haemorrhage. The neck was a mass of bruises, some nearly an inch in diameter and there were bloody, half-moon-shaped indentations from the nails on the fingers and thumbs of the killer.

Thorne's hands drifted towards his throat. He closed his eyes.

Was that chocolate bar his, Charlie? Did he give it you to keep you quiet? Or did he produce it himself, afterwards, and eat it slowly, watching her, while you were crying?

There was massive bruising and abrasion to the floor of the mouth, the epiglottis and the lining of the larynx. The tongue had been all but bitten clean through. The crocoid cartilage was crushed, the thyroid cartilage virtually unrecognisable and the hyoid bone was fractured. It was this internal damage which most clearly indicated the severity of the attack which led to Carol Garner's death.

Did you see it happen, Charlie? Did he shut you out of the room, or did you stand and scream, and beat your tiny fists on his back and watch your mummy's eyeballs bulging out of their sockets?

Thorne leaned down to pick up the coffee that he'd left on the floor by the sofa. It was stone cold. He looked at his watch. He'd been immersed in the details of death for well over an hour. Thorne was as disturbed as always by this . . . capacity he had.

He'd tried reading crime fiction once but it had not suited him at all. He could barely read any so-called thriller for more than a few minutes without starting to drift away, and yet a jargon-filled description of ruined flesh had him riveted. He was confident that there was nothing overly perverse in this. He could honestly say that he had never enjoyed *watching* an autopsy.

The truth was that an intimate knowledge of real killers and real victims made him a difficult reader to please.

Thorne had seen enough wild-eyed gunmen and bloodied blades, and soft-spoken, heavy-lidded perverts. He'd seen plenty of batterers and arsonists and smiling poisoners. He'd seen more than his fair share of damaged bodies: some dead, and others more damaged still, left behind to remember.

He'd seen holes in flesh and holes in lives.

Thorne picked up his coffee cup and was heading for the kitchen to make another when the doorbell rang.

Hendricks was standing on the doorstep wearing a floor-length black leather coat and watch cap. He was brandishing a blue-striped plastic bag that was threatening to break at any instant thanks to the vast quantity of cheap lager it contained. The accent hardly suited dramatic declamation, but he did his best. 'Let us drink beer and talk of death.'

Thorne turned and headed back inside. Neither of them was big on ceremony. 'It sounds like you've already started on the drinking bit . . .'

Hendricks slammed the outer door and followed Thorne inside. 'I've been doing both, mate. I've been with

Dr Duggan most of the day . . .' He closed the inner door and moved into the living room.

'He the one who did the first post-mortem on Ruth Murray?'

'She. *Emma* Duggan. Very good, *and* very fanciable, if you like that kind of thing.'

Thorne shook his head and reached into the plastic bag that Hendricks was now cradling gently. 'Formaldehyde does nothing for me, sorry.'

'And I've spent the last few hours up to my elbows in Ruth Murray myself, so yes,' Hendricks said, dumping the bag on the sofa, 'I *did* have a couple on the way over.'

While Hendricks took off his coat, Thorne opened a beer and picked up the CD remote control. He switched Cash's *Solitary Man* back to the beginning. The guitar kicked in on 'I Won't Back Down'.

Thorne took the chair and Hendricks the sofa. It was a familiar and comfortable arrangement that, bar a few awkward weeks the year before, had been repeated at least weekly since Thorne had first moved in nearly eighteen months ago. He'd rattled around in the big house in Highbury for three years after his divorce, before finally taking the plunge and buying the flat. He still hadn't got used to the place. He *did* like the oatmeal IKEA sofa a lot better now it had a few beer stains, but though the place was at last starting to look worn, it had become no more welcoming.

The person responsible for most of the stains grunted, at home now and ready to talk about death.

'So . . . ?' Thorne was trying not to sound impatient.

'So . . . interesting.'

The phone rang. Thorne sighed, pulled himself out of

the chair and marched across to where the cordless phone stood, near the front door.

'Thorne . . .'

'Sir, it's Holland . . .'

'Nothing so far then?' He could hear the confusion in the silence from the other end. 'Don't worry, Holland, I can always tell if you're excited. Your voice goes up an octave.'

'Sir . . .'

'So, nothing at all? Maybe we need to widen things geographically as well . . .'

'There were a couple that looked likely, but there were arrests on both of them and the only other ones, two assaults . . . and two women stabbed on the same day in July, didn't pan out timing-wise.'

'Sure?'

'Positive. McEvoy double-checked. Couldn't have been the same killer who did both. Even if . . . you know, the times of death were a bit off . . . he'd have needed a helicopter to have done both of them.'

'OK, knock it on the head . . . like you weren't about to anyway. Tomorrow you might have more luck. I'm sure this wasn't his first time. You'll get something. Besides, you won't have any distractions.'

'Sorry?'

'I'm taking DS McEvoy with me to Birmingham.'

It took Holland a few seconds to work out why Thorne might be going to Birmingham, and why he would want Sarah McEvoy to go with him. Once he had, he was grateful that he would be the one stuck in front of a computer all day.

Then, after he'd hung up, Holland started to wonder what Thorne had meant by 'distractions'.

'Tell me about *interesting*.' Hendricks looked up at him and raised an eyebrow. Thorne went on. 'Ruth Murray. "Interesting", you said.'

Ruth Murray. 32. Married with, thankfully, no children. Hers actually the first body to be found, wedged in behind a large metal rubbish bin in a road behind King's Cross station.

Hendricks had helped himself to the meagre contents of Thorne's fridge while he'd been on the phone to Holland, and his reply was broken up as he attempted to swallow an enormous bite of a cheese sandwich. 'I'm writing it up . . . first thing tomorrow . . .'

'I won't be here first thing tomorrow.'

'I'll have it on your desk by midday, all right . . . ?'

'Just give me the highlights, Phil.'

Hendricks wiped his mouth, swung his legs off the sofa and turned to face Thorne. There were important things to be said. 'OK, well first off, don't get too excited about the skin under her fingernails.'

'Because . . . ?'

'Because most of it's probably hers.' He explained before Thorne had a chance to ask him to. 'It's quite common with strangulations. The victim often scratches their own neck in an attempt to remove the ligature . . . or in this case the killer's hands.' As Hendricks explained, his hands automatically went to his neck and Thorne watched them scrabbling at the flesh. 'She had good nails . . . made a right mess of her neck. She might have scratched him as well though, so it's worth looking at.'

'Carol Garner didn't have good nails?'

Hendricks shook his head. 'Badly bitten . . .' Thorne wondered if she'd begun biting her nails after her husband had been killed. Looking at her baby son and seeing his father. Never dreaming that the boy would be an orphan before his fourth birthday.

'But . . .'

'What?' Thorne leant forward, on the edge of his chair. Hendricks had been saving something up. Always the need to show off just a little.

'We might . . . *might*, have another DNA source. Duggan missed something.'

'But you said . . .'

'She was good. Yeah, she is. Just not as good as me.'

Thorne could not keep the irritation out of his voice. 'For fuck's sake, Phil, can we cut the Quincy crap?'

'All right . . . look, once it had been established that there hadn't been a sexual assault, Duggan didn't see any point in looking for bodily fluids. It was a fair enough presumption really, the body was fully clothed, same as Carol Garner. But I'd checked when I did the PM on *her*, so I looked anyway . . .'

Thorne held his breath. He could feel the excitement building in the same place it always did: at the base of his skull. A tingling, a buzzing, a low throb of excitement and revulsion in advance of the detail to come. He hated it when it was sexual. There was always a slightly higher chance of a result, but still, he hated it.

Hendricks was equally excited. 'It was Luminol and UV that did it in the end. Tiny patches all over her face and on her arms. It took me ages to work out what it was; it was actually more about working out what it wasn't . . .'

Thorne nodded. It was good news; if they caught him it almost certainly guaranteed a conviction, but it sickened him just the same. It was no consolation that the killer would probably have done it after Ruth Murray had been killed. If anything, it made it worse.

'Forty-eight hours then?'

Hendricks held up a hand. 'Yeah, hopefully. There's really only a minuscule amount of the stuff and to be honest, I'm not even sure we can get anything. There may be *some* cellular material, but I've certainly never heard of it being done . . .'

Thorne stood up. 'Hang on, Phil, I'm lost here . . . are we not talking about sperm?'

Hendricks shook his head. 'Tears, mate. Dried tears.'

Thorne's mouth actually fell open a little. Hendricks casually reached down for another can of beer. 'Fucker wasn't wanking while he was killing her, Tom, he was weeping.'

1983

Nicklin walked back towards the railway line, his right hand hanging awkwardly, cradling his clammy treasure. In his other hand was the last of a melting chocolate bar. He pushed what was left of it into his mouth, threw the wrapper onto the floor and turned around. He was twenty feet or so away, ready for his run-up, but Palmer had put the bat down.

Nicklin's face reddened. He had a good mind to stroll back and start smacking Palmer over the head with it, but he stayed calm. 'Come on Mart, pick the bat up. This is going to be brilliant.'

The bigger boy shook his head, squinting at Nicklin and raising a hand to shield his eyes from the sun. 'I don't want to.'

'Why not?'

'I just don't want to.' They stared at each other for a while. 'Why can't I bowl? You're much better at batting than me . . .'

'You can bowl next time.'

Palmer looked vaguely sick. 'Are we going to do it again? But how . . . ?'

Nicklin laughed. 'There's loads of them round here. Now stop pissing around, Martin. Pick the bat up.'

Palmer said nothing, thinking about the two more weeks until they went back to school.

The rails began to hum; there was a train coming. They watched as it rumbled past, a knackered old engine pulling a couple of rusty hoppers. Within thirty seconds, the only sound was a distant sizzle and the chirrup of a grasshopper from somewhere close by.

Palmer looked up. He saw the blue and pink splotches of cornflowers and foxgloves against the green of the embankment on the other side of the tracks. He saw mare's tails and periwinkles at Nicklin's feet. He saw Nicklin just staring at him, with the look that made his palms sweat and his head ache and his bladder start to fill.

Still, he didn't want to do this.

It always came down to something like this. Nicklin would find him and they'd spend half an hour or so down by the railway line, chucking stones at bottles or talking about football, until Nicklin smiled that smile and the games would change. Then they'd be dumping turds through letterboxes, or lobbing eggs at buses, or . . . this.

Palmer could hear a rustling in the long grass on the bank behind him. He wanted to turn around and see what it was, but he couldn't stop looking at Nicklin. Suddenly, Nicklin looked really sad. On the verge of tears almost. Palmer shouted to him.

'Look, it doesn't really matter does it? We can do something else . . .'

Nicklin nodded, tightening his fist, squeezing what was held inside. 'I know, course we can. I just thought . . . you were my mate that's all. If you don't want to be mates, just say, and I'll go. Just say . . .'

Palmer felt light-headed. A trickle of sweat was running down his back. He couldn't bear the thought of Nicklin feeling like this. Nicklin was his best mate. He would far rather he was angry with him than feel let down. He felt himself reaching down for the cricket bat, and was elated to look up and see Nicklin beaming at him.

'That's it, Martin. I knew you would. Ready?'

Palmer nodded slowly and Nicklin started running towards him, concentrating, his tongue poking between his teeth.

The frog spread its arms and legs out as soon as Nicklin let it go and for a second it looked as if it was flying. Nicklin began to cheer as soon as he opened his hand.

'Now Mart . . . now.'

Palmer shut his eyes and swung the bat.

It was a wet sound. Dull and sloppy. A small vibration up his arm.

Nicklin watched the whole thing, wide-eyed and yelling. His eyes never moved from the glorious blur of blood and green guts that flew gracefully into the nettles on the other side of the railway line.

He spun round, his black eyes bright in expectation of the sick, shit-a-brick look on Palmer's pale spotty face. The expression that he always saw afterwards. He froze and narrowed his eyes, focusing on something else: something behind Palmer and above him.

Palmer dropped the bat and turned away without looking at the stain on the blade to climb back up the bank. He stopped dead in his tracks. Next to the hole in the chain-link fence, the tall grass past her knees, stood a girl with long blonde hair. She looked the same age as him, perhaps a little older. Palmer had never seen anyone as beautiful in his whole life. The girl put two fingers into her mouth and whistled.

Then she started to clap, grinning her pretty little head off.

THREE

Both Thorne and McEvoy felt distinctly uneasy as they walked across the concourse at Euston station. Neither admitted this to the other and both later wished that they had. Both, as they bought magazines and papers, grabbed last-minute teas or cold drinks, imagined the eyes of a killer on them.

He had watched Carol Garner in this same place, and followed her. Perhaps he'd been standing where they now stood when he first saw her. Reading a newspaper or listening to a walkman, or gazing through the window of a shop at socks and ties. Thorne looked at the faces of the people around him and wondered if Carol Garner had looked into the eyes of the man who would later murder her. Perhaps she'd smiled at him or asked him the time, or given him a cigarette . . .

They walked towards the platform, past their own tattered posters requesting help and information from the public. There were similar posters at King's Cross and these had given them their only real lead thus far – a partial description. A forty-one-year-old prostitute named Margie Knight had come forward and told them about seeing a woman who she thought *might* have been Ruth Murray, talking to a man on York Way, a road running along the side of the station. She'd remembered because for a minute or two she'd thought it was a new girl muscling in on her patch.

It had been dark of course, but there was some light from the shop-fronts on the other side of the road. 'An ordinary kind of face really. He was a big bloke though, I can tell you that. Leaning over her, talking to her about something. He was tall. Not fat, you know, just big . . .' She'd claimed that the look she'd had was not good enough to make it worth her trying to do an e-fit. Helping the police was not something Margie felt particularly comfortable with.

Thorne stared at the poster. Carol Garner's death distilled into a single grainy photograph and a phone number. They'd shown a picture from the Railtrack CCTV footage on the local news and though there *had* been plenty of sightings, nobody had picked up on anyone who might have been following her.

They couldn't be one hundred per cent sure of course, that anyone *had* been following her. The station thing might yet prove to have been pure coincidence. The killer could have picked her up on the underground or on the walk home from Balham tube station.

Somehow though, Thorne was pretty sure that this was where he'd first seen Carol Garner. Chosen her.

He'd sat through that CCTV footage a hundred times, scanning the faces of the people around her, as she and her son walked blithely towards the escalator. Men with briefcases, striding along and braying into mobile phones. Men with rucksacks, sauntering. Some meeting people or hurrying home, or hanging around for one of a hundred different reasons. Some who looked dangerous, and others who looked all but invisible. If you looked at them long enough you could see anything.

Except what you needed to see.

In the end, his eyes always drifted back to Carol and Charlie, hand in hand and deep in conversation. Charlie was laughing, clutching tightly to his book, the hood of his anorak up.

Thorne always found something horribly poignant about these CCTV pictures; these utilitarian clips of people in public places. The figures seemed real enough, close enough, that you could reach out and help them, prevent what you knew was about to happen. The fact that you couldn't, the fact that this recent past would inevitably become a terrible future, served only to increase the sense of sheer helplessness. The fuzzy, jumpy quality of the film touched him in a way that no album of treasured photos or home-video ever could. The jerky footage of Jamie Bulger being led away through that shopping centre to his death; or ten-year-old Damilola Taylor, skipping along a concrete walkway, minutes away from bleeding to death in a piss-spattered stairwell on a Peckham estate; or even a Princess – and Thorne was no great fan – smiling and pushing open the back door of a Paris hotel.

These pictures clutched at his guts, and squeezed, every single time.

The images of the dead, just before death.

Now, Carol and Charlie Garner strolling across a busy station concourse; relaxed and happy in a way that could only ever be captured on film when the subject was unaware they were being filmed at all.

Unaware that they were being watched. By a camera, or by a killer.

What should have been a ninety-minute train journey took closer to two hours, and nobody seemed hugely surprised. Thorne and McEvoy flicked through papers and chatted, and generally put the world to rights. The small talk was easy and enjoyable. It passed the time, and besides, each of them knew instinctively that they would not feel much like chatting on the return journey.

They were still an hour from Birmingham, and McEvoy was on her way back from the solitary smoking carriage for the fourth or fifth time. She caught sight of Thorne, his head buried in the paper, as she weaved her way down the carriage and it struck her how, from a distance, he looked like somebody you would try and avoid sitting next to. Up close of course, once you'd been around him a while, there was a warmth in the eyes; something that drew you in, in spite of yourself. But at first glance, he was, to say the very least . . . intimidating.

As she sat back down and picked up her magazine, Thorne glanced up and gave her the look of the reformed smoker – jealous as hell, but trying to be disapproving. She wondered what their fellow travellers made of the pair of them. They were both dressed reasonably smartly: she in a blue wool coat and skirt, and Thorne in his ubiquitous black leather jacket. She was carrying a briefcase, but she seriously doubted that anyone would mistake them for business types. Not Thorne anyway. Her minder perhaps. Dodgy-looking elder brother, or even her dad, at a real push . . .

'What's so funny?'

She looked up. Still smiling. *Maybe even her slightly older bit of rough.* 'Nothing. Just an article in this magazine . . .'

*

Robert and Mary Enright, Carol Garner's parents, lived a few miles south of Birmingham city centre, in Kings Heath, a ten-minute cab ride from New Street station. Theirs was a purpose-built, two-bedroom house on a modern estate, a short walk from shops and buses. The sort of place that a couple in their early sixties might move to. A quiet place where people like them could relax and enjoy retirement, with little to worry about, now that their children were settled.

Settled perhaps, but never safe.

Mary Enright, whose world had so recently turned upside down, greeted them warmly and showed them into a small and unbearably hot living room. She was a short, contained woman. She produced tea almost instantly.

'Robert won't be long. He's taken Charlie over to the park. There's a nice playground, you know, a roundabout and some swings, it's very popular actually. To tell you the truth, I think Robert gets more out of it than Charlie does at the moment. He needs to get out of the house, you know, breathe a bit. Things have been a bit tense to be honest . . .'

McEvoy sipped her tea and nodded, full of understanding, or the appearance of it. Thorne looked around the stifling room, happy to let his sergeant keep the conversation going. Both just waiting to see the boy. Both dreading it.

The few child's books and toys, arranged neatly next to the sofa, seemed horribly out of place among the ornaments, antimacassars and gardening books. The house smelt of beeswax and liniment. It wasn't a place where a child was at home yet.

Thorne noticed that there were already a few Christmas cards on the bookshelf in the corner. Greetings from those who didn't know. He wondered whether the Enrights would celebrate anyway, for their grandson's sake. Grief often came down to going through the motions.

And often, so did investigating the cause of it.

Charlie Garner had already been interviewed. As per procedure this had been done by specially trained officers under strictly controlled conditions. The interviews had taken place at a house in Birmingham owned and maintained jointly by local social services and West Midlands police. It was a simple modern house much like any other, except for the fully equipped medical examination suite and state-of-the-art recording facilities.

Charlie had been given toys to play with, and officers from the Child Protection Team had chatted to him while the entire process was monitored from an adjoining room. Thorne had watched recordings of all the interviews. Charlie had been a little shy at first, but once his trust had been won he'd become lively and talkative, about everything save what had happened to his mother . . .

Thorne wasn't sure he could get anything out of the boy. He didn't know if there was anything to get. He was certain that he had to try.

He was just summoning up the courage to ask if they might turn the radiator down a notch or two, when he heard the key in the front door. He and McEvoy stood up in unison and so quickly that Mary Enright looked quite alarmed for a moment.

Robert Enright shook hands and said, 'pleased to meet you', but his watery blue eyes told a different story. In stark contrast to his wife, he was very tall and had clearly once been fit, but where she was spry and alert, he seemed merely to drift, hollowed out and vague.

Death hit people differently. She was getting by. He had all but given up.

He slumped on to the sofa while his wife scuttled off to make more tea. 'Charlie's gone up to his room I think. He'll be down in a minute.' His voice was deep and gentle, the heavy Brummie accent lending a weariness to it that it almost certainly didn't need.

Thorne nodded. He had heard the *thump thump* of the boy's feet charging upstairs as soon as the front door had shut.

'Good time in the park?'

The old man shrugged. Stupid question. *Fuck off out of my house, away from me and my family.* 'It's starting to get cold . . .'

Mary bustled in, handed her husband his tea and attempted to kill the time until Charlie arrived with aimless chatter. She talked to Thorne and McEvoy about their journey up and how difficult their work must be, and how her friend had a son who was a sergeant in Leicester, and how she knew all about the pressures of the job.

Thorne thought: *it doesn't get any more difficult than this.*

The old man leaned forward suddenly and fixed Thorne with a hard look. 'What are you going to ask him?' Serious, unblinking . . .

Thorne turned to McEvoy, sensing that this would be better coming from her. This, indeed, was why he'd wanted her along. She picked up her cue. 'We don't necessarily need to ask him anything. We just want to get an idea of what he remembers really. Has he talked about what happened at all?'

'No.' Quickly.

'Nothing at all? I mean he might have said something that just sounded like a joke, you know, or a—'

'I said no.' Louder now, unashamedly aggressive.

McEvoy's eyes flicked to Mary, asking for help if she knew how to give it. She picked up her husband's hand and placed it on her knee. She took her hand away and held it up for Thorne and McEvoy's inspection. 'Bob worked in the Jewellery Quarter for forty years. He made this wedding ring in 1965. Made Carol's as well, four years ago. Sort of came out of retirement for it, didn't you?' She laughed and patted her husband's hand but he said nothing. 'See, we didn't have Carol until late.'

Thorne looked at McEvoy. He knew what she was thinking and he knew that she was wrong. These were not ramblings. These were fragments of a shattered picture that Mary Enright was holding up to the light in desperation, in the hope that Thorne and McEvoy might understand the whole. Might grasp the enormity of it. Now, she just shook her head and said it simply. 'Bob's taken everything very badly you see. Worse than me, really, or differently at any rate. It's often the way, I think, when something happens and there's two of you. One just muddles along, you know, gets on with things, while the other . . .'

Thorne could see them then. The old woman sitting in the corner of an overheated lounge, making jigsaws with her grandson or writing shopping lists, while her husband stands stooped in a back bedroom, shouting, his body racked with sobs.

He stared at Robert Enright until the old man met his eye, then he spoke. 'I want to find the man who did this thing to you. To your daughter and to you. Charlie saw him. We're here to let him tell us anything he feels like telling us. That's all.'

They all stiffened then, at the footfalls on the stairs. Thorne thought he saw Carol Garner's father nod, a second before the door flew open and her son ran into the room.

The boy froze on seeing the strangers, and lowered his eyes. He began to inch across to the sofa from where Mary reached out a hand and pulled him to her. He was perhaps a little small for his age, with longish mousy hair and brown eyes. He was wearing denim dungarees over a red long-sleeved top and his hands were covered in what looked like blue felt-tip pen.

'Some friends of ours have come to see you,' Mary said, her voice not much above a whisper. 'This is . . . ?' She looked across at McEvoy and Thorne, the question in her eyes.

'Sarah,' McEvoy volunteered, leaning forward with a smile. She glanced at Thorne. 'And Tom.'

Charlie looked up, appraising them. He rubbed his grandmother's hand across his cheek for a second or two, before dropping it and racing across to where his toys lay on the floor. He picked up a yellow plastic toolbox and emptied the contents on to the carpet.

McEvoy was flying by the seat of her pants. This was not the same as counselling a rape victim or trying to calm a battered wife. She'd noticed the hushed, almost reverential tone that Mary Enright had used when speaking to the boy and felt instinctively that this was wrong. At least, it was wrong if they wanted to get any information out of him. She knew that she had to gain his trust.

'Are you looking forward to Christmas, Charlie?' The boy picked up a thick, red plastic bolt and began pushing it through a hole in a tiny workbench. 'I'm sure Father Christmas will bring you lots of nice things if you're a good boy.' He pushed the bolt further in, his face a picture of concentration. McEvoy moved from her chair and knelt down, a few feet away. 'It looks like you're a good boy to me.' She picked up the plastic screwdriver and examined it, as Charlie furtively examined her. She tried hard to keep any hint of seriousness out of her voice. 'What would be *very* good is if you could tell me and Tom a little bit about when your mummy got hurt . . .' She glanced up at the Enrights. Mary's eyes were already filling with tears. Her husband sat motionless, his eyes on the floor.

Charlie Garner said nothing.

'What you could do, if you wanted, is tell your Nan about it. Do you want to do that?'

He didn't . . .

McEvoy felt herself sweating and it was only partially due to the temperature. She was beginning to feel out of her depth. She started to say something but stopped. She could only watch helplessly as the boy stood up suddenly, marched past her and plonked himself down at Thorne's feet.

Thorne gazed down at Charlie and shrugged. 'Hello . . .' Charlie produced a small squeaky hammer and began vigorously banging on Thorne's shoe. It might have been nerves or it might have been because the moment was, in spite of everything, genuinely comical, but Thorne began to laugh. Then Charlie laughed too.

'I hammer your shoe . . .'

'Ow . . . ow . . . ouch!' Thorne winced in mock agony, and

as the boy began to laugh even louder, he sensed that the moment might be right. 'Do you remember the man who was there when your mummy got hurt?'

The laughter didn't exactly stop dead, but the answer to Thorne's question was obvious. Charlie was still hammering on the shoe but it was purely reflexive. The intermittent squeak of the toy hammer was now the only sound in the room. Mary and Robert Enright sat stock still on the sofa, and Sarah McEvoy was all but holding her breath, afraid that the slightest movement could spoil everything.

Thorne spoke slowly and seriously. He was not following a different tack to McEvoy for any particular reason. There was no strategy involved. Instinct just told him to ask the child the question, simply and honestly. 'Can you tell me what the man who hurt your mummy looked like?'

A squeak, as the hammer hit the shoe. And another. Then the tiny shoulders gave a recognisable shrug. Thorne had seen the same gesture in a hundred stroppy teenagers. Scared, but fronting it out.

Maybe I know something, but you get nothing easily.

'Was he older than me do you think?' Charlie glanced up, but only for a second before returning to his hammering. 'Was his hair the same colour as yours or was it darker? What do you think?' There was no discernible reaction. Thorne knew that he was losing the boy.

Hearing a sniff, Thorne looked up and could see that the old man on the sofa was quietly weeping, his big shoulders rising and falling as he pressed a handkerchief to his face. Thorne looked at the boy and winked conspiratorially, 'Was he taller than your Grandad? I bet you can remember that.'

Charlie stopped hammering. Without looking up he shook his head slowly and emphatically. Thorne flicked his eyes to McEvoy. She raised her eyebrows back at him. They were thinking the same thing. If that 'no' was as definite as it looked, it certainly didn't tally with Margie Knight's description. Thorne wondered who was the more credible witness. The nosy working girl or the three-year-old?

Eye witnesses had screwed him up before. So, probably neither . . .

Whatever, as far as Charlie was concerned, it looked as though the shake of the head was all they were going to get. The hammering was growing increasingly enthusiastic.

'You're good at hammering, Charlie,' Thorne said.

Mary Enright spoke up from the sofa, she too sensing that the questions were over. 'It's *Bob The Builder*. He's mad on it. It's what he calls you sometimes, isn't it, Bob?' She turned to her husband, smiling. Robert Enright said nothing.

McEvoy stood up, rubbing away the stiffness in the back of her legs from where she'd been kneeling. 'Yeah, my nephew's always going on about it. He's driving his mum and dad bonkers, singing the theme tune.'

Mary stood up and began tidying things away, while Charlie carried on, the hammer now replaced by a bright orange screwdriver. 'I don't mind that,' Mary said. 'It's just on so early. Half past six in the morning, on one of those cable channels.'

McEvoy breathed in sharply and nodded sympathetically. Thorne looked down and brushed his fingers against the boy's shoulder. 'Hey, think about your poor old nan will you Charlie? Half past six? You should still be fast asleep . . .'

And Charlie Garner looked up at him then, his eyes wide and keen, the bright orange screwdriver clutched tightly in his small fist.

'My mummy's asleep.'

In spite of all the horrors to come, the bodies both fresh and long dead, *this* would be the image, simple and stark, that would be there long after this case was finished, whenever Thorne closed his eyes.

The face of a child.

It's been over a week now, Karen, and it's still on the television. I've stopped watching now, in case something comes on and catches me unawares when I'm unprepared for it. I knew that it would be on the news, you know, when they found her, but I thought it would die down . . . I thought it would stop, after a day or two. There always seems to be people dying in one way or another, so I didn't think that it would be news for very long.

They've got some sort of witness they said. Whoever it was must have seen me because they know how tall I am. I know I should be worried, Karen, but I'm not. Part of me wishes they'd seen me up close. Seen my face.

A police officer on the television said it was brutal. 'This brutal killing.' He said I *was brutal and I really tried so hard not to be. You believe that don't you, Karen? I didn't hit her or anything. I tried to make it quick and painless. I don't really expect them to say anything else though. Why should they? They don't know me . . .*

The other one, the one in south London, I can barely bring myself to think about that. It was horrible. Yes, that was brutal.

The scratches are fading, but a couple of people at work noticed and it gave them something else to use against me. Not as if they needed any more ammunition. It was all nudges and giggles and, 'I bet she was a right goer' or, 'did she make a lot of noise?' You know, variations on that theme. I just smiled and blushed, same as I always do.

Oh my God, Karen, if they only knew.

Sometimes I think that perhaps I should just tell them everything. That way it would all be over, because someone would go to the police and I could just sit and wait for them to come and get me. Plus, it might at least make some of them think about me a bit differently. Find someone else to belittle. It would wipe a few smiles off a few faces wouldn't it? It would make them stop. Yes, I'd like them to step back and start to sweat a little.

I'd like them to be scared of me.

But I'm the one that's scared, Karen, you know that. It's the way it's always been hasn't it? That's why I can't ever tell them. Why I can't ever share this with anyone except you.

Why I'm praying, praying, praying that Ruth will be the last one.

1984

They caught Bardsley just outside the school gates. He had a few mates with him but they took one look at Nicklin, at his face, and melted away into the background. Some of them were fifth-formers at least a year older than he was, and it excited him to watch them scuttle away like the spineless wankers he knew they were.

The two of them were on Bardsley in a second. Palmer stood in front of him, solid, red-faced and shaking. Nicklin grabbed the strap of his sports bag and together they dragged him towards the bushes.

The park ran right alongside the main entrance to the school. A lot of the boys cut across it on the way to school and back, and the sixth-formers would hang around with their opposite numbers from the neighbouring girls' school. It wasn't a nice park; a tatty bowling green, an attempt at an aviary and a floating population of surly kids – smoking, groping or eating chips.

Palmer and Nicklin pushed Bardsley towards the bushes that bordered the bird cages. He grabbed on to the wire of the nearest cage. It housed a moulting mynah bird which, in spite of the best efforts of every kid in school, resolutely refused to swear, producing nothing but an ear-splitting wolf-whistle every few minutes. Bardsley began to kick out wildly. Palmer clung on to the collar of his blazer, which was already starting to tear, and shuffled his legs back, out of the range of the boy's flailing Doc Martens. Nicklin stepped in closer and, oblivious to the pain in his shin as he was repeatedly booted, punched Bardsley hard in the face. Bardsley's hands moved from the wire to his face as blood began to gush from his nose. Smiling, Nicklin pushed him on to his knees, rammed a knee into his neck and pressed him down into the dirt.

After a nod from Nicklin, Palmer dropped on to Bardsley's chest and sat there for a few moments, breathing heavily, his face the colour of a Bramley apple.

Bardsley took his hand away from his face and glared up at the younger boy. There was blood on his teeth. 'You're fucking dead, Palmer.'

Palmer's face grew even redder as his big hands reached forward to grab greasy handfuls of Bardsley's dirty blond hair. 'What did you say about Karen?'

'Who the fuck's Karen?'

Nicklin was standing behind Bardsley's head, his back against a tree, his hands in his pockets, his foot pressed against the scalp of the boy on the ground. He pushed his tongue in behind his bottom teeth, opened his mouth and slowly let a thick, globular string of spit drop down on to the bloody face below. Bardsley flinched and squeezed his eyes tight shut. When he opened them again he was staring up at the pistol in Nicklin's hand.

Palmer and Bardsley moaned at almost the same time. Bardsley in terror at the sight of the pistol, and Palmer in disgust as the groin of the boy beneath him quickly began to grow damp.

'Shit . . . he's pissed himself!' Palmer jumped up and pointed down at the dark, spreading stain on Bardsley's grey trousers.

Nicklin giggled. 'Well turn him over then.' Palmer shook his head. Nicklin stopped giggling as the mynah bird let out a shrill whistle from the cage behind him. 'Fucking turn him over . . .'

Palmer stepped forward nervously. Bardsley glowered at him as he tried with some difficulty to scramble to his feet, one hand wiping away blood and spit and dirt, the other covering his groin. His voice was thick with rage and the effort of holding back tears, 'Dead . . . fucking dead . . .' But the fight had gone out of him and Palmer was easily able to yank him over on to his belly.

Nicklin moved round and knelt down next to Palmer at Bardsley's feet. 'Pull his pants down.'

Bardsley began trying to drag himself away until Nicklin leaned forward and pressed the pistol into his neck. Bardsley froze and dropped back into the dirt.

'Right, grab that side . . .' Nicklin took hold of Bardsley's waistband and began to pull. He looked at Palmer, who, after a second or two, did the same, and moments later, Bardsley's trousers and pants were around his ankles.

'He's got fucking blue pants on . . .'

'Stu, that's enough, isn't it?'

'Pissed his pants like a girl. I can smell shit as well . . .'

'Stuart . . .'

Nicklin handed Palmer the pistol. 'Stick this up his arse.'

At these words Bardsley was predictably energised, and his buttocks pumped rapidly up and down in his frantic attempts to get away. Palmer took a step back, staring at the ground, but Nicklin leaned in close to Bardsley, laughing. 'Go on Bardsley, you bummer, shag it. Shag the ground you fucking perv . . . only thing you'll ever get to shag, you spastic . . .'

Palmer turned the pistol over and over in his hand. Nicklin looked up at him, smiling, making certain that

Palmer was reassured by the smile before letting it slowly dissolve. Looking serious. Concerned. Shaking his head.

'He said he was going to do stuff to Karen, Martin.'

Bardsley tried for the last time to tell them that he didn't have a fucking clue who Karen was, but the words were lost as he dissolved into sobs.

Nicklin lowered his voice and spoke slowly. Things he didn't want to tell his friend; things he had to tell him. 'Dirty stuff, Mart. He called her names.' Palmer wrapped his fat fist around the butt of the pistol and dropped down slowly, his knees heavy on the back of Bardsley's calves. 'Said you'd done things to her . . . touched her tits.' Palmer pushed the barrel into the soft, pale flesh of Bardsley's buttocks and held it there. Bardsley whimpered.

Nicklin whispered. 'Go on Martin . . .'

Palmer looked down at Bardsley's soft, spotty backside, afraid to so much as glance at the boy next to him. Afraid of his friend's excitement. He could see the twin rolls of sweaty, girlish fat on his chest shudder as his heart thumped beneath them. He could taste the perspiration that was running into his mouth. He knew that he should throw the pistol away and get to his feet and run through the park, without looking back, down past the bowling green and up and across the playground, not stopping until he was home . . .

Nicklin put a hand on his shoulder and squeezed, and as the mynah bird screeched raucously behind him, Palmer pulled the trigger.

Bardsley screamed as the jet of compressed air fired the tiny lead pellet deep into his flesh.

FOUR

The train journey back to London had been half an hour quicker than the outward leg, but had seemed infinitely longer. For the first twenty minutes or so, Thorne and McEvoy had tried to make conversation, then given up. He picked up the newspaper he'd already read and she made for the smoking carriage.

Thorne had closed his eyes and tried, without any success at all, to go to sleep.

McEvoy hadn't bothered coming back.

It was after six by the time Thorne finally got back to Hendon. Becke House was in the Peel Centre, a vast compound that also housed the Metropolitan Police Training College. Hundreds of fresh-faced recruits buzzing about, learning how to put handcuffs on, learning procedure. Learning nothing.

A BBC film crew had been around for the past few months making a documentary on the new intake. Thorne had spoken to the director one day in the canteen, suggested that he might like to catch up with his subjects again in a year or two; see how those ruddy-cheeked recruits had matured into the job. The director had been hugely, stupidly enthusiastic. Thorne had walked away thinking: that'll be one show they'll need to put out after the watershed . . .

Thorne headed for the office. He decided he wanted to put in another couple of hours. It would be a good idea to save the drive back to Kentish Town until the rush hour had died down a little. That was the excuse he gave himself anyway.

Holland was the only member of the team there, still hunched over a computer screen. In spite of the day he'd had, Thorne didn't envy him. He'd been forced to attend *two* courses and was still a computer illiterate. The only things he could access with any speed were the Tottenham Hotspur FC supporters' newsgroup and the technical support line.

'Where's the DCI?'

Holland looked up from his computer, rubbing his eyes. 'Meeting with the Detective Super.'

'Jesus Christ.' Thorne shook his head. 'We've only just started.'

'Where's McEvoy?'

'Probably soaking in a long hot bath by now . . .' Holland nodded. Thorne noticed how tired he was looking. 'Go home, Dave. Start again in the morning.'

'Yeah, I'd better, before I get RSI. My mouse finger's fucked.' He stopped laughing when he pictured Sophie's expression as he walked through the door. 'I'll just finish what I'm doing . . .'

One week into it, and neither of them wanting to go home. Both afraid of looks on faces.

Thorne pushed open the door to the office he shared with Brigstocke, and waited for a second or two before turning on the light. The room looked a damn sight better in the dark. Who the hell could be expected to work efficiently in an airless grey box like this, or the even smaller one next door that Holland and McEvoy worked out of? Worn grey carpet, dirty yellow walls and a pair of battle-scarred brown desks, like two rectangles of driftwood floating down a shitty river. No amount of potted plants or family photos, or knick-knacks on monitors could stop this room sucking the energy out of him, blunting him.

There were moments in this office, when Thorne almost forgot what he did for a living.

He flicked on the light and saw a post-mortem report sitting on his desk.

When he *almost* forgot . . .

Sarah McEvoy consoled herself with a glass of wine, another cigarette and the thought that crying was easy.

She couldn't think of the boy in Birmingham as anything other than a potential witness and she knew that perhaps she should. She knew that there were feelings missing. Not maternal ones necessarily, or even feminine. Just human. She felt angry at what had happened to the boy's mother all right. Anger was always instant and powerful. It made her feel light-headed. Anger was enjoyable, but sympathy never came as easily.

It wasn't fair. She felt that her behaviour was being judged. Maybe right now, Thorne was telling somebody else, Holland probably, how . . . hard she was. There was no middle ground as a woman. She was used to it, but it still pissed her off. Frigid, or a slag. Girly, or one of the boys. Hard, or emotionally unstable. Actually, hard-*faced* was a favourite with female colleagues. Usually followed by *bitch* or *cow*.

She was sure that Tom Thorne wouldn't be crying about anything.

As it was, there had been quite a few times lately when she'd woken up and been pretty sure that she *had* been crying. She could never be positive of course, however puffy she looked, or fucked up she felt. She certainly wasn't going to ask whoever she might have woken up next to for the details. Conversation of any sort, by that point, would be kept to a bare minimum in an effort to get rid of them as fast as possible.

She knew what those at work who guessed at her domestic arrangements would make of them. For this reason she did her best to ensure that it stayed as guess-work only. She wasn't frigid, so there was only one other option wasn't there? It was a small jump for a small brain from 'sexually active' to 'sexually active with superior officers'. There were still those who suspected that any woman rising through the ranks did so on her back.

Right. Lying on her back and staring at that glass ceiling . . .

It was nobody's business and it was her choice. A regular boyfriend was nice in theory and a bonus at parties, but in her experience it rarely meant regular sex, and she needed that. She needed to feel wanted, and if that occasionally meant *used* then that was fine, because it cut both ways.

All the time she was checking to see what was on TV and thinking about what she might eat, she knew perfectly well that she'd end up going out. She'd been thinking about it all the way back on the train. Staring at her own reflection in the blackness of the carriage window, smoking cigarettes down to the filter and wishing the hours away. She might even walk there. It was only fifteen minutes away. Following the path of the railway line all the way from Wembley Park to Harlesden.

She'd need to get changed first though. The people she was going to see, like those on the train earlier, almost certainly had no idea what she did for a living, but she didn't want to take any chances.

In the single pool of light from a desktop lamp, Thorne sat, trying to keep his mind on death, but distracted constantly by an image that was full of life. Much as he tried to concentrate on Ruth Murray's post-mortem report, he couldn't stop the animated features of Charlie Garner from intruding: staring up at him from beneath the gurney, or peeking around the mortuary door.

He had finally worked out what it was that had disturbed him so much when Charlie had looked up at him in that sitting room only a few hours before. He'd seen it instantly, but it took a while before he *understood* exactly what it was he'd been looking at when he stared into that child's eyes. There, in that face, in those shining brown saucers beneath long lashes, Thorne had seen doubt.

My mummy's asleep . . .

The smile had been broad and beautiful, but in those eyes had been the tiniest flicker of something like uncertainty. The smile hopeful, but the eyes betraying a knowledge Charlie Garner didn't even know he had. Who could blame him? Now, that child could never be really certain about anything ever again. It was too harsh a lesson and learned too early.

And each time Thorne saw that face, the flicker of doubt grew stronger . . .

When the phone on the desk rang, Thorne started a little, and on glancing at the page in front of him, realised he'd been staring at the phrase *blood-spotted conjunctivae* for the past half an hour.

'DI Thorne . . .'

'It's Phil. Have you read it?'

'It's right in front of me. I've . . . had loads of stuff to wade through.'

'How was Birmingham?'

Thorne exhaled and leaned back in his chair. He should have gone home much earlier. Even with a smooth run back to Kentish Town, it would be ten o'clock by the time he got in. Another couple of hours to wind down meant getting to sleep late and waking up pissed off. Hendricks, by contrast, sounded relaxed. Thorne could picture him, legs up on a piece of sixties' black-leather furniture, some skinhead in the kitchen making them both dinner.

'That bad?' Hendricks asked.

'Sorry?'

'Birmingham. Doesn't matter, tell me tomorrow. Listen, bit of good news. Catch the bastard, we'll put him away. There *was* plenty of Ruth Murray's own tissue under her fingernails, but loads of his as well. Profile should come through some time tomorrow.'

It was *very* good news. Now he would at least drive home in a good mood. 'No need to test those teardrops you were so excited about then?'

Hendricks snorted. 'Nah, tell you the truth it were a fuck of a long shot. We might have had a chance if he'd worn contact lenses.'

Thorne was intrigued. 'This sounds good . . .'

'Obvious really. A foreign body in the eye would cause

a certain amount of irritation so the tear fluid would probably have contained more cellular material. See? Even better if he'd cried out of his nose actually . . .'

'I don't want to know . . .'

'It's all academic now anyway.'

'No chance of a Nobel prize just yet then?'

'One day, mate.'

Thorne folded up the post-mortem report and started putting papers into his briefcase. 'Never mind, it told us something about him anyway . . .' There was no response. Thorne heard someone talking to Hendricks. He heard his friend's muffled voice answering, then heard the hand being taken off the mouthpiece.

'Sorry Tom, dinner's nearly ready.' Hendricks's voice dropped to a whisper. 'Got myself a cracker here, mate. Nice arse, *and* handy in the kitchen. Sorry, what were you on about?'

'The tears. I'm not sure exactly *what* they tell us about him, mind you.'

'Well, we know he was in a better mood than when he killed Carol Garner.'

Thorne stood up and closed his case. He might make it home by quarter to, with a following wind. 'Right . . .'

'No, I mean it. Go through the report, it's obvious. He must have calmed down or something. Maybe whatever the fucker was *on* had worn off. It's a very different attack. The hyroid is intact, there's only minimal damage to the cartilage . . .'

Then Thorne could feel the tingle. The small current running up the nape of his neck. Making him catch his breath. Almost sexy . . .

Something that had been nagging at him was coming

into focus, revealing itself. He sat down again, opened the case and pulled out the post-mortem report. 'Take me through this slowly can you, Phil?'

Opening the report now, tearing pages as he turns them too quickly, speed-reading, his breath getting shorter by the second as Hendricks turns their murder case into something altogether more disturbing.

'OK . . . externally, both bodies were much the same, Murray and Garner, but internally it's a different story. Ruth Murray died from a slower, more sustained pressure on the artery. Call it a slow, hard squeezing. Carol Garner was nothing like that. She had bruises on the back of her skull where he smacked her head on the floor as he was throttling her. That was . . . frenzied. With Ruth Murray it was different. Maybe he'd got the anger out of his system. Maybe that's his pattern. You tell me mate . . .'

Then, Thorne knew. No, not *his* pattern . . .

The tears. A big man's tears on a body, outdoors. A body less damaged, wept upon. Elsewhere, a child in a house, nuzzling what was once the sweet-smelling neck of his mother, now bruised, and bloody, and broken inside. The wrapper from a chocolate bar, discarded . . .

Was he taller than your Grandad?

And Charlie Garner slowly, defiantly, shaking his head.

'Phil, can I call you back . . . ?'

Tired as he was, Holland had *still* not left. Thorne's expression, as he burst into the office next door, was enough to wake him up in a second.

'The stabbings . . . tell me about the stabbings.' Thorne's voice low, measured, but with a scream of something – excitement maybe, or horror – lurking just beneath the surface.

'Sir . . . ?'

Moving across the cramped office, talking quickly. 'Two women, both stabbed on the same day. July, I think you said.' Thorne nodded towards the computer, trying to stay calm. 'Call them up.'

Holland spun the chair round and began to type, trying to recall the details. 'One in Finchley, I think. The other one . . . much further south if I remember . . .' The relevant documents appeared on his screen and Holland studied them for a second or two. 'Forest Hill, that's right . . .' He scrolled slowly through the document, shaking his head. 'No . . . no . . . it's not possible. He couldn't have done them both.'

Thorne nodded and glanced out of the window. His eye was taken by the sparks flying up from beneath a tube train passing below on its way south from Colindale; lolling heads in the brightly lit carriages, snaking away from him as the track curved round and out of sight.

'He didn't.'

Holland stared at him, waiting. Thorne stood stock still and spoke slowly, but Holland could see his fists clenching and unclenching at his sides. 'The knives used might have been similar, might not, I don't know . . . not sure it matters. The pattern and depth of the wounds though . . . in all probability the *number* of wounds, on each of the victims, will be at odds with each other. The . . . character of the two attacks will be completely different.'

Holland turned back to his screen and typed again, calling up SOC and pathology reports as Thorne continued. 'One of the women will have died from multiple stab wounds. Vicious . . . indiscriminate . . . savage. The other, probably one single wound, to the heart, I would guess, or . . .'

Holland spun round again. The look on his face told Thorne all he needed to know . . .

Brigstocke answered his mobile on the first ring.

'Russell Brigstocke . . .' The voice low, betraying annoyance.

'It's Tom . . .'

'DI Thorne . . .' Spoken for somebody else's benefit.

The meeting with Detective Superintendent Jesmond had probably turned into dinner. So much the easier.

'We're onto something. Tell Jesmond. Call it a breakthrough, he'll like that.' He turned to share the moment with Holland but the DC was studying the documents on his screen intently. Trying to make sense of it all. 'Tell him it's one hell of a good news-bad news routine . . .'

'I'm listening,' Brigstocke said.

'I don't think we're looking for one man.'

Thorne expected a pause, and he got one. Then: 'Are you saying that these murders might not actually be connected?'

'No I'm not. They *are* connected, I'm certain of that.' Thorne knew the look that Brigstocke would be wearing. Contained excitement, like trying to hold a shit inside. He wondered what Jesmond, no doubt holding a large glass of red wine and studying his DCI's strange expression, would be making of it.

Brigstocke was starting to sound a little impatient. 'So, what is it? A new lead on the killer?'

Thorne kept it nice and simple. 'Kill*ers*, Russell. Plural. There's two of them.'

1985

It was a moment he would always remember. Karen sitting on the bank, pushing a strand of blonde hair behind her ear, and Stuart smiling, mouth full of chocolate as always, his dark eyes focusing on something in the distance, searching for it, seeking out the source of their next adventure.

And him, looking from one to the other, nervous but happy, the sun in his eyes and a small cloud of gnats swirling in front of his face . . .

It was a moment that took him back to a day two summers earlier. That day with the cricket bat. The day when he saw Karen for the first time. That was when he and Stuart were at the same school of course. Before the business with the air pistol . . .

The two of them weren't really supposed to see each other after the Bardsley incident. Following the expulsion, efforts had been made to keep them apart, and for a while Palmer had been happy enough to go along with that. After all, the police had told their parents that it would be better for everybody if they were not allowed to be together. There had been talk of 'influence' and of 'geeing up'. He missed the excitement though, he missed the unpredictability, and he was delighted when Stuart, once they'd started hanging around together again, told him that he'd missed it too. Plus, he always felt better about being around Karen, if Stuart was close by.

Karen was older than he was, closer to Stuart's age, but

Stuart couldn't make her laugh the way he could. He'd always been the one that got her giggling, ever since that day when she'd crawled through the hole in the fence and seen the business with the frog. There were times, when he saw the two of them whispering, or smoking, or watched them walking ahead of him along by the railway line, that he would start to feel like he shouldn't be there. Then Karen would stop and smile that smile at him and ask him to pull some stupid face, or put on a silly voice or something and he would soon have her in fits. Sometimes he thought that perhaps she was teasing him a little, but he didn't really mind. He could see how important he was to her, and to Stuart. He could see the three of them together, friends for good, the long grass of the railway embankment becoming the carefully tended lawn of a college quadrangle and the back garden of one of the big houses that each of them owned . . . and finally, the rambling parkland of that Heath in London his mum had taken him to once, where the three of them would sit together on a park bench, with dogs, and perhaps children.

Palmer knew, as much as he knew anything at barely fourteen, that he was in love.

Karen stood up and looked around for a few seconds before half-running, half-tumbling down the bank. She pretended that she was going to crash into Nicklin, and he pretended to be frightened. At the last minute, she jumped and Nicklin staggered back as he caught her, shouting and laughing, one hand holding tight to her arse.

Palmer laughed too and, swatting the swarm of gnats aside, followed them as they each lit a cigarette and began walking slowly towards the small group of blackened, broken-down railway buildings in the distance.

Once inside the main building – a disused equipment shed – they did the usual quick sweep, searching for signs of habitation. Tramps slept here sometimes. The place still smelt of stale piss and strong lager. They'd found the remains of a fire a few times before now, and empty tins and syringes, and once, a used condom which Nicklin had picked up and chased Karen around with for a while. Today the place seemed even more deserted than usual. The usual fixtures and fittings. A mountain of fag ends, some old newspapers, a soggy, mouldering roll of carpet that had once been a dosser's bed.

Huge bluebottles flew around their heads as Palmer threw stones at the remaining slivers of glass in the rotting window frames. Nicklin stubbed out his fag and looked around for something, anything, to spark him off, and Karen wandered around singing the latest Duran Duran single, her light, high voice echoing off the grimy Artex walls.

'Let's go. Fuck-all in here.' Nicklin aimed a kick at an empty bottle. It skittered across the concrete floor and into the far wall where it smashed.

Palmer cheered. 'We could start a fire or something . . .'

'Let's all have a dump,' Karen said, ignoring him and leering at Nicklin. She began to laugh and Palmer turned away, blushing. He hated it when she talked like that. She would squat down in the long grass sometimes and he couldn't bear it.

'Boring,' Nicklin said. 'Fucking eggs for lunch anyway. Couldn't squeeze one out even if I wanted to.' He lit another cigarette from a packet of ten Silk Cut. Karen took a loose one from the top pocket of her denim jacket and moved over to join him. She took the cigarette from Nicklin's mouth and used it to light her own.

When Palmer turned round, Karen and Nicklin had gone. For a moment he was frightened, but then he heard them just outside, murmuring. He looked out through the broken window towards the embankment opposite. There was a housing estate at the top, where Stuart lived, and he'd seen people emptying their bins down there, using the grassy, green bank as a rubbish tip. Shitting in it, every bit as much as Karen or Nicklin did.

He still loved the place though. He knew where there was a foxes' earth hidden in the roots of a large oak tree. He'd once found a baby jay at the foot of the very same tree, bright blue and puffed-up, miaowing like a cat, calling for its mother. He knew where to find massive blackberries and which species of butterfly were attracted by the buddleia that flourished all over the place, and he knew where he could find slow worms and grass snakes nesting beneath rusting sheets of corrugated iron . . .

He was startled by a footstep next to him, the sound of broken glass being ground into concrete. He turned quickly to see Nicklin at his shoulder, smiling like he'd finally found something.

'Karen wants to do it with you.' His tone, matter of fact. Palmer said nothing. Nicklin took a drag on his cigarette, waited, shrugged. 'I'll tell her you're not up for it then, shall I?'

'Everything?' Palmer's voice, helium-high, his breathing ragged.

'That's what she said. She's had it with loads of blokes, done all sorts, it's not a big deal really. Probably suck you off as well . . .' He ran a hand across his head. His normally thick black hair had been cut suedehead-short for the summer.

'What does she want me to do?'

'Just fuck her, mate.' Then a snort and a laugh. Nicklin's voice high too, his movements jerky. Excited . . .

Palmer turned to look at him, his palm already pressing against the front of his trousers. 'No . . . I want to. I just mean, does she want me to go outside or will she . . . ? Come on, Stu . . . what?' Trying to force a smile. Mates together. Not scared.

'Just get it out. She's probably got her pants off already. I'll go and get her.' Nicklin flicked his cigarette into the corner and strolled outside.

After a few seconds, Palmer could hear him round the side of the building, whispering to Karen. He strained to hear the noise of clothing being removed, listened for the sounds that he always imagined he would hear before sex – a moan in the throat, a catch in the breath. The only breathing he could hear was his own; rapid, desperate, unsexy, as he loosened his belt and reached for his zip. He turned away from the doorway and stared at the wall, trying to calm down. Trying not to think of the things she was going to do to him. Someone had scrawled a cock on the dusty grey breezeblocks. He looked down at his own, far less impressive member and began to rub at the red marks around his belly where his waistband had pinched.

He heard movement in the doorway behind him. Her voice was almost enough to end it before it had even begun.

'Ready then, Martin?'

His hand had moved to his cock without him even realising it. He was moaning softly and stroking himself even as he was turning round to look at her, smiling . . .

Karen and Nicklin stood in the doorway, their mouths

open, clutching on to one another, waiting for the best moment to let the laughter out. Karen was the first to crack, but the laugh died almost as soon as it came out of her mouth and she looked quickly away. Nicklin began to howl, slapping his sides as Palmer had seen people do in films. Nicklin saw the look on his victim's face and spat out his scorn in between the laughs. 'Fuck, Palmer, it was a joke. I was joking . . .'

Karen glanced back. 'Jesus . . .'

Nicklin pointed at Palmer's crotch with a groan of disgust and Palmer's fist tightened instinctively around his soft, shrivelled penis.

Karen leaned against the doorframe. 'Jesus, Martin . . .'

'You've upset her now,' Nicklin said. Karen began to cry softly and the amusement vanished from Nicklin's voice in an instant. 'You really have upset her, you stupid bastard. Because you don't know a fucking joke when you hear one, you pervert . . .'

There was nothing left to do then but run, as he should have done that day in the park, and the summer before that, and a dozen or more times in between.

He ran without stopping to dress himself, clutching his trousers to his waist, bolting through the doorway, between the boy with the short black hair who was tugging with his teeth at the wrapper of a chocolate bar, and the girl in the blue dress who was sobbing.

He ran away towards the grassy, green embankment.

He ran, his head down, towards the housing estate. Wiping the tears away as he charged through the long couch grass and clattered across a rusting sheet of corrugated iron.

He ran far away from the nest of snakes.

FIVE

'How are they working together?'

It was the first question Brigstocke had asked him the previous night on the phone, and it was the first question he put to them now as a group. They were gathered in the bigger of the two offices. Brigstocke, Thorne, Holland and McEvoy. The core of an investigation that had been sizeable before and overnight had become the biggest that London had seen in a long time.

Thorne's answer now was the same as it had been a few hours earlier. He had no idea, but he hoped that together, they might come up with something, anything, that might point the hundreds of officers and civilians working on the case in the right direction. The hundreds working in the industry of killing . . .

'It seems likely that they kill alternate victims.' Brigstocke looked as though he hadn't had a lot of sleep the night before. Thorne hadn't had a great deal himself, but he hadn't had Jesmond giving him grief at the same time. Thorne looked at his DCI and saw, as if he needed another one, an object lesson in the benefits of avoiding promotion. He didn't need a lecture from a desk jockey like Jesmond. He knew full well that those wondrous, imaginary places where the buck stopped and where credit, if any, would be due, were a long way apart.

Brigstocke leaned forward, his fingers interlocked in front of him on the desk, his voice a little hoarse but crackling with urgency all the same. 'The evidence suggests that they are different types, psychologically as well as physically, but we need to know how they . . . interact. Do they attack their victims together and simply carry out the actual killing individually? Maybe one kills while the other keeps a lookout . . .'

'I don't think that's likely.' Holland was the first to speak up. Thorne was as impressed as always at the confidence, at how far he'd come in a year.

Brigstocke nodded. 'Go on, Holland . . .'

'Margie Knight's statement made no mention of a second man . . . of anybody else at all in the immediate vicinity as far as I can remember, and nothing that Charlie Garner has said would indicate that there was more than one man.'

'Have another word with Margie Knight,' Brigstocke said. His eyes met Thorne's.

'I'll give the Enrights a ring.' Thorne was already hoping that he would not need to speak to them again in person. At least not until he had good news. 'Holland's right though, sir, the boy's said nothing at any time about two men . . .'

One was bad enough wasn't it, Charlie?

'I think we're forgetting about the time element here.' McEvoy sounded as tired as Brigstocke. Thorne looked across at her and thought that she didn't look a whole lot better. 'They could have killed Carol Garner and Ruth

Murray together, or at least both have been present *when* she was killed, but the stabbings in July almost overlap timewise and they were miles apart. Each of them has got to be working on their own.'

'I agree,' Thorne said. It was about as much as he *was* sure of.

'OK, so the chances are that, even though they kill on the same day, they kill separately, but we have to presume that they plan these murders carefully. For Christ's sake, they must get together to work everything out, discuss dates . . .'

Thorne shook his head. 'I don't think we can presume anything.'

It was possible that the men they were after might never even have met. Thorne had read about a pair of killers in the United States who did their butchering separately but who got their kicks out of communicating with each other. They discussed the selection of potential victims by phone and over the Internet. They egged each other on and then compared notes after the event. They shared the experience but never actually clapped eyes on one another. Thorne shivered as he recalled reading that one of the murderous pair had used his last breath to send best wishes to his partner in crime, seconds before they'd administered the lethal injection. If it was true, at least financially, that when the USA sneezed, the UK caught a cold, might it not also be the case when it came to one of the biggest growth industries of all?

McEvoy took out a cigarette and lit it. 'You said that the killers were probably different psychologically. What about bringing a profiler in?'

Brigstocke nodded first towards the cigarette and then

the window. McEvoy sighed, stood up and strode across to the window while Brigstocke answered her question. 'I've already been on to the National Crime Faculty . . .' McEvoy opened the window and winced. Third floor, December, it was a little bit more than fresh air.

'Jesus . . .' Holland turned and grimaced at McEvoy. She took another drag, mouthed 'sorry' at him and blew the smoke out of the window.

Brigstocke continued. 'Both the profilers on the current recommended list are busy on other cases . . .'

Shivering, Thorne reached for the leather jacket he had slung across the back of his chair. 'Which kills you quicker, passive smoking or pneumonia? This is ridiculous . . .'

McEvoy took a last drag, flicked the butt out into the wind and closed the window. 'Bunch of girls,' she scoffed, moving back to the desk. As soon as she'd sat down again, she locked eyes with Brigstocke and carried on as if nothing had happened. '*Both* the profilers, you said. Are you telling me that there are only two of them in the whole country? Two?'

'Two that are actually recommended, yes.'

'That is fucking ridiculous.' Brigstocke shrugged. McEvoy shook her head in disbelief. 'Oh come on . . . profilers aren't like psychics, you know. It's a recognised science. Sir?'

She looked at Thorne for support. She'd picked the wrong man. 'I don't think now's the time to discuss the pros and cons of profiling, Sarah. Whatever any of us think, there isn't one available anyway.'

'Couldn't we find our own?'

Holland grinned at her. 'I'll grab the *Yellow Pages* shall I?'

Brigstocke brought the discussion to a close. 'Listen, if we find somebody ourselves, if we use someone who's not on the NCF list and we fuck it up, we'll all be ironing uniforms again the next day. Nobody wants that kind of bad publicity.'

Thorne looked up from the notepad in front of him. He'd been doodling.

Three pairs of eyes. Two drawn in thick black strokes, the eyes big, heavy-lidded, cold. One pair finer, the dark eyes smaller, long-lashed . . .

'Talking of publicity,' he said, 'what kind do the Powers That Be think we *do* need?' Thorne could guess, but the mischief-maker in him wanted to hear the DCI say it. Such decisions of course were not for the likes of him. He just had to worry about catching the people that generated the publicity in the first place.

Brigstocke answered in a voice that Thorne thought was no longer wholly his own. He'd mislaid it somewhere between the squadroom and the Detective Superintendent's office. One on one with Thorne, there was no problem, he would say what he thought, but with lower ranks present, Brigstocke's tone was unreadable. 'I spoke to Jesmond first thing and a press conference is being organised for this afternoon. I gather that he *will* be telling the press about this latest development.'

There was no such greyness in Holland's response. 'That's stupid. Surely we should be keeping this *out* of the press. Knowing that there are two of them is the only advantage we've got . . .'

A small part of Thorne was relieved that Holland could still be so naive. 'There you go again, Holland, thinking like a policeman. Detective Superintendent Jesmond, on the other hand . . .' – Brigstocke smiled at this, in spite of himself – 'has his job to consider and he's realised, quite cleverly, that to the great British public, two *separate* murderers sounds fractionally scarier than *one* pair of them . . .'

Even as he spoke, Thorne could feel an old, instinctive dread beginning to settle over him. He was certain that the two men they were after would prove to be a whole lot scarier than any number of run-of-the-mill, bog-standard murderers.

When the meeting was over, Thorne, Brigstocke, McEvoy and Holland left the room in silence, each in their own ways coming to terms with the importance, the urgency of the job ahead. If there were plenty of unanswered or unanswerable questions, one thing was horribly evident. They needed to catch these men quickly before there were more bodies for Phil Hendricks to deal with.

Because he would be dealing with them two at a time.

Jane Lovell, a thirty-nine-year-old divorcee, had bled to death on a warm July evening on a patch of wasteland in Wood Green, N22, in the London Borough of Haringey. That was why, five months later, on a bitterly cold Monday afternoon, a long weekend of collating, of organising, of *sod all* behind him, Tom Thorne was at the headquarters of the Serious Crime Group (East). The teams based here policed ten boroughs' worth of killing, Haringey included.

Thorne, freezing in a smoke-filled room in Edmonton, sitting opposite one of the most arrogant little gobshites he'd had the misfortune to encounter in a long time.

'Are you saying we should have seen a link? Christ knows why. Buggered if I can see a link between your two . . . what are the names?'

'Carol Garner and Ruth Murray. Sir.'

DCI Derek Lickwood nodded and spat out the smoke from his latest cigarette. 'Right. Yeah, well, it all seems a bit far-fetched to me, but that's your business.' He wore an expensively cut blue suit and leaned back on his grimy plastic chair as if it were a well-upholstered leather recliner. His hair was black and swept back from a face that was almost, but not quite, handsome. Both chin and nose were a little big, as was his Adam's apple, which bobbed furiously up and down as he spoke. He addressed his comments, curiously, to a point six inches above Thorne's head.

'When it starts becoming my business though, I get a bit nervous,' Lickwood said. 'I'm not mad keen on people who are supposed to be colleagues, strolling in here and intimating that maybe my team, and by implication, me, could have done a better job of something. That upsets me.'

Thorne, even after a cursory glance at the file on Jane Lovell, had realised that it would have been hard to have made a *worse* job of it. Everything that needed to have been done, had been, but no more. It was by the book and not from the heart. Two days after Jane Lovell had been stabbed to death, the case was as cold as she was.

Thorne could see that Lickwood's reaction was all pose. A typically spiky and defensive response from an officer who feared that his shortcomings were going to be exposed. Thorne knew that he wanted, very badly, to punch Lickwood in his smug mouth, and he knew that he would have made a very tidy job of it. He also knew that, if he was going to get anywhere at all, a little diplomacy was called for.

Call it diplomacy. Basically it was just bullshit.

'As far as Jane Lovell and Katie Choi, the victim in Forest Hill, go, sir, there was probably no link at all, other than . . .'

'Right.' Lickwood leaned forward and jabbed at the file on the desk in front of Thorne. 'We looked at the Katie Choi murder, of course we did, but she was butchered. Jane Lovell was killed by one single stab wound, clean. The Choi girl was virtually unrecognisable. He'd almost cut her head off. Why should anybody think they were connected?'

Thorne nodded. Connections. When 'sick' connected with 'warped' they gave the job to him.

'Ostensibly they aren't . . . weren't.' Thorne was picking his words carefully. 'The only link is the one we're now seeing retrospectively – the fact that they were killed by two people who, in all probability, are at least known to each other . . .'

Lickwood, eyes wide, parroting. 'In all probability.'

'There aren't so many murders in London that we can put it down to coincidence. Two women stabbed to death on the same evening. Four months later, two women strangled to death, both of whom had passed through main-line stations just before they were killed. I think the killers are narrowing their parameters as they go. Increasing the number of specifics . . .'

Lickwood looked at the spot above Thorne's head. 'Sorry, I'm not with you.' Thorne could guess what he was thinking. *Smartarse.*

'If it's some sort of game, it's as if they're trying to make it harder for themselves.' Thorne couldn't help smiling at Lickwood's nod. The tiny gesture, given to signal his understanding and agreement, indicated perfectly just how obtuse he really was. At that moment, Thorne would have been happy with just one quick right-hander. Break the fucker's nose. A small slap even . . .

'Where d'you want to start then?' Lickwood said, lighting up again.

Thorne had, in fact, started already. McEvoy and Holland were busy re-questioning all the key witnesses, notably Michael Murrell, who worked in the cinema at Wood Green shopping centre, which Jane Lovell had visited just before she was killed. Murrell had given a description of a man he'd seen hanging around outside the cinema who looked as if he'd been waiting for someone. After tracing most of the people in the cinema that night, this man could not be accounted for. An e-fit had been created, which was of course on file, but Thorne wanted to see what difference five months had made to Michael Murrell's memory. He also wanted to see what DCI Derek Lickwood had to say about one statement in particular.

'Tell me about Lyn Gibson.'

Lickwood blew smoke out of his nose in a dramatic gesture of exasperation. He clearly enjoyed using his cigarette as a prop, but he was hammy as hell. 'Mad as a cut snake if you ask me. I think she enjoyed the drama of it all, you know, maybe she had a thing for coppers. She was round here every ten minutes, hassling us, demanding to know what we were doing.'

'She was Jane Lovell's friend . . .'

'So she said . . .'

'She thought that Jane was being pestered by someone at work?'

'Pestered one minute, *doing* the pestering the next. Gibson couldn't make her fucking mind up, which made it obvious to me that she didn't really know much about anything. Basically, she thought that there was some bloke Jane worked with who we should be looking at, but she had no idea who he was. Jane never mentioned his name apparently, which was one more reason not to take it particularly seriously . . .'

'Did you not even check it out? Talk to the people she worked with?'

'It's in the file.'

Thorne knew full well what was in the file. He'd spent most of Saturday and Sunday ploughing through the reports on Jane Lovell and Katie Choi. Patterns of dried blood on wasteland. Stab wounds running into the hundreds. Another weekend of light reading.

He waited Lickwood out.

'Without a name it was a waste of time. It's not a small company. We asked around, got a feel of the place, looked at a couple of people, but short of asking if anybody there was harassing a woman who'd just been found murdered, there was bugger all we could do.'

Thorne was finding it hard to maintain even a pretence of respect for the man's rank. 'What about company politics? There's always rumours. Couldn't you find the office gossip?'

Lickwood leaned back in his chair again, striking a pose, only inches from tumbling arse over tit. 'Well, that was the problem, mate. We'd already found her, hadn't we? Dead as mutton, a hundred yards off the Wood Green High Road. As far as we could tell, Jane Lovell *was* the office gossip . . .'

*

Dave Holland rarely went to the cinema. He and Sophie were much fonder of a night in with a rented video, and if he sometimes wondered whether or not he was missing out on something, one look at the seedy, sticky-carpeted interior of the Odeon, Wood Green told him he was better off with Blockbuster.

Michael Murrell was a tall, unnaturally skinny black man in his late thirties, who coughed to announce his presence, brushed non-existent lint from the sleeve of his blazer, and announced curtly that he could give Holland five minutes of his time at the most. It took a lot less than that for Holland to realise that this man's job as Front of House Manager was pretty much all he had going for him. What he lacked in warmth he made up for in efficiency and an unparalleled knowledge of popcorn sales. He could doubtless have told him how many buckets of salty or sweet had been sold in the last calendar month, and whether men or women were the biggest consumers of cheese-covered nachos. Though not exactly charmed, Holland was relieved. Whatever the cause of this strange devotion to work, he guessed it made Mr Murrell a reliable witness. He still had, or at least claimed to have, a vivid memory of the man he'd seen hanging about outside the cinema five months earlier.

'*Pearl Harbour* with Ben Affleck and Kate Beckinsale. The programme started at eight twenty, the main feature at eight thirty-five and the audience began leaving at twenty past ten. I've got a good memory, Detective Constable, I can still see his face.' Murrell spoke matter-of-factly, staring at Holland from behind thick, oversize glasses. 'You see, what sticks in my mind is that he didn't look shifty or suspicious . . . as much as scared.'

*

Sarah McEvoy could smoke for England, but Lyn Gibson made her look like a lightweight. She worked for a small PR firm in Putney, in a building with a strict No Smoking policy. They'd been standing in the car park, freezing their arses off for twenty minutes and already there were cigarette butts scattered around their feet.

Lyn Gibson's were easy to spot. The ones with the bright red lipstick. Four of them.

The fact that her mouth was otherwise occupied was only one reason why she wasn't saying much to begin with about her friend's death. It was obviously still difficult to talk about in any depth. McEvoy knew better than to push. Five months was a long time in Serious Crime. A lot of bodies. To the friends and relatives of the dead, five months was a moment.

'Jane wasn't a saint, you know, but there was never any malice in her.' When Lyn did speak, she spoke slowly, in a series of disconnected statements, as if seeking some reassurance in this catalogue of *things that were true*, this solid analysis of her dead friend's character.

'She was always laughing. With me at any rate. I know she had a good old cry on her own sometimes though . . .'

It was only when McEvoy mentioned Jane Lovell's job that Lyn Gibson became animated. Then, she spoke passionately about a man that her friend had said was bothering her. Jane had admitted that she'd flirted with him, maybe even led him on a little, but it was only teasing. She'd never really been interested.

'Something about him worried her though. She could never really say what it was and when I tried to find out more she shut up, like it was something spooky. I never even knew the bloke's name. But you should try and find him. I know that wanker Lickwood thought I was some kind of nutter, but I knew Jane. You know . . . ?'

McEvoy was impressed. The woman was angry, but as far as McEvoy could tell, she had no axe to grind. There was a burst of throaty laughter as Lyn Gibson put another cigarette in her mouth, but as she lit it, McEvoy could see the flame reflected in the tears that were gathering, ready to drop.

'I told her to come and stay at mine, you know. Stupid cow was too fond of her own bed.' She laughed again, and the laugh became a cough. She took a deep drag and pressed the heel of her hand to an eye. 'I'll tell you the really stupid thing. The film we went to see that night. It was shit. It was a shit film . . .'

It was amazing how much a simple thing like the Christmas lights in Kentish Town could raise Thorne's spirits. They were a long way removed from the gaudy display of Oxford Street or Brent Cross, just simple strings of white bulbs stretching from one side of the main road to the other, but he found them bizarrely uplifting after two hours in the company of Derek Lickwood.

Thorne liked Christmas. He didn't get as excited as he had when he'd been a kid, but then who did? As an only child, it had always been special. Now, he could afford to be cynical when the decorations started appearing in shops sometime just after Easter, and marvel at how much money was spent, but he always hoped for a white Christmas, and a kids' choir singing *In The Bleak Midwinter* still made him teary.

This brief, early flowering of seasonal cheer was more than a little pissed upon when Thorne arrived home and opened his post to discover that his one and, thus far, *only* Christmas card was from the Bengal Lancer, thanking him for another year of custom. Now seemed like as good a time as any to thank them for their card-cum-calendar, by ringing to order a home delivery.

Moving to get the phone from the table by the front door, Thorne noticed the light blinking on the answering machine. He pressed play and then, a few seconds later, hit the *Stop* button as soon as he heard his father's voice. Thorne knew that the message itself would almost certainly be unimportant; just the latest in a long line of thinly veiled hints about his failure to ring.

Thorne took the hint and picked up the phone.

Since the death of his mother two and a half years earlier, the relationship between Tom and Jim Thorne had settled into one defined by the father's absurd, almost pathological fondness for pointless quizzes and stupid jokes, and the son's grim acceptance of blame for the fact that the distance between them was far more than the twenty-five miles from North London to St Albans.

Forced laughter and instant guilt.

It was usually the joke that came first. 'Tom, what is ET short for?'

'Go on dad . . .'

'Because he's only got little legs.'

Then the guilt, which tonight took the form of the annual amble round the houses to decide where Thorne's father was going to spend Christmas. He'd spent the last two with Thorne in London, *and* the couple before that, when there'd been three of them. The days when there had been *four* of them to exchange socks and perfume, eat dry turkey, argue over the Queen's speech and then fall asleep in front of *The Great Escape*, seemed like a long way away. The days before strokes and hospital visits and a grief that changed people for ever.

The days before affairs.

Now, there was just the father and the son, and it was as if the old man needed to be wooed, like a girl. He had a sister in Brighton, whose name would go unmentioned all year and would then be mysteriously dropped into the conversation around the same time that the first Christmassy Woolworths adverts appeared on television. Thorne knew his dad's 'I know you're busy, let's not bother' routine by heart. Like Santa, it came once a year and Thorne had started off believing it. Yes, he *might* go to Eileen's . . . maybe it would be easier for everybody . . . he didn't want to put anybody to any trouble . . . he promised to tell him as soon as he knew what he was doing . . .

Thorne was well aware that the old sod knew *exactly* what he was doing.

By the time two cans of Sainsbury's premium Belgian lager had washed down a plateful of Kentish Town's finest Kashmiri food, Thorne had stopped being pissed off with his father. It was time to catch up with McEvoy and Holland.

Holland told Thorne that he'd gone through Margie Knight's description with Michael Murrell, and even though they were similar, Murrell maintained that the man he'd seen had been wearing glasses. 'Right, let's get Knight *and* Murrell together,' Thorne said, 'Come up with something definitive.'

McEvoy confirmed that Lyn Gibson's story needed checking out. Something had gone on with somebody at Jane Lovell's office and it was worth looking into. After all, might not at least one of the killers have started close to home? Started with somebody he knew? Thorne had been thinking exactly the same thing and despite what Lickwood had said about it being a waste of time, he'd already decided to see what he could find out. He'd have done it anyway, whatever DS McEvoy had thought of Lyn Gibson, just to annoy Derek Lickwood. If he couldn't punch him, he could at least piss him off.

As he spoke to McEvoy, Thorne gathered up the take-away cartons off the floor. Elvis, his cat, squirmed around his ankles, yowling. He'd inherited her, stupid name and all, a year earlier in unpleasant circumstances, during the hunt for the 'Sleepyhead' killer. Elvis was a nervous moggy, but it never seemed to affect her appetite.

Thorne carried the rubbish through to the kitchen. He couldn't say that he actually *liked* his flat very much, but it was at least tidy, most of the time.

He scraped the dried remains of his dinner into the bin, thinking that it would be nice to hear a woman say how tidy his flat was.

Sarah McEvoy told Thorne that she'd see him tomorrow and switched off her phone. She smiled across at Dave Holland who, not two minutes before, had said and done exactly the same things.

The bell rang for last orders. Holland looked first at his watch and then at McEvoy. She nodded and reached for a cigarette as he picked up their empty glasses and began pushing his way through the crowd towards the bar.

Thorne sat thinking about the day, no crowds keeping *him* from drink.

It had been a day when sirens had wailed. When he'd been aware of the all too familiar noise, more so than usual; every few minutes, moving towards or away from him. The Doppler effect of one barely registering, before another took its place. Perhaps there'd been some horrible incident. A train crash. A fire in a tube station. Or perhaps it was just another day in a city Thorne loved and hated in pretty much equal measure.

Police cars, ambulances, screaming their way around the streets of the capital.

The sound of London.

Thorne stared at the television screen. He was thoroughly unengaged by the brash and jumpy images. Half past midnight, and the programme seemed to consist of a partially dressed woman shouting at complete strangers in the street. Thorne didn't connect with it on any level. He saw only a face that was vaguely familiar. A tired-looking, grey face, dimly glimpsed, floating behind the dusty screen, in the occasional, blessed moments of dark stillness.

Outside, it was cold enough for snow.

Inside, Thorne sat staring at his own reflection. Wondering what Charlie Garner wanted for Christmas.

1986

Even later on, when winter came, he knew that he would prefer to be outdoors. On the street. There were bound to be a couple of days, he knew that, a couple of those really bad days when the cold made your balls ache, when he would need to get into a hostel for the night. He'd heard a couple of the really old ones, the stupid old fuckers, the drunks, talking about nights when your trousers would freeze stiff and stick to your legs, and you'd have to piss in your pants just to thaw them out. Then, maybe, he might go back to the shelter, back for the hot soup and Jesus bit. Otherwise though, unless the snow was at least a foot thick, he'd be sleeping outdoors. I mean that was why they called it 'rough' for fuck's sake.

And he'd always been able to put up with plenty of pain.

This place was genuinely unique. A maze of walkways and underpasses and tunnels. A small city of concrete rat-runs for the human rats. It was only really at night that Cardboard City sprang fully formed to life. In order to appreciate the faces properly – the mad eyes, the running sores, the matted beards – you needed to see them lit by the glow from a fire burning in an oil drum. By day, the skateboarders had the run of the place, but when darkness fell they would pick up their boards and drift away, home for dinner, and then the vermin would come out. The vermin like him.

He'd only arrived here recently. At first he'd been content with a doss-house and had usually made enough each day for a night in the Endell Street Spike in Covent Garden, but he didn't believe in doing things by halves. Outdoors was best, and besides, it tickled him to live here, down below the South Bank, with the Royal Festival Hall and the National Theatre right above his head, in a city built from boxes and fuelled by strong lager and despair.

Begging would do for the moment. There was plenty of time to work out an angle, but for the time being, a couple of quid a day was doing him handsomely. Enough to buy a paper, and a can of something, and always the chocolate to give him energy.

He firmly believed in never doing anything unless you were going to give it absolutely your best shot. He was a very good beggar. He'd picked it up very quickly. He didn't just stand there looking like a puppy who's pissed himself, holding out his hand like some Ethiopian. He made an effort. Yes, he was brighter than most of the others, and him being only sixteen didn't hurt, but it wasn't rocket science was it? It was all about making the punter think that they had no other choice. Not by being aggressive, no; that was stupid and a waste of energy. It just needed to be real, and looking like you had a sense of humour didn't hurt. If I can afford to laugh about this, mate, you can afford to put your hand in your pocket, and if all you've got in there is a pound coin then you might as well toss it my way. Gawd bless you guv'nor . . .

These yuppie cunts could afford it anyway.

Leaving had been the best thing, he was certain of that now. Six months ago, chucking a few things in a bag, nicking the money he'd need to tide him over from his mum's purse. He'd not been a hundred per cent sure then, but he knew he didn't really belong there.

Had to go.

He still thought about Palmer and about Karen. Thought about them far more often than he thought about his mum. He dreamed about his dad, once, but tried not to think about him.

It was stupid really. He didn't exactly miss *them*, he missed the things he could do when they were there, and the feelings he got from doing those things. Palmer and Karen were just like his air pistol or his knives or his cricket bat. They were things he used.

It was a warm night. He lay back, his head on his bag, and stared up through the ramps and stairwells at the thing that flashed and moved on top of the Hayward Gallery. Somebody told him that the colours changed with the wind. Art, by all accounts. Wank, more like . . .

The moon was full above Waterloo Bridge. He could see figures moving slowly across, staring left and right, marvelling at the view up and down the river. Stupid tossers. The best view of London wasn't from up there. London was happening down where he was, among the dopers and the dogshit. It was a city that came alive the lower you went, and he was starting to fit right in.

Martin and Karen . . .

He pictured them, in that blackened shed by the railway line, or in the park or the shopping centre, or traipsing through darkening underpasses, following him, looking. Martin, his huge hands flapping in panic, needing to be soothed, needing to be coaxed. Karen, laughing at him, at his awkwardness and anxiety.

Nicklin drifted off to sleep and dreamed about fucking them both.

SIX

Baynham & Smout was a large accountancy firm whose glass-fronted premises on Shaftesbury Avenue nestled next to those of film companies and publishers, a stone's throw from Chinatown and Soho. If, having spent a hard morning number-crunching, an accountant wanted a bowl of hot and sour soup and a handjob at lunchtime, this was a fantastic place to work.

Thorne sat on a vast black leather sofa admiring the understated but classy artwork on the expansive white walls. He glanced at Holland on the chair opposite, leafing through the style magazine he'd picked up from the glass-topped coffee table in front of him. He wondered how much more it had cost to kit out this lobby than it had cost to furnish his entire flat. Probably more than it had cost to *buy* his flat . . .

He caught the eye of one of the two gorgeous young receptionists sitting at adjacent, walnut desks on the other side of the lobby. She smiled. 'Won't be much longer.' As the words echoed off the marble and glass, her colleague looked up and smiled as well.

Thorne nodded. One of them would only have been there for five months . . .

He closed his eyes and saw an image from one of the photos in his ever expanding gallery. She was lying on her side, her right arm trapped beneath her, and her left thrown high above her head, like a schoolgirl eager to get a teacher's attention. One high-heeled shoe was missing; it lay a few feet away, in a patch of nettles, and the dew glistened on her thin summer skirt. She was yellowy white, like the bone of some giant dog, gnawed and then forgotten. Her clothes hung on her like scraps of flesh, her hair like pale strands of gristle. The single patch of colour – the blood that had poured from the wound in her chest and dried overnight to the shade of old meat.

Thorne looked over at the two girls busy at their computer screens when they weren't answering the constantly trilling phones. He wondered which of them had replaced Jane Lovell.

'Sean Bracher . . . sorry.'

Thorne looked up to see a sharp suit, a proffered hand and a mouth with far too many teeth in it. Holland was already on his feet and Thorne stood up to join him. He picked up his battered leather jacket and moved to follow Bracher to his office, but Baynham & Smout's Assistant Director of Personnel was going to do his talking to the police right there in the lobby. He flopped into one of the chairs, tossed his mobile phone on to the coffee table and called across to the reception desk. 'Jo, a pot of coffee would be good . . .'

Bracher was in his mid-thirties, with rapidly thinning hair, which Thorne guessed he was not at all happy about. Clearly an Essex boy made good, he could probably turn on an acquired sophistication when it was needed. With Thorne and Holland, he'd obviously decided that matey was the way to play it: estuary vowels, laughter, innuendo. One of the boys.

The coffee arrived quickly, and Bracher said his piece. 'I can only really tell you what I told your colleague back in the summer. We're a big company and I tend to pick up on most things that are going on, but there's no way I can be on top of what the people here are up to in their own time. Having said that, there was no-one Jane had a problem with as far as I'm aware. I'm here for people to tell me stuff like that and Jane and I were good mates, you know, so, I think she'd have said something.'

Holland placed his coffee cup back on the table. 'I get the impression that Jane was pretty much the life and soul round here. That she liked to enjoy herself.'

There was a resounding raspberry noise as Bracher shifted on the leather chair. 'I think that's why what happened hit everybody here so hard. It can get a bit dull around here if you're not careful, and since everything went so bloody PC, some people can get a bit touchy if people try to . . . liven things up.'

Thorne glanced across as a motorcycle courier came through the revolving doors, took off his helmet and strolled towards the reception desk.

'Liven things up?' Holland said.

Bracher leaned forward, elbows on knees, fingers intertwined. He had a serious point to make. 'Seventy-five per cent, *at least*, seventy-five per cent of people meet their husbands, wives, or long-term partners at work. That's a fact. But if you so much as ask a woman out these days, you've got to be careful, you know? You used to be able to have some fun, men and women could wind each other up a bit, but now it's all got a bit po-faced. Nobody really talks to anybody else now, except for five minutes when they're making a coffee or whatever. "Water-cooler time" I think they call it in America. Anyway, Jane didn't give a toss about any of that. She just enjoyed a laugh, and if people didn't like it, then sod 'em, you know?'

Thorne watched as the courier pulled a package from the bag over his shoulder and handed it to one of the girls at the desk. She laughed at something he said . . .

'Was there anybody who didn't like it?' Holland asked in such a way as to imply that not liking it, whatever *it* was, would have been utterly stupid.

'Well, there's always a couple of arseholes anywhere isn't there? I bet you've got a few on the force haven't you?' Holland smiled, but only with his mouth. 'Yeah, there was the odd one, you know, couldn't see the joke, but we'd just take the piss. You've got to have a sense of humour haven't you? I mean, we're all fair game at the end of the day . . .'

Thorne tuned Bracher out. The courier and the girls on reception were still flirting. Jane Lovell might have been killed by a complete stranger, and she might have been killed by someone she knew well. A third option was that her murderer was someone with whom she was casually acquainted – someone she saw regularly without ever really knowing. A courier, a shop assistant, someone she met at the tube station every morning.

Call it a couple of thousand suspects . . .

'Jane was always up for it, you know? Up for the crack.' Bracher was still eulogising. 'As far as I know, she got on with almost everybody.'

Thorne spoke directly to him for the first time, his sarcasm undisguised. 'And, *as far as you know*, Mr Bracher, did she ever get *off* with anybody?'

Bracher reddened. He picked up a teaspoon and tapped it against the side of the table for a few seconds. 'Look, I'm here to make sure that people can work together. Who they're sleeping with is really none of my business.'

'Even if it's someone in the same office? I find that hard to believe.'

Bracher's mobile rang and he grabbed for it gratefully. As he murmured into it, he raised his eyebrows at Thorne, an apology for the tiresome interruption. Thorne looked at Holland. Time to go.

Bracher shrugged and stood up. 'I'm sorry, but unless there's anything else . . .'

As they all shook hands, gathering up jackets and overcoats, the thought crossed Thorne's mind that Bracher had primed a colleague to ring him after ten minutes, giving him an excuse to get away. As he and Holland pushed their way out through the revolving door, a second thought entered his mind. A question. Had he developed finely honed, razor-sharp instincts, or was he just a cynical bastard?

'What do you make of him, then?' Holland asked. They were walking along Shaftesbury Avenue, towards the Cambridge Circus NCP on Gerrard Street, where Thorne's F-reg Mondeo was busy lowering the tone. It was bright but freezing. Scarves and sunglasses weather . . .

'I think he was sleeping with Jane Lovell, or had been at some point.'

Holland nodded. 'Worth looking at d'you think?'

Thorne pulled a face. He *was* a cynical bastard, but those instincts he did have told him that Bracher, though an arrogant, unpleasant sod, was probably no more than that. He wondered how many more of them he was going to have to deal with before this case was finished.

★

Back at Becke House, Thorne walked past McEvoy who was on the phone in the Major Incident Room. She waved at him, indicating that she needed to talk. He nodded and carried on through to his own office.

He sat down at his desk, flicked the desktop calendar forward to Tue, Dec 11, and stared for a minute at the psychedelic screensaver that Holland had installed for him. The vivid colours swam and morphed and bled into one another, and he gazed at them until they began to blur and hurt his eyes. They were there, so he'd been told, to stop the computer screen burning out. Thorne wondered if they made something that could do the same for policemen.

He stood up and marched briskly out of the office into the Incident Room, not looking at anybody, not speaking, grabbing a chair and taking it with him.

He wasn't burnt out yet . . .

If he disliked his office, his feelings for the Incident Room were closer to pure hatred. There was so much more of it. A room of sharp corners and dead air. A long, dirty window, the light diffused through an off-white vertical blind, one blade permanently broken and crumpled onto the windowsill, where it lay among the corpses of a hundred long-dead bluebottles. A dozen or more desks. Sharp corners waiting to catch a thigh or tear the back of a hand. There was one in particular that caught Thorne several times a week, no matter how hard he tried to avoid it. The room was a feng shui nightmare. Not that he had any truck whatsoever with that kind of rubbish. The only rearrangement of furniture and personal belongings that he had *any* belief in, involved burglars and fences.

He dragged the chair across the room behind him,

steering well clear of the lethal desktop. He planted himself at the far end, in front of the wall, and stared.

Jane Lovell. Katie Choi. Ruth Murray. Carol Garner. Photocopies of photos on a tatty, cork pinboard.

And file names on a computer, sticky labels on jars in a mortuary . . .

Arrows and swooping lines marked in thick, black felt-tip pen on a wipe-clean chart. Lines that linked grainy prints of the four victims to lists of dates, times and locations. Beneath these was another batch of names in a row of wonky columns. Margie Knight. Michael Murrell. Lyn Gibson.

Charlie Garner . . .

Witnesses. Friends. Family. Figures at the periphery of the case diagram. Thorne stared at the chart. A few nights before, he had sat and thought about the hundreds, the thousands of those whose livelihood depended on killing. Now, he thought about the more unwilling participants. Those who had not chosen to play any part in the process – a process that ended with their names scribbled on a wipe-clean board.

Those hundreds of lives touched by a single death.

Jane Lovell. Katie Choi. Ruth Murray. Carol Garner. Four single deaths. Two twisted killers. Thorne stared at the names and pictures on the wall in front of him and felt it slipping away. The case was going cold. They were losing it.

Thorne turned at a commotion behind him and saw Brigstocke marching across the office in his direction. A step or two behind the DCI was a man Thorne recognised from the press conference a few days earlier. He couldn't remember the name . . .

'Tom, this is Steve Norman, our new Senior Press Officer.'

Norman, that was it. Soberly suited and suitably respectful as he'd welcomed the ladies and gentlemen of the media into the briefing room at Scotland Yard, and smoothed the way for Trevor Jesmond with a few easy jokes. Nothing that might compromise the seriousness of the investigation of course, or distract the attention of the cameras from their intended target. Clearly he was someone who could tailor his demeanour to any occasion.

Thorne stood. Norman stepped smartly forward and reached for his hand. He was a smallish man, sinewy and energised. His black hair was gelled and swept back, and his dark eyes held Thorne's as their hands met.

'Pleased to meet you, Tom.'

There were perhaps forty people in the room – detectives, uniforms and civilian auxiliaries. The hubbub, the noise of phones ringing and printers whirring, was not inconsiderable. Thorne, for reasons he couldn't explain, felt forty pairs of eyes upon him and imagined that the entire place had fallen silent.

Brigstocke gestured towards the other side of the room. 'Let's go into the office shall we. You can't hear yourself think in here . . .'

Thorne led the way. Brigstocke and Norman walked a few paces behind, and despite his best efforts, Thorne could hear nothing of their murmured conversation. As he glanced back over his shoulder, he caught his thigh on the sharp corner of the deadly desktop.

'Fuck!'

The stab of pain was intense. He kicked the leg of the desk. The eyes of the woman behind it widened in alarm, her arms spreading to prevent a tottering tower of paperwork from collapsing.

When Thorne reached the door to his office, still rubbing the top of his thigh, Holland, who was on a coffee run, caught his eye. The DC's raised eyebrows asked the question. Thorne's tiny shrug gave the answer. *Your guess is as good as mine, mate . . .*

Once inside, Thorne poured himself into a chair and was a little disconcerted to see that Brigstocke was still standing and Norman was leaning casually against a desk. They were both looking down at him.

'It's clear that the media are not giving up on this until we've got a result . . .' Brigstocke said. It was the voice he usually reserved for superior officers. 'So it's important that we keep Steve up to speed with everything.' Thorne was hugely relieved that Brigstocke hadn't gone as far as mentioning the fabled hymnsheet that they were all supposed to be singing from.

Norman flashed the smile that Thorne had seen him use to such good effect when he'd introduced Jesmond at the press conference. 'Russell's already filled me in. I just wanted to introduce myself properly, and apologise in advance, because at some point I *will* become a pain in the arse.'

Thorne, who didn't doubt it for a second, did his best to summon up something like a smile in return. 'I'm sure I'll cope.'

Norman nodded, pushed himself away from the edge of the desk, strolled across to the window. 'If a media type says "off the record", my advice usually would be to shut the fuck up very bloody quickly, but off the record, Tom . . .' Brigstocke laughed. Thorne sort of joined in. 'Anything I should know about?'

'Impossible to say,' Thorne said. 'I don't know how many things you don't know.' Norman didn't turn from the window so Thorne couldn't judge his reaction, but Brigstocke's was clear enough. Thorne knew that he'd better play along. 'We'll make sure you're the first to know if anything significant breaks. We're chasing up a few leads . . .'

Norman turned from the window and looked straight at Thorne. 'Listen, I don't really expect to be the first person to know anything, but it's always a good idea to use the press. If you don't, give them a chance and they'll have you . . .' Thorne didn't bother even trying to think of a smart-arse answer, because he knew Norman was right. He'd seen too many good policemen eaten up. If the appetite was to be satisfied, he needed to tolerate people like Norman.

'Right now, they're getting a bit impatient,' Norman said. 'We've made a major breakthrough, no question about it, but we need to follow it up.'

'We should never have made it public. The fact that the killers are working together . . .'

Norman dropped the matey tone as if it was a turd. 'That was not down to me, Inspector, as you well know. My job was, and *is*, to implement the decisions taken at a far higher level than *this*, as far as they affect the Met's relations with the media.' He looked across at Brigstocke, cocked his head.

Was that clear enough?

Brigstocke took a few steps towards Thorne, put his hands on the back of the chair.

'Anything from the meeting with Bracher?'

Thorne was uncomfortable discussing the case *as it*

was actually unfolding with Norman in the room, but he understood that Brigstocke was angling for something, anything, that he might be able to throw to the press office.

'Not really.' He turned to look at Norman. 'But we should be able to let you have a definitive e-fit of the man we think killed Jane Lovell and Ruth Murray very soon.'

Norman seemed inordinately pleased. 'Great . . . that's great. Excellent. I'm going to get us maximum exposure. Every front page in the country, every major news and current affairs show . . .'

There was a knock and Sarah McEvoy stuck her head round the door. 'Sir I . . . oh sorry, I'll come back . . .'

Norman threw up his hands. 'I'm about done here, Russell . . .' He started walking towards the half-opened door.

Brigstocke beckoned McEvoy in. 'It's OK, Sarah.' McEvoy stepped into the room and stood aside as Norman walked past her. Thorne could see him sizing her up, checking her body over, before he turned at the doorway.

'Obviously a DNA match would have been fabulous, but just having a print is the next best thing. If you get him, when you get him, they'll convict him. Media relations can help you get him, Tom.'

Brigstocke nodded, looked at Thorne. 'I'll see you out, Steve . . .'

Norman said something to McEvoy, and Brigstocke said something to both of them as he and Norman took their time leaving the office. Thorne stayed in his seat and watched them go, his mind wandering. He span his chair round and gazed out of the window. A glorious view of the industrial estate on the other side of the A5. Stores with names like Carpet Kingdom and Shoe World and Dictatorship of Leather. Vast, American-style warehouses. Everything becoming more American.

Including the killings.

Thorne watched the little square cars passing the big square superstores. From the windows on the *other* side of the building, he could gaze down at the college parade ground, occasionally see recruits being put through their paces.

Either way, the view was depressing.

'Looked interesting . . .'

Thorne spun round. McEvoy was perched on the edge of his desk, waiting to be told everything. He couldn't be arsed with telling her much more than was blatantly obvious from his expression. 'Not really.'

McEvoy wasn't going to be fobbed off. 'Seemed like a slippery customer.' Thorne said nothing. She had one last crack at him. 'I was especially impressed by the subtle way he managed to give my tits the once over.'

Thorne laughed. 'It wasn't that subtle . . .'

'Trust me, it's relative. Is he going to be a problem?'

'I don't think so, as long as we let Mr Norman think he's keeping the massed hordes of the press at bay. Right now, I've promised him this e-fit as soon as. We need to get Murrell and Knight in here . . .' McEvoy edged herself off the desk. Thorne saw her eyes flick away from him for a second. Bad news. 'What?'

'That was actually what I needed to see you about.' McEvoy tried to sound matter of fact. 'We can't find Margie Knight.'

'*Can't find her?*' Thorne was shouting. He knew that heads would be turning outside the office door.

'Look, she must have freaked out after she talked to us. Maybe she's gone on holiday . . .'

Thorne stood up, stomped across the small office. 'For fuck's sake, Sarah. We should have brought her in here straight away, got an e-fit then.'

'She's a prostitute. She has a natural dislike for the police because most of the time we're trying to arrest her or stop her making a living. You reckon we should have dragged her across London, tied her to a chair?'

McEvoy was reacting aggressively to the anger born out of Thorne's frustration, but he knew that she was right. Co-operation had to be just that. Memory was an untrustworthy thing at the best of times. Never a reliable ally. The last thing it needed was to be forced.

'Couldn't we just go with Murrell's description for now?' McEvoy asked. 'Maybe give the press a couple of options. With and without glasses . . .'

'No.' Thorne knew only too well how much of a difference a description could make. He'd made costly mistakes before. Inaccuracies, inconsistencies, were unavoidable, but keeping them to a minimum could save lives. It was that horribly simple.

'Murrell's description is five months old. Margie Knight had a good look at this fucker two weeks ago.' He walked back towards his desk, stopping opposite McEvoy, making it very clear. 'I want to see the face she's carrying around in her head. We'll put it together with Murrell's and then we'll see what he looks like.' She nodded. He moved across to his chair and sat down. 'So, what are we doing?'

'I've called in a few favours at Vice and every uniform in the area is carrying a description. We'll find her.'

Thorne looked at her. Her face was often difficult to

read, but at that moment it told him that whether McEvoy found Margie Knight or not, she'd tear every dodgy sauna, massage parlour and tin-pot knocking shop in the city apart trying. He leaned back in his chair and tried to sound as if he was still a little pissed off.

'Go on then . . .'

The doubts swept over him with the draught from the door that McEvoy slammed behind her. For a minute or two with McEvoy, when the anger had taken hold, he'd sounded almost decisive. It had almost been as if he actually had an idea what he was doing. Two weeks since Ruth Murray and Carol Garner had died and they were going backwards fast. Scrabbling about for leads from two murders committed five months before that.

Thorne knew that he was going to spend the rest of the day working by numbers and fighting away two horrible thoughts. The first was that probably, no, almost *certainly*, the only thing that would help the case move forwards now, that could provide a springboard that might lift the investigation on to another level, was another pair of bodies.

The second was not so much a thought as a feeling; like a virus or an infection lurking within him, waiting to burst into life, clammy and clinging, and immune to treatment.

A feeling that they wouldn't have to wait too long.

The police came to the office today, Karen. Two of them, hunting in pairs. Like the men they're after . . .

They were just sniffing around really. It wasn't at all dramatic. There was no smashing down of doors or snipers on the rooftops opposite. It's difficult to know just how much they've worked out. I've been racking my brains ever since they left but it gives me a headache just thinking about it. They wouldn't have come if they hadn't made a connection between Jane and the other one, you know . . . Ruth, the one behind the railway station. They must know about that. But how much do they know about the others? About his*? I can't work it out at all . . .*

All the time they were here, I knew that I could have ended it with a word. It would have been so easy to fall on the floor in front of them and confess. This is complete fantasy, I know. If I hadn't been terrified of the police, I would never have begun this in the first place, would I? So, I'm left, as usual, confessing to you, Karen. I must tell you that your face, the face I see in my mind's eye as I'm confessing, is full of understanding, and warmth. Full of love.

My work's really starting to suffer now and people have noticed. I got a warning the other day. I don't think they'd ever sack me or anything but if I want to carry on moving up in the company, you know, the intimation was that I'd better buck my ideas up. How can I concentrate on anything, Karen? How can I think about anything, with what's in my head? I'm amazed that I can still breathe. I'm astonished, all the time, that I can eat, and walk and dress myself.

All I can see are open mouths and red eyes and spit on teeth.

All I can hear are grunts and gulps and the sound of blood bubbling out of holes.

All I can feel is dead flesh against my fingers.

This is not even the worst, Karen. There is something much, much worse. All this, the sensory memories of these acts, might fade I suppose, given time, but time is something I am not being given.

Two weeks, no more, only two weeks since I pushed that girl into the shadows and put my clumsy, great hands on her. It's only been two weeks, Karen. Fourteen days, that's all. Hardly time to catch my breath and already there is a new set of . . . instructions.

Soon, I've got to do it again.

1989

He knew, even before he'd come, that this would be the last time.

He'd glanced down at the head of the man on his knees in front of him and seen the bald patch and the grease and the bits of scurf in his hair, and decided. This was probably as good a time as any to call it a day. He'd put enough money away in the last three years. Now, he could move on.

He'd only spent a short time begging, and even then he'd done it properly. He'd gone about things professionally. It was the same with this. He wasn't doing it to finance a smack habit like most of the other boys in the same line of work. His earnings were not wasted on drink or gambling. He used what he needed for the very minimum of food and shelter, and salted the rest away.

He'd made a lot of money in dirty hotel rooms and executive motor cars. He worked harder and more often than any of the others. He'd always been able to take a lot of pain and his disgust threshold was no lower. It had been easy. Half a dozen a day, ten on some days and all paying in cash. Seven days a week, rain or shine. His customers knew that they could always go to him.

He was like a 7-Eleven.

He had more than enough now, and he'd spent time getting to know the people who could help with the paperwork. Now it was time for all that effort to pay dividends. What he was planning to do made sense of course. He needed to do it to be on the safe side, to make sure they couldn't find him, but he also liked the idea because he was bored. He'd been the same person for far too long. After nineteen years, he fancied a change.

It was time to reinvent himself.

He pulled his cock out of the old man's mouth and started to moan theatrically. The old man gasped and opened his mouth. He had a yellow tongue and sharp incisors and his nice clean work shirt was plastered to his neck with sweat.

He came, and for once it was more than the pitiful spasm and spurt he manufactured for punters on demand. Suddenly, the moan from deep in his throat was long and loud and deeply felt.

He came . . .

Spunking away everything that was left of Stuart Nicklin. Out and away. Ridding himself of himself . . .

The sensation continued long after the ejaculation was finished. He was still moaning as he began to rain blows down on the head of the old man on the floor. He punched and he spat and he kicked, the effort causing sweat to run down between his naked shoulder-blades. He closed his eyes as he continued to lash out, and imagined himself remade, a long way from where he was, and from who he was. It was comforting. It was everything he had ever dreamed about. He saw himself surrounded by people that liked and trusted him. He saw himself in a position of responsibility. He saw himself paid to control other people's lives.

The old man had stopped screaming.

He opened his eyes and looked down at the pathetic figure in a nylon shirt, curled up at his feet, spitting out blood and yellow teeth. He gave him one more kick for good measure and began to gather up his clothes.

He still had some way to go of course, before his vision became a reality. The paperwork was fairly straightforward, but there was training to do. It would not be handed to him on a plate, he would need to work for it. And he would work hard because he wanted it more than anything.

He pulled on his shirt and slammed the door of the dingy flat behind him. He jogged down the stairs and emerged, grinning, into the sunshine. Taking the first steps towards a brand new life.

Considering everything that had happened, it was ironic that there was only one job that he'd ever really wanted to do.

SEVEN

Thorne woke from a dream filled with fountains of blood. He could barely make himself heard over the roaring of the arterial gush, as he shouted at the man with the scalpel. He fought to stop the blood falling onto the face of the young woman in the hospital bed, but she lay there unable to turn her head away, the dark red spots slowly obliterating the pink of her face, like the spatter from a paint roller.

He sat up and waited for the dream to evaporate, which it did, quickly, leaving only the memory, which was far, far worse.

The phone was ringing. Thorne glanced at the clock as he leaned over to grab it. Friday night had only just become Saturday morning. He'd barely been asleep for an hour.

'Tom Thorne . . .'

'It's Russell. Wide awake? Or d'you want to grab a coffee and call me back?'

Brigstocke's tone cleared Thorne's head in an instant. 'I'm fine, go ahead.'

'Our friend in the hotel trade is back.'

Thorne had always known that he would be, eventually.

He guessed there would be bodies. He guessed right.

'A middle-aged couple in the Olympia Grand, been dead since early yesterday evening by the look of it . . .' Brigstocke paused, cleared his throat. For Thorne it was always a relief to hear colleagues hesitate to speak about violent death. A relief and a surprise. 'He tortured them, Tom. There are marks . . .'

'Who's picking this up, Russell?'

Another pause, for an altogether different reason. 'I was hoping you would.'

Thorne sat up, swung his legs out of bed. 'I don't think I like where this is going, sir.'

'Don't go off on one, Tom. There's nothing sinister happening, but this was our case and I just don't want strangers on it. Team Two are already down there but I'd like you to get across, see what you make of it. Hendricks is on his way. Go and give them a hand.'

'What about the Garner case?' He knew it then. He'd named it. Four women dead, but for Thorne it was the Garner case. All the murders distilled into one, the one which for a small child had taken away so much more than just his mother. The case would *always* be about that child, as the case a year ago had been about a woman in a hospital bed, unable to move.

The woman he'd been dreaming about.

'It's been nearly three weeks, Tom . . .'

'Seventeen days.'

'Look, I agreed to let you spend time looking for Margie Knight, to hold back on releasing the e-fit, but we're getting nowhere.'

'Sir . . .'

'I've backed every decision you've made on this . . .'

'Because they've been the right decisions . . .'

'Jesmond's getting fucking jittery, all right? Now, I'm not talking about winding it down, so don't panic, but progress *somewhere* would go down a storm right now.'

Thorne was off the bed, catching glimpses of himself in the wardrobe mirror as he stomped around the room. He didn't look at all happy. He knew that Brigstocke was right of course, but his hackles were up all the same. 'Does he think we're sitting on our arses?'

'The hotel killings will be all over the paper in the morning.'

'What? How . . . ?'

'The bodies were found by a housemaid who went to turn down the beds. She called the papers before she called us.'

'Jesus. Norman must be up in arms . . .'

'He isn't the only one. The couple were Dutch, from Amsterdam. Tourists, Tom.'

Thorne grunted sarcastically. 'Oh, *I* see . . .'

'I don't care *what* you think you can fucking see, Inspector.' The change in Brigstocke's tone was sudden, and shocking. Thorne felt a twinge of guilt. The DCI was clearly under some pressure. 'We could have a decent break here, so while we're waiting for the same thing to happen on the other case, I want you to see what you can do, all right? So get down there and have a look.'

Ronald Van Der Vlugt had spent a fairly unremarkable fifty-eight years on the planet, until the night he answered the door to a stranger in a top London hotel. Now, he lay naked in the bath, an inch of bloody water slopping around his lifeless body, trussed up like a defrosting turkey.

'What about the cuts, Phil?'

Hendricks was kneeling by the side of the bath, measuring wounds, and muttering into a small dictaphone. He grunted, and scratched his head through his distinctive yellow showercap. 'Stanley knife, looks like. Something very sharp and very straight. Dozens of them, all over the poor bastard. Face, torso, genitals. Same in there.' He gestured towards the bedroom where Mrs Van Der Vlugt lay stretched out on the bed, staring up at the ceiling, her body as sliced and chipped and stiff as a chopping board.

'No chance he did it post-mortem is there?' Thorne asked. The dead would stay dead, of course, but the living did no harm in searching for a crumb of comfort to offer the relatives. Thorne glanced down at the cuts on the mottled belly, the floating faeces, the brain matter caked across the overflow. He had no idea whether the Van Der Vlugts had children, or grandchildren . . .

Hendricks shook his head. 'Too much blood, mate. He cut 'em up for a while, then smashed the back of their heads in. End of story.' Hendricks switched his dictaphone back on and returned to work. Thorne turned and wandered into the bedroom, exchanging nods with a couple of the SOCOs who crawled and crept slowly around the room, pressing tape into carpet, dusting surfaces, collecting fibres and hairs; working in a silence broken only by the click of knee joints, the snap of evidence bags and the rustle of white plastic bodysuits.

Thorne stood at the foot of the bed and looked at Sonja Van Der Vlugt. She was younger than her husband, he guessed. Early fifties with a roundish face. Silver hair cut into a stylish bob, a well-kept figure. And torture marks.

Thorne had no evidence to support him, none whatsoever, but he knew without any shadow of a doubt that the man responsible had made each watch as he took a knife to the other; the muffled screams behind improvised gags and the straining against bonds exciting him as much as the feeling of the blade nicking the skin, the blood running.

The small safe in the bottom of the wardrobe had been opened; there might have been jewellery taken, watches and cash perhaps, but this wasn't about theft.

Not any more.

Walking across the lobby towards the manager's office, Thorne was struck by how much it reminded him of the one at Baynham & Smout. The killer must have been impressed by the marble and the leather. Impressed and excited by the expense. If he was going to steal, he'd want to steal from people that could afford the finer things in life.

Thorne knocked on the manager's office door, wondering if the killer was motivated by envy. Dismissing the thought. *No, not about theft . . .*

DI Colin Maxwell of Team 2 at SCG (West) had a wide, thin mouth which turned upwards at each end, giving the impression of a permanent smile, rather like a dolphin. His workmates would have laughed at this anyway, but the fact that he was almost always miserable made it even funnier.

'Tom.' They shook hands. Maxwell turned to the short, plump man standing against the desk. 'Mr Felgate, this is Detective Inspector Thorne.' Felgate stood up and Thorne stepped across to shake his hand. It was only then that he noticed the woman sitting in a chair near the door. 'And this is Mary Rendle, who found the bodies.'

At the mention of her name, the woman raised her head and stared at Thorne. She was in her forties, with short black hair and a scar across her chin. It was Thorne who looked away first.

'How much longer do you think it will be until the bodies are removed?' Felgate's question sounded matter of fact, as if bodies turned up in his hotel on a daily basis.

'We're working as fast as we can, sir,' Maxwell said.

'So . . .' Thorne waited until Felgate was looking straight at him. 'The Van Der Vlugts had ordered room service. Exactly what time was that?'

Felgate opened his mouth and looked at Maxwell. Thorne tried not to sound overly impatient. 'Sir?'

'I've already gone over all this with Mr Felgate,' Maxwell said. 'I'll fill you in later.'

For someone who, theoretically at least, had been sent to help, Thorne was not feeling particularly welcome.

It was a feeling he knew pretty well.

Thorne turned to look at Mary Rendle. 'Tell me about finding the body.' He caught her glance towards Maxwell and took a step closer to her. 'And I'm sure you've already *gone over* this with DI Maxwell.' Another step. 'Go over it with me.'

'I went to turn down the bed at about seven o'clock.' She had a smoker's voice, parts of the top range missing. 'There was no reply, so I used the pass key.' Her eyes flashed. 'It's perfectly normal.'

'Nobody's saying it isn't.'

'That's it, all right? She was lying on the bed, and he was in the bath. I don't know what else you want me to say . . .'

'You could start with why you didn't call the police straight away.'

Thorne could have sworn she smiled slightly, as if this was a question she'd been expecting. One to which she'd rehearsed a good answer.

'They were dead, it was obvious. What difference was it going to make? If they'd been alive I would have called an ambulance, but they weren't, so I sat down and thought about it . . .'

Thorne was gobsmacked. 'You sat down and thought about it?'

She glared at him. 'I get three pounds sixty an hour to pick up dirty towels and scrub toilets. I didn't have to think about it for very long.'

Thorne and Maxwell walked across the lobby in silence.

Thorne was resigned to violent death. Most of his colleagues were, at the very best, resistant to its effects. Now, members of the public were reacting in the same way, and for the third or fourth time since he'd got out of bed, Thorne wondered what it would be like to knock it all on the head; to run a pub, or work in a shop, or maybe just sit around doing fuck all, until concerned neighbours started banging on the door.

They stopped at the lifts. Maxwell lit a cigarette, shaking his head. 'Fucking unbelievable.'

Thorne shrugged. He hoped the newspapers had agreed to give Mary Rendle a decent whack. She was going to need something to tide her over. The look Felgate was giving her as Thorne and Maxwell left the office told him that she wasn't going to be picking up dirty towels for very much longer.

Maxwell pressed the button to call the lift. He needed to go back to the murder scene. 'Listen, you'll be in on it when we get this fucker, all right?'

Thorne looked at the smiley dolphin face, unable to read it. The offer at least *sounded* genuine. 'Thanks, Colin. Anything you need, give us a bell . . .'

'The DCI's given us full access to the files, but you lot have done the donkey work, so it's only fair, you know.'

'Going at the staff first?'

They'd been convinced six months earlier, before the killer had gone underground, that he had to have some sort of contact with someone on the inside. Their best guess was that a member of staff at each hotel was feeding him information. They had no idea how he made these contacts, but they had to be telling him which guests were in their rooms, which had ordered room service, where he needed to avoid CCTV cameras . . .

Now, one of these contacts was an accessory to murder.

'Yes, I think so.' Maxwell nodded, but he narrowed his eyes slightly. Not liking to be told what to do. Not enjoying being patronised, however unintentionally or subtly Thorne was doing it.

The lift arrived and Maxwell stepped inside. 'Cheers then . . .'

Thorne stepped forward and put his hand against the closing door. 'Listen, has anybody looked into a drugs angle here? Just to be on the safe side. The torture, the Dutch connection . . . ?'

Maxwell moved back inside the lift, leaned against the ornately mirrored back wall. 'Ronald Van Der Vlugt was a rare book dealer. Over here for an exhibition of antique books and manuscripts at Olympia. My bet is, only drugs he ever took were sleeping tablets or laxatives. Viagra maybe . . .'

In spite of himself, Thorne laughed a little. He stepped back and waited for the doors to shut.

Maxwell was definitely smiling. His turn to patronise. 'I'm surprised at you, Thorne. Clutching at straws . . .'

Thorne looked at him hard as the doors began to close.

'Always, mate. Always.'

'You look like shit,' McEvoy said.

Thorne took a swig of coffee. 'So do you, and I've been looking at dead Dutch people all night. What's your excuse?'

It was just after nine o'clock in the morning and Thorne had been up eight hours already. He'd got back to the flat at quarter to five, failed to get any more sleep and come into work. The drive in, through the virtually empty Saturday morning streets, had been the best part of his day by a long way. Thorne was guessing that, by the time he got to bed again that evening, it still would be.

Now, he was utterly exhausted and in as foul a temper as he could remember. He obviously wasn't the only one.

'What I look like isn't really any of your business, sir.'

'What?' Thorne wasn't so wiped out that he couldn't start to get angry.

'Forget it.' McEvoy stared at him for a few seconds, her eyes cold and challenging, before spinning on her heels and marching out of the office.

'Jesus . . .' Thorne took a deep breath. He opened his desk drawer, stared blankly at the stapler for a moment and slammed it shut again.

He picked up the paper from his desk, leaned back in his

chair and read the *Tourist Slaying* story for the third time since getting to the office. It was predictable fare, hinting at the unspeakable horror in Room 313 while laying on the 'city no longer safe for visitors' stuff with a trowel. A smattering of gory detail, a heavy dose of outrage.

The newsprint began to dance in front of Thorne's eyes, so he closed them. It might have been a few minutes, it might have been an hour, when he heard Holland's voice.

'Sir . . .'

Thorne didn't open his eyes. 'If you've got fresh coffee for me, Holland, promotion's in the bag.'

'It's better than coffee.'

Thorne sat up as Holland dropped into a chair opposite him. It struck Thorne, looking at him, that maybe he'd had a rough Friday night as well.

'Margie Knight's turned up.'

It was the instant jolt of adrenaline that Thorne needed. 'Where?'

'Uniform found her last night. Noshing off some solicitor in a parked car on the Caledonian Road.'

If it was what Thorne needed, it might also be the bit of luck that the investigation needed. A simple piece of London business after dark. A woodentop with a torch, a working girl cleaning up on a Friday night and a brief who couldn't keep it in his pants. Cases had hinged on a lot less.

'Right, get her and Murrell in here today. I want pictures of this bloke on the streets as soon as possible. Let's move this thing forward, Dave.' Holland nodded and stood up. 'What's wrong with McEvoy this morning, anyway?'

Holland stopped at the door and turned. 'Sorry?'

'Somebody's rattled her bars. I made some crack about what she looked like and she bit my head off.'

'Right.' Holland looked away, shook his head thoughtfully. 'Probably just being over-sensitive. Maybe it's her . . .'

Thorne held up a hand to stop him. 'The mood she's in right now, Holland, if you so much as *suggest* that it might be her time of the month, I'm guessing she'll kill you on the spot.' Thorne was making light of it, but he sensed that it was more than just a bad mood. His original comment *had* been tit-for-tat, but there was no question, McEvoy did look rough.

'I'll try to find out if there's anything up with her.' Holland spoke as if Thorne had asked him to perform an autopsy.

'Are *you* OK, Dave?'

There was a long pause, and the few mumbled words that Holland managed before hurrying out of the office obviously did not come easily. 'Bit of trouble at home . . .'

Thorne had wondered about it before, but this was the first time that Holland had so much as hinted that things between him and Sophie might not be hunky-dory. His reticence told Thorne that now was probably not the time to dig any deeper. Whatever was going on, he hoped they could work it out quickly. Thorne had only met Sophie once; she had seemed nice enough.

Thorne glanced up at the clock. Nearly ten. Brigstocke was due back from a meeting with Jesmond any time, and chances were it would not have been a barrel of laughs. Thorne would bring him up to speed about last night and then give him the good news about Margie Knight's miraculous reappearance.

Take some of that pressure off.

McEvoy . . . Holland . . . Brigstocke. Thorne got up, left his office and walked across to the coffee machine, thinking that perhaps he wouldn't be the first one to crack up after all.

Duddridge always waited for the customer to leave before counting the cash. It was only polite. Besides, knowing that nobody ever tried to rip him off had made him fairly relaxed about payment. People were always told gently that if their accounts weren't settled to his satisfaction, he could find them.

Use some of his own stock.

The money was all in twenties. He counted it without even looking down. He glanced around the pub which was starting to fill up with the afternoon football crowd, the lads with mullet haircuts and loafers, gathering for the last Saturday before the Christmas break. They would crowd around the big screen TV, drink themselves silly and watch the Sky coverage of the day's games, each of them putting away enough lager to pay twice over for a satellite dish at home.

The money, as expected, was all there. Duddridge decided to have a celebratory drink. It had been a nice bit of business after all. A simple referral from someone he knew and a mug punter he could overcharge, one who had no idea he was paying over the odds.

He pushed his way to the bar and ordered a Jack Daniels and Coke.

He'd sold gear to all sorts over the years, but this one had been odd, no question about it. The bloke hadn't got a clue what it was he wanted for a start. It had all been written down for him, presumably by the bloke who'd referred him to Duddridge in the first place. He said he wanted it for protection of course, which was what they all said, trying to make out like they were just responding to the dangerous times they were living in, but just needing it quickly and not wanting to piss about with licences and stuff. Right, and people only did smack to see what it was like, because they were writing a book about it.

Thing was, with *this* bloke, Duddridge could almost have believed it. The fucking great idiot had looked scared to death. Most of his customers were a little nervous, but they weren't buying cornflakes, after all. The bloke who'd handed over the fistful of twenties, one of which Duddridge was now peeling off to pay for his drink, *he* looked like he was going to shit his pants at any moment.

Maybe he *did* just want it for protection. Weirdo certainly didn't look like he could hurt anybody, or *want* to hurt anybody, at least.

It always made Duddridge a little wary selling to people like that. You never knew when it might come back at you. The items he sold were completely untraceable – he had a reputation built on that – but you could never predict exactly what the people who bought them might do. A simple job was fine, they were his bread and butter. He saw himself as someone who sold quality tools to professionals.

But there was no accounting for nutters.

Duddridge felt the mobile phone on his belt vibrate. Another customer. He downed his drink and began making his way through the crowd towards the doors. He pictured his last customer doing the same, just a few minutes earlier, moving awkwardly between the tables, clumsy cunt knocking over a drink, one hand flapping for the door handle, the other clutching on to his purchase for dear life.

He always made a bit more dosh out of the amateurs, but he didn't really like doing business with them. You could never be certain what you were dealing with. It was always the unassuming punters, the funny-looking ones, the ones whose neighbours were always shocked and amazed . . . who you saw on the news, their eyes like puddles of piss, shooting up a playground or walking calmly into McDonald's with an Uzi.

The thought reminded him. Uzis. He needed to talk to his contact in the States, see if he could get his hands on a few.

1999

He shut the door behind him, took off his jacket and slumped down behind his desk. From somewhere down the corridor he could hear raised voices, a door slamming. The temperature must have been well into the eighties; fans on all over the building, the place reeking of sweat and bad tempers. He stared out of the window, perfectly content. He had his own ways of coping with stress.

He reached into his jacket pocket, took out his wallet and removed a small, tattered, passport-size photo. Two young boys, on an afternoon much like this one, pulling faces in a photo-booth. Two boys he used to know, pissing about in Woolworths, more than fifteen years earlier.

Now, he bore only the faintest physical resemblance to the smaller of the boys in the photo. Just the eyes, really. He was a world away.

He was nearly thirty, and considering the somewhat bumpy start, had achieved a hell of a lot. Anybody would have to admit that. Life was good, he was still on the up, and in Caroline, he seemed to have found the perfect wife. She was someone suitable in every sense, the ideal person to have by his side. They'd met seven years before, during training, and clicked straight away. They found the same things funny, they each had their own interests, and in the five years they'd been married, he could barely remember a cross word.

Yes, he felt good about sharing his life with Caroline. Sharing most of his life.

She never questioned the late nights, or the time away from home, or the occasional lack of interest in the bedroom. Perhaps she'd already convinced herself he was having an affair. If so, that was no bad thing.

He was seeking excitement of course; it was what he'd always done, but he'd never have found what he needed in furtive liaisons, in the willing arms of some young tart or other. He needed a hit, a high, a buzz. He needed something far deeper and longer-lasting than he could find in simple adultery.

He wanted no part of anything consensual.

He'd always managed to get what he wanted, eventually, and this had been no different. It had become surprisingly easy actually. He was always careful – travelling widely, never repeating himself, taking no chances. Now, if he was being honest, he was becoming a little bored.

He wondered if perhaps it went in cycles. Exactly ten years before, hadn't he become bored with who he was? He'd made the decision then to start again, to change everything, to become someone else. Now, he was happy with who he was, who he'd become, but what he was doing, for pleasure, had started to excite him less and less. It was a drug to which he was rapidly becoming inured, and it was not acceptable. It was something that needed to change.

Happy with who he was . . .

There was a knock on the door and a colleague put his head round, pale-faced and sweating, to remind him he was needed elsewhere.

He pulled his jacket from the back of the chair and slipped it on.

He picked up his wallet from the desk and slid the small photo back inside.

He stared at the credit cards that carried his name. Not his real name, of course, but the name he'd been known by for more than ten years. His real name belonged to someone he'd last seen in a first-floor flat in Soho, a long time ago. If he was walking along the street now, and heard his old name, heard those two words being shouted at him, he'd know he was being shouted at by someone who didn't know him. Someone he'd been at school with . . .

He looked at his watch. Late for a meeting. His mind racing backwards and forwards in time. Remembering, imagining . . .

Moments later, striding briskly away down the corridor, he reached for his wallet a second time. Smiling, he took out the photo again, and looked at the two young faces.

Fifteen years was a very long time.

EIGHT

```
Date: 16 December
Target: Fem
Age: 20-30
Pickup: Pub, club, winebar etc.
Site: TBA
Method : Firearm (pref not silenced)
```

Sunday. Thorne's first real day off in nearly a fortnight.

Lunch with the old man had seemed like a reasonable idea at the time. A distraction, something to wash over him, a time-killer. Now, driving back down the M1, he really wished he hadn't bothered. Aside from anything, he was starving. Of his parents, it had been his dad who'd done most of the cooking. Once upon a time, he'd enjoyed it, but his enthusiasm for that, along with everything else, had waned at the same rate as his fascination for pointless trivia and old jokes had rocketed.

While Thorne had pushed a lump of overcooked chicken and a few pallid, underdone vegetables around his plate, his dad had waffled on at absurd length about everything and fuck all. He'd quizzed him about what he thought the five top-selling soap powders in the country were, and giggled through countless stories about men walking into pubs. In fact, he'd barely drawn breath for the entire time Thorne had been there, except for a few uncomfortable minutes when, in the middle of a story about nothing, his eyes had filled with tears, and he'd calmly got up from the table, walked through into the kitchen and closed the door.

Thorne could do nothing but sit there, hating himself for thinking that he'd have been happier at a murder scene.

The big Christmas discussion had never really materialised until Thorne was about to leave, and even then, it was just the usual tiresome dance, a frustrating bit of back and forth on the doorstep.

'So, dad . . . are you coming, or what?'

'What d'you need to know now for? It's not for numbers is it?'

'It's only a week away and . . .'

'Nine days.'

'I just want to know what's happening.'

'I don't know . . . it might be good to do something different.'

'Well it's up to you, but . . .'

'I might go to Eileen's . . .'

'Right. Have you asked her?'

'Name the last six Prime Ministers . . .'

'Dad . . .'

'Blair, Major, Thatcher.'

'Have you asked Eileen?'

'They're the easy ones. Callaghan . . .'

It was starting to get dark so Thorne flicked on the headlights. He let the Mondeo drift slowly across into the inside lane. The drive home was relaxing him, calming him down, and he was in no great hurry.

He turned on the radio and tuned it in to Radio 5 Live. The second half of Ipswich versus Leicester City. Hardly a glamour fixture, but the commentary soon engaged him as he pushed on along the all but empty motorway towards north London. Moving: out of the semi-countryside and into the unlovely and reassuring urban sprawl of Brent Cross, Swiss Cottage and Camden. Moving: from one old man's life going slowly down the tubes, to thoughts of four young women who would never even have *that* golden opportunity. Moving, towards the possibility of more . . .

Moving, away from an afternoon and towards an evening.

They rolled apart from each other and lay there, sweating, exhausted, each of them trying to think of a good thing to say. Something that might help. Eventually, Holland came up with something, but Sophie was already turning over, ready for sleep. The sex had been good, better than good, but then it usually was after an argument. They'd spent the best part of the day fighting, then fucked away the rest of it, trying to pretend the fight had never happened.

The row came at them with the slow, graceful horror of a lorry skidding on black ice. With the arse-end of a dull Sunday just around the corner, the boredom had slowly given way to irritation and finally, anger. It was an anger that had been there all the time of course, like a bad smell in a locked room, and, once it escaped, it got everywhere, and into everything. It followed them around the flat, as each of them took turns in chasing the other from room to room, swearing and screaming and pounding on walls. It was still there, all over both of them, two hours later, as they cried and squeezed each other until finally, the kissing began.

Then mouths devoured each other which, only moments before, had ranted and shouted, wounding with words. Some were used far more than others. *Work, job, support, wanker, selfish, bitch, children, choice, Thorne . . .*

Sophie's breathing quickly settled into a pattern that told Holland she was asleep, but he knew that he wasn't going to follow her quickly. There were far too many thoughts rattling around in his head.

He wondered how much damage each of these weekly sessions was doing to them, and if the money they'd spent, the time and trouble they'd taken moving into a new flat, would end up being wasted.

He wondered why, considering that it was usually the other way round, he still fancied Sophie, but didn't much like her any more. Why, if he still fancied Sophie so much, had he spent most of the time they were making love thinking about Sarah McEvoy?

Jacqui had cooked lunch for seven without a word of thanks. Roast beef and the rest of it, for her husband, her mother and her sister's lot. As ever, by the time she'd finished, she wasn't actually hungry herself. Staring at her face in the dressing-table mirror, changing her mind for the second time about which shade of lipstick to go with, she decided that she'd grab something when she was out. Maybe some of the other girls might fancy a meal afterwards. If she ever bloody well got there . . .

It wasn't as if she'd expected any volunteers to help

clear up, certainly not any of her own useless lot, but it would have been nice. Her sister, as ever, sat there on her fat behind not raising a finger, so by the time Jacqui had washed up and cleared away the mess her sister's horrible kids had made in the living room, she was really late. It wasn't the first time.

For heaven's sake, it was only every other Sunday. One night, once a fortnight, when her and a few of the girls could let their hair down and talk about how shit everything was at home, and then get back to it before half past ten. She'd tried to suggest that *maybe*, every other Sunday, her sister could have everybody round to her place. The idea had not gone down well, and that had pretty much been that . . .

Mim stood in her knickers, the iron in one hand, remote in the other, channel-surfing. She stopped briefly when she got to *The Antiques Roadshow.* She knew her mother would be watching it, assuming that she wasn't sulking after the row the two of them had just had, or storming around the house taking it out on her poor father. She carried on surfing, settling finally for a documentary about sharks, and went back to ironing her jeans. It had been a row she'd known was coming, ever since term had ended and she hadn't eagerly hopped aboard the first train home. *Miriam, how could you choose to stay in that dingy bedsit rather than with your own parents in a comfortable house blah blah blah . . . ?*

She'd tried assuring her mother that she *would* be home in time for Christmas, but once the tears had started, it had been a lost cause. It wasn't like she didn't want to go home, but quite a few of the people on her course had decided to stay on for a bit and it was a laugh, just dossing about with them, going to the pub every night.

She pulled on her jeans and moved hangers back and forth along the clothes rail, looking for a shirt. It was quiz night in the pub and she wanted to get there early, make sure she was on a team with that new bloke in the first year with the nose-stud and the green eyes . . .

Jacqui was ready and waiting on the doorstep by the time her husband had got back from running her mother home. He leaned across and opened the passenger door as she came hurrying down the path. This was their routine. She pulled the door shut, placed her handbag in her lap and the car moved away, beginning their conversationless, ten-minute journey to the tube station.

Mim turned off the television before the God Squad began in earnest. There was really nothing else to do on a Sunday night than sit in the pub. Fuck, she worked hard enough, why the hell not? She pulled her door shut, jogged down the stairs and stepped out into the cold. She heard the rumble of a diesel engine and looked up to see a bus coming round the corner. Swearing enough to make her mother faint, she started to run.

Jacqui and Mim lived miles apart. They did not know each other. They would never meet. They would finally come together as two names, the latest *pair* of names, one above the other in capital letters, on a large square of white, wipe-clean plastic.

Two names.

One of them belonging to a dead woman.

★

Hendricks rang while he was feeding the cat, and Thorne quickly realised he hadn't been the only one having a shit Sunday. Mr Handy-In-The-Kitchen, who was actually called Brendan, had turned out to be Mr Unreliable-In-Every-Other-Way.

'So where's the next piercing going then, Phil? On second thoughts, don't tell me . . .'

Hendricks laughed, but Thorne could hear how upset he was. 'Not in a million years, mate. I don't know . . . I wasn't clingy, I wasn't stand-offish, I really . . . tried this time, Tom, you know?'

'Don't forget for a second that you're talking to completely the wrong person here, but for what it's worth, maybe you're trying too hard. That might be what you're doing wrong.'

Hendricks sighed, said nothing for a while, then: 'I know *exactly* what I'm doing wrong. Cutting up dead bodies, removing brains, and hearts and lungs . . .'

Thorne understood straight away. This was a conversation they'd had a couple of times before. 'Right. Another one didn't approve of the career choice?'

'Never said as much, but it was obvious. It's always difficult, but since the start of this year, it's like telling people I'm a terrorist or a murderer or something . . .'

At the start of the year, a scandal about the removal of body parts from dead children had discredited the business of organ harvesting in general and pathologists in particular. The hysteria had died down but damage had been done. Rates of organ donation had dropped dramatically. Transplant numbers were down. Pathologists had trouble making new friends.

'I tell people what I do, there's like this pause, you know?' Thorne did know, very well. Hendricks had started to ramble a little then, and Thorne could tell that he'd been smoking. The dope was something they never talked about, but Thorne had often smelled it. He could all but smell it now, as Hendricks's voice on the phone dropped to a whisper. 'I wonder if . . . what I do, is something that I carry on me. D'you reckon?'

'Phil . . .'

'Not the stink, I know how to get rid of that . . . I mean, more like a shadow or summat. No . . . more like, when you're under UV light, like at a club, you know . . . same as we use with Luminol . . . and you can see all the fluff and bits on your clothes, all that twinkly dandruff, glowing . . . shining white? Maybe it's like that . . . yeah. Little pieces of death starting to show up on me . . .'

Thorne cooked himself scrambled eggs, ate them at the tiny kitchen table. He thought about his father. Why, as the silly old bugger spiralled increasingly away into the distance, did Thorne feel so . . . buttoned up? Maybe *he* needed to do a bit of dope occasionally. Free up his thinking a little. Jan had smoked the odd joint, sometimes. Never in front of him, but he wouldn't really have cared if she had. It wasn't like he had any major objection to it; there was still far too much time and effort wasted in its criminalisation, but ultimately, it wasn't for him. He could always think of something better to spend his money on. Like beer and wine . . .

Suddenly, he could picture Jan and the lecturer she'd been screwing behind his back, skinning up, giggling, incense burning by the side of the bed. He opened a bottle of a different kind of drug and carried it through to the living room.

Abandoning the fruitless search for distraction on TV, Thorne sat for a while, considering what Hendricks had said. Remembering and thinking ahead. Thinking about bodies stabbed and bodies strangled. Thinking about a pair of cardboard coffins in the cargo hold of a plane bound for Amsterdam . . .

Were those who worked with death ever free of it?

He stood and walked across to the stereo. His fingers ran along the rows of CDs and lingered over a boxed set of Johnny Cash, before moving on. He'd treated himself to it the year before, a set of three CDs, each containing songs on one particular theme. *God*, *Love* and *Murder*. Much as he loved Johnny Cash, there was still one of them Thorne hadn't listened to.

Later, lying awake in bed, the lights turned out, the radio on, he couldn't get Hendricks's slurred monologue out of his head. It was dope-induced rubbish. It was paranoia, self-pity. It was cliché masquerading as philosophy.

It compelled him.

It had been over a year since his last relationship. No sign of another one. Was he too carrying a little of the stuff around with him? A handful of sparkling death, visible to those with an eye for it? He pictured his jacket lying across the back of the kitchen chair in the darkness. He closed his eyes and imagined them, luminescent, caught in a beam of moonlight coming through the kitchen window . . .

A few tiny fragments, glittering at his collar and in the folds of the sleeves. Like malignant diamonds.

Karen, I didn't do it.

I wish I could tell you that it was because I refused.

Because I stood up and said no to any more of it. I wish I could tell you that I was strong, that I decided not to go through with it.

The truth is, I tried to go through with it and I failed.

Thank God. Thank God, I failed. Perhaps, a big enough part of me wanted to fail, wanted it to go wrong so badly that I made it happen. Perhaps I just chose the wrong girl. Or the right one.

I sat in the pub and watched her, wanting to run, wanting to stay, counting each drink she had, listening to her laughing and feeling the thing heavy in my pocket. I sipped water and hummed along with the music and willed it all to be over quickly.

It was late when she finally left; they were virtually the last to leave the place and it was horribly perfect, Karen. They could have gone in the same direction, all of them heading home together and me needing to look again, to head into town and find a club, but she went her own way and I could do nothing but follow.

I don't often use bad language, Karen, but when I took out the gun, I was fucking terrified. It hung at the end of my arm like a dead thing and her mouth just opened so wide then, and I stood and watched her mouth and listened to her scream for a while. I don't know how long we stood there for, but instead of doing it quickly, instead of firing, instead of doing it . . . the thing I was there for, I just stared as she ran at me, and I bowed my head as she hit and hit. I backed away and I could see her bending down like she was picking something up. Then she came at me again and it started to really hurt and I know it sounds stupid but I almost laughed, because I suddenly realised that now, the sound of screaming was coming from me.

I watched her running off towards the lights and shouting and I wiped away the blood that was running from my head on to my face.

I put the gun back into my pocket and I left that place.

It has to end now, Karen.

I wish I was brave enough to come to you, but you already know that I'm not. I think the poison inside me has eaten away every ounce of courage there might ever have been.

I need to find just a little more.

2000

One phone call to the loving parents, a few weeks earlier, had been all that was necessary. He wasn't surprised that they hadn't moved. Probably never would. A bit of flannel, the charm turned full on and after a few minutes he had addresses for home and work, phone numbers, everything.

He stood outside the brasserie and peered in through the window. A fashionable expanse of exposed copper piping and deep leather sofas at the front, with tables tucked away towards the back. He couldn't see him. He'd watched him come in alone, but perhaps he'd met someone inside and they were eating . . .

His own lunch was starting to melt. He pushed the rest of the chocolate into his mouth, stuffed the wrapper into his trouser pocket and stepped through the door. The barman looked up and smiled, but Nicklin shook his head, kept walking slowly towards the back of the room, the tables out of sight around the corner.

The fluttery feeling in the pit of his stomach wasn't nerves, exactly. He didn't suffer from that particular condition, certainly not in any fearful sense. He never had. For as long as he could remember, he'd done things that he knew few others would have done, or dared to do, not because he was brave, but because he wasn't scared. He knew there was a very important difference.

What he was feeling now was excitement. The possibility of something new and more intense than anything he'd felt before. And in a way of course, he'd be picking up where he left off a long time ago. Something old and something new . . .

He reached the back of the room, glanced to his left and saw him immediately. Sitting at a table with two others – men without chins, in shirt-sleeves, guzzling wine, yapping – expense account wankers.

He began walking towards the table.

When he was ten feet away, Palmer looked up, clocked him and went back to his conversation. Of course, he hadn't recognised him. Nicklin had been almost certain he wouldn't. He would have been more than a little disappointed if he had. No fucking point if it wasn't dramatic.

He stopped. So did the conversation. He took a final step forward, his thighs flush against the edge of the table, their wine glasses wobbling.

'Can we help you with something?' One of Palmer's friends, nervous but trying very hard to sound edgy. He ignored him, his eyes only on Palmer, waiting for them to be met. When they were, and the tiny spark of recognition flared up into an inferno, it was a moment equal to anything he'd imagined in the preceding weeks.

'Martin? Are you feeling all right, mate?' The second man now, the concerned colleague, pushing back his chair, looking around.

Palmer, eyes wide, mouth dropping, yes . . . actually dropping open. Skin the colour of old newspaper.

Nicklin nodded, showed his teeth. 'Hello, Mart. This is great, isn't it?'

Palmer, struck dumb, his face frozen. Drool running from the corner of his slack mouth and dripping gently down onto the immaculate white tablecloth.

Staring, terrified, at his past.

NINE

Nearly three weeks since Charlie Garner had watched his mother die. A fortnight to the day since the case had officially begun. Eight days before Christmas.

An office full of people waiting . . .

Thorne watched as they moved around him, heads down mostly, exchanging smiles of resignation when pressed. Carrying files, answering phones, tapping at keyboards a little harder than was necessary. Frustrated, bored, some of them pissed-off for reasons of their own, others wiped out by the weekend, but all aware, to some degree, that they were doing no more than going through the motions.

The e-fit of the man seen by Margie Knight and Michael Murrell, the suspect in both the Jane Lovell and Ruth Murray murders, was on the front page of most of the papers today. But Thorne wasn't waiting for the phones to start ringing. He wasn't waiting for helpful punters, eager to pass on the news that the man in the picture might be the brother of a friend, or was like a workmate's husband, or looked a little bit like the man in the flat upstairs.

Thorne was waiting for the bodies.

Since it had become clear that they were looking for two killers, violent crime against women was being carefully monitored right across the city. Monitored and sifted. They were looking for the murder, the attempted murder, the assault perhaps . . . then waiting for its hideous mirror image to appear. Looking for both halves. Thorne remembered a kids' card game: the object was to collect as many pairs as possible.

I've got two stabbings, two stranglings . . . what have you got?

It hadn't been a particularly busy Sunday night, thank god. A lot of stuff had come in, but almost all of it was quickly dismissed. Of those cases that raised even a modicum of interest, none looked very promising. A woman attacked by another woman with a bottle outside a pub in Canning Town. A stabbing in Willesden, almost certainly a domestic. A woman threatened with a gun in Clapham, probably a botched robbery or an attempted rape . . .

The picture was also being shown on every news bulletin and it quickly began generating results. The calls came in. By mid-morning there was a list of names. None of them appeared more than once.

Brigstocke did his best to rally the troops and stop sweating. Thorne tried to stay busy. All of them, wading through treacle. Over two pints and a tomato juice at lunchtime, Holland tried, a little clumsily, to articulate the frustration they were feeling.

'It's like having sex, without ever coming . . .'

Thorne puffed out his cheeks. It was an . . . interesting analogy.

McEvoy grinned. 'Yeah, well now you know what it's

like then.' She laughed, and Thorne joined in. Holland blushed, took a sip of his tomato juice. 'I'm talking generally of course, Dave,' McEvoy added, 'I'm sure Sophie has no complaints.'

Holland said nothing. Thorne heard him say it.

'Sorry. Have I . . . ?' She looked from Thorne to Holland and back again. 'What, am I not talking like a proper lady?' She emphasised the last word comically, as if it were spelt with a 'y' in the middle and two 'e's on the end.

Thorne smiled. 'Well at least you're in a better mood than you were on Saturday. Good weekend?'

It was McEvoy's turn to redden. 'Yeah, I'm sorry about that. Just woke up feeling arsey. Weekend was . . . fine. Great, actually. Thanks.'

Before the silence had a chance to make itself uncomfortable, Thorne caught sight of Brigstocke in the pub doorway, scanning the crowd, looking for them. Thorne waved and the DCI came over. Before he arrived at the table, Thorne could tell from his face that there was news.

Simply a question of how bad . . .

'Got a fax through ten minutes ago. The description of a man who threatened a woman with a gun near Clapham South tube station last night . . .'

Thorne's shoulders lifted. A reflex as the jolt ran through him. The tingle. Not bad news at all . . .

McEvoy could see where Brigstocke was going. 'Not attempted robbery or rape then?'

Thorne answered her, quietly. 'Attempted murder.'

Brigstocke nodded. 'Sounds like our man. Tall, thickset, sandy hair, glasses. Better add *bleeding* as well. Woman he pulled a gun on says she beat the shit out of him with a high-heeled shoe.'

McEvoy swallowed a mouthful of beer. 'Fucking good.'

'When can we talk to her?' Holland asked.

'I'm trying to arrange it. She's being looked after by her family – obviously she's still upset.' Brigstocke moved to sit down. Thorne shuffled along to make room for him. 'Hopefully by the end of the day . . .' Brigstocke sighed and allowed himself the first smile that Thorne had seen for a few days.

Thorne stood up and reached for his jacket. If the man with the gun was one of the men they were looking for, then thankfully, one killer had failed. Thorne felt certain that the other one would not have done . . .

The object: to collect pairs.

Thorne disliked being the one to remove the smile from Brigstocke's face, but didn't hesitate to do so.

In his head it was a scream. It came out like a whisper.

'Somewhere, there's a woman who's been shot to death. I want to find her.'

London was a city of ghosts, some deader than others.

Thorne knew that in this respect, it wasn't unlike any other major city – New York or Paris or Sydney – but he felt instinctively that London was . . . at the extreme. It was probably down to the history of the place. The darker side of that history, as opposed to the parks, palaces and pearly kings' side that made busloads of Japanese and American tourists gawk and jabber. The hidden history of a city where the lonely, the dispossessed, the homeless, wandered the streets, brushing shoulders with the shadows of those that had come before them. A city in which the poor and the plague-ridden, those long-since hanged for stealing a loaf or murdered for a shilling, jostled for position with those seeking a meal, or a score, or a bed for the night.

A city where the dead could stay lost a long time.

Thorne had known about London's skill at concealing its cadavers for as long as he had been a police officer, but it still disturbed him. Those that died peacefully at home could lie rotting in their front rooms for weeks and months, attracting the rats and the flies, and eventually the attention of the neighbour with the well-developed sense of smell.

Those that died violently, those whose killers did not *want* them found, could lie alone and out of sight for far longer. Buried, burned or bricked up, dismembered, dumped or weighted down in water, until those that looked for them were only memories themselves. Until the dead were no more than a page in a yellowing file, or a name on a set of dental records.

Of course, such things happened in small towns and in villages, in places where they were still remarkable, but there was something about London which, Thorne felt, suited anonymous death. There were those that bleated on about how *their* particular area of the city was a little community, no really it was, friendly and welcoming . . . Thorne knew that, in reality, this meant little more than the newsagent calling you by your first name and the barman in your local *maybe* knowing what your tipple was. When it came down to it, you could still lose touch with your best friend if he lived more than two streets away, and the reaction of many Londoners to a woman being raped on their train would be to raise their newspapers a little higher.

Thorne's depressing reflections on the city where he had been born, where he lived and worked, were prompted by the simple and not unexpected fact, that by the end of the day, they had still not found the body they knew was out there. They had of course been monitoring missing persons' reports but nothing had come in. The victim had not been missed yet. There could be a hundred reasons why.

Now, as he and Holland drove towards Wandsworth to question the woman who had survived the attempted murder the night before, Thorne tried to stop thinking about the woman who hadn't. Her body, wherever it lay, might hold vital clues that even now were disappearing as the corpse changed shape, texture, consistency; popping and sighing gently.

The city would give it up when it was ready.

In the meantime, Thorne had a whole list of things to worry about.

A real cause for concern was the fact that the killings were speeding up. It had been nineteen days since Carol Garner and Ruth Murray. Jane Lovell and Katie Choi died over four months before that. A shortening of the intervals between killings was a predictable pattern, but this was dramatic. Unless of course there were murders in between the two sets that they'd missed . . . Thorne quickly dismissed this chilling thought, settling for the slightly less disturbing one that for the killers, the hunger was really starting to take hold.

The killers . . .

Thorne's other major worry. Two killers but one of them was, as yet, no more than theoretical. A shadow. They were on their way to talk to a woman who'd come face to face with one of them. The same one seen by Margie Knight and Michael Murrell. The one whose face was all over every newspaper and TV screen. Was he the careless one? The sloppy one? Or was his partner just so much better at covering his tracks, at killing and killing, and staying invisible?

The killer who had given them their only leads, the one whose blank, bespectacled face now stared out from a hundred thousand posters, was the one who killed quickly and efficiently; the single stab wound, the sustained pressure on the neck . . . the killer that wept. He was not the one who butchered and walked unseen into the darkness covered in blood. He was not the one that throttled the life out of Carol Garner, smashing and squeezing while her little boy watched.

He was not the one . . .

Thorne wanted the killer on those posters. He wanted him very badly. But he wanted his partner more.

Sean Bracher glanced at his watch as he stood at the bar waiting for the useless wanker behind it to bring his drink.

She was late.

He wasn't worried that she wouldn't come, just slightly annoyed that he'd have to get up again to fetch her a drink when she finally deigned to arrive. He handed over the money for his beer without a word, grabbed a huge handful of peanuts from a bowl on the bar and strolled across to a table.

He wasn't planning on sleeping with her tonight. Obviously he wasn't going to say no if he turned out to be wrong, but he guessed that Jo, for all her flirting, was the type to make him wait for it. Jane had made him wait too, only the one more night mind you, and it had certainly been worth waiting for. It was only ever going to be a fling of course – he'd made that clear from the word go and she was cool about it. He didn't want to be tied down to anybody, least of all a receptionist, but it certainly made the working day, not to mention the odd weekend business trip, a damn sight more interesting. She'd turned out to be kinky as fuck . . .

He stuffed a fistful of peanuts into his mouth and looked around. The place was starting to fill up with those grateful to have got another Monday over with, desperate for a quick one before the struggle home on the train or the bus. Somebody had left a rolled-up copy of the *Standard* on the next table. He reached across for it and began idly flicking through the sports pages.

Yeah, it was a nice pub. They would grab a couple here and then head off for an Italian or something. Nothing with too much garlic. He'd done exactly the same thing with Jane on their first date, over six months before.

Jo was actually better looking than Jane, but not as much of a laugh. He missed the piss-taking with Jane, the wind-ups, the crack. He'd encouraged her to flirt with that freak in the overseas section. That had been hysterical. The pillock had fallen for it one hundred per cent. Stammering and blushing. Went fucking ballistic when he found out he'd been had. Christ though, if you couldn't have a laugh at work . . .

He looked at his watch again. Checked his mobile for messages. Why the hell were women always so fucking late? She had been keen enough when he'd suggested meeting. He typed in a quick text message and sent it. *Where r u?* Probably still in the ladies back at the office, tarting herself up. On second thoughts, maybe he *would* end up giving her one later. Her place preferably, no reason to stay the night then . . .

He smiled, mentally in bed with her already, as he flipped the *Standard* over.

He glanced down at the front page and almost choked on his peanuts.

The young student got off the bus on Kingsland High Street. From there it was only a two-minute walk up the Dalston Road to her flat.

The evening was surprisingly mild. He took off his jacket as he went along and threw it across his arm. Walking quickly, looking through the windows of second-hand record shops and Greek cafés, thinking about the way she'd looked at him the night before.

She'd smiled a lot, raising her eyebrows, the tip of her tongue just visible against her top teeth. She had a laugh that made people on the other side of the pub stare. They'd all been a bit the worse for wear, celebrating their team's quiz win by drinking the first prize. Then the pair of them had stood at the bus stop at Highbury Corner, talking, letting three or four buses come and go before walking home – her off towards Dalston and him, in the other direction, towards the small, damp cupboard he rented in Tufnell Park.

They'd agreed to meet for lunch today at Pizza Express. He'd slept until really late and in the end he'd had to rush to get there on time, arrived out of breath and sweating. He'd waited for over an hour.

It had been a casual sort of arrangement, maybe far more casual than he remembered – he had drunk an awful lot of Guinness – but he had expected her to come. She didn't have a phone at her flat so he'd rung her mobile a couple of times during the afternoon, left messages. He was halfway through dialling her number again when he'd decided to go round. It was only ten minutes away and the bus was virtually door to door. He was sure she'd be glad to see him. Yes, they'd *both* had a lot of Guinness, but he was pretty sure she would be.

It was a dirty white door between a shoe shop and a cut-price travel agency. Three bells, her name underneath the top one.

He rang.

He put his jacket back on; she'd said she liked it last night. Looked up at the windows above him. An old man peered down at him from the first floor. Maybe they could go and have a pizza *now* – there were loads of places in Islington. Or they could just sit around, smoke a bit maybe, order something later. Whatever, it would just be really nice to see her.

He rang again . . .

'Don't let Bracher go anywhere. Just keep him there . . .'

Thorne and Holland had been heading south towards Blackfriars Bridge when Thorne's mobile had rung and he was informed that Sean Bracher was currently annoying the duty officers at Charing Cross, shouting about how he was one hundred and ten per cent certain that the man in the e-fit was someone he worked with, someone from Baynham & Smout . . .

Thorne had all but yanked the wheel out of Holland's hands. The woman in Wandsworth, Jacqueline Kaye, could wait until tomorrow. This was someone who they needed to talk to right now. They'd been to the office . . . Jesus, even Lickwood had been to the office, and the fucker had been there all the time . . .

Now, Thorne was talking to a DI at Charing Cross as well as trying to give Holland instructions on the new route they were taking.

'What's the name?' Thorne nodded solemnly as he was told, then began waving his arm in front of Holland's nose. 'Go right, we'll cut through Lincoln's Inn Fields.'

Holland smacked a palm angrily on the wheel and did as he was told, keeping one eye on Thorne, watching his reactions, desperate to be told the details.

'Has Bracher told anybody else? Anybody at work? Good . . .'

Thorne pointed some more, grunting into the phone, meeting Holland's sidelong glance and nodding. This was major.

As the unmarked Rover roared along the Strand, Thorne began to shout into the phone, as if he was losing the signal. 'We'll be there in about ten minutes . . . yes, ten.'

He punched the button to end the call and turned to Holland. 'Sean Bracher . . .'

Holland's phone began to ring.

'Fuck . . .' Holland groped inside his jacket for the mobile.

'Bet you it's for me,' Thorne said, 'I could hear the call-waiting signal on mine . . .'

'Fiver?' Holland asked, pulling out the phone. Thorne nodded.

Holland answered. 'Hello? Right . . .' He handed the phone across. 'McEvoy.'

Five pounds to the good, a smiling Thorne took the phone. Sarah McEvoy was out of breath. She'd run to make the call.

'We've got a man fitting our description, a man named Martin Palmer . . .' The smile froze on Thorne's face. It was the same name he had heard a few moments before; the name Bracher had given. 'Palmer walked into West Hampstead nick half an hour ago, dropped a gun on to the desk and confessed to two murders.'

'OK, we're on our way.'

Holland grimaced, unsure which direction to head in now. Thorne pointed north. *Keep going.*

'Slight problem,' McEvoy said. 'West Hampstead doesn't have a custody suite.'

'Fuck.' Thorne thought fast. 'Right, Kentish Town's about the nearest. Get somebody to run him over.'

'I'll call them and get straight down there.'

'Good. We should be with you in about fifteen minutes.'

McEvoy was already there by the time Thorne and Holland arrived. The three of them stood outside the room where Martin Palmer was being held. McEvoy filled them in on the details. He had walked calmly into the station to give himself up at around about the same time that Bracher had barged into Charing Cross, shouting his name out. Palmer hadn't been cautioned. He was there of his own volition.

Holland sat down on one of the green plastic chairs that were bolted in a row along the wall. 'He saw the picture too, must have. Knew somebody was going to recognise it. Thought he'd be doing himself a favour.' McEvoy looked across at him, nodded her agreement.

Thorne stared at the door. 'Maybe . . .'

'Reckon he'll give up his mate?' Thorne turned and

stared at McEvoy. She'd asked, knowing it was what he was thinking, watching the tension take hold as he glared at the scratched grey door, imagining the man on the other side of it.

Give up his mate . . .

It had been the question Thorne had been asking himself since he'd heard Palmer's name for the second time. Christ, it could be that simple. Perhaps there was a chance, if he was hit quickly, and hard.

'Is Brigstocke coming?' Holland asked.

McEvoy took a few paces back towards the main reception area, smiled politely at the small collection of gawping uniforms gathered around the desk. 'On his way.'

'Should we wait for him?'

'Probably,' Thorne said, and opened the door.

In the couple of seconds he spent marching across to the tape recorder on the far side of the room, he took it all in. The uniform in the corner, jumping slightly as Thorne slammed the door. The cold. Palmer, his white collar grubby, sitting at the brushed metal table, head bowed. The wad of bandage clumsily plastered to the top of his head, the blood dried brown.

Thorne picked up two fresh cassette tapes and began tearing roughly at the plastic packaging, his eyes never leaving the figure seated at the table.

Palmer was a big man, that was obvious, slumped and hunched over as he was. Wispy, sandy-coloured hair and metal-framed glasses. Murrell and Knight had done a good job. The picture was spot on.

'I'm Detective Inspector Thorne and I'm in no mood to piss about, is that all right with you?'

Palmer said nothing. He didn't even move.

Thorne slammed the tapes into the recorder, hit the red button and waited. Once the buzzing had stopped and the recording had begun, he cautioned his interviewee. He spoke the caution quickly, spitting out the words like pips from something gone sour. He told Palmer he was free to leave, that he was not under arrest, that he was entitled to free and independent legal advice. He said these things because he had to, without thinking about them, or caring a great deal. The only moment of hesitation came when he looked across at the uniformed statue in the corner, to ascertain his name for the tape.

The constable's eyes widened and he spoke his name as if he was confirming it from the dock.

Thorne stood opposite Palmer, his hands on the dull metal tabletop, staring hard. He was aware of Constable Stephen Legge in the corner, shifting his feet nervously. Good, Thorne thought. I'm scaring you, I must be scaring this fucker . . .

Palmer didn't look up.

'Now then, these two murders you're so courageously putting your hand up to. That's two murders out of four, if we're being accurate, isn't it? Four murders all told. There's another man, isn't there?'

Nothing. Thorne let a few seconds become thirty. Moved in that bit closer.

'Actually, we'd better make that five murders. You fucked up last night, fucked up or bottled out, doesn't matter which, but I'm bloody sure *he* didn't.' Slowly, asking it again, 'There's another man, isn't there?'

Palmer nodded. Sniffed. He was about to cry.

'Who is he?' Casual. Like asking the time. *Just give me a name . . .*

Thorne moved round the table, stood behind him. Only a cliché because it was true, because it worked. Leaning down, close enough to smell the sweat, to see the first, fat teardrop plop onto the fag-browned table edge.

'There's a woman's body . . . somewhere. At the moment, she's only missing. I'm not sure it's even been reported yet, but people are missing her. There's people somewhere who are starting to feel it in their guts about now, just *starting* to feel it. That flutter of worry, turning to concern and then eventually to panic. That's when it really starts to hurt, like a cramp that's squeezing the inside of them, making it hard to breathe. Crushing the pipes and valves, *there*, in the gut. All of them, all those people, friends and relatives, huddling together because they all feel the same, and all of them feeling like parts of them are starting to shut down bit by bit. To stop working. Feeling as bad as anyone could ever feel, ever . . .'

Palmer's head drooped slowly down until his cheek lay flush on the table. There were still tears, pooling beneath the side of his face, but no sound at all.

Thorne's voice got lower, quieter. 'But it isn't. It isn't as bad. It's nothing like. When their missing wife or daughter or mother becomes their *dead* wife or daughter or mother, that's when the real pain begins.

'Hearing the news, there's a hammer blow to the skull, and the blows don't stop coming. Identifying the body. Waiting while it's stared at and quantified and filleted. The funeral to arrange, the loose ends, the belongings to sort through. The clothes to bag up for Oxfam. To bundle up and bury your face in . . .

'The lives that have got to be carried on with, while the pain settles, inside and out. A scalding in the belly, a scab to be picked at. Rage and guilt. That's agony a long way beyond the physical, Martin.

'That's not better in the morning, or in a week's time or a month's. That's terminal . . .'

Everybody and everything perfectly still. The room, freezing but suddenly airless. Finally the question, on a slow, shallow breath.

'What's his name?'

Thorne actually flinched, as Palmer raised his head with surprising speed. His eyes were red-rimmed beneath the thick lenses, and desperate. His voice came from somewhere a long way away.

'I don't know.'

Thorne pushed himself away from the table with a roar and charged back across the room towards the door. He wanted two things, badly. He wanted to punch a hole in Palmer's fleshy face and he wanted Palmer to think that he was going to.

'You had your fucking chance . . .'

'No, *please*.' There was terror in the voice, and helplessness. Thorne stopped at the door and turned. 'You don't understand. We were at school together . . .'

Thorne shrugged, raised his palms, waiting. *And . . .* ?

Palmer turned his face slowly away from him. He cast his eyes back down to the wet tabletop. Down to his own indistinct reflection in the scarred and dirty metal.

'No . . . I don't know who he is. But I know who he was.'

PART TWO

FOR THE CHILDREN

TEN

Detective Superintendent Trevor Jesmond smiled like he was sucking on a lemon.

'Let me see if I've got this straight. There's a double murderer sitting in the cells at Kentish Town right now, and you're suggesting that not only do we keep the fact that we've caught him to ourselves, but that we start filling the newspapers with stories of other murders that haven't even happened? Murders that we . . . make up?'

Jesmond raised an eyebrow and looked to the men on either side of him, Russell Brigstocke and Steve Norman.

The fourth man in the room rubbed at a mysterious white patch on the sleeve of his black leather jacket.

'In a nutshell . . . yes.'

Thorne was watching Brigstocke and Norman as well, looking for a reaction, trying to gauge just how much, how many, he was up against. He thought that Brigstocke looked non-committal, the slight shake of his head unreadable. Norman, the oily media merchant, just looked bored.

Thorne spoke again, thinking: I've beaten tougher opposition than this. 'We didn't *catch* him.'

Jesmond stared. 'I'm sorry?'

'We didn't catch Palmer. He wandered in off the street.'

Brigstocke leaned forward. 'Tom, splitting hairs isn't . . .'

'It makes a difference.'

The DCI leaned back again, the head movement loud and clear this time. *Don't go getting cocky and fucking up your chances, Tom. This whole idea sounds stupid enough as it is . . .*

It was two days since Palmer had walked a little unsteadily into a police station with a head wound, a revolver and a few dark secrets to whisper. The idea had lodged itself in Thorne's head from the moment Palmer had first spoken to him.

I don't know who he is . . .

The idea grew, rolled around his brain like a snowball being pushed around a field, making more noise as it gained weight, groaning, until it was massive and immovable, impossible to ignore.

Palmer had been like a man in a dream, terrified of waking up to the nightmare of an agonising reality.

He told Thorne all he knew. About the past and the messages and the terror, and *Jesus*, the excitement. He told him all he'd done. With his knife and his hands and the tears that had to be wiped away, so that he could see their faces properly as he killed them. Now, he wanted no more than to be punished for it. To be put somewhere secure. To be removed.

Thorne though, wanted much more and as soon as the plan had become fully formed in his mind, he had offered Palmer a way, surprising and simple, to make the waking up more bearable. To end the nightmare . . .

Palmer had agreed in principle to all of it.

Now, he sat waiting, as Thorne waited, for approval of what at the very least was an unorthodox move, and at the very worst, would end a career or two.

Jesmond shuffled his chair a little closer to the table, sat up straight. 'I have to tell you, I'm not convinced.'

You don't have to tell me anything, thought Thorne. It's written all over your pointless, pinched face. Spelt out in the red veins across your nose and cheeks . . .

Jesmond continued. 'Palmer is a multiple murderer, a serial killer if you want to be sensationalist about it . . .'

Norman nodded. 'Why not? It's what the press want.'

'Right. Now, we can give him to them. Now, we have a chance to ease what I assure you, Detective Inspector, is a great deal of pressure to get some results, and I must say I'm inclined to take it.'

Thorne tried to make it as clear-cut as he knew how. 'If we announce that we've got Palmer, we lose a far more dangerous killer.'

Jesmond flicked a finger across his thin lips, glanced down at the notes in front of him on the table. 'Stuart Anthony Nicklin. As was.'

Was . . .

Thorne nodded. 'Yes, sir.'

'"Far more dangerous" is a little bit over the top isn't it? Nastier, agreed, but he and Palmer have each killed twice, so . . .'

'That we know of, sir.'

Brigstocke nodded. 'I have to agree with DI Thorne, sir. Nicklin seems to be the more predatory of the two. Certainly the more violent.'

Thorne thinking, thank fuck, about time. 'Nicklin is the one that has arranged these killings. Without *him* the killings would stop. Without Palmer . . . I think he'll simply go to ground.'

There was a pause. Thorne looked over at Brigstocke but the DCI was looking at the table. Thorne shifted his gaze to the window. The sky was the colour of a long-dead fish. It was quietly drizzling.

It was Norman who spoke up. 'And that's . . . bad is it? Nicklin just disappearing?'

Thorne tried to sound informative, tried not to make Norman feel too stupid. 'He won't disappear for ever. He'll wait until he thinks it's safe, then start again. He'll do it differently. Maybe he'll move and start killing somewhere else.'

Norman nodded, but Thorne caught something in his look that told him he hadn't tried hard enough. Norman felt stupid . . .

Brigstocke took off his glasses, rubbed the bridge of his nose. Thorne had a sudden, disconcerting memory of seeing him do the same thing, right before he punched the front teeth out of a paedophile's mouth. 'I'm not sure the papers'll go for it, Tom. Knowingly running false murder stories could get them into deep shit with their readers later on. They'll only play along up to the point that their circulation gets hit.'

'Nicklin needs to think that Palmer's still out there killing for him. Can't we make the papers print what we want them to?'

Jesmond glanced at Norman. 'Steve?'

Norman looked across at Thorne. *Now who's asking stupid questions?* 'There's something in what DCI Brigstocke is saying. A balance would need to be struck. We'd have to let them feel that they were being altruistic, at the same time as offering them the big story if it works. If we get Nicklin.'

Thorne nodded. It sounded like a way forward.

Norman hadn't finished. 'There would of course be other, bigger problems. There could be . . . almost certainly *would* be, leaks from within the investigation, not to mention the odd, slightly unusual journalist with a strange compulsion to tell the truth.' He smiled at Thorne a little sadly, and shrugged.

'Perhaps I'm being a bit dim,' Jesmond said, flashing sharp incisors, 'but I'm still not quite sure why we don't just print the truth in the papers. About the failed attack on Ms Kaye I mean.'

Norman was nodding halfway through Jesmond's speech, and didn't stop. 'Right. "Twin killers strike again. One strikes out."'

'Or something of that sort,' Jesmond agreed. 'Might not reporting the failure frighten Nicklin a little? Prompt him to contact Palmer perhaps?'

All eyes on Thorne now. He seriously doubted that much would frighten Nicklin, but despite seeing some sense in what Jesmond was saying, he stuck to his guns. 'I'm convinced that the most dangerous thing would be to disrupt the pattern.'

Jesmond was stubborn as well. Stubborn, and with pips on his shoulder. 'He might know about it anyway. He might have watched Palmer mess it up. He might have seen him *fail* to kill Jacqueline Kaye. What then?'

'Obviously, we can't rule that out completely until the missing body turns up and we establish time of death, but the Lovell and Choi killings would indicate that isn't part of his pattern. I think Nicklin does his bit and then gets another jolt from sitting back later, and watching the reports of Palmer's killings on TV and in the papers. Sir.'

Jesmond shook his head, slowly. 'We must have other options. More conventional avenues of investigation. We have a description for a start and it certainly sounds as if a decent description is what got us Palmer in the first place.'

'You're right, sir,' Thorne said, thinking, *Yes, and who was that down to?* 'Unfortunately, the description Palmer has given us, based on the single meeting the two of them had in the brasserie, is hardly decent. Nicklin had a beard. For all we know he doesn't have it any more. All Palmer really has is an impression of this man, a description based on his memory of him, rather than on the way he looks now.' Thorne pictured the look of confusion on Palmer's face, as he'd tried, with very little success, to recall how the boy he used to know had looked that day he'd strolled up to his lunch table and turned his dull little world on its head. 'Palmer can describe the fifteen-year-old boy like he saw him yesterday, but he can't give us an accurate picture of the man who walked into that brasserie six months ago. We've got height and a rough idea of weight, clothes, colouring, but we don't have a face. We sat him down with the CCTV footage from Euston, but he couldn't pick Nicklin out.'

'Or *wouldn't*,' Jesmond said. 'We can't be certain he wants his friend caught as much as he says he does.'

Thorne shook his head. 'I am certain of that, sir.'

And yet . . .

There was *something* that Palmer was keeping hidden. He appeared to be co-operating fully, to be answering every question, but Thorne sensed there were secret places he was unwilling to go, pictures he was wary of painting too fully.

Thorne would keep digging. If they'd let him . . .

'What about these e-mails?' Jesmond opened a green folder and began pulling out copies of the messages Nicklin had sent to Palmer. The tech boys had printed them out from Palmer's home PC.

'They're untraceable,' Thorne said, emphatically. 'Anonymous servers. Accounts set up on stolen credit cards. He was very careful.'

Jesmond quickly re-read a couple of the mails, clenching his jaw at the most chilling – the ones that had issued Palmer with his instructions: the dates, venues and methods of the killings.

'Can't we just monitor his e-mails?' Jesmond asked. 'Have them forwarded on to one of our computers?'

Thorne leaned forward. 'We will be watching for any communication from Nicklin, of course, *and* using the description we've got, but I still don't think it's enough, sir. It's got to be all or nothing.' He pulled one piece of paper away from the others, slid it in front of Jesmond.

'Look at that one, it pre-dates the first killing by a few weeks.'

Jesmond picked it up, started to read.

```
Received: (qmail 27003 invoked by alias);
28 Jun 2001 11:35:29 -0000
Date: 28 Jun 2001 11:35:29 -0000
Message-ID:
<921065729.27000@coolmail.co.uk>
To: martpalmer@netmail.org.uk
Subject: THINKING OF SUMMER
```

```
From: Old Friend.
Martin. Any thoughts yet? I can see
you're thinking about it. You look miles
away sometimes and I know that you're
picturing it. Soon it will be a lot more
than a picture. I'm presuming (as I could
always presume with you) that you're on
board. I will give you details in the
fullness etc etc. Your face tells me that
you're remembering those summers. Think
about the summers to come ...
```

Jesmond looked up, and across at Thorne, his face giving nothing away. Stupid, or just *playing* stupid, Thorne was finding it hard to tell.

'He's watching him, sir. He says so. "I can see you", "you look miles away", "your face tells me". He's watching him.'

'It sounds like he *was* watching him, granted,' Jesmond said.

'I think he still is. He likes to be in control.'

Norman was keen to show that if his last question was a little . . . silly, it was a long way from typical. 'If he *is* watching, then what are we talking about? You've said yourself that we can't be sure he didn't see Palmer screw up with Jacqueline Kaye? He might also have watched him walk into that station on Monday. If he already knows we've got Palmer, Detective Inspector, what you're asking would be an enormous and potentially dangerous waste of time. Wouldn't it?'

It was the obvious question. The one Thorne had been most afraid of. He knew his response was hardly convincing, but it was the only one he had. 'It's a risk worth taking. It's why we need to do this quickly.' Jesmond stared down at the papers in front of him. Norman put away his pen. Thorne thought of something else. 'I'm not saying he watches Palmer all the time. He can't. He gave Palmer the impression that he had a full-time job . . .'

Jesmond started gathering up his notes, like he'd already made up his mind. 'Risk, you said. Risk is a very good word for it, Thorne. We take a murderer, a man who has killed at least two women, and just put him back on the street . . .'

Thorne sighed in frustration. 'That isn't what we'd be doing. I told you . . .'

'What would you call it, then?'

'Just leaving him . . . in vision. Not frightening Nicklin off. One way or another, when it's over, Palmer goes away.' Thorne looked back to Brigstocke, searching for backup and not getting it. He knew he couldn't rely on the DCI's support. Brigstocke was still smarting from Thorne going it alone two days earlier. Interviewing Palmer without waiting for him. The bollocking he'd dished out was still being talked about by anybody who'd been within half a mile of his office.

Back to Jesmond. 'Organised Crime do this sort of thing all the time, sir,' Thorne said. 'When they need a witness on the inside. I don't see why we can't do the same. We release Palmer on police bail, pending further enquiries. It's a common enough procedure . . .'

It was probably as close as Jesmond came to losing his temper. 'I'm perfectly aware of the procedure, Thorne, but Palmer is not a fucking loan shark. He's killed two women, and we don't normally go around releasing murderers on police bail.'

There was little Thorne could say and Jesmond quickly relaxed. The advantage was his. He took out a handkerchief and pushed one corner up a nostril, digging around, his face contorting with the effort. 'So, hypothetically, Palmer's walking about, we're watching him. Then what? Nicklin makes a silly mistake? He hasn't made too many so far has he? So, we wait for him to kill again?' Thorne said nothing. He knew it might come down to just that. 'I'm not sure you've thought this through, Inspector.'

'With respect, sir . . .' The volume rising now. Precious little respect anywhere.

Brigstocke leaned across the table. 'Listen, Tom . . .'

Thorne narrowed his eyes and opened his mouth far too quickly. 'That fence you're sitting on must be playing havoc with your arse, Russell.'

Jesmond raised a palm but Thorne carried on. He looked at each of them as he spoke, knowing he only had the one chance, if that. 'Yes, Palmer is a killer, a fucking freak, and when this is all over, whatever we decide to do, he's going away for the rest of his life. He *wants* to go away, he's not angling for anything, he's not trying to make a deal.' He stopped, took a breath, carried on. 'I firmly believe, however, that if this investigation continues *along the lines I have suggested*, he will not be a danger to anybody . . .'

Jesmond was ready to come in. Thorne didn't let him. 'I think this is our only chance to get Nicklin and if we don't take it, we'll regret it down the road. Now, as things stand, with a killer in custody, we all get patted on the back or promoted or whatever. Later there'll be blood.'

He stared at Jesmond. *Why the fuck should you care? You'll probably be long gone by then.* He had drawn the line at talking about 'taking full responsibility' but something in Jesmond's small, ratty eyes told Thorne that it would be a given; that should it prove necessary, the grip he was barely maintaining on his career would be loosened by a few strategically placed boots on fingers. Something else told him that it was all academic anyway. They weren't going to go for this in a million years . . .

Thorne stood up. 'I've said my piece I think, sir.'

Jesmond looked to his colleagues, straightening his papers like a newsreader for want of anything better to do. 'Thank you, Inspector. Obviously, this needs discussing and not just by us. I've got a conference call with the Deputy Assistant Commissioner arranged and he may want to take it even higher. So . . .'

So . . . Thorne sat in the office next door, fighting a childish urge to put a glass against the wall, and cursing the tiny strand of DNA somewhere within him that made him do . . . these things. Made him incapable of settling for anything.

He had never been one for war stories. He could prop up a bar with the best of them and swap tales, but when stories of who put who away were told, he would smile, slap backs and retreat inside himself to where he could silently revisit failure. Success did not occupy him a great deal, but failure was always around, waiting to be given the nod.

He was English, after all.

It wasn't the ones he caught that Thorne remembered. That he *always* remembered. It wasn't the ones he finally got to see in an interview room or through the peephole of a holding cell, or across a courtroom. It wasn't them.

It wasn't the Palmers.

Thorne had forgotten the faces of a dozen convicted killers down the years, but he still saw, clearly, those killers for whom he never had a face at all. He would do whatever was necessary to prevent Stuart Anthony Nicklin *as was*, taking his place in that particular gallery.

Bloody-minded, stubborn and pig-headed were easy words to use. Guilty on all three counts. Yes, yes and yes again. But they were not the *right* words.

It would have been so easy to accept the plaudits and take what had been handed to him on a plate. Easy to look at a picture of Martin Palmer on the front page, to prop up that bar for a night or two. Easy to pose with the victims' relatives, to shake hands and look into grateful faces, then turn away, ready to go to work again, to begin the next hunt.

Easy to crack on, smug and satisfied.

So hard to dismiss a small boy with a squeaky hammer.

Can you *forget his face, Charlie? I hope so . . .*

Now Holland and McEvoy were moving across the incident room towards the open doorway of his office. He watched them getting closer, taking an age to get to him, wondering at the expressions on their faces, tight and dark, the piece of paper in Holland's hand, the fist clenched at the end of McEvoy's arm. Then they were in his office and the sheet of paper was on his desk, and he was trying to take in what it said and McEvoy was talking.

'The body of Miriam Vincent was found this morning in her flat on Laurel Street in Dalston. She's been dead a couple of days. Shot in the head.' McEvoy's tone had been professional, calm and informative. Now, in a reddening rush, she let the anger come through. 'She was a student at

North London University. She was nineteen for christ's sake . . . a fucking teenager . . .'

Holland looked at her, alarmed at the sudden display of emotion. Thorne took it, used it, let her anger clear his head. Where a few moments before he had felt woozy and disorientated, now he was suddenly bright and focused. He knew exactly what to do.

'I haven't seen this.'

McEvoy cocked her head. 'Sorry . . . ?'

'You couldn't find me. Clear?' He handed the piece of paper to Holland, pointed towards the office next door. 'Go and tell *them*.'

Holland hesitated for a second and McEvoy snatched the paper from him. 'I'll do it . . .'

Thorne held out his hand. 'No you won't, you're too . . . charged up. They've already had me.'

McEvoy handed back the piece of paper, grunted and turned away. Thorne passed it on to Holland, caught his arm, squeezed. 'Calm . . .'

Holland nodded and quickly marched out. Without looking back he walked straight up to the door of the adjoining office, knocked and went in without waiting to be asked.

McEvoy went back to the incident room and while he waited, Thorne watched her, moving among her fellow officers, fired up about Miriam Vincent's murder, blazing with the knowledge of it. He liked her anger. He understood it. He worried that lately, she seemed a little less able to control it.

McEvoy and Holland were the only people, aside from the three next door, who knew what he was proposing to do. The rest of those working on the case were still flushed with the success of the Palmer arrest. There was suddenly a lot more laughter around the building, and those not laughing were only nursing the hangovers that came from too much celebration. He knew that if his idea was to stand any chance of working, the celebration would need to stop. The lid needed to come down hard and stay on tight.

Thorne suddenly saw how unutterably stupid he was being. Stupid to think that the powers-that-be would agree to releasing Palmer and stupid for wanting them to. He started to feel relieved, light and free of it, anticipating their polite but firm refusal.

He knew that what he was planning would have gone down like a cup of cold sick anyway, for all sorts of reasons, not least the time of year. He wondered whether he owed his colleagues a chance to wind down a little, to level out, to have a life with their families.

It only took a second or two to remember that there were others, dead and alive, to whom he owed a lot more.

Those that would pull faces if Thorne got his way, those that would mutter in corners and ignore him in the pub after work, had not met Carol Garner's mother and father. They had not met her son. Perhaps he should invite what was left of that family down for the day, show Charlie around the station and sit every single officer, every member of the civilian staff, down with them for fifteen fucking minutes.

He wondered whether Carol had bought Christmas presents for Charlie before it happened. Would her mum and dad give them to him, and would they tell him who they were from . . . ?

Thorne heard a door open and looked up to see

Brigstocke emerge from the office next door, eyes scanning the incident room, looking for him.

'Russell . . .'

Brigstocke turned to look at him. When their eyes met, it was clear to Thorne that his earlier comments, which he had meant but now regretted, had neither been forgotten, nor forgiven. They would need to talk.

Suddenly, Thorne wanted it more than anything. Wanted the go-ahead. In those last few seconds, while he waited for some sign from Brigstocke, he wanted the chance to stop Stuart Nicklin, to be rid of him, and bollocks to careers, and pissing people off and celebrating a job only half done. Less than half done . . .

Brigstocke closed his eyes and nodded. All right.

Thorne acknowledged the nod with his eyes, then spoke the words quietly, but out loud.

'Oh, fuck.'

ELEVEN

The man who used to be called Stuart Nicklin was not a big fan of Christmas shopping, but these things had to be done. He'd nipped out at lunchtime and was pretty pleased with the progress so far. He wouldn't be able to face the coming weekend, the last before the big day, the crowds of zombies milling around. Everyone pretending they were happy about handing out cash for disposable shit and shiny paper. His wife would brave the crush of course, but then she had that many more things to buy. For parents and friends, people at work. *His* colleagues never really bothered. Christmas was a time to forget about work for a while . . .

He carried his coffee to a table by the window and dropped his bags down beside the seat. She would like the necklace, he was certain, and the smelly stuff, but the sweater was a bit risky. He'd got the receipt: she could always take it back. They usually spent the morning of the twenty-seventh, or twenty-eighth, queuing up with dozens of others at the M&S exchange counter, everyone silently seething, horrified at what they'd become.

This was a time of day he looked forward to immensely.

Normally he'd retire to his room about now, and maybe he'd get half an hour of peace with the papers. A chance to go through each story, each version, update or piece of breaking news. He watched the television as well, of course. He was a slave to Teletext in the days after one of his adventures, but there was nothing like getting it fresh. Seeing it laid out on the page in front of him. Feeling it on his fingertips for the rest of the day. He always bought two papers. A tabloid and a broadsheet. Needing both breadth and brevity, the detail *and* the distaste.

He'd been waiting four days now for the latest . . . coverage. The stories would always appear eventually, cheek by jowl with political analysis in the broadsheet, or jammed up against some piece of pouting, top-heavy jailbait in the Red Top. He fucking loved it all. The anticipation, as in the act itself, growing keener, almost unbearable as each day without news of what they had done, passed.

Now, the waiting was over. Today was the day, and he was really looking forward to what they had to say this time. This time it was going to be very interesting.

He took a sip of his overpriced cappuccino and reached down for the two newspapers in the purple WH Smith carrier bag. An *Independent* and a *Mirror* today. An old woman sitting opposite tore a chunk away from a pastry with her teeth and grinned at him. He smiled back as he unfolded the *Independent* . . .

There it was. There they were.

He looked at his watch. He didn't have to be back for at least a quarter of an hour. Fifteen blissful minutes in which to switch off, enjoy his coffee and immerse himself in the coverage of two brutal murders. One of which he had first-hand knowledge, of course. One was so real, was so fresh in his memory, that he could still smell the girl's vomit. Acrid and boozy. She'd puked the second he'd raised the gun. Opened her mouth as if to scream and heaved instead. He'd had to step back smartish to save his shoes, then stretch to step over the stuff, and put the gun to her head.

The other one, Palmer's murder . . . well, that was one the silly bastards had gone and made up.

The detail was good, it sounded convincing enough, but they had wasted their time. Palmer was motivated by fear, pure and simple, always had been. He was scared enough of Nicklin to kill in the first place, but what he was *really* scared of was letting him down. Fucking up would be the only thing that could possibly have scared Martin enough to turn himself in. After Nicklin had shot the girl in her flat, he'd watched Palmer all the next day. He'd seen him come out of his flat like a man in a dream and followed him all the way to the station. Watched him totter inside like a drunk, failure as visible about him as the stained bandage on his fat head.

So, now they didn't want him to know that they had Palmer in custody. Too late. The real question of course, was just how to respond . . .

He'd think about it more later, while he was supposed to be working. Now he had ten minutes left to read all about the two murders.

One true, one false . . .

He wondered which one he was going to enjoy reading about more.

Thorne watched the rest of the world moving round him, overwound, frenetic, going about its business. He saw people, running around like blue-arsed flies, buying presents they didn't want to give, heaving bags crammed with food they wouldn't eat. Unable to stop themselves. Caught up in it. Peace, goodwill and socks to all men . . .

He saw some absurdly happy.

He saw those that hated it, battening down the hatches.

He saw a set of shell-shocked parents organising their daughter's funeral.

While all this was going on, Tom Thorne spent the last few days before Christmas working at his own speed. Slowly but very surely pissing off virtually everyone who knew him.

To most coppers 'overtime' was a magic word, right up there, and in some cases well above, 'conviction'.

But not at Christmas.

Coppers got a bit huffy come Christmas. Self-righteous and sentimental, and salt-of-the-earth indignant. Jesus . . . (not used in any religious sense of course) . . . didn't they deserve a break, them and their families, after the shit they waded through for the other fifty-one weeks of the year? To Thorne, it was a moot point. He didn't get overtime anyway. DIs and above had been bought out with a few grand extra on the annual salary. It was cases like this one that made it obvious how much they'd been shafted. As it was, despite gripes of his own, Thorne didn't blame anybody for feeling tired, for needing a rest from it, but there was one major stumbling block . . .

Killers didn't stop for Christmas.

Suicide was the well-known one of course, but it wasn't the only pastime which became popular once the novelty singles began clogging up the charts. Crime figures tended to go up across the board during the seasonal period and murder was no exception. Domestics, incidents involving alcohol – all increasing, all leaving victims and the relatives of victims, demanding action. None of them giving a toss if your parents were coming down from the North, or if you'd put a reservation on a cottage in the Cotswolds, or if it was your kid's first Christmas.

Especially if their own kid was not going to see another one.

Easy to think like that of course, when you were the one cancelling the holidays. No meticulously worked-out rota, no amount of overtime, was going to make the majority of officers on this case think any differently of Tom Thorne. Not Brigstocke. Not McEvoy. He wasn't even sure about Dave Holland. The simple fact was that, thanks to him, they would all be spending Christmas babysitting a double murderer.

Palmer would not be going back to work until the New Year now, but Sean Bracher had been well briefed, so that there would be no problem when he did. Palmer's absence just before Christmas would be put down to illness, and the issue of his resemblance to the man police were seeking would not be ducked. He had come forward and been immediately eliminated from enquiries. End of story. Bracher would assist in disseminating this information as well as smoothing the passage for the new Baynham & Smout employee who would be working very closely with Martin Palmer. One unhappy DC, seconded from SCG (South), would be spending *her* Christmas ploughing through *Accountancy For Idiots* . . .

Palmer's domestic situation would be easy to monitor. He lived on the second floor of a fifties mansion block in West Hampstead. There was one entrance. He would be followed to and from work, with permanent surveillance maintained outside his flat and at least one plain-clothes officer inside at all times, though at *no* time would Palmer be accompanied as he entered the building.

According to Palmer, he seldom went out anyway and had *never* invited anybody to his flat, so comings and goings shouldn't be a problem. Thorne was keen that Palmer's movements appeared normal and so, to a degree, this side of things would be played by ear. If he was asked out for a drink (which he had told them *had* happened, but not often), they'd decide at the time whether to cry off or not. Similarly, at work, he'd be accompanied to lunch by the undercover DC, with a backup team on hand should this start to become suspicious in itself. In fact, the only break from any kind of routine involved Palmer ringing his parents to tell them that he couldn't make it home for Christmas Day. This was also the only part of the whole complex arrangement that Palmer seemed remotely uncomfortable with.

Thorne wanted everything tied down tight. No mistakes. The man he was after was clever. He would, Thorne felt certain, be watching at least some of the time. He might well of course have seen enough already to tell him that Palmer was in custody. Stable doors and horses . . .

As Thorne had told Jesmond, it was a risk he felt they had to take.

There were certainly plenty of risks . . .

Norman had spotted a couple of them straight away. He himself would handle the media, but the team had not responded well to the lecture Thorne had delivered, that he felt *needed* to be delivered, on leaking ships. He'd wanted Brigstocke to do the honours, but the DCI was still in no mood to do Thorne any favours. In terms of the bad feeling coming his way, the atmosphere that followed his speech was pretty much the icing on the cake, but Thorne knew that it was necessary. Besides, normally he only alienated the top brass. Now he was getting on *everybody's* tits. At least this was a change . . .

Thorne wanted this to go right. He wanted nothing in the public domain, *nothing*, unless it could have come from a source other than Martin Palmer. They could, for example, go with Palmer's description of Nicklin – they could always invent a witness who might have come up with that – but any avenue of investigation that could only have originated with Palmer needed to be walked with the utmost care and discretion.

Thorne could handle the black looks, the comments subtle and otherwise, but the only real moment of doubt had come at the press conference on the Saturday, less than forty-eight hours after Miriam Vincent's body had been discovered.

It was the *lies*, naked in the light from a hundred flash guns and boldly sharing the stage with Miriam Vincent's grief-stricken mother, that were hard to bear. Someone, it might have been Steve Norman, had actually suggested that they hire actors to play the parents of Palmer's fictitious victim. Thorne was glad he'd drawn a line and said no to that one. This was bad enough . . .

Norman had led out an impressive looking party, consisting of Jesmond, Brigstocke, a young DC acting as Family Liaison, and Mrs Vincent. After the predictable rhetoric from Jesmond, Norman introduced Rosemary Vincent. She was in her early fifties, tall and slightly awkward, with a face that had probably been open and easy to read until two days ago, when it had become the mirror of emotions that were alien to it.

The scalding in the belly, the scab to be picked at. Rage and guilt . . .

She spoke movingly of her only daughter, clutching Miriam's picture and trying not to break down as she remembered their last conversation – a row about her not coming home. Thorne stood at the back of the room, behind the journalists, away from the cameras, unable to take his eyes off this woman. He had seen people in the same situation a hundred times, but rarely had he seen the freshly dead part of them so clearly. It was there in every nervous smile, every pull at the hair and quiver of the lip. He winced when she spoke about the grief that the parents of the other victim must be feeling. He felt the shame, like a cold hand at his throat, when she sent them her love and support, when she sympathised with their pain; an agony so crippling that they hadn't felt able to come along themselves . . .

Thorne had made a promise to himself then that, whatever happened, when it was all over he would visit Rosemary Vincent and tell her the truth, and explain why he had done what he had done.

That night, he watched the highlights of the press conference on half a dozen different channels and felt the fingers at his throat every time.

He was just about ready for bed when the phone rang.

'Yeah . . .'

'Tom? Is that Tom?'

'Who's this?'

'This is Eileen, love. Your dad's sister.'

'Oh . . .'

'Sorry if it's a bit late, but we were watching a film. You know, waiting for it to finish.'

'It's fine . . .' Thorne had actually been carrying a half-empty wine bottle and dirty glass back to the kitchen when the phone went. Now, he sat down on the sofa, stuck the bottle between his knees and yanked out the cork again.

'So how are you, love?' She spoke as if he was ill, or a little slow.

Thorne was about to fill his glass when he decided that, actually, he was in no mood to have this conversation. He knew what she wanted and he couldn't be arsed waiting for her to say it. Christ, how long had it been since he'd seen this woman? It was certainly before Jan had left. A funeral, but he couldn't remember whose. Maybe one of Eileen's husband's parents . . .

'Listen, Auntie Eileen—'

'I was sorry to hear about you and your wife . . .'

So Thorne poured the wine and made the tedious small talk, and waited for her to get to the point; to say what she'd obviously called to say. He'd warned his dad against ringing her, silly old bastard. Now it was going to be embarrassing. He started prompting her, getting tetchier, waiting to hear that she was ever so sorry but she *really* couldn't have Jim at Christmas. She had a houseful after all, and there wasn't the room to put him up and maybe if he'd given her a bit more notice . . .

Stuff you, Thorne thought. We'll be fine, the two of us . . .

'So we've talked about it and decided that your dad's coming to us this year.'

Thorne held the wine glass halfway between his knee

and his mouth. He knew he'd heard correctly, but couldn't think of anything to say. 'Sorry? But . . .'

'If you drop him at Victoria, we'll pick him up at the other end.'

Thorne felt himself starting to redden a little. 'Listen, maybe I'd better have a word with dad . . .'

'Don't worry, it's all been organised, love.'

'But you'll have a houseful. You haven't got the room . . .'

'We'll be fine. Look, we'd love to have him and I dare say it'll be a bit of a break for you.'

Then five minutes more of this and that, until Thorne heard the call-waiting signal on the line and dropped a hint. Auntie Eileen took it, announcing that now it *was* past her bedtime and telling Thorne how lovely it would be to see *him* sometime, too . . .

Thorne had told Phil Hendricks the whole thing before he'd really had a chance to decide how he felt about it. It was probably rash of Hendricks to make the invitation and Thorne couldn't decide whether it was stupidity or desperation that made him accept, but either way, two days later, here he was . . .

Christmas Eve. Playing gooseberry. Sitting in a pub and not listening.

'Tom? For fuck's sake . . .'

Thorne felt as if he were emerging at speed from a long, long tunnel. Gold, silver and red coming into focus. Cheap decorations, catching the light, dangling from fake wooden beams. He blinked. 'Sorry Phil. Is it my round, mate?'

Hendricks stared at him. 'Hello! Brendan's up there, getting them in. You haven't heard a word, have you?'

Thorne downed the last of his pint. 'Yes, I have.'

'So? What d'you reckon?'

Thorne puffed out his cheeks, just needing a second or two. He began to recall bits of a one-sided conversation. Brendan and Phil were an item again. Yes, that was it. Hendricks wanted to know whether taking Mr Didn't-Turn-Out-To-Be-A-Bastard-After-All back was a good idea.

'What's definitely *not* a good idea,' Thorne said finally, 'is having me dossing on your sofa like a spare prick at a wedding.'

Hendricks sighed. 'Look, we've been through this. It's not a big deal.'

Thorne looked around. The place was packed. It was hard to make themselves heard over the hubbub and the loud Christmas music. Slade, Wizzard, Mud. Utterly predictable and hugely reassuring. He glanced towards the bar where Brendan was handing over money for the drinks. 'Have you asked him?'

'It's fuck all to do with him. I'm not daft anyway – I know he's only back because he can't face being at home. His mum and dad don't know he's gay and he's got nowhere else to go . . .'

'None of us is exactly spoilt for choice.'

'Don't go on about it, all right? You're staying. It's either you for Christmas or some old tramp from outside the soup kitchen.'

Thorne grinned. 'Wouldn't the smell bother you?'

Hendricks gleefully supplied the punchline. 'I'm sure you can clean yourself up.'

They were still laughing as Brendan arrived with the drinks, but as soon as he put the glasses down on the table,

Thorne was out of his seat and pulling on his jacket.

'Listen, I'm going to get out of your way . . .'

Brendan held up Thorne's new pint. He looked pissed off and was about to say something, but Hendricks put a hand on his arm to stop him. He knew there was little point in arguing.

'See you later, yeah?'

Thorne said nothing. He squeezed round the table, put a hand on Brendan's shoulder. 'I'm sorry about the beer . . .'

'Tomorrow for lunch, then?' Hendricks asked.

Thorne nodded, but knew instantly that his friend could tell he didn't mean it. He took the hand from Brendan's shoulder and held it out towards Hendricks. 'Have a good one, Phil.'

Hendricks stood, took the hand and pulled Thorne into a slightly awkward hug.

'You too. Now, fuck off . . .'

So, Thorne did.

TWELVE

A DC answered the door and Thorne held up his warrant card. If the officer, who was ginger, pudgy and only an inch or so above minimum height, could smell the beer on Thorne's breath, his face wasn't letting it show. It showed only the same blank truculence that Thorne had seen on the faces of the two muppets in the car outside.

Parents coming . . . the cottage . . . the kid's first Christmas . . .

'I'll not be long.' Thorne nodded back over his shoulder towards the chair in the hallway. The officer stepped outside and sat down, muttering and disgruntled. Thorne shut the front door behind him. He probably *had* smelt the booze. It didn't matter.

Thorne noticed a copy of the *Sun* on the table just inside the door. He opened the door and offered it to the constable who took it with a grunt. *Fuck you*, Thorne thought, pulling the door shut again.

He turned and walked through into the living room. Palmer stepped out of the kitchen carrying a mug of tea. He had evidently not heard the knock on the door and started slightly when he saw Thorne.

They looked at one another for a few seconds. Then Palmer spoke, his voice deep and slightly nasal. 'Has something . . . ?' Thorne shook his head.

Palmer held up his mug, the steam fogging his glasses for a second or two. 'Can I get you one?'

Thorne said nothing, walked across to where the computer sat on a small desk near the window. It was logged on to a server twenty-four hours a day. The second Nicklin got in touch, they'd know about it.

Thorne stared at the screensaver – a series of multi-coloured clocks which swam about, bouncing all over the screen, buzzing and ticking, chiming on the hour. He leaned forwards and moved the mouse so that the clocks disappeared. He pulled the chair away from the desk, turned it round so that it faced into the room and sat down.

He hadn't taken his jacket off.

'What d'you do? Surf the Net? Chat? Play Scrabble on it?'

Palmer sat straight-backed on the sofa. He held his mug of tea in two hands against his chest. 'Yes. The Net. Sometimes.'

'And . . . ?'

'Well, with a police officer in constant attendance, I'm hardly likely to spend the hours of darkness trawling through porn sites, am I?'

'But if you were on your own?' Thorne asked, quickly.

Palmer stared down into his tea. 'I see. What would a filthy degenerate seek out? Well, I'd be looking for something perverse, almost certainly. You know, sick.' He looked up and across at Thorne. His head was tipped slightly back, his nose wrinkling slightly to stop his glasses sliding off. 'Bodies perhaps. Autopsy photographs, they're out there if you know where to look.' He started to talk faster, his voice getting louder, his breathing harsh and faintly wheezy; the best impression he could do, he could *give*, of excitement. 'Perhaps even a video or two, with sound if at all possible to pick up the noise . . . the howl of the buzz saw. You know the sort of thing, danger and dissection, the usual saucy mix for the pathetic, the sexually dysfunctional—'

'Stop.'

Palmer had. Thorne silently admonished himself. He should never have got into this. At best, it was prurient. At worst, it smacked of the kind of cheap psychology that was also to be found on the bits of paper which would spill from crackers round lunch tables the following day. He glanced across at Palmer who clutched his tea and stared straight ahead. Thorne couldn't quite read the expression. Sad? No, disappointed.

The screensaver had kicked in again, and the growing silence was now broken only by a series of distant, electronic ticks.

'I might go out tomorrow,' Palmer said suddenly. He turned to look at Thorne, his upper body leaning forward, his face now keen and animated. 'Just for a walk, get a bit of air. Going a bit bonkers in here . . .'

Thorne snorted. Palmer started to nod thoughtfully even though it was strangely comic. 'I know, I'd better get used to it. Won't be many creature comforts when all this is over. Actually . . .'

He stood up quickly. Reflexively. Thorne did the same. Palmer looked over at him, nervous. 'I've got some cans of beer in the kitchen.' He took a step forwards, then stopped. 'Have one. You could have one.'

Thorne nodded without thinking and Palmer was away towards the kitchen. 'It's bitter, I think. Is that all right?' Thorne said nothing, sat back down again.

He looked around the room. As usual, there was nothing out of place. The layout was simple, the furnishings modern and functional. The first time Thorne had walked into the place, he'd been reminded of somewhere, and then after a few minutes had shivered slightly as he'd realised that the flat was like his own. A few more books and plants maybe, an absence of family photos or souvenirs. Little evidence of a life lived with much enthusiasm. There was nothing homely . . .

Through the open kitchen door, Thorne could see Palmer moving around, hear him getting glasses from a cupboard and rinsing them out. He was a big man; a man that lumbered and loomed and yet he was oddly graceful. Considering his height and weight, he had very small hands and feet, and looked on occasion as if he must surely tumble forwards on to his pale, fleshy face.

These were observations Thorne had made in the beginning when they'd spent many hours going over it all. Getting the story. Then they'd spent days and days planning, working out how they could make it work; giving Palmer a last taste of freedom so that Nicklin might . . . *might* show his hand. All those hours in overheated interview rooms and yet they had never talked, not really.

Thorne thought about this now, as he sat in Palmer's living room, not with any sense of regret – he had no desire to get to know this man – it was just interesting, that was all, considering where they were.

And still he had that lingering sense that Palmer was holding something back. Saving something up . . .

Palmer returned with two glasses of beer, an odd look of pride on his face, as if he were delivering the heads of a pair of conquered enemies. Thorne took the glass that was offered and placed it on the floor by the side of his chair. Palmer stayed standing, staring out of the window and nodding slightly. He smiled. 'Quite lucky, actually. All these police officers everywhere, especially the one outside the door . . . at least I haven't been bothered by carol singers.'

Thorne stared up at him. Palmer was wearing baggy grey tracksuit bottoms, blue moccasin-style slippers and an orange hooded top. The clothes looked cheap, not a natural fibre anywhere. And not for the first time, Thorne wondered what Palmer spent his money on. He had a good job, but his car wasn't flashy and there were no signs of extravagance.

'Where does all the money go?'

Palmer moved across to the sofa and sat down. He looked across at Thorne, squinting at him, as if trying to grasp every nuance of meaning in the question.

Thorne tried again. 'What do you spend money on?'

Palmer shook his head, shrugged. 'I save it.'

'Holidays?'

'I save it. It's all in the building society. I send some home occasionally, well I *did*, but my parents don't like taking it, so now I just buy them things. You know, when they need them. I bought them a new boiler a couple of months ago.' He nodded again, a series of small nods, like he gave all the time. As if he was agreeing with himself, trying to confirm something.

Thorne thought again about that first meeting, when he had spoken and shouted about a disease called bereavement and Palmer had first spoken about Nicklin. Later, he'd been taken to have his head wound stitched – Jacqui

Kaye had done a fair amount of damage with that shoe – and when he'd returned he'd talked more, and with more ease, about Nicklin – the meeting in the brasserie, the proposal, the instructions for the killings. Early on in that conversation, when they were talking about how he and Nicklin had first met, Palmer had mentioned a name. Twice, perhaps three times, a girl's name had bobbed into view. She, or at the very least, her name, had appeared briefly, like a shape dredged up; something which you could almost place, appearing just below the surface of water before disappearing back into the depths. Now, that name floated to the surface of Thorne's swampy consciousness.

'Tell me about Karen.'

Palmer took a drink. He held the beer in his mouth for a few seconds before swallowing it down. 'Karen died.' More nodding. Thorne waited. 'She got into a car and died. On a sunny day, she climbed into a blue Vauxhall Cavalier – it was on the news, you can probably get the video. That was it. She was fourteen.' He downed nearly all that was left of his beer in three enormous gulps, put the almost empty glass carefully down on the floor and then looked up at Thorne. 'A blue Vauxhall Cavalier. Driven by a murderer. Like me.'

There was only one way Thorne could fill the pause that followed. He'd spoken the words aloud on a hundred different occasions. He'd felt the same sour taste of loss and longing then, hanging in the air, tart on his tongue.

'I'm sorry.'

Instinctively, he meant it. Then another instinct every bit as strong swept over him and he felt the need to qualify what he'd said.

'Not for you. For *her*, for her family. Not for you, Palmer.'

Then silence, and a nod or two, and the ticks and beeps from the swarm of animated clocks seemed suddenly much louder, filling the space between them.

Thorne jumped a little at the chorus of computerised chimes and turned to look at the screen. He glanced down at his watch. Midnight. Christmas day. When he looked back round, Palmer had shuffled forward to the very edge of the sofa. He was smiling awkwardly at him, holding his all but empty glass, just half a mouthful of beer in the bottom.

'Merry Christmas, Detective Inspector Thorne.'

Thorne stood up quickly, feeling as if he was going to be sick. The moment passed but he strode quickly across the room towards the door, belching the taste of vomit into his mouth and then swallowing it away again.

He opened the front door. The officer outside put down his newspaper and stood up. Thorne hovered for a second in the doorway, feeling a little woozy despite his untouched glass of beer. Behind him, in the living room, he heard the sofa creak and was aware of Palmer standing up.

'What did you come for?' Palmer asked.

Thorne beckoned the constable back inside. He leaned forward to take in a gulp of air from the hallway outside before stepping into it.

'Fuck knows . . .'

Palmer pressed his face against the window. Below him, Thorne emerged through the set of double doors and stood on the grass outside, breathing deeply.

He took a mouthful of beer from Thorne's glass and then another. As he drank it down, his enormous Adam's apple bobbed up and down and a little beer dribbled down his chin, and he closed his eyes to prevent the tears that were pricking at the corner of his eyes from forming.

When he opened his eyes and looked down again, Thorne had gone.

He'd always cried easily, even before he'd met Stuart Nicklin. Crying and blushing – he'd had little control over either of them for as long as he could remember. He recalled Stuart dancing around him in the playground, singing, chocolate smeared around his mouth.

Cherry ripe, cherry ripe . . .

And him, moving slowly towards the wall behind him, driven backwards by the heat coming off his own face, growing redder and redder . . .

He recalled the voice of an older Stuart, six months ago, that lunchtime in the brasserie; after those two from work had skulked away and Stuart had spoken to him, and it had all begun again. The voice deeper now, and weathered, but still that laugh in it, the laugh that made you want to be near him, and still that ice inside the laugh.

'Do you ever think about Karen? I never told them you know, Mart. Not everything I mean. There was no need was there? It wasn't your fault, what happened. Her going off with that bloke was nothing to do with that other business. The business with you.' He'd stopped then and leaned in close, his face creased with concern. 'Do you think it was your fault? Course it wasn't. Yes, she was upset, but that doesn't mean anything, does it? Mind you, I wonder what people would think, now, if they *did* know? Do you think they'd blame you? You know what it's like these days, everybody going on about sex and protecting the kids. People getting hounded . . .'

Palmer had tried not to let the terror show on his face as Nicklin finished speaking, but he knew he'd failed miserably.

'I'm not saying I'd ever tell anybody Martin, but you know, some people have got fucking sick minds . . .'

Sally from Glasgow: 'We only do it for the children anyway, don't we?'

Arthur from Newcastle: 'Why shouldn't it be commercial? Shopping means a damn sight more to a lot of these kids than Jesus Christ . . .'

Bridget from Slough: 'How can we celebrate anything with the world the way it is? People starving. Drug addicts. Folk living on the streets. What about the families of those two poor women shot dead a couple of weeks ago? What sort of Christmas are they going to have?'

The man who used to be called Stuart Nicklin stuck a small gold bow on to the final parcel, leaned across and turned the radio up. This was a bit more like it. Bridget, up there on her high horse, had every right to be angry of course: it was a very nasty business. Even if one of the so-called 'poor women' was completely fictitious.

Bob, the phone-in host, agreed with the caller. Absolutely. He said a big thank-you for the call, but he was keen to move on to Alan from Leeds who wanted to talk about the shocking increase in the cost of first-class post . . .

He turned the radio off, stood up and rubbed away the cramp in his legs from squatting on his heels the last half an hour, busy with Sellotape and scissors. This had become something of a tradition – Caroline in bed nice and early, and him up late, wrapping presents.

Just a few more hours now until it all kicked off. They'd have a houseful tomorrow: Caroline's parents, her sister, her sister's three kids running around like maniacs.

Maybe, this time next year, they'd have one of their own. Not if he could possibly avoid it of course, he was doing his best to duck the issue, but Caroline was bringing it up all the time. Not now though. Not yet. He had a great deal he wanted to do before he went down *that* road. When he saw himself as an observer might, when he imagined himself in his mind's eye, he was standing, straight and tall over a body, the blood fizzing through him, the light breaking over him like clouds across the wings of a powerful jet. He was cutting through life, slicing through it, capable of anything. He was mercurial. He would not be . . . lumpen. He would not potter around, hunched over a baby-buggy with milky sick on his lapel. Fucked. That was not him.

He carried his wife's presents across to the tree and slid them underneath. He straightened up, leaned forward and studied his dim, distorted reflection in a large silver bauble. He still got a shock seeing himself without the beard. He'd been a little worried shaving it off, but he needn't have been. The dramatically different hairline, the filled out cheeks and the nose-job he'd saved up for all those years ago, still gave him a face significantly different from the one he might be expected to have sixteen years on.

As it was, he could probably have kept the beard anyway. The pictures he'd seen in the papers and on TV had been so wide of the mark as to be laughable. Palmer's description must have been all over the shop. Maybe the hormone, or the endorphin or whatever, that was stimulated by fear – was it adrenaline? – maybe it fucked up the memory circuits.

Perhaps that was how dictators thrived. A line from Robespierre to Pol-Pot, all using terror to keep themselves safe. Make your enemies, and better yet, your friends, so afraid of you that they forget all the terrible things you're doing to them. The question was, did it work the other way around?

If they stopped being afraid, would they remember?

He knelt down to the plug, switched off the lights and stayed there, breathing in the gorgeous smell of the tree and thinking about Palmer.

He imagined him now, frightened and alone. Some boot-faced bobby keeping the watch, glaring at him, resentful, fantasising about hurting him and doing everybody a favour. He pictured Palmer's wide, soft, cushion face, his mournful, wide-eyed expression. Staring out into the night, thinking about Karen and waiting to be saved. Chewing on his fat bottom lip and blushing like a girl.

What do you want from Santa, Martin?

My head on a plate? My name on an arrest sheet, so that you can slope away to prison, just that little bit less guilty?

Sorry, Mart . . .

He thought about sending him a message to cheer him up. Christmas e-cards were very popular after all. Something seasonal and simple. A picture of a robin perched on the handle of a snow-covered spade and a short message.

I'm thinking about you . . .

It was a tempting idea but he knew he was just being dramatic. There was no way they could trace it, he was sure about that, but even so it was probably not the right time. He'd get Christmas out of the way first, let things settle down a bit. Then he'd decide what to do next.

Assuming that the decision wasn't made for him.

*

It was starting to rain.

Thorne flagged down a black cab on Abbey Road. He was not a million miles from the zebra crossing the Beatles had so famously strolled across more than thirty years before, McCartney barefoot and out of step.

He opened the door. 'Kentish Town . . .'

The driver didn't even look at him. 'Triple time now, mate. That all right?'

Thorne smiled at the strip of tinsel wrapped around the cab's aerial. Maybe the gesture was ironic. He nodded and climbed in. 'Yeah, whatever . . .'

'I Wish It Could Be Christmas Everyday' was blasting out of the radio. It was a song Thorne loved, one guaranteed to have him rushing out to buy holly and advocaat, but for the first time in his life, he wanted Christmas to be over and done with. Christmas *and* New Year, condensed, compressed. He wanted, no, he *needed*, to be shot of them . . .

He thought about Charlie Garner.

Would the boy be lying in bed now, listening out for reindeer on the roof, unable to sleep? Or had he been unable to sleep for the last month, and was he lying in bed now listening to his mother screaming?

The taxi rumbled through Swiss Cottage, down damp, deserted streets, towards Chalk Farm. The cabbie was talking to him, throwing meaningful glances over his shoulder, but Thorne wasn't listening.

A boy called Stuart Anthony Nicklin . . .

Thorne wished the fortnight ahead gone not because of how he was likely to be spending it, nor because of his father, nor Charlie Garner. He needed a leap forward in time to move the case on.

There was an outside chance that there *might* be a break over the Christmas period but he seriously doubted it. What he *was* sure of was that there would be pressure from Jesmond, and from Brigstocke on his behalf. The Powers That Be would demand to know what was happening. When was this stupid idea of his going to yield anything significant bar an astronomical overtime bill?

The taxi squealed to a halt at some lights. A gaggle of drunken revellers crossed the road in front of them, waving and singing. The cabbie waved back, muttering, 'Wankers.'

The cab roared away from the lights and swung right into Camden. Thorne leaned back and closed his eyes. Two weeks mollifying the PTB would at least kill the time, and he wanted it killed. He wanted it stone dead.

If he was going to get pro-active, he couldn't do it while the rest of the world was on holiday. And some people took longer holidays than others . . .

Thorne had decided that in order to move forward, he needed to go back.

He was going to go back to where it had all started.

PART THREE

THE FACE TURNED AWAY

THIRTEEN

The school stood in a quiet, leafy part of Harrow, only a mile or so from a slightly more famous school – one with its own theatre, farm and golf course – which boasted Byron, Nehru and Churchill among its former pupils. As the car moved slowly up the drive towards the main building, Thorne knew that King Edward IV School for Boys would soon have even less reason to be proud of *its* Old Boys.

A week into 2002. The investigation in dire need of a kick up the arse.

The fortnight or so since Christmas had gone much as Thorne had feared: very little progress, lots of grief. The holidays *had* covered a multitude of sins – the inactivity in the case would have been exposed to a far greater degree at any other time, but coupled with the demands on manpower, it still drew unwelcome attention from the Powers That Be.

Brigstocke was clearly copping it from above and he seemed to take great delight in passing it on to those beneath him.

'Patience is running out, Tom.'

'Theirs or yours?'

'Same thing.'

'Right. Got it. Look, as soon as the schools go back, I'm—'

'What? Going to check Nicklin's truancy records? See if he got into detention much?'

'You got any better ideas?'

'You're the ideas man, Tom. We're just waiting to see one of them fucking amount to anything . . .'

'Is this still about the arse on the fence remark? Look, I'm getting tired of saying sorry.'

'Well I'm not tired of hearing you say it, OK?'

Pupils were moving aside to let the car through as Thorne drove slowly up the long drive and swerved into the car park. The boys looked smart in grey trousers and blue blazers trimmed with claret piping. If the school had an inferiority complex, it didn't show from the outside.

Holland stepped out of the car, widening his eyes.

'Not like my school . . .'

Nor mine, thought Thorne. He pictured a short, stocky lad jumping off the bus, thoroughly delighted with his feather cut, his new, five-button bags and his star jumper. Thorne watched him trudging up the hill singing 'Blockbuster' and 'Mama Weer All Crazee Now', wearing platforms instead of beetlecrushers, needing that extra inch or so. He smiled as the boy swaggered into the playground and chatted to his mate. Making up stuff about the weekend, swearing, talking about music and Saturday's results.

The school bell rang, and as Thorne followed Holland towards the entrance, he glimpsed the same boy again, disappearing into the distance. Thirteen-year-old Tom Thorne was hoisting his dirty green rucksack across his shoulder. The canvas was emblazoned with the names of bands and footballers – Slade and Martin Chivers – the bag crammed with games kit and Marmite sandwiches, and maybe even the odd exercise book covered in wallpaper . . .

The school secretary was like every school secretary that Thorne remembered or had ever imagined. Maybe they bred them somewhere, taught them how to put their hair in a bun and look down their pointed noses, before sending them out into the world with a pair of big glasses, a fondness for tweed and something uncomfortable up their backsides.

'Mr Marsden won't be a minute. He knows you're here.'

Thorne smiled at her. 'Thank you so much.'

He and Holland were seated on brown plastic chairs outside the headmaster's office. Opposite them sat a boy of about twelve, looking absolutely terrified. Thorne made eye contact, but the boy looked away.

'This takes me back,' Holland muttered.

'What, sitting outside the beak's office? Can't imagine you were ever in too much trouble, Holland.'

'I had my moments.'

'Come on, a policeman's son?'

Holland laughed a little but then began to think of something and the laughter quickly faded. Thorne thought about his own father. He found it hard to remember him as a teenager's dad. Jim Thorne was in danger of becoming for ever associated with worry and duty, and strange conversations.

'Happy Christmas, Dad. Is Eileen looking after you?'

'She overcooked the sprouts . . .'

'Right. Did you like the video? I didn't know what else to get you.'

'Name all the reindeer.'

'You can watch it later maybe . . .'

'There's nine of them. Nine reindeer . . .'

'Dad . . .'

'Go on. I'll give you Rudolf, that's the easy one. Dasher, Vixen, Comet . . .'

Thorne closed his eyes and searched for an image of his father from his childhood. He could smell disinfectant, taste semolina, hear the squeak of a plimsoll on a gymnasium floor, but a picture of his old man as a young man was temporarily unavailable.

He opened his eyes to find the frightened boy staring at him before quickly looking away again.

Thorne didn't see fear on the faces of kids any more. Not the ones he had cause to talk to. Maybe they just hid it very well or maybe they just weren't scared. What he saw was arrogance and scorn, sometimes even something like pity, but he couldn't remember the last time he'd put the fear of god into a kid.

Thorne looked at the clock above the secretary's door, then back to the boy. 'It's only just gone nine, son. How can you be in trouble already?'

The boy looked up at him and opened his mouth but Thorne would never get an answer to his question. At that moment the door opened and a ludicrously tall man with a shock of white hair stepped from the room.

'I'm Brian Marsden. Come in.'

Thorne and Holland did as they were told.

The next ten minutes were among the most bizarre of the entire case. Marsden knew full well why they were there, knew about Palmer and Nicklin, and yet proceeded to treat Thorne and Holland more like prospective parents than police officers on a murder investigation. He handed them each an expensively produced brochure containing an outline of the current syllabus, details of the school's impressive array of sports facilities and even a sample lunch menu. Before either of them could stop him, he launched into a potted history of the school. It had been a basic state grammar until the late eighties when it became grant maintained. This confirmed several things Thorne already knew: Palmer and Nicklin had both earned their places at the school on merit; Nicklin, despite being brought up by a single parent on a nearby council estate, had passed the necessary exams to get into the best state school in the area. He was a very bright boy.

Things Thorne already knew . . .

A knock at the door stopped Marsden in full flow. He stood up as another teacher entered the room. This one was short and hesitant, and Thorne thought he looked a little embarrassed to be there at all. Marsden marched across to the door to usher them all out again.

'Andrew Cookson is our Head of English. He'll be showing you round, answering your questions. Perhaps you'll pop in again before you leave . . .'

Cookson led Thorne and Holland back past the secretary's office and into the main reception area. The place stank of floor polish mingled with a hint of sweat.

'Actually,' Holland said, 'we don't really need the tour.'

Cookson nodded slowly. He looked a little confused.

Thorne had other ideas. 'No, it's fine . . .' Holland looked at him as if he were mad, but Thorne just shrugged.

He thought getting a feel of the place couldn't hurt and he actually quite fancied having a look round.

'Right, follow me,' Cookson said. 'There's something you'll want to see in the main hall, then we'll have a quick scoot round and then I'll hook you up with Bowles.' He held out his hands. *Fair enough?* Thorne nodded and Cookson smiled. Thorne could see instantly that he'd be a popular teacher. The smile was huge and infectious. Thorne also saw, suddenly, that Cookson's dark eyes were mischievous, and that even though he must have been in his late twenties or early thirties, he still had the energy, the vigour, of a child.

As he'd thought he might, Thorne hugely enjoyed being shown around. Cookson's wry commentary was highly entertaining, as was the look of boredom on Holland's face.

'I think your sergeant must have bad memories of his time at school,' Cookson said with a grin. 'What about you?'

Thorne shook his head. 'Sounds a bit swotty, and trust me, I really wasn't, but I bloody loved school.'

'Me too,' Cookson said. 'Still do . . .'

King Edward IV had clearly modelled itself on a public school; unavoidable probably, considering the proximity of such a celebrated one. The imitation was a good one, right down to the fives courts, the house system and even the mortar boards and gowns which, Cookson was relieved to say, were strictly reserved for the big occasions.

Speech day, prizegiving, school photos . . .

'These are the ones you'll be interested in . . .'

The entire back wall of the school hall was covered in framed photos, some dating right back to the forties. There were dozens, row upon row of them. Cookson led Thorne and Holland to a group of photos covering the late seventies and early eighties.

'Here we go. 'Eighty-two, 'eighty-three and 'eighty-four.'

Each photo was about three-and-a-half-feet long; the sort where the entire school lined up, kneeling, sitting, or standing on chairs, and the camera panned slowly down the line. Thorne remembered *his* school photos and a boy named Fox who used to take great delight in waiting until the camera had begun to move, and then legging it round the back to pop up on the other side, so as to appear on both ends of the final photo. He got detention every time, but he always did it anyway . . .

Thorne stared at the first photo. He spotted Palmer almost straight away. He was a head taller than the boys around him, with the same hair, the same thick glasses. He studied the list of names at the bottom and eventually found Nicklin. The boy had moved as the shot was taken and his face was blurry, but it looked as though he was grinning. By nineteen eighty-three, Palmer and Nicklin were standing together. Palmer stared straight at the camera, his face flat. Nicklin's head, at the level of the taller boy's shoulder, was bowed slightly, but his eyes were up, dark and full of challenge.

Thorne leaned in close to the photograph.

'Hello, Stuart . . .'

After a moment, Thorne moved on to the 'eighty-four picture, pressing his nose up to the glass. Again, Nicklin's head was looking away from the camera as he whispered something to Palmer who stood stiffly beside him wearing an odd smile.

Thorne moved on, scanned the 'eighty-five picture, but of course, neither Palmer nor Nicklin were there. He moved back, looked again at the blurred features, the face turned away. He knew that it wasn't possible, but he couldn't help imagining that seventeen years before, Nicklin had been deliberately trying to hide. Even then, as a thirteen-year-old boy, he'd somehow foreseen the day when someone like Thorne would be staring at the picture, looking at him.

Looking for him.

Cookson turned to Holland. 'Probably a stupid question, but . . . this is the first time you've seen him, right?' Holland nodded. 'Well, couldn't you have got pictures off his family?'

It wasn't a stupid question.

Nicklin's family had been traced quickly. Only the mother was still alive; nearly seventy and living in warden-controlled housing. Holland had made the call. The old woman's voice had been a little quivery, but clear. Holland had introduced himself and explained that her son's name had come up in connection with an enquiry and that he had a few simple questions. Her answers had been all but monosyllabic. Had she seen him? *No*. Had she had any contact with him? *No*. Holland had had no doubt that she had been telling the truth, but found it disturbing that she seemed to have no interest whatsoever in what her son, missing these last fifteen years, might have been doing or where he might be. She had asked nothing.

It was her answer to Holland's last question, which he had thrown in as if it were an afterthought, that had been oddest. Chilling, even. He'd asked if she wouldn't mind letting them have a few photographs, she'd get them back of course, the most recent would be best, something taken just before Stuart had left home maybe . . .

That would not be possible, she'd said. Mrs Nicklin had explained calmly that she didn't have any photographs at all of her son Stuart. Not one.

It was strange, but not the end of the world. Thorne had been unconvinced, in light of what Palmer had said, that a fifteen-year-old picture would have been a lot of use anyway.

Holland asked the teacher where he could find the nearest toilet and excused himself.

Cookson wore a moleskin jacket, button-down shirt and chinos. Thorne thought he looked rather preppy. The sound of expensive American loafers kissing the polished floor echoed as Cookson led him up a flight of stairs and down a long, straight corridor. It was a far cry from the lumbering sadists in corduroy jackets or tracksuits that Thorne remembered.

Cookson stared through the window into every classroom they passed. They were looking for Ken Bowles, a maths teacher, and the only member of staff who'd been here in the early eighties, at the same time as Palmer and Nicklin.

Thorne wondered why so few teachers from that time were still here. It wasn't much more than fifteen years, after all.

'Teachers used to stick around a lot longer in one place,' Cookson said, 'but not any more. It's easy to . . . stagnate, and money's always an issue. This is a good school. If you've done a couple of years here, there's a fair chance you can double your money in the private sector. The place up the road poaches a few every couple of years . . .'

Thorne was leading the way. He looked into the next classroom, saw an old man with tufty white hair, sitting at a desk and staring out of the window. 'What about you?'

'Been tempted, but . . . well, I'm still here. Seven years this year, and I'm already one of the old farts.' Cookson looked past Thorne into the classroom. 'Yep . . . here we go . . .'

He knocked on the door, pushed it and held it open for Thorne. 'I'll maybe see you later then . . .'

Sarah McEvoy took another swig from the bottle on her desk. She'd already got through a couple of bottles, but the water couldn't get rid of the dry mouth or the sour taste at the back of her throat any better than the cigarettes could.

She was still feeling guilty, having barked at a DC five minutes before. She was taking it out on a junior officer, as it had already been taken out on her. She'd arrived late, feeling rough, and a bollocking from Brigstocke had done nothing to help her feel better. The bad mood was being passed around the investigation like a virus, while the man who'd caused it was off at some school chasing ghosts.

They should all have been on a high since Palmer had fallen into their laps, but that would have been far too easy for Tom Thorne. It was as if he had some aversion to a morale that was anything except down in the fucking dust. As if every minute that passed without catching the second killer was their fault. As if he wanted to see shame etched onto the face of every officer and a hair shirt hanging in every locker. While he was content to let a murderer walk about, breathing the same air as normal people.

She screwed her eyes tight shut; tried to calm herself

down a little. She knew that Thorne was only doing what he believed was right.

She'd been feeling edgier by the day since the holiday. A couple of long, long days trapped in her parents' house in Mill Hill. Like she gave a toss about Chanukah anyway, with her tedious brother and his dull-as-ditchwater family. She had been desperate to get out, needing to be among strangers.

She'd found all the strangers she'd needed over New Year. The faces, strobed in white or lit up by the flashing reds and greens, had been reassuringly unfamiliar and the nights had become longer and louder, and altogether fucking fantastic, and suddenly – not in terms of the time, but in terms of her *realising* it – suddenly, dragging herself into work in the morning . . . some mornings, had become painful.

And Thorne and Brigstocke didn't fucking well like her anyway. The pair of them, commenting on her clothes and the way she looked, which she knew damn well they would never have done if she didn't have tits.

She reached for the water bottle and unscrewed the cap. Her mobile rang.

'McEvoy.'

'It's Holland . . .'

She took a mouthful of water while she waited for Holland to say what it was he wanted, but he didn't. She listened to the hiss on the line, swallowed, and wiped her mouth on the sleeve of her shirt. 'What?'

Another few seconds of hiss. 'Nothing urgent. Just touching base.'

Touching base? 'What cop show did you see that in?'

'Sorry?'

'Forget it. Just being a sarky cow. Where's Thorne?'

'Trying to track down Nicklin's old teacher . . .'

As McEvoy listened, the DC she'd shouted at earlier walked past her desk. McEvoy smiled – an attempt at an apology. The DC gave her nothing back. 'You sound all echoey.'

'I'm in the toilets,' Holland said. 'Nice to see that posh kids piss on the floor as well.'

'They're not that posh, are they?'

'I didn't see many of them playing football in the playground.'

'Yeah, but not like . . . Biscuit Game posh.'

'Eh . . . ?'

McEvoy laughed. 'I'll tell you later.'

'That's one thing they'll miss out on though,' Holland said. 'Being an all boys school . . .'

'What?'

'The sheer, unbridled pleasure of running into the girls' toilets and screaming your head off.'

McEvoy remembered the very same thing happening at her school. She suddenly pictured herself, twelve going on twenty-five, shaking her head in disgust as she listened to the whoops and cheers of half a dozen testosterone-crazed, adolescent boys. She grinned at the memory. This phone call was doing her a lot of good. 'Why did you do that anyway? I could never work it out.'

'I think it was a genetic thing. Marking your territory or something . . .'

McEvoy glanced up. On the other side of the incident room she could see Brigstocke talking to Steve Norman. Brigstocke looked across at her, then Norman. Weaselly little fucker. She wondered whether they'd heard her laughing. She took another sip of water, her mouth still sticky. 'So, anything of interest?'

'Not really, you?'

'Nothing. Derek bloody Lickwood's been on the phone again, demanding to know what's going on. He reckons he's being kept in the dark, keeps threatening to come over and make trouble. Why should I have to deal with him?'

'Short straw. Lovell was his case so we've got to work with him. The boss reckons you'd be better at it than he would . . .' McEvoy grunted. 'What about Palmer?'

'At work.' She said no more than that, but there was an edge to her voice. The unspoken bit was obvious. *At work, totting up figures and drinking coffee, when he should be sitting against a rough stone wall listening to keys turning in locks; his knees pulled tight against his chest, his heart thumping, his belt and shoelaces taken away.*

She would never criticise Thorne to Holland. Besides, she knew, somewhere, that her judgement was perhaps a little off these days. Her thinking was maybe a bit extreme . . .

'Right,' Holland said. 'Do you want to grab a beer later?'

She looked across at Brigstocke. He and Norman were still deep in conversation. 'I've never been propositioned by a man in a toilet before.' She could *hear* Holland blush. 'I'm joking Holland.'

'Yeah . . .'

She murmured huskily into the phone. 'I've been propositioned by men in toilets *loads* of times.'

Holland didn't laugh.

McEvoy puffed out her cheeks, blew out the air noisily. She reached for the bottle of water. It was empty. 'Listen, Dave . . .'

'I just meant . . . a beer. That's all.'

She tried not to snap at him, but couldn't help herself. 'I know.'

'If they were in my class it's because they had a particular aptitude for mathematics, but I don't remember either one of them covering himself in glory.'

Thorne nodded patiently. Ken Bowles didn't seem to remember a great deal about anything. He knew that teaching was a stressful profession but Bowles could not possibly be as old as he looked. He had hair the colour of confectioner's custard and leathery grey skin. Behind the wire-framed spectacles the eyes were watery, and he had big discoloured teeth, like old-fashioned sweets in a jar, which clacked noisily together when he spoke and sometimes when he didn't.

'You do remember Palmer and Nicklin being close?' Thorne asked.

Bowles pushed himself away from the edge of the desk with a small grunt and moved across to the window. His tie was askew and there were chalk marks around his crotch. 'I don't recall a great deal about them at all. I don't think I liked either of them very much but that isn't unusual. Maths is the lesson where the most disruption occurs. The taller one . . . was that Palmer?' Thorne nodded. 'He let himself get distracted by his friend. *There* . . .' He pointed to a corner of the room. 'The two of them messing about at the back. Passing notes and laughing. Palmer's homework was good, I think, but in class he was . . . somewhere else.'

'Could you not have split them up? Moved Palmer to the front . . . ?'

Bowles shrugged, stared out of the window. 'I never really had them for that long, you see. They would probably have gone into different streams anyway that September, but of course they got expelled.' He raised his hand, rubbed with a finger at a dirty spot on the window. 'An older boy, can't remember his name. They grabbed him outside the school gates, dragged him into the park, I think . . .'

Thorne knew the story. Palmer had told him. His eyes filling behind his glasses, the nodding slow and sorrowful as he looked back at himself down the wrong end of the telescope, sweating as he relived it. Each detail preserved in the hideous aspic of shameful memory. The big feet in scuffed brogues, rooted to the spot, refusing to carry him away. The thick fingers, closing slowly around the brown, pimpled grip of the air pistol.

Thorne knew then that this had been the moment when everything had changed. From then on it had been unavoidable. He thought about what Bowles had just told him. A couple more months and Palmer and Nicklin would have been in different streams, moving along different paths; Nicklin's influence on the younger boy not as strong. Would they have drifted apart then? Might a few months, all those years ago, have saved the lives of five women?

At *least* five women . . .

There was a knock at the door and Holland entered. Thorne nodded in his direction. 'This is Detective Constable Holland . . .'

Bowles peered theatrically across the room, feigning shock. 'Looks like a bloody sixth former.' Holland shrugged and smiled at the feeble joke.

'Did you follow their progress after they'd been expelled?' Thorne asked.

The teacher shook his head vigorously. 'Didn't miss either of them for a second. Nicklin was nothing but trouble and Palmer was just a big blob. Not his fault, I suppose. Boys his age can be terribly awkward, find it difficult to fit in. Like a lump of Plasticine that needs shaping. Palmer just got shaped by the wrong person, I think.'

Thorne nodded at Holland. Time to make a move. 'Thanks Mr Bowles.' Thorne handed over a card, which Bowles took without looking at it. 'If there's anything else that occurs to you . . .'

'I taught myself to juggle when I was younger,' Bowles announced. 'I'd do a bit for the class. Last day of term, that sort of thing. I can remember doing it for their class – Palmer and Nicklin's class. Cascade of five balls, six on a good day. Balancing a chair . . .' He pointed at a heavy looking wooden chair behind the desk on the platform. '. . . one of *those* chairs, on my chin. Do you know that Marsden's younger than I am?'

Thorne was itching to get away. 'Sorry, sir?'

'Headmaster. They brought Marsden in a couple of years ago, from outside. I'm ten years older than he is.' He threw his arms wide, as if the sense of what he was saying was obvious for all to see. 'Be glad to get out of here to tell you the truth. Can't even manage three balls these days . . .'

Holland opened the door, and Thorne gratefully took a few steps towards it. 'We'll be on our way, sir.'

Bowles nodded and spoke quietly. 'What's Nicklin done?'

'I'm afraid we can't . . .'

'Of course not, I'm sorry I asked. Do you know, I hadn't

thought about either of those boys in years until I was told it was them you wanted to talk to me about? I've taught hundreds of boys. I can't remember most of them to be honest. I can recall the *work* sometimes, but not faces. Ever since I heard those two names again, I've been thinking about them a good deal. Thinking about *him*. There's a look on your face, Inspector Thorne, whenever you talk about him, did you know that?'

Thorne knew it would be pointless to deny it, to express surprise. His face hid nothing. It never had. Not the scorn he felt for some, not the pity for others. The creases in his face folded as naturally into genuine expressions of horror, disgust and rage as those of a bad actor might shape themselves into their phoney counterparts. His face fell easily into darkness; the scowl more at home there than the smile. Though the smile was the rarer, it was arguably the more powerful.

Both had got him into plenty of trouble.

Bowles moved to the door to show them out. 'I suspect that now I shall be thinking about Stuart Nicklin often.' The watery eyes studied Thorne's face. 'The boy's moved on from air pistols, hasn't he?'

Thorne thought about Rosemary Vincent: the memory of an argument on the phone, the photograph turned over and over in her hand that day at the press conference. The hole in her precious daughter's head.

The shadow moved across Thorne's face as he answered the teacher's question.

'Yes. He's moved on.'

He was thinking about something that had happened a long time ago.

Years earlier, back when he'd still been Stuart Nicklin and supporting himself by tossing off sad old men and confused young ones, he'd learned about making the appropriate response to a situation. Another rent boy, a spiteful little prick who was older and uglier, had stolen some of his customers. Not his regulars, they were loyal, but some of the passing trade. The fucker was undercutting, a tenner here, twenty notes there, a bit more cash and we'll forget about the condom – poaching punters to make some last ditch money before his looks went altogether. Understandable, but very bloody annoying.

He was furious. He wanted to do something to punish the thieving toerag, the little bitch, but he knew that the sensible thing, the *appropriate* thing to do would be to ignore it. Let it go and move on. There were plenty of punters to go around and there was no need to risk trouble with the police. No need to rock the boat. That would be stupid.

He was also thinking about what was happening right now.

They were afraid he was going to disappear. Scared shitless that, with his partner taken, he would pack up and head for the hills. If that was what they were afraid of, he knew that it was exactly what he should do. It was the appropriate response. They didn't want him to melt away and then resurface when the time was right to start again. So, that was the right thing for him to do. It was simple and sensible. It was self-preservation.

It would be hard, there was no question of that. He loved what he was doing. He was very good at it and he loved that too. It was a rush like nothing he could remember, and even without the added buzz of the other, even without Palmer playing along for real, he knew that not doing it would be like dulling all his senses. Stopping would be like cutting off the oxygen to the very best part of himself. Giving it up would be like going to sleep for a while. It wouldn't be for ever, it might not even have to be for very long, but it would be very bloody hard. Still, it made sense. It was the appropriate thing to do, so he would have to try.

He would try to stop.

Years earlier, back when he'd still been Stuart Nicklin, having decided not to do anything stupid, he'd made a few calls and lured the thieving rent boy to an empty flat he sometimes used off Glasshouse Street. It was February and freezing. From the small window he could see the crowds in scarves and heavy coats, moving across Piccadilly Circus. He could just make out the icicles dangling from the bow of Eros and the frost on the steps leading up to the statue, sparkling in the multicoloured neon from the vast signs above.

When the boy arrived, Nicklin beat him unconscious with a housebrick, stuck a funnel in his mouth and poured a gallon of bright blue anti-freeze down his throat.

In its own way, an appropriate response. After all, it was a very cold night.

He was thinking.

He would *try* to stop . . .

Thorne, too, was thinking about something that had happened a long time ago . . .

The boy he'd last seen trudging towards school sporting a feather cut, though he wasn't an awful lot taller, had at least filled out a little.

It was three years later. It was twenty-five years ago.

Boxing Day. Nineteen seventy-six. A two-all draw at home against Arsenal, ground out on a snowy pitch with an orange ball. An acceptable result in a season that was going from bad to worse.

His dad had stayed up near the ground for a pint with his mates, leaving him to make his own way back. He trudged up the Seven Sisters Road, the dark slush soaking through his boots, filling his turn-ups. The black and white scarf worn as much for warmth as to declare allegiance.

They looked like grown men from a distance, but as they got close, he could see that they were only a year or two older than he was. They were bigger too, with green Harrington jackets, and red and white scarves.

He brushed shoulders with one as they passed and a look was exchanged. He had shrugged slightly and smiled.

Two apiece. A fair enough result, don't you reckon?

A few minutes later he heard the footsteps thumping behind him and before he had a chance to react, the first of them was on his back, an arm around his neck, driving him face first on to the icy pavement.

Cars roared past, spraying water and light across the three figures, but not slowing down.

He pushed himself up on to his knees and got the first of several punches in the face. As the fists came down, he deflected some with his arms, feeling something crack in his hand at the same time as something long and heavy smashed across his shoulder blades. He was crying and straining to get down on to the floor so he could pull his knees up to his chest. He could no longer tell which were the grunts of pain and which were the dull sounds of fists clubbing into cheekbone and shoulder.

He heard a voice and saw the shadow of an arm reaching across him. The biggest of the Arsenal fans stepped over him, cursing, and finally, he was free to drop back to the floor. He rolled over, moaning, and as he began to crawl away, he turned to see them laying into an older man in shirt sleeves. One of them had him by the hair while the other casually brought his forehead down into the man's face. The man was Greek, he thought, maybe Cypriot. Difficult to tell with all the blood. Perhaps he was a shopkeeper who had heard the noise and stepped out to intervene. He shouted and swore as the two thugs pushed him down into the wet gutter and drew back their feet.

Tom Thorne began to shout too, then, for someone to come. Shouting for help as the first kicks went into the groin and stomach. Shouting even louder than the man on the floor as the boots flew in again and again. Shouting for help and running away, fast . . .

He moved around the flat, turning off the lights, very ready for bed. He smiled, remembering the way his dad had ranted from the terraces: foul-mouthed and usually wide of the mark. '*Hoddle, you're fucking useless!*'

He wondered what had become of the man who'd tried to help him and got a good kicking for his trouble. He probably hadn't made the same mistake again.

He still felt guilty that he hadn't gone back. He'd scanned the papers for days afterwards but found nothing. The man was probably not seriously hurt, but the boy couldn't forget the pain and fury on his face. Twenty-five years on and Thorne could still see it, and hear the soggy thump as the man had crashed down on to his back in the slush.

Thorne closed the bedroom door, sat down on the side of the bed and started to undo his shoelaces. Twenty years a copper and he still couldn't understand why they'd attacked him.

He'd only smiled at them.

FOURTEEN

Thorne thought: so this is old age.

A heavy chair near the television, with its shit-coloured seat covered in plastic and panic buttons everywhere. Handles around the bath and piss-soaked knickers in the sink, and a woman who couldn't really give a toss, popping round twice a day to see if you're dead yet.

'Do you take sugar, Mrs Nicklin?' McEvoy stuck her head round the kitchen door.

Annie Nicklin shook her head at nobody in particular and Thorne relayed the answer to McEvoy with a more obvious gesture of his own. Though she hadn't said a lot, the woman in the heavy chair, with her clawed hands resting on top of a green blanket, was still fairly sharp mentally, but her body was on the way out. Arthritis, diabetes, angina . . . the catalogue of diseases had been reeled off cheerfully by the warden – a hard-faced article named Margaret – as she'd shown them into Annie's flat and explained that they wouldn't get a great deal out of her. Nobody ever did.

McEvoy brought the tea through, and as she handed round the mugs, Thorne continued to ponder the question that had absorbed him since he'd walked through the door. Which was preferable? A good brain and a body that was fucked? Or hale and hearty flesh and bone, with nothing left up top? Obviously, nobody ever really got the choice, but still, Thorne couldn't help weighing it up. Considering the options. It looked as if his old man was heading down the second road, but Thorne reckoned that when it came to it, he'd prefer to go to pieces upstairs *and* downstairs. At least that way, if he were sitting in his own mess, he'd be blissfully unaware of the fact . . .

He sipped his tea and thought about meeting Ken Bowles the day before. There was a man who could see pain and loneliness just up ahead. He took a biscuit and thought about the Enrights. As if the everyday agonies of old age weren't bad enough.

He had the same old thoughts about the boy, Charlie Garner, who was no age at all. His life still ahead of him and already blighted. His mother taken away by the son of the old lady sitting a few feet away, slurping tea in a shit-coloured chair covered with plastic.

Thorne stared at Annie Nicklin. When she had looked at her son, at Stuart, back when he was no older than Charlie Garner, what had she seen in his future? What had she dreamed he might become?

'That all right for you, Annie?' McEvoy asked.

Mrs Nicklin nodded again, slurped a bit more, continued to stare at the television screen, even though it wasn't switched on.

Thorne hoisted his behind from the depths of the soft, springless sofa and leaned forwards. 'We just wanted to ask you about Stuart.'

Nothing. Just the noise of the drinking. The endless *beep beep* of a lorry reversing somewhere. A dog howling in one of the other flats.

Thorne looked across at McEvoy, raised an eyebrow. *You have a crack, and keep it nice.*

McEvoy, much to her annoyance, had won that morning's toss-up. Thorne had not been able to decide which would work better with the old woman – Holland's boyish, floppy-haired charm or the empathy of a younger woman? The coin had picked McEvoy and in the car on the way out to Stanmore, with Thorne driving *and* trying to coax any kind of warmth out of the Mondeo's knackered heater, she'd not been shy about why she was pissed off about it . . .

'I don't particularly feel like wheedling stuff out of a sweet old lady whose son happens to be a psychopath. You don't need to have read a lot of textbooks to figure that she might have something to do with that.'

Thorne hadn't read a single textbook and he was having none of it. 'What? Did she lock him in the coalshed? Make him wear women's clothes and lipstick? We need to talk to this woman, and frankly, I couldn't be less interested in a debate on nature versus nurture . . .'

McEvoy clearly didn't care whether he was interested or not. 'Nurture, every time. Every time.'

Thorne stopped at traffic lights and yanked up the handbrake. 'Supposing you're right. You aren't, but supposing you are . . .' – McEvoy said nothing, stared out of the window – 'what about Nicklin's father? Why can't he have been the one who beat poor little Stuart with a coathanger or whatever?' Palmer had already told him that Nicklin's father had left home when he was still a toddler.

Nobody knew, or by all accounts cared, if he was alive or dead.

For a few moments, McEvoy thought about what Thorne had said, or at least pretended to. 'No. Mothers and sons. Fathers and daughters . . .'

Thorne leaned on the horn as a white van roared away from the lights and swerved in front of him. 'You've never met my father, have you?' McEvoy didn't laugh, so Thorne stopped being nice about it. 'Listen, if there's anything this woman can tell us that might help, I want to hear it OK? You're a copper, not an amateur shrink, so go in there and do your job . . .'

McEvoy had been laying it on with a trowel ever since they'd got there.

'Maybe we could start with when Stuart left home, Annie.'

The old woman cleared her throat. Her chest rattled for a second or two after she'd finished. Then she spoke. 'That's where it starts and where it finishes. He left. The end.' It was her longest sentence so far. Thorne looked at McEvoy. *Carry on . . .*

'So you never heard from him?'

Annie Nicklin picked up an empty teacup, looked at it, put it down again. 'There was a letter once, from London.'

'Do you still have it?'

She turned her head slowly round to look at them and smiled, though she was clearly in some pain. 'I never opened it.'

'Did you not want to know where he was?' Thorne asked.

He couldn't be sure whether she was choosing to ignore him or the question. Either way, she wasn't answering.

McEvoy moved on. 'He left in September 1985, is that right?'

The old woman nodded.

'Just like that? Out of the blue?'

'I wasn't . . . hugely surprised.'

Thorne thought: *or bothered . . .*

'This was a month or so after the disappearance of Karen McMahon?' Mrs Nicklin licked her lips, stared ahead. McEvoy tried again. 'When Stuart left, that would have been about a month after . . . ?'.

With a small moan, Mrs Nicklin reached for the stick that was propped against her chair and, grunting with the effort, she pointed with it to a bottle of pills on top of the television. Thorne stood up and fetched the bottle. 'These?' He opened the bottle. 'How many? Just one?' Mrs Nicklin nodded and he handed her a tablet. There was a glass of water on the tray attached to her chair and he passed it to her. She swallowed.

Thorne sat down again. Pills for Annie's body which was giving up the ghost. Still sharp up top though. Sharp enough to understand everything. To decide when might be a good moment to take a tablet in order to avoid a question she didn't want to answer . . .

'Was he upset about Karen? Was that why he left?' McEvoy was craning her head round, trying to make eye contact. 'How much was he seeing of Martin Palmer before he left?' Somewhere, the dog was still crying, and now, Annie Nicklin was avoiding McEvoy's questions as well.

Thorne pushed himself up, stepped in front of her. She began to click her tongue and tried to move her head. Thorne stood solid, between the old woman and the television that wasn't on.

The gentleness had gone from Thorne's voice. 'Tell me about Karen, Mrs Nicklin.' There was a low moan from deep in her throat but that was as communicative as she was getting. Thorne leaned down close to her, very little patience left. 'Tell me about Karen McMahon.'

The case had begun to ring a bell when Palmer had first mentioned the name. Thorne remembered it of course, but not well – a missing girl, a nationwide search – the details were vague. When he found out the date he realised why. The summer of 1985. He had been . . . absorbed by a case of his own at the time. *Johnny Boy*. Francis John Calvert, a killer of gay men, who felt that the police were getting too close. So close that he had had no choice . . .

The nightmare a young DC called Thorne had walked into . . .

'Tell me about Karen.'

He could see the pale, paper-thin flesh around her jaw constrict across the wasted muscle as she gritted her false teeth. With what little movement was left in her clawed fingers, she grasped at the blanket across her lap, pulling it close to her.

'Tell us and we'll go, Annie,' McEvoy said.

'She got into a car.' She spoke slowly and with emphasis, as if explaining something terribly complicated. Just to make sure Thorne understood, she said it again. 'She got into a car.'

'When she was with Stuart?'

'After. A bit after that. She was ahead of him and the car pulled up.'

'The blue Vauxhall Cavalier . . .'

She stared down at her blanket, clutched at it. 'You know all this.'

Thorne shook his head. She looked away. 'Stuart must have been very upset. He saw it all happen, didn't he?'

She turned back to him quickly. 'Yes. He was upset. He never stopped crying afterwards. Stuart saw everything. He saw her get into the car. He saw the man who was driving it. He told the police what the man who was driving the car looked like, you can check.'

'He told the police? Or he told you and then *you* told the police?'

'Both, both.' She tut-tutted and one liver-spotted hand began to rap lightly on the arm of her chair.

McEvoy was on her feet now, standing directly behind Annie Nicklin's chair. 'This man, the man that Stuart saw, did he grab Karen? Did he get out of the car? Force her?' McEvoy might just as well have been talking to herself. She stared at Thorne across the white hair of Annie Nicklin's bowed head. She shrugged. *Enough?*

Despite what Thorne had said to McEvoy in the car on the way over, he had an urge to shout at this old woman, to bully her. He raised his voice only slightly, but as soon as he began to speak, Annie Nicklin raised her head. She met his gaze for the first time, and held it.

'Did Stuart have any idea why? If this man didn't force her, did Stuart have any idea *why* Karen McMahon got into his car? Did he tell you that, Annie?'

Thorne could feel his hard stare being returned with interest. Then, as if the movement was painful, she dragged her eyes away from his and down towards the floor, one hand clasping the blanket for dear life and the other reaching for the walking stick.

It was only after a few seconds that Thorne became aware of what was happening and glanced down. The knocking of the stick against his shin was almost imperceptible. The impact of the rubber tip against the bone was feeble, but the impulse behind the movement was anything but. Annie Nicklin was poking and prodding, trying to push him away, to poke and push him away. Jabbing and pushing at him . . .

In time with the jerky movements of her withered arm and knotted stick, she spoke. Her voice was clear and high, and the tone of it took on a strange sing-song quality as she spoke the same five words over and over again.

'She got into a car . . .'

Urging the Mondeo back towards Hendon, along the bizarrely named Honeypot Lane, Thorne pictured a girl in a white dress – he had no idea what Karen McMahon had really been wearing, but it had been a summer's day – pulling open the door of a blue car, pushing a strand of hair behind her ear and climbing in.

At the edge of the picture stood a boy called Stuart Nicklin, blurry, with his head slightly bowed, but with those dark eyes taking in every detail. Absent, but very much there, like a phantom image or a double exposure, was a man named Martin Palmer, still utterly fucked up nearly twenty years later.

There was something wrong with the picture . . .

'So, nature or nurture?' McEvoy said, as they got near to Becke House.

Thorne smiled. 'I'm saying nothing.'

'A lot like the old woman then . . .'

Thorne had to agree. 'I've known armed robbers, rapists . . . I've interviewed axe murderers who gave it up easier.' McEvoy laughed, but Thorne was being deadly serious. 'If Nicklin's got a fraction of that determination, or that . . . cunning, we're in trouble.'

'What about Palmer's parents?'

Thorne shook his head. There was really no need, and besides, they would know what was happening soon enough. One phone call from Palmer, a day or two after he'd given himself up, had established how Nicklin had tracked him down. 'Oh yes, a nice boy you were at school with called, trying to get hold of you . . . didn't leave his name . . . wanted it to be a surprise, I think.' Beyond that, there was nothing useful to be had out of them. Eventually, it would just be about giving them the bad news.

He was intrigued, but also a little relieved that Annie Nicklin had shown no interest in news of any sort about *her* son or his whereabouts. That would have been decidedly tricky.

'*Oh yes, he's turned up . . . But . . .*'

At the Peel Centre, they pulled up to the security barrier and Thorne fished around for his ID. McEvoy leaned across him and showed hers to the officer on duty. After a moment, the barrier lifted and Thorne nudged the car towards the parking bays.

'Got plans this evening?' Thorne asked.

McEvoy turned away and stared out of the window. There were a dozen or so recruits working with dogs on the far side of the compound. 'Not really. Early night, I think. You?'

'Myself and Mr Philip Hendricks have a hot date with Sky Sports and a Chinese takeaway.'

'Sounds good . . .'

'Yeah, if you don't mind being a relationship counsellor when you're trying to watch the match.' He pulled a face for McEvoy's benefit, but really he was looking forward to Hendricks coming over.

Unwinding. Letting a little of it go . . .

Thorne guided the car into a space next to Brigstocke's Volvo estate and killed the engine. He stared up at the dun-coloured walls and peeling olive paintwork of the three-storey sixties' monstrosity they had the misfortune to work in. If management had any sense, and a desire to maintain levels of recruitment, they would have instructed the film crew to make sure they kept the cameras well away from Becke House.

'It's a phenomenally ugly building,' McEvoy said, after a few moments.

Thorne nodded, thinking: *We're in it, trying to catch people who do phenomenally ugly things.*

McEvoy pushed in the button to release her seat belt. 'What's on this afternoon?'

Thorne took a deep breath. 'Well, I'm going to make a few calls, try and find out what's going to cost more, fixing the heater or replacing the car.'

'About bloody time. I'll be spending the next half an hour trying to get some feeling back into my feet . . .' Thorne laughed. 'It's ridiculous. Why don't you use the car you've been assigned?'

Thorne shrugged. 'I don't know . . . it's brown.'

McEvoy was gobsmacked by Thorne's answer, and by how much he suddenly looked like a confused and sulky teenager. 'So, get another one . . .'

'I like this car,' Thorne said. 'It's got all my tapes and stuff.'

'Oh right, yeah. Dolly Parton and Tammy Wynette.'

Thorne sighed and opened the door. 'I'm going to kill

Holland. No, I'm going to make him listen to some proper country music and *then* I'm going to kill him . . .'

McEvoy climbed out of the car, snickering like the cartoon dog in *Wacky Races*. 'It wasn't his fault. He didn't say . . .'

'Actually, fuck that, the music would be wasted on him anyway. I'll just kill him.' Thorne turned the key in the lock, looked at McEvoy across the Mondeo's roof. 'While I'm busy killing Detective Constable Holland, I want you to do something for me.'

'I think I'm already doing quite enough keeping Derek Lickwood away from you. He knows you're avoiding him.'

Thorne smiled. 'Don't worry, it's a lot easier than that.' McEvoy waited. 'Get on the phone for me, and find out who was in charge of the Karen McMahon case.'

Alf from Stoke-on-Trent: 'Hanging's too good for these bastards. I'd happily pull the lever myself . . .'

He shook his head and broke off another big piece of the chocolate bar, thinking: *Come on, Alf, you can't have it both ways*. Still, he knew that this was how a fair proportion of the British public thought that he, and others like him, should be dealt with. This was what they considered an appropriate response.

The phone-in host, who was normally there to play devil's advocate, agreed wholeheartedly with Alf, and the two of them began to gleefully discuss whether or not, if we ever came to our senses and brought back capital punishment, we should stick to the noose or perhaps move into the twenty-first century and go for lethal injection.

He closed his eyes, tuned out the chat.

Others like him . . .

He couldn't say that he'd ever actually met *anybody* else like him. Not really. He'd run into his fair share of those for whom respect for the law was a luxury, and some whose moral framework had never existed or had been eaten away. He'd known plenty of men desperate enough to consider anything, but never an individual who was happy to consider *every*thing. This fact didn't disturb him, but neither did it give him any great comfort. He just accepted it as the way of things. He wasn't arrogant enough to believe that he was completely unique. He accepted that one day he might stare across a street, or along a station platform, or even at a television screen and recognise a look in someone's eye.

It was a look he'd certainly never seen in Martin Palmer's eye. Now it was time to get in touch with his old friend again.

He got up from the armchair and crossed the room to where the laptop computer, bought for cash in Dixons the day before, lay on the dining table. He switched it on, and while it was booting up, he fetched the freshly cloned mobile he'd picked up in south London on the way home. He'd ditch the computer and the phone the next morning on the way in to work.

He had always been careful to vary his methods. Opening up any one of a hundred free e-mail accounts was easy, and he always took care to make the hardware as near to untraceable as possible. The first few times, he'd simply walked into an Internet cafe. He preferred the smaller places – converted greasy spoons that advertised cheap photocopying, and had a couple of grubby, first-issue iMacs lined up in a back room. These places were tucked away, almost invisible between massage parlours and dodgy minicab firms: places that even the backpackers didn't know about, where no-one served cappuccino or gave a toss about what porn sites you accessed. These were places without CCTV.

He'd moved on to laptops which were, of course, ideal for his purposes, and then it had just been a case of where to plug the things in. This wouldn't be the first time he'd used a stolen mobile – he had a contact who knocked them out for next to nothing – but in the past, he'd also enjoyed the telecommunications facilities offered by a number of shitty hotels in and around central London. Just a matter of checking in, logging on and fucking off. If, and it was a very big *if*, the place was ever traced, nobody would have any memory of the anonymous businessman with the small leather carrycase.

He connected the phone to the laptop and sat down in front of it. He began to give some thought to what he was going to write. He always liked to get the wording right.

It was funny, he'd almost predicted that something like this would happen, that in some strange way his hand would be forced, his mind made up for him. Now, he had no choice but to respond. The response, appropriate or not, was pretty much the only one he could make.

He logged on and the computer began to dial. In a matter of minutes he'd opened a new account, invented a name and created a password. He enjoyed assuming fresh identities whether they lasted many years or just a few hours in a dingy hotel room. He even relished those which, like this one, he would only ever need to assume in cyberspace for the few short minutes it took to send a handful of words across the city.

Pretty much the only response he could make . . .

He wasn't sure exactly *what* Thorne had been hoping to

gain by going to the school, but there it was. He snapped off another chunk of chocolate. The Detective Inspector was clearly not a man whose actions were predictable or immediately explicable. That was all right.

Neither was he.

He laid out his instructions in the e-mail with the usual care. There was to be no misunderstanding. He had always strived to make it straightforward for Palmer, to make everything clear. Martin had always needed that.

Do this, now. Do that, only when I tell you.

What was *less* clear, at least right now, was exactly why he was bothering to do this at all. Why was he sending these details to Palmer in the first place? Why was he issuing instructions which would never be followed, except in the creation of a newspaper story about a murder that had not taken place? Mind you, once the murder that *would be* taking place was discovered, they wouldn't bother making up any more stories anyway.

So why was he going through the motions like this? Why was he playing their game?

Palmer had chosen to remove himself from the equation and in doing so had taken away with him some of the . . . mustard. Dulled that extra buzz. Maybe he could get a little of it back this way. He *needed* to get it back, to go along with their not-so-clever bit of let's pretend, and see where it led all of them.

But that wasn't the only reason.

If he was being honest, he liked his routines and only *he* would decide when they changed. So, yes, it was a refusal . . . an *absolute* refusal to relinquish control, but it was also, he had to admit, because of a perverse desire to . . . carry on as normal. Business as usual, at least for the time being. He'd always had a sneaking admiration for that very British breed of nutcase who treated flood, fire or pestilence as no more than a minor inconvenience and refused to adapt. There was never any need to move house, or see a doctor or make a scene. Stubborn and stupid. Brave and barking mad. It worked the other way round, of course. It was only ever in this country that people could win millions on the lottery and decide to carry on working in a factory. Of course, in the end, those morons always *did* adapt, and so would he, when he absolutely had to. It wasn't rocket science, after all. Go with the flow, or rot where you stood. Adapt or get caught.

For now though, he'd suck it and see.

He heard Caroline coughing in her sleep upstairs. Poor thing had been feeling rough for a couple of days. As he checked his typing for spelling errors, he made a mental note to pick up some Benylin for her the following day.

He popped the last square of chocolate into his mouth and pressed 'send'.

They rolled apart from each other and lay there, sweating, exhausted.

Holland leaned up on one elbow and whispered mock-seductively into the ear of the woman next to him.

'So, come on, tell me about this mysterious Biscuit Game.'

McEvoy was still getting her breath back and marvelling at how, just an hour and a half before, she'd arrived home to find Holland on her doorstep, clutching a bottle of wine and stammering like a poor man's Hugh Grant.

Seven thirty: awkward exchanges as keys were fumbled for. Twenty past eight: second bottle opened, lying around like students. Nine o'clock: the pair of them, smiling, naked and slippery.

She had definitely been a lot more impulsive lately.

'Come on then . . .'

Was she actually blushing? 'It's just this stupid— It's probably not even true, it's like an urban myth, about this game they play at public schools.' She turned on to her side. He was staring at her, grinning, waiting for her to carry on. 'OK, basically, all the boys stand in a circle wanking.'

'Wanking?'

'Yes, apparently. There's a biscuit in the middle, and they all come on it, and whoever comes last has to eat the biscuit.'

There was a pause worthy of a great comedian before Holland let out a groan of disgust. 'You're making it up.'

McEvoy started to giggle. 'I swear . . .'

'Whoever comes last?'

His look of confusion made her laugh even more. 'I said it was stupid . . .'

'So they're actually being trained to come quickly?'

'I know. Mind you, it certainly explains why all the public schoolboys I've ever shagged have been shit in bed.'

They lay there for a minute, saying nothing, laughing now and again and trying to get their new, rather odd picture of the world into some sort of focus. McEvoy wondered how long he was planning to stay. Holland had just decided that he should be getting home, and was thinking about Sophie for the first time since McEvoy had put her tongue in his mouth and her hand on his cock, when she spoke.

'What about you?'

'What?'

'Were you a public schoolboy?'

Holland raised his head up off the pillow. 'Was I fuck!'

McEvoy's leg slid across his, and her hand began to creep across his stomach. 'Calm down, Holland. I'm kidding. You've already made that *very* obvious.' She smiled as she hoisted herself across him and began wriggling into position.

Holland put a hand on each of her shoulders and looked deep into her eyes. 'What sort do they use?' She looked down at him, confused, so he explained. 'The biscuit. Digestive, custard cream, bourbon . . . ?'

She was still laughing when they'd finished.

Thorne had been right about the relationship counsellor bit. Within ten minutes of the kick-off, he'd learned that Brendan had not, as predicted, buggered off as soon as Hendricks had given him his Christmas presents, but had actually stuck around and was now, miracle of miracles, dropping hints about moving in.

At half time, Thorne got up and threw the remains of the Chinese takeaway into a bin-liner. There wasn't a great deal of anything left, Elvis having licked both plates clean within moments of them putting down their forks for the final time.

He returned with two more cold cans from the fridge. 'So you're happy about this, are you? Brendan staying?' Hendricks looked decidedly unsure. Thorne handed him a can. 'Oh, for fuck's sake, Phil.'

'It's just unexpected. I need to think about it a bit . . .'

'Not easily pleased, are you?'

Thorne opened his beer and slumped back into his

chair. In the studio, some bald bloke who'd won three caps in the early seventies was attempting to make the previous forty-five minutes sound interesting. Aston Villa and Leeds United grinding out a nil-nil draw in the pissing rain was proving to be far from riveting.

'So what does he make of this then? Brendan . . .'

'He's not a football fan, well, not beyond thinking Thierry Henry's got nice legs anyway, so he's not really bothered.'

Thorne took a sip, stared at the TV. 'No, I meant, you know, you coming over here . . .'

For a minute, Hendricks said nothing and Thorne wondered if, like him, he was thinking about what had happened between them a year before.

They had fallen out badly in the middle of a case. Hendricks had told him he was gay, at the same time as telling him what a selfish bastard he was being. Thorne had been gobsmacked by the confession and shamed by the accusation – he knew that Hendricks had a point. His friend had gone out on a limb for him and suffered for it. Thorne hadn't been there to speak up on his friend's behalf when he should have been.

Back then, with the bodies piling up, Thorne hadn't even been there for himself.

It was the death of strangers that had eventually brought them back together, as it had brought them together in the first place.

'You want to know what Brendan thinks about you?'

Thorne shrugged, gestured with his can towards the slow-motion replay on the screen. 'Look, he should have scored, he was clean through. Couldn't hit a cow's arse with a banjo. No . . . just, you know . . .'

'Why is it that eventually, you always get round to asking if my boyfriends fancy you or not?'

'That's bollocks.'

'Don't get me wrong, you're usually quite subtle about it, but there's always some comment, some bit of fishing . . .'

'All in your twisted mind, mate . . .'

'He thinks you're a bit chunky.'

Thorne's show of mock annoyance, the raised voice and wounded expression, barely masked how genuinely pissed off he really was. 'Chunky? What does he mean, "chunky"?'

Hendricks sniggered and reached for the remote. The teams were coming out for the second half. 'Shut up, you tart . . .'

They watched in silence as twenty-two thoroughly bored-looking individuals with bad haircuts jogged half-heartedly out into the rain. Hendricks picked up the remote again and pressed mute.

'What about you anyway? Much going on horizontally?'

'Sod all. Turn the sound back on . . .'

'You never rang Anne Coburn, did you?'

Thorne shook his head and pictured the woman he'd been involved with a year ago.

'Why don't you call her?'

A question Thorne had asked himself often enough. 'No, mate. Far too complicated.'

'Don't worry about it, you're better off on your own.' Hendricks made a wanking gesture. '*That's* . . . not complicated.'

'Right, but the conversation's awful.'

Hendricks turned the volume back up, but not very

high. They said nothing for a minute or two, listened to the pundits doing much the same thing.

'You haven't said a lot about the case . . .' Hendricks said.

Thorne hadn't even mentioned it, but he didn't need to. It was there all the time, the synapses sparking, the associations bursting into life in his brain and forcing themselves upon him, in spite of his best efforts.

Katie Choi's mother and father owned a Chinese restaurant in Forest Hill . . .

The programme on television, sponsored by Vauxhall . . .

Would Charlie Garner grow up supporting Aston Villa now that he lived in the Midlands? Or had he already begun to cheer for a London club? Was Charlie an Arsenal fan like the man lying on the sofa? The man who performed the post-mortem on his mother . . .

Thorne shifted in his chair, looked across at Hendricks. 'Not much to say.'

Hendricks nodded. 'Just waiting . . .'

'Yep, for a lot of things. Some tiny piece of fucking luck. Waiting for them to run out of patience and hand me back my uniform. Waiting for a body to show up.'

'Make it a warm one, will you?'

Thorne raised his eyebrows, snorted. 'We'll do our best, Phil.'

'I want the bastard fresh on her, you know?'

Thorne did know. A warm body, a crime scene crawling with evidence. That was what they all wanted.

He nodded at Hendricks and raised his can to him. His friend was someone you could measure yourself against. Someone Thorne *did* measure himself against. Hendricks's voice was flat, and the words could often sound harsh and ill thought through, but they sprang from somewhere deep and very clean, somewhere passionate and honest.

'Do you think he's still around?' The tone was casual, as if he was asking whether Thorne could see a goal on the cards, second half.

'Oh yeah . . . he's around,' Thorne said. 'It's just a question of whether he decides to let us know about it.'

Hendricks considered this for a moment. 'I think we can count on it. Man who enjoys slicing and dicing as much as he does . . .'

Thorne almost spilt his beer. Even for Hendricks, that was a good one. 'Slicing and dicing? Fuck, and they let you near grieving relatives?'

'Only when they're very short-staffed.'

'Turn it up.' The teams were about to kick off. They let a silence fall between them as they stared at the television, both trying to think about anything but warm bodies and cold slabs.

After about ten minutes Thorne turned to Hendricks again.

'Fucking "*chunky*"?'

The second forty-five minutes was, if anything, less entertaining than the first. This, combined with beer and central heating, and the general level of fatigue that was creeping over everybody on the case, ensured that they were both asleep at just after eleven, when the phone rang.

It was Martin Palmer.

'There's more instructions. He wants to do it again.'

It was as if Thorne had been jolted awake with a cattle prod. 'When?'

'Tomorrow.'

'Fuck.' He looked across at Hendricks who was already walking towards the kitchen mouthing 'coffee'. Thorne nodded.

'He's going to do it again tomorrow.' Palmer sounded as if he was on the verge of tears. 'Can you stop him?'

'Just shut up, Palmer, OK? Shut up. Shit . . .'

Thorne could hear the beep on the line. That would be the boys in IT trying to reach him. They were monitoring Palmer's computer and would have seen the e-mail at the same time he had.

'Palmer . . .'

The beep on the line stopped, and immediately the landline began to ring. Hendricks came through from the kitchen and picked up the phone.

Thorne could have hung up and talked to the technicians, but he wanted to hear it now, that second, from the man it had been sent to. 'Palmer, is there anything else? What does the message say *exactly*?'

Palmer held back the sobs just long enough to tell him.

FIFTEEN

Date: 9 January
Target: Male (Let's not be predictable)
Age: You're as old as you feel
Pickup: Immaterial
Site: Indoors, target's home
Method: Blunt instrument ... in conjunction with a *sharp* mind

The man had once observed the same routine every morning. Moving from room to room and getting himself ready for the day with great care and precision. These days, the effort was all too much. Where once the clean white shirt would have been laid out ready the night before, now he just grabbed another un-ironed one from the pile and often turned the previous day's socks inside out. He put on the kettle and radio, cut himself shaving, then pulled on his rumpled cardigan in front of the heavy, free-standing oak mirror that had been a wedding present, many years earlier. He placed his battered and bulging briefcase next to the front door, made himself a slice of toast and settled down to listen to ten minutes or so of *Today* on Radio 4.

The knock at the door was puzzling, but nothing to be alarmed about. He checked his watch. It was too early for the post. Perhaps it was a neighbour, or the man to read one or other of the meters. He put down his toast, rose slowly from the kitchen chair, and moved towards the front door.

His wife had always used to tease him about his passion for routine, and the way that any disruption to the order of things could put him in a bad mood. Then, perhaps, it had been true, but not any more. These days, a surprise of any sort could be an unexpected fillip. Something to be welcomed with open arms. There was a second knock, a fraction louder, just before he reached the door.

'Just a moment . . .'

When the door was opened, the man with the leather sports bag at his feet smiled, cleared his throat, and punched the man in the creased white shirt, full in the face.

Then he picked up his bag and stepped inside.

The man on the floor held his hand to his shattered nose, but the blood ran through his fingers on to his shirt and on to the carpet. The blood felt strange and warm. It was oddly smooth against his freshly shaved cheeks. He was crying, which annoyed him greatly, and he was desperately trying to clear his head just a little, so that he might reach his shattered spectacles and work out where the noise was coming from. The noise that was like a drumming, like a thumping, like a train passing beneath the floor. The noise that drowned out the sound of the sports bag being opened.

Zzzzzzip . . .

Then a gentle rustle as something was removed from

the bag, and the man on the floor suddenly realised that the mysterious noise was the sound of his own heart smashing against his chest like a trapped animal. He was pleased that he'd worked it out.

Now, there was just the pain in his face, and the terror . . .

He glanced up and his body spasmed, and he cried out a girl's name as he saw the long, dark shape coming down. His eyes screwed shut and his hands flew from his face to his head. Every one of his fingers was broken, a fraction of a second before his skull was shattered.

The man with the cricket bat in his hand needed to get about his business quickly and that annoyed him. It distracted him. With him, the looking . . . the *considering*, had always been as much a part of it as anything. After he killed, he could rarely remember the details of the act itself. His mind had been elsewhere when that was happening.

Today, there wasn't much time for enjoyment.

With a grunt, he swung the bat.

The man on his knees seemed to jump then, and he screamed a name which the man with the bat knew belonged to his dead wife, and the noise of the bat making contact was like jumping on egg boxes.

The man who used to be simply *Stuart*, lifted up the bat which came away wet and a little sticky. He hoisted the dripping wooden blade high above his head and brought it back down again with every ounce of strength in his body. He felt the shudder up his arm and across his shoulders. He closed his eyes, and the colours and shapes that swam about in the blackness were like the blood flying into the dirt, and the pulped body of the frog sailing gloriously across the blue and into the long grass . . .

The man who was variously *First Friend* and *Blast From The Past* and occasionally *Ghost Of Summer*, lifted and swung, lifted and swung, and each time he thought would be the last, but each new contact, each vibration, shook loose some new desire in him, liberated the hunger again and he felt the urge in his head and the action down his arms . . .

Finally, after many minutes, the man who had signed his most recent e-mail *Night Watchman* stopped and looked down at the swirls of bone and brain and blood making new patterns in what was already a somewhat garish carpet.

It took him thirty seconds or so to regain his breath, and then he was moving, quickly. He removed the gloves, wiped down the bat and put it back into the bag, having already taken out the fresh set of clothes. He stepped away from the body, taking care to mind his shoes. He didn't want to be walking bloody footprints all round the place for the rest of the day.

In less than ten minutes he was changed and ready to go, with plenty of time left to get to work. As he closed the front door behind him he checked his wristwatch. He tut-tutted at his carelessness.

The face of the watch was flecked with blood.

Someone, he wasn't certain who, had once said something Thorne was particularly fond of. A phrase he'd heard and never forgotten.

Knock hard, life is deaf.

It was a sentiment he did his best to live by, but there were occasions, many of them in fact, when those around him might have been happier had he tried to keep the noise down a little. Times when they seemed unwilling to discover what might be on the other side of the door.

Usually, this would only make Tom Thorne knock harder, bang louder. Today, even he was not sure he wanted to see that door opened.

Today, a man was going to die a violent death. A man who, but for Thorne, but for the course *he* had chosen to follow, might otherwise live. It was pretty much that simple, and it was not a pleasant thought to be bouncing around in your head from the second you opened your eyes in the morning.

Thorne rushed into work like a madman, but if he had imagined it might be . . . easier, with people around him, among the team – at the heart of things – he was wrong.

It was as if his colleagues, no, not just his colleagues – the woman in the newsagent, the postman, every driver he'd cut up on the North Circular on the way into work – all of them, could see his guilty thought, his dark admission. It was as though it had become visible, like a tiny spot floating across his eyeball. They all saw the terrible thought and processed it, and instantly, they all produced their own thought to keep it company:

You're right. It was/is/will be your fault . . .

Wednesday, 9 January. A wet and windy and godforsaken fucker of a Wednesday, when it was easy to see why its children were full of woe. A shitty, dreary, dry wank of a day. A day for watching clocks and losing tempers, and listening for phones.

A day for talking about it.

Thorne, Brigstocke, Holland and McEvoy. Sitting around a table, the rain beating against the windows. Talking about it.

'A man, this time. Is that important?'

'Like he said in the mail, ringing in the changes.'

'It feels like he's playing a game.'

'With Palmer, or with us?'

'What the fuck does "Night Watchman" mean anyway?'

'Like a security guard . . .'

'Or in cricket, you know? Someone they send in late on. Someone who's dispensable.'

'Sounds a bit odd. Does he think he's dispensable?'

'I doubt it . . .'

'I'm not sure how seriously we should take any of it.'

'Any of it,' Thorne said, '*except* for the killing.'

Talking about it, because that's all they *could* do. Everybody keen to make their contribution.

Jesmond on the phone to Brigstocke: 'This will probably be our only chance, Russell. Make sure you don't blow it.'

Steve Norman, who Thorne was disliking more and more each time he encountered him, on a cheery visit from the press office, annoyingly only spitting distance away above the station at Colindale: 'Well, everything's geared up at our end, Tom.' He laughed then. 'Bloody press have been making up stories for years anyway, about time *we* had a go.' Thorne neglected to laugh along, but Norman seemed not to notice. 'Just to let you know, ready and waiting when it goes off . . .'

Waiting.

To an extent of course, they were *always* waiting: Thorne, Brigstocke and the rest of them. Those at the shitty end of it. Waiting for the next call, the next case. Waiting for the one that would do their heads in, or fuck their lives up. Waiting to open the wrong door or pull over the wrong motor – the one with the mad fucker in it.

Waiting for the knife or the bullet, or if they were clever and lucky, just waiting it out. Waiting for the pension.

This was a different kind of waiting though. This was far crueller. Now they had been given . . . parameters.

They knew when, sort of. They knew the sex of the victim. Christ they even knew *how* he was going to be killed – the death to which this man, whoever he was, had been doomed. They had been shown what few have seen, and yet, at the same time they were powerless to change the picture. It was like being some not quite all-knowing, not quite all-seeing force, hamstrung by the missing pieces of the jigsaw. Omnipotent and impotent.

Like being God with Alzheimer's.

It was just a matter of *exactly* when and *exactly* where. Then, yes, then, they would move. Then, the springs tightened beyond endurance would be released and they would move like streaks of fucking lightning, blazing to wherever this man's violent compulsions led them, praying that it would turn out to be worth it.

Thorne sat at his desk wondering whether *anything* could be worth this, remembering the conversation he'd had a few short hours earlier. He stared out through the rain-streaked windows into the glowering, grey sky. Into the face of Phil Hendricks, those dark eyes lit up.

Make it a warm one, will you?

At lunchtime, a fleet of mopeds delivered a mountain of pizzas. Thorne and Brigstocke shared an extra large Spicy Meat Feast, but not equally. Brigstocke's reply when this fact was pointed out was not one Thorne felt like arguing with, even if the DCI did have a broad grin plastered across his greasy chops as he spoke.

'If I'm going to sit on fences, I'll need a fatter arse, won't I? So stop moaning.'

Thorne wasn't very hungry anyway.

The small talk didn't feel forced or awkward, just a little inappropriate. Like a bad joke at a funeral where everyone's turned up way too early and they're standing around waiting for the body to arrive.

Which was, of course, exactly what they were doing.

'How're the kids?'

Brigstocke's eyes widened as he slurped up a string of red-hot mozzarella. He had four kids under six and was often to be found spark out at his desk in the middle of the afternoon. Often, but not during this case.

'Little bastards,' Brigstocke mumbled. 'Glad to be here if I'm honest, whatever the circumstances.'

Thorne knew what he meant. He'd come into work more than once for pretty much the same reason, except that in his case, the only person he was escaping from was himself.

'Everybody reckons it gets easier, but fucked if I can see when. The time they're old enough to start making their own breakfasts and sticking on Cartoon Network, so you can stay in bed for a bit longer, is just about the same time they start bunking off school and doing crack. Just a different set of things to worry about. Do you want that last bit?'

Thorne shook his head and watched as Brigstocke pushed the entire slice of pizza into his mouth. He grunted with satisfaction, then started looking around and waggling his oily fingers.

'I'll grab some paper towels from the Gents,' Thorne said. He could hear Holland and McEvoy laughing about something in the adjacent office as he moved across to the door.

He stopped and turned, his hand on the metal door handle. His palm slippery with sweat and grease. 'I know this was what I wanted. Flushing him out.' He took a deep breath. 'It still feels shit though.'

Brigstocke swallowed the last of the pizza, pushed up his glasses with a clean knuckle. 'Course it does, and you're not the only one feeling bad.'

'I know, but . . .'

'I'm the only DCI in this room, Tom. Nobody's got a gun to my head on this one. Jesmond gave me the chance to say no.'

'Why didn't he just say no himself?'

Brigstocke stood, jammed the pizza box into the wastepaper basket and crushed it down hard with a size eleven brogue. 'Fear.'

Thorne opened the door. 'I'll get us a couple of coffees while I'm out there . . .'

All day at work he thought about what the police might be doing.

He imagined them in their offices, in their incident room. Some of them staring at the carpet, waiting for the news to come in. Others reacting differently, scurrying about the place, trying to feel useful, keeping themselves busy. Just another day on the investigation.

He pictured them in their toilets. The joshing, pudgy types at the stinking urinal, heads bowed and cocks out. Other less experienced, alone in cubicles, elbows jammed on knees and legs going to sleep after too long on a warm lavatory seat. Staring at a cracked tile floor, breathing heavily. The shit pouring out of them like water. Arseholes red, raw.

Plenty of lame jokes to ease the tension. The bog door kicked as their colleagues took the piss, the echoing sound of jeers and hollow laughter to chase away the feeling of dread.

Hopefully, yes, a feeling of dread . . .

He saw the pale and puffy faces of these men and women who were so very desperate to catch him. These police officers – fat and unhappy, skinny and dried-up, soft as puppies or hard as housebricks. He saw them all, as they sat at their desks and stared out of windows, and spoke into the grubby mouthpieces of grey telephones. As they passed in corridors and shared illicit cigarettes by open windows. The smell of the fags never quite managing to cover up that sour smell of sweat, trapped, rich and rank in the weave of cheap shirts and rumpled jackets.

All day at work he imagined it, alone or with colleagues, at his desk or about the place. Each new thought, each fresh image, entertaining the hell out of him.

He couldn't quite conjure up an image of Thorne, though.

His face, yes, but not its expression. Not the *set* of him. Thorne was definitely not the headless chicken type, but neither was he the sort to brood and wait, powerless and hog-tied. He knew that Thorne would be the one to feel it the most when the body was found. When the call came through and the sparks started to fly.

That certainly couldn't be too far away.

For him, the day was just rushing by. He doubted that it was passing quite as quickly for Tom Thorne.

*

'Fuckfuckbollocksfuck . . .'

On the way back to his office with two steaming cups of coffee, Thorne had been ambushed by the lethal corner of the desk that hated him. The pain of a bloody graze across an already existing bruise along with the scalding to both hands was intense. For a second, he felt as though he was going to be sick.

'Hand me that fucking Sellotape.'

The passing uniform did as he was told while Thorne grabbed a handful of paper from the desk and sank grimacing to the floor.

Brigstocke, alerted by the industrial-strength exclamations, emerged from his office to find Thorne on his knees, screwing up wads of A4 and taping them clumsily across the corner of the offending desk.

'I'll get my own coffee then, shall I?'

'Bollocks!'

Brigstocke laughed. This was a piece of slapstick that would probably do them all a lot of good. 'I hope you've checked that isn't important . . .'

'What?'

Brigstocke pointed to the corner of the desk. 'That paper. Six months from now we don't want the prosecution case collapsing because a vital witness statement is taped to the corner of a desk in Hendon.'

'I don't care . . .'

There was more laughter, this time from Holland and McEvoy, who stood giggling like children in the doorway of the smaller office. Thorne stood up and threw them a filthy look. He rubbed his leg.

Christ it hurt . . .

Thorne realised abruptly that this pain, laughable though the cause of it might be, was actually the first thing he'd really *felt* in hours. The agonising stab woke him up and reminded him where he was. All at once, the sting of the graze, the tingle of the burn, shook something loose in his brain and shoved it roughly into focus. A jumble of indistinct words and blurred images formed themselves into a question. Something slippery became graspable and he seized upon it.

Suddenly, Thorne was knocking hard.

'Keeping Palmer on the outside, keeping him visible, was so as the pattern wouldn't change. So that the other killer wouldn't panic and bolt. So that he might carry on as normal. Now he's changed the way he does things. Why?' Gritting his teeth, Thorne marched back into his office. Brigstocke, Holland and McEvoy followed him.

'He hasn't changed it really,' Brigstocke said, shutting the door behind them. 'I mean the details have always changed, from one killing to the next. The murder weapons, the locations . . .'

Thorne crossed to the far side of the office. He leaned back against the window, looked hard at the other three. 'Always a woman though.'

Holland shrugged. 'Three times, yeah. I suppose that's always.'

'Yes, Holland, that's always.' He spoke slowly, emphatically, his next sentence as complete a description of the man they were after as he needed or cared about. 'He kills women. He got Palmer to kill women. So why a man suddenly?'

McEvoy sniffed, then replied, her voice casual, her answer much the same as it had been earlier. 'I think he likes to vary things, keep them fresh. He makes that stupid joke about being predictable in the e-mail . . .'

'That's another thing. The joke feels wrong. The tone of the whole thing is forced. None of what he's doing is casual. He wants us to think it's random, like it's whimsical, like it doesn't matter to him who he targets. He doesn't want us to know that maybe, for the first time, he's got an agenda.' He made eye contact with each of them. 'I think there's a good reason for this, for today . . .'

McEvoy was the first to see it. 'Fuck!'

Brigstocke and Holland looked at her, desperate to know what she was thinking, annoyed they weren't already thinking it.

'We were too late,' McEvoy said.

Thorne nodded, pushed himself away from the window and moved quickly across to his desk. 'He's pissing around. He knows we've got Palmer.'

Brigstocke stiffened. 'What?'

Thorne grabbed his jacket from the back of the chair and headed quickly for the door. The pain in his leg was gone. 'I got it wrong. He knows all about Palmer. We need to get him away from work *now*, get him home. It's Martin Palmer who Nicklin's planning to kill today . . .'

Brigstocke picked up the phone, shouted after him. 'Hang on, Tom. There must be at least half a dozen officers there . . .'

Thorne walked out without looking back.

'*I'm* not there.'

SIXTEEN

Thorne thought that Palmer looked scared, then realised it was the way he always looked. Certainly, Palmer's laughter when Thorne told him what was going on – why he'd been forced to take the rest of the day off 'sick' – seemed genuine enough.

He'd taken off his thick glasses, wiped his eyes and squinted at Thorne. 'Whatever else he is, Inspector, he's still my friend. I'm sure he still thinks of himself that way at any rate. He wouldn't try to kill me . . .'

Thorne had said nothing, dragged a chair across to the window.

That had been many hours ago. Since then they'd sat, or moved slowly around each other, saying virtually nothing as it grew dark, Thorne occasionally talking on the radio to the officers in the unmarked cars at the front and rear and to those on foot. Six officers were present, seven including Thorne. Still, the sudden crackle of static from the radio, the shrill ring of the telephone or a shout from an adjacent flat were enough to tighten something momentarily in his guts, to increase the beats per minute by a couple.

'What do you think of me, Mr Thorne?'

Palmer had been perched close to the television. Thorne had turned the sound right down. Palmer leaned forward, switched the set off and swung round to look at Thorne who was sitting straight-backed on the sofa, eyes closed. He had his mobile in one hand, his radio in the other.

He spoke without opening his eyes. 'Nothing. I think . . . nothing of you.'

'Sorry, I'm being dim. You think nothing of me or you don't think of me at all? It's confusing. Which do you mean?'

Now Thorne opened his eyes and his voice was tight with what might have been irritation. 'Either. Both. Turn the television back on . . .'

Palmer got up and moved across to take the chair opposite Thorne. As he sat down, Thorne stood and stretched, produced a yawn from somewhere. 'I'm going to get another coffee . . .'

'You must have seen a lot of killers, Inspector.' Palmer's voice was quiet, a whisper almost, but as always, he sounded like he had a heavy cold: nasal and laboured, the chest faintly wheezy between phrases. 'You've been in rooms with plenty of people who've done the same as me. Breathed the same air as a few who've done a lot worse I should think. I don't know, kids . . . what have you.' Thorne said nothing, but the coffee seemed forgotten. He wasn't going anywhere. 'So why do I make you so uncomfortable?'

Thorne took a step towards Palmer, annoyed suddenly that he seemed so relaxed. Palmer drew back in his chair a little. 'You know that I'm here to catch *him*. Not to protect *you*. You do fucking well know that, don't you?'

Palmer nodded. Thorne stayed angry, groping for

words. 'By the way, my dodgy knee makes me uncomfortable, one or two of my superiors often make me uncomfortable, *wind* makes me fucking uncomfortable. You . . .'

'What? I make you sick? I make you want to hurt me?'

Thorne turned away and walked towards the window. He checked his watch as he went. It was a little after half past nine.

He stared down at the courtyard outside, at the high green fencing and the quiet street on the other side of it. He could see one of the cars sitting a hundred yards or so away, could just make out the figures of the two officers inside. He imagined their tiredness, their irritation, and his own began to vanish, like dirty water down a drain. He waited a minute or two. 'I'm impressed you waited so long.'

Palmer pushed up his glasses, shook his head a little. 'Waited for what?'

'To give me the "I'm not like him" speech.'

'I wasn't . . .'

Thorne didn't take his eyes from the street below. He held up his hand to cut Palmer off. 'If that's what you're building up to here, you needn't bother. I don't care, and for what it's worth, I think you're actually worse.' He turned to see Palmer lowering his head, clasping his hands to his chest. 'Nicklin, you know, the one you reckon still thinks of himself as your friend, is a maniac. Psychopath, sociopath, whatever. I don't know why he kills. Not exactly. He likes it, he gets off on it, it's the only way he can express himself, sad little fucker. And he gets an extra kick out of getting you to do it as well.

'So, with you it's a bit easier isn't it? We know exactly why you kill.' Palmer raised his head, blinked slowly behind his glasses. Thorne acknowledged the small plea he saw in Palmer's eyes.

'All right, past tense, we know exactly why you *killed.* You killed because he told you to. Pure and simple. To my mind, that makes you worse than he is.'

Thorne turned back to the window. 'He slaughters women in front of their children, and you're worse.'

It was several minutes later that Thorne heard the sigh of the armchair as Palmer stood up, and a few moments after that when he saw the shadow creep across the floor at his feet, and felt the presence of the man behind him.

'Have you ever been really afraid, Inspector Thorne?'

Outside it was cold and clear, but as he stared out at the night, the thoughts came against his will.

Thorne saw the rain suddenly begin to come down in sheets, and he was driving too fast along the dark, wet streets of south-west London, following a car with tail-lights like the eyes of a monster . . .

He was moving through the corridors of a house full of whispers, the voices of those for whom it had been the last place they'd spent any time alive.

He was climbing, blind into an attic, rising up through the floor of a room that would soon be drenched in blood. What he saw when his eyes adjusted to the bright light stopped him dead like a palm pressed hard into his chest, took the breath out of him as effectively as any fist . . .

Now, one year on, the night was cold but clear, and as the memory receded, Thorne felt his heartbeat start to slow. While his breathing grew less shallow, he watched unmoving as the reflection of the man in the window grew larger and a killer drew closer to him.

Palmer spoke slowly, the deep nasal voice emotionless,

almost robotic. He gazed straight ahead, as if talking to the distorted image of himself in the windowpane. 'Whatever it is you're thinking, however bad it is, or *was*, imagine living with it. Not now and again. Not when you've had a few too many and it comes rushing at you out of nowhere. Not in the middle of the night when you wake up sweating and you thank God or whoever as mercifully it drifts away from you, but *all the time*.

'I'm talking about living with something that paralyses you, that turns your skin to something wet and unknown, even to your own touch. Something that makes your bowels boil and your blood freeze, that ties you up and cuts you off utterly, from *every* person but the one who frightens you, the one who generates the power of the fear itself, the one to whom you are bound and beholden.

'Now, imagine living with it to the point where, in spite of how much you hate and dread it, eventually it becomes something that you cannot bear to be without. It becomes a thing that you crave – the tightening in the chest, the rush as it hits you, the jolt as it does its work. The spidery touch of it, delicate and deadly, climbing up your body, from your toes to somewhere just behind your eyes, and yes, in your groin, always down there . . .

'By now, you need to be afraid to feel alive. The fear is the worst feeling in the world, the very worst, until it isn't there any more and you realise that there's a worse feeling.

'These aren't excuses, though I'm sure they sound like it. It isn't as simple as I'm making it sound, I'm not saying it is. What I did was not just . . . a reaction. There was obviously some foul and desperate part of me that wanted to turn the tables, that wanted to make others afraid.'

Palmer shook his head, as if arguing politely with the

other him on the dark side of the glass. 'No. No, I didn't do the terrible things I've done *just* because I was afraid. I don't even know if it was him I was afraid of, or whether I was being afraid *for* him, on his behalf.

'He was frightened of nothing, you see. He *is* frightened of nothing . . .'

Thorne did not want to turn to look at Palmer. Instead he looked hard at the reflection: the mouth turned mournfully down, the tears obvious despite the dirt on the window and the low light. At that moment, and Thorne would always be amazed by this, Palmer reminded him of nothing so much as one of those giant bears in some eastern European shithole. A lumbering thing, de-clawed and degraded, dancing in a collar and chain while idiots threw coins and those who watched it on the news at home threw bigger ones to try and put a stop to it.

Thorne was equally surprised by his own tone of voice when he spoke. It was, if anything, *reassuring*, so at odds with his anger of a few minutes ago. He was speaking for Palmer's benefit, as much as for his own.

'If he's out there,' Thorne said, 'he *should* be frightened.'

Palmer moved slowly forwards and placed a huge hand against the window, the fingertips whitening as he pressed against the pane. Thorne glanced sideways and watched Palmer staring out into the darkness at his past: distant, recent and somewhere in between.

'He's out there. He's always been out there.'

Holland woke and looked at his watch, panic-stricken.

'*Fuck* . . .'

He'd told himself he needed to get up an hour and a half ago but it had been so easy to drift off. Now he'd have some explaining to do. He needed to get showered and get the hell out of there.

He needed to get home.

When he opened the bathroom door and saw her bent over the sink, his first thought was that she was being sick. He moved towards her, an arm outstretched.

'Sarah . . .'

She turned, the white powder obvious above her top lip.

They stared at each other for a while. He was naked, goose-pimply, his arms wrapped around himself. She was wearing a white towelling dressing gown, her hair wet, her mouth hovering somewhere between two very different expressions.

Finally, she smiled. 'Want some?'

Holland barked out a laugh. His mouth formed itself into a question, a *why* or a *what*, but it wouldn't come out. He just wrapped his arms tighter, gritted his teeth and stared hard at the tiles around the bath, at the grout greying and flaking off, until he had something to say.

'Well, looks like I'll be making Sergeant a lot quicker than I thought . . .'

McEvoy's smile vanished and she turned away from him. She looked at herself in the mirror, leaned in close and blinked. In one quick, practised movement she wiped away the coke around her nostrils and slid the powdery finger into her mouth. She ran her tongue around her gums and spoke to his reflection, the anger not far below the surface.

'I don't need a fucking lecture, Holland. All right?'

'You're not going to *fucking* well get one,' he said. 'I just want a shower and I'm away . . .'

The smile came back then, of a different sort entirely. 'Right, back off home to her indoors, once you've washed the smell of me off your cock . . .'

Holland reached for a towel, wrapped it around his waist. 'Yeah, right. Change the subject, whatever.' He reached into the shower, turned on the taps, held his hand under the water waiting for it to get hot. 'Do you get high at work?'

McEvoy laughed and coughed at the same time. She spat something out into the sink. '*High*? Jesus, Holland, you sound like my dad . . .'

The water was suddenly red-hot. Holland pulled his hand away quickly. He wanted to hit her. He wanted to shout, so he shouted. 'OK . . . slaughtered, wankered, off on one, monged, fucked up . . . whatever bit of stupid, fucking druggy jargon is the most current. Fair enough?'

'Well, we have been reading our pamphlets haven't we?'

'Answer the question.'

'What do *you* think? Do you think I take drugs at work? Do you not think I can do my job?'

'Not if you're using at work, no.'

McEvoy cocked her head, as if she was thinking about his answer. For a few moments they stood there, saying nothing, the small bathroom starting to fill with steam. She ran a hand through her wet hair and sniffed. 'So, now what happens, Constable?'

Holland had no answer. Her dressing gown was starting to gape and his eyes dropped, just for a second, to her breasts. He felt himself harden immediately. She saw it at once and smiled, opening the dressing gown completely.

'Well, I'm still up for it if you are. I mean cocaine doesn't make you *quite* as horny as ecstasy but still . . .'

Before he could stop himself, Holland was moving across the bathroom, ripping the dressing gown from her shoulders and pushing her down on to the floor.

It was far better than when they had done it an hour earlier, better than it had ever been. Their voices, as they moaned and shouted and swore, echoed off the tiles. The hiss and spatter of the shower was not loud enough to drown out the noise.

In Martin Palmer's bathroom, Thorne stared at himself. Weighing up his options if, *when*, he walked away.

Thorne the pub landlord. Quite a few went down that road anyway, why not sooner rather than later? A couple of extra pounds and a beard maybe. Early mornings, changing the barrels, a free bottle or two for the local uniforms. Piece of piss . . .

Thorne the shopkeeper. Why the hell not? The greying hair slicked back and someone else to do the accounts. No need to kowtow either. Curmudgeonly, characterful, with a faithful clientele . . .

Thorne, forty-one and fucked. The copper who was fooling nobody.

He leaned forward slowly until his forehead was flat against the cool mirror. Opening his brown eyes wide, he stared at the long, thin snakes of blood crawling across the whites, the creamy crumbs of sleep still trapped in the lashes and the lines underneath, up close, like the skin of an old man.

Like his father's skin.

Thorne opened his mouth. A long, low moan escaped

and was swallowed by the splash of the cold water that poured into the sink. The breath he pushed out to follow it rose and fogged up the mirror. He pushed himself away from the glass, raised a hand to wipe away the condensation and looked at the face of a man who was dead-on-his-feet tired. Tired of waking up and needing a minute or two. Of bodies in baths and in student bedsits, of chit-chatting to killers and of needing to remind himself who and what they were.

Tired of being on his own. Tired of being so fucking angry. Tired of waiting.

The noise of the running water faded away until it was no more than a faraway hum, and for a moment his mind was wonderfully clear and empty. It was just a moment . . .

Then, in a rush: the gulp and rumble of the plumbing, the shock of the ice-cold water on his hands and face, Charlie Garner still there, hammering when he closed his eyes, and somewhere, the sound of a phone ringing . . .

When Thorne ran back into the living room, Palmer was holding out the chirruping mobile like an extremely bright dog with a stick of dynamite in its mouth. As Thorne reached for it, the ringing stopped.

'Shit . . .'

He snatched the phone, punched at it, called up the last number received. It wasn't one he recognised.

The voice that answered was terse, professional. A man's voice. A police officer's voice.

'Yes?'

'This is Tom Thorne. You just . . .'

'Oh, right. This is DS Jay from Harrow Station here. I'm in attendance at a murder scene, and I know some of your lads are on their way, but I thought I might as well try you, because my victim has got your card in his jacket pocket.'

Thorne's mind began to race. 'Have you got an ID on the body?' He looked across at Palmer whose fingers were entwined across the back of that thick neck, his head shaking, his eyes glassy.

'Yes, nice easy one,' Jay said. 'Everything here in the wallet, which is handy. The poor bastard's head has been battered into the middle of next week. Looks like he was a teacher at a local grammar school.'

The realisation was instant then, and dreadful. Something that did not belong, dropping, slapping, crunching into place. Like a coffin toppling from the shoulders of pallbearers and smashing onto a concrete path. For no particular reason, Thorne saw the smiling face of the English teacher who had showed him and Holland around the school.

'Cookson . . . Andrew I think . . .'

'What?'

'Medium height, dark hair, mid-thirties.'

'Sorry. This bloke's a damn sight older than that . . .'

The telephone line crackled, but Thorne heard only the terrible noise of the coffin hitting the ground, the deafening sound of the wood splintering as it hit. Before DS Jay had a chance to speak the name of the dead man out loud, Thorne knew that Ken Bowles had been right to be afraid of the future.

Now, so was he.

SEVENTEEN

This time, Thorne wasn't even allowed at the meeting . . .

There are dozens of pubs in London with what can only be described as a less than salubrious past. Places where strong drink and acts of violence have come together, often infamously, to create moments of history.

The Ten Bells in Spitalfields, which used to be called The Jack the Ripper. Where the man himself is thought to have drunk, where several of his victims plied their trade, where, over a hundred years after five local prostitutes were butchered in three months, you could buy Jack the Ripper books, mugs and baseball caps and, most bizarre of all, you could watch strippers a couple of lunchtimes a week.

The Blind Beggar in Bethnal Green, where, if people are to be believed, at least a hundred thousand East Londoners saw Ronnie Kray shoot George Cornell, allegedly for calling him a 'big fat poof'.

And the Magdala Tavern in Hampstead, where Ruth Ellis put five bullets into the pointless prick of a man who told her he loved her, three months before she became the last woman in Great Britain to go to the gallows. The

Magdala Tavern, where Tom Thorne was sitting, early on a Monday evening, nursing a pint, waiting to hear what *his* sentence would be.

It was a pub he was fond of anyway; somewhere to pop into after spending an hour tramping across the Heath and marvelling at the stupidity of grown men wanting to spend their free time flying kites. The beer was good, the landlord was amiable enough and the food was passable. It was the dark history of the place though, its associations, that drew Thorne, that engaged him. He could never resist putting a finger into those bullet holes that still cratered the tiling on the wall outside. It made him feel connected somehow. He would inevitably turn then, and imagine her.

Always in black and white.

The bleached hair, the pale, powdered skin tight against those perfect cheekbones, her long nails scraping against the heavy Smith & Wesson revolver. Twenty-eight years old and nowhere left to go. Fingers in the bullet-holes – as spiritual moments go, it was hardly thrusting a hand into Christ's wounds, but fuck it, when you've had a few of a lunchtime . . .

Easter Sunday, 10 April, 1955. A moment of madness, of judgement, on a Hampstead pavement: the first step on a journey to the long drop in the execution chamber at Holloway Prison. Forty-seven years later, nearly half a century after they hanged Ruth Ellis, and life for those who kill for pleasure didn't always mean life.

Now, Thorne sat and waited for DCI Russell Brigstocke, wondering just how tight they were going to tie the noose around his neck. Staring into his glass and looking at a few highlights of the past few days.

The pre-sentence proceedings.

The early hours of Thursday morning: gazing down at bits of a teacher's brain on the carpet, Jesmond making his grand entrance, his face set in a reasonable facsimile of horror and grim determination. The smile that the Detective Superintendent had saved just for him. 'I think it might be best if you took things easy for a couple of days . . .'

'Best for who?'

Thursday evening: Hendricks ringing with the results of the post-mortem. As usual, nothing of any real use, but a reference finally explained. 'The tiny wooden splinters embedded in what was left of Bowles's skull. They were willow.'

'A cricket bat . . .'

'Right. Night Watchman. Ha, fucking ha . . .'

Friday afternoon: His father. 'Oh . . . I didn't think you'd be there. I was going to leave a message on your machine . . . I need a bit of info. By body count, who were the three greatest killers in British history?'

'Greatest? Jesus, dad . . .'

'It'll be a trick question see, to wind up some of the lads down the Legion. I ask them for the greatest killers. They say Christie or whoever, and I tell them the greatest killers were actually bubonic plague or smallpox or what have you. See?'

'Right . . .'

'But I need the names. I reckon Shipman's got to be first hasn't he . . . ?'

Saturday morning: Holland with an update. 'Nobody knows what the hell's going on to be honest. There's one or two new faces around, but everything's all over the place. There's a meeting on Monday, the DCI, Jesmond, you know . . .'

'Right, thanks. McEvoy OK?'

'How the fuck should I know?'

Thorne looked up to see Brigstocke walking quickly towards him. He downed the rest of his pint. What had Holland been so tetchy about anyway?

Brigstocke slid in next to him, leaned in close. The quiff had looked better. His breath smelled of the cheap cigars he was so fond of.

'You owe me a drink. You owe me *lots* of drinks.'

Fighting the urge to punch the air like a goalscorer, Thorne nodded, made his way to the bar and bought them both a couple of pints each. Halfway through the second, Brigstocke gave Thorne the headlines.

'You're still on the case. Just.'

'Why do I get the feeling that's the only bit of good news?'

'Depends how you look at it. People are very pissed off.'

'I assume you're including Ken Bowles's family?'

Brigstocke struck a match, held it to the end of one of his cheap cigars. 'I'll ignore that, but strictly as a mate, shut your silly mouth, Tom.'

'Sorry, Russ.' Thorne was. He knew that Brigstocke had stuck his neck out for him. He would try to remember it. 'So, what's next?'

'Damage limitation.' Thorne opened his mouth, remembered, shut it again. 'The case proceeds as normal,' Brigstocke said slowly. 'Emphasis on *normal.* No more fucking about. We work crime scenes, we make enquiries, we gather evidence. It proceeds, as in *procedure.*'

'What about Palmer?'

'Martin Palmer was taken into custody and charged

with the murder of Ruth Murray this morning. Highbury Corner Magistrate's Court this afternoon. Belmarsh or Brixton by teatime. By the numbers, Tom.'

Thorne had no argument. There simply wasn't one. Nicklin had killed Bowles as a warning. He must have. He knew that Thorne and Holland had gone to the school and that they could only have been led there by Palmer. There was no point in any further pretence.

Having said that . . .

'Why did he send the e-mail to Palmer, when he knew we had him?' Thorne asked this question of Brigstocke, as they had all asked it of each other, as he had asked it of himself a hundred times in the last few days. The reply he got was pretty much the best that anybody could come up with.

'He's playing some kind of game. Dicking us about.'

'Dicking *me* about. It was me that went to the school. Me he must have been watching . . .'

Brigstocke leaned forward to flick ash into a vast plastic ashtray. He shook his head. 'He's a clever sod, that's all. He wants us to be doing this, to be asking these questions.'

Thorne shrugged, picked up his pint, looked at it. He couldn't help feeling that in killing Ken Bowles, somebody *he* had spoken to, Nicklin had been sending him some sort of message. He wasn't sure whether thinking this was ego or instinct. He'd confused the two before.

He emptied his glass, put it down. He didn't know whether he wanted to stay at that table and swallow down beer until he couldn't feel anything any more, or rush home and shut the door tight. 'Are they giving Palmer to the press?'

'That's still being decided. Jesmond and a few higher up

are in with the press office. It would be a good move in some ways, you know – killer in custody, get a few old dears worked up, ready for a bit of banging on vans outside the Bailey come the trial. Do us all a bit of good, so soon after . . .' He left an appropriate pause which Thorne filled in in his head.

. . . I got Ken Bowles killed.

'It's hard, without admitting we fucked up.'

Thorne scoffed. 'Thanks for the *we*.'

'Don't blame yourself for Bowles, Tom.'

'Why not?'

Brigstocke blinked, reached for his drink. He hadn't got an answer. Thorne asked the only appropriate question. 'Another pint?'

Brigstocke finished off the one he was drinking, shook his head as he swallowed. Thorne reached behind for his jacket. It looked like he was going home.

'You're off the hook for the same reason they let you get on it, you know,' Brigstocke said. Thorne raised his eyebrows, asking the question. 'Fear. They were afraid of being wrong, afraid of fucking up. Now they're afraid of being *seen* to fuck up, which is a thousand times worse.'

Thorne stood and pulled on his jacket. Brigstocke stayed seated, his cigar down to nothing. 'They've got sod all to be afraid of. I'll be taking responsibility.'

Brigstocke ground out his nub-end. 'Oh, don't worry, you have.'

They both laughed, a little louder and longer than was necessary. 'What happened to being off the hook?'

'You are,' Brigstocke said. 'But it's only a matter of time until you're on it again . . .'

'A stay of execution.'

Brigstocke looked at him, smiling, not understanding the reference. Thorne was already wondering how many more he would need to drink. How much before he would be able to wrap himself inside his duvet and crawl deep down into the darkness without seeing Ken Bowles, eyes open and swimming in blood, hands clawing at the carpet, bits of his own cerebellum beneath his fingernails.

Without seeing Martin Palmer, huge and hunched against the white wall of a cell.

When the adverts came on – cheaply made soundbites for pension or blame-and-claim companies – he got up and went to make himself tea. The show wasn't very interesting tonight anyway, which was a shame. He'd been looking forward to the calls even more than usual.

He'd had a pig of a day at work. It was a busy time: lots to do and he, as usual, the one to do most of it. It was his own fault if he was honest. He was something of a control freak. While he complained of the workload, he didn't trust anybody else to do it as efficiently as he would, so he got on with it himself.

He'd actually been glad of the extra work. He'd needed something to focus his mind a little for the past few days. He'd been struggling to adjust, to adapt to the new way of things.

Palmer was gone: it was just him again.

However much he'd wanted to be in control, to be the one to change things, he couldn't be too angry about what had happened. Palmer was always going to be taken out of circulation after this last murder, and that, after all, had been his choice. He had decided to kill Bowles. Just when he'd been getting into Thorne's little game, enjoying it even, it had become necessary to change direction and now he had to live with the repercussions.

Back on his own. He liked it like that, yes, but *still*, he'd have to find some other way now to up the ante. He couldn't bear to be bored, to be still. Stillness meant sinking, and he'd do anything to avoid that. He needed to find the next thing quickly, the something, the *new* thing, the bright spot on the horizon. He'd found it with Palmer, but now, with him out of the picture, he'd need to find some different way to jack up the rush a little. While he waited for inspiration, he got his head down at work.

Work work work, home, chat, dinner with Caz, and then an hour or two next to the radio with a bottle of wine, enjoying the wit and wisdom of the country's more opinionated insomniacs. Later, he might wake Caz up and fuck her. Stick it in and move it around, while he closed his eyes and thought about Bowles's brain like undercooked porridge, or the nice neat hole in the student's head, or perhaps the way the woman with the little boy had stiffened when he put his hand over her mouth.

While the kettle boiled, he thought about Thorne.

He wondered how the Detective Inspector relaxed after a tough day. After a tough *few* days. It couldn't get harder than a fresh body could it? The body of someone he'd connected with. How quickly did a man like Thorne get over that, especially when it was . . . unnecessary? Who did he talk to about those things? Family? Friends? He was suddenly hugely amused by the idea of turning on his radio and hearing Thorne himself phoning in.

'*We're going to Tom in London, who has a problem. How can we help you Tom?*'

Then that voice, recognisably London. A little rough around the edges, just like the man himself. Deep and impressive, certainly. Soothing or stentorian, depending on his mood, or the impression he was trying to create. Tonight though, the voice a little higher, nervous, a catch in it . . .

'*Well, Bob, it's a bit embarrassing.*'

'*Tom, are you a first time caller?*'

'*Yes, I am, sorry . . .*'

'*Just relax, you're among friends.*'

'*The thing is, I was wondering if any of your listeners might be able to help me. I'm trying to catch a multiple murderer you see, and it isn't going at all well . . .*'

He picked up his steaming mug of tea and carried it back into the sitting room, still chuckling to himself. On the radio, a new caller was broadcasting to the nation. Not Thorne of course, but he sounded equally interesting.

Leonard from Cheshire: 'This bloke who was battered last week, this teacher? They say on the news it was that pair, the ones who've been doing all these murders, but I reckon it was just some little bastard, pardon my French, what hadn't done his homework. I mean it could have been, couldn't it, you know what they're like now in some of these schools . . . ?'

He was laughing so much, he had to hold on to his tea with both hands.

When Thorne arrived at work the next morning, the last thing he was mentally prepared for was a bust up with Steve Norman. The press officer, on the other hand, who was waiting for Thorne in his office, seemed well up for it.

'You've made us all look very stupid, Thorne.'

Thorne cocked his head and crossed to his desk, thinking, *how hard can that be?*

Norman followed him, standing at his shoulder as Thorne, without looking at them, picked up a pile of reports from his desk. 'Alienated most of your fellow officers already, now you're making a pretty good job of pissing the rest of us off as well.'

Thorne carried the sheaf of papers across to the window and began pretending to read them. He wasn't sure why Norman was here and why he was in such a bad mood, but he *really* wanted him to leave and guessed that it might be a good idea if when he did, it wasn't with a broken nose or any teeth missing.

He dropped the paperwork down onto the window ledge and turned to face him, trying his damnedest to look tired rather than angry. 'What's your problem, Norman?'

'No problem. I just wanted you to be aware just how much trouble you've caused. We worked our bollocks off, liaising with the press, getting close to the journos . . .'

'That must have been hard. All that expense account wine to get down your necks . . .'

Norman laughed in mock confusion. 'Sorry, don't you remember whose idea this was? An idea which, for the record, most of us thought was half-arsed at the time.' Thorne shrugged. He hadn't forgotten. 'Yeah, well this time it was people like me at the sharp end of it. You wanted false stories planted in the press, you needed a lie perpetrated and we did it. Brilliantly. Now, it's all gone tits up because *you* were wrong, and we've got to sort the mess out.'

'Let me get this straight,' Thorne said, starting to fray a little round the edges. 'You're shouting your mouth off, because basically, you've got to do your job.'

'I'm not . . .'

Thorne took a step closer to him. 'Well, why don't you shut up and go and do it?'

Norman showed no inclination to retreat. He raised a finger, jabbed it towards Thorne's chest. 'I will, and you'd better be bloody thankful that someone round here's good at their job. I might, *might*, just be able to put things right with the press. I might be able to get this operation out of the mess it's in with half a decent reputation left.' He turned away and strolled towards the door, stopped when he got there. 'When I say *this operation*, I'm not including you of course. You're already down the shitter and there's no way to get you out again . . .'

Thorne laughed, moved to the chair behind his desk. 'Listen Norman, I'm busy, and if you're just going to stand there stating the obvious . . .'

Norman opened the door. 'Later, Thorne . . .'

Thorne spoke calmly, straightening things on his desk, lining up the pens. 'Oh, just to let you know, if you point that finger at me again, I'll break it. Fair enough?'

Norman turned around. Thorne saw the colour rise to his cheeks and was quietly delighted to see a little of the cockiness disappear from around the eyes. They looked at one another, unblinking, for a few slow seconds.

'There's a theoretical equation of ranks between officers and civilian staff. Did you know that, Thorne?' Thorne did, but said nothing. 'It's a courtesy thing really, but most people tend to observe it. A press officer on my team equates with a Detective Inspector such as yourself. I'm a *senior* press officer, which if I'm not wrong, *and I'm not* . . . equates to a DCI – the rank immediately superior to yours. Are you listening, Thorne?'

Thorne looked up, the desk nice and tidy, the eyes nice and dead.

'Like you said, it's theoretical. Now fuck off.'

Norman did as he was bid, and was replaced almost immediately by a far friendlier face. Holland leaned against the doorframe and watched Norman as he made his way across the incident room.

'Cheer me up,' Thorne said. 'Tell me the Desk of Doom has got him, gouged a big hole in his leg. Better yet, taken one of his bollocks off.'

'Sorry, no luck. You padded it with all that paper anyway.' Thorne grunted. He'd completely forgotten doing it. 'What was all that about?' Holland asked. 'I could hear it from next door.'

Thorne got up and walked across to join Holland in the doorway. 'Your guess is as good as mine. Something got up his arse though.'

'Well, whatever it is, it looks like it's gone now . . .'

The two of them watched as Norman stood talking to Sarah McEvoy. He was smiling, gesturing with his hands. She smiled back, leaned towards him, briefly placed a hand on his arm. Her eyes darted towards Thorne and Holland. Half a second later, they were looking at the floor in front of her.

Holland moved into the office. Thorne followed him.

'Oh, listen, I'm sorry about the other morning on the phone,' Holland said. 'You asked about McEvoy, how she was doing, or something, and I was a bit stroppy. Didn't get much sleep . . .'

Thorne had been wondering if Holland would say anything. His reaction had been so out of character. He shrugged. 'I don't know what you're on about.'

Holland breathed in, let it out. Like he'd got something out of the way. 'Norman got it in for you then?'

'Looks that way,' Thorne said. 'Buggered if I know why though. Worst thing about it is, I can't really argue with him. Most of what he was saying was spot on.'

Holland opened his mouth to argue but Thorne cut him off. 'He's a little tosser, don't get me wrong, but he knows what he's talking about.'

'No need to make it personal though, is there?'

Thorne sat down. 'He's a small man, you know? All got big chips on their shoulders.' Holland looked at him, eyebrows raised, a grin threatening to appear. Thorne's face crinkled, sarcastically, in return. 'He's smaller than *me*, OK? I'm average . . .'

Holland held up his hands. 'I'm not arguing. What about chips though?'

Thorne thought for a second, then smiled, like he'd suddenly remembered an old friend.

'Me? More than Harry Ramsden, Dave.'

Holland laughed loudly, and at that moment, Thorne would have been happy, Jesus, he would have been deliriously happy, to just close his eyes and listen to the sound of it all day. He would have been delighted to shut the door and do fuck all of any use to anybody and just sit and wait for the darkness outside the window. To let the night come and grow thick around him. To sit in his office and drink tea and talk to Holland about nothing: about Sophie, his girlfriend and his last holiday, and Tottenham's pointless push for a place in Europe, and what films he'd seen lately and how bloody awful they both thought public transport was . . .

Whatever.

But he knew that every few seconds, his voice, even as he spoke, would grow quiet to his ears, as if the Mute/Fade button on his brain's remote control were being fingered, and a new sound would take its place. A sound that he had to invent. One that could only exist in his imagination. A sound that very few people, very few people *living*, could ever have heard. The dull, wet smack of a bat striking a skull.

Over and over again.

I got Ken Bowles killed.

The phone rang. Thorne reached for it absently, picked it up without looking, said nothing.

After a moment or two, a voice. Tight, impatient, a faint Midlands accent.

'Is this Thorne?'

'Yes . . .'

'This is Vic Perks. You've been trying to get hold of me.'

'Have I?'

Perks sighed. 'Well *somebody* there has. Ex-DCI Vic Perks. I was in charge of the Karen McMahon investigation in 1985.'

Thorne grabbed a notepad and began to write . . .

As he jotted down details, as he and Perks made arrangements, an image began to form at the back of Thorne's mind. There one second and gone the next. Then back again, like the picture glimpsed in a cloud formation or an odd arrangement of shadows.

He saw a stranger leaning down and reaching out a hand to pull him up – to drag him from the cold, dark water at the very moment he was about to go under.

EIGHTEEN

They met in a pub called The Mariners' Arms on the Isle of Dogs.

It was a basic kind of place. Thick nylon carpets, a dart board, beer. Wednesday lunchtime, and aside from Thorne and Perks, there were only two people in there: the barman – a student by the look of things with dyed blond hair and bad skin – who stared intently at the small television above the bar; and a wizened old man in a battered brown trilby who sat in the corner with a newspaper, half a Guinness and a fierce-looking Alsatian at his feet.

While they worked their way through their beers and waited for two cheese rolls to appear – there must have been *somebody* else there, in the kitchen, because the rolls materialised eventually – they talked about their respective journeys. The pub had been Perks's idea. He hadn't wanted to travel too far from the small flat in Epping to which he and his wife had retired. When the older man mentioned where he lived, Thorne had glanced up from his pint, only for a second, but Perks still knew what he was thinking. That part of the world did have something of a reputation.

'That's right. Retired to the same place where most of the villains I spent all those years chasing ended up. I see one or two of them now and again. Buying the paper or down the garden centre. We say hello . . .'

Thorne had been right about the Midlands accent: Birmingham was his best bet, or Coventry maybe. Perks was a tall man. His face was thin and deeply lined, but Thorne guessed that laughter was probably just as responsible as worry. He was in his early sixties, with his grey hair cut short and a neatly trimmed moustache, a collar and tie beneath the padded car coat.

Perks finished his last mouthful of cheese roll, wiped the crumbs from around his mouth with a wax-paper serviette and looked Thorne in the eye.

'You haven't found her. You haven't found Karen, else you'd have said by now.'

Thorne was still eating. He swallowed quickly. 'No. But I intend to.'

Perks stood up, scanned the room for the entrance to the toilet. He looked down at Thorne before making a move.

'So did I . . .'

Later, they walked east, along the river. The fine rain was annoying more than anything – not enough to warrant an umbrella, but enough to necessitate screwing up the eyes and hunching the shoulders. The Thames was wide here. They walked within feet of cheaply built sixties' council housing, drab and depressing. On the other side of the river, at the top of the hill was Greenwich Observatory, the Royal Naval College and the *Cutty Sark*.

They walked slowly; Thorne moving a little slower than he might normally have done. The river belched and slid and slurped beneath them, oily and gunmetal grey. Ahead and across from them, the bizarre monstrosity that was the Millennium Dome rose up through the drizzle, rusting and ridiculous. A million and more a week, so they reckoned, just for it to sit empty.

'That's a decent hospital every couple of months,' Perks said. 'A school every few weeks.'

'Did you think she was alive?' Thorne asked. 'When you were looking for her?'

Perks turned his face away towards the river, towards the wind. When he finally spoke, Thorne had to strain to hear the words. 'For a week, perhaps a fortnight, we hoped. I probably thought so longer than anyone else. That was my job I suppose.'

Thorne went another step or two before he realised that Perks had stopped. He turned and walked back towards him. 'There were sightings weren't there?'

'Several. Always plenty of sightings though. People are well-meaning or else they're being plain malicious. Hard to tell at the time. One though in particular . . .'

'Carlisle?'

Perks nodded, wiped rain from his face with the back of a brown leather glove. 'A few miles outside actually. Three days after she went missing. That one was hard to ignore. The clothes were spot on – we never released everything but the description was perfect. Hair, clothes, the car. That one felt right.' Perks said something else but it was lost as a screaming gull passed just overhead, its cry mingling with the clatter of a nearby helicopter. Thorne looked up and saw a bulky, tomato-red chopper swooping down towards City Airport.

Perks moved past him. Thorne followed, but kept an

eye on the helicopter, unable to explain the sudden, morbid thought, but not wanting to miss a moment should it burst into flame and plunge into the river.

'So that's why you never searched locally?' Thorne asked.

'We searched everywhere . . .'

'Sorry, I mean . . . looked for a body, looked for it in the area where she disappeared. The country park, the railway line . . .'

'The sightings were one reason, certainly. Didn't make sense for whoever took her to kill her and bring her back to dispose of the body. Not that these animals do anything normal . . .'

Perks's gaze was steady but despite the disgust in his voice, Thorne thought that there was something missing from the eyes. It was something Thorne saw in the bathroom mirror every morning, flickering into life. On a good day he might call it passion. On a bad one, panic.

'Then there was the lad's statement,' Perks said. 'The boy that saw her get taken. We had an eye witness who watched Karen get into that car.'

'Stuart Nicklin.'

Perks's eyes narrowed for a moment. 'Yes. Nicklin.'

They walked on in silence for a few minutes. A varied panorama of heavy riverside industry moved slowly past them on the other side of the water, some of it flourishing, some of it long dead. All of it pig-ugly. A disused power station, a grain processing plant, the scrapyard where the *Marchioness* was finally broken up and melted down, wharves piled high with gravel and aggregates, rusting cranes poking skywards.

The sky, the shore, the water, the buildings. Black, grey and brown . . .

'Tell me about Nicklin.'

'He was a strange kid . . .'

Thorne nodded, thinking, *Jesus* . . .

'You don't know how much things like that are going to affect kids down the road, do you? He was really upset. Seeing her get into that car. He knew it was wrong, you see. I think he knew he should have done something to try and stop it. He never said that but . . . he knew. Seeing her taken like that, it shook him. They were close, not boyfriend and girlfriend, but close. Best friends, you might say. Actually there was another kid, Martin Palmer. They were a bit of a threesome. They'd all been together earlier that day, but then they'd had some kind of falling out and Palmer had gone home.'

'Any idea what they'd fallen out about?'

Perks squinted at him, his mind racing ahead, aching to work it out. 'No . . .'

'You knew that Nicklin had been expelled from school before this? Him and Palmer?' The look on Perks's face – the confusion, the desperate desire to know – made Thorne feel suddenly guilty. He was going round the houses. Pissing a decent ex-copper around for no good reason he could think of. He should have just said what he had to say back there in the pub, told Perks what he wanted – what he wanted *confirmed.*

Thorne put a hand on Perks's arm. 'I wanted to talk to you about Stuart Nicklin. Palmer as well, but really . . . this is about Nicklin. I wanted to check that his statement was the only reason why you didn't look for Karen closer to home; how much what he said to you at the time had to do with that . . .'

They couldn't walk any further. They'd reached

Saunders Ness, the end of the riverside walk. A spit, or *nose*, of land formed by the huge curve of the river as it swept round the Isle of Dogs and out towards the estuary.

Perks leaned on the handrail and stared out across the river. 'The Thames was more or less dead a couple of years ago. Did you know that? Bugger all could live in it.' Thorne was not surprised. All manner of shit got dumped in the river and most people didn't know or didn't much care. To the average Londoner, the Thames was just something you had to cross sometimes. Perks looked at him as if reading his thoughts. 'The few people who gave a toss did something about it though. There's nearly a hundred different types of fish in there now – sea trout, salmon, jellyfish. They found seahorses up past the Dartford crossing. They've brought this thing back to life. Nice you can do that, isn't it?'

Thorne nodded, acknowledging that yes, it was nice.

Perks smiled and pointed towards the water. Thorne peered at the shoreline and saw what he was so pleased about; his tale of life after death being illustrated for him, right there. White against the dark water, a heron, standing motionless in the shallows, looking for lunch.

Thorne took a breath, and started. 'Stuart Nicklin has murdered at least four people. He . . . manipulated Martin Palmer into killing another two. I'm sorry if this is hard for you to listen to. I can only say that I want to catch him, every bit as much as you wanted to catch the man you thought abducted Karen McMahon. Nicklin, whatever he calls himself now, whoever he is . . . he's a man who kills for pleasure.' He waited just a second or two before saying the hardest thing of all. 'That said, you won't be surprised when I tell you that I don't think he told you the truth about what happened to Karen.'

Thorne stopped, waited. It was impossible to gauge exactly how Perks was going to react. In most cases, being told, however sensitively, that something you had done was wrong, or at the very best, a touch misguided, was likely to provoke a defensive reaction. Thorne remembered Lickwood's anger: a predictable response to allegations of incompetence. This was far from that, but still, a similar reaction would be entirely understandable.

Perks turned and looked at him, looked at his eyes. Thorne had been wrong in thinking he'd get an angry response. The tone was gentle, comforting almost. Vic Perks did no more and no less than voice thoughts that were familiar to him. These were words that passed through his mind daily: simple and straightforward words he'd heard many years before, and now spoke easily and without hesitation. As Perks talked, Thorne knew that he'd been wrong about something else. The passion wasn't missing at all.

'She got into a blue car, sir. A Cavalier, I think they're called. Blue with rust on the front bumper and a sticker on the back window, and a six and a three in the number plate. She had a strange look on her face. I remember wondering what she was thinking, but she didn't seem frightened. Just before her head disappeared, down behind the door, I think she might even have waved at me. Just a little wave. Either that or she might have been pushing the hair back behind her ear. She did that a lot. It was hard to tell because the sun was in my eyes . . .'

Perks stopped, screwed up his own eyes. He was trying to remember something else, or perhaps he was simply recreating the face of the boy who'd first spoken these words. Thorne couldn't be sure.

'He was fourteen, Thorne. A few weeks older than she was, that's all. Karen had just turned fourteen. 17 July, 1985.' He blinked twice, slowly. 'Karen would be thirty-one this year.' Thorne nodded. It was clearly a calculation Perks could do in his sleep. 'He was still a child. I had no reason not to believe him.'

'I know.'

'Christ, people saw the car. Bloody idiots thought they saw the car, thought they saw Karen . . .'

Thorne was a fraction of a second from reaching out a hand and placing it on the old man's arm, when Perks turned away, shaking his head. He leaned on the wall, fixed his gaze on the shoreline.

The tide was almost fully out. Thorne stared down at the assorted detritus revealed by the retreating water, squatting in the sludge. Tyres, dozens of them, broken crates and of course the ubiquitous supermarket trolleys. How the hell did these things get here? He couldn't imagine anybody unloading the weekly shop into the back of the car and then merrily hoiking their trolley off the nearest bridge. Yet here they were, probably deeply symbolic of something or other, but to Thorne, right at this minute, just a bunch of old trolleys stuck in the mud.

This was a fairly typical bankside treasure trove, though Thorne had often come across more exotic items. A number of artificial limbs. A 1968 Harley-Davidson. A dead white bull-terrier, bloated and snarling like a hideous spacehopper.

And of course, the occasional body.

Every so often the river gave them up. Gently laid them

out on a sandy bank, coughed them up into a tangled bed of weeds or spat them onto the mud. Most were never identified, never claimed, remaining as anonymous as the supermarket trolleys. Many still waited to be discovered, moving up and down the river far below the surface. Their eyelashes and fingernails, the flakes of their skin, snacked upon by sea trout, salmon and seahorses.

Thorne wondered how quickly, if at all, the body of Karen McMahon would be given up, released into his care so that he could learn things from it . . .

'Two things,' Perks said suddenly. Thorne turned to him, waiting. 'I know I won't be the first person you call, or the second. Probably won't be high up on the list at all. Get to me as quickly as you can though, will you? When you find her?'

Thorne nodded. He hadn't needed to be asked.

'What's the other thing?'

Perks turned to him, shivering, tucking his scarf down inside his car coat. 'I want to be the one that tells Karen McMahon's mother.'

Holland stood in the doorway, blocking it. McEvoy moved to go past him. He moved to prevent her.

She laughed without a trace of humour. 'This is stupid.'

'Yes, it is,' Holland said. 'If you come into the office and I'm here, you turn around and leave. I come in when you're already here, you get up and go . . .'

'So, ask the DCI if you can move offices.'

'Right. What am I supposed to tell him?'

'Anything you like.'

'. . . that we're suddenly not getting on?'

Holland sighed and stepped forwards, giving McEvoy

little choice but to move back a step or two. He closed the door.

'We're not doing our jobs properly, Sarah.'

McEvoy narrowed her eyes and lowered her voice. 'You're on that one again, are you?'

'I said *we*, Sarah. Both of us need to sort this out before it goes too far.'

'Is that a threat? Going to grass me up, Holland?'

Holland brushed past her, sank into a chair. 'Jesus, Sarah, you're so paranoid.'

'Yeah? Well you should see me when I've done a few lines.' She glared at him, standing her ground but wanting more than anything to throw open the door and run. Wanting to bolt into the toilets and open her bag and sniff up a little confidence . . .

It was almost as if Holland could see the need in her face. 'And have you? Done a few today?' McEvoy said nothing, but felt the burning start behind her eyes. 'Where do you keep it? When you're here I mean. In your bag is it? In here somewhere . . . ?' Holland's eyes scanned the room. 'Better pray none of the trainee sniffer dogs ever gets loose in here . . .'

She cried easily these days. The tears could come at almost any time. They were just gathering in the corners of her eyes, only a drop or two, and easily pressed back with the heel of her hand, but still enough to stop Holland dead in his tracks.

'Sarah . . .'

'*No!*'

Her hands dropped back to her sides and she raised her head. Not a trace of softness remained in the set of her features. The anger always followed the tears and she welcomed it. She was on safer ground then. A clenched fist and a tightness in the chest felt more comfortable than the taste of saltwater in her mouth.

'Listen, I don't want your help and I don't need your advice. I certainly don't need telling what's good for me, work-wise or any other fucking-wise.'

'Nobody's trying to tell you . . .'

'A few fucks and a grope in the car park does not give you any rights at all, OK? And I didn't hear you complaining the other day when you were giving me one on the bathroom floor. Grunting and pushing me into the side of the toilet . . .'

'I only want . . .'

'Just leave it alone. I don't do it at work.'

The single knock was followed instantly by the noise of the door opening and they both turned at the same time. McEvoy instinctively took a step towards the door. Neither she nor Holland had a clue whether the man in the sharp suit with the slicked-back hair who was walking into the office had heard any of their conversation, but it was all either of them was thinking during the exchange that followed.

'I'm looking for McEvoy.'

'I'm DS McEvoy. Do you not know how to knock?'

'I knocked.'

'You knock, you wait, you get asked to come in, you come in. It's pretty bloody straightforward.'

'Who's got time? I'm DCI Derek Lickwood from SCG east.' He dropped an overcoat on to a chair, held out a hand. 'You're nothing like you sound on the phone.'

Thorne got on to the Docklands Light Railway at Island Gardens which straddled the Greenwich Meridian. Here, a tiled Victorian walkway ran right under the river, connecting with the south shore near the *Cutty Sark*.

In no time at all, the train was rattling through the heart of Canary Wharf; the view as breathtaking to Thorne as any he had just seen staring across the Thames.

It was a bizarre journey. A matter of minutes separated one of the oldest parts of London from the brand new developments that were changing the skyline for ever: from nineteenth-century tea clipper in Greenwich dry dock to forty-foot yacht in Limehouse Basin; from the classical elegance of the Queen's House to the very different beauty of the new skyscraper, days away from becoming the tallest building in the city; from stucco and slate to steel and mirrored glass in a couple of minutes.

The DLR was as close as the city got to a time machine.

Now Thorne needed to make a far shorter journey back in time. Just the tiniest hop back, seventeen years to the summer of 1985.

A hot summer. Live Aid, French nuclear testing, Brixton ready to boil over. DC Tom Thorne, newly married, standing in a stuffy interview room with a man named Francis Calvert, everything about to change.

And a young girl who, while Thorne was fighting to get the smell of death off his clothes, may or may not have climbed into a car. A girl whose picture grew smaller and finally dropped off the front pages as bigger stories exploded on to them. A girl who almost certainly died alone and afraid on a warm night when perhaps people danced at Wembley stadium or threw petrol bombs on Electric Avenue, or sat at home like Tom Thorne, trying to keep the rest of the world well away.

Thorne put his head back and looked out of the

window. Walls and windows and endless stretches of spray-painted metal moved past him in a blur. Seventeen years ago when Karen McMahon had disappeared, he'd been somewhere else. Now, perhaps they could finally help each other.

The train rumbled on towards Bank where he would change: Northern line back to Hendon and a few hours in the office before driving back out to south-east London again later on.

He closed his eyes and pictured himself twenty years down the road – being sat down in a grotty pub or walked along the river by some spunked-up wannabe; a fast-track thirtysomething DI only too eager to tell him how he'd got it so very wrong all those years before, how he'd screwed up and how they were re-opening the case and how, finally, now, they could put his mistakes right . . .

He pictured himself smiling and saying, fair enough mate, but you'll have to tell me which case you're talking about. Which particular fuck-up.

It's a bloody long list . . .

Later, approaching HMP Belmarsh, Thorne's mind turned to DIY or gardening as it usually did. The place couldn't help but put him in mind of a B&Q, or any one of those other shop-cum-warehouse monstrosities he could see from his office window, if he was unlucky and it was a clear day. Belmarsh looked as if it had been modelled on an American-style penitentiary: utilitarian, functional. Though the big old Victorian prisons like Strangeways and Brixton were doubtless grimy and overcrowded, Thorne couldn't help thinking that they had a little more . . . character.

Not that character was really the point, of course.

That bizarre London mix of old and new was there again, sandwiching Thorne on his drive south, from the Greenwich marshes, through Charlton towards where the prison squatted, somewhere indistinct between Woolwich and Thamesmead. It was a straight road running alongside the river, and though the scenery on either side was hardly picturesque, it was certainly contrasting. On the right, set back from the road, were a number of converted Victorian barracks and army buildings. Dark and dirty, and on land most probably poisoned by a hundred years of oil and ordnance. To Thorne's left as he drove along beneath a sky already dour and darkening at four o'clock, stood plot after plot of new housing developments. They were the sort that used to be advertised by that bloke with the square chin and the deep voice who swooped down in a helicopter. Red bricks and green roofs, which would almost certainly fall down long before the somewhat darker buildings on the other side of the road.

Then there was the prison itself. Its security level was as high as anywhere in the country. Home at one time or another to Jeffrey Archer, Ronnie Biggs and any terrorist worth their salt. Nobody had ever escaped. Low and grey and grim, and itself overlooked by yet another housing development. Thorne wasn't sure who had the worst view: the unhappy families in their lovely new red-brick houses, or the prisoners . . .

It took a little over half an hour from when Thorne first showed his warrant card at the desk in the visitors' centre to when he was sitting in the Category-A legal visit room, waiting to see Martin Palmer.

It was a drawn-out and regimented procedure. From the visitors' centre, where Thorne had to leave all personal belongings in a locker, on to the main building where his authorisation was checked again and an ultraviolet mark stamped onto the back of his hand. Then out into a courtyard where his pass was re-checked, through an X-ray portal, a maze of glass and air-lock type passages – one door shutting before the next one opened. And then the wait for the van that transported visitors to the separate Category-A compound. Once there, a third check on credentials, another X-ray machine and a good deal more grunting and staring before Thorne was finally ushered into the small, rectangular visit room.

Then another wait that depended on nothing but the mood of the prison officers concerned. It was always the same and it always pissed Thorne off. Police officers and prison staff were old enemies. The finders and the keepers resenting each other. Screws were seen as failed coppers. Coppers were thought of as delivery boys with smart suits and clean hands. On a prison officer's territory, if anything could be done to make things that little bit more tedious and difficult, it usually was.

Ten minutes later, a heavily tattooed and deeply depressed prison officer led Martin Palmer into the room. Palmer walked across and took a seat at the table opposite Thorne. The prison officer, who Thorne thought looked like a shithouse with right-wing leanings, left to take up his position behind the door from where he could observe through the window.

Palmer was pale. He was wearing the orange hooded top that Thorne had seen him in at his flat on Christmas Eve. He stared at Thorne, blinking slowly. He looked more like a man who'd just woken up than one who, as a matter of policy, would be on suicide watch.

Despite the time and trouble he'd taken to get there, Thorne wanted to keep it quick and simple. He was only really there to deliver a message.

'I'm going to find Karen,' he said.

PART FOUR

NEED

NINETEEN

Palmer looked lost.

He stared around in search of something that might anchor him, some familiar landmark from which he could navigate, but everything felt alien and unknown.

Thorne watched, trying to imagine the man as a boy in this place when the world was very different, but he was no more successful than Palmer at recapturing the past.

It was understandable, of course. The embankment was unrecognisable compared to how it must have been almost twenty years earlier. This stretch of line, which a mile or so further on ran past the bottom of the King Edward's playing fields, had been disused for years. It had been earmarked for a development which, luckily for this operation, was never quite funded properly. The railway buildings – maintenance sheds and equipment stores – had long been demolished. The track was overgrown and in pieces. In patches, the grass was over eight feet high. Palmer was a stranger in this place he had once known so well.

The handcuffs he was wearing hardly helped.

Thorne moved across to him, stood at his shoulder.

'Something tells me this isn't going to be easy.'

'It's not the same place. It's completely different.'

'Nowhere's ever the way we remember it.'

'I know. But this . . .' Palmer began to move towards a clump of trees. Thorne went with him. The sky was clear, but it had rained heavily overnight and the wind, which had picked up, blew water off the brown ferns and grey sycamores. The long grass clinging to their legs as they walked was heavy and wet. Thorne was wearing waterproof over-trousers and Palmer's jeans were already soaked.

'The curve of the bank, maybe,' Thorne said. 'A particular arrangement of trees. Anything that might at least narrow it down for us.'

Palmer nodded. 'I'm looking.'

Thorne saw the confusion etched across his face, but beneath it, Palmer wore the same base expression, his *key* expression, that Thorne had seen often. The one he had seen staring out at him from the front page of most of the papers that morning. Palmer, six months earlier, blinking and blurry, cradling a soft drink at some doubtless horrendous office party or other. Snapped hiding in a corner, his eyes wide, the pupils reddened by the flash; doing his best to look as if he was enjoying himself and failing dismally.

Thorne's money was on Sean Bracher as the source of the photo. If the slimy wanker had been in front of him at that moment, he might have given him a dig, but he couldn't summon up the energy to be too pissed off about it. Bracher, like that cleaner in the hotel, cashing in on killing, making a little something. One person's tragedy and all that. One dog-eared snap. One nice new sports car and a couple of weeks in Antigua with the girlfriend. It was only a picture. Fuck it, why not . . .

Palmer with that same expression now as he stared around him.

All at once, Thorne recognised the expression for what it actually was: embarrassment. Embarrassed to be at that party. To be walking into a police station confessing to murder. Embarrassed to be here. Palmer was, Thorne realised, embarrassed to be pretty much wherever he was.

Palmer let out a small groan, his disorientation growing, and it struck Thorne that even the seasons were conspiring against him – against both of them. Palmer would have remembered this place as it was in summer. Then the trees would have been heavy with fruit and flower. Today they dripped, dark and skeletal.

'It might help to think of the place in relation to the houses,' Thorne suggested. 'Can you remember which estate Nicklin used to live on?' They both looked up towards the top of the embankment. A healthy crop of TV aerials and satellite dishes blossomed, just visible, beyond the treeline.

Palmer shook his head. 'They're different. Newer.'

'What about the bridge? Can you get your bearings from that?'

Palmer looked up at the metal footbridge, a quarter of a mile away, high above the embankment valley. 'That wasn't even there. They were still building it. I can remember the noise . . .'

Thorne suddenly felt wetter and a damn sight colder as the thought hit him. How devious and clever could the fourteen-year-old Stuart Nicklin have been? Was Karen McMahon buried under a hundred tons of concrete bridge support? If she was, they'd almost certainly never find her. Not that Jesmond or those above him would even agree to looking. He'd had enough of a job getting a search on *this* scale organised. The three magic initials had done the trick in the end. Having spoken to Hendricks he was far from sure whether it was even possible, but the outside chance of the killer's DNA being salvageable had swung it. They'd got nothing from any of Nicklin's recent victims, but maybe he'd not been quite so careful back when he was still a beginner.

DNA – a huge breakthrough in the struggle to catch and convict murderers. A useful weapon when it came to getting the better of one's dimmer superiors . . .

Palmer's eyes moved from the bridge to the slopes that rose up on either side of them. He studied the small troop of uniformed officers, positioned at various points along the bank on his right-hand side. Some stood perfectly still, radios in hand, and some of them were moving slowly, their steps mirroring those of himself and Thorne.

'What's going to happen?' Palmer asked. 'How's this going to work?'

'As soon as we get a fix, whenever you can give us somewhere to start, a team will come in to clear the area – get the grass cut, bring in machinery to make it a bit more manageable. For a while, it'll be more like *Ground Force* than anything.'

Palmer nodded quickly. This wasn't what he wanted to know. 'I mean what about afterwards? The actual searching. The digging . . .'

Thorne puffed out his cheeks. Not having been involved in an operation like this for a number of years, he wasn't a hundred per cent sure himself. 'A team of specially trained officers. With dogs probably . . .' Palmer flinched. Thorne wondered how on earth they trained dogs for this . . . speciality. It wasn't something he bothered to think about for long. Sniffing out drugs was one thing, but sniffing out death? 'Cadaver dogs' they called them in the States.

A vivid image caught him off guard for a second, took a little breath away . . .

Lolling, leathery tongues, and paws scrabbling away at soil. Tearing through delicate cobwebs of skin and pressing down through chalk sticks of powdery bone.

Thorne waited a few seconds. 'Then, if we find a body, we'll bring in a forensic archaeologist . . .'

Palmer cut him off. 'You won't find anything.' He stopped and looked down at Thorne. His wrists were cuffed in front of him and his naturally stooping gait had become almost absurdly exaggerated. He looked like a hunchback. 'Why would she be here?'

The question, seemingly genuine and heartfelt, prompted Thorne to ask one of his own. One he'd asked before. Why had Palmer not considered the possibility that Nicklin might have had something to do with Karen McMahon's disappearance? 'Not back then, maybe,' Thorne said. 'That's fair enough. But *now*, since he came back, and the killing began, now that you know about him. Don't you at least think it's possible?'

Something like a smile appeared on Palmer's face, as it had when Thorne had pressed him on this before, and he more or less repeated the only answer that he seemed prepared to give.

'Anything is possible, I suppose. If either of us was responsible for what happened to Karen that day, it was me . . .'

'Tell me why.'

Palmer leaned forward as if he might fall, but at the last second he took a huge step and his momentum carried him away. Thorne watched him go for a second or two, thinking. Was it something about Karen, the thing which Palmer seemed to be keeping back? Or was there something else? Something he wasn't saying about Nicklin?

Thorne moved off after him, following in his wake as Palmer noisily stamped down a path. The rust-coloured couch grass wind-whipped and sopping. Sharp enough to draw blood. The ground itself was sodden underfoot. Muddy water squelched up and into Thorne's boots as they walked.

'I talk to her sometimes,' Palmer said suddenly. 'I know that sounds very stupid.'

Thorne didn't think so. He'd enjoyed, or more accurately, endured, a number of conversations with the dead down the years.

'What do you talk to her about?'

'I don't so much now, but before, I used to tell her what I'd done.'

'Confessing?'

Up ahead, Palmer grunted. 'She knew anyway, of course.'

'Did she forgive you?'

'You could never be sure what Karen was thinking. I don't think even Stuart knew a lot of the time . . .'

Palmer began to move well ahead of Thorne. He veered off sharply to the left, away from the embankment that climbed steeply up to the new housing estates and towards the gentler slope on the other side. At the top, high metal fencing separated this wild, untended patch of wilderness from a shiny new industrial park. Thorne glanced towards the embankment on his right. The officers were still tracking their movements, one or two moving gingerly down the slippery bank.

'She knew what *I* was thinking all the time, of course. All the time . . .' He said something else. Thorne strained to hear, but it was lost on the wind.

Palmer's strides were getting bigger, the distance between himself and Thorne growing with every step. Thorne started to move a little quicker, but they had come through the grass now and were heading into an area where progress, for him at least, was rapidly becoming far trickier. Though the ground was suddenly drier, the undergrowth was denser, his feet heavier. He couldn't raise his legs high enough to step over the huge expanses of bracken and briar. He stumbled through masses of bare bramble, across a tangle of spiky dead thistle-heads. He swore as he caught his hand on something sharp, and bringing it to his mouth, he lost sight of Palmer for a second or two. He looked round quickly, in time to see a uniformed officer a hundred or more yards away, sliding down the embankment on his backside. He was on the verge of calling out, when he heard Palmer's voice . . .

'That's because I loved her, I suppose. I always loved her . . .'

Thorne pushed aside the overhanging branches of a dead blackberry bush, and saw him standing thirty feet away. Thorne was breathing heavily. He suddenly felt rather stupid. He looked at Palmer up ahead of him, stock still. What on earth had he been worried about?

He followed Palmer's tracks through a shin-high patch of dried-out ferns until he was standing alongside him.

'Was Karen the only woman you ever loved?'

'Yes. The only *woman*.' He turned to Thorne and smiled sadly, like an idiot. 'I always loved Stuart, of course.'

Palmer raised his handcuffed wrists and pointed as best he could towards the gnarled black roots of a sorry-looking oak tree a few yards away.

'This is it. I found a baby bird here once.' He turned around and began looking excitedly in different directions. 'The sheds we used to mess about in were over *there*. Stuart's house was up *there*.' He looked at Thorne, nodded. 'It was around here, where we used to come, the three of us. This was the last place I saw Karen.'

Thorne turned around. After a few seconds, he made out the figure of Dave Holland at the top of the embankment, talking to two uniforms, drinking tea. Thorne stuck two fingers in his mouth and whistled loudly to attract Holland's attention. When he had it, he started pointing.

Holland waved and began to speak into his radio.

Checking in his rear-view mirror, Thorne saw that Palmer's head was bowed, as if he was looking down at the metal around his wrist and around that of Dave Holland who was sitting next to him, and quietly reminding himself how the handcuffs came to be there. How *he* came to be in the back of this particular car. The detective driving the Vectra behind them caught Thorne's look and flashed his lights. Thorne raised a hand in acknowledgement.

The small convoy turned left off the southern approach to the Blackwall Tunnel and made for Woolwich, heading back towards Belmarsh Prison.

Palmer spoke casually, as if he were asking to have a window opened, but even over the rattle of the Mondeo and the roar of other cars on the road, Thorne could hear the need in his voice.

'It will be life, won't it? I'll not be coming out . . .'

Thorne always tried to put the trial to the back of his mind. He'd need to give evidence of course, but his real job, if he'd done it properly, was over by then. He was usually on to the next one. Occasionally, *more* occasionally in the last few years, some moron of a judge – some fossil, who didn't know what rap music was and thought that women in short skirts were asking for it – might fuck things up for everybody: make headlines and undermine months, maybe years, of police work by sentencing a murderer as if he'd neglected to take his library books back . . .

'It will be life?' The emphasis on *will*. 'Do you think . . . ?'

A glance in the mirror told Thorne that, now, Palmer's head was raised, his eyes fixed straight ahead. Thorne gave the only honest answer he could. 'I hope so, yes.'

Palmer nodded a few times to himself, to Holland. Thorne thought he looked relieved. 'The other thing is, they'll separate me as well, won't they? When I'm in there? They do that, I read it somewhere, for prisoners who've killed women. They isolate them, because the other inmates, the honest, *decent* thieves and armed robbers, and contract killers will hurt the likes of me inside, if they get the chance. That's true isn't it?'

Thorne saw little point in denying it. 'Sometimes, yeah. It's normally sex-offenders, stuff with kids . . .'

'I know, but I would be a target though.' It wasn't a question. Thorne shrugged, let Palmer continue. 'There's no way they can keep you apart all the time though, is there? Even if you're with . . . other prisoners who are the same as you, the special ones. There's a pecking order of some sort, I imagine. If you're a pervert who's killed a schoolgirl, you're obviously worse than the animal who killed the old age pensioner. The man who's battered his wife to death is not quite as hated as the one who's murdered two women he didn't even know . . .'

Thorne did not want to listen to any more of this. In the beginning, it had sounded like an attempt at self-assurance. Now, it was sounding like self-pity. 'Listen Palmer, if you want me to tell you it's going to be tough inside, I'll tell you. Yes, you're going to hate it. Then again, you're not a stupid man are you? Isn't that sort of the point?'

'Yes, of course . . .'

'If you're asking me to feel an ounce of anything like fucking sympathy . . . ?'

'No. Absolutely not.'

'Good.' Thorne stuck his foot down, gambled on amber and roared across a mini-roundabout onto Woolwich Church Street, the river to the left of him. He checked in the mirror to be sure that the Vectra had made it through the lights behind him. His eyes flicked across to Holland who'd said next to nothing since they got into the car. He stared out of the window, lost in thought. Just a body to handcuff a prisoner to.

'Something else you need to think about, Palmer. Yes, you're quite right, you'll be hated because you killed women. Doesn't matter *why* you killed them, the ones who'll want to hurt you for it will think it was a sex thing, whatever. They haven't really got a lot of time for psychology. Well they *have*, of course, loads of time, but they just can't be arsed. They'll just make presumptions.'

Palmer raised up his wrist, Holland's moving with it,

and scratched the side of his head with a thumbnail. 'I suppose it would be stupid to ask if anybody ever puts them straight. Tells them the truth.'

'Very stupid. It gets a lot worse as well. They'll have two reasons to hate you.'

'What . . . ?'

'Two reasons to smash your face into a sink. To push you down a couple of flights of stairs, or knock something up in the tool shop to stick into you while you're queuing up for your dinner. Don't get me wrong, these people have *got* a moral code, it's just not a normal one.' Thorne caught Palmer's eye in the mirror and held it. 'They hate men who hurt women, or *pretend* to hate them, doesn't much matter which, and if you're lucky, they might only piss in your tea. But if there's one thing they really *do* despise even more than that, it's a grass. With you, they'll be getting two for the price of one.'

Slowly, in the mirror, a clear view of the Vectra emerged, as Palmer's head dropped and he slumped down in his seat. Pleased as he was with his little speech, Thorne couldn't help but feel like a grown man who's played games with a small child and refused to let him win.

Ten minutes later, Thorne swung the car round and pulled up at a T-junction. The Vectra came alongside him, the four officers exchanging looks, both cars waiting for a gap in the traffic coming from his left. A thousand yards away on the other side of the road, across the expanse of reclaimed saltmarsh, lay the prison. The slouching concrete warehouse . . .

Cons R Us. Kingdom Of Killers.

The driver of the back-up car gave Thorne the thumbs up and accelerated away into the stream of traffic heading back towards the city. Thorne pulled across the road and drove slowly towards the prison's main entrance, feeling the first twinges of a headache kicking in behind his eyes.

He looked at the clock on the dashboard as he rolled up the drive towards the barrier. It was just after half past one. He began to think about where he was due to be in less than an hour.

The day was not going to get any better.

TWENTY

If someone told Thorne that he had a nice singing voice, chances are they'd be wearing black . . .

He *did* have a good voice, surprisingly high and light for someone who looked and spoke like he did, and usually coming as a shock to anyone who heard it for the first time. As he sang, it struck him, as it usually did on these occasions, that such events were actually the only time that he ever really sang, the only time *most* people sang properly: weddings, or more likely in his case, funerals.

They finished singing 'The Lord Is My Shepherd' more or less together, and sat down. As Brian Marsden, the headmaster, made his way to the lectern, Thorne looked at the people around him.

It was a large congregation. Sixty-five or seventy people maybe. The majority were friends and colleagues, several generations of teachers and ex-pupils, but a number of those who sat shuffling feet and orders of service were there in an official capacity.

There were more police than family.

Thorne and McEvoy were there, representing the key investigative team. Malcolm Jay, the DS from Harrow, was in church, and Derek Lickwood. Steve Norman was around somewhere, to liaise with any unwelcome reporters who might try to grab a few words with grieving relatives.

While respects were being paid, the mourners were being closely watched in case the killer himself decided to pop along and sprinkle soil on the coffin of his victim. He wouldn't be the first, but as always, Thorne thought it unlikely that he or anybody else would be able to spot him if he were to show up. He would hardly be the one dressed in bright colours or sniggering during the eulogy. He was unlikely to be looking shifty or coughing nervously when the vicar talked about the deceased being 'taken from us'. Nevertheless, it was a useful thing to do. They would ask discreetly for a guest list and, even more discreetly, someone would be filming those guests as they filed out of the church.

Thorne craned his head round. There was a row of six or seven schoolboys in the rearmost pew. They were sixth-formers probably, sitting stiffly and wearing what in Thorne's day would have been called 'lounge suits'. One of them caught his eye and smiled. Thorne inclined his head non-committally and turned away. The teachers, at least fifteen or twenty of them, sat together on the left-hand side. Some were wearing gowns and mortar boards. All of them watched the tall, white-haired man at the lectern. The headmaster's voice echoed round the church, as it did every morning round the main hall at King Edward's. Thorne looked at the sombre expression on Brian Marsden's thin face and guessed that he looked the same every day in assembly.

The family sat on the front row. The teenage nephew and niece. The sister in her forties. The father . . .

Thorne looked at the old man and saw the shadow of Charlie Garner's grandfather. Thirty years older perhaps, and a sight more frail, but with the same haunted expression. Like he'd been hollowed out and there was nothing of substance to hold the bones in place any more.

The congregation was rising to sing again, the organist playing the opening bars of 'Abide With Me' badly. As Thorne stood, he caught the eye of the headmaster who had just returned to his place, his tribute to Ken Bowles paid. Thorne opened his mouth to sing and realised that he hadn't heard a word of what had been said.

Later, outside the church, people watched the coffin being loaded into the back of the hearse. With McEvoy away somewhere re-applying make-up, Thorne was joined by Malcolm Jay and Derek Lickwood. They both lit cigarettes hungrily and the three of them stood around, not knowing what to do with their hands and trying not to look too much like police officers.

'Inspector Thorne . . . ?'

Thorne turned at the familiar voice and found himself face to face with a smiling Andrew Cookson, the teacher who'd shown him around the school. The teacher who, two weeks earlier, Thorne had mistakenly assumed to have been the body they had today come to bury.

'Here mob-handed then?' Cookson said, laughing.

Thorne nodded and turned to his colleagues. They had obviously not been doing a great job of blending in. 'DS Jay, DCI Lickwood . . .'

'Andrew Cookson. I worked with Ken.'

While handshakes were exchanged, Thorne looked at the man who was hovering at Cookson's shoulder. His head was completely bald and spotted with brown patches.

He leaned on a walking stick and stared at something in the distance, his lower jaw moving constantly, as if he were chewing something everlasting.

He turned his head suddenly, looked at Thorne. 'Thank you for coming.'

'I'm sorry about your son,' Thorne said.

Cookson stepped back and took the old man by the elbow. 'This is Leslie Bowles, Ken's father.'

Thorne saw Jay and Lickwood exchange an uneasy glance. Before they had a chance to mumble an awkward response, the old man spoke.

'Very kind of Andrew here, to look after me . . .'

'Don't be silly,' Cookson said.

'Doesn't know me from Adam.'

'I knew Ken . . .'

'Not as well as some.'

Cookson shrugged and shook his head. Bowles took a slight step towards Thorne and the others. 'It's supposed to stop isn't it?' he said. 'Everybody says it switches around when you get old and they have to look after you. The parent becomes the child . . .' He sounded well educated. The voice was surprisingly strong and deep. Thorne knew that the old man was a lot tougher than he looked. 'It's nonsense though, it really is. Even when they're cooking for you and getting your shopping in, you know? Even when they're doing up the buttons on your pyjamas and pretending to listen to your stupid stories, even . . .' His eyes twinkled and he lowered his voice conspiratorially. '. . . Even when they're wiping your arse, you're still the father—' His voice faltered suddenly. He swallowed, took a breath and continued, the sentences now shorter, the words spoken between gulps of air. 'It never stops, never. You're still the father and he's still the son. Still the son . . .' He turned his head away from them. His jaw began its chewing movement again.

'Dad. They're ready . . .' Leslie Bowles's daughter appeared behind him. Thorne watched them move slowly away towards the line of cars, and saw McEvoy pass them on the narrow gravel path, walking towards him.

'He's amazing,' Cookson said, looking towards the old man. 'He must be pushing ninety.'

McEvoy arrived. She nodded to Lickwood and Jay, stepped in close to Thorne. 'Lippy re-applied. All's right with the world. What's happening?'

Thorne caught a look from Cookson and made the introduction. 'Andrew Cookson, he teaches at King Edward's. This is Detective Sergeant McEvoy . . .'

McEvoy and Cookson shook hands. 'I was wrong,' Cookson said. 'You don't all look alike.'

'Oh, you've noticed that, then?' McEvoy said, smiling sarcastically. 'And you're a *teacher*, are you?'

The cars were rolling sedately away from the church. The mourners began to drift after them, putting up umbrellas as a light rain began to fall. Thorne was pleased. He was still damp anyway from tramping about on the railway embankment and his feet were freezing, but he thought that, all things considered, it *should* rain at a man's funeral. There should be flurries of black umbrellas and rain hammering down on to the lid of the coffin, and a mysterious woman who nobody can identify, weeping . . . and a dirty great shitload of alcohol.

Maybe he was just thinking about his own funeral . . .

'Come on,' Thorne said, and he and the others began to move towards where the cars were parked. It was three or four miles to the cemetery. Graveyard of course, never crematorium. Always burial, in case the body should ever need to be exhumed and looked at again.

'*I mean what about afterwards? The actual searching. The digging.*'

He remembered what he'd been doing that morning, thought about the dogs again. Barking, howling, pawing at the ground, sniffing out the stench of something long-dead below the Coke cans and the fag ends and the weeds.

The rain was really starting to come down by the time they reached the cars. Thorne and McEvoy climbed into the Mondeo. He started the engine, remembered that he still hadn't got the heater fixed, flicked on the squeaky wipers. He pulled the car out on to the main road and followed the line of bigger, blacker cars up ahead.

I got Ken Bowles killed.

And Thorne knew that he *had* – that he would always be sorry for it, that he would catch the man who had done the killing. He knew that standing at the graveside, he would feel his guilt, hot and heavy inside him, curling round his innards and settling down to sleep fitfully in his gut.

He also knew that as he watched the coffin going down into its grave, he would be thinking about Charlie Garner's mother Carol, in *hers*. About Katie Choi and Miriam Vincent in *theirs*. As they lowered Ken Bowles down, he would be thinking about Karen McMahon, in a grave as yet unknown and never tended.

A grave a good deal shallower.

He sat there shaking. Across the table from him, Caroline was crying, and in truth he wasn't far away from it himself . . .

She had cooked pasta. They'd been sitting and talking

about their respective days, neither of which had been particularly easy, and suddenly, she'd brought up the subject of kids again. It surfaced every few months, and for him, it was usually just a question of making the right noises. He'd nod and smile, and point out how far she could still go career-wise. He'd question whether now might be *exactly* the right time and squeeze her hand, and assure her that yes, of course he wanted children too, but that they needed to be sure. They needed to decide *together* . . .

Tonight he'd been unable to conjure up even that piss-easy piece of flannel.

His mind was racing, as it was every second of the day. There was so much to consider, so many avenues to explore. He was still searching for the idea that would excite him, that would fire his imagination. He knew what he had to do, but he had yet to succeed in visualising it. The big idea. The concept that would replace the short-lived adventure with Palmer.

Caroline was talking about crèches and maternity leave . . .

It would involve creating a new scenario. A new backdrop to the act itself, which after all was the easy bit, the unsophisticated part. He *had* toyed with juicing up the killing. He'd visualised new and interesting ways of doing it, but it ended up like the script to an old Hammer movie, with Vincent Price knocking off people who'd upset him in the manner of Egyptian plagues or Shakespearean tragedies.

No, he needed to mould the context, to shape his environment in a way that would stimulate and spark, that would challenge and charge him.

Above all, he needed to keep moving forward. Never still and never back.

This was what *should* be occupying him, but there was

anger in the way. He couldn't think creatively while that was clouding his thoughts, preventing any real focus.

He was furious that they were looking for Karen.

Caroline leaned across the table and took his hand. Would there be a better time than this? Their jobs were secure, there was enough money coming in. It wouldn't be plain sailing, of course not, there was bound to be a period of adjustment, but they could make it work . . .

He'd watched Thorne and Palmer down by the railway line. Thorne cajoling, suggesting, Palmer looking forlorn in his handcuffs. He'd watched them strolling along the embankment like a pair of old poofs with a taste for S & M. What the fuck did Thorne think he was going to gain, even if he did find her?

Her family would help. Giving them stuff, babysitting. They would still be able to go out, have their own lives . . .

It was *his* past and he wouldn't have it messed with. He didn't want it altered. When, *if*, he wanted things discovered, he was the one who would lead them to discovery. He was the one that controlled things.

It was about working together, supporting each other . . .

He needed to put the anger aside, in one part of his brain. Yes, that might do it. Let the other side concentrate on the future – on finding a new motor.

Caroline didn't want to leave it too late. She wanted to enjoy being a mother while she was still young . . .

He would find it, course he would, if he just had some space to work it out, but Thorne and the rest of them were really starting to needle him.

A child would bring them close, bring them closer . . .

He could see it in his mind's eye, almost – unformed and not quite reachable.

Didn't he want a child? He'd said he did.

Like something on the tip of his tongue, nearly there, nearly . . . but what the fuck did Thorne think he was up to?

Didn't he love her any more . . . ?

He leaned forward and slapped her.

It wasn't his fault. She wouldn't shut up, wouldn't be quiet for just a few seconds so that he could compartmentalise. Probably not her fault either, course not, she didn't know, did she? She couldn't see past the smile, the face that gave nothing away, but even so, I mean *bloody hell . . .*

He just needed a bit of space to deal with things. To separate the anger from the creativity.

He looked at her. The handprint was clear, a livid scarlet across her jaw and the top of her neck.

Silly bitch. Waffling on about babies. When he needed a bit of peace and quiet so that he could think about death.

For Thorne, the mug of tea before bed had become something of a ritual. The stroll down to the late-night grocers, after discovering he'd run out of milk, was not uncommon either.

He was in this shop half a dozen times a week, minimum. The three brothers that ran it were Turkish, he thought, maybe Cypriot. He didn't know any of their names. They smiled, sometimes, when he bought his bread, paper and beer, but they didn't seem that interested in getting to know him.

As Thorne reached into his pocket to pay for the milk, he imagined finding that he'd left his wallet at home. He wondered if they'd let him owe them the money until next time. Seeing as he'd been in their shop six times a week for the past eighteen months. Would they? Probably not. Maybe if he produced his warrant card, showed them he was a policeman.

Outside the shop, Thorne stood waiting for the lights at the pelican crossing to change, studying the adverts in the window. The one that caught his eye was scribbled in red felt-tip on the back of a postcard. It was misspelled, but the services offered were plain enough.

It had been a long time.

Thorne took out a pen and scribbled down the number on the side of the milk carton.

TWENTY-ONE

They'd found Karen McMahon within twelve hours.

From the top of the embankment it was obvious where the team was working. The white tented-off area around the grave stood out starkly against the browns and dark greens of the long grasses and tangles of fern. A white square billowing above the bones.

Holland began to move down the hill towards the site, McEvoy ten feet or so away. The two of them had driven there together, along with another DC and a trainee detective. The conversation in the car had been sparse and far from sparkling. Now they moved slowly down the slope, their white plastic bodysuits rustling. Aliens descending, unsure of their footing.

The grave had been found in one of the drainage ditches that ran alongside the embankment at the foot of each slope. Once the overgrown and overhanging greenery had been cut back, it had not been hard to see or to reach. The ditch was about four feet wide but movement was restricted. The sides were muddy and in danger of collapse, and hours of hard work which had revealed the remains of Karen McMahon could be undone by one clumsy step.

Holland and McEvoy pulled up their masks and ducked down inside the tent. It was cramped and crowded. There were already half a dozen people in there, crouched or stooping, the tent not high enough to stand up straight in. The sun had not been up long and the morning wasn't warm, but the heat beneath the canvas was stifling. Though the lamps had been turned off outside the tent, there were still two powerful ones inside and the temperature was climbing all the time. Inside the bodysuit, Holland could already feel the sweat trickling down his back as he stepped carefully past Phil Hendricks who was on his haunches at the graveside, and moved towards where Thorne was deep in conversation with Doctor James Pettet.

Thorne glanced towards Holland and McEvoy as they entered the tent. Instantly, and for a second or two, he wondered if something might be going on between them. There was an atmosphere . . .

He dismissed the thought, and returned to a conversation about death and decay.

As forensic archaeologists went, James Pettet was probably as good as they came, but he was no great shakes as a human being. If Thorne never saw him again, he wouldn't lose a great deal of sleep.

'. . . moisture is the enemy of composition. Moisture and heat together is just about as bad as it gets. Or good of course, depending on which way you look at it.'

Behind his mask, Thorne let out a long slow breath and very quickly took another one in. *Which way you look at it?*

'Buried in a drainage ditch, as you say, at the height of summer, it's remarkable we have anything at all.' Pettet's voice was deep and he spoke as if he was constantly on the verge of nodding off, worn out by the effort of explaining things to idiots. 'There is a complete absence of fleshy matter and you can see that the bones themselves are mushy.'

Thorne had never met Pettet before and could only guess at what lay beneath the plastic hood wrapped tightly around the face and the mask that covered the nose and mouth.

'The non-organic material has been better preserved of course.' As Pettet catalogued it, an assistant moved carefully around the grave, occasionally dropping to his knees or onto his chest to gather up a fragment with long forceps and drop it into a plastic evidence bag. 'The material of the dress, the refuse bags, what's left of the carpet she was wrapped up in. The rope, or cord, around the neck remains remarkably intact . . .'

Thorne imagined Pettet to be balding, perhaps with a Bobby Charlton comb-over and very bad skin.

Thorne turned away and looked down into the grave, the buzzing arc lights casting a harsh and unforgiving light across its grisly contents.

Mushy was about right. Tea-coloured bones sunk down into mud and slime. Tattered remnants of a blue dress, *not white, thank heavens*, and matted clumps of carpet, all floating in a brown soup. Tufts of hair, plastered to the bobbing skull like worms.

The white bleached bones of the human skeleton existed nowhere but under the skin, where they belonged, and in the imaginations of television scriptwriters. *Dem bones dem bones*, hanging, grinning and unreal in doctor's surgery sketches.

Not like this. This human stew.

At the foot of the grave, Hendricks stood back to let one of the team come in close, to stoop down and pluck something long and greasy from the mud. Thorne caught his eye. Hendricks winked at him. He turned back to Pettet.

'What about DNA?'

The archaeologist puffed out his cheeks. 'Don't hold your breath.'

Thorne grunted – as close as it was possible to get to a laugh. The smell inside the tent was overpowering, and, masks or not, holding their breath was exactly what everybody around the grave was trying to do. Everybody but Pettet, anyway. The archaeologist failed to see any irony in what he'd said. 'The victim's DNA, yes, perhaps. Get me some comparable material – hairs, fingernail clippings. Sometimes the parents hang on to those things for sentimental reasons.'

Of course they'd go through the motions, run the tests, but Thorne knew he was looking at what was left of Karen McMahon. 'Any chance of anything from the killer?'

Pettet almost managed a smile. 'Always a chance. There's a chance you'll win the lottery isn't there? Only possibility is the rope. Bits of skin caught in there, perhaps, but any cellular material will have been destroyed by the creosote.'

Thorne turned, raised his eyebrows.

Pettet explained, slowly. 'Creosote is used to weatherproof the railway ties. Same stuff you put on your garden fence. Over the years it's leached into the water running along these ditches. Ironically, if she'd been buried on higher ground, somewhere drier, the creosote in the soil might have acted as a preservative and we might have had a lot more of her left.'

To Thorne, the disappointment in Pettet's voice sounded strictly professional. Not sentimental like those silly parents with their jewellery boxes full of hair and fingernails . . .

Thorne glanced over to the other side of the tent where a small pile of dirty rocks stood in the corner. Pettet caught Thorne's look. 'At least all the bones are there. The killer took the trouble to make sure the foxes didn't get at them.'

A layer of rocks laid carefully on top of the grave. Rocks too heavy to be shifted by the snout of something hungry. Rocks, then a layer of mud two feet or so thick and underneath it all, the body of a 14-year-old girl shrouded in bin-liners, rotting beneath an old carpet. Safe from foxes. Safe from everything.

A few minutes later outside the tent, Thorne dropped a hand on to Phil Hendricks's shoulder. 'Don't get big-headed, but it's a treat to talk about death with someone who doesn't behave like he's suffering from it . . .'

'Wish he was,' Holland muttered. 'Miserable sod.'

Hendricks grinned. 'He *was* hard work, wasn't he?'

'Like I don't know what fucking creosote is!' Thorne shook his head, the wounded expression just what was needed to set them off. They all laughed then, as they desperately needed to. They laughed and shook their heads as they stepped clumsily out of their bodysuits. McEvoy lost her footing and her hand reached out to Holland for support. The laughter stopped quickly after that, and they all stood in silence for a few moments, taking in lungfuls of wonderful dirty London air.

'I don't understand,' Hendricks said, looking around. 'He obviously didn't want her disturbed, you know, by animals . . .'

Holland nodded. 'Must have taken him ages to find all those rocks. There's not many of them anywhere round here.'

'. . . but he didn't seem to much care where he buried her. She wasn't very well hidden.'

'She wasn't hidden at all,' Holland said. 'She wasn't hard to find. Nobody'd ever bothered to look for her, that's all.'

McEvoy lit a cigarette, spoke as she exhaled. 'Obviously he didn't think anyone *would* look for her.'

'Oh, he *knew* they wouldn't,' Thorne said. 'He made sure of it.'

She got into a blue car, sir. A Cavalier I think they're called . . .

'He did this when he was fourteen,' McEvoy said. 'Then he disappears, and pops up again over fifteen years later. Fifteen years.'

Thorne nodded. He knew what was coming. He asked the question out loud, the one he'd asked himself as he'd stared down at Karen McMahon's remains. 'How many more bodies are there out there?'

It was warming up. There was no wind at all where they stood at the foot of the embankment and the smoke from McEvoy's cigarette rose straight up, blue against the concrete-coloured sky.

'No chance on the DNA then?' she asked.

Thorne shook his head.

'I told you,' Hendricks said.

Thorne shrugged. *Worth a try*. It was all academic anyway. They knew who it was lying back there inside the tent, in a hole they dignified with the word *grave*, and they knew who had put her there. There would be nothing in the way of concrete evidence on the Palmer–Nicklin case, on the *Garner* case, to present to anybody. But they had found a body. Bullseye. Thorne had a corpse to offer up to his superiors. He saw himself rather like a cat, dropping a dead bird at the foot of its master. *Stroke me. See? Look at how clever I am.*

Thorne had never felt less clever in his life.

They turned at a rustle of canvas from behind them, and saw Pettet emerge from the tent carrying a small plastic evidence bag. He pulled down his mask and strolled across to them. Thorne was pleased to see that he had been right about the bad skin.

'I thought you might want to see this.'

He held out the bag, and Thorne and the others clustered around, staring at what was inside. Whatever it was had once been a bright colour, but was now faded and thick with black mud. It was Holland who first made sense of the broken down and barely legible lettering.

'Bloody hell, I used to love those. Can you still get them?'

Hendricks leaned in a little closer, peering at the plastic bag. Its sides were streaked with muck. The bottom filled with dirty water, gritty with tiny stones and traces of bone marrow. 'What is it?'

'It's the wrapper off a chocolate bar,' Thorne said. 'And no, I don't think you *can* get them any more.' He guessed not anyway, unless Nicklin's tastes had changed. It wasn't the same brand as the one they'd found licked clean and clutched in Charlie Garner's hand, but its presence chilled him every bit as much.

Thorne took a few steps up the slope of the embankment towards the cars, stopped and looked back. He spoke to Pettet, staring over his head at the small white tent. 'Be careful taking her out of there, will you?'

Pettet opened his mouth to reply, but Thorne was

already turning and climbing away up the hill. He clutched the white plastic bodysuit in his fist, wondering just how much protection it provided against what Hendricks had called the little pieces of death. Back in that tent, there would have been millions of them floating around, settling unseen against the bright white material. Some would have got through and ended up sitting on the skin, nestling in the cuffs and trapped on the soles of shoes. Waiting to sparkle when the time was right.

When it was dark enough.

Thorne took a breath and started to climb faster. He was starting to feel the ache in his thighs as he took out his phone and dialled Vic Perks's number.

He would have liked to have stayed and waited until they brought her out. That would have been interesting. He wondered how she would look. Probably just one more stain on that manky old carpet he'd wrapped her up in and tossed across his shoulder. The outline of her reduced down and imprinted on it. Bodily fluids marking out her skinny frame in the cheap nylon pile.

He would have liked to have stayed, but he needed to get to work.

He was annoyed but he was not letting it get to him. He was angry that his past was being disturbed, examined, when he had taken such great care, *always*, to ensure that to all intents and purposes, it had never really existed. He was in control of what lay behind him, every bit as much as he was of what lay ahead. It wound him up to see them taking a little of that control away. He felt usurped.

But he wasn't going to let it spoil things.

Let them uncover a small piece of who he used to be. It

wouldn't do them any good at all. He was about to take another leap into the future.

He'd felt close to it the night before. It had been there, almost within his reach when Caroline had been going on about kids. Then afterwards, as she had sobbed and shouted, as he'd reached out to draw her into an embrace, it had come to him.

The way forward.

Two major changes to the way he was going to go about things, now that he was working alone again. Two. And each *on its own* enough to ratchet up the excitement, to get whatever it was that spewed out adrenaline working overtime. Even as he considered what he had decided to do, his exhilaration was tempered by the thought that he would never be able to top it. How could he?

He was being far too modest, of course. Hadn't he thought the same thing with his hands around a woman's neck, imagining Palmer's hands around another doing as he'd been instructed? When he'd put the gun to that young girl's head and pictured another gun being raised? A gun, as it turned out, in somewhat shakier hands.

Now, things were about to change. He had his new motor.

Never stay still and never go back.

This time, the victim would not be chosen at random. She, and it would be a *she*, would not be plucked from the crowd. She would be carefully selected.

The second change was the breathtaking one – the part of his plan that really raised the stakes. It was so beautifully brazen.

The woman who he was going to kill next would be *invited* to die.

Now it was just a question of deciding on a guest list.

★

Sarah McEvoy slammed the door behind her with such force that Holland braced himself, waiting for the sound of shattering glass, which thankfully never came. The windows were equally lucky to survive the onslaught of McEvoy's fury, which moved in front of her like a swinging bludgeon as she stomped across the office.

'*You wanker!* You self-righteous, tight-arsed little wanker!'

'Listen . . .'

'What was it? WD40? Motor oil?'

Holland felt like he'd been punched in the stomach, winded by the force of her anger, sick because of what had caused it. Gutted that what he'd done had been proved to be necessary. 'It was cooking oil. Just cooking oil . . .'

A thin layer across the top of the cistern in the Ladies, invisible unless you were looking for it. The cocaine gone in a second. A trick they used in some of the more drugs-conscious clubs. He'd picked up the oil on the way to work. He hadn't wanted to be seen taking the bottle from the cupboard at home . . .

'Think you're clever, don't you?'

'No.'

'Any idea what it costs? Come on smartarse, you've got your finger on the pulse, haven't you? Any idea how much it is a gram?'

Holland had had quite enough of being lectured at. He stood up, took a step towards her. 'Listen to yourself . . .'

'I can't afford to waste it . . .'

'I don't think you can afford not to.'

McEvoy laughed. It wasn't a pleasant sound. 'Which fucking seminar did you pick that one up at?'

Holland looked at her. She was shaking her head, breathing heavily. Her speech had been machine-gun fast. Though the oil had stopped her, it clearly hadn't held her up for very long. She'd probably just done a line off the back of her hand.

'You said you didn't do it at work.'

'You really think I've got a problem, don't you?' She was laughing again, looking anywhere but at him. 'You go on like I'm some fucking junkie. It's just an occasional thing. Just now and again, *Jesus* . . .'

'You said you didn't do it at work, Sarah.'

She coughed, wincing a little as something came up into her mouth. 'Yes, well, it hasn't exactly been a normal sort of day, has it?' She pushed past him and dropped into the chair behind her desk. 'I needed something after spending all morning staring into that hole, all right with you?'

Holland realised that at that moment there was almost nothing about this woman, whose body he knew intimately, that he recognised. 'No. It isn't all right.'

She glanced up, threw him a twisted smile. 'Are you still here?'

'That is the sickest piece of self-justification . . .'

'Bollocks! I don't need to justify what I do to you.'

'No, but you obviously need to justify it to yourself . . .'

McEvoy picked up a sheet of paper and studied it. 'The gun that Palmer failed to shoot Jacqui Kaye with. He says that Nicklin delivered it, left it outside his door. The boss thinks that's bullshit, reckons Palmer's lying for some reason . . .'

'I know. Sarah—'

'So we don't know why Palmer's not telling us, but he

must have got the gun from somewhere. From somebody who made it very clear that he better keep the *whos* and *wheres* to himself.'

Holland wasn't listening. He wasn't sure she was. 'This is stupid—'

'If there's a connection to Nicklin we've got to start chasing it, so this is a list of known, or suspected dealers which I've divided up, A, because it's depressingly long, and B, because we should probably work separately, I mean, I wouldn't want to compromise you . . .'

'You need to talk to somebody.'

Her look was one he would remember. 'Or *you* will?'

There was a small knock and Paul Moorhead, a trainee detective, poked his head round the door. His expression said that he knew full well it was about to be bitten off.

'Sorry . . .'

'What for?'

'DCI Lickwood on the phone for you. Do you want me to put it through?'

'Yeah, thanks.'

McEvoy put her hand on the phone, picked it up the instant it began to ring.

'Derek.'

She laughed at whatever it was Lickwood said, placed a hand across the mouthpiece and stared at Dave Holland until he left.

'*There's something else I want to tell you.*'

On TV, half a dozen dull, unattractive people sat about in a house, each trying to avoid being voted out. Thorne bit unenthusiastically into a sandwich and prayed for something interesting to happen. Like a meteor striking the house, or maybe a knife fight. He thought it was ironic that this was called fly-on-the-wall television. The morons that enjoyed it would have got as much entertainment out of capturing a real bluebottle in a jam jar; watching it smack into the glass over and over again.

The sound was turned down. *Folsom Prison Blues* provided the soundtrack.

Thorne was almost certain that there would be nothing jaunty about Belmarsh Prison Blues. No *boom-chicka-boom* two-beat. Just feedback. A tuneless dirge screamed over the monotonous thumping of boots on stairs and heads against walls. Martin Palmer had walked into the visiting area a few hours earlier looking like it was a song he'd been hearing a lot in the last week.

Thorne had said nothing. He'd put the plastic bag down on the table, slid it across. Palmer had leaned forward and stared at the wrapper, much as Hendricks and the others had done earlier. Palmer had seen what it was straight away. He'd recognised it.

'Nicklin killed Karen, Martin. He killed her and buried her in a ditch, then told everyone she'd been abducted.' Thorne had only glanced away for a second but when he'd looked back, Palmer's face had been wet. 'Come on, did you never even consider it?'

Palmer had reached forward and put his hand over the plastic bag. Obscured it.

'Karen was his first,' Thorne had said. 'At least, I think so. There isn't much of her left to test, so we'll never know for sure, but I'd guess he assaulted her as well. Some kind of sexual activity before he killed her . . .'

Palmer had looked away, poking two fingers behind his glasses to wipe his eyes. 'How did he do it?'

'He strangled her. Wrapped a rope around her neck. Stuart, who you loved.'

'I don't believe he did anything to her like that. Anything sexual, I mean.'

Thorne had scoffed. 'You're right, I'm only guessing. We'll just stick with murder and dumping the body in a shallow grave, shall we? Did you ever ask yourself how many more he might have killed, Martin? How many more Karens there might be?'

Palmer had turned back to him suddenly. 'I want to see where she was.'

'You know where she was. At the embankment. I told you, we found the body in a drainage ditch . . .'

'I want to see exactly. I'd like to see exactly where he put Karen.'

Thorne had heard similar requests before from friends and relatives of victims. *Show me where he died. Take me to the spot they killed her. Where did the accident happen?* Location was important to people. Somewhere to leave a marker, to visit. Increasingly, thanks to Diana and the emergence of a shrine culture, a place for complete strangers to leave bunches of flowers or teddy bears.

Palmer was not a victim though. Palmer was on remand, charged with murder.

'Sorry, no. What's the point, anyway? They've taken the body away, she's not there any more. There's nothing there any more . . .' Thorne said this, but didn't know for sure. The body would probably have been removed by now, but he didn't know what else might be happening at the site.

'I don't care. I want to see.'

'Forget it.' Thorne stood up, took a few steps in no particular direction. 'Before, you were helping us locate the body, fair enough, but this is pointless. Even if I was in favour of it, which I'm not, I couldn't get it authorised.'

'Please.'

'Shut up.' With Palmer, it always seemed to go the same way. He made Thorne feel something that was *almost* like sympathy, whatever it was turning quickly to something that was *definitely* anger. 'Why the fuck should I try to . . . ?'

Palmer shoved back his chair and stood up fast. Through the window at the far end of the room, Thorne could see one of the prison officers moving to check that everything was all right. He had been about to signal that there was no problem when Palmer had said what Thorne had been desperate to hear since those first few days after he'd handed himself in.

'*There's something else I want to tell you . . .*'

Now, in his flat, the phone was ringing.

Thorne got up, turned off the television and stereo en route and fetched the phone from the table by the front door. Stepping sideways to avoid the unfinished sandwich on a plate on the floor, he dropped backwards over the arm of the chair leaving his legs dangling, and hit the button.

It was his dad. They hadn't spoken for a week or so.

'Tom . . .'

'How's it going?'

'Fine, you know.'

'Gags tonight, or quizzes?'

'Tom, it's Dad.'

'I know.' Thorne laughed. 'You all right?' His dad breathed heavily down the phone at him. 'Listen, you never told me how it went down the Legion.'

'What?'

'The trick you were going to pull. You called me and asked me about the worst killers.'

There was a pause. 'I didn't . . .'

'That smallpox thing. It was a joke to play on your mates. Remember? It was a couple of weeks ago, I think.'

'No. Sorry. No idea what you're on about. Smallpox?'

'Come on, yes you do. You asked me for the names of the worst killers . . .'

'What, you mean diseases?'

'Yeah, that was the point, I think. Forget it. Wasn't one of your best anyway.'

'Is this a wind-up?'

Thorne laughed again, pulled a face. 'Well if it is, it's not me that's doing it . . .'

'Just piss off, all right . . .'

'Dad . . . ?' Thorne swung his legs over the arm of the chair, sat up straight.

'Who the hell d'you think you're talking to? Talking to me like that . . .'

Thorne was suddenly concerned, but tried his very best not to sound it. 'Look, calm down, Dad. It doesn't matter OK. OK?'

There was silence then, save for the laboured breathing. Ten, fifteen seconds . . .

'Dad, I—'

'Go to hell, you little fucker!'

An explosion of rage, then the dialling tone.

TWENTY-TWO

Karen McMahon's parents hadn't been informed about the finding of a body, at least, not officially. That wouldn't be done until tests had been completed, but being asked to provide material for a DNA comparison must have given them a fair idea. A call out of the blue fifteen years down the line, and suddenly they would be thinking about finally laying their daughter to rest.

Karen McMahon's parents would not yet have visited the site of this, her first grave. When they did, they wouldn't have a great deal of trouble finding it.

Over forty-eight hours now since they'd found the bones, the bin-bags and the carpet. The equipment, the paraphernalia, was already long gone. Now it was just a muddy hole, its location marked by footprints, a few scraps of crime-scene tape, and the small pile of rocks which Nicklin had used to keep the animals away which now stood like some parody of a headstone.

They'd probably come down with Vic Perks, the parents, when they came . . .

Perks had been very clear about wanting to visit. He'd

sounded grateful when Thorne had told him – grateful and devastated.

'Would it have been quick, do you think?' Palmer had been staring down into the drainage ditch for several minutes, saying nothing. The sudden question took Thorne a little by surprise.

'To bury her?'

'To kill her.'

Thorne pictured the rotten black rope hanging loose around the bones of the neck where once it had bitten tight against the flesh. He remembered Carol Garner's post-mortem report. 'Not quick enough,' he said.

Palmer stepped back from the ditch and turned away. He looked up towards the top of the embankment where the back-up officers sat in their car – the Vectra parked up next to Thorne's Mondeo. It was raining gently. Both cars were splattered with mud. At the foot of the slope, Holland, in a yellow waterproof jacket, wandered up and down, glancing across occasionally at Thorne and Palmer, looking like he'd rather be anywhere else.

'Stuart lied to me,' Palmer said.

Thorne had heard stranger things said, but he couldn't remember when. 'Did he?' he said, thinking: *he did a lot more than fucking lie to you . . .*

'Something happened the day Karen went missing.' He cleared his throat, corrected himself. 'The day she was killed. When the three of us were together down here.' He began to move, each step taking an age, as though he were walking in slow motion.

Thorne moved after him, taking two steps to each one of Palmer's. They'd cut the grass and the earth felt spongy beneath his feet. He was aware of Holland away to his right at the edge of his vision, the bright jacket vivid against the dark bank behind him.

'It was a trick,' Palmer said. 'I don't know for sure whether they were both in on it. It doesn't matter now anyway. I thought Karen . . . wanted me, and I felt excited. She wanted *me*, you see. Not Stuart.' His voice was a little higher than usual, as if the memory were forcing it closer to the way it had sounded fifteen years before. He shrugged. 'Like I say, it was a joke. I was being made a fool of, but I didn't know that then. I was excited, more than I'd ever been, more than I *have* ever been. What happened wasn't intentional. I'd tell you if it were, you could hardly think any worse of me, but it genuinely was not.' He took a breath. 'I exposed myself to her.'

Palmer had stopped moving and turned to look at Thorne as he arrived at his shoulder. 'I'm well aware of how . . . insignificant this sounds now. Then, *at that moment*, I would have taken my life in a heartbeat if I'd had the means. If I'd had the courage. When I turned round I saw the joke, I could see that they had probably been conspiring, but the look on Karen's face was horrible. She was disgusted. Not comic disgust, real horror, like she was reminded of something . . .

'I've wondered since if perhaps she was being abused, if the sight of me brought something back.' He nodded to himself. 'Useless to speculate now, I know . . .

'Whatever, I ran from that place, from *this* place, terrified that I had done something to Karen that day. Later, after she had disappeared, Stuart did his best to confirm it.'

Thorne looked down. He saw that Palmer's fists were clenched. They bobbed in front of his groin, forced forwards by his elbows, pressed tightly together by the handcuffs.

'He told you that it was your fault she got into the car, didn't he?'

Palmer nodded. 'Like I'd disturbed her so much she needed to get away. He told me he would keep it secret. He told me he was protecting me. He reminded me of it, that day when he walked into the restaurant. Hinted at things . . . made threats.'

'He was using you to protect himself.'

'Yes I know that now,' Palmer said, irritation creeping momentarily into his voice. He lowered his head for a second, raised it. The irritation had gone. 'I'm sorry.'

Thorne said nothing.

'Over the years I gave it all a slightly spooky twist. I thought about it all the time, and it got hammered into this bizarre shape in my head. I convinced myself that what I'd done to Karen had somehow contaminated her. Like I'd put the smell of it on her. The victim smell. Something . . . powerful. The perversion of it lingering around her, attracting that man in the car, drawing him to her . . .'

Thorne waited a few seconds, making sure the story was finished.

'What else did you want to tell me about Nicklin, Martin?'

Palmer's eyes slowly closed. His head drooped. As Thorne watched, he half expected to see Palmer's bulk begin to sink into the soggy ground, pushed into it by the force of the invisible weight that was pressing down on him.

'What else were you going to tell me?'

Thorne turned and signalled to Holland, shaking his head. It was getting dark anyway. They might as well try and beat the rush hour.

Martin Palmer wasn't saying anything else for the time being.

Two cars driving nose to tail from north-west London in a long diagonal down to the south-east. In the dirty blue Mondeo, three men, lost for the majority of the journey in their own thoughts. Looking for solutions.

Nursing desperate ideas.

Martin Palmer. Remembering lies, considering the nature of betrayal, praying in advance for forgiveness.

Dave Holland. Weighing up his options and finding each of them in their own way unpleasant, sickening. Beyond him.

Tom Thorne. Running out of time and ideas. Wondering if this was to be one of the ones he'd be doomed to remember. Would Stuart Nicklin's be a face he'd never see and so never be able to forget?

For each of them the answers would come sooner than they could have guessed.

'I want this sorted before we get back to Belmarsh, Martin.' Thorne spoke casually, as if resuming a conversation. They were passing through Maida Vale, down towards Paddington. Twenty minutes without a word and he'd had about enough.

'I took you to see Karen's grave. Believe me, I went to a great deal of trouble . . .' Brigstocke's face had been a picture. Thorne couldn't begin to imagine the rictus that must have distorted Jesmond's deathmask features when the request was passed on.

'You led me to believe there was something else you wanted to say. That's what I told people. Something about Nicklin.'

Palmer sat handcuffed to Holland, unmoving.

'I want to hear it, Martin. It felt like an agreement to me.'

'*Quid pro quo*, Doctor Lecter,' Holland whispered.

'Right,' Thorne said. Fuck knows what it meant, but he'd seen the film. He turned and threw Palmer a look. *Well?*

If Palmer knew what it meant, it didn't appear to make a great deal of difference.

Five minutes later, just past Victoria Station, Thorne yanked the wheel sharply to the left and put his foot down. Behind them, the Vectra flashed its lights.

'Sir,' Holland said, 'Vauxhall Bridge, Camberwell, Peckham, New Cross. That was the agreed route . . .'

Thorne raised a hand, acknowledging the Vectra. He raised his voice a little to answer Holland. 'Lambeth Bridge, Elephant & Castle. That's the new route. I've changed it.'

'The Elephant?'

'Dropping you off home, Dave.'

Holland leaned forward looking concerned. Palmer did likewise and not just because of the handcuffs. 'I appreciate the gesture, but in terms of the amount of shit we're all likely to be in, this really isn't one of your better ideas. Sir.'

'Probably not, but there's no need for anybody to know about it, is there?'

'No, but I still think . . .'

'Look, we're virtually driving past your place anyway. Besides, I think Martin's come over a little shy.'

Holland looked at Palmer, looked behind to the back-up car. One of the detectives raised both his palms. *What the fuck are we doing?*

They drove on through Victoria, across the river and past the huge twin guns outside the Imperial War Museum. Ten minutes later they were cruising slowly up Holland's road.

'Get the handcuffs off, Dave. Unless Sophie wants an extra body for dinner. Second on the left isn't it . . . ?'

Thorne watched, amused, as Holland slammed the door and walked back to the Vectra. The two detectives were out of the car before he got there. A couple of minutes of shrugging and headshaking later, they were back inside, waiting.

Holland came round to Thorne's window, leaned down. 'Are you sure, sir?'

'Go inside, Holland.' He nodded towards the back seat. 'Look at him. I don't think he's going to be giving me a great deal of trouble. We're just going to be chatting . . . hopefully.'

Holland stepped aside as the Mondeo pulled away and sped off towards the Old Kent Road.

Inside, Thorne was playing cabbie. 'Look at this traffic, not even four o'clock and it's mental. I bet it's already snarled up round Deptford. You've got about fifteen minutes I reckon, twenty, tops.'

Thorne checked the rearview mirror. Palmer was staring at the back of his head, breathing hard. Was what he had to say *so* difficult to spit out?

'A quarter of an hour until we get back to the prison, Palmer. That's all. Now fucking speak up . . .'

Nearly going-home time.

The place was starting to empty but he was staying behind. He had one or two things to catch up on. Above all, he wanted to sit alone for a while and enjoy his cleverness.

He never thought about what he did as being particularly clever. What he did with his knives and his hands and his friends. It was something he needed to do, it felt more instinctive than anything else. Yes, of course there was planning, more when he was manoeuvring Palmer, but none of it was really difficult. It was straightforward stuff, mostly. Surviving was easy. It was making it interesting that was the tricky bit.

This was clever though, no question. He wondered whether it had been lodged in his subconscious for a while, waiting to pop out, fully formed. It was so perfect. *She* was so perfect. She fitted the plan and the plan fitted her, so snugly that he wondered if perhaps it was her, the idea of her, the things she made him think, that had been responsible for it in the first place.

He had finally selected his guest and really, there could never have been any other.

He could not be certain of course, not yet, that she would come, or if she did, that she would do precisely as she was invited to do. Whatever happened, he was protected. That was the brilliance of the scheme. As things stood, he was quietly confident. He knew he had made a wise choice.

A wise choice. Like ordering an expensive bottle of wine in some up-its-own-arse restaurant. A wise choice if I may say so, sir . . .

It quickly became apparent to him that he was not going to get any work done. He could concentrate on nothing but the enterprise ahead.

How was he going to kill her? Where? Jesus, so much

excitement ahead, so many brilliant bits of it all left to work out . . .

No wonder he couldn't be bothered with paperwork. That had always been his way though: scan the horizon, find the source of the new adventure and then forget everything else. Throw yourself into it, take others with you if they had the bottle to come, wring each last ounce of life out of it, every drop of juice . . .

He'd pick up a nice bottle of something on the way home, Caroline would like that. She'd forgiven him for Monday night, suggested that maybe he was working too hard, getting stressed out. He'd agreed, said that yes, perhaps he *had* taken on a bit much, laughed to himself about that when he was alone.

Dinner and some TV, and then the radio later, after Caroline had gone up to bed. He was thinking about it already, but later, alone, he'd decide on the final wording. The wording of this first part at any rate. It wasn't going to happen immediately, of course. He'd need to make it irresistible and that would take time. The time frame was still a little vague. He only had a provisional date in mind for the big event itself, but he would start tonight.

Sending out the invite.

'We'll see the fucking prison in a minute, Palmer. It's less than half a mile.' Thorne was trying not to shout. 'Once I pull up to the barrier, that's it. You can forget anything else you might want to say to me, ever. If I don't hear something from you in the next few minutes, I stop listening. Do you understand?'

Thorne wasn't sure he understood himself. He wasn't certain what he was threatening Palmer with. All he knew was that Palmer had seemed keen to tell him something. He always had. He suddenly wondered if all this time it had simply been the confession about exposing himself to Karen McMahon. That was certainly something about which he'd been obsessed. Thorne's hands were clammy on the wheel. Had he seen salvation or inspiration in what was nothing more than a teenager's guilt about getting his cock out?

No, there had to be something else. Something that could point Thorne towards Nicklin.

'What is it, Palmer?'

Palmer, bouncing his handcuffed wrists on his knees, those annoying little nods . . .

'For Christ's sake, you walked into a police station with a gun. You walked in bleeding. I saw how desperate you were, how fucked up. You said you were sick of it, you said you would do anything to help. You said you wanted to stop him.'

'I do.'

Thorne almost jumped. Palmer's first words since the railway embankment.

'So tell me, then. What is it? What was it you were talking about in the prison the other day?'

As Thorne asked the question, the car turned a corner and Belmarsh came into view, the lights of the perimeter fence just a thousand yards away, dancing as the light dimmed.

'Here we go, Palmer, home sweet home.' Palmer made a noise, something like a growl. 'Not very nice is it? Why not go back in feeling like you've done something useful. You can't make up for the women you killed, but you can help me try and stop any more dying . . .'

Palmer shaking his head, wrestling with something. Thorne no longer trying not to shout.

'Come on!'

They slowed down, stopping at the point opposite the main drive, the T-junction where they had to wait before crossing the main carriageway. Headlights sped towards them from their left, a gap in the traffic maybe half a minute away. The Vectra pulled out to come up alongside them.

'I fucking mean it. I'm walking away . . .'

The driver of the Vectra looked across at Thorne, waiting for the confirmation that everything was hunky-dory, looking for the signal that they could go.

'Give me something on Nicklin. I know there's something you aren't saying . . .'

Just a couple more cars.

Thorne glanced to his right. 'How much more guilty do you want to feel? How much more fucking guilty?'

Thorne waved. The Vectra nosed forward, waiting for the gap.

Palmer's body tensing, reaching for something.

'Tell me about Stuart. Tell me what you're thinking. Please . . .'

The Vectra sounded its horn, the detective nearest Thorne's window raised an arm.

'*Come on!*' Thorne shouted, as the car alongside him roared away to the right. Thorne watched it go, slammed his hands on the dashboard, took his foot from the brake. 'Too late . . .'

The voice from the back of the car: '*I think he might be a police officer.*'

Thorne's left foot slipped from the clutch. The car

stalled and lurched forward. He rocked back in his seat, and was about to turn round when his head was pushed violently forward.

Thorne was still conscious as his face bounced off the worn vinyl of the steering wheel, but not for very long.

Might be seconds . . . might be minutes . . . how long?

Thorne looked at the clock on the dash, waited for his vision to clear.

Minutes. Just a few . . .

He turned round slowly. He felt like cement had been poured in through both his ears. Palmer was gone. The back door was open.

Where . . . ? What was it he said . . . ?

Thorne looked around wildly, each eye movement like a punch as he scanned the area, desperate to see Palmer lurching away into the distance. Headlights from the cars that continued to rush past lit the darkening stain down his shirt, the string of scarlet snot that dripped from the steering wheel.

A hundred yards behind the car was a fence maybe six or seven feet high. Up onto the telephone junction box there and over. Away into the building site.

Piece of piss. Could he climb the fence with cuffs on? Probably. Taken the key anyway. Away and gone . . .

Thorne opened the door and all but fell out onto the road. He stood up and stumbled a few feet forward. He raised an arm and waved at the oncoming traffic.

Nobody stopped.

Nobody gives a fuck. No trust in anyone these days. Six days a week, for the past eighteen months in that shop. Maybe if I produced my warrant card, showed them I was a policeman . . .

The Mondeo's headlights were still on. Thorne winced as he brought a hand to his shattered nose and stepped into their beam. The car that rushed past him blared its horn as Thorne staggered across the carriageway through a tunnel of light, towards the prison.

TWENTY-THREE

'Jesus, Tom. Do you feel OK?' Brigstocke looked shocked and concerned.

The nose had swelled grotesquely almost immediately, and now, two days later, the rest of Thorne's face had caught up. He had huge dark rings under his eyes and blue-black bruises along each cheekbone.

'I feel fine,' Thorne said. 'I look like a fucking panda, but I feel fine . . .'

The concern vanished from Brigstocke's face. 'That's very fitting, because pandas are an endangered species as well, aren't they? What the fuck did you think you were doing?'

There had been occasions in the past when Tom Thorne would have fought his corner a little at this point. Stood his ground and made a speech about ends and means. Today, he couldn't be arsed.

'I fucked up.'

Brigstocke had stood up on Thorne's appearance in the doorway. Now, he slumped back down behind his desk. 'Listen, I've got to serve you with this.' He handed Thorne a piece of paper. 'It's a Regulation 7 notice. The DPS want to see you . . .'

Thorne had expected nothing less. The Directorate of Professional Standards – another stupid American name for what had used to be the CIB, the Complaints Investigation Bureau: the team that was there to root out corruption, to weed out the bad apples. The same organisation that had recently been involved in a well-publicised operation to deal with officers moonlighting as extras on *The Bill*, and were currently investigating a complaint that an officer had broken wind during a raid and failed to apologise.

'I can't wait,' Thorne said.

'What about the nose?'

'No picking, no sneezing. I go back in a week or so when the swelling's gone down. Depending on how it looks, they either do nothing, or break it again, re-set it.'

'Do they need volunteers?'

Thorne crossed to the other desk and sat down. 'What are you doing about Palmer?'

'What are *we* doing? You're priceless . . .'

'Sorry. I know that sounded . . .'

'We're doing what you'd expect, which is more than you did, isn't it? The media are all over this and we'll have to play along a bit if we want to use them. Somebody knows where Palmer's gone and the only way we're going to find them is through the papers, the TV . . .'

As if on cue, Steve Norman strolled into the office.

'Russell . . . DI Thorne . . .'

Brigstocke stood up. Thorne, for no good reason, found himself wearily doing the same. 'I'm going to get coffees,' Brigstocke said, moving to the door. 'Everybody want one?'

Thorne nodded. Norman grunted his assent as he

dropped a pile of newspapers onto the desk. He picked off the top one and turned to Thorne, holding it up.

'You certainly know how to generate a good story, Thorne.'

The front page of the tabloid was almost filled with a photo of Martin Palmer. The headline was simple and dramatic. What the Americans called a 'scarehead' . . .

KILLER ON THE RUN.

Thorne stepped around the desk. He was tired, in pain and in no mood for another shouting match. 'Listen, Norman . . .'

Norman raised a hand to stop him and looked surprised when it did the trick. 'Look, before this kicks off, I want to apologise for the argument the other week. I was being an arsehole, OK? I've been meaning to come in and sort it out, but work's been piling up.'

Thorne was completely on the back foot. 'Right . . .'

'Things had been a bit tricky at home to tell you the truth, and I was just on a short fuse. It was out of order, and I know we're not going to be best mates but there's no point us being at loggerheads, is there? Especially not now. Fair enough?'

Thorne nodded, wondering if he was suffering with delayed concussion.

Norman thrust a finger at the front of the paper. 'Actually, *this* is exactly what we need. The phones have been ringing all morning. We'll probably have him back in custody by tea time.' Norman's expression darkened a little as he pulled out another paper from further down the pile. 'Did you see yesterday's?'

Thorne shook his head. He'd been lying in a darkened room most of the day, waiting to stop feeling like somebody had their boot on his face. This time the picture on the front page of the paper was far more indistinct. Two figures, shot with a zoom probably, from hundreds of feet away, like one of those blurry photos of Bigfoot or the Beast of Bodmin.

Thorne and Palmer at Karen McMahon's grave.

'This one we *didn't* give them,' Norman said. 'Somebody did though. Somebody who's getting a bit too pally with the press.'

Distasteful as it was, Thorne had to agree. Bracher was probably responsible for the early stuff the papers had got hold of, but this had to be down to someone on the team. 'I'll find out who it is.'

'Good. I have to say, though, that it's doing us more good than anything else at the moment. We've actually started feeding them a bit more on Karen McMahon.' Thorne looked slightly confused. 'They formally identified her thirty-six hours ago. Around the time this was taken.'

Thorne needed to catch up fast. He'd been out of the loop since he'd put Palmer in the back of the Mondeo on Thursday afternoon and driven him back to the railway embankment.

'*I think he might be a police officer . . .*'

'There's a lot of human interest there,' Norman said. 'Which they love of course. Fifteen years of torment for the parents, all that. Plus, the simple fact that a murder's been solved. Finding that body has done everybody a lot of favours. We can claw back a bit of lost ground.'

The stabbing pain that ran across Thorne's face cranked up a notch. He reached into his jacket pocket for the painkillers. 'I found one body, then lost another.'

Norman laughed, a wheezy snicker. 'Right. But they

kind of cancel each other out.' Norman had a newspaper in each hand. He held them up in turn to illustrate his argument. 'Thanks to the brownie points we earn for finding Karen McMahon, we can let them go to town with Palmer's escape, and hopefully we can keep one or two of the less impressive procedural details out of it.'

Less impressive procedural details?

'Right,' Thorne said. 'Obviously I'd be grateful . . .'

Thorne poured himself a glass of water. He needed it to swallow the pills and to take a very unpleasant taste out of his mouth. As he threw his head back, he caught sight of Brigstocke heading towards them across the incident room with three plastic cups.

'Coffee's here . . .'

'Great.' Norman's mobile rang. He looked at the screen. 'Excuse me, I need to take this . . .'

Thorne watched as Norman took the call, turning away and murmuring into his phone. He was finding it hard to distinguish between the pain and disorder colliding in his head like a pair of very long trains, ploughing endlessly into each other. Norman apologising . . . one body lost, one body found . . . a leak on the investigation . . . the DPS . . . Palmer's tone of voice in the car when he said what he said about Nicklin.

Then, there was the one less-than-impressive procedural detail he hadn't told them about at all . . .

McEvoy was logged on to the Internet. Holland hadn't recognised the page she'd had up on screen, but the glimpse he'd caught before she saw him and quit, gave him the idea it might be a mail server. They were not supposed to use the system to send or receive personal e-mails, but Holland said nothing. In the scheme of things it was pretty trivial, and besides, he knew how any comment of that sort would be taken.

'At least you're not leaving when I come into the office. We must be making progress.'

McEvoy shrugged, not looking up. 'Can't let you accuse me of not doing my job properly.'

Holland saw no point in pussyfooting around the issue. He opened his mouth and said it. 'I think one of us needs to transfer off this team.' Her face told him that he'd shaken her. 'Come on, you must have been thinking about it, it's—'

She cut him off. 'Well *I'm* not fucking going.'

'Sarah . . .'

'Right, course. By *one of us*, you mean me. Well?'

Now would be the time to walk away if he was going to; to forget he'd brought it up and make the best of it. He hesitated. 'Yes.'

'Forget it.'

'You're the one with the problem, not me.'

'Are you sure?'

'Don't psychoanalyse me. I'm not the one snorting away my wages, fucking everything up, putting the lives of my colleagues at risk . . .'

The colour sprang into McEvoy's face. She could feel tears pricking at the corners of her eyes. 'When? Tell me when?'

'Maybe never. Maybe half an hour from now . . .' Holland wanted so much to cross the five feet of space between them, right then, and take hold of her. He couldn't.

'Nobody else knows about this, Dave.' McEvoy watched

herself, feeling like a ditzy blonde trying to avoid a speeding ticket. Loathing it. 'Let's just forget all the shit that's happened. Dave . . . ?'

'Nobody else knows for now. I don't think you're doing a very good job of hiding it.'

McEvoy changed tack in a second. 'You go to Brigstocke and I'll be right behind you. I'll tell him you've been harassing me. They'll think you're making it up because I wouldn't fuck you . . .'

Holland could see that she was desperate, backed into a corner. He knew that she was clinging to the ledge by her fingernails, saying things she didn't mean and would never carry through, but still his temper got the better of him. He marched across the office, picked up the newspaper from the top of a filing cabinet and threw it down in front of her.

McEvoy stared down at the picture of Thorne and Palmer at the drainage ditch.

'You talk to *anybody*,' Holland said, 'and you'll be opening a major can of fucking worms.'

McEvoy looked up at him, confused. 'You think I'm the leak?'

'*I can't afford to waste it*, you said.' Holland snatched up the paper, screwed it into a ball. 'Shit, this is easy money, isn't it? A tip here, a photo opportunity there, that's you sorted for the week. For all I know, they probably fix you up with the coke themselves, save messing about with cash.'

'Dave . . .'

'Just admit it, you did, didn't you? Just fucking well admit it . . .'

Holland saw McEvoy's eyes flicker, saw her body tense. He turned to see Thorne standing in the doorway. There was no awkward pause, no meaningful silence. McEvoy was up and moving towards the door, wisecracking to Thorne on her way out as if nothing had happened.

'Some people around here are obviously feeling as shitty as *you* look . . .'

Then there was a silence.

Thorne closed the door, moved into the room. 'Dave, is there a problem between you and Sarah?' Holland said nothing. Thorne felt hot and hassled. He did not want any more uncertainty, any more disorder. 'DC Holland, is there a problem between yourself and Detective Sergeant McEvoy?'

Holland looked at Thorne. Later, standing at bars or staring up at a striplight, he would remember this moment. In the months and the years to come, sitting on the side of the bed in the middle of the night, Sophie stirring next to him, he would look back and picture this instant. He would recall every detail of Thorne's bruised face, every nuance of his bruising voice. He would remember, and wish to God that he'd told the truth.

Holland looked at Thorne. 'No, sir.'

Thorne let out a long slow breath and moved across to the window. He looked down, hoping to see something that might raise his spirits. Some cadets marching badly would do the trick. Better yet, a group of them forming a human pyramid, mounted on the back of two motorbikes like they used to do on those displays when he was a kid . . .

There was just a pair of civilian staff smoking in a doorway.

Thorne turned and walked back across the room. He was feeling aimless, untrusted, unnecessary. He opened the door of the office, looked out across the incident room. In the far corner he saw Norman standing over McEvoy's desk. She said something that made him laugh.

'McEvoy and Norman are getting friendly, aren't they?'

'He's probably trying to talk her into going on to the next press conference,' Holland said. 'He's been telling her she should get some media training. Says he thinks she'd come across well on camera.'

Thorne turned back into the room. 'What about me? How camera-friendly am I looking?' Holland said nothing, trying to decide how diplomatic to be. 'Does it really look bad?'

'Once the bruising's gone it'll be fine. A broken nose is quite cool actually. Women go for that sort of thing . . .'

'Please, God . . .'

'I should look on the bright side,' Holland said. 'Fact is, with all due respect, sir, you were quite an ugly fucker before.'

No picking, no sneezing. The pain told Thorne that they definitely needed to add laughing to the list.

Thorne waited until the office was quiet before making the call.

His heart was pounding as he dialled, as it had each time he'd tried the number from home. A dozen times or more since getting back from the hospital. A dozen times or more, he'd got the answering machine.

He waited for the connection.

He should have told them about this, there were things they could have done – traces – but he felt instinctively that their efforts would be fruitless, that this was the right thing to do.

The phone rang.

This was the way he *might* make up for his mistake . . .

Ten, twelve rings as usual, then the familiar message. 'Shit . . .'

'*This is Tom Thorne. Leave a message or try my home number, which is . . .*'

Then suddenly Thorne remembered the call he'd seen Steve Norman take earlier. He pictured the press officer as his phone was ringing. *Looking* at the screen before answering.

Caller ID . . .

This number, the office number, was withheld, as was his own at home. Both would show up on the screen as private numbers. The calls would go unanswered. He needed a number which was registered, which would show up and give the man who had his phone a good idea who was calling.

Thorne opened the door, scanned the incident room, hoping that Dave Holland hadn't left yet.

Minutes later he was dialling the number again on Holland's borrowed mobile. The name would show up on his phone. He had programmed it in himself.

The phone began to ring . . .

Whoever was holding it would be seeing HOLLAND MOB come up on the small screen and would surely be able to guess who was calling. Would perhaps risk taking the call.

The phone was answered.

'Palmer. This is Thorne.'

Fifteen seconds. Thorne was starting to wonder if maybe it wasn't Palmer on the other end. Then that voice, the nasal tones even more pronounced over the phone. 'I'm really sorry, Mr Thorne . . .'

'You broke my fucking nose . . .'

'I'm sorry, I didn't mean to.'

Thorne moved across to the window, stared out at the lights of Hendon, the cars speeding north on the M1. 'Why did you take my phone?'

'I won't be on long enough for you to trace this. I presume you're tracing this . . .'

'Did you take it to give yourself more time to get away, or because you knew I'd call?'

Thorne could hear Palmer breathing, considering the question. 'A little of both, probably.'

'This is so stupid you know. We'll find you. You've given yourself up once, you should do it again.'

Palmer laughed, but it sounded desperate. 'Why? Is it going to make a difference to my sentence?'

'Why should you care about that? You wanted to be locked up for life anyway. What's changed, Martin? Why are you doing this?'

'I should go . . .'

'Is it because of what I said about what might happen to you in prison?'

'Not really. Yes, sort of . . .'

Thorne looked at himself reflected in the blackness of the window, the bruises dark shadows across his face. For half a second he forgot that he was chatting to a murderer. He felt like a character in some noirish pop video, his mouth miming these disconnected sentences – strange snippets of conversation dropped into a dark ballad about loss or the impossibility of forgiveness.

'What did you mean in the car? What did you mean about Nicklin being a policeman?'

'I didn't mean anything. I was just saying it. I needed to distract you . . .'

'That's bollocks, Martin. You could have done anything, said anything. Why did you say *that*?'

'I had a feeling, that's all. It was just an impression, like he was used to people doing what he told them . . .'

'Wasn't he always like that?'

'I told you, it was just a feeling. Something about him that day in the restaurant. It's nothing I could put into words. I have to go now . . .'

'Wait. I want you to think about stopping this. Wherever you are, we'll find you. What's the point of it?'

'I really can't talk to you any more . . .'

'Wait a minute. I'll call again. I'll let it ring three times first, and then hang up, so you'll know it's me. Three times, Palmer. OK?'

The line was dead.

McEvoy lay on her back, holding her breath, staring up at the mirrors.

Her heart was going bonkers in her chest. Her face was tingling, the gorgeous numbness spreading across her mouth and teeth, the buzz dancing its way up into her skull.

She froze as she heard a car pull up outside. Every muscle tensed, waiting for the footfall outside the door. She could get to the mains switch in ten seconds . . .

She was flat on the floor beneath the window ledge in the living room, out of sight. She'd moved the free-standing mirror in from the bedroom, positioned it to the inch, tilted it until it gave the optimum view. Now she could lie here safely and watch the back garden. She would see any of them coming immediately. There was another mirror halfway down the garden – a big one she'd hung from a fence post. From this position, she could see around the side as well.

When she'd first bought the flat, the garden had been great. She'd enjoyed sitting out there on summer nights, with a man sometimes, sharing a bottle of wine before bed. These days it was a bloody liability. It would be the way they would come. It was the place they watched her from most of the time, though the officer in the cherry-picker pretending to fix the lamp post on the street outside was a clever idea. But she was cleverer. She knew all the tricks, didn't she? The surveillance game. She knew the car that was following her was probably the one in front. She knew all the tricks because she was one of them.

Holland must have been talking. Everybody knew, she was certain of it. She'd caught two people at it in the space of five minutes, earlier in the day. Talking about her, clamming up when she came into the room. Watching her and judging. Well she was watching *them* as well. As she re-applied make-up using the small mirror she kept in her bag. She could see what they were thinking. Same as Holland. Same as everybody. All of them thinking that she couldn't do the job.

She froze. A shadow moved across the garden. She could be at the mains switch in less than *five* seconds at a push, plunge the place into darkness, turn everything off. She'd done it before when she'd heard them coming. It was a pain to spend the time re-programming the video and re-setting clocks, but she'd had no choice.

They were out there, listening. The bastards weren't going to hear or see anything tonight. She slid across the floor until she was away from the window before standing up and inching her way around the wall. She dropped into the chair by her desk, woke up her computer.

There were those she could talk to who *knew* how good an officer she was. Who thought she was probably better at the job than anybody else. Who challenged her to prove it.

She had e-mail.

The ringing phone punched its way into Thorne's dream where it became the bark of a hungry animal, scrabbling at a door, digging its way beneath it. Behind the door stood a small boy, rooted to the spot, terrified, until a girl arrived and took him by the hand. Thorne woke then and leaned across, fumbling for the phone.

'Palmer?'

'Thorne? It's Colin Maxwell. You in bed?'

Thorne blinked hard and looked at the clock. It was just after eleven. He'd been asleep less than half an hour. 'I was reading. Trying to get an early night . . .'

Maxwell. The hotel killings. More bodies . . .

'Which hotel is it?'

Maxwell sounded surprised. 'The Palace, in South Kensington. How the hell did you know?'

Thorne was wide awake now. He needed some more painkillers. 'Why else would you be calling? How many dead?'

'Nobody's dead. Listen, I think we've got our wires crossed here, mate. This is good news, and I reckon you could do with cheering up. Our man isn't as bright as we thought he was.'

The painkillers could wait. 'You've got him?'

'He delivers bar supplies. Drives a fucking beer wagon. Delivery once a month, gets friendly with the catering managers, chats up a few waitresses. Who've you got staying? Who's throwing their money about? Bungs them a few quid for the right bit of information . . .'

'What's the Palace hotel got to do with it?'

'A witness comes forward, a cleaner, gave the suspect information last year when she was working at the Regency, back when our murderer was still just a thief. The suspect approaches this girl again last week, only now our cleaner's read the papers hasn't she? She knows all about him. We've told her she's in the clear if she plays along.'

Thorne was growing irritated. They could go over it all in detail later. 'Colin, just tell me about the Palace hotel . . .'

'That's the best bit, mate. What are you doing next Tuesday night?'

TWENTY-FOUR

Thorne looked down at his new phone. It was smaller than the one it was replacing and flashier. He'd spent most of the day making sure that everyone who mattered had the new number. He hadn't discontinued the account on his old phone. He wanted that number active for the time being.

While it was quiet, while they were waiting, Thorne messed around with some of the new phone's features. This one had a predictive text function. He had never been one for sending text messages, it always seemed easier and quicker to make the call. This might be fun, though. He typed the message. There were probably all manner of symbols and shortcuts he could be using – he knew this stuff was hugely trendy with kids – but he just kept it straightforward. He pressed the send button and looked up, smiled at a couple of the others. Nobody was saying a great deal.

Thorne was pretty sure that what he'd sent would be read. There was no risk in opening it, even if the number that sent it wasn't familiar. It was a simple enough message.

GIVE UP . . .

A stomach rumbled, breaking the silence, dispersing the tension. They all had a good laugh. Somebody suggested calling room service, ordering up a bit of dinner on expenses.

Holland and McEvoy pushed through the revolving door and made their way across the lobby towards reception. Holland was wearing a blue suit. McEvoy wore a soft leather jacket over a black dress.

They were hand in hand.

'Room 133, please,' Holland said.

McEvoy took a small hand mirror from her bag and checked her make-up.

The woman behind the reception desk plastered on a fake smile that was almost, but not quite, the same fake smile she plastered on the rest of the time. The tremble in her hand was almost imperceptible as she handed over the key.

'Do you need a call in the morning?' she asked.

McEvoy shook her head.

'Would you like a newspaper?'

Holland smiled. She was very good. 'No thanks. Goodnight . . .'

They waited for the lift. McEvoy stared at her reflection in the metal doors. Holland turned round casually, had a quick look. A man smoking a cigar on the armchair by the main entrance, fifty-ish, waiting for someone. A party of noisy business types spilling out of the bar. A younger man on the phone.

The lift arrived, bringing with it half a dozen more jabbering businessmen. Holland and McEvoy stepped inside. Holland pressed the button for the first floor.

It was only when the doors had closed fully that they stopped holding hands.

Jason Alderton moved quickly along the corridor, his feet in soft black training shoes that made no noise on the deep carpet. A woman came around the corner. He grinned as they passed each other, got a smile in return.

He stopped outside the door and readied himself. He placed the bag soundlessly at his feet, looking left and right every few seconds, pulling on the gloves. It was important to step up close to the door, to get your face right up against the spyhole. The clothes were utilitarian enough anyway, but up close all anyone could see was the smiling face that looked away unconcerned, whistling.

Jason breathed in and out very fast a dozen times, then knocked. It gave him a little kick that inside the gloves, his palms were perfectly dry. He was getting very good at this.

Footsteps from inside the room. He tensed up, ready for it. It was the surprise that gave him the edge. They were always so completely stunned. He saw that expression on every face. They'd felt safe.

'Who is it?'

'Hotel maintenance, sir. Problem with one of your radiators . . .'

When the door was opened, in the half a second before he struck, Jason took in every detail necessary.

Fucker in a suit, about thirty, here for the conference like the girl had told him . . . average size, not big . . . fit-looking, but that wouldn't matter . . . full of himself most probably, but he would cry like a baby when it came to it . . . the look on his face, the shock, starting to sense much too late that something isn't right . . . a woman, the wife or girlfriend, behind him, sitting on the edge of the bed . . .

He raised both hands and pushed the man in the suit hard in the chest, shoved him back down on to the floor. He was moving in then, picking up the bag and shutting the door in one clean, quick movement, and the man in the suit was on his hands and knees moaning, and as Jason stepped forward to kick the fucker in the stomach, he saw the woman on the bed jump up, *really jump up in the air*, just like the old Dutch woman had done.

She jumped up in the air and screamed . . .

McEvoy screamed.

The scream of the terrified wife. The scream of the good copper giving the signal for everyone to move.

Thorne stepped quickly out from his hiding place behind the right-angle formed by a line of built-in wardrobes. He saw the look of sudden panic on the suspect's face, watched it grow as he turned, looking for a way out, only to see two more men bursting out of the bathroom behind him.

It would be five seconds, no more, from the moment Thorne stepped out into plain view, to the moment he would find himself staring down at the man on the floor, amazed at the fact that he wasn't punching him into unconsciousness.

As Thorne moved towards him, the suspect tried to run but Holland moved fast from his hands and knees, tackled him around the waist and drove him back across the room. McEvoy moved out of the way, and Holland and the suspect crashed down onto the edge of the bed. Thorne and Maxwell were right behind them, and together they lifted the suspect clear off the floor and threw him across the bed into the wall on the other side.

Before the suspect had hit the carpet, Thorne was stepping round the bed after him.

Up for it.

Ready to do some damage to that face.

The face not hidden by a balaclava, because the fucker hadn't been planning on leaving anybody alive to identify him. The bag over his arm – the bag that contained the knife and the tape, and Christ alone knew what else . . .

Thorne remembered the last time he'd been in a hotel room. He thought about the bodies in the bath and on the bed. Now he was ready to kick and punch and smash away a little frustration. Half a yard behind him, Maxwell and Holland moved just as quickly, reading the look on Thorne's face, ready to stop him.

They wouldn't have to.

Thorne saw something like amazement on the face of the man lying crumpled on the floor between the wall and the bed. In the tussle, his trousers had got pulled down to the top of his thighs, exposing grey underpants. A livid scratch ran across his forehead. His hair, thick with gel, lay plastered to his scalp like the legs of fat black spiders. Beneath, a thin, bland face, the small eyes wide, the mouth hanging open as he panted for breath. Thorne came around the bed at him, his fists clenched, his discoloured face a disaster area. Thorne could see the man on the floor wondering if *his* was going to end up the same way . . .

Thorne stopped dead. He stopped and stared down at the pig-shit-thick piece of pond scum, who'd more or less handed himself over to them. The vicious moron who wasn't quite careful enough and who would grow old in prison thinking about it. A tick in a plus column, a feather in a commander's cap. A killer caught for the same simple reasons that most of them got caught.

Blind luck and stupidity.

Sutcliffe, West, Nielsen, Shipman. Virtually everybody on that list his father had asked for. All of them tripped up by a piece of good fortune, or coincidence, or carelessness. Not just the big ones either: Killer A and Rapist B too. Everyday maniacs on any street corner, and the majority of them a long way from the bright, refined psychopaths of popular fiction. All killing for ordinary, dull reasons. Anger, envy, lust, greed. Malign individuals, yes, but also every bit as stupid as some of those that hunted them . . .

Thorne and the rest of them stumbling around, having good days and bad. Hot streaks and shitty patches. Following procedure or not following it, depending on who they were and how much they gave a fuck. Detectives hoping that *this* one wanted to get caught and failing that, praying for the sharp-eyed witness, the conscience-stricken relative, the dim-witted accomplice.

Needing all the help they could get.

Thorne knew it, of course. He knew it very well, but once in a while it would slap him in the face. A moment, an image, would remind him. How lost he was. How much he was reliant on fortune and fuck-ups.

Detective? They needed to invent a new name for it.

Thorne couldn't remember the last time he'd detected anything but the smell of bullshit or beer on a colleague's breath.

It was five seconds, no more, since he'd stepped out of his hiding place. Thorne felt an arm on his sleeve, heard something high-pitched and unpleasant. Came out of it . . .

The man on the floor was not looking at him, but *past* him, across the room at something else. The arm on his was pulling him away – not from the suspect, there had been no violence – but towards something else, something that demanded his attention.

Thorne turned at the same time as he started to really hear it. He turned, wincing, and looked in the same direction as everybody else in the room. They had their hands over their ears. They stared at where Sarah McEvoy sat slumped against the wall near the door.

She was still screaming.

TWENTY-FIVE

When she lifted her head up to look at him, Holland could see that his shirt was sopping, with snot, and tears.

McEvoy had been crying for over an hour.

She'd kept it together until moments after they'd climbed into his car and driven away from the hotel. She'd been hysterical from there, all the way back to Wembley, and when he'd pulled up outside her flat, she'd leaned across, crying so hard she was almost unable to speak, and demanded to be held.

They hadn't moved since.

At the hotel, the two of them plus Thorne had moved downstairs once Jason Alderton had been taken away. They'd gone silently down in the lift and moved to a sofa and chairs in the deserted reception area. Thorne had found somebody, ordered coffee and then looked at them, demanding answers. Holland had been gobsmacked at how quickly McEvoy had recovered her poise, how easily she was able to look Thorne in the eye and lie to him. She told him that her mother was ill, that she was finding it hard to cope. She laughed and said that the business up in the hotel room was probably just down to her subconscious getting a lot of pent-up shit out of her system. Just a one-off thing. A bit of a wobbler, sir . . .

Thorne had fucking believed her. Talked about her taking a bit of time off. Asked a bit more about her mother.

Or maybe he hadn't believed her. Holland had looked in the rear-view mirror as they'd pulled out of the hotel car park and seen Thorne standing there, watching them leave. It struck him then, watching Thorne standing with his hands in his pockets, *that look on his face* . . . perhaps he was just leaving it all for another day.

Holland tried to shift his position a little. McEvoy was all but on top of him, her weight making him uncomfortable, but every time he tried to move, she began wailing again. It had started and stopped half a dozen times since they had arrived at her flat, unbearably loud; the noise dredged up from somewhere deep down in her guts. An emotion so raw and unformed that it screamed when it met the fresh air. Each time, the sobbing seemed to tear through her whole body, and through *his*, for long minutes at a time until it finally settled down.

With the engine off, the clock on the dashboard wasn't lit, but it must have been well after midnight. A man walking his dog looked into the car and quickly looked away again. Holland didn't know if he understood what he was seeing.

'Sarah . . .'

She moaned and raised her head. She looked like she'd been dunked in paint-stripper. When Holland opened his mouth, she pushed her tongue into it and he felt the stirring in his groin. It took a major effort to pull away from the kiss.

'Sarah, let's get you inside.'

'No . . .'

She squeezed his neck so hard that he had to fight not to cry out. He reached up and wedged a hand between her fingers and his skin. 'You need to stop this. You need to get to bed and go to sleep.'

Her voice was hoarse and punctuated by desperate, absurd intakes of breath. 'Was it nice . . . to be proved right? To see me . . . fuck up at work . . . ?'

'Don't be stupid.'

'In front . . . of everybody . . .'

'What you said to Thorne was . . . good enough.'

'If he believed me . . .'

Holland realised that he'd been stroking her hair for a while. 'Listen, what you said about me being proved right. I don't give a toss about that, but maybe it's enough of a warning for you to want to do something about it . . .'

She burrowed her head deeper into his shoulder. She might have been nodding, but he couldn't be sure.

'Sarah?'

She whimpered. It sounded like there might be another attack of hysterics on the way. His hand stopped stroking her hair, grabbed a handful of it. 'This might be the last chance you get, you know?'

She raised her head and stared at him, with something strange in her bloodshot eyes which he couldn't come close to reading. She looked up at him for maybe fifteen seconds. Challenging . . . apologising . . . accepting . . . saying *something* without words; something he would spend a long time afterwards trying to interpret.

Then, in the early hours of the morning, with the first few drops of rain crashing onto the windscreen, he could say very little which didn't sound pat and pointless. 'I'll be here to help you, if you try and change things . . .'

He pulled her head gently back down on to his shoulder, and the two of them sat there, holding on to each other for all the wrong reasons.

McEvoy needing to go through this but wanting him to go. Wanting to get inside, on her own, and turn on her computer.

Holland shushing her like a child. Changing his position ever so slightly, moving his arm just a little to get a look at his watch.

Mary from Rickmansworth: 'He should never be let out. What about the life sentence the parents have been given? What about the parents of that little girl?'

Alan from Leicester: 'It isn't about vengeance, Bob, it's about justice. It's just too soon.'

A child jailed for the murder of a little girl now a grown man eligible for parole. The debate had raged eight months before, over the parole for the boys that killed Jamie Bulger. It was raging again. The phone-lines, as Bob kept reminding everybody, were red-hot . . .

Susan from Bromley: 'That boy should be kept in prison for his own good. If he comes out, someone will find him and kill him.'

That one was his favourite. Let's not talk about releasing our own demons back into society. Let's not say we want them locked away for the rest of their lives because it makes us a bit less guilty about not protecting our children. Let's pretend we're concerned for the safety of the murdering bastards. Priceless.

He weighed up the arguments, as he always did, and in the end, he was firmly with the majority on this contentious issue.

The man should never be set free. Killing kiddies was evil.

Caroline had gone to bed nice and early, and he'd had most of the evening to sit and think, and assure himself that he'd thought of everything.

He'd considered abandoning the whole thing when Palmer had escaped. He thought about trying to find him, starting their little partnership up again. He bore him no ill will for weakening the last time, for turning against him. That was the way it went with characters like Martin. The fear could be harnessed, but it was sometimes a bit unpredictable.

After due consideration, he'd decided to press on. Never still and never back. Palmer was part of his past now, let him flounder and drown. *His* future was far more exciting. It did give him a laugh though, Palmer escaping the way he did. Thorne was so arrogant. Thorne, who never suffered fools. Now he'd fucked up very badly.

Now, Thorne was the fool.

He poured himself another glass of wine. He wondered if McEvoy would fuck up. It wouldn't be the end of the world if she did – he'd be covered – but it would be disappointing after the effort he'd put in so far. On balance, he decided he had good reason to be optimistic.

She was the perfect choice after all.

The first time he'd met her, he'd recognised something. He'd seen a need, and not just the obvious one. He'd spotted the drug dependency immediately, of course: he'd seen it many times when he was on the street. It was probably the coke that had first put the idea in his head, but he quickly found out that McEvoy's need ran far deeper.

So, all being well, they would *both* get something out of

it. He would know if he had made the right choice very soon, but if all did not go well, he had already decided that he would kill her later anyway.

He leaned across to the radio and turned it up. Some idiot was wittering on about how it would be impossible for this boy to hide who he used to be, even if he was released. They'd said the same things about Venables and Thompson. They'd have to become different people; they'd need to hide their past from everyone. They'd have to lie, for ever, to close friends and future spouses. It wasn't possible. *Someone* would find out, surely. How could you keep your past so secret?

He smiled at that. He knew it could be done.

Thorne pressed the *Play* button on the answering machine, and a day that had ended badly got even shittier.

'Hello . . . Tom, it's Eileen. Auntie Eileen, from Brighton . . . I hate these things. Listen, we need to have a chat about your dad. I've been in touch with him a fair bit, you know, since Christmas and, well . . . it's not good. You wouldn't really remember, but your grandad was the same . . . later on. Sometimes I think he forgets to eat anything. Anyway, I've been nagging him and he says he's going to see the GP. I think he'll probably get referred, you know, for proper tests, but anyway, give us a call and we can put our heads together. You should tell him yourself as well, make sure he keeps the appointment . . .'

He hit the *Stop* button and went to put the kettle on.

He banged down the mug on the worktop. It had been a week since the row with his dad. He should have called him back the next day, sorted it out. What was Eileen getting involved for anyway? She'd never been arsed before.

Christ, they always came out of the woodwork when there was something to get worked up about. Busybodies like that loved a fucking crisis didn't they?

That KFC he'd picked up on the way home had been a mistake. He was starting to feel a little sick.

Proper tests? What did that mean . . . ?

He looked at his watch. It was far too late to call his dad now. He tore at the milk carton roughly enough to spill milk everywhere. Fuck it, the tea would only keep him awake anyway. Wasn't there supposed to be more caffeine in tea than coffee?

He stomped back into the living room and sat there in silence, cradling his phone.

Who was he kidding? If he slept at all it would be a miracle. The adrenaline that had rushed through his bloodstream in the hotel room earlier was still around, looking for something to do. The feelings that had taken hold of him, knocked him around a little, as he'd looked down at Jason Alderton, had gone back to wherever it was they hid most of the time, but he was still feeling bruised.

And McEvoy . . .

What the hell had all that been about? He'd need to talk to Brigstocke about it in the morning. Maxwell would probably write it up in his report, but Thorne knew it would be good if he could get in first. He hadn't a clue what he was going to tell Brigstocke though. Probably the same bollocks McEvoy had given *him* . . .

He'd need to talk to Holland as well.

He looked at his watch. Only five minutes later than the last time he looked.

He let it ring three times, hung up, dialled again. It rang for a very long time.

'Palmer?'

'I was asleep . . .'

'Give me an address.'

'What . . . ?'

'Give me the address where you are, and I'll come and get you.'

'I can't.'

Thorne hadn't expected it to be that easy, but he was still genuinely annoyed. 'Why don't we just get this over with, Palmer? You're not someone who escapes. You're not even someone who runs. You're just a fuck-up, you're just weak.'

There was a pause long enough for Thorne to get up and move through to the bedroom. He lay down on the bed. Then Palmer spoke again.

'I know . . .'

'So what do you think you're doing?'

'I'm not sure.'

He wasn't the only one. Thorne stared up at the ceiling and asked himself why an escaped killer was the only person he could think of ringing at half past midnight. There was no need to answer the question of course – it was bollocks. He was tired and thinking all sorts of strange shit. Holland wouldn't have minded, he was probably still up anyway. Hendricks as well. He could have called Hendricks . . .

'Is there any news on Stuart?' Palmer asked.

'Worried he might find you before we do, Martin?'

'No . . . just, you know, any news?'

Thorne grunted. 'Only if you've got some.'

'Sorry . . . I don't know anything about him.'

'Except that he might be a policeman.'

'I did say, before, that it was just a feeling. It was nothing I can back up with anything. I've never lied to you, Inspector Thorne.'

'I'm supposed to be impressed with that, am I? Supposed to think that counts for something?'

'I never said that.'

'You've stabbed one young woman, strangled another . . .'

'Please . . .'

'But deep down you're pretty honest!'

'I'm sorry if I don't fit into a convenient pigeonhole for you.'

'Bollocks . . . shut up. That's crap.'

Thorne could hear the distant rhythms of an argument from somewhere down the street. A man and a woman. He couldn't tell if they were getting closer or moving further away.

'You aren't the only one who would like to know,' Palmer said. 'What I am.'

'Don't make any mistake about this, Palmer, I *know* what you are . . .'

'I'm sorry if I got you into any trouble . . .'

'And stop fucking apologising. It's pathetic.'

Thorne needed more of his painkillers. He took a deep breath and swung his legs off the bed, the undigested chicken rising up his throat.

'Inspector Thorne . . . ?'

He stood and walked slowly across to the wardrobe. He kicked open the door, stared at himself in the full-length mirror on the back of it.

'Jesus Christ . . .' He hadn't meant to say it out loud.

'Inspector Thorne . . . ?'

The swollen distorted face looked back at him and reminded him of what he was supposed to be. It asked him, politely but firmly, what the fuck he thought he was doing.

'Are you all right, Inspector Thorne?'

Then the explosion of rage. The one that ran in the family.

'Don't talk to me. Not like that, do you understand? Not *are you all right*? Not *sorry* . . .'

'I don't . . .'

'Talk to me like a murderer.'

TWENTY-SIX

Thorne arrived at work feeling hollow, certain that little would happen during the day that could fill the empty space.

The sleep following his conversation with Martin Palmer had been surprisingly deep – a welcome side effect of the painkillers. This time, the animal had worked longer and harder at the space beneath the door. Digging down, forcing its snout into the gap. This time, behind the door, Karen McMahon had not been there to take Charlie Garner's hand.

The day ahead would, Thorne knew, be almost surreal considering the state of the case.

The hunt for Palmer was going nowhere.

The hunt for Nicklin was going backwards.

Thorne and the team would probably spend the day celebrating . . .

A bottle or two and a backslap or three to put the lid on last night's result at the hotel. A session of whistling in the dark that would only be interrupted – right after lunch, according to his Regulation 7 notice – by Thorne's initial meeting with officers from the DPS.

A day when nothing was going to happen. A day when *everything* was going to be settled . . .

Tom Thorne was not the only one arriving at work, and in the head of the man who used to be Stuart Nicklin, a clock was ticking.

Thorne's assessment of how the day would pan out was pretty much bang on. The only thing he hadn't foreseen was quite how early the party was going to start. The word had gone out: a bit of a drink at lunch-time to toast a job well done. Morale, however, was not exactly through the roof anywhere in Serious Crime. Not among Team 3, not among the team that had taken over the hotel killings, nowhere. A couple of pints in the pub at lunch-time would certainly be welcomed, but there was always going to be a need to push the boat out a little further than that.

The first bottle of scotch had appeared before the morning cups of tea and coffee were finished.

Thorne and Brigstocke watched from their office as paper cups were filled and the stories that had filtered back about the events the previous night were exaggerated and passed around.

'It's a bit early isn't it?' Thorne asked.

Brigstocke raised his eyebrows theatrically. 'Bugger me, are you feeling all right, Tom? Maybe that smack in the face did more damage than we realised.'

Thorne said nothing. Looking out, he noticed that Holland was nowhere to be seen. He wasn't joining in the celebrations.

Brigstocke shrugged. 'I think we need this to tell you the truth. As long as it stays controlled, it's no problem. As long as nobody's too shit-faced when Jesmond pops over to bask in his bit of reflected glory . . .'

The volume of noise from the incident room dropped.

It was clear which bit of the hotel story was being repeated.

'I spoke to McEvoy first thing this morning,' Brigstocke said.

'How did she sound?'

'Half-asleep. Embarrassed about what happened. Said she was fine to come in, but I've told her to leave it until the end of the week. What do you think?'

Thorne nodded; that sounded about right. 'She's got some personal stuff to sort out.'

'With Holland?'

Thorne wasn't surprised that Brigstocke had noticed something – he always had a good handle on the relationships between the members of his team. 'Holland says not,' Thorne said.

'It's not the end of the world. Shift one of them across to Belgravia or the West End . . .'

'Make it McEvoy.'

'Problems?'

'No, not really.' *Not really.* Nothing beyond a loyalty to Dave Holland, and a slight unease about Sarah McEvoy. Nothing he could even name, beyond a vague suspicion he had no intention of voicing.

'Anyway,' Brigstocke said, 'if Holland says not . . .'

'Right.'

'Hello . . . your best mate's here.'

Thorne watched as Steve Norman strolled into the incident room, a slim leather bag slung across one shoulder. He greeted the officers like old friends and held up a hand to gently turn down the offer of a drink.

'What's he doing here? Doesn't he have his own office?'

'I think he's one of those that likes to feel part of the team, you know?'

'Oh fuck . . .'

Norman was on his way towards the office. There was nowhere to hide.

'Hi, guys. Just stopped in to say well done for last night. More work for *me* . . . but that's the nature of the beast, I suppose. Right . . . I'll no doubt see you for a quick one at lunch-time, but I'd better be off. On the move a lot today, loads to do . . .'

He patted his shoulder bag as he turned to leave. Thorne realised that it contained a laptop computer. Norman was clearly one of those that liked to remind others just how important he was. Just how *very* busy. He probably used it a lot on the train.

'Tosser,' Thorne muttered as Norman closed the door behind him.

'I think DCI Lickwood said he might stick his head in later on, just to say hello and have one on our team's tab.' Brigstocke grinned at Thorne's expression. 'Thought you'd be pleased.'

'So no chance of trying to catch any murderers today, then?'

'Come on, Tom. People will be coming and going all day, and we had a good result last night. It's the first one for a while.'

Thorne didn't need reminding.

'Business as usual, of course,' Brigstocke said. 'But with a good feeling round the place for a change. A positive atmosphere. Don't you remember what it was like, last day of term?'

Thorne knew what Brigstocke meant, but it still felt wrong somehow. He walked out of the door, grumbling.

'I'll fetch the party hats . . .'

Then the desk got him.

Thorne swore loudly and kicked at the offending corner – the ball of screwed-up paper he'd taped to it long gone. As he rubbed his thigh, he decided that while the rest of the place was celebrating the end of term, he was going to do something useful. He shouted to no-one in particular:

'Right, get me a fucking saw . . .'

A couple of regulars sat up at the bar, nursing grudges and pints, moaning to the landlord and throwing dirty looks over their shoulders, but the place belonged to Serious Crime. There were a hundred or more officers and civilian staff crammed in to the back bar. Though it was officially just a lunch-time thing, Thorne was pretty sure, based on the morning, that there wasn't going to be a fat lot of work done in the afternoon.

'Fancy a drink, big boy?'

Thorne actually started slightly. Despite the noise and the crush, he'd actually drifted away for a moment, thinking about the generations either side of himself. Young boys and old men . . .

'Only you've been stood here with that half for twenty minutes,' Hendricks said. 'Wishing you were somewhere else.'

'That obvious, is it?'

'I was going to say you've got a face like a smacked arse, but, looking at it, *kicked* arse would be a bit more accurate.'

Thorne raised his glass, took a sip and then gestured with it, pointing at nothing in particular. 'This is fucking nonsense though, isn't it?'

Hendricks shook his head, leaned on the bar. 'Don't

agree, mate. We all need to let our hair down, this lot more than most. You as much as anybody . . .'

'A copper with a pint pot in his hand is not my idea of a good time. Christ, it's rough enough *working* with them.'

'Not been flattened in the rush for a matey chinwag then?'

Thorne finally smiled. 'Most of them stay away . . .'

'Are you having another one?' Thorne shook his head. Hendricks turned to the bar and raised his hand to attract the attention of a barmaid.

Most of them. Steve Norman had marched straight up and bent Thorne's ear for ten long minutes. Keen to impress upon him just how hard he was working. Delighted that after the depressing weeks on Nicklin and Palmer, he finally had some positive material to work with – the McMahon discovery and the hotel murders. He'd drunk two tomato juices before rushing away, as he told Thorne excitedly, to prepare a press release detailing the brilliant operation that had resulted in the arrest of Jason Alderton.

Hendricks was back at Thorne's elbow with a pint of Guinness and a disgruntled expression. 'We've got to *pay* for these now. How much did Brigstocke put behind the bar?'

'Two hundred and fifty. It lasted about fifteen minutes.'

The two of them said nothing for a minute or two. They stood and watched as police officers of all ranks and ages enjoyed a momentary triumph. Battered bomber jackets and fleeces with bottles of lager. Shirts with grimy collars and Christmas ties, spilling pints of bitter. Sharp suits on spritzers. Women who were harder than they looked and men who were a damn sight younger. Old stagers from the squads, a squeak away from their pensions, and West End wannabes with Audis on double yellows and dialogue from a Guy Ritchie movie.

A couple of hours to pretend, to forget. Then back to it.

The Met was haemorrhaging. It was losing officers at the rate of five a day. Thorne was surprised it wasn't ten times that number. He was amazed he was too stubborn, or stupid, or scared, to be one of them.

'It'll all still be there tomorrow, Tom,' Hendricks said. 'A couple of hours on the piss isn't going to make a blind bit of difference. Have a drink, catch the fucker another day . . .'

Thorne smiled and finished his drink, thinking: *Tomorrow is another day nearer the next body. A couple of hours might make all the difference in the world.*

Lunch-time was excruciating. Talking to people, and eating and smiling. Looking like he was interested in their pointless drivel. It was so hard today, when such excitement was so close.

He managed it every other day of course, but that was just routine. And didn't everyone dissemble to some degree or other? Saying you're not bothered about getting the stupid job when you'd happily kill for it. Saying that you just want to be friends when actually you're already fucking somebody else. Wearing a mask. Pretending to care.

On the days he killed, though, it was always like this to some extent. He remembered the tedious meeting at work on the day he'd killed the Chinese girl; the expression of concentration stuck on to his face when all he could think about was what she might look like, how it was going to feel. He could still feel Caroline's mouth against his freshly shaved cheek as she kissed him goodbye on the morning he'd paid his visit to Ken Bowles. He'd smiled and kissed her back, they'd talked about what they might have for dinner later, and all the time he could feel the wonderful weight of the bat in his bag . . .

This one was going to be even better. This time, he was having trouble keeping himself from grabbing people and shouting into their faces. Telling them exactly what he was planning to do, how brilliantly he'd arranged everything, how superb it was going to feel. The buzz was already building. He could almost feel the mask beginning to slip.

Somebody spoke to him. He said something back. He stuck something tasteless into his mouth, glanced at his watch.

He needed a little time on his own. Just half an hour or so, for a coffee and a bar of chocolate. To gather himself before the adventure started.

Thorne looked up to see Holland pushing through the tables towards him. He could see by his face that Holland was having about as good a time as *he* was. The fact that he'd been stuck in a corner with Derek Lickwood couldn't have helped.

'Thanks for that,' Holland said, squeezing in between Thorne and Hendricks.

'Privilege of rank, Holland. I get to inform the next of kin, you have to talk to DCI Dickwood. Did he do that thing of looking over your head while he's talking to you?'

Holland smiled and shook his head. 'He's *such* a wanker. Kept having little digs about Palmer escaping. Asked if you'd ever worked for Group 4.'

Hendricks snorted into his Guinness. Thorne turned to him. 'Shut it.'

'He's off,' Holland said. Thorne looked across in time to see Lickwood at the door on the far side of the room. Just before stepping through it on to the street, he turned and cocked his head towards Thorne. It was a hard expression to read, but Thorne would have put good money on smug.

'I've got a good idea why he was here, though,' Holland said. 'He seemed very disappointed that DS McEvoy wasn't around. A bit confused . . .'

Hendricks enjoyed this sort of intrigue hugely. 'What? Lickwood has the hots for McEvoy?'

'Oh yeah, fancies the pants off her.'

'What did you tell him?' Thorne asked.

'I just sort of ducked it really, made out like I didn't know where she was myself. He was pissed off about it, though, definitely.'

Hendricks downed the rest of his Guinness. 'She's a popular girl is McEvoy.'

'That's true,' Thorne said. 'Problem is, I'm not sure she likes herself very much.'

If Thorne had had a problem reading the expression on Lickwood's face, the one on Dave Holland's at that moment was well beyond his reach. He stared at it for a second or two and then turned away, his heart sinking at the screech of feedback from across the room. Some idiot had got hold of a microphone.

'It's Jesmond,' Hendricks announced.

Thorne knew a cue to leave when he heard one. 'Come on, Holland. Let's get the hell out of here.'

'Where are we going?'

'Happily, I have a pressing engagement in Colindale

with the Directorate of Professional Standards. You can hold my hand.'

As the first distorted platitudes rang across the bar, Thorne and Holland pushed their way towards the exit. Thorne wondered whether the beer on his breath might count against him at his meeting.

Behind him, Holland was remembering how cold it had been at half past three that morning. Sitting naked on the edge of his bed. Whispering into his mobile with Sophie stirring next to him, disturbed by the phone, but not fully awake yet.

McEvoy's voice had been strained, garbled . . . raised just enough to reach him over the noise in wherever the hell she was calling from; as heartbreaking a mixture of helplessness and arrogance as he could ever have imagined.

'I'm fine. OK? I just wanted to tell you that. I really am absolutely fine.'

TWENTY-SEVEN

The voice was getting quieter, line by line.

She hadn't slept in nearly thirty-six hours. She hadn't been straight for a good while longer. It was hard to work out exactly which of these things was responsible for the various things her body was now subject to every few minutes. She was overtired. She was shaking. She was out of it. She was wired, hysterical, comatose, terrified, buzzing, fearless . . .

The night before, as soon as Holland had gone, she'd done the last of the coke in the flat and rushed to her computer. She'd written a few e-mails, received a few and then she'd gone out to score. Walking, running most of the way, she hadn't stepped on any of the cracks in the pavement, as per usual. That way she knew that her dealer would be there, that he'd have something for her.

For the rest of that night she'd been awake – drinking and chain-smoking, opening up the wrap made from a folded lottery ticket, chopping out a line every half an hour or so. Since the sun had come up, she'd been doing one every fifteen minutes.

The fucker was ripping her off, must be. She'd always got

four lines out of a quarter, and now, suddenly, she was getting no more than three. She was needing to make the lines thicker. The bastard must be cutting her stuff . . .

Still, cut or not, the stuff was doing the trick. It was silencing the voice. The voice in her head – so much posher and more attractive than the one that came out of her mouth – had been growing quieter with each new line. The voice that told her she was stupid, that what she was planning was insane, that she was risking her life. Each hit was turning it down another notch.

There were other voices she could still hear, that she *needed* to hear. Holland's voice, telling her she couldn't do her job any more. Her mother's voice. The voice she had never heard, but which she imagined when she read the e-mails. These were the voices that, for the time being, she didn't want to tune out, that were making her do this thing, that she would soon silence once and for all.

A wave of rage swept over her as she imagined them all taking the credit for what she was going to do; praising her initiative and then taking all the glory. Fuck that. She imagined Holland coming back to her, walking out on his dim girlfriend and trying to start things up again . . .

She moved to the table. The empty vodka bottle. The empty wrap.

Fuck, fuck, fuck . . .

She opened up the lottery ticket, pressed it flat on the table and licked. She got down on her knees and began dabbing at specks on the carpet, rubbing equal amounts of cocaine, dirt and dead skin into her gums.

Christ alive, how much had she got through? Bastard must have cut it half and half. Must have . . .

She lit a cigarette, put on her coat.

There wasn't a great deal of time. There was still that one crucial piece of information she needed. The one thing he'd held back while he was sending his cryptic little messages. He thought he was being so clever this last week or so, but he had no idea how good she was. None of them did. She was one step ahead of them, all the time. And she was one step ahead of *him*.

She sent an e-mail, and when she didn't get an immediate reply, she sent another, telling him she had to go out. Telling him how he could contact her. It was the only thing she could do, other than sit and wait until lunch-time which was when he usually came on line. She couldn't wait another second.

She grabbed her bag, and after making sure there was nobody on surveillance outside, she closed the door behind her, shivering as she stepped into the cold air.

McEvoy walked quickly away down the greasy pavement, making quite sure she didn't step on any of the cracks.

'How did it go?'

Holland had been waiting for Thorne in reception, chewing the fat with an old mate on duty behind the desk. He waved goodbye as he and Thorne pushed out through the doors and started the ten-minute walk back to Becke House.

What little sun there was up there was having no luck breaking through a solid blanket of cloud. The sky was the colour of pewter. There were already one or two cars with sidelights on.

It was a little after three o'clock.

'How was it really?'

'I think I got lucky,' Thorne said. 'A pair of rubber-heelers with a sense of humour.'

Holland smiled. Rubber-heelers. *You couldn't hear the buggers coming*. 'What was it that they found funny . . . ?'

It hadn't begun well.

DCI Collins (short and overweight) and DI Manning (tall and overweight) did not look like they enjoyed a laugh. Both had that strange expression – a mixture of boredom and seething resentment – which Thorne had previously seen only on the faces of men standing on Oxford Street with signs reading GOLF SALE.

Manning had shuffled papers while Collins had leaned forward across the table to deliver the caution. It had begun and ended with much the same words that Thorne had used to caution Martin Palmer. In the middle, they had detailed the neglect of duty – the procedural lapse that had allowed Palmer to escape – speaking slowly and seriously. These officers were doing their job of work so much better than Thorne had done his.

'I'd like a number of other serious incidents noted for the record,' Thorne had said. 'Incidents where I neglected my duty.'

Manning had thrown a sideways glance at Collins and then at the tape recorder to check that the spools were turning. 'Go ahead, Inspector.'

Thorne had cleared his throat. 'I have, on a number of occasions, farted without apologising, and though I have never actually *appeared* in *The Bill*, a woman who was drunk told me I looked a bit like the bloke who plays DI Burnside . . .'

Manning and Collins had looked at each other and then pissed themselves.

'So, how did it finish up?' Holland asked. They were approaching the pub where, doubtless, Serious Crime was still busy inside, pursuing various lines of enquiry.

Thorne wasn't certain what would happen next, but for a change he had decided to think positive. 'I'm not exactly off the hook, but I don't reckon they're sorting me out a uniform just yet.'

Holland stopped and nodded across the road towards the pub. 'Are we going back in?'

Thorne kept on walking, shouted back over his shoulder. 'You can do what you like, Holland, I'm going to go and pick the car up. I thought I'd go and see how McEvoy's getting on. Find out if her mother's any better . . .'

At three thirty, they pulled up outside Sarah McEvoy's flat in Wembley.

Thorne got out of the car and walked up the steps to the front door. He turned and looked at Holland who was still sitting in the passenger seat, staring forwards. 'Come on, Dave . . .' Holland got out while Thorne rang the bell. He arrived next to him as Thorne rang again.

Nothing.

Thorne took a step back, peered to his left at the dark blue curtains drawn across the bay window. 'Is that her flat?' He'd picked McEvoy up outside the place on a few occasions, dropped her off on a couple more, but he'd never been inside.

Holland's answer was non-committal. 'Maybe she's in bed,' he said.

Thorne shrugged, thrust his hands into his jacket pockets and trudged back down towards the car.

Holland watched Thorne moving away, wrestling with it, knowing how easy it would be to jog gently down the steps after him. His voice when he spoke was louder than he'd intended it to be – more urgent.

'I think we should go in . . .'

Thorne turned, twirling the car keys around a finger. 'I don't think I want the Funny Firm doing me for breaking and entering as well, Dave . . .'

'I've got a key,' Holland said.

Thorne came up the steps two at a time and took hold of the arm that was already reaching forward to push a key into the lock.

'We'll need to talk about this, Holland . . .'

It was as dark and gloomy inside the flat as it was outside on the street. As well as the curtains at the front, in McEvoy's bedroom there was a blind pulled down over the back window, the one that looked out on to the garden.

'Well, she's not asleep,' Holland said, coming back into the living room.

Thorne wasn't listening. He was staring at a dozen reflections of himself. He counted at *least* a dozen of them. Mirrors were suspended from the ceiling, propped up on the floor, leaning against the walls at a variety of strange angles. Heavy and ornate, plain and unframed, round, square, all highly polished . . .

'What the fuck is this . . . ?'

Holland moved past him to the window, raised the blind, then turned around. He opened his mouth to answer the question but nothing came out.

Thorne moved slowly around the room, every glance bringing some new reflection, some bizarre perspective on himself. The back of a leg, the top of his head. His fading bruises appeared straight on and profiled at the same time.

On the table, Thorne saw another, smaller mirror, and the creased lottery ticket. He knew at once what he was looking at.

'How long have you known about it?' he asked.

'About three weeks.'

'You're a fucking idiot . . .'

Holland raised a hand to shut Thorne up. Yes, he *was* a fucking idiot, he was much much worse, but he had to stop Thorne going off on one. Not now. He could bow his head and accept the bollocking another time. Now, there was something else . . .

'Sir, I think McEvoy's in some sort of trouble.'

'*Some sort* . . . ?'

'Real trouble.' Holland couldn't say why he was worried. He didn't know what it was that was nagging at him, couldn't explain where the feeling came from. It made him shiver and it kept him awake, and he needed to tell someone. It was there in McEvoy's eyes and the things she said, and the way she'd been acting for a while.

It was as if she had a secret. *Another* secret . . .

'What?' Thorne said.

Holland shook his head, looked around the room, searching desperately for something that might bring this indistinct unease into sharp relief. His gaze settled on the computer.

The look on McEvoy's face a few days before, when he'd walked in to the office and found her on the Internet. Panic, and something else. Defiance? Triumph . . . ?

Thorne watched Holland walk across, pull up a chair, hit the button to wake the machine up.

'What are you doing?'

'I'm going to check her e-mails.'

'You think she's been ordering drugs by e-mail?'

'No . . . maybe. I don't think this is about the coke . . .' Holland began moving the mouse, clicking, opening windows.

'Don't you need some sort of password?'

'I would if I was actually going to sign on to her account, but I should be able to check her filing cabinet – see what she's been sending out, what she's received . . .'

Thorne nodded, letting Holland get on with it, whatever it was.

Cocaine. Thorne had suspected as much. He'd known a few coppers who liked a sniff. It was usually the older ones who should have known better, the ones that couldn't be doing with Ecstasy because it involved dancing. Whatever their reason for doing it, some of them got seriously messed up.

Thorne wondered how far into it McEvoy had got. He looked up and saw the answer reflected around the room, from one mirror to another . . .

'Fuck . . . oh fuck, no.'

'What?' Thorne felt the change in his body straight away. He sensed a livening in the nerve endings, a heightening of the senses as he moved rapidly across the room, reacting instinctively to the panic in Holland's voice. 'What is it, Dave?'

Holland ran his fingers through his hair, scratching hard at his scalp, staring in disbelief at the screen. Thorne leaned in and looked over his shoulder. He couldn't immediately work out what he was looking at.

'I can't . . .'

'She's been getting e-mails from the killer,' Holland said. 'From Night Watchman . . .'

Thorne felt something prickle around the top of his shoulders, heard his heartbeat quicken. 'Getting them, or getting them and replying? How long . . . ?'

'Wait . . .' Holland clicked, sorting the mails by date. He began to scroll slowly through them, and Thorne watched it move down the screen in front of his eyes. A correspondence between a woman on his team and the man they were trying to catch. A man who killed more brutally than anyone Thorne had ever lost sleep over.

'A week or more,' Holland said. 'Shit, there's fucking dozens of them . . .'

It had begun tentatively, like an exchange of letters between lovers-to-be. He told her he thought she was special, that there was something about her. He wondered how far across the line she would go to get the right result. His words were cryptic, teasing. Thorne could tell that, at least initially, he had been fishing, trying to find out how much she knew, how much any of them knew about him. He was wooing her. Thorne could see it, clear as day. He wondered if McEvoy had seen it. Her responses were open and forthright. She had fallen for it, or was letting him *think* she had. Thorne couldn't tell which.

'What the fuck is she playing at . . . ?' Holland's panic was increasing with every minute that passed, with every e-mail opened.

As Thorne read on, the answer became horribly apparent. The round-the-houses stuff had given way, in the last day or two, to something specific. An invitation. Did she want to meet him? Was she the individual he thought she was? McEvoy had replied. She was *everything* he thought she was, and more.

'When? There's got to be something that gives us a time . . .'

'Got it,' Holland said, opening another mail. 'Jesus, it's today. Four o'clock . . .'

Thorne looked at the time flashing at him in the top right-hand corner of the screen. Whatever the hell McEvoy thought she was doing, she probably had about twenty-five minutes to live.

'Where?'

Holland clicked, scrolled, jabbed viciously at the keys. 'His last e-mail was . . . just after one this morning.' He opened the file and they stared at the killer's words on the screen.

```
Let's make it the place where Martin
was told the Jungle Story. Looking
forward to it, Sarah ...
```

'What the hell does that mean?' Holland put his finger against the screen and pressed hard, as if he was trying to push through it, rub out the words floating on the other side.

'What about McEvoy's last mail?'

Holland called it up. 'She sent two, one after the other, just before midday today . . .'

```
No idea what that means. Should I? If
you want me
to come, you'd better spell it out.
```

'Let's see the second one.' Thorne dared not hope. He already knew there was no reply from the killer, nothing that spelled anything out. Would McEvoy's final message be to cry off, to suggest they rearrange? She would have no choice, surely. She didn't know the place he was suggesting . . .

```
Going out now. Not sure when I'll be
back. Need
to know where to meet.
```

Then, two words that jumped off the screen, sent the guts shooting up towards the throat.

```
Text me.
```

Holland's body spasmed. 'Shit. He's sent a text message telling her where to meet him.'

'We don't know if he contacted her at all,' Thorne said. 'We don't know anything. She might come breezing back in here any second, off her tits with a bag full of Charlie.' Holland's look told Thorne that he didn't believe it any more than he did.

Thorne grabbed at the phone on the corner of the desk, thrust it at Holland. 'Call her mobile.'

He walked away, across to the window and stared out into the garden. The wind was coming up. He watched the overgrown grass sway slightly, and the long, rusty mirror bump gently against the fence post. Watching, hoping to hear Holland's concern translate into anger when he got through. *Where the fuck are you?* Hearing instead a long, frustrated breath, the crack of the phone going down, two more words he could really have done without.

'Switched off . . .'

Thorne turned around, walked back to the desk and picked up the phone himself. He dialled, waited, then hung up.

'Who are you calling?'

Thorne said nothing, his hand never leaving the receiver. He snatched it up again and dialled the number. He looked away from Holland, waiting for an answer . . .

'It's me. Tell me about the Jungle Story . . . never mind that, *just tell me*! Listen, Palmer, there isn't time for this, tell me what it is. No . . . forget that, just tell me *where*. Where was it . . . ?'

Holland couldn't believe what he was hearing. *Palmer?* What the hell was Thorne playing at . . . ? He stopped thinking about anything at all when Thorne's face changed. Even the bruises on his face seemed to grow momentarily pale. He thought that perhaps Thorne let out a long, low moan, though it might actually have come from him . . .

Thorne hung up with his finger. Gently but quickly he passed the receiver to Holland.

'It's at the school. He's meeting her at King Edward's.'

'Where are you . . . ?'

Thorne was on his way to the front door, his voice getting louder as he moved further away. 'Get on the phone and get it organised, right now. Tell Brigstocke I want an armed response unit. Keep trying McEvoy's mobile, or get somebody else to.'

'Sir . . .'

By now Thorne was shouting.

'And get a message through to the school . . .'

TWENTY-EIGHT

McEvoy walked into the playground in slow motion.

Stop. Just move backwards. Out of here the way you've come. Only he *will ever know you bottled out. You don't have anything to prove, Sarah . . .*

It was that strange time between darkness and light, the half an hour or so that can't quite make its mind up. As McEvoy pushed herself through the air, she felt like she was wading through a sticky, viscous liquid.

Adults and children milling around. Their movements impossibly fast. Their voices ringing through her, setting her teeth on edge. The squeals of the younger children, the honking voices of those a year or two older, the shouting of teachers. A braying cacophony fighting for space in her head with the voice.

The voice was back with a vengeance.

She thought about turning round, getting away to somewhere she could do a line and shut herself up. Getting away was just what the voice was telling her to do, though, so she kept moving forward. Maybe, if she just dived inside the school, found the toilet . . . She couldn't do it out here, not with children around. It would only take a minute. The teachers had to have their own toilet, surely . . .

What the fuck do you think you're doing? Think why you've come here. Worrying about where you do your next line is neither here nor there, considering.

She just kept walking. She'd decided that when she reached the far side of the huge playground she would turn around, walk slowly back again. They hadn't agreed on anywhere more specific. His text message hadn't narrowed the location down.

Silly bitch. Hard-faced bitch. Hard-faced as you like . . . not going to do you any good now. What's he going to do to you?

Her bag was over her shoulder. She pulled it in close to her body. Was there anything in there she could use against him if it came to it?

Run. Get out. Call Thorne . . .

Most of the boys smiled as they walked or ran past her on their way out. In a hurry to get home, but still polite as they had been taught to be. Deferential to adults, well-mannered, especially with ladies.

He *was a pupil here, wasn't he?* He *isn't very well-mannered with ladies.*

She raised her head and looked up at the school building on one side of her, the trees in the park high up in the distance on the other. Was he watching her from somewhere? Would there be some sort of signal? The weight of all the things she didn't know felt suddenly unmanageable. She felt stupid. Trapped and stupid. Even fifteen minutes before, she was so in control, so ready for this.

Now she walked across a playground, her grip loosening with every step.

*

He could see that she was scared.

Probably nobody else who saw her would have spotted it. She looked like she was out for a stroll. Adjusting her route to avoid collision with a burly sixth-former, turning side-on to miss a gaggle of first-years. She looked like she was in control.

He knew what to look for, though. He recognised fear. He would have seen it even if he'd been a long way away. He could see it coming off McEvoy like a heat-haze.

Her being scared was good, but it was less important than the fact that she was here. And that she'd come alone.

That had been the gamble all along, and it was one he couldn't really lose. He'd been able to watch her arrive. From his vantage point he'd been able to verify absolutely that she'd done as he'd asked. If she hadn't, if at the last moment she'd double-crossed him, gone to Thorne, he'd have known it. Even if they'd sent her in *as if* she'd come alone, using her as bait, he'd have seen it. He'd have spotted them, however well hidden they were.

They would never have recognised him.

Even if she'd stood him up he would have coped, taken her to task over it later.

But she was here, as ready for him as she was ever going to be. He felt a surge of pure excitement that, but for these moments just before he killed, he hadn't felt since he was a child.

He grinned. He could still taste the chocolate. Was that what all this was about? Getting in touch with his inner child?

`cu @ 4 @ plygrnd :o)`

The text message had been simple. The childish shorthand was proof, if she needed it, of his sense of fun.

Now it was time for the real fun to start.

Driving like an idiot through Wembley Park, horn blaring, lights flashing; one eye on the dashboard clock, and a speech forming itself in his mind. The words tumbling into sentences with each busy junction, every queue at traffic lights. The speech he would be giving to Sarah McEvoy's parents if he was too late . . .

Why had the killer targeted McEvoy? *How* had he targeted her?

Thorne leaned on the horn, swerved inside to accelerate noisily past a Transit van. He knew he wouldn't get the answers to these questions, not yet. Not until the fucker was in a chair opposite him, shitting himself in an interview room in the early hours of the morning.

There were other questions, though. Questions a little closer to home that got into his head and stayed there like a jingle he couldn't shake. Why hadn't he noticed? Why hadn't he seen a senior member of his team getting into this? The drugs, the lies, the descent into something warped and deadly . . .

He drove north across Fryent Country Park, the school now maybe less than five minutes away. The minute hand moving another notch past the vertical. The speech almost fully formed.

DS McEvoy was a fine officer, who gave her life in the line of duty . . .

Thorne hammered the Mondeo across a roundabout and turned left towards the centre of Harrow. He bellowed at the windscreen as the car that should have had right of way missed him by a matter of inches, the face of its driver murderous. Thorne returned the look with interest and stamped on the brakes, catching his breath through gritted teeth as a line of stationary vehicles appeared in front of him.

All of those who worked with her, of whatever rank, will miss her dedication and good humour . . .

The school was no more than a quarter of a mile away. Thorne's knuckles were white on the steering wheel, his foot pumping the accelerator as he raced the engine in neutral. The shriek of the complaining engine was almost as loud as the scream inside his head.

Nothing was moving. There were no lights ahead, no sign of an accident. Nobody was going anywhere.

The fucking school run.

McEvoy reached the far side of the playground, turned and looked around, thinking come on you fucker, where are you? Moving back towards the centre now, saying it out loud, like a madwoman on a bus. I'm here, why the hell aren't you? There's a big surprise coming your way, coming everybody's way . . .

Then a few words from the voice, and she stopped, because she needed to evacuate the playground. Of course she did. After all, she had no idea what was going to happen. There were still plenty of kids around – the slower ones, the stragglers, a group kicking a ball around. Christ he'd used a gun before, hadn't he? Thoughts of Dunblane, of Columbine High . . .

How messed up are you? Protecting the public should have been your first thought, would *have been a few months ago. If this is about showing how good you are at your job, it's not going very well so far . . .*

She reached into her jacket pocket for her warrant card, opened her mouth to start shouting . . .

What if they panicked? If he was nearby, it might provoke him into something. No, she might scare him off. She needed to do what they'd agreed. Besides, if he *was* nearby, she was going to take the fucker before he could hurt anybody.

That was her last thought before she felt the knife in her back and heard the voice, close to her ear.

'You are alone, aren't you, Sarah?'

'Yes.'

'You're not lying. That's good. Walk with me, and please be sensible . . .'

She gasped as the point of the knife pressed through her jacket and shirt, and into her skin. A hand was placed in the small of her back and began to guide her forwards towards the exit.

His voice. Did she recognise it? Yes, maybe, couldn't remember. Fuck it . . .

McEvoy almost laughed. *She was going to take the fucker*. She knew exactly what she wanted to do, *needed* to do, but couldn't for the life of her remember how. She was suddenly all but asleep on her feet. Helpless. If she hadn't felt as weak as a baby already, the words whispered into her ear would have taken away any last vestige of strength in her body.

'If you scream or try to run, I will kill a child.'

Thorne thought that from somewhere a few streets back he could still hear the horns that had blared at him as he'd got out of the Mondeo and begun to run. Now they were being sounded in pure rage and frustration at the abandoned car.

Oh Christ . . .

He began to slow down, his hands flying to his head, legs suddenly leaden.

Fuck . . .

Where were they coming from? Which direction would the back-up vehicles come from? Brigstocke, Holland, the Armed Response Unit? The traffic had been impossible before. Now, thanks to him, it would be gridlocked. If the cars were coming the same way he had . . .

Suddenly, Thorne was aware of schoolboys moving past him: in ones and twos at first and then in bigger groups. Jabbering and clowning around. Blue blazers, trimmed with claret. The ties taken off for the journey home.

He was nearly there.

He took a painful breath and picked his legs up again, drove himself forward.

We can only hope that more young women of her calibre will come forward and offer their services to the public . . .

The tree-lined streets around the school now thick with blue and claret, alive with shouts and taunts, and boasts.

Hitting the ground. Dragging his knees up . . .

His stomach began to burn, the judder of each step sending an agonising shockwave through his shattered nose and up into his forehead. His chest rattled and clattered. Beneath his jacket, the sweat had plastered his shirt to his back. It froze as it met the cold air blowing down his collar.

Christ they were big, some of them. A pair of lumbering teenagers, striped ties wrapped around their foreheads, blocked the pavement ahead of him. Thorne put his head down and charged at them, ignoring the shouts and jeers as he crashed through the middle and began sprinting for all he was worth up the school drive.

As he ran, as his feet smacked the ground beneath him, he remembered the car crunching slowly over the gravel. He remembered the last time he'd come up this drive. He and Holland comparing educations in the car.

Then inside the school, the first time he'd got a look at Stuart Nicklin. The face turned away.

In making the ultimate sacrifice, this brave officer has increased the determination of those she leaves behind, to continue the fight . . .

Was he about to see that face in the flesh?

He was only a hundred yards or so away. The drive curved sharply to the left and then narrowed suddenly, a bottleneck forming at the high, narrow gate that was the main entrance to the playground.

He began to slow down as he approached it.

Everything seemed normal. Kids coming out smiling. There was no noise, no *abnormal* noise. He slowed to a jog and then a fast walk. Getting his breath back. Everything *seemed* normal, but he had no idea what was waiting for him inside that gate.

He was suddenly very worried – sweating every bit as much as he had been when he was running.

If the message, whatever it was, however it had been worded, had got through to the school, then surely things would *not* have been so normal. Wouldn't the kids be inside? Kept away from any danger, held inside the building?

Thorne put out an arm, brushed past a boy hovering at the gate and stepped through.

He stood there, his guts churning, his eyes flicking across the expanse in front of him, trying to take it all in quickly. The main building to his right. The huge windows of the gymnasium, lined with wallbars. Up ahead, the newer buildings – the sixth-form block, the music rooms – and beyond them the playing fields. Still plenty of kids about. Singing coming from somewhere. A few teachers moving around . . .

McEvoy . . .

He took a step in her direction and then stopped. Her eyes bulged, terrified, out of a bloodless face. What little breath Thorne had left was gone in a moment.

'Sarah . . .'

Then Thorne got his first look at the face of the man immediately behind her. The man who was guiding her gently but firmly towards him. The man who stopped and looked straight at him, scowling, as if he were no more than a hindrance.

Then Thorne knew exactly why Ken Bowles had been killed.

TWENTY-NINE

'You're out of breath,' Cookson said. 'What *have* you been doing?'

It was a moment of terrible clarity. The sort that only ever comes hand in hand with terror, or great pain. Thorne embraced it as he would the sting of the flame that cauterised a wound.

Andrew Cookson . . .

'You killed Bowles because he recognised you,' Thorne said. 'It wasn't random. It wasn't a message. You *needed* to do it . . .'

Cookson casually placed a hand on McEvoy's shoulder. 'Silly old sod should have retired years ago. Could barely do his sums any more. Then after half an hour with you he takes one good, hard look at me without the beard and . . . bang! Cobwebs well and truly blown away. Corners me in the staff room. Pointing his finger and making melodramatic speeches. *I know who you are.* Fucking idiot . . .'

Thorne pictured the chalk on Bowles's crotch, the soil dropping down on to the lid of his coffin. Why hadn't he called the police? Why, when he'd recognised Cookson as

Nicklin, hadn't he used the card that Thorne had given him, the one that Jay had found in his jacket pocket?

The answer was a painful one to acknowledge. It wasn't heroism, it was desperation. It was Ken Bowles's last chance. A crack at balancing that chair on his chin one final time.

'Enjoyable as this is,' Cookson said, 'the situation is a little tricky, wouldn't you say? I think we need to resolve it quickly. So, any bright ideas?'

His tone was easy and faintly amused. Not hard when you were the one with a knife in a woman's back.

'Not really,' Thorne said.

'I thought not.'

There was a silence that should have been heavy with threat and danger, but with children filing past smirking, it felt no more than awkward or embarrassing. Thorne wondered what the three of them looked like. Cookson and McEvoy might have been lovers, and he the ex-boyfriend, bumped into at an inopportune moment . . .

Cookson smiled, as if working something out that pleased him enormously. 'You've come on your own as well, haven't you?'

Thorne thought about lying but wasn't quick enough. Cookson leaned forward, ready to move on. 'Well, you have somewhat gatecrashed things, but we're not going to let it spoil our enjoyment, are we, Sarah?' McEvoy winced as the knife nudged through another layer of skin. Thorne was close to rushing at him, hammering fists into his face. 'So, we're just going to carry on as if we never saw you. Excuse me . . .'

There was nothing Thorne could do. He had to step aside to let Cookson walk away. He didn't have a shred of doubt that he would push the knife into McEvoy's spine at the slightest provocation. He turned side-on, giving Cookson the room to get past, to manoeuvre McEvoy through the gate and away. Thorne noticed that in his free hand Cookson was carrying his briefcase with him. His cover was perfect. This was territory he'd felt safe on. Just a tired teacher heading home with a friend at the end of a long day . . .

Cookson froze suddenly, looked right and left. Then Thorne saw what was happening. Children were moving back towards the building, some running. Teachers had appeared silently around the edge of the playground and were gathering in those pupils still around.

The message had got through.

Hissing instructions, beckoning, gesturing, the teachers emptied the playground in as orderly a way as they could. Following the directives that they had been given – that were standard in such situations – they were trying to do it without alarming anyone, least of all the killer they'd been told might be nearby.

He was nearer than they realised and he *was* alarmed. Thorne could see the hesitation, the tension in Cookson's face and in the hand that squeezed the back of Sarah McEvoy's neck.

'Please,' McEvoy said. It was more of a moan than a word.

'I think we're stuck with each other,' Thorne said. 'Half the Met is waiting for you out there. Plenty of them are armed and looking for an excuse . . .'

Cookson shook his head, and in an instant he had brought the knife round to McEvoy's throat. Smiling, he began to move backwards, towards the centre of the playground. Thorne followed slowly, praying that what he'd just told Cookson was, or would very soon be, true. As they neared the middle of the playground, McEvoy's eyes locked on to Thorne's. He couldn't begin to guess what they were trying to tell him.

Cookson stopped and took a deep breath. He adjusted his position, leaving the knife exactly where it was, the blade biting into McEvoy's neck, but moving round a little to stand next to her.

'You know I'll kill her, so why don't we stop pissing about. One way or another, I'm leaving here. If I'm in the back of a squad car, then she'll be leaving in a body bag.'

'Fuck you,' McEvoy said.

Cookson opened his eyes wide in mock surprise. 'It speaks,' he said. 'I was wondering where you'd got to. I reckon your blood must be about ninety-eight per cent Colombian.' He laughed, and McEvoy grunted as a line of blood an inch or so long sprang onto the flesh of her throat and began to drip.

'Sorry,' Cookson said. 'Accident . . .'

Thorne twitched and Cookson's look told him to keep very still. It told him that the next time there would be a lot more blood.

'What did you do with the boy when you killed Carol Garner?' Thorne said. 'Did he see it happen?' Cookson narrowed his eyes and pursed his lips as if confused by the question. 'Did you make her son watch while you killed her?'

Cookson shook his head, blew out a breath through tight lips. 'Sorry, you'll have to help me. Which one was Carol Garner again?'

Thorne knew then that as things stood, none of them

were likely to leave that playground alive. He was willing his feet to stay where they were, but he knew that at any moment he would fly at this man, that rage would simply stop him caring any more. He knew that McEvoy's throat would open and cover the two of them with blood as she dropped away while he and Andrew Cookson murdered each other with cuts and clutching hands on the cold asphalt . . .

Thorne became aware of a low buzzing noise. He realised that the sound was coming out of McEvoy's mouth.

'I'm sorry . . . I'm sorry . . . I'm sorry . . .'

'McEvoy . . .'

Thorne's voice just seemed to activate some switch in McEvoy's brain. Now the words gushed out of her. She shook her head violently as if trying to dislodge something, shake it out of there; her neck moving back and forth across the blade of the knife, the blood running down Cookson's fingers.

'I'msorryI'msorryI'msorryI'msorryI'msorryI'msorry . . .'

Thorne could have sworn that the scream that followed came from him, or was at the very least inside his head, but if it *was*, why was Cookson spinning round? Why was he looking so astonished . . . ?

The figure came running from around the side of the main building, shouting and waving. Thorne blinked, looked again.

The figure was waving a gun.

Martin Palmer lumbered towards them, and the things that Thorne was seeing seemed to happen in slow motion at the same time that the thoughts in his head started coming faster than he could make sense of them.

Cookson pushing McEvoy away, dropping the knife . . .

McEvoy turning, running straight at Palmer . . .

Cookson bringing up his hands to protect his head as the first shot rang across the playground . . .

As Thorne went down hard, he heard the second shot, and at the edge of his vision he saw McEvoy stumble and crash heavily to the ground. An instant before he closed his eyes, he saw the look of astonishment frozen on Cookson's face, and a look there were simply no words to describe on Martin Palmer's.

It was no more than a few moments, but when Thorne opened his eyes, it seemed to have become considerably darker. There were a few spots of sleet in the air.

Thorne raised his head. Twenty-five yards away, McEvoy lay on the floor. He had no idea where she'd been hit, how badly she was hurt. He heard her moan as she tried to move the leg that was twisted awkwardly beneath her.

She was moving at least.

Thorne slowly got to his feet. His eyes, and those of Andrew Cookson, never moved from the figure of Martin Palmer. He stood no more than a few feet from them, his head bowed, the hand that held the gun twitching spastically.

'What the fuck are you doing, Palmer?' Thorne said.

Palmer looked up. His eyes seemed huge behind his glasses. The gun was smacking against his leg. 'I'm sorry.'

Behind Palmer, McEvoy cried out. Thorne couldn't make out whether it was pain or anger.

'Sorry?' Thorne shouted. 'Fucking sorry . . . ?'

'You're full of surprises, Martin,' Cookson said. 'I *tell* you to shoot someone, you throw a wobbly and run to the police . . .'

Palmer shook his head. 'Shut up, Stuart . . .'

Cookson didn't even draw breath. 'Then up you pop out of the blue, and fuck me if you don't put a bullet in one of them.'

Palmer raised the gun and pointed it at Cookson's chest. 'I told you to shut up.'

'Not deliberately, of course. I think we know who the bullets were meant for.' He nodded his head towards McEvoy. 'She was just a lucky accident.'

Thorne looked at Cookson, no more than two paces away, and promised himself that whatever else happened, he was going to hurt him.

A noise came up from Palmer's throat, a low growl which erupted out of his mouth as a roar. His knuckles were white against the grip of the gun, his finger twitching against the trigger. He nodded once, twice. Those little nods. Urging himself to do it, telling himself to shoot.

Cookson looked unconcerned. 'I always had to get you riled up, didn't I?' he said. 'Do you remember? There was a small window of opportunity if I was going to get you to do something, because you never held it together for very long. So, what's got you so excited now? Specifically?' He asked the question casually, as if checking some trivial fact. 'Was it Karen?'

Palmer swallowed hard. He brought his left hand up to steady the gun.

'Yes, of course it was.' Cookson smiled. '*Was* is right, isn't it, Martin? You've lost it already. You *want* to kill me, but whatever made you brave enough to actually *try* has vanished, hasn't it? Run out of you like watery shit. Now you're just scared again . . .'

Thorne looked at McEvoy. She was getting harder to

make out clearly. The clouds were lower now, and blacker. The light was dirty, diffuse. The whole scene seemed lit by a thousand dusty, forty-watt lightbulbs.

He had to make a move. 'I need to get to my officer,' he said. Palmer didn't appear to be listening. Thorne took a step forwards, and in a second the gun was levelled at him.

'*No!*' Palmer shouted.

Thorne was genuinely surprised. 'What are you playing at, Martin?' Palmer said nothing. He looked lost. Lost, confused, and with a gun pointing at Thorne's belly.

Thorne tried to keep his voice low and even. 'There are armed officers watching us right now. They're slightly better at this than you are. Do you understand, Martin?'

Palmer nodded slowly.

Thorne knew damn well that there was nobody watching them – not yet. If the Armed Response team had been there, then Palmer would not be standing and pointing a gun. He would almost certainly be dead by now.

'Throw the gun away and let me get across to my sergeant. Martin . . . ?'

A light came on to Thorne's right. His eyes flicked across and he saw that there were children at the windows of the gymnasium, watching.

The sleet started to get a little heavier.

'Martin?' Thorne said.

Cookson shrugged. 'It's a toughy, Mart . . .'

Thorne's head whipped round and he spat gobbets of spittle and hatred into Cookson's face. 'Shut your fucking stupid cunt's mouth. *I* will kill you, is that clear? *I'm* not afraid, certainly not of you. I don't care what happens. He can shoot the pair of us, I don't give a fuck. But if I hear so much as a breath coming out of you before this is finished, a single poisonous whisper, I'll rip your face off with my bare hands. I'll take it clean off, Nicklin. I'll make you another nice, new identity . . .'

Cookson's face was blank. He was very still. Thorne thought he'd shaken him, but he couldn't be sure whether the stillness was that of the prey that seeks to protect itself, or the predator that is conserving its energy, preparing to strike.

Palmer spoke and the thought was gone.

'I'm sorry about your officer.' His voice was lower than usual, certainly calmer than it had been a few minutes before. 'I need to tell you something,' he said. 'I got the gun from a man in a pub. The first gun I mean.' He pointed with the gun to Cookson. '*He* knows, he can tell you. It's a pub in Kilburn, I'm sure you could find it . . .'

Thorne stared at him. *What the hell was he on about?* 'We don't have to do this now, Martin . . .'

'I got this gun from the same man. I followed him from the pub. He's got a lock-up garage in Neasden, near the railway works, just across from the tube station.'

Thorne was confused, but his mind raced, made connections. *Neasden, four or five stops from where they were on the tube. Fifteen minutes, no more. Palmer, easily able to get here quicker than he had.* 'Martin, this isn't important . . .'

'Please, you have to listen. I took the gun, and there was a great deal of cash . . .'

Cookson snorted. 'He'll fucking kill you.'

'He's dead.' Cookson's eyes widened. Palmer's looked like they were ready to bulge out of his head as he craned his neck towards Thorne. 'He was a bad man, though, so maybe I did a good thing. I had no choice anyway.' He glanced at the gun in his hand. 'I needed . . . this. I needed somewhere to stay for a while. I stayed in the garage. With the body. It was starting to really smell in there . . .'

Palmer blinked slowly, his eyes closing almost, but not for quite long enough for Thorne to think about lunging . . .

'We can sort all this out later, Martin. There'll be loads of time. Just get rid of the gun. You must get rid of it . . .'

Palmer lowered his arm.

'That's good, Martin, but you have to drop it. Let it go.'

Palmer shook his head. Thorne sensed movement away to his right, and turned his head to see the children in the gym being led away from the windows. One by one the faces disappeared.

Thorne blinked. The last face pressed up against the window, eyes wide and full of doubt, belonged to Charlie Garner . . .

There was other movement, indistinct and fleeting, somewhere above and to the right of him. Finally, Thorne knew that back-up had arrived. Positions were being taken up, targets identified, sights fixed. A momentary glance told him that Cookson had seen it too.

'I don't want you to be afraid,' Palmer said suddenly.

Thorne looked away from the rooftop. As he brought his gaze back round to Palmer, he checked out Cookson, who was standing stock still, arms by his sides, eyes narrowed.

Palmer's expression was bizarrely earnest. 'Really. You don't have to be afraid.'

'Guns make me afraid, Martin. Throw it away.'

'You know fear has a taste, don't you? It's actually the taste of your adrenal gland. That's what you can taste, that's the flavour of it . . .'

Thorne saw Palmer's fingers moving. He watched, afraid to breathe, as the finger moved away from the trigger.

Should he move now? Go for the gun . . . ?

'It's a very strange taste. Like chewing on a bit of tinfoil. That suggestion of metal in your mouth. It's actually the chemical that's in adrenaline . . .'

Palmer slipped his finger out of the trigger guard. Rested it against the outside. Safe.

He needed to do it now. He wasn't sure he'd seen McEvoy move for a while . . .

'It's called adrenochrome. Did you know that?'

Thorne shook his head. He didn't know the name, but he knew the taste very well.

As Palmer screamed and raised his arm, Thorne saw what was happening. As Palmer levelled the gun at him, Thorne saw exactly what he was trying to do.

He saw everything, far, far too late.

The bullet from the marksman's rifle had ripped through Palmer's throat before any of them had even heard the shot.

Palmer dropped to his knees with an odd slowness, but then pitched forward fast on to his face. Thorne thought, or perhaps imagined, that he could hear nose, cheekbones and glasses shattering as the face hit the ground.

Thorne went down quickly, put his hands on the gun that was lying a foot or so away from Palmer's corpse. He looked across towards McEvoy, hoping . . .

'Congratulations on being alive, Thorne.' Cookson smiled, slowly raising his hands into the air. 'Being alive's the easy bit though, isn't it?'

From somewhere behind them, a distorted voice

boomed through a loudspeaker. Cookson took a step towards it, his arms high and straight. 'It's *feeling* alive, that's the hard part . . .'

In one smooth movement, Thorne stood up and whipped his arm round hard, smashing the butt of the gun across Cookson's mouth. He could feel the lips burst. He saw the teeth shatter and split the gums an instant before the hand moved to stop the gush of blood.

Thorne heard the thump of feet behind him. He turned to see officers pouring in through the gate, and Dave Holland sprinting across the playground towards Sarah McEvoy's body.

THIRTY

The pitch was frozen. A lot of mistimed tackles, flare-ups, silly mistakes. All the game needed was a dubious penalty and a sending-off, and Thorne would feel that this month's subscription to Sky had been justified.

He wondered whether his dad would be watching, shouting at the screen as if he were still on the terraces. His dad who had taken him to his first Spurs game over thirty years before, back in the days of Martin Chivers and Alan Gilzean. Thorne wondered how much longer his old man would be *able* to watch, able to follow the game.

The call had been typical of him. He'd dealt with the situation in a predictable way.

'Remember the joke I told you about the bloke who goes to the doctors?'

Thorne laughed. There had been plenty. 'Which one?'

'The doctor says to him, "Bad news I'm afraid. You've got cancer *and* Alzheimer's disease . . ."'

Thorne felt something tighten. 'Dad . . .'

'So the bloke looks at the doctor . . .' The voice on the phone, starting to waver a little. 'He looks at the doctor and says, "well, at least I haven't got cancer."'

'What are you on about, Dad?'

There was a long pause before the old man repeated the punchline, said what he'd called to say.

'*At least I haven't got cancer, Tom.*'

Then Thorne had understood what it was his father *did* have.

The hiss of a ring-pull brought Thorne out of it, and he turned to look at Hendricks. He was stretched out as usual, shoes off, feet up on the sofa.

'You said something interesting once,' Thorne said.

'Only once?'

'You said you thought the smell of formaldehyde put people off. You don't reckon your feet might have anything to do with it?'

'Piss off,' Hendricks said.

Things were pretty much back to normal.

Nearly a month since Thorne had walked away from the playground at King Edward's. Watching the stretchers sliding into ambulances. The arms of teachers wrapped around crying children. The look on Dave Holland's face . . .

Nearly a month since he'd walked back up that long drive, wondering idly what might have happened to his car.

How long it would take to scrub blood off asphalt . . .

Palmer had known exactly what he was doing, when he'd pointed that gun. Thorne should have seen it coming earlier – when Palmer had been so keen to tell him where the gun had come from. A last attempt at a good gesture, before the most desperate one of all.

Was suicide, which is what it was, the act of a coward or a brave man? Thorne thought, in the end, that Palmer had done what he did, not out of self-disgust, but simply because he knew, emotionally at least, that he would never survive prison.

The school's former Head of English, on the other hand, was made of sterner stuff. Of far stranger stuff.

Andrew Cookson would do very nicely. While the true-crime cash-ins were being scribbled, he would carve out a niche for himself in Belmarsh or Broadmoor. Number one nutter in the nick. Fear was all-important in prison. In a place where getting through a day unscathed was hard enough, robbers and rapists would probably scare just as easily as Martin Palmer had done.

Palmer, scared stiff all his life, whose one act of anything like bravery had gone so tragically wrong.

The words of the speech, the platitudes that had rattled around in his head that day, were close enough to those that were needed. To those that were eventually used.

'*All of those who worked with her, of whatever rank, will miss her dedication and good humour . . .*'

The faces of Lionel and Rebecca McEvoy had joined those of Robert and Mary Enright, Rosemary Vincent and Leslie Bowles. The flaking portraits of those that had lived to bury their children.

Leslie Bowles had put it simplest, and best.

It never stops. Never.

'By the way,' Hendricks said. 'If Brendan rings, I'm not here . . .'

Thorne turned and stared at the scruffy article sprawled on the sofa, at the open and expectant face of the man who had performed the post-mortem on Sarah McEvoy.

Who afterwards had somehow managed to misplace the toxicology report.

'Oi . . . I'm not here. If he rings. Is that OK?'

'I see another piercing coming,' Thorne said. 'What's happened now?'

Hendricks swung his feet on to the floor and sat up. 'You remember when I thought he was freaked out by the job, yeah? Well, it turns out he actually quite likes it.'

'So?'

'So, now *I'm* the one that's a bit freaked out . . .'

'You're never happy.'

'Me! What about you?'

Thorne stood and strolled towards the kitchen to get a couple more beers. 'I'm fine.'

Hendricks leaned back grinning, his hands behind his head. 'Yeah, well, so you should be. Fantastic mate like me, beer, Spurs one-nil up away from home. It doesn't get much better than this really, does it?'

With his back to him, Hendricks had no way of knowing if Thorne was smiling as he spoke.

'Christ, I sincerely hope so . . .'

EPILOGUE

23, Dyer Close
Kings Heath
Birmingham
B14 3EX
West Midlands

28 February, 2002

Dear Inspector Thorne,

I know it's taken a while to drop you a line, but I'm sure you appreciate that there's a lot going on and that it's been quite difficult for us since the arrest.

We were very sorry to hear about Detective Sergeant McEvoy. She must have been about the same age as Carol. Please pass on our condolences to her family.

Charlie is really starting to do well now. He's settled in very well at school and is sleeping a lot better. The child psychologist is very pleased with him. My wife thought you'd like to know.

The real reason I was writing, was to say a belated 'thank you' for the tool set you sent Charlie at Christmas. It was thoughtful. I hope you don't mind, but we didn't tell him that the present came from you. We're not sure if he remembers you anyway and we thought it best, considering, to just tell him it was from us. I'm sure you understand.

Yours sincerely,

Robert Enright

Robert Enright